A DARK ROMANCE THRILLER

ALL THE WAYS I'D LIVE FOR YOU

B.W. LACEY

All the Ways I'd Live for You

© 2026 B.W. Lacey

All rights reserved. No part of this publication may be reproduced, distributed, or transmitted in any form or by any means, including photocopying, recording, or other electronic or mechanical methods, without the prior written permission of the publisher, except in the case of brief quotations used in reviews, articles, or other non-commercial uses permitted by copyright law.

This is a work of fiction. Names, characters, places, and incidents are either products of the author's imagination or are used fictitiously. Any resemblance to actual events, locales, or persons, living or dead, is entirely coincidental.

ISBN: 979-8-9948565-1-2

Imprint: Independently published

First Edition: 2026

Contents

Playlist

1. Goodbye Horses – Q Lazzarus
2. Hunted Down – Soundgarden
3. Romance – Varials
4. Kill4Me – Marilyn Manson
5. Cherry Waves – Deftones
6. CPR – Summer Walker
7. Ambrosia – Siaynoq
8. Seven Nation Army – The White Stripes
9. Hush – The Marías
10. N.h.i.e – 21 Savage ft. Doja Cat
11. Sienna – The Marías
12. Angel – Massive Attack
13. After the Storm – Kali Uchis
14. Lovesong – The Cure
15. Nothing's Gonna Hurt You Baby – Cigarettes After Sex
16. Sextape – Deftones

Trigger Warnings

This novel contains explicit content and mature themes that may be disturbing or triggering for some readers. Please proceed with care. This is the darkest installment in the trilogy. Reader discretion is strongly advised. Your mental health matters.

Content Includes:

Graphic violence and murder, torture and physical abuse, graphic gore and dismemberment, execution-style violence and mass casualty events, cannibalism, necrophilia, sexual assault and rape, dubious consent and non-consensual situations, power imbalance and coercion in romantic relationships, obsessive and controlling behavior, psychological manipulation and gaslighting, stalking and surveillance, captivity and loss of bodily autonomy, poisoning and biological harm, profanity and strong language, explicit sexual content, mental illness, PTSD and emotional breakdowns, miscarriage and pregnancy-related trauma, medical procedures and trauma, loss of a loved one, suicide and implied self-harm, drug and alcohol use, blood play, knife play, primal play, BDSM and other kink elements.

This is a dark romance novel featuring morally gray characters. The narrative intentionally explores uncomfortable and extreme subject matter and is not intended for sensitive readers or those seeking a conventional love story.

This is book three of the Psychotic Devotion trilogy.

This story continues directly from the events of book one: All the Ways I'd Kill for You and book two: All the Ways I'd Die for You. For the best reading experience and to fully understand the characters, relationships, and consequences that follow, it is strongly recommended that you read Books One and Two before starting this novel. This book does not recap prior events. It assumes you already survived them.

For the final girls who became the villain
They made you into this
Make them choke on it

Prologue

The first siren rips through the forest, bouncing between the trees and closing the distance they bought with blood and panic. Wet snow sticks fast, heavy enough to slow them down, cold enough to burn.

Liam snaps his head toward the sound, eyes blown wide, breath tearing out of him in uneven bursts that fog the air. Sweat and melted snow plaster his hair to his forehead. His lungs burn. His legs shake inside thin sweats soaked through to the skin. They've been running far too long for hope to still feel real, and the siren confirms it. Whatever grace period they were given was finished.

"Move!" Chris shouts, his voice cracking under the strain. "Go, go, GO!"

Beth runs at his side, feet slapping against slick mud and half-frozen leaves, the hem of her dress heavy with water and clinging to her thighs. The cold bites at her exposed skin, numbing her fingers even as her heart hammers violently against her ribs. Behind them, Cindy and Liam struggle to keep pace, Cindy's dress tangling around her legs, Liam's feet skidding on roots and stone, branches tearing at fabric and skin as they push deeper into the dark Oregon woods.

They can barely see more than a few feet in front of them through the darkness. The snow makes the ground unpredictable, sometimes soft, sometimes slick, sometimes hiding something sharp.

The second siren wails. The hunt has begun.

"Oh my god, they're coming," Cindy whimpers behind her, hair whipping across her soaked face.

Liam doesn't see the trap until it snaps shut.

Metal slams together with a violent crack that echoes through the trees. Liam screams at the same moment, a raw, tearing sound forced out of him without control. His body jerks sideways as the force rips his foot out from under him. His leg folds beneath him at an impossible angle, twisted past the point joints are meant to allow, and he hits the ground hard enough to knock the air from his lungs. Snow bursts up around him as his body strikes the frozen earth.

Beth stumbles to a stop, her balance slipping as her bare feet hit fresh blood that wasn't there moments ago.

The bear trap snaps shut around Liam's ankle and locks in place. Steel teeth tear through skin and muscle before biting down hard against bone. Blood spills out in heavy, steaming surges, seeping through the jagged teeth and soaking into the snow below. Splintered bone presses against the metal, some pieces snapped clean, others crushed inward, all visible through torn flesh that no longer resembles a leg.

"OH GOD," Liam screams. His hands fly to his ankle, fingers smearing blood everywhere they touch. "GET IT OFF. GET IT OFF. AAHHHH. PLEASE. PLEASE!"

Chris drops beside him, slipping on blood-slick snow, hands shaking as he grabs Liam's shoulders and tries to lift him. "Don't move," he shouts, his voice cracking, even though Liam can't stop shaking or screaming. Cindy lunges for the trap with bare hands, fingers immediately burning from the cold metal and the heat of fresh blood. She strains with everything she has. The jaws stay locked, teeth driving deeper as Liam's weight shifts, pressure crushing bone and tearing what little structure the leg still has.

Liam's scream collapses into sobbing gasps. Foam gathers at the corners of his mouth. His eyes roll, unfocused, white showing. Blood keeps pumping, pulsing in time with his heartbeat, each thud spraying more red into the snow.

"Please," he chokes, reaching for Cindy. His fingers tremble violently. "Please don't let me die. Please."

Another convulsion tears through him. The trap grates again, and something inside his ankle gives way. Liam screams once more, then his voice shatters into a hoarse, animal whine as shock begins to crawl in.

Slow footsteps crunch through the snow.

Beth freezes so hard it feels like her bones lock in place. The others follow her stare. A figure slides out from between the trees, their outline warped by drifting snow, almost indistinguishable from the trunks behind them.

The figure carries a harvesting blade that is long and curved, designed to cut down whatever stands in its path. Moonlight slides along the edge and catches on patches that are already wet and dark. The figure stops just far enough away to watch, head tilted slightly.

"No. No. No," Liam sobs as panic tears through him.

He tries to drag himself backward, palms scraping at the snow while his heels dig uselessly into the ground. The bear trap yanks him short with brutal force, jerking his body back toward it. Steel teeth shriek as he moves, the sound high and grating, and his ankle grinds again inside the locked jaws. Fresh blood spills out immediately, pooling beneath him and soaking through his sweats until the fabric clings to torn flesh underneath. His breaths come in choking bursts as pain rips through him faster than he can process.

The figure kneels beside him with ease. They slide the curved blade beneath Liam's chin and lift slowly, applying just enough pressure to force his face upward. His jaw shakes violently as his head tilts back, his throat exposed without resistance.

"Please don't," he whispers, his voice barely holding together. "Please."

The blade moves.

It cuts his throat clean and wide in a single smooth sweep. Skin splits, muscle parts. Blood explodes outward in a violent arc, slapping across Cindy's face and neck. Liam's body jerks hard enough to rattle the trap. His hands fly to his neck, fingers plunging into the open wound, coming away coated and dripping.

He gurgles. Thick bubbles push through the ruin of his throat. His legs kick, reflexive, wild, heel hammering uselessly against the steel jaws that still hold him. His eyes roll back, then flutter violently. His body convulses again, then again, then stills.

Beth screams so hard it tears through her, her throat burning as her voice starts to give out.

The killer stands. They snap the blade once, sending a fan of blood into the snow, then turn and vanish into the storm as if the forest swallows them whole. The distant siren fades into nothing.

Beth stumbles, vision smeared red, skin slick with blood. Behind her, Cindy sobs as she runs, breath hitching hard enough to steal air from her lungs. Her hair is plastered to her face and neck, legs trembling as she tries to keep moving.

"There it is," Cindy gasps, panic forcing the words out too fast. "I can see the gate."

There is a thick, ugly crack that splits the air and cuts the sentence short. Beth turns just in time to see the bolt hit. It punches through the side of Cindy's neck and tears out the other side in a violent burst of flesh and arterial spray. Blood erupts in a hard, pulsing stream, splattering the snow and striking Beth's exposed arms and hands.

Cindy's eyes go wide as her body staggers. Her mouth opens and closes without sound, jaw working uselessly as her throat fails her. Blood bubbles between her lips, spilling down her chin and soaking the front of her dress. She reaches for Beth with shaking fingers, hands slipping in her own blood as her knees begin to give way. Cindy collapses mid-step, knees buckling, body slamming into the snow. She tries to breathe. The sound that comes out is wet, choking, wrong.

Beth drops beside her, hands shaking, pressing uselessly at the wound, whispering over and over, "Cindy, no. Stay with me. Please."

Cindy's eyes flutter. Her chest hitches once more. Blood spills from her mouth and runs into her hair as her body finally goes slack.

On the ridge above them, a silhouette lowers a crossbow with mechanical calm.

Then it is gone.

Beth doesn't remember standing up. Her body just goes, pushed forward by panic she can't stop. Her legs feel numb, the cold doesn't register, and the burn in her lungs barely reaches her. All she hears is Chris yelling her name behind her and the heavy crunch of boots tearing through the snow.

Chris catches her arm and spins her around hard enough to make her stagger. His hands are shaking violently. His face is streaked with blood, smeared across his cheek and jaw.

"Hey, look at me," he says, his breath hitching with every word. "We can make it. Just keep going."

He turns to run. Branches snap hard to their right, followed by the heavy rush of movement cutting through the snow. Beth barely has time to register the shape breaking from the trees before the killer hits him.

The axe is driven straight into Chris's stomach with full force. The blade buries deep, tearing through fabric, muscle, and organs in a single violent motion. The impact knocks the air out of him instantly. His body jerks forward, then locks in place, back arching as his mouth opens in a silent scream. Blood spills immediately, pouring down over his hands as he instinctively clutches at the handle lodged in his abdomen.

"CHRIS," Beth screams as she lunges toward him. "Chris!"

His eyes are wide with shock, pupils blown out as his body begins to tremble. His lips quiver as he tries to breathe. He coughs hard, and blood bursts from his mouth, splattering Beth's bare arms and the snow between them. Red flecks cling to his teeth and run down his chin.

"Beth," he wheezes, his voice thin and broken. "Baby. Run."

The word barely makes it out. His knees buckle as his strength gives way. The killer stays close. Gloved hands wrap around the axe handle still buried in Chris's stomach. Chris feels it before he sees it. His entire body seizes as a strangled sound tears out of his throat.

"No," he gasps. "Stop."

The axe is ripped free and driven in again with brutal force. The blade tears deeper through his torso, shredding what little resistance remains. His body collapses forward as blood pours freely now, soaking his shirt and spreading beneath him.

Beth stumbles backward as her legs buckle beneath her. The air leaves her lungs in a single rush and her vision narrows until there is nothing but Chris on the ground. His body twitches once and then goes still.

The killer lifts their head and turns toward her. Snow clings to their clothes and blood coats their hands. They raise one finger and point straight at her.

Beth's mind blanks under what she's seeing. Whatever thought she had falls apart, and her body moves on instinct alone.

She turns and runs.

She runs until her chest burns so badly it feels close to splitting, each breath shallow and frantic. Her calves scream with pain, muscles tightening and threatening to fail as her bare feet strike frozen ground, roots, and rock. Trees blur together as she pushes forward, her breaths breaking into panicked sobs that barely keep her upright.

The chainsaw starts behind her. The engine catches with a rough, uneven roar that cuts through the forest and the storm. The sound climbs rapidly, growing louder and more aggressive as the motor revs higher. Metal screams against metal as the chain spins faster, the noise tearing through the air and closing the distance behind her.

"No. No. No. Please," Beth cries, words tumbling out of her in raw sobs as she crashes through branches that tear at her face and arms. She slips on ice and mud, goes down hard, rolls, slams into a tree, then staggers back up.

The chainsaw roars again, closer this time.

Beth's foot comes down wrong as she runs. A jagged rock punches straight through the sole of her foot. The impact steals her balance instantly. Her ankle twists as her weight collapses onto the injury, and she goes down face first. Her chin slams into frozen dirt with a muffled crack that rattles through her skull. Pain detonates up her jaw and into her ears, leaving her stunned and gasping. She tries to scream and only manages a wet sob.

Beth scrambles backward, palms digging frantically into the ground as she fights to put distance between herself and the sound. Broken sticks drive into her hands and wrists. Blood smears across the snow in streaks as she drags herself away, her injured foot trailing uselessly behind her and leaving a thick red trail wherever it touches.

The chainsaw revs again.

Boots crunch closer, each step pressing into the snow. The figure steps into view. They are tall, shoulders broad beneath dark clothing dusted with snow. Their grip on the chainsaw is relaxed. The blade is still running as it drags behind them, chewing into ice and stone. Sparks burst where metal strikes rock. The air fills with the stench of fuel and hot oil layered over blood and pine.

Beth crawls backward in terror, heels slipping, hands sliding through her own blood as she stares up at the figure closing in.

"Please," she begs, her voice breaking as terror shreds what little control she has left. "Please. Don't do this. Please."

The killer lunges.

The chainsaw slams into her side, the impact knocking the breath out of her lungs. It doesn't cut cleanly or deep enough to end her. The teeth bite into her ribs and tear sideways, ripping flesh apart in a grinding, violent drag. Bone cracks and splinters under the blade. Part of her side is cut open in an instant, replaced by a spray of hot blood that bursts outward and strikes the snow in steaming sheets. Beth screams as the vibration tears through her body, the force shuddering through her ribs and spine, rattling her teeth in her skull.

She rolls blindly across the ground, shrieking, hands clawing at her side in panic. Her fingers slide into tissue that shouldn't be exposed, slick and loose beneath her touch. Pain tears through her torso in blinding waves.

"Stop. Please. Stop," she screams, her voice breaking down into raw, hoarse sounds that barely resemble words.

The killer lifts the chainsaw overhead.

For a brief, frozen moment, Beth sees her own reflection warped across the metal. Her face is streaked with blood, her mouth open in a silent plea, her eyes wide and glassy with shock.

Then the saw comes down.

It strikes her pelvis first. The teeth chew through bone with a brutal, grinding force, splitting her hips apart as flesh tears open around it. Blood erupts upward as the blade climbs, ripping through her abdomen and shredding muscle and organs in its path. Her body convulses violently, back arching off the ground as the last of her strength spasms through ruined nerves.

Everything inside her gives way at once. A final, soundless scream twists in her throat, strangled before it can escape. The chainsaw tears up through her with unstoppable force, and she feels every second of it.

Pain overwhelms everything, sight, sound, breath, until her mind snaps and her vision floods with blinding, merciful white.

The killer finishes the cut in one long, deliberate motion, dragging the saw up through the center of her body.

The chainsaw sputters once. Then it goes silent.

Beth's body collapses in two broken halves. Steam rises from the ragged ends of muscle and bone as blood pours freely, pooling thick beneath her and soaking into the snow. Her limbs twitch once before falling still. Snow continues to fall, settling gently into open wounds and pooling in the recesses of her destroyed torso.

The forest falls quiet again.

Figures slip out from between the trees, one after another, filling the clearing. Some clean their weapons while others check and reset their gear. Blades are inspected, traps are set again, and bodies are hauled across the snow, leaving long, smeared trails behind them.

The next hunt is ready to begin.

PART ONE

Chapter 1
Brooke

I wake up choking on air, my body jolting as I drag in breath after breath. The room drifts in and out of focus, and the ceiling seems to tilt no matter how hard I try to lock onto one point. Beige walls box me in. Heavy curtains smother the windows, shutting out daylight and time. Recognition comes slow, then hits hard. This is John and Mary's house in Fresno.

How the fuck did I get here?

My head aches in a deep, relentless way that presses behind my eyes and crawls into my jaw. My mouth feels dry, coated with a bitter taste. I try to remember how I got here, but my thoughts slide away from each other, refusing to connect. I remember Colorado, the hotel, the chaos. I remember Grant's voice and the sound of a gunshot that doesn't stop echoing in my mind. I remember seeing Seth go down, and the moment my brain tries to reject what my eyes saw. After that, there's nothing.

There's no memory of travel. There's no memory of time passing. One moment I am there, and the next I am here, with nothing in between. Someone drugged me. That is the only explanation that makes sense, because I can't lose two states of time without help.

I try to move, needing to get out, needing to get back to Seth. When I lift my hand, metal clinks softly. The sound snaps my attention downward. Cold circles my wrist, and I see thick handcuffs biting into my skin, bolted into the wooden armrest of the chair.

I yank against the cuff. The chair scrapes across the floor until the wood groans. The noise feels too loud in the muffled room. I search for a weak point, for a loose screw. If I can loosen one, I can tip the chair. If I can tip the chair, I can run. If I can run, I can find a phone, or a neighbor, or a way out. I can't sit here and wait for whatever comes next.

The door creaks open, and the sound cuts straight through me. Mary steps inside and closes it behind her with careful hands, as if quietness could make this less frightening. Her smile is soft and concerned, the same one she has worn my entire life when something is wrong and she wants me calm.

"Sweetheart," she says gently as she moves closer. "You're awake. I was so worried about you."

Relief hits so fast it makes me lightheaded. For a second, my brain grabs onto the only normal thing in the room. She wasn't there. She didn't see what John and Grant did. She doesn't know who John really is.

"Auntie, please," my voice shakes with desperation. "You have to help me. John isn't who he says he is. He tried to kill me. He tried to kill Seth. Grant shot him. They drugged me. Please get these off me."

Mary slows to a stop a few feet away from the chair. Her expression shifts. It isn't shock or confusion. A tired look settles over her face instead, like she has been waiting for this exact moment and already knows what she is going to say.

"It's for the best, Brooke," she says quietly. "You don't understand what's at stake."

The words don't register at first. They don't fit the version of her I know. The understanding hits anyway, hard and brutal. She isn't confused. She knows. She has always known who John is, and she stayed.

"What are you talking about?" My voice shakes harder.

John walks into the room. He doesn't look surprised to see me awake. He doesn't glance at the restraints. He put me here.

"Brooke," he says calmly. "You're finally awake."

I jerk against the cuff again, harder this time. "Where is Seth?"

The last image of Seth crashes through me without warning. I see him on the ballroom floor. I see blood spreading beneath him too fast. I feel Grant's hands dragging me away while I scream Seth's name until my throat burns. I still don't know if Seth is alive, and the not knowing is its own kind of hell.

My stomach twists, and I fight down the nausea that rises with it.

Fuck, I'm pregnant.

My body has been drugged, restrained, and hauled across state lines. I barely had time to process it before everything collapsed. I found out, and then the hotel turned into a slaughterhouse, with bodies everywhere, people screaming, people running, people hiding, people dying.

Seth and I barely got to talk about it. We didn't get to decide anything. My mind keeps circling back to him on that floor and the possibility that if he's gone, this baby is the only piece of him I have left. Losing him and losing this baby would destroy me.

John exhales slowly. "You don't need to concern yourself with him."

"Who the fuck are you?" I fight against the restraints. "Let me go."

"Brooke," he says sharply. "Enough."

"Is he alive?" My voice cracks. "Is Seth alive?"

John pauses. The silence stretches long enough to make my anxiety peak even more.

"If he is alive," he says evenly, "he'll be charged with every murder at the Everspring. Ours and his included." His gaze stays on me. "They'll attach every kill tied to Stratford too."

I glare at him, shock and anger rising fast.

"He'll be taken into custody," John continues. "He won't remain there long. We have people inside. Guards, administrators, men who understand what loyalty demands." His tone doesn't change. "They've already decided what will happen next. He's going to die publicly."

My throat tightens, and swallowing feels difficult.

"Nick's family wants their name restored, Amber's family does as well." He sighs. "This is how the Collective keeps itself clean. They give the public a single monster to fear. Then they remove him."

He looks at me directly. "That is how the Collective functions."

I shake my head. "What the fuck is the Collective?"

John drags a chair across the floor and sits like he's about to lecture me.

"The Collective," he says calmly, folding his hands together, "is not new. It didn't begin with Grant. It didn't begin with me." His gaze stays fixed on mine. "It has existed for generations. Wealthy families. Political dynasties. People who have always understood how power actually works."

My mouth goes dry again.

"We aren't pretending the world is innocent," John continues. "We see it as it is. Violent. Competitive. Unstable." His voice remains calm. "We also understand that violence doesn't vanish because certain people refuse to acknowledge it. Someone always directs it somewhere."

I try to follow him, but my thoughts keep racing.

"I train our men," he says. "I prepare them. I teach discipline, restraint, and obedience. Not everyone can kill on command. Not everyone can live with it afterward. I decide who can."

He pauses, then adds in a tone that makes my skin turn cold, "The men Seth killed at the hotel were mine."

The men in the animal masks. The ones with the machete, axe, and crossbow. The ones that attacked me and Seth.

"They were yours? The ones in the masks?"

"Yes."

"One of them tried to kill me."

John shakes his head once. "No." He doesn't even blink.

"He wasn't trying to kill you. He was trying to take you." His gaze stays on mine. "The instructions were to bring you back to me. Alive"

Nausea rises sharp and sudden, and I swallow it down.

John leans back slightly. "The Collective doesn't exist just to indulge violence. It exists to direct it. Chaos already exists. We decide where it goes. Order requires structure. Structure requires sacrifice."

I force air into my lungs. "You murdered a hotel full of people, for a fucking tech company?"

John nods once. "Trinity Tech interfered with interests controlled by our faction, they refused cooperation. They assumed public ethics would shield them." His voice stays calm. "They were wrong."

For a moment, my thoughts slow. Then they line up in a way that feels worse than panic.

I remember John pulling me out of the freezer. I remember the freezer door slamming shut again.

Is Travis still inside?

The thought hits like a gut punch. Travis alone in the dark, locked behind metal that is turning colder by the second. His breath will get thinner as the temperature drops, and nobody will find him in time.

"Is Travis alive?"

"If he is, he shouldn't be." John folds his hands in his lap. "He works for Trinity Tech. That means he had to die. Everyone in that building should be dead."

My vision blurs as the thought hits, both of them gone.

I stare at him, trying to match this man to the one who drove me to school, corrected my homework, told me discipline mattered more than talent.

"What is wrong with you?" My voice shakes, but the words come out clear. "You weren't like this. You raised me. You watched me grow up."

John exhales through his nose.

"You knew the version of me I showed you. That was all you needed."

My breath stutters.

"You killed my parents."

"Your father was one of ours. He knew the rules, and he decided they didn't apply to him anymore." He tilts his head slightly. "That's when he became a problem."

I shake my head, but it isn't denial. It's my body refusing to accept it.

"People like this don't come out of nowhere, it runs in families, and you see it early." His eyes stay on me. "Your father had it. That's why he was brought in. That's why it mattered when he stopped listening."

He smirks. "And you have it too."

My throat burns. My hands curl into fists as much as the cuffs allow.

"We were instructed to kill you as well, Mary begged me not to. So you became somewhat of an experiment."

I shake my head, refusing it even as the truth starts to settle in.

"You were compliant," he continues. "You showed promise. You learned quickly. You endured without collapsing. You adapted when others would have broken. You were never meant to be sheltered. You were meant to be shaped."

I grip the edge of the chair, fingers tightening against the wood.

"All those years," he adds, "I was preparing you. Conditioning you for what this life requires. The training, the discipline, the exposure. Nothing you survived was accidental."

"What the fuck?" I yell. "What the fuck are you talking about?"

I lunge forward on instinct. The cuff snaps me back hard. Pain shoots through my arms as the chair tips and slams down again.

John leans forward slightly, resting his forearms on his knees.

"You could've lived quietly," he says. "I would've continued smoothing things over. You would've finished school. You would've married strategically."

"Married who?" I ask. "Nick?"

"Yes."

John gives a tight-lipped smirk, as if I missed a fortunate opportunity.

"Being married to a Talbert would've saved you," he continues. "Their name carries weight in the Collective."

I press my lips together, forcing them to stop shaking.

"You were manageable," he goes on. "You weren't drawing attention. Seth was."

I draw in a breath and hold it, then let it out slowly.

"He killed members. He killed his own father. He disrupted things that are meant to stay contained." His eyes lower to me. "He was marked long before Stratford."

My mind flashes to masked men again, to blood on tile, to Grant's face.

"When you chose him, you attached yourself to instability." John moves his hands in a small gesture, as if weighing options. "But then you killed Nick and Amber."

"They tried to kill me."

"That is irrelevant to them."

"You made yourself expendable," he continues. "And you placed me in a position where I had to answer for you."

A broken sound leaves me. "You're insane."

"No." He tilts his head slightly. "I'm practical."

My mind struggles to keep up with it, with how easily the man who once felt like a father can talk about me like I am nothing but a pawn.

"They want you and Seth dealt with. Killed if possible. Locked away if necessary. Public consequences matter when certain families are involved." He shakes his head. "You force their hand."

I stare at him. I look at his face and understand I have never known him.

What unsettles me more is the realization that I don't know what I have been living inside of all these years, and I don't know what part of me has been shaped by it.

Mary steps closer, hands lifted in a careful gesture that tries to look gentle. "John, that's enough for now." Then she turns to me, and her voice slides back into the softness she uses when she wants me calm. "Brooke, sweetie, you need to eat."

"Did you know about this?" I ask.

She blinks once. "When was the last time you ate, Brooke?"

"No. Answer me." My voice shakes. "Did you know he killed my parents? He killed your sister."

Mary exhales. "Brooke, there is nothing I could've done. Your father brought this on himself."

"What the fuck do you mean you couldn't stop it?" I demand. "If you knew, you could've warned them."

"Some choices have consequences," she murmurs. "And some outcomes can't be changed."

Something inside me snaps.

"Shut the fuck up, Mary."

John stands abruptly. "Do not speak to your aunt like that."

"Shut the fuck up!" I scream. "Both of you. You are liars. You are murderers. You are fucking insane!"

His hand strikes my face before I can react. My head snaps to the side, and the cuffs jerk my arms back hard enough to sting. The taste of copper fills my mouth.

"I don't know what's gotten into you," John says, his voice tight with contained rage, "but it stops now. You have never spoken to us this way. Not once. We aren't starting now."

"This isn't real," I whisper. "This isn't real. This isn't fucking real."

"It is real," John steps back as if nothing has happened. "And you need to accept what comes next. If you don't, you won't survive."

Mary hovers beside me. "Please don't cry, sweetheart. You're overwhelmed. The trip was long. You must be hungry."

"Don't touch me," I say as I jerk away from her touch.

John clears his throat. "She's disoriented. Give her space."

They call it disoriented. They don't call it restrained. They don't call it kidnapped.

Mary leaves and returns with a tray of scrambled eggs. Toast cut into triangles and a glass of orange juice. It looks like a normal morning in a house that has turned into a prison.

"Eat," she says gently.

I stare at the food, and my stomach lurches with disgust and hunger at the same time.

"Eat." John doesn't look away. "You're going to need your strength."

"Brooke," Mary whispers. "Please. Your uncle is trying to help you."

"He is not my fucking uncle."

I shift my wrists slightly, testing the restraints again. The bracket bolted into the chair arm feels weak.

John's eyes drop to my hands. "Don't."

He bends closer until I can smell his cologne, and the familiarity makes my skin crawl. "If you break that chair, I will put you on the floor and make sure you can't move. Do you understand me?"

"Fuck you."

"We will fix that attitude." His mouth tightens. "One way or another."

He moves behind me, his hand pressing into the back of the chair. He doesn't need to touch me to make his threat clear.

"If you want to survive, you will cooperate." His grip on the chair tightens. "You will eat. You will listen. You will learn."

Then he steps away and leaves the room. The door closes.

Mary stays, standing close enough that I can feel her presence even when I don't look at her.

"How could you let this happen to my mother?"

"I loved my sister," Mary says, and her voice wavers. "Once the decision was made, there was nothing I could do. If I interfered, they would've killed me too. They would've killed you."

I let out a harsh sound that isn't a laugh.

"John spared you." Mary steps closer.

"No." I shake my head. "You spared me because you felt guilty."

"No." Her eyes harden. "I love you."

"Stop."

She falls silent.

I let her believe there's still a version of me she can reach. I need her distracted. I need her watching my face instead of my hands. I shift in the chair again and test the bracket. If I pull the armrest at the right angle, it will give.

Mary slides the tray closer. "At least eat something."

I keep my eyes on the plate until hers follow. When her gaze drops, I twist my wrist carefully. The screw shifts slightly.

Mary lowers herself into the chair across from me. "You were out for a long time. The medication was strong."

"How long?"

She pauses, and her throat moves as if she has to swallow the answer.

"Two days," she whispers. "Almost three."

My mouth goes dry again.

"What did they give me?"

"A strong sedative," she says carefully. "From one of our doctors. You were hysterical. We had to keep you safe."

Safe is not the word for drugged and transported and hidden.

"Can I have water?" I ask.

Relief flashes across her face so fast it makes me sick. She wants signs of cooperation.

"Of course," she says quickly.

The moment she steps out, I yank the armrest hard. The chair groans, and the screw turns another notch. I stop moving the second I hear her footsteps return. I let my shoulders sag and force my breathing to slow.

Mary comes back with a glass of cold water, condensation slicks the outside.

Mary steps close, steadies the glass and brings it to my lips. "Drink slowly."

I drink carefully, taking small sips while she watches my face. The water tastes clean, and it makes me realize how dehydrated I am.

Mary exhales. "Once this settles, once you see how important this is, you'll understand."

I flex my fingers against the armrest again, hiding the motion in the small tremor of my hands. One more screw. One more. Then I'll be free or I'll be dead. Either way, I won't stay here.

I pull back from her and swallow. "I will never understand any of this."

She smiles. "You will."

Chapter 2

Brooke

I feel like I'm in a nightmare I can't wake up from. Every instinct in my body wants to move, to fight, but none of that will help me right now. Panic burns energy too fast, and I can't afford to waste any. I focus on breathing, on keeping my expression calm, on remembering that John watches everything. He always has. He likes patterns. He likes compliance. He likes thinking he is ahead.

If I want out of this, I need him to believe I am already where he wants me.

The door opens again. John steps back into the room with his phone still in his hand. He glances at Mary first, then at me.

"So what's it going to be, Brooke?"

Mary straightens immediately, her spine stiffening like she's been called to attention. I tighten my grip on the armrest, angling my wrist to keep the loosened screw out of view.

John sets his phone down on the dresser and folds his arms.

My gaze drops to the tray in front of me. The smell of eggs makes me nauseous. I look at the toast that is untouched. Then to the glass of water Mary brought.

"Fine," I whisper. "I'll eat."

Mary lets out a breath of relief. John gives a single nod, already satisfied.

I lean forward slightly. The movement shifts the chair.

Mary reaches for the fork like she is about to feed me herself.

"I'm not an infant," I snap. "I can feed myself."

She recoils, then nods quickly and places the fork in my hand. My cuffed hand. The metal presses into my skin.

I lift the fork, scoop a bite of eggs, and bring it halfway to my mouth.

The smell hits me. My stomach lurches violently. Heat rushes up my throat and I gag, twisting my head away just in time as bile burns my tongue. I bend forward, dry heaving, eyes watering, breath tearing out of me.

Mary is at my side instantly. "Brooke," she says softly. Watching me too closely now. "Are you nauseous?"

I swallow hard, fighting it down. "I'm fine."

"You're not." Her gaze flicks to the plate, then to my face. Something clicks behind her eyes. She picks up the tray and steps out of the room.

John watches from across the room.

Mary comes back with a warm biscuit and a little jar of honey. She breaks the biscuit in half with her fingers and drizzles honey over it.

"Here," she says gently. "Eat this. It'll settle your stomach."

I stare at it for half a second too long.

Refusing will draw attention. Eating will buy me time.

I take it.

The biscuit is soft and sweet, the honey sticky against my fingers. I chew slowly, keeping my breathing calm, forcing my body to cooperate.

Mary smiles, relieved. "That's better," she murmurs.

I nod, swallowing the last bite. I wipe my fingers on the napkin, lower my gaze, and let my shoulders slump.

The screw shifts again under my palm. Almost there. I shift hard in the chair. The armrest groans, wood complaining under pressure.

"Brooke." John's voice cuts through the room.

I freeze.

"Don't," John warns. "Do not do something stupid."

Too late.

I throw my weight sideways and wrench the armrest with everything I have. The wood cracks and the bracket holding the lower cuff tears free from the chair with a loud snap. The cuff is still locked around my wrist, but the armrest comes with it, splintered wood and chain hanging from my arm as I shove the chair aside and scramble to my feet.

Mary screams behind me as I shove the chair aside.

John is already moving.

I swing the broken armrest and catch him across the side of the head. It is not clean enough to drop him, but it staggers him long enough for me to run.

The cuff still circles my wrist, the chain dragging the jagged piece of wood behind me as I tear into the hallway.

"Brooke!" Mary cries. "Stop!"

"Stay the fuck away from me!"

I reach the kitchen door and yank the handle.

Fuck, it's locked.

John slams into me from the side and drives me into the wall hard enough to knock the air out of my chest. I fight anyway. I claw at him, kick his ribs, twist against his grip.

"Stop it," he shouts. "Stop it right now!"

I drive my knee into his side and tear loose for half a second.

It is not enough.

He grabs me again before I can run and slams me back against the wall. A gun appears in his hand, the barrel pressing hard against my temple.

"Settle the fuck down," he says coldly. "Or I walk into that garage, shoot the dog and the cat first, and then come back here and put a bullet in your head."

My body goes completely still.

Krueger.

Luna.

The fight drains out of me all at once.

"That's better," he mutters.

He forces me into the bedroom and slams me back into the chair. The broken cuff still dangles from my wrist, the splintered armrest dragging with it.

John grabs it, yanks the wood free with a sharp crack, and tosses it aside. The loose cuff snaps against my skin as he drags my other arm forward. Cold metal bites down as he locks the second cuff around my free wrist, forcing both hands together in front of me.

Then he reaches for the rope.

It winds tight around my torso and the chair slats, pulling me back until my shoulders strain and the wood cuts into my ribs. He cinches it harder, testing it once, making sure there is no give.

Mary hovers near the doorway, panicked and shaking.

"John, please," she whispers.

He ignores her and crouches in front of me.

"The Collective wanted you executed years ago," he says. "I could've killed you that night."

My jaw locks, but I don't look away.

"You were supposed to die with your parents," he continues. "Mary begged me not to do it. She is the only reason you're still breathing."

Mary's voice trembles. "She's still your niece."

John's expression hardens.

"No," he says calmly. "She's a liability."

He leans closer, his voice dropping.

"So here are your only two options. I can send you to Elliot's manor where The Collective will decide how useful you still are."

His gaze locks onto mine.

"Or I execute you right now and finally finish what should've been done years ago."

The room goes very quiet.

He straightens and adjusts his sleeve as if the decision means nothing to him.

"Think carefully about which option you prefer."

Then he turns and walks out, leaving the rope tight around my ribs and the cuffs locked around my wrist.

Mary lingers a few feet away. Her eyes are wet, rimmed red.

"Brooke," she says softly, "why would you do that? You are only making this harder than it needs to be."

I don't answer. I force my breathing to slow, drag it down into my chest until the shaking eases. Panic won't save me. It never has.

Mary watches me too closely.

"Brooke," she tries again, gentler now, coaxing. "Please. Say something."

I lift my head slowly and meet her gaze.

"Where's Luna and Krueger?"

"In the garage, we shut them in there so they wouldn't run when we brought you in. They're safe."

"Did you hurt them?"

Her brows knit together, almost offended. "Of course not. I would never. We aren't monsters."

I almost laugh. The sound lodges in my throat and burns there.

My wrists throb where the cuffs bite into skin. I take a shallow breath.

"Mary," I say quietly, "I'm pregnant."

She goes still. Her expression shifts, eyes narrowing slightly as if she is fitting a final piece into place.

"Oh, Brooke," she murmurs. "I knew it."

My stomach drops. "How?"

"The biscuit," her voice softens. "With the honey. That's what your mother craved when she was pregnant with you. She couldn't keep anything else down."

"You have to help me," I beg, leaning forward as far as the restraints allow. The rope cuts deeper into my ribs. "Please. I can't stay here."

Mary's gaze drops for a second, like she's weighing something she already decided.

"Sweetheart, this is bigger than you and me. Decisions are already in motion." Her voice lowers. "There are things I can't interfere with."

"Auntie," I whisper. "Please."

Her eyes flicker, just once. Pity maybe, or regret, then it is gone. She looks at me as if she has already made her choice and learned to live with it.

The door creaks.

Mary straightens instantly, hands folding neatly in her lap, composure snapping back into place like a reflex.

John enters with the calm of a man delivering a verdict.

"Your best option is not a pleasant one," John continues, "you're being transferred to Elliot's Manor."

Mary's composure wavers. "John...she's pregnant."

John turns toward her slowly. "What?"

"She's pregnant," she repeats. "That changes things, right?"

John stares at her for a long moment. Then his gaze slides back to me.

"You should have told me."

I glare at him. "And what would you have done? Give me a baby shower?"

"How far along?"

"I don't know."

He nods once.

"This complicates things," he says.

Mary steps closer, her voice tight with hope. "Does that protect her?"

John looks at her.

"No."

My grip tightens against the chair until the wood digs into my palm.

"If Brooke is just another capable young woman, they can find ways to use her for a long time," he continues. "But pregnancy changes that. She'll slow down. She'll get tired. Eventually she'll be too far along to do much of anything."

My jaw tightens.

"They are not the kind of people who enjoy maintaining complications," he adds. "They prefer efficiency."

John slowly paces in front of me, hands behind his back.

"If Brooke is compliant and keeps her head clear, they may decide she is worth keeping alive for a while."

"And if they don't?" I ask.

"Then they will eliminate you." He adjusts his sleeve as if the conversation has already ended.

"You leave in the morning," he says. "Grant will handle the transfer."

He looks at me one last time.

"Do not mistake this for mercy. It's a negotiation."

John walks out. The door closes behind him.

Mary lingers in the doorway, hands folded neatly in front of her. Whatever guilt lives on her face never reaches her eyes.

"Try to breathe, sweetheart," she murmurs. "It's all for the best."

The way she says sweetheart makes my blood run cold.

Then she turns off the light, closes the door, and locks me in.

And the last family I had left chooses The Collective over me.

Chapter 3

Brooke

The house stays too quiet, every small sound carrying farther than it should. I work at the cuffs until my wrists throb, pulling, twisting, testing for anything that might give. Nothing does. The rope digs into my waist each time I shift. My legs go numb, then sting as feeling comes back. My shoulders ache from being held in place.

My thoughts continue to spiral until it lands on one thing. The thought finally settles but my mind refuses to see it properly. My father, Greg. The man who baked cookies on Sundays and drove me to softball practice. The man who told me to question everything and trust my instincts. A killer. Just like John. Just like Seth.

The connection is there whether I accept it or not.

If John is right, if violence runs through blood the way he believes it does, then this isn't chance. It was always there. Not something I turned into. Something I started as. The thought hits hard enough that I have to force myself to breathe through it.

And my baby.

If killers make killers, if this thing is passed down instead of learned, then what does that mean for the life growing inside me? Is it already marked? Already destined to be a killer. Or is that the lie John needs to believe so he can justify everything he's done.

I don't know which answer terrifies me more.

Sometime deep into the night, the door opens again. Light spills in as Mary steps inside carrying a tray. A bowl of grits sits in the center, steam rising faintly from the surface, butter melting into pale swirls, salt dusted across the top. A glass of cold water rests beside it. She closes the door behind her with the same careful quiet she always uses.

"You need to eat." Mary sets the tray down with careful hands, her voice still soft.

The smell hits me and my stomach twists hard. Hunger claws upward.

I shake my head weakly. "I don't want to eat."

"Stop." She straightens, fingers tightening around the spoon. "You're pregnant. You can't afford to be stubborn."

She dips the spoon into the grits and stirs once before stepping closer. She lifts it toward my mouth.

I turn my head away. A cramp seizes low in my abdomen, stealing my breath.

"Brooke." Her tone lowers. "Don't make this harder than it already is."

I try to resist, but the room tilts. Dark spots crowd the edges of my vision. Hunger wins.

I open my mouth.

The grits are warm and thick, salted just enough to taste good. The butter coats my tongue. I swallow with effort, forcing it down while every instinct tells me not to take anything from her. She feeds me slowly. Between bites, she lifts the glass and presses it to my lips.

"Drink." She tips the glass slightly.

The water is cold. It slides down my throat and settles in my stomach.

When the bowl is empty, she wipes my mouth with a napkin as if I am a child. Then she lingers, watching my breathing even out.

I stare at her. "Did you ever love me?"

Her hand stills midair.

"Of course I did."

"Did?"

She lowers the napkin. "I love you like a daughter."

"Then how can you let this happen to me?"

"This is the only way you survive." She folds her hands together. "Any other way and they kill you."

"And what you're doing right now isn't killing me?" I lean forward as far as the restraints allow. "Sending me where you're about to send me isn't killing me?"

Mary's face tightens. "If there was any other way, I would've begged John to make it work."

"John doesn't give a fuck about me." I hold her gaze. "Do you?"

She doesn't answer.

"John told me he wanted me with Nick." I swallow hard. "That means you both knew. You knew what Nick was. You knew what Amber was. And you let me trust them anyway."

Mary's throat moves as she swallows.

"John believed being close to the Talberts and the Vosses would make you harder to touch." She shifts her weight, avoiding my eyes for a second. "Nick's family has power. Being tied to them would have put you under their protection."

"I was raped." The word breaks on the way out. "That was your idea of protection?"

"That was not supposed to happen." Her jaw tightens. "Nick stepped out of line."

I let out a sharp breath.

Her shoulders sag. "He was supposed to be the best option. After you killed him, The Collective stopped seeing you as manageable."

"What about when I first brought Seth over?" I press. "You said he was good for me. You said you hoped he'd help me find my voice."

Something shifts across her face.

"I did hope that." Her voice softens despite herself. "I hoped he'd take you far enough away that none of this could reach you."

Her voice cracks.

"He couldn't." She looks down for a second before meeting my eyes again. "And now he's most likely dead, sweetheart."

"And you still stayed with John...after all this?" I scoff. "Knowing what he planned to do?"

"I stayed because leaving wouldn't have protected you." Her tone sharpens. "Staying gave me access. It gave me leverage. It gave me a way to keep you alive."

Tears slide down my face and I can't wipe them away.

"You're sending me there." My voice breaks. "You're letting them take me."

Her jaw clenches. "You don't understand how close they are to deciding you aren't worth the trouble. There are men who think killing you would be easier. John barely kept that from happening."

"And you?" I ask. "What are you?"

She pauses.

"I'm the reason he argued for you." Her voice lowers. "I'm the reason you're not already dead."

A cold dread creeps up my spine. "What is Elliot's Manor?"

She pauses again. Just long enough to make me think she might actually change her mind.

"It's a place the Collective uses...For discipline."

"Discipline?"

Her gaze drops, then lifts again. "All I can tell you is this. You need to survive."

My voice cracks. "How the fuck am I supposed to survive?"

"You endure." She leans closer, eyes locking onto mine. "You don't provoke them. You don't challenge them. You don't test their pride. You make yourself useful....That's how you live through it."

The way she says it tells me she knows exactly what that means.

"You survive first." Her voice softens again. "You hate me later."

Tears slide down my face. The silence that follows is worse than shouting.

"Grant will be here soon." She steps back toward the door. "Get some rest."

She touches my arm once then she steps back and waits by the door until John calls her name from somewhere down the hall. She leaves without looking at me again.

The house goes silent.

My thoughts keep circling back to Seth. I try not to imagine him dead.

I don't sleep. My arms ache, my legs go numb. Every time the chair creaks, my heart jumps. I count breaths until I lose track.

Morning arrives without warning.

I hear a vehicle pull up outside the house. An engine cuts off. Car doors open and shut. Voices murmur somewhere beyond the walls.

Then the front door opens and footsteps cross the entryway.

They move through the house, down the hallway, getting closer with every step until they stop just outside the bedroom.

The door opens.

Grant steps into the room first, filling the doorway before walking fully inside. His eyes sweep the space once slowly, before settling on me. Still tied to the chair where they left me.

A small, satisfied smile touches his mouth.

John appears a second later behind him, lingering near the doorway instead of stepping fully into the room. Mary hovers in the hall.

Mary speaks first.

"John... please." Mary steps closer, her voice low. "Tell Grant to remind Elliot not to harm her."

John doesn't answer.

She moves another step in, fingers twisting together. "Please."

He exhales, jaw tightening, then shifts his attention to Grant.

"You will remind Elliot that she is not to be killed. Not to be harmed. No mysterious accidents."

Grant glances over his shoulder, one brow lifting.

"You talk about my brother as if he's a monster."

John meets his eyes. "He is."

A slow breath leaves Grant's nose, amusement flickering across his face.

"He'll make her obedient." His gaze drifts to me. "That much I can promise."

"Don't let him kill her." John's tone stays flat.

Grant tilts his head, studying him. "Protective. That's new."

John doesn't react.

Something in me snaps.

"Where's Seth?" I lunge forward as far as the restraints allow, the chair jerking violently. "Is he alive? Where is he?"

Grant turns toward me, unhurried.

"Someone is loud this morning."

Mary lingers just inside the doorway, hands clasped tight. She says nothing.

"Answer me," I shout. "Where the fuck is he?"

Grant crosses the room in two calm steps. He pulls a gag from his pocket and shoves it into my mouth. Leather presses hard against my teeth as he ties it tight behind my head until the corners of my lips burn.

"That's better. Women should be quiet when men are talking," he smirks.

Before I can react, John grabs the back of the chair and drags me across the floor. The legs scrape loudly over the wood as he hauls me out of the bedroom and into the hallway.

Mary follows behind them. She doesn't protest. She simply closes the bedroom door as we pass it.

Her voice comes again, thin and strained.

"John... please make sure she—"

"She'll survive," John cuts in. "She's strong. We raised her to be."

Something cold slides through my chest at that.

The tension between the men hangs heavy in the air. I don't know the full history of Grant and Elliot, but the way their names are spoken makes one thing clear.

Elliot is not someone people trust. He is someone people endure.

Two men step forward and cut the rope binding me to the chair. The tension snaps loose all at once, and my body pitches forward. My legs buckle the second the pressure releases, but they catch me before I hit the floor.

John steps in, grabbing my wrists. The cuffs dig into my skin as he unlocks them, the metal clicking open one after the other. He doesn't give me time to react before shoving my arms forward.

One of the men takes over immediately, snapping thick black zip ties tight around my wrists. Plastic bites into my skin as he yanks them smaller, tighter, until my fingers tingle. Another cinches one around my ankles. A third wraps around my waist, securing my wrists close to my body so I can't lift my arms more than a few inches.

Grant approaches me. I strain against the restraints until fire tears through my wrists. I scream behind the gag.

My vision blurs from the pressure of fighting. Hands lock me in place. I lean forward again, trying to force the words out, but Grant reaches into his coat and pulls out the hood. He slides it over my head and cinches it tight at my neck.

My breathing sounds too loud, trapped beneath the fabric. Panic creeps in despite my effort to control it.

They drag me out of the house, and cold morning air bites into my exposed skin. I am lifted into a vehicle and forced down onto the floor. The door slams shut, and the engine starts.

Time blurs into motion. I feel turns, stops, and uneven roads while sweat collects beneath the hood until the fabric clings to my face.

At some point the vehicle slows, and the engine drops into a low idle. Gravel crunches beneath the tires while doors open and close outside. Boots strike the ground, and voices drift in and out.

Hands grab me again.

They haul me upright and drag me forward. The ground shifts beneath my feet before smoothing out, and the air changes, cleaner, colder, more open.

Then I feel it.

The hollow echo of a large space and the overpowering scent of fuel.

They push me forward again.

My steps falter as they force me along, and then I am lifted and shoved into a seat. Straps snap tight across my body, locking me in place. A door slams shut, sealing me in.

For a moment, everything goes still.

Then a low rumble kicks on beneath me, deep and mechanical. It builds fast, the vibration spreading through the floor and into my spine. The seat hums under my body, the sound growing louder, heavier, until it fills the space around me.

The movement starts slow, then picks up. The pull drags me back against the seat as speed builds, the force pressing into my chest. The noise climbs with it, loud enough that I feel it in my teeth.

My grip tightens against the restraints.

The pressure shifts. The ground drops away. Weightlessness hits for half a second, just enough to make my stomach flip and my body tense against it.

We're not on the road anymore. We're in the air.

Grant reaches forward and rips the hood off my head.

Light burns my eyes as the inside of the private jet comes into focus. Leather seats line the narrow cabin, clean and polished in a way that makes everything feel wrong.

Grant sits across from me, relaxed, one arm draped over the back of the seat as if this is nothing more than a routine trip. He looks at me like a man unwrapping something he has waited a long time for.

I stare back without looking away. There is no fear left, only hate.

"Well, looks like good old Seth got you knocked up, huh?"

His eyes move over me slowly.

"I can't say I don't get it," he adds, his mouth curving. "You filled out real nice from that little twelve-year-old we used to watch."

Disgust crawls up my spine. I lean forward as far as the restraints allow and hold his stare.

He laughs.

"Yeah, you take after your mom. She had a great body too."

Something inside me fractures.

"If we had more time, I was planning to have some fun with her before Richard slit her throat." He shrugs. "I mean, I still could've. But the job was done. Your dad was dead. So we had to go."

I scream against the gag.

Grant tilts his head as if listening.

"What was that?"

He leans closer.

"I can't hear you."

He reaches forward and loosens the gag.

I don't hesitate. I spit straight into his eye.

He jerks back with a curse, wipes his face, and then laughs under his breath. He leans forward and spits at me. The saliva slides down my cheek, and I wipe it off on my shoulder without breaking eye contact.

"I'm warning you," he says quietly. "Don't piss me off."

He pulls out his phone and taps the screen. The glow lights his face as the call connects.

Grant angles the phone toward me.

Kristie Talbert, Nick's mother, the mayor, appears on the screen.

"You're on."

"Brooke Sinclair," her gaze drags over me slowly. "The little slut who thought she could touch my son."

I don't look away.

"We're almost there," Grant says. "Everything's arranged."

"Good," she replies. "I don't give a fuck what John told you. He doesn't have the money or the standing to pull rank. Not with me."

Grant chuckles softly.

"You killed my son," she continues. "You humiliated our family. You made us look weak."

Nick's face flashes in my mind, his weight pressing down on me, his voice in my ear, the way he laughed when he said he would split me open.

He had it coming.

"The Manor is the best punishment," she smiles. "I'm going to love watching you suffer."

Grant's grin widens.

"See you soon, Brooke" she murmurs. "I can't wait to see you break."

Grant ends the call.

Only then did the jet change, the vibration shifting as the nose dipped. The engine tone drops into a deeper grind. My stomach rolls with the descent.

I twist against the grip on my arms. The zip ties bit. My shoulders burn.

"What happens in Elliot's manor?" I ask.

Grant's mouth curves. "The only thing you need to know is you follow what he says."

My eyes burn. "Or what?"

Grant's gaze stays calm. "Men like us decide if you breathe or if you don't. We're gods. If I were you, Brooke, I'd fall in line."

Time stretches after that. The engine noise settles into a constant roar that fills the cabin while my body remains locked in place as the plane carries us farther away from anything familiar.

Grant shifts in his seat as if remembering something.

"Oh. I almost forgot."

His eyes move over me again, slower this time.

"Elliot likes his girls to look clean."

A faint smile touches his mouth.

"Obviously we can't do anything about all those tattoos right now. But we can at least get rid of the piercings."

Before I could lean away, he reaches forward and shoves the gag back into my mouth. The fabric forces my jaw open and presses against my tongue as he ties it tight behind my head. The pressure cut off any chance of speaking.

Then his hand comes up to my ear.

His fingers catch the first earring along the shell. He twists it free with quick, careless movements. The small piece of metal drops into his palm. He moves down the row without pause, unscrewing each one and pulling it out. The cold air brushes over the empty holes as he clears the last of them.

Grant rolls the little cluster of jewelry in his hand, studying it.

"Oh yeah," he looks back at me. "The footage my PI got."

His tone carries a thin edge of amusement.

"It also showed you have piercings in a few other places."

He grabs the front of my shirt and yanks the fabric down just far enough to expose my breasts. The movement is rough enough that my shoulders jerk forward.

Grant looks at the barbell through my left nipple.

"Thought so."

His fingers close around the metal.

He doesn't warn me. He doesn't slow down.

He twists the first ball loose in a quick, impatient turn. The metal shifts inside the piercing, dragging painfully through the tissue as he pulls the bar out. The sudden movement sends a sharp sting through my chest.

A muffled sound pushes against the gag as my body jerks against the restraints.

He drops the piece of jewelry into his palm with the others.

"Let's see the other one."

He grabs the fabric again and pulls it lower.

The jet rocks slightly as it cuts through the air, but Grant doesn't seem to notice. His fingers close around the second barbell.

Again he twists the end off quickly, careless with the angle. The metal catches as he pulls it free, sending another hot flare of pain through my nipple before it slides out.

He holds both pieces up for a second, turning them between his fingers like he was inspecting them.

He sighs, "shame we're about to land."

His hand returns to my chest before the words even finish leaving his mouth. His fingers close around my nipple and twist hard.

Pain rips through me.

My back jerks against the restraints as a muffled sound pushes against the gag. The movement only makes it worse. My breasts had already been swollen for days, heavy and sore from the pregnancy, my nipples tight and painfully sensitive even before he touched them. The pressure of his fingers sends a sharp, nauseating jolt straight through my chest.

Grant watches the reaction closely.

His eyes lift to mine.

A raw scream tears out of my chest, trapped behind the gag. The sound comes out strangled and furious, my body jerking against the restraints as rage surges through me. My teeth bite down hard into the fabric while the jet roars around us.

Grant doesn't react.

His fingers tighten again, grinding the sensitive skin before finally letting go.

"I could've had a lot more fun with you. But Elliot doesn't like sloppy seconds." His mouth lifts slightly. "He prefers to ruin them himself."

He leans back like the moment is over, like none of it matters.

The engine pitch shifts under us. The steady roar dips lower, the vibration changing as the plane starts to descend. My body tilts forward slightly against the restraints, pressure building in my ears. The movement turns uneven, subtle drops and corrections as we cut through the air.

Then the landing hits.

The impact slams up through the seat and into my spine, hard enough to jar my teeth. The wheels screech briefly against the runway before the plane stabilizes, still moving fast but grounded now. The roar fades into a lower rumble as we slow, the vibration easing in waves beneath me.

The engine idles low, steady now. A latch clicks somewhere behind me. Then the cabin door opens and cold air floods in.

I barely get a second to process it before the hood is dragged back over my head, sealing me in darkness again.

Rough hands grab me. They haul me out of the seat and push me forward. My boots hit metal first, then shift to narrow steps. I stumble as they drag me down, the angle steep, their grip the only thing keeping me upright.

Wind cuts through my clothes. I feel gravel under my feet.

They don't slow. They pull me across uneven ground, stones shifting and crunching with every step.

A car door opens.

I'm shoved forward and forced down onto the floor again, my shoulder slamming into something hard as the door shuts behind me.

The engine starts. The second drive feels shorter but rougher, with fewer turns and longer stretches of silence that press in around me.

When the vehicle finally stops, no one speaks.

The door opens, hands pull me out again. My boots hit the ground, and the air feels different here, colder and heavier.

"Come on."

They haul me forward. Even through the hood, I feel it before I see it. Then the hood is ripped off.

The building stands in front of me.

Dark stone stretches upward. Rain slicks the walls, turning them black and reflective. Tall pines crowd close on every side, cutting off the horizon and swallowing any sense of escape.

Only a few small windows glow, their yellow light weak against the mass of shadow swallowing the rest of the structure. Most of the house is dark, its shape fractured into wings and towers that suggest too many rooms and not enough ways out.

Grant smirks. "This is Elliot's Manor."

The doors open. They haul me inside. And the darkness closes around me.

I already know I won't leave here the same.

Chapter 4
Brooke

The men drag me through the front doors, and the inside of the manor is nothing like the outside. Black and white marble gleams beneath my feet, reflecting the chandelier overhead in broken shards of light. Gold trim lines the walls. A sweeping staircase curves up through the center of the foyer, with dark banisters polished to a shine. Everything looks expensive, pristine, carefully placed. It should feel beautiful. Instead it makes my skin crawl.

They haul me deeper inside and into a study. Dark wood shelves climb from floor to ceiling, packed with books in perfect rows. The desk is broad and polished, the leather chair behind it untouched.

They force me into a straight-backed chair facing the desk. The zip ties stay tight around my wrists. One of the men yanks them once more, testing the tension until the plastic bites deeper into my skin, then steps back.

Grant stands near the doorway.

"Outside," he tells the others.

They all file out without argument, Grant smirks as he follows them out. The door closes with a firm click.

I look around the room.

The desk, a leather blotter, a closed laptop, a heavy glass paperweight. A fountain pen resting in a holder. My eyes lock on it for a second. The metal tip is sharp enough to stab. But not strong enough to cut through industrial plastic.

I scan lower.

No scissors in sight. No letter opener within reach. The drawers are closed tight. Behind the desk, a glass-front cabinet displays nothing but rows of books.

My gaze moves to the corners of the room. A bar cart stands against one wall. Crystal decanter. Glass tumblers. No corkscrew visible from here.

Think Brooke.

The bookshelf to my left has decorative bookends made of solid metal. If I could reach one. If I could get close enough to grind the plastic against an edge.

I keep scanning. Nothing loose. Nothing I can use to escape.

Their voices continue outside, clear through the wood, and I force myself to listen while my eyes keep moving, cataloging every object, every surface, every possibility.

Grant speaks first. “She’s pregnant.”

There's a pause.

Then a voice answers. “And?”

“So John wants you to be careful with her,” Grant replies.

A soft sound follows, almost a breath of amusement.

Grant continues, “John said don’t kill her. No permanent damage. Discipline her if you have to. But don’t kill her.”

“John says?” the voice repeats.

“Yes.”

Another pause.

“And Kristie?” the voice asks.

Grant lets out a quiet laugh.

“She doesn’t believe John has the standing to override her,” Grant adds. “Her words, not mine.”

A faint shift, like someone leaning back against the wall. “So whose request am I supposed to follow?”

Grant sighs. “That’s up to you.”

The voice responds. “You know me. I make my own rules.”

“I know,” Grant says. “Which is why I’m telling you. Kristie will contact you soon.”

there's a brief pause.

“Don’t do anything too extreme before she calls,” Grant finishes. “She wants to see it.”

A low hum of acknowledgment answers him.

"I'll decide what we do with her for now," the voice says.

Grant's footsteps begin to retreat down the hall. "I figured you would. Have fun brother."

The space outside the study goes quiet. A single set of slow footsteps approaches the door. I straighten in the chair as much as the zip ties allow. My pulse hammers in my ears. The handle turns. The door opens.

A tall man walks in. His posture is relaxed, and his expression is calm. His hair is sandy blond. He wears a light-colored polo and pressed pants. His face is clean-shaven. His movements are polished and relaxed. He looks like he comes from old money. He closes the door behind him and looks at me as if he is examining a new object.

"You're Brooke," he says. "It's nice to finally meet you."

I keep my eyes on him.

"I'm Elliot, I run the Manor. I want you to understand this clearly. The Manor is a safe place. I'm here to watch over you and guide you through your stay."

He speaks gently.

"You'll meet my colleagues who live here," he adds. "They help me maintain structure."

He opens the door and steps to the side. Three people stand waiting in the hallway. The first steps forward. He is tall and lean, with light brown hair slicked neatly back from a high forehead. His face is narrow, almost boyish, with pronounced cheekbones and a mouth pulled into an eager, unsettling smile that shows too many teeth.

"Hey, I'm Knox," his tone is friendly, but it sounds forced.

The next is a young woman with dark hair pulled high into a tight knot, a single braid falling over her shoulder. She wears a fitted black top and black slacks. Her makeup is flawless, dark liner sharpens her green eyes, and her lipstick is a deep muted red. She looks over me before she speaks.

"Hi, I'm Sophie." Her smile is restrained, professional, and cool. "I'll help you settle in."

The last man steps into view. He has a buzz cut and a thick, muscular build. His posture is relaxed, shoulders loose, head slightly angled as if he is listening more than watching. His expression holds a faint, unreadable calm, neither friendly nor hostile.

"I'm Asher," he says.

All three watch me, but none of them show open hostility. Their politeness feels fake, like they have been taught to greet people this way.

"They're here to assist you," Elliot explains. "You'll learn the routine. Everything is scheduled. Once you understand the structure, your days will feel predictable."

A guard approaches the doorway. "Her room is ready."

Elliot nods. "Good. We'll take her there now."

He looks back at me with the same light expression. Nothing in his voice carries threat. Everything about him feels designed to appear calm and approachable.

"You've had a long trip," Elliot murmurs. "It's best to get you settled."

Knox steps to my left, and Asher steps to my right. Sophie walks just ahead of us. Elliot leads the way through the hall at a comfortable pace, as if this is a tour instead of a transfer. I follow because the restraints give me no other choice.

"I want you to feel comfortable here. If you follow the routine, everything will run smoothly."

Nothing in his tone reveals what Grant warned him about. Nothing in his expression shows anything violent. But something in him doesn't sit right, and I can't ignore it.

The guard opens the door and guides me inside. The room looks nothing like a cell. The walls are painted a soft neutral color. There's a large window with curtains pulled open to show the courtyard lights below. A small dresser stands against the wall. A matching desk sits in the corner with a bottle of water already placed on top. A rug covers most of the floor. The lighting is soft and warm. The bed looks comfortable with a thick blanket and two pillows arranged neatly at the headboard. Everything looks expensive and neat.

That makes me more nervous.

The guard comes behind me and cuts the restraints. I rub at my wrists with numb, clumsy hands, trying to soothe the sting. It only makes the bruises flare. My limbs feel both too light and too heavy, shaky in a way that makes me furious.

The door locks behind them. I sit on the bed and keep my hands in my lap. My mind spins. I last about ten seconds before the tears come.

I press my palm to my mouth, but the sob pushes through anyway. My chest aches. My throat tightens. I fold over and cry into the blanket. Everything hits at once. The terror. The confusion. The ride here. The restraints. John's words. Mary's. The Collective. Grant. Elliot. All of it.

But nothing hits harder than the thought of Seth.

I cry until my eyes burn. I cry until my head throbs. I hold my stomach because the pain there scares me. I think about the life that Seth and I created. I think about him never being able to meet our child. I think about him dying in that ballroom.

If he is dead, I have nothing left to lose.

That breaks me again. I curl on the bed with the blanket clutched in my hands. The room stays silent. The walls give me no sound, no hint of anything outside. Time drags. My body shakes. My breathing keeps slipping out of control. I try to slow it, but the grief stays heavy. My chest hurts. My stomach tightens in waves.

Hours pass like minutes. I barely move. When the knock finally comes, it startles me so badly I almost fall off the bed.

I wipe my face with the blanket. "Yes," I whisper.

The door opens. Sophie stands there with a fitted red silk dress folded neatly in her arms. Her expression looks friendly at first glance, but something in her eyes doesn't match it.

"It's time for dinner."

My voice barely works. "I need a minute."

"You don't have a minute." She interjects. "You need to change."

I stand slowly. My legs feel weak. My face is still wet, but Sophie acts like she doesn't notice. She hands me the red silk dress. I change with her waiting inside the room. She watches without discomfort. She watches like it's routine.

When I finish, she steps back and looks me over. "Good. Come with me."

Asher and Knox stand outside the door. Asher gestures for me to walk ahead of him. Knox gives me a calm nod, as if this is normal.

We walk to the dining room. The table is long. The plates are set. The lighting is warm. Elliot sits at the head of the table with a small smile that looks practiced.

"Brooke, join us."

I sit slowly. Sophie sits beside me. Knox sits on my other side. Asher takes the seat across. Elliot raises his hand slightly, and a servant enters with a tray of steaming food. He places plates in front of us with quiet movements. Roasted chicken. Vegetables. Bread. Water. My body reacts before my mind does. My stomach cramps with hunger.

Elliot notices. "Eat, Brooke. You need it."

I pick up the fork. My hands still tremble, but I eat. My body pulls everything in fast. I try to slow myself, but hunger takes over. I breathe through the tightness in my chest and keep going.

Sophie pours water into my glass.

Knox leans back in his chair and takes a sip from his cup. "We were just talking earlier about tomorrow's schedule. Breakfast at seven. Tasks at eight. Outside work if the weather stays clear."

Asher nods. "If not, indoor rotation."

Elliot smiles slightly. "You won't be expected to do anything strenuous yet. Your first few days are for observation."

I swallow hard. "Observation for what?"

"For how you adjust."

Their table manners are perfect. Their voices stay relaxed. It creates a false calm that makes my skin crawl.

Sophie tilts her head. "You should know that we eat together every night. It helps with discipline. It also keeps everyone accountable."

"Accountable for what?" I ask.

That earns a short laugh from Knox. "You'll learn."

Asher cuts into his chicken. "We have fun here...You'll see."

Fun. The word feels wrong.

Elliot rests his hands on the table. "Brooke, I want this transition to be smooth. You aren't exactly a prisoner. You're a participant."

I hold his stare. "I didn't volunteer to be here."

"You're right," he chuckles. "But you're here now so why not make the best of it?"

My palms grow sweaty. I force myself to breathe evenly and eat more.

Sophie speaks again. "There are house rules, but nothing unreasonable."

I glance at the television mounted on the wall. "Can we watch the news?"

There has to be coverage by now. The Everspring Hotel massacre. 50 something people dead. A public tragedy. A bloodbath. If Seth is still alive, I'll see it in a headline.

If he isn't, I'll know that too.

Elliot shakes his head. "No. Not tonight."

"Why?"

"Because tonight is about us," he says. "We are getting to know you. And you're getting to know us. The outside world doesn't matter right now."

He sets the drink down and picks up the remote. "How about some music instead?"

He clicks it once.

"Goodbye Horses" by Q Lazzarus starts playing over the speakers—smooth, eerie, and instantly unsettling. I know this song. *Silence of the Lambs*. The skin suit scene. They are playing it on purpose. My skin crawls, heart pounding harder with every note, like the room is closing in, like someone is watching and waiting for me to break.

The door opens.

A guard enters and leans down to whisper something in Elliot's ear. Elliot nods, eyes still on me.

"Bring tonight's entertainment."

The guard leaves without a word.

Knox turns slightly in his seat, studying me. "So John. He's not your blood uncle, is he?"

I shake my head once.

He smirks. "Figured."

Sophie leans in, elbows on the table. "I heard he trained you. What kind of training was it?"

I don't respond.

Asher grins. "Was it combat? Or something more... personal?"

The implication is foul. Revulsion crawls through me as I understand exactly what he means. John never touched me like that, but he still fed me to monsters. That line barely matters in a place like this.

None of them look away. That is when I know they aren't asking to learn. They are asking to see how much I will tolerate.

That's when I make my decision.

I push my chair back slowly, careful not to give them the satisfaction of panic. The scrape of wood against tile echoes too loud in the room.

Sophie arches an eyebrow, amused. "Where are you going?"

"I need to go to the bathroom," I say flatly, even as my pulse roars in my ears.

Knox's chair creaks. "We'll take you."

I turn and run.

Chair legs shriek behind me. Someone shouts my name, but no one follows. Their footsteps don't pound behind me. All I hear behind me is the sound of quiet laughter.

They aren't chasing me. They're enjoying the show.

I sprint into the hallway, legs already shaking. My shoes slip slightly on the tile, but adrenaline keeps me moving. I turn the first corner blindly, no destination in mind—just escape. Every door I pass is closed, identical, unmarked.

Somewhere behind me, echoing through unseen speakers, "Goodbye Horses" is still playing. It follows me through the halls.

I run harder.

The hall stretches long and sterile. I turn again and find another corridor. I don't know where I'm going, I only know that I can't stop.

Then I see the door. It is heavier than the others, framed in metal. I grab the handle and yank. It opens with a groan. The door swings inward, and I freeze.

And it is covered in blood.

The smell hits me first. Then the details follow. A severed leg on the floor. A hand near the dresser. The sheets soaked through, red, wet and clinging to the mattress like glue. A girl's head—mouth open, eyes wide, rests crooked on the pillow like some fucked-up display.

Then a girl half-naked, bruised, bleeding, stumbles forward from the far side of the room. Her wrists are shredded, skin hanging in strips where restraints have torn her open. Her body is shaking, chest heaving. She barely looks at me before crashing into my shoulder and shoving past.

I stumble back, hit the wall, barely keeping upright as she runs. I want to go after her. I can't move. I stand there, breathing hard, bile rising in my throat, vision swimming. I can't look away from the bed. From the head. From the way her mouth is still open like she died mid-scream.

I recover and follow, half from instinct, half from the sick realization that if she knows the way out, I have to stay close. Her footsteps pound against the tile. Blood drips behind her. She nearly slips twice but doesn't stop. The hallway opens ahead.

And there it is. An exit door. A real one. Metal bar across the center. Narrow window near the top. Freedom.

She sees it and lets out a ragged sound, something between a sob and a gasp and sprints faster. I chase her, breath ripping out of my lungs, chest aching. I'm only a few feet behind. I can see her hand reaching for the bar. She pushes it.

A mechanical click echoes above us.

I don't understand the sound until I look up. A mounted shotgun drops from the ceiling. It snaps into position directly above her head.

It fires.

Her head comes apart in a violent bloom of meat and bone. The force flings her backward. Blood sheets across the walls and ceiling, spattering the lights. Wet heat slaps my face. Grit hits my cheek. A chunk of skull skips across the tile and spins to a stop near my foot.

Her body hits the floor hard. One leg jerks, then another, then nothing. Blood pours out fast, pooling under her.

A scream rips out of me. I drop to my knees and my hands sink into it, coating my palms and wrists. The smell, iron and flesh scorched, thick enough to taste.

My stomach heaves. My body shakes so hard I can't push myself up. I stay there, staring at the space where her face had been.

Guards appear from both ends of the hallway. One kneels beside her body. Another begins collecting fragments of her skull. A third brings a bin.

I stare as they sweep up pieces of her, mop her blood off the walls, zip her into a black body bag like it is just another part of the routine.

Elliot strolls into view. Sophie, Knox, and Asher follow. All three look relaxed and unbothered. Like they have seen this before.

"Damn," Knox chuckles. "There goes tonight's entertainment."

Elliot stops in front of me. I am still on the floor. Blood is smeared across my face. My dress is soaked. I can't stop shaking. He looks down at what is left of the girl, then back at me.

He sighs. "This is what happens when people don't follow the rules."

I stare at him, chest heaving, tears burning down my face.

He smiles.

"Welcome to the Manor."

Chapter 5
Brooke

The water hits my skin and runs red in thick streams.

I stand under the showerhead with both hands pressed to the tile. The blood on me doesn't move easily. It clings to my arms, my neck, my chest, and the front of the dress I've peeled off. My chest feels tight. Every inhale scrapes the back of my throat.

I scrub my arms until my skin burns, but pieces of her still stay on me. My hair is stiff with dried blood. I run my fingers through it, trying to untangle the knots, but something catches between my fingers. I pull it free.

A tooth sits in my palm.

It is small and white with blood around the root. My breath rips out of me. I drop it into the shower floor and watch the water push it toward the drain. My stomach lurches so hard I have to grip the wall to stay upright.

My vision blurs. The ringing in my ears gets louder. I wipe my face again, but more blood smears across my cheek. My hands shake so badly I can't hold the soap.

I fold to the tile and press my forehead to it, skin burning against the cold. Water runs over my spine, but none of it matters. I can't stop seeing Seth. Couldn't stop thinking about what was growing inside me. Whether this level of fear could hurt it. My palms press against my stomach.

This place is built to overwhelm people just long enough to kill them. That won't be me.

I wipe my face and breathe through the adrenaline still crawling up my neck. I don't need everything to make sense right now. I need one opening. If I can separate them, I can dismantle them. If I can turn their confidence against them, I can get out of this.

The bathroom door opens without warning.

Sophie steps inside and pauses, her gaze moving over me like she is assessing damage.

"Wow," she tsks. "You really went for it."

I keep washing, dragging my hands over my arms like I can scrub it all off if I just keep going.

She moves farther in, heels clicking against the tile.

"You know," she goes on, "most people don't even make it after breaking rule one."

I swallow hard. "Can I finish washing?"

She doesn't answer.

Instead, she cuts the water off. Before I can react, her hand wraps around my arm and yanks me forward. My feet slip against the tile as she drags me out from under the shower.

"Stop. Please—"

"You already took more time than the girl before you," Sophie says flatly. "You get nothing."

My knees buckle slightly when she lets go. I catch myself against the wall, my hand slamming against the sink to stay upright. Pain pulses under my ribs as I try to steady my breathing.

Sophie straightens, her expression shifting back into something bored.

"Get dressed. Elliot wants to meet with you in the study."

She turns and walks out.

I stand there for a second, dripping water onto the floor, my body still shaking as the cold settles into my skin.

I grab a towel, and wrap it tight around my body before stepping into the bedroom.

Sophie stands near the bed with a dress draped over her arm. She holds it away from herself like it offends her.

"You destroyed the other one," she sighs. "Do you know how irritating it is to scrub blood out of silk?"

She shoves the dress into my hands.

"Put it on."

I pull it over my head.

The fabric stretches tight across my chest, pressing painfully against my breasts that feel heavy and sore. The fit clings in ways I can't hide.

Sophie notices immediately.

Her gaze drags over me, taking its time. "Hmm, Elliot's going to clock that the second you step inside."

Heat climbs up my neck.

She smiles. "He has a habit of breaking things that stand out. And right now, you stand out."

I turn away to adjust the hem.

"Hurry," Sophie says. "You already wasted enough time crying in the shower."

I smooth the dress down with shaking hands. Sophie leans against the wall, arms crossed, watching me with open contempt.

"Let's go."

A knock hits the door. Sophie opens it. Knox and Asher stand in the hall. Both look at me the way someone looks at an animal that needs training.

Knox smirks. "You clean up fast."

Asher's eyes stay on my face. "Move. He's waiting."

They escort me down a staircase I hadn't seen earlier. The Manor feels larger at night. The hallways are colder, the lights dimmer. Every step I take feels heavier as they lead me toward a room with double wooden doors.

Sophie opens one door and gestures for me to enter. Elliot stands inside, leaning against the desk with both hands rested on the edge. He looks calm, collected, and freshly showered. Not a drop of blood anywhere on him.

"Brooke, come in."

I step inside. My feet feel unsteady. My throat still burns from earlier. Knox, Asher, and Sophie line up behind me, silent. Elliot stays focused on me.

"We need to talk about what happened...Sit."

I sit in the chair across from him.

He studies my face for a long moment, then nods slightly.

"You can't escape this. Running is not allowed. Opening unauthorized doors is not allowed. Approaching exits is not allowed."

His tone is slow and stern, each line delivered with the patience of someone lecturing a stubborn child.

"What happened tonight should make that very fucking clear."

I clench my hands in my lap. "You told me I'd be safe."

He lifts his gaze to mine.

"I said the Manor is safe," he chuckles. "No one in and no one out."

My stomach drops.

He continues. "The woman you saw tonight broke three rules. The Manor responded. It will respond the same way every damn time."

My jaw tightens. "What did she do?"

Elliot tilts his head slightly. "She made a choice. Choices have consequences here."

I swallow hard. My hands tremble again.

He leans forward, resting his elbows on his knees. "If you attempt to run again, or break the rules, the result will be worse."

Knox lets out a soft laugh. Sophie smiles. Asher shifts his weight, watching me closely.

My heart pounds, but I force the words out anyway. "I don't know the rules."

"I'll tell you now," Elliot says.

I hold his stare.

He stands slowly, pushing off the desk with both hands. His posture shifts, and the room feels smaller as he steps in front of me.

"There are three rules," he continues.

Elliot raises one finger. "You do not try to escape."

A second. "You follow the instructions you are given, exactly as they are given."

A third. "And you do not try to fight us. Ever."

His eyes stay on mine. His voice stays calm, which makes it worse.

"You break any of those," Elliot adds, "and the response will be immediate. You saw the first example tonight. That wasn't even the harshest outcome we have."

A tremor runs through me.

He leans down just enough that I have to look up at him. "Do you understand what I'm saying?"

I nod.

"Use your words, Brooke."

"I understand."

He steps back. "Good. Tonight, your initiation begins. You will follow what we say, when we say it. And you won't test boundaries again."

He gives a small nod toward Knox.

"Knox will take you to your room. We'll call for you when we're ready."

Knox steps forward and grabs my arm. His grip is tight and unyielding, a silent reminder that I have no control here. Asher opens the door. Sophie follows behind me calm and composed, as if this is just another routine part of the night.

Elliot watches me leave with the same casual smile on his face, completely at ease, like he is commenting on the weather instead of delivering a threat.

The study doors click shut, and Knox steps in close behind me, his mouth near my ear.

"You better follow every rule in this house," he murmurs. "Or you end up just like the last girl."

Asher lets out a low chuckle.

Knox shoves me through the open door and slams it shut behind me without a second thought.

I lean back against the wall, too exhausted to move, too on edge to sit down. Every part of me feels stripped bare.

I can't stop thinking about the girl who ran. I can still see her face before the shot went off. I can still hear the sound of her body hitting the ground.

And then there's that room.

The severed limbs. The head on the bed. The blood that painted everything like it was done with intention. It isn't random. It is staged. It is meant to shock, to unnerve, to leave fear inside me.

Now I understand exactly what kind of people I am dealing with. They aren't just dangerous. They are methodical, cruel, and sadistic. They don't want me scared, they want me broken.

Whatever this initiation involves, I know it will not end with them earning my loyalty. It will end with them trying to destroy every part of me. And I have no idea how much of myself they plan to take.

I take a seat on the edge of the bed with my palms pressed into the mattress, forcing myself to stay upright.

The exhaustion runs deeper than muscle or bone. My limbs feel heavy, my thoughts slow and thick, like I'm moving through water.

My hand slides to my stomach before I can stop it. I still don't know how far along I am. I don't know if it has been days or weeks. All I know is that fear has been living in my body nonstop, and the stress feels relentless. I can't stop thinking about whether all of this is already hurting the baby.

I keep trembling. The movement is small but constant, a quiet shaking in my hands and legs that I can't control.

Seth's voice cuts through my head. He always said to find something, anything to use to fight.

I push myself to my feet and search the room. The space is intentionally stripped of options. There are no loose objects. There are no cords. There is no exposed metal. The lamp on the dresser is the only thing with enough weight to matter. I grab it and pull hard.

It doesn't move.

I yank again, panic flaring when I feel the resistance. The base stays fixed in place.

It is bolted down.

I move into the bathroom. The toilet lid is secured tightly to the base. I try anyway, fingers straining until my knuckles ache. It doesn't shift.

My eyes lift to the mirror.

My heart begins to race. I grab a towel and wrap it around my hand, folding it tight. I raise my fist, jaw clenched, bracing myself for the impact and the pain that will follow.

Then the bedroom door opens.

I freeze.

I drop the towel and step back just as a guard fills the doorway. His face is blank, almost bored, like I am an errand he has already completed a dozen times.

"It's time to go. Elliot wants you for your initiation. Come now."

My stomach drops so hard that my vision swims.

He doesn't wait for a response. His hand closes around my arm and drags me forward. I stumble but stay upright. I don't fight him. Not yet at least.

As we move through the manor, the sounds reach me before I see anything. Low moans echo through the halls, broken by wet, choking noises and laughter. Asher's laugh carries easily. Knox's voice follows, amused and cruel. Elliot's tone sounds calm and pleased.

The door opens into a game room flooded with harsh, unforgiving light that leaves nothing to the imagination. A pool table sits in the center like a stage.

Sophie is on her back, stretched across it, her bare legs spread wide, her body tense but responsive, her breath coming fast and uneven. The bruises on her skin don't slow her down. They seem to fuel her. Her back arches higher when Elliot stands between her thighs, his hands locked around her hips, holding her open while he thrusts into her with force. She meets him every time, gasping, her mouth parting in sounds that are not pain.

Knox stands at her head, his fingers twisted into her hair, guiding her mouth exactly where he wants it. His cock fills her mouth, her lips stretched around him as he sets the pace, using her throat without restraint. One hand stays tight in her hair while the other moves over her chest, squeezing her breasts, pinching her nipples until her body reacts sharply and she moans around him.

Asher stands close at her side, his pants undone, his cock hard in his hand. He guides Sophie's wrist, showing her how fast, how tight, how to stroke him exactly the way he wants. She follows without resistance.

Sophie isn't fighting them. She is leaning into it. Her body moves with theirs, her pleasure obvious in the way she spreads her legs wider for Elliot and hollows her cheeks for Knox. This is control given and taken by choice. A shared language of dominance and submission that they all understand.

And standing there, watching, I realize this isn't meant to shock me alone. It is meant to show me what kind of initiation they believe in, and exactly how far they expect me to go.

Asher shifts first. He steps back and trades places with Elliot without breaking the rhythm of the room. Elliot steps back, giving space as Asher moves in behind her.

Asher grabs Sophie's hips and drags her forward, folding her over the edge of the pool table, her chest pressed to the felt table, her back arched.

He reaches for a pool stick resting along the table's edge. He angles it against her ass and pushes it inside her with a rough, steady force.

Sophie cries out, her fingers gripping the table as her body reacts. Her hips press back against him instead of pulling away, breath breaking as she adjusts, spine curving deeper as he sets the pace, keeping her exactly where he wants her.

Elliot turns away from her and walks toward me.

His cock in his hand, his expression relaxed, almost amused. "You ready to join?"

I can't answer. My mouth won't work as I try to process what I'm witnessing. Fear locks my jaw in place, and my pulse roars so loudly I can barely hear anything else.

"This is how women survive the manor," Elliot says calmly. "You give us what we want, and you stay comfortable."

His hand brushes over my chest, his fingers grazing the curve of my breasts through the silk. My body reacts before my mind can stop it, and I flinch hard, stepping back.

He smiles wider. "You've got some nice tits. I'm going to have a lot of fun with you."

I shake my head, breath coming fast and shallow.

"I don't rape," Elliot says, his tone almost bored. "Look at me. Does it look like I need to beg for pussy?"

He steps closer again. "It is in your best interest to meet our needs if you want your stay here to be as pleasant as it can be."

I swallow, my throat tight, and shake my head again. "No."

He laughs softly. "Really?" His eyes flick over me with open contempt. "I thought you'd be more of a cock-hungry slut. I saw the videos of you and Seth. I figured you'd be desperate by now, especially since your boyfriend is probably dead."

The words knock the air out of my lungs. I gasp despite myself.

Elliot strokes himself slowly as he watches my face. "Last chance to make yourself useful, I promise you won't like the alternative."

I weigh everything in a split second. Fear, survival, Seth, the baby, my own body. Then I shake my head again. "No."

Elliot chuckles, "Suit yourself."

He turns, opens the door, and calls to the guard to bring in another woman. Then he walks back to the pool table like nothing has happened.

Sophie is fully open now, riding Asher as he sits back against the table, his hands gripping her thighs. Elliot positions himself behind her and pushes into her asshole, filling her completely while Knox moves to her mouth. Knox shoves himself deep between her lips, thrusting until her throat strains around him. She gags and chokes, tears spilling from her eyes, but she doesn't pull away. Knox groans and comes hard, holding her head in place until he is finished.

The guard returns with another woman. She is shaking so badly her knees nearly buckle. Her eyes are wide with terror.

Elliot stays inside Sophie as he looks over his shoulder. "Take Brooke back to her room."

The guard grabs my arm and pulls me away.

As I am dragged out, I lock eyes with the terrified woman being pushed inside. The door closes between us, and the sounds swallow her whole.

The guard doesn't say a word as he drags me back down the hall. His grip stays tight on my arm, fingers pressing into my skin like he wants to leave a mark. I stumble once on the carpet runner and he yanks harder, like I have done it on purpose. When we reach my room, he opens the door and shoves me inside without slowing down.

I hit the floor hard, my knees slamming the wood. The door shuts behind me with a heavy thud, followed by the unmistakable click of the lock sliding into place.

I stay there for a second, frozen.

Then I hear it.

Screaming.

It's her. The woman who has taken my place.

The sound is high and panicked, pure horror tearing out of her throat. And I know without question, that it is coming from the game room. From the pool table. From the men who didn't get what they wanted from me.

Another scream follows, this one cracked and gurgled, like it has been ripped apart in the middle. Then something heavy hits the floor. The room spins, and my stomach turns over hard. I stagger to my feet and clutch the edge of the dresser for balance.

And it hits me.

The room with the severed head. The limbs. The blood smeared like someone had tried to crawl out. The woman who ran past me and got her head blown off. Those weren't just horrors meant to shock me.

They are messages.

Those were the women they no longer had use for.

The only comfort I have is the thought of Seth's arms around me. The warmth of his skin, the weight of his body trying to shield mine. My heart kicks hard.

No. I can't go there. I can't believe he's gone.

I swallow the panic down like poison. Seth is stronger than that. He has to be.

My hand presses against my stomach again. If I lose him... if this baby is all I have left of him... I won't let anything happen to it. Even if I had been unsure before, even if the timing terrified me, the thought of losing both of them makes it feel like there would be nothing left of me at all.

If Seth is alive, he will come for me. He always has.

But for now, I can't count on anyone but myself. I wipe my face with the heel of my hand and force myself to breathe.

I won't let them break me.

Not for The Collective.

Not for anyone.

Chapter 6
Brooke

I wake up before the sun.

The door snaps open, the lights flip on, and Asher's voice cuts through whatever fragile sleep I've managed to fall into.

"Get up."

I'm hauled to my feet and marched through the halls, still half-dizzy, still feeling the fear from the screams I heard last night.

The Manor grounds are freezing. Morning fog hangs low across the yard, blurring the treeline into a gray smear. Dew soaks the grass under my bare feet. My breath puffs clouds in the air. Knox, Asher, and Sophie surround me like I'm a prisoner on display.

Elliot waits in the center of the yard. His hands are tucked behind his back, his posture relaxed, as if this is a morning yoga class and not whatever fresh hell they have dragged me out here for.

"Bring him," Elliot says.

The back door opens, and two men drag someone out into the yard, a man I have never seen before. His shirt hangs in shreds from his shoulders, soaked through and clinging to his skin. His face is badly swollen, one eye nearly sealed shut, his mouth split and dark with dried blood crusted along his jaw. Deep purple bruises spread across his ribs and trail down his arms in ugly patterns. Each breath comes out of him with a harsh rattle.

He looks barely conscious until they shove him down onto his knees.

Then his eyes fly open. Panic tears across his expression as if a switch has been flipped. He tries to stand, but his strength fails him, and he pitches forward into the wet grass, palms slipping as he claws for balance.

"Please," he gasps, voice breaking. "Please, don't do this. I'll do anything. I swear."

His voice cracks in terror.

Sophie watches with disinterest. Knox and Asher smile. Elliot doesn't react at all. He steps forward, pulls something from behind his back, and holds it out to me.

A gun.

My stomach drops.

"Brooke," Elliot says softly. "Shoot him in the head."

The man sobs. He presses his forehead to the dirt, whispering please over and over like a prayer.

I glare at Elliot. "No."

Elliot's face doesn't change. "So you're not following the rules?"

"I'm not killing him." My voice shakes, but the words come out anyway.

"I'll only ask one more time," Elliot extends the gun again. "Shoot him."

My fingers curl. My brain screams. The man begs harder, crawling toward me on shaking elbows, leaving streaks of red in the grass.

I step back. Sophie grabs my shoulder to keep me from retreating farther.

Elliot shouts. "Now!"

My hand feels like it doesn't belong to me as I reach for it.

I lift it with trembling hands, pointing it toward the man who is begging for his life. His eyes are wild. His breath hitches between sobs. Every inch of him pleads.

My vision blurs.

Elliot watches me with that unreadable calm, like he is grading a test I am destined to fail.

My finger hovers over the trigger.

I shift the gun away from the man and turn it on Elliot.

His brows lift the slightest bit.

"Brooke," Sophie hisses behind me.

I ignore her. I aim right between Elliot's eyes and pull the trigger.

Click.

Nothing.

I pull it again.

Click.

My stomach drops. I pull it again, frantic now, desperate—

Click.

Empty.

Of course.

Elliot steps closer, taking the barrel of the gun with two fingers and lowering it like I'm a child holding a dangerous toy incorrectly. He holds it loosely at his side.

Then with the same steady posture, he reaches behind his back with his other hand and pulls out a second gun. Black metal catching the gray morning light.

The kneeling man sees it and wails, his voice shredding itself in panic. "No—no, please, please, I'll—"

Elliot doesn't let him finish.

He aims and fires.

The shot cracks across the yard like lightning. The man's body snaps backward, collapsing into the wet grass. His blood spreads fast, mixing with dew, turning the ground into mud.

My ears ring, Knox grins, Asher wipes his boots in the grass and Sophie just watches me.

Elliot finally looks up from the corpse and meets my eyes with terrifying calm. Then he steps in close. Close enough that I feel the warmth of the gun he has just used. He lifts the empty pistol I tried to fire and taps the barrel lightly against my chin.

"Now," his tone lowers, "you've broken Rule Two."

My throat locks.

"You didn't follow instructions."

His voice isn't angry. It is clinical and precise. As if this is just data for him. Brooke Sinclair: noncompliant, defiant, requires correction. He lets the cold barrel slide down from my chin to my collarbone before lowering it completely.

"You won't like the consequences," he adds.

And behind him, the dead man lies facedown in the grass, punishment for a rule I hadn't even known existed yesterday. Now I am about to learn mine.

"Oh and by the way," Elliot smirks. "No one is coming for you. You're ours now. Grant just confirmed a few hours ago, Seth is dead."

Chapter 7
Brooke

Dead.

Dead?

No.

The word detonates in my skull, relentless and brutal, stripping everything. It doesn't make sense. It doesn't stop. My lungs fight for air, but nothing moves right. My thoughts scatter like broken glass.

Seth is gone?

Knox's hand clamps around my arm before I can get a full breath. I don't even register the pain, just the rush of panic swallowing me whole. A sound escapes my mouth, wrecked and desperate.

No. No. No.

This can't be happening. He can't be gone. Seth can't be—

Knox yanks me forward. My body folds, overtaken by grief so violent it shatters my control. Sobs tear out of me in waves.

"Move," Knox snaps, dragging me when I can't keep up.

Tears blur everything. My head spins. The corpse Elliot left on the grass lies behind us. But all I can see is Seth bleeding, lifeless.

"No—no—no—" I choke on the words as they break apart in my mouth. They aren't even words anymore, just sound.

Behind me, Sophie exhales sharply. "Pathetic."

Asher lets out a quiet laugh.

My legs stop working entirely. Knox doesn't pause. He just yanks harder, my feet scraping against the ground. My wrist throbs from how hard he grips me, but I barely notice. All I can feel is the nothingness growing inside me, swallowing everything in its path.

He's not dead.

He can't be.

The sobs rip out of me louder now.

Sophie's footsteps accelerate. Then—

CRACK.

Her hand slams across my face, snapping my head sideways with enough force to blur my vision.

"Enough," she barks. "Get up!"

I drop again, chest heaving, body trembling from the inside out.

My vision swims, but the words don't stop screaming in my head.

He's gone.

Seth is gone.

Knox drags me up again, this time managing to get me mostly upright. My legs barely support me, my body a shaking wreck. I can't stop crying. I can't ground myself. I am outside of it now, half-watching, half-dissolving.

He wouldn't leave me. He wouldn't.

But the voices keep replaying it, until everything inside me shorts out. The numbness sets in like ice beneath my skin.

My world has been reduced to a single word.

Dead.

Knox hauls me across the yard toward the house, Asher walking behind like he is herding something beneath him. Sophie brings up the rear, her face bored, like none of it touches her at all.

Inside, the Manor is silent and freezing. The lights in the hallway flicker overhead. Knox drags me down a narrow passage and through a side door I haven't noticed before. The room inside is bare. Concrete floors, a drain in the center. No furniture. No windows. A space built for pain.

Asher shuts the door. Knox shoves me into the center.

My sobs fade into tremors. My skin burns where Sophie hit me. My throat tastes like blood and bile. I stand there shaking, breath shallow and erratic, the word still burning behind my eyes.

Dead.

Sophie steps forward, hands clasped calmly in front of her.

"You dumb bitch. Do you understand what you just did?"

I stay silent, breathing erratically.

Sophie smiles without warmth. "You fucked up, really bad."

"He gave me the gun, what the fuck did you think I'd do?" I snap, voice trembling from leftover sobs.

"Well, you could've made the correct choice. Instead, you decided to be a disobedient brat."

I back away a step. Knox and Asher don't move, they just watch, bored and curious, like this is entertainment.

Sophie takes one slow breath. "He told you the rules and you've already broken two."

"If you're going to kill me just fucking do it," I say, even though fear and heartbreak are tightening every muscle I have left. "I'm not afraid of you."

She tilts her head. "We'll see about that."

Her hand moves faster than my eyes can track. Her fist cracks across my face so hard my vision goes white. The sound echoes across the concrete. My head snaps sideways, and I stumble, catching myself on my hands. Pain lights through my jaw. I stand back up.

Sophie's brows lift.

I swing at her. Just raw, wild momentum tied to grief and rage and disbelief. My fist connects hard with her cheekbone. She staggers half a step.

Knox lets out a low whistle. Asher grins. Sophie touches her cheek with her fingertips. A smear of red appears. Her expression shifts—still calm, but colder, almost offended.

She doesn't wait. She lunges, grabbing the front of my dress, slamming me against the wall. Air bursts out of my lungs. I claw at her arm, trying to wrench free, but she shoves her knee into my stomach. Pain curls me forward.

I swing again. I catch her in the ribs this time. Her breath hitches. She snarls. She grabs my hair and yanks me upright, slamming the back of my head into the wall.

"Stop fighting bitch," Sophie grunts.

"Go fuck yourself bitch," I choke.

She twists me away from the wall and shoves me toward the center of the room. I hit the ground hard, but I kick out, catching her shin.

She grabs my right arm and wrenches it behind my back without warning.

For a second, I don't feel anything except the weight of it all—

Seth is dead, Seth is dead, Seth is dead—echoing louder than breath or thought. The floor beneath me feels detached. My body is a shell, nothing registers.

Then the angle changes.

The burning pain slices through the numbness like a blade. My shoulder jolts forward on instinct, but Knox steps in, planting a boot beside my knees, blocking any chance of movement. He is a wall. I barely notice. My brain is still stuck in the loop.

He can't be gone.

He wouldn't leave me.

He wouldn't.

Sophie leans in, her breath disturbingly calm against my neck while mine stutters out in choked bursts.

"You think you're strong?" she whispers. "Let me show you what strength actually looks like."

She yanks my arm higher, forcing it toward an angle it was never meant to reach.

My grief-flooded mind doesn't catch up in time. Something inside my wrist strains. Then it gives out.

Pain shoots up my forearm—white-hot and immediate.

"Don't," I gasp, the word crashing into a sob. "Please don't—"

She twists.

SNAP.

The sound comes first, sickening and sharp. Then the scream rips out of me, too loud to hold in. My vision shatters into white. The pain tears straight through my wrist and blooms into my chest, my throat, my skull. I collapse forward onto my knees, curling around the broken joint instinctively.

The world swims in and out, doubled and warped. Every pulse feels like glass grinding through bone.

Somewhere off to the side, Knox mutters, "Ouch," like it is a joke.

But my wrist is broken. I know it. I can feel the shape of it, wrong, twisted, useless. Sophie has shattered it like she is snapping a twig.

Asher shakes his head like he is disappointed.

But their voices feel far away, muffled under the roar in my skull:

He's dead. He's dead. Dead. Dead. DEAD—

Sophie stands over me, breathing evenly, wiping her palms on her pants.

"When you break the rules, I break bones."

Everything sounds underwater. My heart is breaking in a rhythm I can't stop. My breath shakes out in shallow, panicked bursts. My body trembles around a grief too large to fit inside my ribs.

Seth is dead. Grant confirmed it.

No.

No, he's too strong.

He promised he wouldn't leave me. He promised.

Sophie crouches, face level with mine.

"You point another weapon at Elliot, and I'll break more than your wrist."

I try to glare at her, but my vision blurs, edges pulsing, pain and grief crashing into each other until I don't know where one ends and the other begins.

She stands and turns to Knox and Asher like she's bored with the whole performance. "Take her downstairs, she's done being a guest."

Something inside me cracks.

"No," I whisper, voice trembling. "Please—John said—"

"I don't give a fuck what John said," Knox cuts in. "You broke the rules. You're not a guest anymore."

He grabs me under the arm and yanks me upright.

My broken wrist dangles, useless and screaming with pain. I sob as white-hot agony lances through my entire arm. My legs give out, but Knox doesn't pause. He drags me forward like I'm just deadweight.

Seth is dead.

He can't be dead.

But what if he was? What if I felt it the second that shot rang out? What if the last time I saw him in the ballroom was it?

Asher opens a door at the end of the hall. The air changes immediately, it is colder, damp. A narrow staircase leads into the dark, and every step down makes it harder to breathe. My mind drifts in and out, tumbling between grief and panic, like drowning in slow motion.

The basement door slams shut behind me. The sound echoes like a vault locking.

Three figures turn to face me from the shadows.

The first is a man in his thirties. He stands with effort, like every movement hurts. Bruises shadow his jaw and collarbone, and his eyes look dead behind the exhaustion.

Beside him, on a cot pressed against the wall, sits a woman with tangled blond hair, wrapped in a threadbare blanket. Her arms hug her torso like she is trying to stay inside her own body. She doesn't speak.

Further down the room, in the far corner, two bodies are curled up together on a thin mattress. A guy and a girl. The guy has one arm wrapped around the girl protectively, his chin tucked over her head, her face hidden in his chest.

The man steps toward me. "They broke it?" he asks, nodding toward my arm.

"Yeah," I choke out. My voice barely works.

"They like doing that." He doesn't sound surprised. "I'm Miles."

I nod, dizzy. "Brooke."

He gestures toward the younger pair in the corner. "That's Jared and his girl Emma."

Jared shifts slightly, his eyes cracking open at the sound of his name. He doesn't speak, just tightens his hold around Emma, who doesn't stir.

Miles glances toward the woman on the cot nearby. "This is Sarah."

Sarah gives a small nod. Her face is sunken, her knuckles scabbed.

I try to respond, but the words catch in my throat. I stumble, and Miles crouches beside me.

"Sit before you pass out."

I slide down the wall and collapse onto the freezing concrete. The cold hits instantly, slicing through my legs and spine. My wrist burns in time with my pulse.

Miles watches me. "What did you do?"

"I... I tried to shoot Elliot."

Sarah doesn't react. Her gaze stays forward, blank.

Miles flinches. "Jesus," he mutters.

I glance around. "Do you... do you all know what this place is? Are you part of them?"

Miles frowns. "Part of what?"

"The Collective," I say. The name feels like poison in my mouth. "The people running this."

Sarah lets out a brittle, almost-laugh. "What the fuck is that?"

"We were abducted and then we just woke up here," Miles adds.

"They treat us like animals," Sarah says quietly. "Like prey to hunt."

I hold my wrist, trying to keep the shaking at bay.

"A physician will come," Miles confirms.

"For this?" I lift my broken wrist, the motion making me suck in a breath.

"Yes."

I stare at him, confusion clawing through the pain. "Why bother fixing it if they're just going to keep torturing me?"

"Because it's not about killing you. Not yet. They patch us up so they can break us more," Sarah adds.

Miles nods. "You're no fun to them if you can't move."

My stomach turns. My lungs feel too small. My fingers go numb.

Seth isn't here. No one to ground me. No one to talk me down.

Sarah curls deeper into herself and looks down at the floor again.

Miles is quiet for a moment, then says, "They want us ready."

"For what?" My voice barely sounds like mine.

He looks at me, eyes flat. "The games."

A scream echoes through the vents above.

Miles doesn't flinch. "They're warming up."

My voice shakes. "Warming up for what?"

He doesn't look away. "For whatever part of the show we're in today."

My chest rises too fast. I can't slow it. I can't steady it.

Seth's voice cuts through the panic. The memory of it:

Slow it down, baby. Breathe in through your nose, out through your mouth. Look at one thing in the room. I've got you.

I squeeze my eyes shut. One breath in. One breath out. It hurts. It doesn't fix anything. But it keeps me from falling apart completely.

"I'm not dying here," I whisper, even though it comes out broken.

Miles's expression softens.

"Good," he murmurs. "You'll need that."

Another scream echoes, louder this time.

No one reacts.

They are used to it. They are dead inside in a way I refuse to be. I wrap my good arm tighter around my ribs.

Seth.

Please don't be dead.

Please don't leave me.

Because if The Collective wants to break me, they haven't met the part of me that refuses to give up.

The part Seth sharpened.

The part Seth loves.

The part of me that will make them pay.

Chapter 8
Brooke

The basement door scrapes open without warning. Light spills down the stairs.

"Brooke," a voice calls. "Come."

Miles stiffens. Sarah's eyes snap open, dread already blooming there.

Knox appears behind the man in the white coat. "Get up."

I don't move fast enough. My body isn't really here. Knox grabs me anyway, yanking me upright. My wrist screams. My pulse skitters painfully in my throat.

The physician turns and walks, expecting me to follow. My feet follow out of instinct while my mind floats somewhere else. It feels like moving through a nightmare I can't wake from.

The hallway is too clean, too sterile for a place like this. My vision shimmers, as if my eyes can't decide what is real. Images flicker behind my eyelids:

Seth falling. Seth bleeding. Seth not getting up.

And this time the ache doesn't spike, it sinks. A hollow carves out inside my chest where warmth used to be.

The physician leads me into his quarters. A stripped-down infirmary with a cot, a tray of metal tools, shelves of supplies that feel more threatening than helpful. The door clicks shut behind us.

"Sit."

I sit because my body understands obedience better than my mind right now.

He takes my arm without asking and examines it with quiet focus.

"Clean break," he says. "Nasty, though."

"No shit," I rasp.

He barely looks at me. "Swelling's manageable. You'll need it immobilized. It'll function—assuming you last that long."

His words feel like they are aimed at a version of me that isn't in the room.

"How... how long would it take to heal?" My voice feels thin.

"Six to eight weeks. More if it sets badly," he mutters with a small shrug. "But I doubt you have that kind of time."

I swallow against the tightness in my throat. "Are they going to kill me?"

"Most likely," he replies, wrapping my wrist. "Not many survive this place. Not once they outlive their usefulness."

The hollowness in my chest grows heavier. It is hard to breathe around it.

"Please... help me," I whisper.

"Absolutely not."

It is the calm certainty of his voice that guts me. There is no anger or fear. Just the simple truth that I am not worth saving.

"My uncle—" I start, and my voice cracks.

"I know about your family," he interrupts. "Your father was killed for trying to help victims. For killing Collective members. Even though he was a part of it."

His tone doesn't change.

"He went rogue. That got him and your mother killed. And now you're here."

Another weight presses into the hollow space in my chest. It's another betrayal, another loss that has never been my choice to carry.

"I'm not putting myself or my family on the line for you. The most I'll do is stabilize your wrist."

My eyes burn as my body trembles uncontrollably. I try to steady my breathing, but my gaze drifts toward the tray beside me. A scalpel rests there, its metal catching the overhead lights.

My breath falters.

One motion would be enough. One quick slit of my wrists.

I could stop all of this. I could end the terror, the pain, the endless waiting, and the grief that feels like it's swallowing me whole. There would be no more games, no more screaming, no more desperate hope for someone who will never come.

My fingers twitch toward the instrument.

Then another memory surfaces. Seth's hand resting on my stomach. The sound of his voice when I told him. Almost stunned in a way I had never heard from him before.

A shaky breath tears out of me.

I can't kill myself. I can't kill us.

Our child is inside me. The last piece of him this world hasn't stolen from me.

If I die, our baby dies too. If I give up now, everything Seth fought for ends here on a cold metal table under fluorescent lights.

He would have wanted our baby to live.

And he would have wanted me to keep fighting.

My hand slides away from the scalpel, trembling.

The physician's clinical and detached voice cuts back in.

"If Elliot kills you before the terms are carried out, it will fracture things between him, Grant, and John."

I blink, forcing myself to focus on him. "Fracture them how?"

The physician adjusts his glasses and finally meets my eyes. "It would cause problems. Things have already been on shaky ground between them for some time. Elliot resents being told what he can and cannot do, and John is increasingly frustrated with how often his instructions are ignored."

My pulse pounds in my ears.

"If Elliot disregards what John asked for and kills you anyway, it will almost certainly deepen those tensions," he continues. "Grant tends to sit somewhere in the middle of that conflict, which only complicates the situation further."

I swallow hard. "So that protects me?"

The physician hesitates before answering.

"Not necessarily," he says carefully. "I am not convinced John cares enough about the outcome if he sent you here in the first place. What seems to frustrate him more is the pattern of people disregarding his authority."

My chest tightens.

"In other words," he adds quietly, "your survival is less important than whether Elliot chooses to challenge him."

"And Seth?"

The physician pauses for a moment before answering.

"The only thing all three of them agreed on," he continues, "was that Seth needed to be removed."

The air leaves my lungs.

"He's..." My throat closes. "Seth is dead."

The physician's expression doesn't change.

"That is what is being reported."

My breath escapes me as if my body has forgotten how breathing works.

He is gone.

He is not coming back.

The world around me loses its center. I force myself to inhale, then again, even though every breath feels like it scrapes through my chest.

I remember Seth's voice, how he guided me through panic:

Breathe. Hold. Exhale. Slow it down, baby. Focus on something real. I'm right here.

But he isn't.

And that is the part that hurts more than the wrist. More than anything Sophie can break.

Before I can respond, a chime buzzes overhead. Then a voice crackles through the intercom:

"It is time for our first game. All participants report to the game room."

My stomach turns.

The physician steps back and wipes his hands with a cloth. "You've been summoned. Don't keep them waiting."

Knox reappears in the doorway and jerks his chin. "Move."

I follow him, heart racing, wrist throbbing under the fresh bandages. He leads me down a different hallway, one I haven't seen before, toward a set of double doors painted with ornate gold designs.

He pushes them open. The room inside looks like a twisted version of a living room. Comfortable chairs, soft lighting, a fireplace burning low. The chairs form a circle like something out of a therapy session, if therapy sessions were held in hell.

The others are already there. Miles, Sarah, Jared, and Emma—silent, unmoving, eyes fixed on nothing.

In the corner sits someone new. A man I haven't seen before. Late twenties, maybe. One eye swollen shut, dried blood on his lip.

Elliot stands near the mantelpiece, hands folded behind his back, smiling like a host welcoming guests to a party.

"Good," he says. "Everyone is here."

My pulse skitters.

Elliot's smile widens. "Welcome, to our first game."

He gestures to the chairs. "Let's sit. Since Brooke is new, we'll start with introductions. It's important you all get to know one another before we play."

Miles avoids my eyes. Sarah stares at the fire, hollow. Jared and Emma sit rigid, jaws clenched.

Elliot stands in the center, hands folded, eyes glittering. Sophie leans against the wall. Asher rests a steel baseball bat on his shoulder. Knox flicks a dart between his fingers, spinning it lazily. The victims sit stiffly around me. We all stare straight ahead like soldiers waiting for execution.

Elliot smiles. "Okay, let's start with introductions."

Dead Silence. Empty. No one dares speak.

Elliot raises an eyebrow. "Well?"

No one moves.

Elliot's voice snaps through the air like a whip:

"NAMES. NOW!"

Everyone flinches.

Sarah jolts upright. "S-Sarah."

Emma's voice is barely a whisper. "Emma."

Jared's cracks. "Jared."

The new guy—the one I don't recognize—speaks next. "Carl."

Miles is last, his voice ragged. "Miles."

Elliot claps slowly, mockingly. "Excellent. Now that we're all friends..."

My stomach twists so hard I think I might throw up.

"Let's begin our first game," Elliot says, pacing behind the chairs like he is warming up for a performance. "Would You Rather."

He stops behind Sarah's chair. His shadow spills over her shoulders.

"Sarah," he says gently. "Would you rather have your finger broken, or your toe?"

Before she can answer, Carl shifts in his seat. "What if we refuse?"

Elliot turns slowly toward him. "Then you're eliminated."

Carl stares. "What does that mean?"

Elliot raises the pistol and cocks it with a single click. "This, is elimination."

Carl doesn't wait for clarification. He bolts up from his chair and runs for the door.

Two shots crack through the room.

Carl's body hits the ground face first. Blood spreads fast beneath him.

Elliot lowers the gun, unbothered. "Shame. Such an early elimination."

My pulse roars in my ears. I can't breathe. He is serious. This isn't just torture. This is an execution dressed up as theater.

They are going to kill us. Not all at once, one by one. Game by game.

"So Sarah," he says calmly. "Would you rather have a finger broken, or a toe?"

Sarah shakes her head frantically, terror tearing through her face. "Please. I can't. I can't choose. Please—"

Elliot smiles. "You already did." He tilts his head toward Sophie. "Go on."

Sarah's breath hitches. "Finger," she nods, barely, her whole body shaking.

Sophie steps forward. She reaches down, seizes Sarah's hand, and yanks it flat against the arm of the chair. Her grip is tight. She isolates Sarah's index finger between her own fingers and bends it back.

Too far.

The sound is a wet crack, like snapping a chicken bone.

Sarah screams. The noise rips out of her, raw and high, as pain tears through her hand. She convulses forward, clutching her finger to her chest as it twists at the wrong angle, already swelling, already turning dark.

"Oh my God," she sobs, rocking violently. "Oh God—"

Sophie lets go and steps back.

Elliot watches with quiet satisfaction as Sarah curls in on herself, whimpering.

"See?" Elliot says mildly. "That wasn't so hard."

Elliot's smile widens as he turns to the couple.

"Emma, would you rather have a plastic bag held over your head for one minute... or allow Jared to take a cattle-prod shock?"

Emma freezes.

Jared shakes his head immediately, panic breaking through his voice. "Emma, no. No. Just choose me."

Miles leans forward. "A minute... Emma, you can—"

Elliot cuts him off without looking at him. "Miles. Silence."

Emma looks at Jared, fear and love colliding in her expression. Her throat moves as she swallows.

"I'll take the minute."

Jared lets out a broken sound. "Emma, please don't."

Asher is already moving. He grabs her arm and hauls her to the center of the room. Sophie follows, pulling a thick, clear plastic bag from a drawer and shaking it open. The material crackles loudly in the quiet space.

Emma's breathing turns rapid and shallow. "Wait. Please. Wait—"

Asher doesn't respond. He forces her down onto her knees and yanks her head back by her hair. Sophie steps in front of her and pulls the plastic bag down over Emma's head in one swift motion. The thin material clings instantly to her face, sticking to her lips and nose as she inhales.

Emma screams. The sound comes out muffled and distorted through the plastic.

Asher twists the open end tight at her neck and holds it there, sealing it with his fist. Sophie grips Emma's shoulders and forces her upright so she can't collapse. The bag sucks inward with every desperate breath, flattening against her mouth and nostrils as she tries to pull in air that isn't there.

Elliot checks his watch. "One minute. Begin."

Emma thrashes immediately. Her hands fly to her face, fingers clawing at the plastic as she tries to tear it open. The bag stretches and snaps back, crinkling loudly. Her chest heaves violently, ribs expanding against nothing. The oxygen inside the bag thins within seconds. Her movements grow frantic, uncoordinated. She makes choking sounds that don't fully escape.

My heart pounds so hard it drowns out everything else. Jared stumbles forward, hands shaking. "Stop. Stop. Let me do it. Let me."

Elliot blocks him with a single arm. "Move again, and I'll shock you anyway."

Emma's body convulses as carbon dioxide builds inside the bag. The plastic fogs with her breath, then clears, then fogs again as she fights for air. Her legs kick out wildly, heels scraping against the floor. Her fingernails tear at the material until one splits and begins to bleed. She gags inside the bag, her breath growing louder and more ragged.

Sophie holds her steady while Asher keeps the seal tight at her throat. At fifty seconds, Emma's movements slow. Her hands drop from her face and twitch weakly at her sides.

Elliot lifts his hand. "Time."

Asher rips the bag off in one quick motion. Emma collapses forward, dragging in a violent, broken breath that turns immediately into coughing. She sucks in air and chokes on it at the same time, her body shaking uncontrollably as oxygen rushes back in. Her eyes are bloodshot, tiny vessels burst around the whites. Saliva and tears soak her face.

Jared breaks free from Elliot and drops to his knees beside her. "Emma. Emma, look at me."

He pulls her into his arms, brushing damp hair from her face with trembling fingers. "I'm right here. I'm right here."

Emma can't answer. She coughs and gasps against his chest, her body shuddering as she tries to regain control of her breathing.

Elliot watches with calm satisfaction, his hands clasped neatly behind his back. "Very good, Emma."

Emma is still shaking when Elliot shifts his attention to Jared.

"Well, since the two of you are so devoted... it's only fair Jared gets a turn."

Jared's shoulders stiffen. He looks up slowly, eyes wide with dread.

"Fuck, please," he whispers. "Please don't—"

Elliot smiles gently, like this isn't torture but a fond conversation.

"Jared, would you rather..."

Silence tightens around the room.

"...have Emma take the bag again for another full minute..."

Emma makes a tiny terrified sound, part inhale, part sob.

"...or would you prefer to take the cattle-prod shock yourself?"

Jared freezes.

Emma reaches blindly for him, fingers trembling. "Jared—no—no. Please. I can't—I can't breathe—I can't—"

Her voice breaks again into a violent cough. Jared's face crumples.

He cups her cheek. "I won't let them do that again. I won't."

Elliot tilts his head. "Your choice must be spoken, Jared."

Jared doesn't look at Elliot. He only looks at Emma. And whispers, voice shattering, "...shock me."

Emma sobs and grabs at his shirt. "No—Jared—no—no—"

But Knox already steps forward. He presses the cattle prod into Jared's ribcage and fires. The sound is a brutal crack. Jared's entire body seizes, back arching violently, muscles spasming under the current. A strangled cry tears out of him, before he collapses sideways on the floor, trembling uncontrollably.

Emma reaches for him, crawling with shaking limbs.

"Jared—Jared—baby—" She holds his head, sobbing into his forehead. "I'm sorry—I'm so sorry—please, please breathe—"

Jared gasps weakly, chest spasming, eyes glassy, fingers twitching.

Elliot watches them like a delighted spectator.

"Beautiful loyalty, you two will give us excellent entertainment."

The rest of the room falls silent. A silence full of dread. A silence full of the understanding that every choice they give us is designed to break us far deeper than bone.

Jared collapses into Emma's arms, still twitching from the shock. Emma holds him tightly, pressing her forehead to his, whispering apologies through broken breath. Watching them hurt. Watching how far they will go for each other.

It hits something raw inside me.

Because for all the terror in this room, for all the screaming and shaking and begging, Emma and Jared still choose each other. Again and again. Even when the choices are designed to tear them apart. Their loyalty isn't just love. It is survival glued together with desperation and hope.

And I can't stop the thought that Seth would've never let them put me here. Seth would've burned this entire house down before letting someone put a bag over my face until I couldn't breathe. Seth wouldn't kneel helplessly beside me.

He wouldn't sob while someone else suffered for his sake. He would've killed everyone in this circle and every guard outside before they laid a hand on me. And I would've done the same for him.

A cold pit settles in my stomach. Because unlike Emma and Jared...Seth isn't here. Seth is dead.

And I am alone.

Elliot turns next, hands clasped in a mockery of courtesy.

"Miles."

Miles lifts his head slowly, as if every ounce of strength he has left is draining through his fingertips.

"Please..." he whispers. "Please don't."

Elliot crouches down in front of him, voice gentle.

"Would you rather, have three of your fingernails removed..."

Miles's face twists.

"...or shall we remove three of Brooke's?"

My heart lurches.

Miles's haunted eyes meet mine—full of horror, guilt, apology.

I shake my head quickly. Don't choose me. Please don't choose me.

He blinks slowly, pain filling the spaces between his breaths.

Then he whispers:

"Me."

Sophie steps forward with the pliers. Not the tooth-extraction kind, but the flat, heavy ones meant for gripping and tearing. Miles grips the chair arms so tightly his knuckles strain. Sophie grabs his left hand, pins it against the wood, and slides the pliers beneath his first nail.

Miles shuts his eyes.

She rips it up and off in one brutal pull.

Miles chokes, not quite a scream, not quite a cry, the sound of someone whose pain has nowhere to go. Blood wells immediately.

She takes the next finger. Tears the nail away.

Miles jerks hard, a strangled gasp ripping out of him.

Emma turns away, hand over her mouth. Sarah stares at the floor, blinking rapidly. Jared groans weakly from Emma's lap.

Sophie removes the third nail slower, peeling it back with steady pressure before ripping it free.

Miles slumps forward, trembling violently, forehead resting against his knee. A drop of blood hits the floor.

Elliot straightens, dusting off his hands lightly.

"Wonderful, everyone is making such thoughtful choices today."

Then his eyes shift to me. Predatory, pleased, curious.

My pulse thunders in my chest.

"Brooke," Elliot says warmly.

The final round. The worst one.

"Your turn."

Chapter 9
Brooke

I keep my gaze locked forward, even though my hands tremble.

Elliot gestures with a casual sweep of his hand.

Asher steps forward carrying a steel baseball bat, cold, heavy, dented with old damage. Knox approaches behind him, holding a set of darts, metal tips gleaming under the firelight.

Elliot clasps his hands behind his back.

"Would you rather, take three strikes from Asher with the bat, or allow Knox to throw three darts into your back?"

My pulse roars in my ears.

The bat means broken ribs. The bat means bruised organs. The bat means the kind of internal damage you don't get to walk away from. I have already been kicked there once, and I can't gamble on a second hit. Not with what I am carrying. Not with the only part of Seth left in the world.

But darts will stay on the surface, mostly. Darts will tear skin and muscle. The pain will still be mine, my back, my flesh, my nerves lighting up. But it won't be a direct strike to my stomach. It won't be a gamble with the tiny life inside me.

Seth would've taken the pain for me a thousand times over. I have to do the same.

Elliot tilts his head. "Choose, Brooke."

Asher smirks and lifts the bat. Knox twirls a dart between his fingers, like he is warming up for a game at a bar instead of a punishment.

My breath hitches.

"I choose," I say as my voice wavers, "the darts."

A soft ripple moves through the room. Shock, a murmur of pity. A flicker of something like understanding from Miles.

Elliot's smile tightens. "Excellent."

Knox steps behind me, light on his feet, almost cheerful as he gestures towards the fireplace. Asher lowers the bat with obvious disappointment, like he was looking forward to hitting me.

I stand and walk slowly to the fireplace.

"Face the fireplace," Knox says.

My legs tremble, but I turn. Heat from the flames brushes my front. Cold dread presses into my spine.

"Lift your hair," Knox adds.

My hand shakes as I gather my hair and pull it over one shoulder. The exposed skin across my back tightens under the air, every nerve alert and waiting.

"Lift the dress," he says.

I reach for the fabric of my dress and raise it slowly, fingers clumsy with tension. The material drags up over my hips and ribs. My broken wrist throbs sharply in protest, pain pulsing up my arm, but I don't stop. Cold air hits my bare skin and prickles along my spine and sides, leaving me fully exposed from shoulder blades to waist.

"Restraints," he says casually.

Asher grabs a leather strap from a hook near the fireplace, dark, worn, stained in a way that is not heat or decor. He wraps it around my upper arms and hauls them above my head. The pressure rips through my broken wrist and makes my vision jump. Then he kneels and clips my ankles together with a short metal cuff so I can't brace, can't twist away, can't run.

I'm upright, but barely. A single shove would drop me. A single dart would drive into unprotected flesh with nowhere else for the pain to go.

Knox stands behind me, humming quietly, testing the weight of a dart between his fingers like he is appreciating the balance.

Elliot leans against the mantel, arms folded. "Three darts. Consequence of choice."

Fire heat licks at my front while cold dread crawls down my spine. My heart hammers against my ribs like it wants out.

I close my eyes and try to keep my breathing under control. I do it for the baby. I do it for Seth. I do it for us.

Knox shouts. "Round one."

The silence before the throw is unbearable, and every sound stretches wide. Firewood pops. Sarah breathes in shallow little pulls. Miles whispers something that sounds like a prayer. My own pulse is pounding so loudly that I nearly miss the motion itself.

A faint whoosh cuts the air. Then the impact lands.

The first dart punches into my lower back with the force of a metal wasp. Skin splits instantly. Tissue tears. Pain flares hot.

A raw and shaking scream rips out of me without permission. The dart sinks deep. The metal trembles with my heartbeat, and blood starts to roll down my side in thick, hot trails.

Knox chuckles under his breath. "That landed nicely."

I clench my jaw. Breath shakes in and out of me. The restraints dig into my arms every time I try to inhale.

Elliot's tone is almost bored. "Breathe, Brooke."

I try. I force air into my lungs and hold it until spots swim behind my eyelids.

In the mirror I see Knox reaching for the next dart. He flicks it once, letting the metal catch the light like he is admiring his own aim.

"Round two."

He throws harder.

The dart strikes high, just under my shoulder blade. It goes deep enough that I feel the point scrape against bone. The agony hits like a burst of electricity. My knees buckle, but the restraints hold me upright, leaving my muscles to convulse with nowhere to go. A broken sound tears out of my chest, part gasp, part sob. Pain radiates outward, searing, numbing, then searing again. My vision goes dark.

Knox leans close enough that I can feel his breath. "That one is deep," he murmurs. "Do you feel it when you try to inhale?"

My breath hitches in jagged bursts. Each inhale sends shocks up my spine, and each exhale feels like my body is giving up something it needs.

Sophie clicks her tongue. "She's probably going to pass out before the last one."

"No," Elliot says calmly. "She won't. She knows better than that."

Knox steps back and rolls the dart between his fingers. "Final round."

I clench my hands until my nails bite into my palms. Tears slide down my face without warning, not from fear, but from my body trying to survive the overload.

Knox holds the third dart longer. He doesn't rush. He lets anticipation crawl up my spine and sit there.

Then the air moves.

The third dart embeds itself left of my spine, too close, far too close. I feel the point scrape between muscle, slicing as it forces its way deeper. White bursts behind my eyelids. My legs give out completely. A choked scream tears out of me, held upright only because the restraints keep my arms locked above my head. My broken wrist jostles and screams with me, sending pain up my arm and into my chest like a hot wire.

Blood coats my back now, soaking into the waistband of the panties I have on. I can feel each drop sliding down, sticky, gathering at the small of my back.

Knox steps around me, admiring what he has done.

"And that, makes three."

Sophie walks over, crouches, and grabs the end of one dart between two fingers. She wiggles it, slowly testing, like she wants to learn exactly how much it takes to break me.

Pain detonates through my back so violently that I gag.

She smiles. "Careful. I would hate for you to bleed out before the next game."

Miles surges halfway out of his chair. "Stop, she needs help, just stop."

"Sit down!" Asher snaps.

Emma can't hold her tears back anymore. They stream silently down her cheeks as she presses shaking hands to her mouth. Sarah stares fixedly at the floor, jaw locked, shoulders trembling. No one speaks.

I can't hold myself upright. My legs tremble hard enough that my whole body sways.

Sophie lets out a low laugh.

The restraints are the only reason I haven't collapsed flat onto the floor. My head hangs forward. Hair falls into my face, and it sticks to wetness I can't tell apart anymore. Sweat, tears, blood, it all feels the same.

Elliot claps once, bright and cheerful, like he is ending a dinner toast instead of torture.

"That concludes the games for tonight, Asher, remove her."

Asher unbuckles the restraints. My arms drop like dead weight. Pain tears through my wrist and my back at the same time, and I collapse to the ground with a broken cry. Asher hooks his hands under my armpits and drags me across the floor. My knees scrape the rug, then hit tile, then concrete. Every bump sends shocks through the darts lodged in my back. Blood smears behind me in long streaks.

The world tilts and blurs as the pain drags me under.

But even as darkness closes in, one thought stays clear.

I am not dying here.

Chapter 10
Brooke

I feel cold at first. Then pain—deep, slicing, pulsing in three places along my spine. Then the feeling of fabric sticking to my skin. I blink slowly and realize I'm lying face-down on a cot in the physician's quarters, cheek pressed to a thin pillow already smeared with my blood. Something tugs at the puncture near my shoulder blade. I jerk instinctively.

"Don't move," the physician says dryly. "Unless you'd like permanent nerve damage."

My breath shakes out in short, panicked bursts. "Stop—stop, please—"

"Hysteria won't speed anything up."

His tone doesn't change at all. He keeps working.

My fingers curl into the pillow, nails scraping fabric as he prods the wound. Pain tears down my back like lightning.

I grit my teeth so hard my jaw aches. "It—hurts—"

"Of course it does. It's been in there long enough to swell around it."

His hand presses harder. I cry out, body arching despite myself. Every movement makes fire shoot up my spine. My legs tremble uncontrollably. I can't breathe. For one heart-stopping moment, panic threatens to swallow me whole. And then a memory slides in. Soft, warm, nothing like this place.

Seth behind me in bed, his breath on my neck, his hand covering mine.

Baby, you're okay. Breathe with me.

I squeeze my eyes shut.

Inhale.

Hold.

Exhale.

I repeat it until my lungs obey.

The physician grunts. "Good. Stay still. Almost there."

He twists the dart once. White-hot agony spikes through me. My scream tears through the room, muffled only when I bite down on the pillow until fabric fills my teeth.

Then a sickening wet pop as the metal slips free. Warm blood flows instantly.

"One down," he says.

I am shaking so hard the cot rattles.

He doesn't wait. The second dart tears even deeper when he probes for it. His fingers press directly into the torn muscle, searching for the barbed edge.

A thin, broken sound escapes me. "Please—"

"Quiet."

He finds the dart and pulls.

My vision blacks out for a second. My body arches off the cot, nerves screaming. My tears soak the pillow. My breath stutters.

Seth's voice echoes again in my mind:

Focus on one point. Block everything else out. I've got you.

I stare at a crack in the wall.

Breathe.

Hold.

Exhale.

The physician moves to the third wound.

"That one is deep," he murmurs. "Don't move unless you want me to rupture something important."

I dig my nails into the cot frame and brace myself. When he pulls the final dart free, I nearly black out again. Heat flushes through my body, followed by cold, followed by a hollow dizziness like I am not fully in my skin anymore.

By the time he finishes cleaning the wounds and stitching them closed, sweat soaks my hairline and the cot sheet beneath me.

He straightens with a sigh. "You'll live."

I can't answer. My throat won't work.

"But," he adds, gathering his tools, "Elliot has asked for you to attend dinner."

My head lifts weakly. "Dinner?"

He gives a thin smile. "This house has... routines."

The intercom crackles.

"Everyone to the dining room. Now."

The physician wipes his hands and steps aside. "Up you go."

I push myself upright. Pain shoots down my back with every twitch of muscle. My broken wrist throbs mercilessly. My vision swims. But I stand.

Asher appears in the doorway. "Let's go."

He grabs my upper arm, dragging me through the hallway. Every step sends a shock through the stitches. I clench my jaw and keep moving. Because stopping isn't an option.

The dining room is too warm. Too elegant. Too civilized for a place built on torture. A crystal chandelier glows above a long polished table set with silverware and linen napkins, like a family dinner scene from a magazine, except everyone here looks starved and hunted.

Elliot sits at the head, calm and composed, like a man presiding over a celebration. Sophie lounges beside him, one leg crossed over the other, sipping red wine like it is the easiest night of her life. Knox leans against the doorway, arms folded, bored. Asher circles the room slowly, smiling like he is waiting for someone to slip up so he can enjoy it.

Next to me sits Miles, Sarah, Jared, and Emma. Every one of them looks like they have been drained hollow. Their cheeks have sunk inward, their hands tremble against the table, and their eyes carry the dull, exhausted glaze of people who have gone too long without real food.

Two servers enter the room carrying silver platters.

The smell reaches me before I even see the food.

It is hot and greasy, thick with rendered fat and something sweet that has burned too long under heat. Beneath it lingers another note that makes my stomach twist. The scent carries the faint copper tang of blood mixed with the heavy odor of cooked skin and marrow. There is something unmistakably wrong about it.

My stomach clenches violently.

The servers lift the lids. Steam rolls upward in dense waves. The platters hold roasted vegetables and thick slices of browned meat, the surface dark and glistening with juices that pool along the edges of the tray.

Miles leans slightly toward me and speaks barely moving his mouth.

"They never feed us like this," he whispers. "It's always shakes or soup. Never this."

I shake my head once, hard.

Every instinct in my body screams at me not to touch it. I don't know exactly what it is, but I know with absolute certainty that it is not food.

Sarah's breathing hitches. She lunges forward first, grabbing at the meat with shaking fingers. Miles blinks rapidly as if he is trying to hold back tears while reaching for his plate. Emma tears into the food with both hands. Jared follows silently, chewing so fast that he nearly chokes.

None of them question it. None of them slow down.

I don't move. I don't touch the plate sitting in front of me.

The smell thickens in my throat, heavy with that same burned sweetness that makes bile rise in the back of my mouth. It doesn't smell like beef or pork or anything that should have been served at a table.

I shake my head.

"Don't eat it."

Miles stares at the plate.

His hands hover above the meat, fingers twitching as steam curls upward. Hunger has hollowed him out so badly his body leans toward the food without him realizing it. His throat works as he swallows, eyes fixed on the glistening slices.

Around us, the room fills with the sound of chewing. Sarah tears through her portion with shaking hands. Emma eats with grease slick across her fingers. Jared stuffs pieces into his mouth so quickly he barely chews.

Miles' hand starts to lower toward the plate.

Then his eyes flick to me.

I shake my head once.

"Don't."

He looks back at the food. His jaw tightens. His stomach growls loud enough for me to hear.

Miles drags in a breath and shoves the plate away.

He leans back in his chair and closes his eyes, fists tightening against his thighs like he needs them there to stop himself.

Elliot lifts his glass.

"To fun and games," he then turns his eyes directly on me. "And Brooke... I'm so glad you could join us for dinner. You took those darts like a champ."

The others barely react. They are too busy eating. Too hungry to notice the smile curling at the corners of his mouth.

I glare at him, silent.

My back still aches from where the darts hit. My wrist throbs like the bones are splintering all over again. Blood sticks to my skin under the dress. And now I'm supposed to sit here, like this is dinner. Like this is normal.

I don't touch the food. I don't speak. I just stare at Elliot and hold my glare, refusing to let him see what I am really feeling.

Elliot claps softly. "Is everyone enjoying their meal?"

He checks an imaginary watch. "And look at that—it's Wednesday. You know what that means."

Sophie grabs a remote and turns on the TV mounted on the wall. The news clicks on. A headline stretches across the bottom in bold white letters:

MISSING COLLEGE STUDENT BETH JENNER STILL UNACCOUNTED FOR.

"The search continues tonight for missing college student Beth Jenner," the news anchor says, her voice calm as she looks into the camera. "Authorities say Jenner disappeared earlier last week under circumstances that remain unclear."

I hear Sarah inhale sharply beside me.

A photograph of Beth appears on the television screen.

"Oh look, Sarah," Elliot says pleasantly. "It's Beth."

The anchor continues, glancing briefly down at her notes. "Investigators say Jenner was last seen with her boyfriend, Chris, who has also not been located. Both individuals remain unaccounted for as the investigation continues."

Sarah's hand freezes halfway to her mouth.

Another photo appears beside Beth's.

"Police are now confirming that Beth Jenner's sister, Sarah Jenner, is also missing," the anchor says. "Sarah was last spotted on Saturday. Authorities have not released additional details but say they are working to determine whether the disappearances may be connected."

The words SARAH JENNER — ALSO MISSING appear across the bottom of the screen.

Sarah's face crumples.

Elliot tilts his head as he watches her reaction.

"Look at you. Basically a celebrity, huh."

My pulse drums inside my skull.

"And we have a surprise guest... your sister is here with us."

Sarah blinks, confused, tears streaking her cheeks. "Beth—she's here—where?"

Asher leans over her shoulder. "She's right here, sweetheart."

He taps the roast with the end of his knife.

A cold wave washes over me. The room seems to tilt sideways.

Emma shakes her head violently. "No—no, no—Oh my god—"

Jared stares at his plate. "No... What the fuck—no—"

Sarah looks from the TV to her plate, lost, trembling. "What—"

Elliot leans closer, his voice soft and cruel.

"You're eating Beth."

The moment the words settle...Everything shatters.

Sarah screams, a high, throat-tearing wail that makes my skin crawl. She shoves the plate away and vomits instantly, collapsing out of her chair. She claws at her tongue, sobbing, gagging, retching like she can somehow erase the taste.

Jared pushes his plate away so hard the ceramic shatters. He staggers up, choking, spitting, crying without sound.

Emma gags into her napkin, shoulders heaving, full-body shaking, tears streaming as she presses both hands over her mouth.

Miles stares straight ahead, eyes empty, refusing to look at the plate.

Sophie claps, delighted. "Now Beth lives in all of you."

Asher bends down to Sarah, whose entire body is trembling so violently she can barely breathe.

He whispers loudly enough for all of us to hear, "Next time, eat slower. Really savor the family recipe."

Sarah screams again raw and broken.

The rest of the victims cry in varying degrees of horror:

"Stop—please—"

"Oh God—oh God—"

"No—NO—NO—"

I can't move or speak. I can barely breathe. The room spins. The screaming doesn't stop. The smell of roasted human meat mixes with vomit and iron and makes my stomach twist violently.

Everything inside me feels cold. Like something essential has been scooped out by these monsters and replaced with nothing but shock.

Elliot stands at the head of the table, looking absolutely delighted.

"What a heartwarming family reunion."

Sophie laughs and wipes a tear from her eye, like she has just heard a good joke.

Sarah wails again and curls into herself on the floor. No one tries to comfort her. No one can.

I swallow hard, bile burning at the back of my throat. The cruelty is suffocating, thick as the warm air in the room. It presses down on all of us.

And suddenly, the physician's words flash through my mind:

Most likely, they'll kill you. Very few survive this place. Everyone dies here eventually.

I had tried to pretend he was wrong. That I was different. That I had enough fight in me to outsmart an entire manor built on terror.

But watching Sarah crumble, watching Jared vomit, watching Emma break, reality hits me like ice water.

I probably won't survive this.

I'm pregnant, injured, exhausted, surrounded by killers who treat human life like a game. And if I do die, it won't be clean or quick. It will be twisted. A spectacle they'll enjoy. A sick, brutal ending—just like Beth's.

I am not naïve enough to deny it anymore. But if I go out, I will take as many of these sadistic bastards with me as I can. Every last one I can reach. Every throat I can tear open. Every bone I can break.

They have no idea who they're fucking with.

I lift my head slowly, jaw clenched, breath shaky.

Elliot opens his mouth to speak.

Then the television blares to life with a sudden BREAKING NEWS ALERT.

Everything stops. Every sound dies in place. Even the killers go still, attention dragged toward the screen.

The anchor leans closer to the desk, eyes flicking down and back up again, voice raised with urgency.

"We're just receiving information out of Colorado. This is developing right now," she says. "Seth Kincaid, the suspected spree killer connected to the Everspring Hotel massacre, has escaped federal custody."

My heart slams against my ribs, and my breath stutters like my body can't decide whether to collapse or run.

A grainy hospital security image appears on the screen. The footage shows Seth moving down a hospital corridor under harsh fluorescent lights. His shirt clings to his body, darkened with blood.

He is walking on his own. He looks pale and badly wounded, but there is no mistaking him.

Seth is alive.

A sound tries to claw its way out of my throat, half sob, half laugh, and I swallow it down hard. My knees go weak.

The anchor's voice rushes to keep up.

"Kincaid was being held at a Colorado medical center under twenty-four-hour armed guard. Moments ago, hospital surveillance footage confirmed his escape. Authorities now believe he was assisted by an accomplice, believed to be extremely dangerous."

Another clip replaces it.

A tall man moves through the frame in hospital scrubs, pale blue fabric streaked dark along one sleeve. His broad shoulders crowd the narrow space as he advances with controlled urgency. A gun sits steady in his hand, a long barrel fitted with a silencer. He moves with purpose, body angled to shield Seth as they advance down the corridor together.

"Law enforcement confirms multiple officers were killed during the escape," the anchor adds, almost stumbling over the words as they come in.

The camera angle changes as alarms begin to wail faintly in the background of the footage.

"At least five fatalities have been reported at this time. Authorities are urging the public to remain indoors as this situation continues to unfold."

The room goes silent again.

Sophie straightens slowly, her wineglass forgotten, knuckles whitening around the stem. Her eyes stay locked on the screen.

Knox stops moving entirely, shoulders squared, attention sharpened into focus.

Asher freezes mid-step, jaw locked, gaze fixed forward.

Elliot's smile twitches, just slightly. He reaches for his glass, and takes a slow sip—buying himself a second to think. When he sets it down, his hand lingers on the stem a beat too long. The corners of his mouth lift again, but the shine in his eyes has dulled. He is calculating now. Reworking whatever script he thinks he is in charge of. Trying to look unfazed.

I laugh.

The sound bursts out of me before I can stop it, too loud for the room, pitched on the edge of hysteria. It scrapes its way up from my chest and spills into the air, breathless and shaking, refusing to be contained. My body trembles with it, as if my nerves have finally shorted out after holding too much for too long.

My chest shakes as the laughter keeps spilling out, raw and uncontrolled, tears burning at the corners of my eyes. I had mourned him. I had felt the hollow certainty that he was gone. They had watched me carry that weight. They had wanted it to break me. They had wanted my hope dead before my body followed.

They failed.

They all stare at me.

Elliot.

Sophie.

Knox.

Asher.

The other victims.

I drag my hand across my face wiping away the tears, the laughter still bubbling out in uneven bursts, and lift my eyes to Elliot.

Seth is alive.

And now I know, with absolute certainty, that he is coming for me.

"You know," I laugh, voice shaking, "whether you kill me or not...you're all so incredibly fucked."

Chapter 11
Seth

Three Days Earlier

I open my eyes slowly and find Brooke beside me in our bed. Morning light filters through the curtains behind her, soft enough to blur everything except her. She smiles, her smile always eases every part of me I never knew how to quiet.

I lift my hand and rest it against her stomach. Her skin is warm beneath my palm, and the gentle swell beneath it makes my heart stutter. Her fingers brush along my jaw, like she is trying to memorize me. She shifts closer and presses her mouth to mine with the quiet confidence that we have all the time in the world. For a moment, I believe it completely.

The dream scattered instantly.

A sudden jolt lifts my body, tearing the warmth away like the bed is ripped out from under me. Harsh light slams into my eyes. Cold air hits my chest. Hands press down on me, pinning me against a surface that isn't soft or familiar anymore.

Voices rise around me in frantic bursts.

"We're losing him—keep pressure there—move!"

Pain shoots through my chest as someone presses down. Another hand forces my head to the side. My breath catches behind a mask I didn't even realize was there until it's already over my face. The world shifts hard, and I realize I'm being lifted onto a stretcher.

A voice right above me shouts,

"Pulse is faint—he's hypovolemic—get the line in now!"

I gasp like I've been drowning. I try to focus as the ceiling of the hotel blurs above me. Sirens wail outside. Medics crowd around me. Blood covers my chest and soaks the sheets beneath me. Every movement sends another wave of heat tearing through my side.

The memories of what just happened slam into me.

Grant yanking that black bag over Brooke's head. Her screaming my name until her voice gave out. I tried to move, but my body wouldn't cooperate. I was on the ground, forced to watch as they dragged her through the service door.

Another image cuts in.

John turned and looked straight at me. He tossed the engagement ring I bought for Brooke into the blood pooling beneath me like it meant nothing.

The same man I trusted enough to ask for his blessing to marry his niece.

My stomach twists as medics push me through the hallway. One of them shouts something about my pulse. Another demands more pressure on the wound. My vision narrows until everything shrinks to a thin strip of light.

Cold metal rattles beneath me as the ambulance sways down the road. Red lights flash against the walls, throwing everything into rapid pulses. Each bump jars my body, sending pain from my shoulder down my ribs in heavy, suffocating waves.

Two medics work over me, one adjusting the mask on my face while the other pushes fluid through the IV in my arm. Their voices cut through the noise in tight, urgent bursts.

"I want another unit of blood ready," one says. "He's not stabilizing."

The other shakes his head. "He lost too much on scene. If he crashes again, I need you on compressions."

Neither of them looks at me. They talk around me like I'm already dead. Then their voices shift.

"Do you know who he is?" the medic near my shoulder says quietly.

"Yeah," the other answers. "Kincaid. He's the one they think did all of this."

My pulse pounds louder than the siren.

"They're saying he killed everyone. Hotel guests, officers. Even that snowplow driver on 38."

"They think he killed the Rangers too?" the other asks.

"That's what the lieutenant said. The FBI wanted him alive for questioning. Looks like he tried to shoot his way out."

They think I did it.

The poisoning.

The massacre.

The chaos.

All of it pinned on me.

I try to speak, but the mask presses tight against my mouth. Pain surges through my ribs when I try to sit up. The medic shoves me back down.

"Let the sedatives work. You're lucky to be breathing."

I ignore him.

None of this matters. None of these accusations matter. Only one question cuts through the pain like broken glass.

Where is Brooke?

I try to force myself up again, but my body won't move the way I need it to. Every instinct in me screams to fight, to claw, to rip out the IV line, to break the restraints on the stretcher, to get out of this ambulance before they take me farther away from her.

If I stay here, I'll lose her. If I stay here, she dies alone.

I push against the straps again. The medic curses under his breath and forces me back down.

"Hold still, you're making this worse."

I don't care about the bleeding. I don't care about passing out again. I don't care about the charges they're stacking on me.

Brooke is out there, and I'm wasting time strapped to a bed in an ambulance.

I need to get out. I need to get to her. I need to kill every single person standing between us.

The thought settles in my head with complete clarity. I will burn through anyone who tries to keep me from her. I will tear apart every agent, every guard, every piece of shit between me and the woman they took.

If this ambulance somehow gets me to a hospital alive, I'm not staying there. Not for one second longer than it takes to stand up and walk out.

The medics keep talking over me. My vision blurs again, but I hold on to one thing with everything I have left.

Brooke needs me.

And I'm coming for her.

My eyes snap open.

Cold fluorescent light floods my vision, and the sterile hum of machines fills the room. Plastic tubing tugs at my arm, and a monitor beside the bed marks time with slow, uneven beeps. The air smells like antiseptic and dried blood.

I lie flat on my back in a hospital bed, my chest wrapped tight, my shoulder burning deep beneath the bandages. Oxygen feeds into my nose, and an IV line runs into my arm.

I try to move, and something pulls hard at my wrist.

A restraint.

Someone shifts near the bed.

A nurse leans into view, her expression changing the moment she realizes I'm awake. "Mr. Kincaid. You're conscious."

Her voice stays calm. She checks the monitor, makes a note on the chart, then carefully lifts the edge of the bandage near my shoulder.

"You were very lucky," she says. "The bullet passed close to your subclavian artery. A couple of centimeters difference, and you wouldn't have survived."

I say nothing.

"You lost a significant amount of blood," she continues. "Do you remember anything about what happened?"

Still nothing.

She studies my face for a moment, then nods as if she expected silence. She lowers the bandage and steps back.

I look down at myself. Bandages wrap my chest. Lines snake across my skin. My shoulder throbs with a deep, pulsing pain.

Something is wrong.

My hand goes to my neck.

Nothing.

The necklace is gone.

The room tilts.

No. No. No.

Panic surges hot and fast. I pull against the cuff and try to sit up, and pain tears through my side hard enough to steal my breath. The IV rips partway out of my arm, blood welling immediately.

"Where is it?" I rasp. My voice sounds shredded. "Where is my necklace?"

The nurse rushes back in, alarm flashing across her face before she forces it down. "Sir, you need to stop. You're going to injure yourself."

"Where is it?" I shout, clawing at the monitor leads. Adhesive tears from my skin. "The necklace around my neck. Where did you put it?"

"You need to calm down."

"Don't fucking tell me to calm down!" My vision tunnels. "Where is it? What did you do with it?!"

Two agents push in behind her without knocking, eyes already hard. One looks me up and down with open contempt. The other stays near the door like he expects me to lunge.

"My necklace. The vial, where the fuck is it?" I snap.

The agent closest to the bed gives a humorless smile. "You mean the creepy little blood chain you were wearing? Was it one of your victim's?"

I lunge forward against the restraint. The cuff bites deep.

He doesn't flinch. "Yeah. We took it. Standard procedure when we bring in a homicide suspect."

The nurse glances between them, then back at me. "All personal items are collected during trauma intake. It's probably been logged with—"

"Probably?" I bite out. "If it's gone, I swear to god—"

"You'll what?" the first agent cuts in, stepping closer to the bed. "Add another body to your list?"

Rage burns through the pain. "We'll look into it," the second agent says tightly. "Right now you need to answer some questions."

"I'm not saying shit until I get it back."

He tilts his head. "You're not in a position to make demands."

They exchange a look that isn't uncertainty. It's calculation.

Brooke is out there, and I don't even have the last thing I have left of her. The thought hits hard enough to make my hands shake. I yank against the strap again. Metal tears into skin. Blood slides warm down my wrist.

The nurse inhales sharply but doesn't reach for the call button this time. Instead she steps closer to the bed, eyes on the agents. "If it's logged, I can call intake myself and confirm the item number."

"Stay in your lane," one of the agents says without looking at her.

She straightens anyway. "He just came out of surgery. Elevated stress can cause complications. Let me verify it."

"Now," I warn, voice low.

One of the agents steps forward until he is within arm's reach. "That's enough, Kincaid."

My head snaps toward him. "Get me the fucking necklace!"

"It's not lost," the second agent says firmly. "It's in evidence or personal effects."

My eyes lock on his. He holds my stare like he is daring me to try something.

The necklace isn't just some keepsake. It's her blood. Her gift. The last thread between us. I can feel the absence of it like something torn out and left open.

"Then go find it," I growl. "Now!"

The first agent gives the nurse an irritated look. "Fine. Get a catalog of his personal items. Make it quick."

She nods immediately and steps toward the counter, already reaching for the phone. "I'll call intake and security. I'll get the item number and have it brought up."

The nurse speaks into the phone with clipped urgency. "Yes, this is ICU. I need immediate verification on patient Kincaid's personal effects... A necklace with a vial attached... Yes... Priority."

I don't relax. I can't. The room tilts again. Black creeps at the edges of my vision. I sag back against the pillows, barely catching myself before I rip another line free.

The nurse moves quickly, pressing gauze to my arm, adjusting the IV with careful hands. "We'll find it."

One of the agents gives a dismissive snort. They mutter to each other as they back toward the door, still watching me like I might break loose and charge. The door shuts behind them with a harder click than necessary.

The nurse who had been monitoring the line finishes checking the bag and steps back from the bed. "I need to grab another kit," she says before slipping out of the room.

Then the door clicks shut.

I stare at it, my chest rising too fast as I wait for it to swing open again with the only answer that matters. Every muscle in my body stays wound tight. My eyes stay fixed on the handle as seconds drag past. I expect another agent, another round of questions.

Instead, a different nurse steps into the room.

She keeps her eyes lowered and holds a cell phone in one hand.

"You have a call," she says before setting it on the rolling tray beside my bed.

She turns and walks out without another word. The door closes behind her, leaving the room quiet again.

The screen glows.

Incoming call. No number.

I pick it up. I don't speak. Silence breathes on the other end for a second.

Then, calm and amused, "Still alive, huh?"

My grip tightens until my knuckles go white.

"Grant."

A soft exhale. "Well you won't be alive for long."

My jaw locks. "Where's Brooke?"

He gives a slow sigh. "That girl has some fight in her. You should be proud. But if I were you, I would stop worrying about her and start worrying about what is about to happen to you."

"If you touch her," I say, each word forced through clenched teeth, "I promise you will regret it."

His voice dips lower. "Oh, Seth. I'm gonna do more than touch her."

Something inside my chest tightens hard enough to make it difficult to breathe.

Grant chuckles. "Rest up, Seth. Prison's not going to be easy for you."

The line goes dead.

For a second, I just hold the phone to my ear, waiting for the click to reverse. Waiting for anything.

Nothing. The silence presses in.

He has her.

And he's going to hurt her.

My chest tightens so fast I think the sutures have split. My pulse roars in my ears.

The door opens, a federal agent steps inside. He shuts the door behind him and slides his phone into his jacket pocket.

"You."

He arches a brow. "Me?"

"You set that up," I snap. "You're in on it."

He gives a short chuckle. "In on what?"

"Don't fucking play dumb," I trying to shove myself upright. Pain rips through my side. "You know Grant."

He looks almost amused. "You're not making your case any better, Kincaid."

"You're working with him. You're in on it. Where is Brooke?"

"Fifty people dead," he steps closer to the bed. "And you're acting erratic. Not a good sign."

My hand flies to the IV. Rage surges so fast it feels electric. I grab the line and yank. Pain explodes through my arm. The tape tears. Blood spills warm down my skin and drips onto the sheets.

The nurse rushes in behind him. "Stop," she demands sharply, already moving toward me.

The agent doesn't help her. He just watches.

"Go ahead," he says. "Keep thrashing. It only reinforces what we already suspect."

"I didn't do this," I grind out.

He shrugs. "That's what they all say."

The nurse presses gauze to my arm. "You're going to tear your stitches," she tries to push me back against the mattress.

I barely hear her.

The room tilts. The fluorescent lights above me flicker, buzzing louder than they should. The agent's face blurs.

And Luke stands near the foot of my bed. He leans against the wall with his arms folded.

"What are you gonna do?" he asks, head tilting. "You can barely even walk. They just had to take a bullet out of your chest."

My throat goes dry.

"You're not real," I mutter.

Luke smiles. "Face it, Seth. You're not gonna be able to save her."

I try to sit up again, but my body refuses to cooperate. The pain pins me down.

"She's gonna die because of you," he goes on. "Just like Natalie died because of you."

My breathing goes uneven.

"And your baby's gonna die with Brooke too."

The words hit harder than the bullet ever did.

My fingers tremble. My vision tunnels.

The nurse's voice sounds far away. "He's not responding to me."

Luke steps closer and crouches beside the bed, eye level with me. "You kill everything you touch."

I see it.

Brooke alone somewhere in the dark. Calling my name and getting nothing back. I see a tiny heartbeat on a monitor flicker once, twice, and then nothing. I see a casket lowered into the ground while I stand behind glass, shackled, unable to move. I see myself rotting in a cell while dirt hits a coffin lid.

My breath hitches and stutters. The rage drains out of me. In its place comes something colder.

Not anger.

Certainty.

Certainty that maybe this is the pattern. That maybe Luke is right. That maybe I am the common denominator.

The nurse's hands are still on my arm, applying pressure. The agent is saying something about psychiatric evaluation.

The room is there again.

But the future Luke paints doesn't fade.

I lie back against the pillows, staring at the ceiling, chest rising too fast, feeling the weight of a future where I fail her.

Not fighting.

Not winning.

Just watching everything I love die because I'm not enough to stop it.

Chapter 12

The man in scrubs moves through the hospital as if he clocked in hours ago.

The fabric hangs over a body that doesn't belong in a hospital uniform. His shoulders are broad, his chest thick and powerful, and his arms fill the sleeves with the dense muscle of someone built for violence rather than medicine.

The surgical mask covers the lower half of his face, but his eyes are impossible to ignore. They hold a cold focus, the kind of steady attention that makes people instinctively uneasy without understanding why.

A clipped ID badge swings lightly against his chest, catching the harsh hospital lights as he moves.

No one questions him.

Nurses hurry past with charts clutched in their hands. Orderlies push gurneys down the corridor without looking up. Doctors speak into phones while walking quickly between rooms, too distracted by their own urgency to notice the danger moving calmly among them.

He slips into the rhythm with ease.

That is his talent.

He can mimic any environment, match its pulse, and disappear inside it.

He steps into the elevator and presses the button for the third floor. The doors close behind him with a soft hiss, sealing him in with his reflection. Sun-warmed skin. Eyes calm and undisturbed by the violence he is minutes away from unleashing.

He rolls his shoulders once, muscles shifting beneath the scrub top, and adjusts the extra set of scrubs in his hands.

The doors slide open.

The third-floor hallway is quiet except for the soft beeping of monitors behind closed doors. Two FBI agents guard the room at the end of the corridor.

The intruder approaches with a clipboard tucked under his arm, posture loose and unbothered.

"Wound check on the detainee," he says, muffled through the surgical mask.

One of the agents steps in his path, eyes hard. "Bullshit. We didn't authorize shit."

The other cocks his head, already sizing him up. "What are you, new? You think we don't check credentials?"

The first agent jabs a finger toward the badge. "This look real to you? Doesn't look real to me."

"You've got about five seconds to explain who the fuck you are before we put you face down," the second adds, his hand hovering near his holster.

The intruder doesn't answer.

Instead, he shifts the scrubs in his grip, unfolding them just enough. A large hunting knife slides free from the fabric. The blade flashes under the fluorescent lights.

He steps in before either man fully understands what is happening.

The knife tears across the first agent's throat in one brutal sweep. The blade opens him from one side of the neck to the other. Skin splits wide, and the cut peels open as blood surges out in a thick, violent rush. The man's voice collapses into a wet choking sound as he grabs at his throat. Blood pours between his fingers, spilling down his chest and splattering the floor as his knees give out.

The second agent finally moves, his hand dropping toward his weapon.

He doesn't get it out.

The intruder drives the knife straight into the man's eye.

The blade punches through the socket with a sickening crack of bone. The agent's body convulses as the knife sinks deep into his skull. Blood and fluid stream down his face as his legs buckle beneath him.

The intruder wrenches the blade free. Both bodies hit the floor. He steps over them without even looking down. To him, killing is not an event.

It is a task.

He pushes into the room and closes the door behind him.

The third guard inside the room stands up immediately, his chair scraping hard against the floor. "Hey, who the fuck are you supposed to—"

The intruder's hand slides behind his back again and pulls a pistol fitted with a suppressor.

He raises it and fires.

The muted shot pops through the room, the bullet punching straight through the guard's skull before he can finish the sentence. The impact snaps his head backward and blows blood and bone against the wall behind him.

The guard collapses back into the chair and slides sideways, his body folding awkwardly as blood runs down his collar and drips onto the floor.

Now the room is silent except for the rhythmic beep of the cardiac monitor.

Seth lies on the hospital bed, pale beneath the harsh lights. Wires drape over his body. Bandages wrap his chest. A handcuff bites into his wrist, chaining him to the bedrail.

His eyes open slowly, tracking the intruder with a mixture of pain, recognition, and relief that he doesn't waste energy trying to hide.

The man lowers his mask, revealing sharp cheekbones, a strong jaw dusted with dark stubble, and eyes that are colder up close. His hair is swept back in a loose tie, a few strands falling around his temples. The clean cut disguise hasn't dulled the lethal energy he carries like a second skin.

"Wow. You look like shit," the intruder says dryly.

Seth's lips twitch despite everything, the faintest ghost of a smile pulling at the corner of his mouth. "Missed you too."

The intruder crosses the room with the calm of someone walking through a grocery aisle instead of a hospital room with three fresh bodies. He bends over the dead guard, pulls the keys from the man's belt, and unlocks the cuff around Seth's wrist. The latch snaps open with a quiet metallic click.

He straightens, flicks the blood from the knife onto the floor, then gathers the extra scrubs in his hand and tosses the folded bundle onto the bed.

"Get changed."

Seth stares at the clothes for a second, then forces himself to swing his legs over the side of the bed.

Pain rips through his side immediately. His body folds forward, breath leaving him in a rough grunt as the bandages across his shoulder and ribs pull tight.

He tries to stand anyway.

His knees wobble under him, and for a moment it looks like he might collapse back onto the mattress.

The intruder catches him by the arm before he can fall.

Seth shakes him off and forces himself upright again. Every movement looks stiff and wrong, his body fighting him with every step as he strips off the blood-stained hospital shirt and pulls the scrubs over his bandaged torso.

Seth steps into the scrub pants, bracing one hand against the bed as another spike of pain shoots through his ribs. When he finishes changing, he looks down at the floor.

His boots are gone.

All that waits there are the thin gray hospital slippers.

Seth stares at them with visible irritation before stepping into them anyway.

The intruder looks down at Seth's feet and huffs out a quiet laugh.

Seth shoots him a glare.

"They took her," Seth says. "We have to get her back."

The intruder studies him for a moment. Seth can barely stand without bracing himself against the bed, sweat already gathering along his hairline.

"You can barely stand."

"I don't care," Seth snaps. "We're finding Brooke."

The intruder lets out a slow breath that sounds halfway between annoyance and reluctant amusement.

"Alright, let's go before the entire Bureau realizes their agents are dead."

He slides Seth's arm over his shoulders and hauls him upright with practiced ease. Seth forces his legs to cooperate, the hospital slippers dragging against the floor for a moment before he manages to move.

They head for the door.

Two more armed agents round the corner at the far end of the hallway.

They stop the moment they see them.

Their eyes move past Seth first, then shift behind him. Both men spot the bodies in the hospital room and the blood spreading across the floor just beyond the doorway. The recognition hits their faces all at once. Hands drop toward their holsters.

The intruder doesn't hesitate.

He raises the pistol and fires twice in quick succession.

The first bullet strikes the nearer agent high in the chest, snapping his body backward into the wall. The second shot hits the other man a fraction of a second later, punching through his throat and blowing blood across the pale hallway tiles.

Both men collapse almost immediately. One slides down the wall, leaving a thick smear of red behind him. The other drops straight to the floor, his weapon clattering uselessly from his hand.

Seth barely glances at the bodies.

He steps over one of them without slowing.

They turn the corner toward the stairwell. That is when the nurse steps out of a side room.

She stops cold. Her gaze drops to the blood streaking the tile. Then to the agents sprawled across it. Then to the gun in the intruder's hand. Her mouth parts. In her hands is a clear plastic belongings bag.

Inside it, coiled at the bottom, is the necklace. The vial catches the light.

For a second, no one moves.

Seth's pulse kicks hard in his throat. He steps toward her.

She flinches, back hitting the wall.

"I was just bringing this to—" Her voice trembles. "They told me to log it, but I thought—"

Seth doesn't answer.

He takes the bag from her hands. His fingers tear the plastic open. The thin hospital seal snaps. He pulls the necklace free.

The chain is cold against his skin as he loops it over his head. The vial settles against his sternum, right over the bloody bandage.

He looks at the nurse. She is staring at the bodies again, shock overtaking her training. Her hands shake. She looks like she might drop.

Seth doesn't offer reassurance. He doesn't threaten her either. He simply walks past her.

The intruder follows, stepping over another agent without breaking pace.

Behind them, the nurse slides down the wall slowly, still clutching the torn plastic bag, staring at the blood pooling across the sterile floor.

Seth doesn't look back.

They enter the stairwell. The intruder clears each landing with methodical precision. Seth stays quiet, conserving strength for violence.

When they reach the bottom exit, he pushes the door open and guides Seth into the cold night air.

A dark SUV idles near the curb. Travis is in the driver's seat, wide-eyed, gripping the steering wheel so tightly his knuckles turn white.

"Shit—Seth—get in—quick," Travis shouts, voice cracking.

The intruder eases Seth into the backseat. Seth collapses against the upholstery with a sharp hiss of pain.

Travis looks back at Seth. "Is he okay? Is he—"

"He'll live," the intruder closes the passenger door. "Drive."

Travis hits the gas so hard the tires screech.

The intruder leans back, finally letting the tension leave his shoulders. He looks back at Seth, whose eyes are half-lidded but still burning with purpose.

"You're welcome," the intruder says.

Seth hisses as he adjusts in the seat.

"Thanks, Beau."

Beau nods once.

Seth watches Beau reassemble his pistol with effortless precision and feels a cold, focused clarity settle in his chest.

They had once turned entire operations into rubble when they worked side by side. They had once wiped out threats their commanding officers swore were "unmanageable."

There were reports that never made it past internal review. Photos that were sealed. Debriefs that grew quiet when certain details came up.

Men left gutted in alleyways after refusing to talk.

One insurgent found without his scalp because Beau needed the others to understand he was done negotiating.

Interrogations that ran long enough for other Marines to step outside and light cigarettes they didn't even want, just to avoid hearing what was happening in the room.

Other Marines called it excessive. Seth and Beau called it efficient.

Command called it a problem.

They were not discharged for incompetence. They were removed because mercy had never been their strength.

Beau checks his weapon without looking down and slides it back into place.

"We'll get her, Seth. Those motherfuckers are in for a rude awakening."

Seth stares out the windshield, the night reflecting faintly in his eyes. The panic that had nearly drowned him in the hospital has burned off. What remains is cold and focused.

His jaw tightens. "They have no idea what hell they just brought into their lives."

It is not a threat. It is a promise already set in motion.

They had once been warned to rein it in. To remember optics. To consider consequences. They didn't. They adapted.

Whoever has Brooke believes they are holding the leverage. Believes they have the upper hand. They don't understand what it means to corner men who no longer care about survival, reputation, or aftermath.

Restraint had been the only thing that ever kept Seth and Beau contained.

And restraint is gone.

Chapter 13
Seth

"Okay—okay—okay," Travis mutters, shaking so hard the wheel rattles. "Now I'm officially a getaway driver. This is a felony, I can't go to prison, man. I'm too good looking. They'll take one look at me and—boom—I'm somebody's bitch by breakfast."

I press a hand against my chest where the stitches are already pulling apart. "Travis."

He keeps rambling. "I swear to God, Seth, I'm not built for prison. They'll pass me around like—"

"Travis!"

He snaps his mouth shut, breathing like he just ran a marathon.

I lean forward between the seats, gripping Travis's headrest as the SUV tears down the road.

"Do you know where they took Brooke?" I ask.

His face crumples instantly. The panic that flashes across it is real, not the dramatic nonsense he usually throws around.

"No. By the time I crawled out of that freezer, both of you were gone. Hence"—he waves frantically toward Beau—"why I called him. I had no idea what the fuck was going on."

I let my head hit the seat, exhaustion and rage scraping through me.

"As soon as you locked us in the fridge," Travis continues. "Some masked asshole in a goat mask showed up. Grabbed her. Locked me and Naomi inside. And turned the freezer all the way up."

My hands clench.

"That man in the mask," I say, "was Brooke's uncle."

He whips around so fast the SUV swerves. "John? What the fuck? What the actual fuck? Why would her uncle try to kill her?"

"I don't think he wants to kill her. He wants to kill me. But they didn't finish the job because they wanted me to go down for the whole massacre."

Travis stares at me, eyes huge. Beau watches him calmly, like this entire conversation is a mild inconvenience.

"And John is not alone," I add. "He is working with Detective Grant. And there's a group of other masked psycho fucks who helped stage the hotel massacre."

"Jesus Christ," Travis whispers.

"It's all tied to Nick and Amber's families," I continue. "The entire thing is connected."

Travis presses both hands to the wheel, his voice climbing. "What the fuck is this, Seth? Why is every rich psycho in California part of some murder cult? And why would they want Brooke? She didn't do anything!"

I push myself upright again, ignoring the pain ripping through my shoulder.

"We're going to Fresno, John probably took her there."

Travis chokes on his own breath. "You're still bleeding! Shouldn't you—I don't know—lie down before you go full Rambo? You're dripping all over the seat."

"Get me to Fresno," I snap. "Right fucking now!"

"Seth, it is an eighteen-hour drive! You are going to bleed out and die in the back seat, and then I will go to prison because they will think I killed you!"

"I'm not dying," I snap. "I'm getting Brooke back."

Beau glances at me, an almost approving look passing over his face. "He's fine. He's been more injured than this."

Travis shoots a look at him. "How is that comforting?"

Beau looks over his shoulder at me, calm as ever. "Plane?"

"You still have it?"

"Yep."

Travis makes a strangled noise. "You two have a plane? Like a real one? Since when?!"

Beau doesn't look up from loading a magazine. "Since always."

"Here's the directions to the hangar. You're an accomplice," he adds dryly. "And if you don't want to be someone's bitch in prison, you better floor it like the man said."

Travis makes a dying whale sound and slams his foot on the gas.

I slump back and close my eyes, pressure throbbing through my shoulder, but my mind isn't on the pain.

It's on Brooke.

Her face. Her voice. The way she looked at me right before Grant's bullet hit.

I should've fought harder. I should've crawled after her if I had to. I shouldn't have passed out. I shouldn't have—

Beau glances back at me. "Stay awake."

"I'm awake."

"Good. Because if you die, I'm not babysitting Shaggy here."

"HEY!" Travis shouts.

I grip the door handle hard enough it creaks.

"We get to Fresno," my tone hardens, "we tear that house apart."

Beau nods. "Good plan."

Travis mutters, "I'm gonna need to smoke so much weed to get over the stress of these two weeks," but he keeps driving.

Fast.

We arrive at the private jet waiting for us on a dimly lit airstrip outside Denver. No explanations needed. Beau has a pilot friend. That friend doesn't ask questions. People like Beau collect favors the way normal people collect phone numbers, and this one happens to fly a jet without scanning passports or running background checks.

Beau doesn't waste time once we are in the air. As soon as the jet levels out, he cracks open the med bag and pulls on gloves. His movements are clean, practiced. This kind of efficiency only comes from doing this a hundred times before, probably on himself.

He peels back the blood-crusted gauze, cleans around the wound with antiseptic that burns deep into my nerves, and mutters something about how I tore it open worse trying to stand earlier. He repacks it tightly, pressing down with more pressure than necessary, and tapes it up again with a new roll.

"Antibiotics," he fishes a prescription bottle out of the bag. He twists off the cap and shakes out two pills, pressing them into my palm. "And take this with it. Oxy. Don't make a habit of it."

I swallow both without asking for water. "You still got that doctor?"

He nods. "Yeah. Why?"

"I need Risperidone. Haven't taken it in weeks."

Beau stops moving. "You hallucinating again?"

I meet his gaze. "Yeah. Luke this time."

He doesn't ask for details. Just gives one slow nod. "I'll make the call."

I lean back against the headrest. My mouth is dry as sand, my tongue heavy. I hadn't realized how dehydrated I felt until Travis's voice cuts in from the aisle.

"Here," he holds out a half-empty bottle of blue Gatorade he raided from the minibar. "Electrolytes. This should help, right?"

I take it without a word and drink until it is gone. It isn't cold, but I don't care. My body pulls it in like it has been waiting for days. I don't realize how dizzy I still am until the sugar hits.

Travis sinks into the seat beside me. His leg bounces restlessly, like he is trying to shake the panic out of his body.

"We're gonna get her. Don't worry."

I stare at the floor for a second, then force the words out.

"She's pregnant, Travis."

His head whips toward me. "What?"

"She told me... right before everything went to hell."

He stares like he can't decide if I'm messing with him. Then he leans back and drags a hand over his face.

"Holy shit."

"Yeah," I sigh.

"She's strong, Seth. Brooke's a survivor."

Luke's voice comes from the opposite seat.

"Tick tock, Seth. Your girl's running on borrowed time."

Luke leans forward, elbows on his knees, eyes fixed on me.

"You're gonna be late. You're always late."

"I'm not," I mutter.

Travis glances at me. "What?"

"Nothing."

The engines hum beneath us. The cabin lights flicker faintly.

"Tsk tsk, Seth," Luke whispers. "By the time you land, she could already be bleeding out somewhere. You can barely keep your head straight."

I force my breathing to slow.

"You're not real," I mutter under my breath.

Luke's grin sharpens. "Doesn't make me wrong."

I blink, and he is gone.

The jet cuts through the night, the vibration settling into my bones. The medication Beau gave me dulls the worst of the physical pain, but it does nothing for the hallucinations.

Brooke is somewhere down there. Alone. Afraid. Carrying our child. Fighting through everything on her own while I am stuck miles above her, useless and furious.

I force my breathing to steady. To stay in control. To keep from putting my fist through the window.

We're closing the distance. Every minute in the air is another step closer to her.

And when we land, I am going to tear apart every person who thinks they can take her from me and live.

Chapter 14
Brooke

I don't feel like I'm in the room anymore.

Seth's alive.

My breath shatters in my chest. Something inside me cracks wide open, too hard to contain. I can't stop laughing. It echoes through the dining hall, cutting straight through the heavy silence.

All of them turn to stare.

Elliot's face twitches, first in confusion, then irritation.

"What's so fucking funny?" he rises slowly from his chair. "You think he's coming for you? We're off-grid, sweetheart. Even John doesn't know where this place is."

I keep laughing. It claws its way out of my chest like relief and fury twisted into one. They told me he was dead. They wanted me broken and hopeless.

But he isn't dead.

He's fighting. He's coming for me.

Sophie leans in across the table, her smirk venom-sharp, arms folded like she is already bored. "That's cute. You really think your boyfriend's going to come save you."

I look her straight in the eye, my laughter finally dying down, my voice hoarse from the scream that wants to follow it.

"Even if he is too late to save me," I laugh. "He's gonna fucking kill all of you."

Elliot moves toward me slowly, savoring every step like he has all the time in the world. His boots click against the marble floor, the sound echoing through the cavernous dining hall. Every step closer feels like a countdown.

"Look at me," he says.

I try to hold it in, but the laughter keeps bleeding out, shaky, broken, too loud in the silence he is trying to control. It isn't joy. It is defiance scraping its nails down the walls of my throat.

He doesn't like that.

His hand comes down hard on my back, right across the line of fresh stitches.

Pain explodes through my ribs, white-hot and instant, blinding enough to suck the air out of my lungs. A gasp tears from me before I can swallow it, and the laugh chokes off into silence.

He presses harder.

"There you go," he murmurs. "Back with us."

Tears sting at the corners of my eyes. One of the sutures has torn, I can feel it. A slow, hot burn blooms beneath the skin.

"Since you think Seth is coming to save you," Elliot goes on, circling behind me, his voice low and disturbingly calm, "that puts a little fire under me. Makes me want to move things along."

He leans down, and I feel his breath brush against the side of my face.

"John may act like he cares about you," he whispers. "But he doesn't. If you die, he'll be annoyed. Maybe he'll say something poetic about wasted potential. But one dead bitch isn't going to topple The Collective."

His fingers drag slowly up my spine, right over the torn sutures, making sure I feel every inch of it.

"You need to understand something, Brooke. No one is coming for you."

My jaw locks. I don't give him the satisfaction of an answer. I won't.

"You're mine now," he continues, his voice softening. "Mine to break. Mine to cut open. And when I'm finished with you—"

He bends lower, his lips brushing the shell of my ear.

"I'll send what's left to Seth. In pieces... I wonder which parts he'll want to keep."

My stomach turns. A wave of nausea crawls up my throat.

But I still don't look away.

Before I can react, Elliot strikes me again. His hand snaps across my back, landing directly over the torn sutures. Pain detonates through me, shredding through nerves until sound collapses into a strangled cry in my throat. My body jerks forward, helpless against it.

Elliot straightens and wipes his palm against his pants, like touching me contaminated him.

"Take them downstairs," he says to the guards. "Cleaning time."

Elliot pauses at the doorway and looks back at me.

"And Brooke," he smiles, "I hope you're ready for tomorrow's game."

Then he turns and disappears into the corridor, his laughter echoing faintly before the hall swallows it whole.

I stay where I am, shaking, pain ripping through my back, my wrists, my ribs.

But beneath the agony, beneath the terror, one truth burns through everything else.

Seth is alive.

And he is coming.

They can hurt me. They can cut me open. They can stitch me wrong and drag me through hell itself. But they have not broken me.

Guards seize us by the arms and shoulders, dragging us toward the stairwell. No one fights. No one can.

They drag us from the dining hall like animals. Two guards herd us through the corridor and down a narrow stairwell, the air growing colder and heavier with each step.

The basement reeks of mold, rust, and old suffering. The kind that lingers long after the screaming stops.

One of the guards, Enzo, waits at the bottom of the stairs, looming like a monument. He is tall, thick through the shoulders, his black tux stretched clean across a frame built like a butcher's block. His face is blank and cold, like emotion has been carved out of him years ago. The kind of man who doesn't blink when things scream.

In his hands, he holds an industrial hose designed to strip concrete, not people.

"Strip!"

No one moves fast enough.

He tears clothing away with brutal efficiency, fabric ripping, skin exposed under harsh lights. We are shoved into a line along the wall, naked and shivering.

The hose roars to life.

He turns it on Jared first.

The water hits him so hard he gasps, stumbling back as the spray hammers raw skin. When Enzo angles it between his legs, Jared folds to the floor, hands shaking in instinctive defense.

"Get up!" Enzo barks, kicking his ribs until he does.

Sarah is screaming, the hiccuping, manic kind that comes from someone whose mind finally snaps. She keeps choking out her sister's name.

Emma is crying so loudly it echoes.

Miles leans toward me. His voice trembles. "Who's Seth Kincaid?"

I swallow hard. The hose hits Emma beside me and she shrieks, her skin going red instantly.

"That's who's going to save us," My voice cracks, but I keep going. "Seth won't stop until he finds me. He won't leave you guys either."

Miles stares at me like hope hurts.

"If he broke out," I continue, "that means he's in Colorado. It'll take him a day or two to get here."

Miles shakes his head. "I don't know if we have a day or two. The others that were here before...they told me. The next is the card game, and the day after that is the last hunt."

My stomach twists. "The last hunt?"

He nods grimly. "That's when they get rid of most of us. They let us out into the forest wearing bright colors so we're easy targets. Crossbows, guns, knives, chainsaws... anything. It's how they clear space before the next shipment of victims."

A cold wave rolls down my spine.

Miles leans toward me again, his voice shaking. "We're running out of time."

Seth has to get here before that.

Enzo reaches me.

"Come on," he demands.

I don't move fast enough. He grabs my arm and yanks me forward, ripping the last scrap of fabric from my body. I try to cover my stomach.

The hose hits my legs first. The pressure is so strong it feels like knives carving upward along my shins, my thighs, my hips.

"Move your hand."

I don't.

He steps closer. "Move it, or I'll move it for you."

I bend forward instinctively, trying to shield the small swell of my lower abdomen with my ribs, turning so the full force won't hit my stomach.

He doesn't like that. He angles the spray up my torso.

The water slams into my breasts and white-hot pain explodes through my chest. The spray makes me scream before I can stop myself.

Enzo laughs, amused.

I bite my lip so hard blood fills my mouth.

He walks behind me.

"No," I whisper, bracing.

The pressure hits the stitched wounds across my back.

Agony rips through me so sharply my vision blurs. I drop to my knees as one of the stitches snaps.

"Oops," Enzo chuckles lazily. "Physician's going to love me today."

Water pools around me, red swirling into pink as it washes off my skin. My whole body trembles from the pain and the cold and the humiliation.

I close my eyes.

Seth, please—Find me.

Chapter 15
Seth

By the time we land in Fresno, the sun is already climbing the horizon. We jack a black SUV from a long-term parking lot near the airport, Beau hotwires it in under thirty seconds like it is just another Tuesday. No plates, tinted windows, half a tank of gas. Good enough.

The drive to John and Mary's neighborhood is quiet. When we finally turn onto their street, the houses look washed out in the early morning light. Peaceful, like nothing has ever happened here. Like Brooke isn't missing. Like we aren't about to turn this place inside out.

Travis kills the engine and wipes a hand down his face. "Okay. We're here. Just... maybe no murder unless it's absolutely necessary?"

Beau's already opening the door. "Only if they make us."

Travis lets out a strangled noise that might be a whimper.

I step out last. My shoulder burns with every movement. The gauze at my ribs is soaked through again, sticking to my skin. It doesn't matter. Pain doesn't matter. Not when Brooke is still out there.

"Let's move."

Beau falls in behind me without a word. Travis stays rooted in place, sweat beading on his forehead, his hands twitching against his thighs.

"I don't think I can do this," he says. "Can I stay out here? I'll keep watch. I swear. I'll scream if I see anything."

"Yes," Beau says, not even turning around. "Please do."

Travis bolts to the corner of the house, muttering something about heart attacks and federal charges and dying young.

We keep walking. Straight toward the house that is about to stop being peaceful.

I walk straight to the door. I don't knock. I lift my boot and kick with everything I have. The door buckles inward and slams against the wall with a bang loud enough to shake picture frames in the hallway. Beau steadies it with his boot, suppressor already raised on his Glock.

Mary stumbles out of the hallway, hand over her mouth, eyes huge.

"S-Seth? Oh my—"

"Where is she?" I demand.

No warm-up. No easing into it. I'm not here to talk.

"I—Seth—sweetheart, I don't—"

"I'm only going to say this once."

I cross the room and grab her by the front of her shirt, dragging her into the living room until her back hits the wall with a crack.

"Where. Is. Brooke?"

She cries instantly. "I swear, I don't know!"

I shove the barrel of my gun under her chin. "You know, Mary, I have been falling for this sweet, innocent aunt act since the day I met you. And I hate being lied to. You are going to cut the bullshit now unless you want your brain to coat the fucking wallpaper."

Mary's voice shakes so violently it breaks apart. "I'm telling the truth! John—John let Grant take her!"

The world goes silent. John let him take her.

"Why?" My voice drops to something quiet and violent. "Why would he let him take her?"

Mary's chin trembles. "That was The Collective's decision. They sent her to Elliot's Manor."

Everything in me goes cold.

"What the fuck is Elliot's Manor?" I ask.

"It is where they send... the ones they want to punish," Mary whispers. "It's like a correctional facility for The Collective."

I tighten my grip on her shirt. "Where is it?"

"I don't know," she sobs. "I swear I don't know. I only know what it is."

I shove the muzzle of my Glock under her chin. "If you lie again, this gun is gonna answer for you."

She sobs harder. "I'm not lying."

"Where is John?"

"He left right after Grant did," Mary says, tears streaming down her face. "He said he had to prepare. I don't know where he went."

I stare at her. "Did you know about any of this?"

Mary nods miserably. "I did. I knew there were... expectations, plans. I didn't know it would happen this soon."

"You knew everything," I snap. "You knew what he planned for her."

She shakes her head weakly. "I... didn't want Brooke to die like my sister."

"You let them murder your sister," I say. "And you let them take your niece to whatever fucked up prison they have hidden."

Mary breaks into full sobs. "I begged John not to kill Brooke. I begged him. He spared her. So we raised her."

"You call that raising?" I hiss. "Letting her grow up in the house of the man who killed her parents?"

Mary cries harder, like that is supposed to buy her mercy. "I didn't want them to do this to Brooke. I couldn't stop them."

My jaw locks. The thought hits me all at once. John had Brooke in this house her entire life. He watched her grow up. He trained her. Men like him don't keep that kind of access without crossing lines, and the idea of him putting his hands on her makes something vicious tear loose in my chest.

I step closer. "Did he ever touch her?"

She understands the implication immediately.

"No," Mary says quickly. "No. Never. Never anything like that. He thought of her as his prodigy. John watched her grow up. That is the closest he has ever come to raising a child. He didn't want one, but he always believed Brooke would be useful."

My jaw tightens. "So you were complicit. You knew all of this all along, and you let John kill your sister."

Mary glares at me. "Didn't you kill Luke?"

I shift the gun slow enough for her to hear every millimeter of metal moving.

"Say his name again."

She freezes.

I lean in closer. "Do you know she's pregnant?"

Mary nods immediately, terrified. "She told me right before they took her. I tried—I begged them not to hurt her—"

"You didn't do enough."

"I swear—"

"If Brooke is dead," I whisper, "I'm coming back to kill you."

She collapses against the wall, shaking.

"But if she's alive," I continue, "I'm saving you for her."

Her eyes widen. She understands what that means.

I let go of her shirt and step back. "Now, where the fuck is my dog and cat?"

She points toward the hallway with a trembling hand. "In the—guest room."

Beau goes immediately to open the guest room door.

Krueger sprints out, nails scraping the floor.

Luna comes out last, slow, terrified, her tail tucked tight against her body. When she sees me, she darts forward and presses her trembling body against my shin, letting out a small, broken chirp before climbing into my arms.

I hold her against my chest, even as my stitches burn and blood soaks through my shirt. Her purring is frantic and uneven, a sound cats make when they are terrified but clinging to the only safety they know.

"You're pathetic," I tell Mary. "You deserve everything coming to you. And if Brooke decides not to kill you, you'll never see her again. You'll never meet our kid. And you'll die with the monster you chose."

Mary's legs give out. She slides down the wall, sobbing into her hands.

I turn away from her and walk toward John's office. Because I'm not here for her. I'm here for answers.

"Office," I tell Beau.

The moment we step into John's office, the smell hits me.

Cigar smoke, old paper, floor polish.

Beau starts pulling open drawers immediately. "Half of this shit is empty."

I look around. Gaps on the bookshelves. Dust outlines where boxes have been. Open safe, hollow and scraped clean.

"John pulled almost everything."

Beau glances over. "Which means?"

"He knew we were coming."

He has prepared for this moment. We tear through the room anyway. Two filing cabinets are empty. The third is too heavy.

Beau frowns. "That drawer's wrong."

"Move."

He steps aside, and I yank the drawer out so hard it hits the ground. A false bottom pops loose.

Underneath the drawer sits a thick black leather binder with worn edges and creased leather that looks like it has been handled for years. The symbol burned into the center of the cover makes something heavy drop straight into my stomach the second I see it. A ring of horns wrapped around a faceless silhouette.

I know that symbol the moment my eyes land on it.

My father had it tattooed across his chest, right over his heart. I remember seeing it when I was a kid while he stood in the bathroom mirror shaving. When I asked him what it meant, he pulled his shirt back down and told me to mind my own business.

Luke had the same one inked along his ribs.

At the time I figured it was some stupid matching tattoo. Luke never explained it when I asked him about it.

He always avoided the question.

A memory from the basement pushes forward. My father had Luke pinned against the concrete wall by the collar, demanding to know if he had talked. I thought he was about to kill him. I grabbed a knife and drove it into my father's side. When he came at me, I picked up the tire iron and swung until he didn't have a fucking face anymore.

At the time I believed I had just stopped my father from killing Luke.

Standing here now with the binder open in my hands, something finally clicks into place.

My father and Luke had been in The Collective together.

I open the binder.

Photographs fill the pages along with printed lists, coded assignments, and organized entries that read like a ledger built to track violence. Victims are cataloged with dates and locations. Rankings are recorded beside names that mean something inside this organization. Every page shows the same level of cold structure. This is not chaos or random brutality. This is a system.

This is The Collective's record. Their playbook. Everything they have done, everything they plan, written down.

And John left it here.

Not by accident.

For me.

My mind moves back through every moment I have spent inside John and Mary's house, and the pattern is suddenly obvious. The way they watched me when they thought I was not paying attention. The way their conversations sometimes stopped the moment I walked into the room.

They knew exactly who I was the entire time. They knew whose son had been standing in their living room. They knew about my father. They knew what my father and Luke were involved in.

They knew what they were planning to do with Brooke.

Every visit. Every conversation. Every time they looked at me across that house suddenly feels different now that I understand the truth. They have never been surprised by my presence. They have been studying me.

They've been waiting.

My jaw tightens harder while the weight of it settles in completely.

I turn another page and feel something in my chest twist when I see the next section.

Forum screenshots. Encrypted message threads. Usernames that I recognize immediately.

Luke's name sits in the conversation logs. Nick's name appears in multiple threads.

I read through the messages and feel the full weight of what I'm looking at settle into place piece by piece. Luke and Nick had been in The Collective together. They trade ideas with other members about killing methods and targets. They talk about violence the way some people talk about hobbies or art. They debate techniques. They plan meetings. They treat murder like a competition.

Luke didn't fall into this by accident.

My father had been preparing him for it his entire life.

Every violent lesson. Every twisted expectation. Every moment my father tortured us suddenly makes sense.

And Luke chose this.

That realization sits in my chest.

Every time Luke said people were watching Brooke, I thought he was trying to get under my skin. He was telling the truth. And he had been reporting back.

The Collective has been watching Brooke through him the entire time.

The muscles in my jaw tighten until the pressure starts to ache.

Luke didn't try to kill me because I locked him in the basement. He tried to kill me because The Collective told him to.

Because somewhere inside this organization my name had already been marked.

Beau flips through another set of papers. I stop when I recognize someone in a photo. A man we know from the hotel.

Connor. The dumb one. The one who split off from our group during the massacre. The one we assumed died.

He is smiling in the photo with a VossTech badge clipped to his shirt.

I exhale once. "You've got to be fucking kidding me."

A sinking realization hits. "He wasn't trapped with us. He was planted."

I grab the binder and march toward the front door.

Travis scrambles up from the side of the house when he sees me. "What—what did you find? Why do you look like that? Why is the binder so—oh God, did you find something bad?"

I shove the page with Connor's photo into his hands.

Travis stares. His face goes from confused to horrified to offended. "You mean to tell me that Connor—lazy, asshole, always-stealing-my-energy-drinks Connor—was a plant? He's not dead? He works for VossTech? And he was part of this murder cult shit?"

"Yup," I say.

Travis rubs his face hard. "Great. Amazing. Perfect. Now I get to deal with work problems and murder problems at the same time. Fucking Fantastic."

I walk past him. "We are heading to Silicon Valley."

Travis groans.

Beau pats him on the shoulder. "I'd drive quickly if I were you."

Travis whimpers.

And I walk toward the car with the binder under my arm, my pulse thundering.

They marked me. That was their first mistake.

The second is letting me live.

Chapter 16
Brooke

They drag me upstairs like a corpse.

My heels scrape along the stairs. Every jolt sends a lightning bolt through my spine and tears something fresh open in my back. By the time they shove me through the physician's door, I can feel warm blood sliding beneath my dress.

The physician doesn't bother greeting me. He doesn't bother acknowledging I'm a person.

His gaze goes straight to the wound like it's a puzzle he's impatient to solve.

He touches the torn edges with two fingers. He isn't gentle. Just clinical pressure that sends a hot shock ripping through my torso so violently my knees nearly buckle. Something metallic floods my mouth, copper and spit and the instinct to bite down on my own tongue before I scream.

"She tore several sutures," he gestures. "Hold her still."

The guards seize my arms, forcing me still, back exposed. My shoulder joints scream. My breath stutters.

The physician threads a needle the length of my damn finger. The metal flashes under the light. A thin, silver threat that promises nothing but suffering.

He doesn't say a word before he pushes it in.

The needle punches through torn skin and muscle, sliding through me like wire through raw meat. The sting is immediate, hot enough to make black spots burst behind my eyelids. My spine pulses, nerves firing in frantic, wrong directions. The pain isn't sharp, it's invasive.

He pulls the needle through in one long drag. I feel every millimeter of it scraping through tissue that isn't ready to be touched.

My jaw locks so tight my teeth ache. I breathe through my nose.

He stitches me with cold precision, tightening each pass until it feels like my skin is being cinched shut with barbed thread. A butcher treats meat with more respect than he treats me.

"You have excellent tissue integrity," he says dryly.

"Good, she won't die before tomorrow's events." Elliot's voice drifts from the corner.

"She's a fighter, I like that," he says. "Fix her properly. I need her functional tomorrow."

The physician finishes the final stitch and wipes the blood away with antiseptic-soaked gauze. It burns like acid. My vision blurs hard enough to double the room.

"She's stable. Take her back."

They drag me down the hall and throw me back in the basement as if dropping off a piece of equipment.

The others look less like people and more like shadows pretending to still be alive. Bruises have bloomed into thick, mottled purples. Lips split. Eyes sunken. Every breath seems like it costs them something they can't afford.

Miles shifts first. He crawls toward me slowly, one palm dragging across the concrete, his other arm wrapped around his ribs.

"Are you okay?"

I let out a brittle laugh that scrapes my throat raw. "As okay as I can be in this hellhole."

He gives a weak nod.

"I'm pregnant."

Miles blinks. "How far along?"

"I don't know." My voice wavers despite myself. "I didn't even have time to find out. We barely knew before we were taken."

"Does Seth know?"

"Yeah."

Pregnancy had never been part of the plan. Years ago my gynecologist warned me that PCOS might make it impossible. I convinced myself that was a blessing. I told myself I would never bring a child into a world where I had watched my parents die in front of me. Now the possibility of a baby growing inside me feels even heavier, because if I survive this place, that child will be born into something far darker.

The thought tightens painfully in my chest.

"What if I'm still here?" I whisper. "What if Seth never finds me?"

Miles shakes his head immediately. "Don't think like that. From everything you told me about Seth, he's coming."

I wipe at my face, irritated by the tears that have slipped free, and force myself to nod.

"I love him so much. I miss him. This is the longest we have ever been apart."

My voice cracks despite my effort to steady it.

"He's a murderer," I say with a weak breath of laughter. "He's also a little psychotic. But he's the most kind, considerate, affectionate man I have ever been with."

"My husband's name is Alonzo," Miles murmurs. "We're both nurses. We met during residency at the same hospital on the same shift." A faint smile appears and then fades. "All we ever wanted was to help people. That was the whole dream."

Miles looks down at his hands.

"Alonzo hates horror movies," he says. "He says they stress him out too much. He cries during medical dramas. He overcooks chicken because he is terrified of food poisoning."

His voice softens.

"I used to tease him about it."

He looks toward the wall instead of at me.

"I just want to see him again."

"You will."

The silence between us grows thick and suffocating.

After a moment Miles speaks again, his voice steady but quieter.

"If I don't make it out of here, I need you to tell him what happened. I don't want him sitting at home wondering if I'm still missing or thinking that I left him."

My throat tightens.

"Tell him that I died with him as the last thing on my mind," Miles continues. "I want him to know that I never stopped loving him."

He swallows and then speaks carefully, making sure I hear every word.

"Our address is 24781 Riverbend Lane in Eugene, Oregon."

I repeat it immediately under my breath.

"24781 Riverbend Lane. Eugene, Oregon."

Again.

And again.

I press it into memory like it is code I will need later. I keep repeating it softly, lips barely moving.

I start to say my own address, in California. The house Seth and I were not even finished settling into.

I stop.

The thought lands quietly and hurts more than I expect. We were already planning an escape. A different place. A clean slate. A future that now feels like something from another life.

If I die, Seth will hunt down everyone responsible. And then he will kill himself, because living without me is not something he believes in.

The image hits me hard and sudden. Seth alone. Seth bleeding. Seth choosing death because I'm not there to stop him.

I bite down hard, forcing the tears back. I refuse to let that future take shape.

Miles reaches out before I can pull away, his hand closing around my wrist.

"Hey, look at me."

I do.

"We're going to figure out how to get out of here," he says. "Okay? I don't know how yet. But we're not just waiting to die."

I nod.

But I don't believe it, not really. This place isn't built for survival. It's built for spectacle. For blood, for endings people watch.

But there is one thing I know with absolute certainty.

I'm not going out quietly.

Chapter 17
Seth

Connor's Silicon Valley apartment looks exactly like the kind of place a smug, overpaid tech-bro would live in. An architectural flex with floor-to-ceiling windows that offer no privacy but scream wealth.

The front door is framed by a top-tier security system, motion sensors, camera feeds, keyless entry. It probably costs more than the SUV we stole.

Beau doesn't even glance at the keypad.

He steps forward, raises his suppressed pistol, and fires two clean shots straight through the wood. The soft thump of the silencer barely masks the heavier sound of bodies hitting the floor on the other side.

Travis nearly faints. "Beau! What the fuck? How did you even know—"

Beau opens the door. "I didn't know. I assumed."

Beau steps over the bodies like they are nothing more than clutter on the floor. Travis freezes behind him, staring down at the blood pooling beneath the guards like he's stumbled into a murder scene he isn't ready for. Beau doesn't even blink.

I shove past both of them.

Connor is on his feet, already moving toward a drawer in the sleek kitchen, probably where he keeps whatever designer weapon makes him feel powerful in his gated, oversecured world. His three glowing monitors light him in cold light as he reaches, frantic.

He doesn't make it.

Travis crosses the room with a burst of momentum none of us expect and cracks his fist across Connor's jaw hard enough to send a shockwave through the glass-topped table. The sound echoes through the marble and steel interior like a gunshot.

Connor collapses to the floor, blood pouring from his split lip, one hand fumbling at his side like he still believes he has a shot at control.

He doesn't.

"You piece of shit," Travis growls, storming toward him. "You killed all those innocent people in that hotel. You almost killed me."

Connor sits up slowly, blood streaking down his chin, and lets out a hoarse, smug laugh.

"Well, you were collateral Travis."

Travis staggers back half a step, like the air has been knocked out of him. His jaw clenches. His expression twists. Anger, disbelief, betrayal all crashing together.

"You're a fucking coward," he snaps. "You stood next to me every day and pretended to be my friend."

"It's called strategy Travis," Connor says, wiping the blood from his lip with the back of his hand. "I didn't need to pretend. You were easy to fool. That's why they put me there. And I understand how to stay useful."

His eyes flick between us, smug despite the blood leaking down his chin.

"And it looks like you cheated death. Again."

He reaches toward the table and grabs a remote. One click, and the flat screen on the wall blinks to life.

News footage. An old mugshot of me fills the screen. Then aerial shots of the Everspring Hotel. First responders dragging out bodies. Police lines. The aftermath.

The headline burns across the bottom in bold red: NATIONWIDE MANHUNT – SUSPECTED MASS KILLER ESCAPES CUSTODY

Connor leans back, smiling through the blood. "You're public enemy number one, Seth," he says. "Congratulations."

I step closer, my boots crunching softly on the pristine floor. The muzzle of my gun finds Connor's forehead.

"Where is Elliot's manor?"

His smile returns, smug, bloodied, mocking. "You really think you're getting Brooke back after the manor? You'll be lucky if you find her in one piece."

I tighten my grip on the gun and push it harder against his skull. "Where the fuck is it?"

His throat bobs as he swallows. Some of the bravado bleeds out of his eyes.

"No one knows. It's off-grid. No satellites. No maps. No digital footprint. Only rumor is... it's somewhere in Oregon. That's all I've ever heard."

"I'm running out of the little patience I have left," I snap. "If you don't get on that fucking computer and find something useful, Victor Voss is going to need a sponge to clean what's left of your face off these monitors."

Connor looks up at me. And at that moment, he knows I'm not bluffing. He climbs into the chair without another word.

Travis shoves a chair next to him and leans in. "Open every encrypted directory. Now."

Connor mutters something under his breath, fingers flying across the keyboard. The monitors light up with code and file structures, hidden servers, dark web comms, payment channels buried behind proxy networks.

Travis jams a USB into the nearest port. "Copy everything."

Connor rolls his eyes. "You don't even know what half of this shit is."

"Keep talking," Travis snaps, "and I'll make sure your jaw's wired shut."

Connor clicks faster, still trying to posture, but his hands tremble slightly.

Then Travis freezes. Eyes lock on a folder as it opens.

"Stop."

Travis points at a photo on the screen, his finger trembling slightly.

"That's Grant."

The image is grainy but clear enough. Grant, standing beside two uniformed officers outside a precinct in Colorado. Same cold smirk. Same dar eyes. The badge on his chest looks official, but it's all theater.

"He wasn't the police," I say quietly. "He bought the police. That's the cop who tried to shoot me in the hallway. Brooke killed him. He wasn't following orders, he was the order."

Next to Grant stands another man. Taller, younger, but unmistakably connected. Same sharp cheekbones, same dead stare, same snake-coiled stillness.

Connor smirks through bloodied teeth. "And that... is Elliot. Grant's brother. He runs the manor."

Travis clicks again.

The screen lights up with another file, this time, interior surveillance footage. A concrete basement, chains dangling from steel beams, stained floors. One frame shows a woman hanging upside down by her ankles, her skin mottled and bruised. Another shows a man split open from groin to chest, ribcage cracked wide. In the corner, someone kneels with their teeth removed, hands bolted to the floor by nails driven through their wrists.

I look away. Not because I can't stomach gore. I've seen worse. I've done worse. But because I can't bear the thought that Brooke might be in a place like that. Right now. Alone.

Travis keeps scrolling. His face drains of color, the light from the monitors painting him a sickly gray. "These are victim logs. There's a schedule: rotations, feeding times, torture intervals. Jesus Christ, Seth..."

My grip tightens.

Another click. A video opens without warning. It's Elliot again, grinning like a game show host, holding a blood-slicked blade over a woman's face while she screams. The camera shakes as someone laughs behind it.

Travis gags. "Fuck. Fuck, I can't..."

I say nothing. My shoulder throbs, pulse hammering through every stitch. But all I can see is Brooke. Somewhere in the dark, near that hell.

"Who's that?" I ask, pointing to the last unfamiliar face in the surveillance footage.

Dark hair, gold chain, lazy grin. He looks like a man who doesn't get his hands dirty unless it amuses him.

Connor snorts through blood. "Dante Valero. He's their supplier. Cocaine, Fentanyl, girls, weapons. Whatever they want, he brings it. He's the only outsider Elliot allows inside the manor."

Travis is already typing, keys clicking fast. "Got something. He's based in Oregon."

He zooms in on a shipping manifest and an encrypted delivery log. "City called Blackridge. Real rural. Looks like he's got a property on the outskirts."

Colorado.

Fresno.

Silicon Valley.

Now Oregon.

We are chasing ghosts across three states while Brooke is locked in a torture palace with monsters who see her as entertainment.

I take a step closer to Connor, my voice low. "Anything else you need to tell us? Anything useful I can actually fucking use?"

Connor leans back in the chair, bleeding, lips curling into that smug, tech-prick smirk he wears like armor.

"How about you go fu—"

I shoot him before he finishes.

The silenced round blows through his temple. His body snaps sideways, collapsing onto the floor in a heap. Blood sprays across the monitor in an arc. The chair rolls back into the glass dining table with a soft bump.

Travis recoils so hard he nearly falls over. "Seth! Jesus fuck!"

"He had nothing else useful to say," I say coldly.

Beau crouches beside the body, nudging Connor's shoulder. "Welp. He's very fucking dead."

"Good," I mutter, wiping the blood off the gun's grip. "Dante is next."

Beau stands and holsters his weapon. "Blackridge is backwoods. I've got a safe house nearby. Another just across the border in Washington if shit gets loud."

Travis exhales shakily, face pale. "We're really going to Oregon."

Connor's blood is still leaking across the floor, soaking into the grout of his designer tile. We walk out of the condo and onto the driveway.

"We need to ditch the SUV," Travis says. "It's already flagged, probably by half the state."

"It is absolutely flagged," Beau replies, unbothered. "We should abandon it somewhere quiet."

We cut through two blocks of overpriced Silicon Valley condos, each more sterile than the last, until we find a side street with no traffic, no porch lights, and no cameras we can see. The SUV's headlights sweep across manicured lawns, mailboxes with corporate logos, and sleeping houses that all look exactly the same.

Travis pulls to the curb and slams it into park. "Okay. We ditch it here and pray nobody checks the Ring cams."

I throw open the back door. Krueger leaps out immediately, landing with force, muscles bristling, head up and ears forward. He scans the dark like he is ready to rip apart anything that moves. Luna stays curled in the carrier beside him, wide-eyed and vibrating with fury.

"Easy," I mutter, reaching out. "We're just switching cars."

Krueger nudges my side with his snout.

Beau moves efficiently, popping the glove box, wiping the steering wheel, pulling out anything with prints or identifiers. He tosses burner wrappers, pockets the USB, and slides the last gun magazine into his coat.

"Hurry," he says calmly. "We shouldn't linger in a stolen, blood-soaked vehicle in a neighborhood where everyone owns a drone and a doorbell camera."

Travis groans and climbs out. "This is so fucking illegal."

Beau shuts the door behind him. "You're deep in the illegal part, my friend. We passed misdemeanor six corpses ago."

We cut through a line of hedges leading to the underground parking garage beneath Connor's building. Concrete columns, dim overhead lighting, the distant buzz of a faulty fluorescent.

Connor, being a tech-bro narcissist with more cash than sense, owns three vehicles. Each one flashier than the last.

A matte black Audi with custom rims.

A silver Tesla that practically screams I overpay for convenience.

And a cherry red BMW convertible that deserves to be pushed off a cliff.

"We're not taking the BMW," Travis says immediately.

"No shit," Beau adds. "Only assholes drive red cars in a manhunt."

We choose the Audi. Sleek, quiet, spacious enough for three fugitives and two animals once the back seats are folded down. Beau pops the trunk while I open the rear door and drop the seats.

"Load them up."

Krueger leaps in, turning once before lying down. I slide Luna's carrier in beside him. She hisses low under her breath, glaring at Krueger.

"They fit," Travis mutters. "Barely."

"They'll manage," Beau says, climbing into the passenger seat.

Travis slides behind the wheel and starts the engine. "I still can't believe we're stealing a dead guy's car."

Beau buckles his seatbelt without looking at him. "He won't be filing a report."

I ease into the backseat beside the animals. Krueger shifts and presses his massive head against my thigh like he can sense the storm building under my skin. I rest a hand on his fur, grounding myself.

Travis backs the Audi out of the garage, mouth tight, knuckles pale against the wheel.

He exhales sharply. "We've gone from Colorado... to Fresno... to Silicon Valley... and now Oregon. What's next, Alaska?"

"Just drive, Travis."

Beau looks back at me. "Hang in there, Seth. We'll get to her."

Every highway we cross, every state line, every hour without her feels like it is pulling me apart thread by thread. There's a limit to how much distance I can take before something inside me snaps.

I keep one hand on Krueger's head, the other on Luna's carrier. Their warmth keeps me tethered. Keeps the worst thoughts from eating me alive.

I've seen enough of Elliot's manor to know what it's built for. What kind of men walks its halls.

And I know this, every second I'm not there is a second he could be destroying her. Hurting her. Breaking her down piece by piece.

And I'm running out of time.

Chapter 18
Brooke

I can't sleep.

The light buzzes overhead. The concrete stays cold. The air feels heavy and stale, and every sound comes from someone else struggling to keep breathing.

My stomach cramps again.

I press a hand low over my abdomen, fingers trembling against the thin fabric of my dress. I don't know how far along I am. Weeks maybe. Barely anything. Just a cluster of cells fighting to become something more. Every cramp feels worse. The nausea comes in heavier waves. Every hollow twist of hunger feels louder than the last.

What if they are starving me on purpose? What if they already know this is killing it?

I swallow hard and keep my palm where it is. I try to breathe evenly, try to imagine something small and stubborn hanging on inside me.

Across the room, Miles lies on his side, arms wrapped around his ribs. The others are sprawled where the guards left them. No one has the strength to talk. No one has the strength to cry.

They only give us protein shakes. No real food, just enough to keep our hearts beating.

Then I remember. Sophie on the pool table with Elliot, Knox, and Asher. The three of them using her, and her letting them. Sophie uses sex as currency. That is how she climbs into their circle. She lets Elliot, Knox, and Asher do whatever they want with her. In return, she gets a room upstairs, clothes that aren't stained, food, hot water, knives. Access.

If I pretend I will do the same, then maybe I will get close enough to find a way out. Or close enough to kill as many of them as I can before they kill me.

I push myself up until I can stand. My back pulls tight where the physician restitches it. Sweat slides down my spine even in the cold air.

"Enzo."

The guard sits at the bottom of the stairs, bored, massive, his hands resting on his knees. He looks over at me without interest.

"I need to speak to Elliot."

He snorts. "Do you?"

"Tell him I want to cooperate," I murmur. "He'll understand."

Enzo stares at me for a long second, then taps the earpiece at his collar and speaks quietly. I can't hear the words. I only hear the short reply on the other end.

Enzo stands. He grabs my arm and drags me up the stairs. Every step makes the sutures pull. By the time we reach the main floor, my breath comes out in tight, careful bursts.

The hallway outside Elliot's study is elegant and warm. The walls hold expensive art.

Enzo knocks once.

"Send her in," Elliot calls.

Enzo shoves the door open and pushes me inside.

The study smells like whiskey and polished wood. Shelves line the walls. A decanter and two glasses sit on a side table. The desk in the center of the room is large and solid, edges neat, papers stacked in clean piles.

Elliot sits behind it, shirt sleeves rolled up, collar open.

Sophie's head moves under the desk. Her shoulders stay visible, her hands braced on his thighs. Her head lifts and lowers in a steady rhythm. She is sucking him off and doesn'teven slow down when I walk in.

Disgust crawls up my spine.

"Brooke," Elliot says, voice smooth. "Sit."

He gestures to the chair in front of the desk.

Sophie pulls back and rises from the floor in one quick motion. Her lipstick is smudged. She wipes her mouth with the back of her hand, eyes flicking over me once, assessing. Then she moves to the side of the desk, close to him but out of the way.

"I'm here to take you up on your offer."

Elliot tilts his head, amused. "What offer?"

My throat tightens.

"When we were in the game room," I force the words out. "When I saw you with Sophie, Knox and Asher on the pool table. I'm here to take you up on that offer."

A small laugh escapes him. He glances at Sophie, then back at me.

"You said I wouldn't like the alternative," I repeat, "and you were right."

His eyes brighten, pleased. "I need to hear that again."

"What?"

"That I was right."

I swallow. My face feels hot. My hand twitches in my lap.

"You were right."

His smile widens. "What else should you say?"

My stomach turns.

"I'm sorry."

His eyebrows lift slightly. "Sorry for what?"

I force myself not to look away. I feel every word scrape through my chest.

"I'm sorry for pointing a gun at you," I say. "I'm sorry for refusing you. I'm sorry I tried to escape."

He watches my face the entire time.

"Better," he smirks. "Now, what are the magic words?"

My nails dig into my palms. I know what he wants.

I swallow the last of my pride.

"Please."

His eyes narrow. "Please what?"

The humiliation tastes sour in my mouth.

"Please let me make myself useful," I say. "Please let me please you."

Sophie gives a short laugh. Elliot joins her.

"That's not very specific," he raises a brow. "I want to hear you say 'Please Elliot, give me your big cock.'"

Heat crawls up my neck. He wants to hear me beg in detail. He wants the words themselves to stain.

I meet his eyes anyway.

"Please, Elliot... give me your big cock."

Sophie watches me closely. There is no pity in her face. Only a quiet, interested focus. She is measuring how far I will go.

Elliot walks around the desk and leans against the front edge, inches away from my knees. His hands rest on the wood. He looks relaxed. His eyes don't. He pauses, then smirks.

"You must think I'm fucking stupid, Brooke."

He pushes off the desk and steps in closer. His gaze drags over my face like he knows exactly where it hurts.

"If I put my dick in front of you, you would most likely bite it off."

I keep still. I don't give him anything.

"And your back is a mess now. Darts, restitching. Scars don't turn me on."

His eyes drop to my stomach.

"And if we kept you long enough, you'd start showing," he adds. "That ruins the entertainment value."

He straightens and slides his hand through Sophie's hair. She leans into it like this is normal.

"You should've kept yourself useful," he gesture to Sophie. "Like Sophie here."

His tone shifts again.

"Sophie wasn't born into this. Her father owed The Collective. He refused to pay. He thought he could disappear."

His grip in her hair tightens for a beat.

"We took his daughter instead. She came here as collateral."

Sophie's jaw tightens, then smooths out.

"She had the same choice you had," Elliot says. "Fight the system or learn it."

He smiles as he says it, like it amuses him.

"She learned it. She listened. She followed every rule. She did what we wanted. She made herself very useful to me, to Knox, to Asher."

His attention flicks back to me.

"Now she has a room upstairs. Freedom to move. She kills well. She entertains well."

He steps toward me again.

"You had the same opportunity. You chose to fight. You chose to be difficult."

His eyes harden.

"You could have been upstairs. You could have been like Sophie. Instead, you pointed a gun at me, you ran, and you made yourself a problem."

He gives a short, dismissive nod, already bored.

"So you'll go back to the basement. You'll sit in the dark. You'll get bigger and more tired and more desperate. You'll stay there until we decide we are ready to play with you again."

He looks at Enzo.

"Take her back."

Elliot picks up a pen from the desk, already done with me.

The study door closes behind us. The warmth of the room vanishes into the colder hallway.

Enzo drags me back down the stairs. Each step sends a line of fire through my back. By the time he shoves me onto the concrete, my vision has started to blur.

The light buzzes overhead again.

Miles lifts his head. "Brooke?"

"I'm fine," I lie.

I shift onto my side, drawing my knees up as I wrap my arms around my stomach. My face burns from what I just said upstairs. My chest aches from how much I hate myself for saying it.

I begged, and he still sends me back to the basement like I am nothing.

Something inside me sags under the weight of it. The humiliation. The hunger. The dull ache in my stomach that I can't stop thinking about.

Maybe Seth will find me. Maybe he won't.

Either way, I am not going to end this place on my knees.

I am not going to become Sophie. I am not going to learn their rules or play their game.

I press my forehead to the concrete and try to breathe through the pain twisting in my stomach.

Seth has to find me.

If he doesn't, I'm not going to survive much longer.

Chapter 19

Seth

The low-fuel light had been on for fifteen miles, somewhere between Silicon Valley and Fresno. We're running on fumes and adrenaline, and only one of those is renewable.

Travis squints at the dashboard. "Yeah, we're stopping. I'm not pushing a luxury car through rural California."

"We should've stopped twenty minutes ago," I mutter, shifting to ease the pressure in my shoulder. The ache is deep and insistent now, a reminder that I'm still stitched together by rage, willpower and Oxy.

He takes the next exit and pulls into a gas station that looks abandoned. A squat concrete box wedged between a sagging chain-link fence and a sun-bleached billboard. The canopy light flickers overhead, bathing the pumps in a jaundiced glow. Two pumps. One cracked glass door. One security camera mounted crookedly above the entrance, its casing yellowed with age.

"Of course it's one of these," Travis mutters. "No pay-at-the-pump. Just vibes."

Beau scans the lot with the focus of someone assessing a kill zone. His gaze moves from the dark corners of the property to the highway entrance, then to the building itself. His hand hovers near his waistband.

"This'll do. Get what we need and get out."

He looks at me. "Stay in the car."

I don't argue. Pain is flaring again, radiating down my ribs and into my back.

Beau cracks the door.

Then freezes.

Inside the store, two cops stand at the counter. Coffee cups in hand. Laughing with the cashier. Relaxed and unhurried like they have nowhere else to be.

Beau shuts the door without a word.

Travis follows his line of sight through the windshield and lets out a pained groan. "Are you fucking kidding me?"

Beau doesn't blink. "We need fuel. If we stall on the highway, we're dead. You know that."

"So we just hang out until Donut Patrol clears out?"

"We're not making a move until they're gone," Beau says. "Or one of us ends up in cuffs."

Travis leans back against the seat, scrubbing a hand over his face. "This is actually insane. I was supposed to be coding right now. Drinking overpriced matcha. Not dodging murder charges and highway patrol."

Beau ignores him, eyes still locked on the store. "They're not leaving."

"They're nesting," Travis says. "This is nesting behavior. They're building a fucking home in there."

We wait.

The cops linger. They laugh. They sip their coffee like it is a social hour instead of the edge of a manhunt.

Beau leans forward slightly. "They don't recognize us, yet."

Travis shifts in his seat. "So we're just supposed to wait?"

Beau turns his head slowly. "You're the only one in this car without a nationwide APB and a felony record."

Travis blinks. "You want me to go in there?"

"Pay for the gas. Don't be weird."

"I'm literally the definition of weird under pressure."

"Then fake normal," Beau says flatly. "Buy a Gatorade while you're at it."

Travis groans and shoves the door open. "If I get arrested, I'm snitching."

He crosses the lot with careful casualness, shoulders loose, pace unhurried. Inside, he goes straight to the register, offers the cashier a stiff half-smile, and hands over cash. Beau and I watch from the car.

Travis finishes the transaction, grabs a bottle of Gatorade from the cooler, and steps back outside. He walks straight to the pump on the driver's side and starts fueling the car.

He has just squeezed the handle when one of the cops inside looks up.

And locks eyes with me through the windshield.

The officer says something to his partner, then turns and walks out of the store, heading straight toward the passenger side of the vehicle.

Toward Beau.

Cold spreads through my chest.

Beau sees it at the same time I do. He exhales once and opens his door, stepping out before the officer can reach him.

The cop slows as he approaches, his hand already hovering near his holster.

"Is there a problem, officer?" Beau asks, posture relaxed.

The officer's eyes flick between Beau and the interior of the car, trying to get a better angle on me through the glass.

"You got ID?" the officer asks.

Beau smiles, calm and faintly amused. "I'm giving you a chance to walk away."

The officer's hand shifts closer to his weapon.

Beau tilts his head slightly. "Think real hard before you go for that gun."

For half a second, the officer hesitates.

Then his hand drops.

Beau moves first.

The suppressed shot cracks through the night. The officer jerks as the round hits him in the center of his chest. Shock flashes across his face before his knees give out and he drops hard onto the concrete.

Everything snaps into motion.

The second cop shoves through the door of the store, sees his partner go down, and immediately turns to shoot.

Beau pivots and fires.

One clean shot.

The second officer collapses mid-stride, his body hitting the pavement a few feet from the entrance.

Silence slams over the lot.

Beau moves immediately. He crouches beside the officer, reaches down, and rips the handcuffs from the man's belt in one clean motion.

Then he stands and walks straight into the store.

Inside, the cashier lets out a broken sound and drops behind the counter, hands over his head, shaking so badly the register drawer rattles.

"Please don't kill me."

"I don't want to kill you," Beau says calmly. "Which is fortunate for you."

He raises his weapon and shoots out every security camera in the store, one by one. Glass shatters and scatters across the tile.

"Are you going to play hero?" Beau asks.

The cashier shakes his head violently. "No. I'm not going to do anything."

"Good."

Beau steps behind the counter, grabs the man by the arm, and hauls him up just enough to snap one cuff around his wrist. He secures the other end to the freezer handle, locking him in place.

"When the police arrive, you will tell them nothing. If you mention us even once, I will come back."

The cashier swallows hard. "I won't say anything."

"You won't get a second warning," Beau says. "I'm a professional assassin. My victims die before they know I'm in the room."

He tears the receipt from the printer and walks out.

Outside, Travis stands at the pump, forcing himself to stay steady as the tank fills. He keeps his head down and his hands on the nozzle, like nothing has happened.

Beau returns to the car without looking at the bodies.

Travis replaces the nozzle, closes the tank, and gets into the driver's seat.

Beau slides back into the passenger seat.

I push myself upright, breath shallow, pain flaring as the engine turns over.

Then we're moving again.

The gas station disappears behind us.

Only twenty minutes to the hangar. Twenty minutes until we meet the plane. Twenty minutes until we are in the air and headed for Oregon.

Beau stares straight ahead.

"That was our one mistake, Seth. We don't get another."

He is right.

But I can't think about the consequences. Not about bodies or headlines or surveillance footage. All I can think about is her.

Brooke doesn't have time for caution.

And I will tear through every cop, every state line until she is safe again.

Beau and I used to have a code. Only kill the ones who deserved it.

But right now? If someone stands between me getting to Brooke, they are already fucking dead.

Chapter 20

Brooke

When dawn splits the basement with harsh fluorescent light, the guards storm in. Sarah screams when they grab her ankle, dragging her across the floor. No one helps because no one can.

They haul us like cargo toward the pool room.

The pool room is a white tile nightmare, bright, clean, too mocking for what it is built to contain. The water steams faintly, but the air has that wrong cold, the sterilized kind that seeps into bone.

On the table, a neat fan of laminated cards.

Elliot stands beside them grinning, a host welcoming contestants to their final episode. Sophie stands nearby, smile stretched thin, eyes hungry. She looks like she is ready for someone to bleed immediately.

"Good morning," Elliot says cheerfully. "I hope you slept well. That luxury is about to expire."

He takes a slow step forward, hands clasped behind his back. "Today is our card game. A long-standing tradition. One of my personal favorites."

Miles mutters, "Fuck."

"Here's how it works," he continues, tone still polite. "In a moment, each of you will step forward and draw a card from the deck. When it's your turn, you'll reveal your task. And then..." He smiles wider. "You do what the card says."

He gestures toward the guards stationed at the corners of the room. "Some tasks are physical. Some are... behavioral. Some require endurance. A few may require assistance."

Sophie's eyes light up at that.

Elliot keeps going,. "Most tasks are survivable. But not without... modification."

He lets the silence sit for a moment, then steps in closer, lowering his voice.

"If you refuse your card, you're flagged for elimination. In case you've forgotten, elimination is not symbolic."

He looks toward Enzo, who remains motionless with the gun raised at his side. Enzo cocks the gun with a slow, deliberate click and raises it without a word. Elliot gestures casually toward him, like presenting a show prop.

"You will complete your task, or you will be eliminated. There are no redraws. There is no opting out."

His gaze sweeps over them, assessing. "Let's begin, shall we?"

"First up, Sarah!" Elliot announces cheerfully, as if he is calling roll in a classroom instead of orchestrating a goddamn torture game.

Sarah flinches at the sound of her name. Her entire body trembles as she steps forward, arms wrapped around herself like they might keep her from falling apart. Her fingers barely hold the edge of the card as she turns it over.

A picture of shattered glass, scattered across blood-streaked tile.

She goes pale.

Elliot grins. "Walk it."

Her lips part, like she might beg or argue, but nothing comes out. Just the shallow rasp of her breathing.

She takes one step toward the strip of jagged glass waiting on the floor.

The first shard pierces the arch of her foot. She gasps, body jolting, blood beading immediately, then spilling down in a hot line. Her toes curl instinctively, but there is no safe place to step.

Another step.

A shard lodges between two toes and slices upward as her weight shifts. Her breath hitches. Her teeth clench so hard her jaw visibly locks. Blood smears across the tile as she keeps going.

By the fourth step, her heel slips in her own blood.

She goes down hard.

Her knees slam into the glass. The crunch is wet and immediate, shards driving through skin and straight into bone, slicing deep until they stick. She screams, the sound bouncing off the cold, concrete walls.

She tries to crawl.

Her hands meet the glass, and it tears straight through the pads of her palms, puncturing the skin until red drips steadily from her fingertips. Her breath comes in panicked bursts as she drags herself forward, sobbing and bleeding.

She doesn't make it far.

Her arms give out. Her body collapses onto the pile of glass, twitching.

Two guards step forward, grab her by the elbows, and drag her away. Her blood streaks across the tile in long, broken smears. Small shards cling to her skin, embedded too deep to fall free.

Elliot claps once, slow and sarcastic. "Well, she gave it her best shot."

No one else moves. The silence is heavy. Dread thickens the air like smoke.

"Jared. Come on down," Elliot says, like he is hosting a game show.

Jared doesn't move.

Then, trembling, he wipes his nose on his sleeve and steps forward. When he flips the card over, he makes a sound that doesn't belong in any living human.

Teeth. The number five. Pliers.

His knees give out.

"No," Jared whispers. "No, no, please—"

Two guards are on him instantly. One slams him onto the tile, pinning his chest with a knee. The other grabs his jaw and forces his head back against the floor.

"Please don't—please wait—" Emma's voice cracks as she screams, but another guard shoves her back.

Jared fights, but it doesn't matter. His hands are wrenched above his head in one violent motion, wrists locked down. His sobs turn frantic. "Don't do this, please, please—"

Sophie steps forward with a pair of heavy pliers in her hand.

The steel tips catch the light as she kneels beside his head.

Jared screams before the metal even touches him.

The first tooth is one of his front incisors. She grips it tight. The pliers scrape against enamel before locking in place. Then she twists. Not a clean pull. A wrenching, grinding turn that cracks something deep in his jaw before the root tears free.

Blood pours instantly, filling his mouth and spilling down his cheeks as he shrieks.

He thrashes, but the guards hold him steady.

The second tooth comes slower. A canine. She rocks it back and forth first, loosening it, stretching the ligament until his screams turn into choking sobs. Then she yanks. The root tears free in one long, sickening rip, trailing tissue with it.

Blood pools under his head, darkening the grout between the tiles.

By the third, Jared is gagging on his own blood. Sophie shoves her fingers into his mouth, feeling blindly, selecting the next victim. She clamps down on a molar this time.

It doesn'twant to come out.

She twists harder. The cracking sound echoes. The crown shatters under pressure, and she has to reposition, digging the metal deeper into the broken stump.

When it finally tears free, he screams so hard his voice gives out mid-cry.

The fourth and fifth come in brutal succession. Another incisor. Another molar. Each one wrenched loose with a violent jerk, each one accompanied by that same sickening pop and a spray of blood that coats Sophie's fingers and the front of Jared's shirt.

His jaw hangs slack by the end of it. Blood runs in thick streams down his chin and neck. When the guards let go, he doesn't sit up. He just lies there, hands twitching, mouth flooding red.

Sophie stands, expression calm, then drops the pliers onto the cart beside her.

Jared sobs so hard his whole body shudders. Blood bubbles at his lips.

Elliot claps once, cheerful.

"Look at that. A brand-new smile."

Emma makes a broken sound beside me and folds in on herself, arms wrapped tight around her knees.

I stare straight ahead, nails digging into my palms until my hands ache.

Elliot claps once, the sound sharp and pleased. "Wonderful. Emma."

Emma breaks before the name even finishes leaving his mouth. Her hands shake as she grabs the card, nearly dropping it. When she flips it over, she freezes.

A metal plate. A hand. Flames carved into it.

Her breath stutters. "No. No—no."

Elliot watches her, head slightly tilted, like he's working something out. Then he almost smiles. "You know what, Emma," he says, voice calm, almost reassuring. "It's actually not that bad after a bit. First part's rough, yeah. But give it a few seconds..." He shrugs lightly. "Your nerves die. Stops you from feeling all of it."

She shakes her head harder, panic spilling over. "Please—don't—please—"

He meets her eyes, steady. "You just have to get through the beginning."

The guards grab her before she can pull away. They drag her across the floor toward the wall. The plate glows orange-yellow, heat rolling off it in waves that warp the air. Sweat breaks across Emma's skin instantly, dampening her hair, streaking down her neck.

She fights them, heels scraping, sobbing so hard she chokes on it. They wrench her arm straight and slam it against the metal.

The sound hits first. A wet, violent sizzle.

Then the smell.

Burnt flesh, thick and choking, sinking into the back of my throat.

Emma screams.

It tears through the room, high and jagged, loud enough to make my ears ring. Her skin blisters on contact, swelling and stretching before splitting open. Clear fluid spills down her arm, hissing as it hits the plate. Parts of her skin stick there, pulled tight against the metal.

Elliot doesn't look away. "Very good, Emma. That's probably the worst of it."

Beside him, Sophie inhales slowly, like she's savoring it.

"Mmm," she murmurs, a faint smile pulling at her mouth. "Smells like Beth in here."

Emma thrashes, howling, her voice cracking raw.

When the guards finally tear her away, her arm does not come free cleanly. Strips of skin peel off and stay behind, stretched and torn. Patches of raw muscle glisten beneath, red and exposed, trembling as air hits it.

Emma collapses to the floor, sobbing and rocking on her knees. She clutches what is left of her hand and forearm against her chest, fingers curled around something no longer recognizable as her own.

The smoke drifts upward.

Elliot finally turns his attention to Miles.

"Miles," he says with enthusiasm. "You're next."

Miles steps forward, but he moves like his body is on a delay, like whatever keeps him anchored has already slipped loose. His hand shakes as he draws his card and turns it over.

An eye. A needle.

A broken sound escapes him before he can stop it.

The guards grab him immediately. One yanks his arms back and locks them high behind him. Another clamps a hand around his jaw and forces his head still, thumb grinding into the side of his skull until his face angles just right. Miles kicks and twists, breath coming apart in short bursts, but the hold is firm. He is positioned for precision, not mercy.

Elliot steps forward. He takes the needle himself.

Miles sees it coming and starts to sob, a thin, frantic sound that shakes through his whole body.

"No. Please. Please!" he yells, words slurring together.

Elliot brings the needle to the inner corner of Miles's eye.

The tip presses in slowly. The surface gives under the pressure, bowing inward before it finally breaks with a soft, wet pop.

Miles screams.

The sound tears out of him, loud enough to scrape along the walls. Elliot keeps pushing. The needle slides farther in, forcing its way deeper as blood spills instantly, running hot and fast down Miles's cheek. Clear fluid follows, dripping and streaking as his eye shifts helplessly around the metal.

Miles thrashes harder, legs buckling as his scream cracks into choking sobs. His voice fails him, breaking down into breathless, animal sounds as Elliot continues unbothered and unhurried.

When the needle finally comes free, it is slick and dark.

Elliot steps back and hands it off without comment.

The guards release him.

Miles collapses immediately, curling onto his side. He clutches his face, fingers pressing uselessly against an eye that leaks and bleeds between them. His body shakes in sharp, uncontrollable spasms while small, broken noises slip out of him.

Elliot looks down at him for a moment.

Then he lifts his gaze.

"Next."

Then he smiles at me.

"Brooke."

My legs feel boneless, but I force them forward.

My card flips over.

Blue water. Lungs. 120 seconds.

Sophie actually bounces on her heels.

"Ohhhh," she croons. "This is going to be fun."

Elliot gestures to the pool.

"Let's see how long you can keep that pretty head under."

The water ripples like it knows exactly what it is about to take from me.

Chapter 21

Seth

I stand close behind Brooke, one arm around her waist, the other hovering near her chest as she holds our daughter. I am careful not to crowd them, careful not to break whatever fragile calm has settled over the room.

Our daughter is warm and small against Brooke's chest. Her breath moves in faint puffs. Short dark curls rest against her scalp. One tiny hand flexes in her sleep before relaxing again.

Brooke presses her lips to the baby's forehead and stays there. When she looks up at me, she leans back just enough to kiss me too. Her smile is tired, but content. I can't look away.

They are real.

They are alive.

They are here.

They are everything I have never been allowed to keep.

Brooke lifts her eyes to mine, and I see things we were never promised sitting there anyway. Peace, safety, a life that doesn't orbit violence. A future that doesn't end soaked in blood.

"She's got your eyes," Brooke whispers, drawing our daughter closer to her chest.

I reach out, brushing my fingers along the baby's cheek.

I want to hold them both closer. I want the world to stay quiet.

And then it takes everything away.

I shoot upright in the back seat of the SUV, lungs locking as pain tears through my ribs. My chest flares so violently it feels like something has split back open. The air inside the car is cold, and my pulse slams hard enough that I taste iron at the back of my throat.

Travis twists around in the driver's seat, eyes wide. "Jesus. You okay?"

My breath comes fast and uneven, refusing to settle. The dream clings to me, like it followed me out of sleep. Brooke's smile stays embedded in my mind. Our baby's face. Then the hollow silence when they disappear.

Beau doesn't turn from the front passenger seat. "You were talking in your sleep."

"What did I say?"

"Brooke's name," Beau says. "And something about not taking her. Then you hit the window."

I look down at my hand. A spiderweb crack splits the glass beside me, pale lines branching outward, quiet evidence of what I can't remember doing.

Travis exhales. "That's... deeply unsettling, but also very on brand."

I ignore him and lean my head back against the seat. I force my breathing to slow. My heart refuses to cooperate.

The dream replays vividly. Brooke is safe. Our daughter is there between us. A family exists in a place my mind retreats to when it allows itself to hope.

I close my eyes.

She felt real.

Now Brooke is somewhere locked inside a torture compound, alone and terrified, carrying the future I was just shown and had ripped away.

The dream is not comforting.

It is a warning of what I have to lose.

Travis turns down a narrow gravel road carved through dense, unmarked woods. There are no signs or lights. Branches scrape the sides of the SUV. Mist clings to the trees. My ribs ache with every jolt of the ride. I keep one hand pressed against my side, eyes fixed forward.

At the end of the winding path stands a structure that looks like it has been condemned. A crooked hunting shed. Gray paint flakes like sunburnt skin, tin roof rusted through in patches, and a warped metal door barely hanging from its hinges.

Beau gets out first. He doesn't say a word, just yanks the rusted door open with one sharp pull, hinges squealing, and motions for us to follow.

The moment we step into the pitch-black interior, he hits a switch embedded in the wall.

The floor clicks, then shifts.

With a low mechanical hum, the section of floor beneath us begins to descend. An industrial lift dropping into the earth, smooth and silent despite the weight. My boots stay planted, but my body tenses anyway. It feels like being lowered into a crypt.

The deeper we sink, the colder the air becomes.

A panel hisses open.

When the lift doors open, it feels like stepping into a luxury panic room.

The bunker stretches wide and deep, reinforced concrete wrapped in matte black soundproofing panels. A pristine kitchen sits to one side, slate countertops, brushed metal appliances. The living area has low leather furniture. A wide digital fireplace. Mounted screens with feeds Beau can access from anywhere.

A hallway branches off to four private rooms, each sealed with fingerprint scanners.

Behind bulletproof glass, a floor-to-ceiling weapons case stands like a private armory. Rifles, handguns, knives, explosives, tactical gear, everything arranged with obsessive precision. You could wage a war from this place and never run out of options.

Travis steps off the lift and stares around the bunker, mouth parting as he slowly turns in a full circle. "How the hell does one even afford something like this?"

Beau doesn't look impressed. "Do you know how much it costs to complete a hit on an elected official?"

Travis blinks. "No. What the fuck?"

"Exactly," Beau says. "Between that, a long list of favors people owe me, and an architect friend who owed me his freedom, this place was a gift. I just renovated it."

Travis drags a hand down his face. "So you received the batcave as a gift. An assassin and a renovator." He lets out a sharp laugh. "Unfucking believable."

Beau shrugs. "Welcome to my happy place."

Krueger leaps before any of us can react, paws landing solidly on the bunker floor. He gives a low, satisfied chuff, then takes off down the hallway like he is clearing the perimeter. Tail high, back to soldier mode.

Luna, on the other hand, is still screaming.

Her carrier vibrates violently, the sound muffled but furious. I crouch and unlatch the crate. She shoots out like a missile, claws out, bolting under the nearest couch without looking back.

"Nice to see she's thriving," Travis mutters, rubbing his ear.

I straighten slowly, pain pulling tight through my side.

I have one job now. Get cleaned up. Get armed.

Get Brooke back.

"Animals are safe here," Beau says, already heading down one of the side hallways. "Back room's soundproof. Climate controlled. They'll be fine."

Krueger pads after him. Luna peeks out from under the couch, eyes wide and curious.

I hate leaving them. They are the last pieces of home Brooke and I have left. But Beau is right. Out there, they are liabilities. Here, they are protected.

Beau turns to me. "Shower. My doctor is on the way. He's bringing more oxy for the pain and your risperidone."

The private bathroom is larger than most apartments. Matte black tile. Stainless steel fixtures. Steam-proof mirror. The shower is enclosed in frameless glass. Black slate lines the walls and floor, lit by harsh overhead spots. Water pours from a ceiling-mounted rainfall head in a steady stream.

I peel off the blood-stiff hoodie, the fabric ripping away from scabbed edges. Pain flares across my ribs and shoulder, deep enough that spots dance in my vision. My skin is mottled with purple bruising, dried blood clinging like cracked paint.

The moment I step under the water, heat slams into me.

The water hits the bullet wound first, and white-hot agony shoots down my arm. I brace a hand on the tile and let it happen. It burns, but it also clears something, like the pain forces everything else out of my head.

Brooke's scream. The black hood over her head. Her body dragged away. My daughter's face from the dream.

All of it blurs with the steam until the world narrows to a single point.

Get to her.

I dry off, ignoring how my shoulder protests every twist, and dress fast. Black jeans that don't restrict movement, boots with quiet tread.

The doctor arrives in under twenty minutes.

Beau has one on call. Discreet, off the books. You don't survive long in Beau's world without contingencies.

The doctor moves with quiet confidence, already assessing me as he guides me into a chair. He peels back the bandages with careful fingers, unfazed by blood or scar tissue.

"Stitches are holding," he says. "You tore some scar tissue, but nothing that needs to be redone."

He cleans the wound thoroughly. The antiseptic burns, sharp enough to pull a breath from my chest. He works fast, rewrapping everything with practiced ease.

He hands me two pill bottles.

"Oxy for pain, Risperidone for mood stabilization. Take them separately."

I swallow the oxy.

He checks my vitals, gives Beau a nod, and packs up. "Avoid unnecessary strain."

"Define unnecessary," Travis says.

The doctor ignores him.

The second he leaves, I am already on my feet. I pull on a shirt, ready to go.

Beau is leaning against the opposite wall, arms crossed, evaluating me like he is deciding whether I pass inspection.

"You need to look presentable. We're going to a strip club, not a morgue."

"Same thing the way we do it," I mutter.

Beau's mouth twitches. "Still. Dress well. They notice sloppy men."

I roll my shoulder. Bone shifts under the strain, gauze pulling tight. Pain spikes, then eases back into a steady burn.

"How's the pain?" Beau asks.

"Manageable."

Beau tosses me a black button-down, a suit jacket, and a loaded pistol. Two extra clips follow, lining up on the table like silver teeth.

Beau notices me eyeing the setup and raises a brow. "You wanna get in, you gotta look the part. Black Ridge ain't the kind of place you walk into dressed like that."

I grunt and pull on the button-down. The fabric is crisp, expensive, and stretches tight across the bandages.

"You think they're gonna recognize us?" I ask, fastening the buttons.

"Oh, I'm counting on it," he says. "But we'll give them a good five minutes of doubt. Long enough to put a hole in someone."

Travis paces near the bunker's steel exit, glancing nervously at a matte-black rifle propped against the wall like it is whispering his name. He looks entirely out of place in this world, too twitchy, too normal.

"So..." he begins, hesitating as he steps closer to us. "What exactly is my role in this? Because I'm feeling real bullet-magnet adjacent right now."

He points vaguely toward the guns. "Do I get a weapon? Or am I just moral support? Maybe hold the coats?"

Beau doesn't answer. He just turns, reaches into the wall-mounted weapons case, and tosses him a compact Glock like he is handing over a pack of gum.

Travis catches it with both hands and stares down at the pistol like it is a bomb. "Cool. Great. Love that for me. Definitely ready for this."

"Keep the safety on," Beau warns, checking his own gear. "You panic and you will shoot yourself."

Travis groans and flips the gun over awkwardly. "Please tell me I at least get a bulletproof vest?"

Beau shrugs. "Sure. But with your face, you're probably getting shot in the head."

Travis freezes. "Why would you say that?"

Beau tilts his head slightly. "Accuracy."

I stand and walk past them, adjusting the holster at my side until it clicks snugly into place.

"Try not to miss," I tell Travis. "And maybe don't die."

Travis blinks. "Seriously? That's the game plan?"

Beau slings a coat over one shoulder, brushing invisible lint off the lapel. "If you're lucky, they'll shoot Seth first. He's prettier."

"Gee, thanks," I mutter.

Travis points at both of us, exasperated. "I hate how casually you say things like that."

"He's right," I say. "If they spot us, don't try to be a hero. Just get to the car."

Beau turns back toward the main hallway. "Honestly, you might want to just stay in the car anyway."

Travis exhales. "I love being excluded."

Beau looks at me as he grabs his keys. His expression finally sobers. "You sure you're ready?"

No.

"Yes."

Because it doesn't matter if I am ready.

Pain doesn't matter. Timing doesn't matter. The odds don't matter.

Only Brooke does.

I check the pistol's chamber, slide a full clip into place, and tuck the weapon under my jacket.

"Let's go."

The drive to Black Ridge cuts through forest and shadow, the road narrowing until the trees press in close. Headlights skim bark and fog. The bass from somewhere far ahead pulses faintly through the night, a low thud you feel more than hear.

Beau drives with one hand on the wheel, relaxed, eyes forward. Travis sits behind us, fidgeting with the gun like it might bite him.

"Either of you ever consider therapy?" Travis asks.

Beau doesn't look at him. "I have a bunker."

"That's not therapy."

"It is for me."

I close my eyes for a second, jaw tight. The dream keeps trying to crawl back in. I shove it down. There will be time for grief later. Right now, there's work to do.

Travis exhales hard. "So... what's my role here?"

"Don't die," Beau says.

Travis glances at the gun in his hands. "I haven't done this before."

Beau finally turns, reaches back, and takes the weapon from him. He checks it one-handed, smooth and fast, the kind of movement that comes from muscle memory.

"Well," Beau slides the magazine in and racking the slide with his thumb, "there's a first time for everything. But I don't want you shooting your dick off."

He hands it back.

Travis stares at the gun, then at Beau. "I'm sorry. I'm not a psycho. I've never killed anyone."

Beau shrugs. "Good. Try to keep it that way."

The club sits at the edge of the lot, lit up in red. The parking area is packed with SUVs and luxury sedans.

Men gather near the entrance in fitted jackets, cigarettes glowing between their fingers.

Black Ridge.

A place built to swallow guilt and spit out profit. Money moves fast inside those walls. Flesh moves faster.

Beau pulls into a spot under a flickering security light.

"Here we go," he kills the engine.

Travis stares up at the building like it might bite him. "So... I'm staying here, right?"

Beau claps him on the shoulder. "That's the smartest thing you've said in two days."

"You sure you don't need backup?"

"If we do," I say, "it's already too late."

I check my gun, then step into the night. The air smells like oil, cologne, and cigarette ash. Music from inside thuds like a heartbeat.

The bouncer spots me the second I step into range. His eyes pause, recognition settling in without surprise. He glances at Beau, then back at me. No greeting follows. No questions. No hands come up to search us.

He opens the door and steps aside.

Heat rushes out to meet us, layered with perfume, sweat, liquor, and something sour underneath it all. The room is packed wall to wall, bodies pressed together. Strobe lights tear through the dark, bouncing off mirrored walls and catching fragments of movement that never fully settle.

Men in tailored suits lounge in red velvet booths, watches flashing at their wrists as they lift crystal tumblers. Women move through the space around them, skin glittering under the lights. Heels tower. Smiles stay fixed. Their eyes look empty, trained to look past everything happening to them.

I keep walking.

Beau veers toward a booth tucked back in the shadows, partially walled off, ropes marking a line that doesn't need enforcing. We slide in. From here, I have a clear view of the stage, the bar, the entrance, and the staircase that leads to the second floor. Dante's office will be up there.

Beau looks like he belongs. Relaxed posture. Lazy smile. He tosses hundred-dollar bills onto the stage like confetti, each one fluttering to the floor beneath gyrating legs and flashing lights.

A server in fishnets and smudged lipstick drifts over. Beau orders a whiskey. I don't care what mine is. I take one sip and set it down.

My focus stays up.

I don't look at the stage. I can't. I have been too close to what places like this actually are to pretend it is entertainment. Every flash of skin feels like a warning. Every smile feels like a threat.

"Beau," I mutter. "Focus."

"I am," he replies, eyes still forward. "I multitask."

He pulls a pen from his pocket, uncaps it, and writes something on a crisp bill before sliding it across the edge of the stage. It stops at the feet of a girl in red heels and fishnets. Her makeup is flawless. Her eyes are not. Bruises shadow the inside of her thighs. She bends, reads the bill, and freezes.

Beau doesn't look away. "Go to the back. Call the number. Tell him Beau sent you."

She blinks, swallows. Then nods once and disappears into the crowd like smoke.

"That your number?" I ask.

"No," he says. "Rescue line. Safe house in Portland. First contact gets her out."

Movement near the bar catches my attention.

The bouncer from the door stands rigid beside a bald man in a slate gray suit. Wired into something. The man presses two fingers to his earpiece and glances up.

The bouncer follows his line of sight.

So do I.

The upper hallway glows with low gold light, throwing long shadows across velvet curtains. Dante stands at the center of it, leaning against the railing. Rings catch the light as he moves. His face is calm.

His gaze finds mine.

And stays there.

I slide my hand beneath the table, fingers closing around cold metal.

"Beau, get ready."

He finishes his drink in one swallow, sets the glass down with a soft click, and rolls his knuckles.

"I stay ready."

The crowd shifts. Security tightens. Someone moves toward the stairs.

I stand slowly, one hand still inside my jacket. Beau slides out of the booth, Glock already in hand.

"Here we fucking go."

Chapter 22
Brooke

Blue water. Lungs. One hundred twenty seconds.

Elliot leans forward the moment he sees the shift in my face. His smile widens slightly, like this is something he's been waiting for.

"You know, professional swimmers can hold their breath for what, five, six minutes?" He tilts his head, thinking it over. "Average person?" A small shrug. "Not even close. Maybe a minute. Less, if they panic."

His eyes lock onto mine.

"So... how long do you think you can hold yours?"

Then his gaze drifts past me, toward the pool a few feet away.

"Before we start," he adds lightly, like it's an afterthought, "we have a guest."

He reaches for a remote on the table beside him and clicks it.

A massive screen on the far wall blinks to life. The image sharpens, and Kristie Talbert appears.

Perfect hair. Perfect makeup. Diamonds at her ears. She looks like she is sitting in a private office somewhere warm and expensive. Like this is just another meeting on her calendar.

Elliot gestures toward me. "Kristie specifically asked to see how you are adjusting to the manor."

The guards force me upright so I face the screen.

Kristie's eyes travel slowly down my body. She takes in the bruises, the torn fabric, the way the guards hold me like a prisoner.

"Brooke," she smiles, her voice smooth and vicious. "You stupid bitch. You're lucky my son even looked twice your way."

My hands clench despite the guards' grip.

"And now you're going to suffer," she continues. "As soon as we find Seth, we are going to kill him on sight. We don't need to wait for some public execution in a prison cell."

She leans slightly closer to the camera.

"After he's dead, we'll let you see the footage. Then we'll kill you too."

Her lips curve.

"You fucked with the wrong family, you little slut. Now let's see if that mouth can stay shut long enough to not drown."

The room feels colder.

Elliot gives a satisfied nod. Kristie settles back in her chair, watching.

I don't realize the guards have shifted until their hold tightens.

One yanks my arms behind my back. Another locks an arm around my waist and drags me toward the pool.

"Don't fucking touch me!"

I twist hard and drive my heels into the tile, but my legs give out almost immediately. Pain rips through my ribs and spine. I kick once, but I can't break free.

They haul me forward. My wrists burn. The restitched skin along my back pulls tight with every step.

I can't do this.

Not with her watching. Not with Seth's life hanging in their hands.

Not with our baby inside me.

The edge of the pool looms closer. The water glows an artificial blue beneath the fluorescent lights. It looks clean. It looks harmless. It isn't.

I turn my head toward the screen. Kristie is still there watching.

Before I can scream, the guards shove me forward.

I hit the water hard. The cold slams into me and knocks the breath from my lungs before I can seal my mouth.

I break the surface choking, hair plastered to my face, arms scrambling for balance.

"Hold her," Elliot says calmly.

Sophie steps in and grips the back of my head.

"Hold your breath," Sophie calls sweetly.

Then she shoves my head under.

The water seals over me like a tomb. I thrash once, instinct, but then I force myself still. No oxygen. No wasted movement. I clench my jaw tight and hold it.

The cold bites into every inch of exposed skin, turning pain sharp. My spine arches as the temperature shocks my system, but I lock down.

Hold. Just hold.

The lights beneath me shift and shimmer, warping my reflection into a thousand broken pieces. The pool is beautiful. It doesn't look like somewhere someone should die.

But it can be.

My chest burns immediately. A heavy ache behind my sternum, like something is slowly inflating where air should be. My heart kicks harder, faster, already frantic.

Seth's voice slides into my head like muscle memory.

You're okay baby. You're still here. Slow it down. Count your heartbeat.

I count.

One.

Two.

Three.

The water muffles everything. The room becomes distant, distorted. Sound reduces to a low, hollow hum. My thoughts float strangely, detached, like I'm watching myself from somewhere else.

I can do this.

I have to.

Then my lungs twitch.

A reflex hits, small and involuntary, like my body is testing me.

No.

Not yet.

Water slips past my lips. My throat clenches violently, sealing shut. Panic flares.

I thrash once.

Sophie tightens her grip.

Muffled voices reach me, warped through the water.

"—thirty seconds left—"

Thirty.

My lungs are already screaming.

The burn intensifies fast and sharp, spreading outward like fire licking the inside of my ribcage. My diaphragm spasms again, harder this time, trying to force an inhale that can't happen.

I kick.

Another set of hands joins hers.

Elliot.

His grip is brutal, his palm pressing the back of my skull. They force my face deeper, angling my mouth downward so if I gasp, I inhale water instead of air.

My chest convulses. My body stops listening to me.

The need to breathe becomes everything. Louder than pain. Louder than fear. Louder than thought. My throat burns. My ears ring. Pressure builds behind my eyes until it feels like they might burst.

Seth's voice slides in my head.

I try to picture him. The way he presses his forehead to mine when I can't breathe through a panic attack and says, *I've got you baby. You're not dying.*

My lungs seize again, harder this time. I can't stop it.

My mouth opens.

Water floods in.

It pours down my throat, tearing at my airway as I gag. My body arches against the hands forcing me down. My chest convulses, trying to pull in air, and only drags in more water instead.

No.

The baby.

Panic rips through me, sharper than the burning in my lungs. I try to clamp my mouth shut. I try to curl inward, as if I can shield something inside me from what I have already inhaled. I can't think of anything except that my body is failing, and I am taking it down with me.

Fire explodes in my chest.

I swallow again and again, reflex after reflex betraying me. Water fills every space that should hold air. My vision flashes white, then shatters into dark spots that swarm and multiply.

I can't breathe. I can't think.

My limbs thrash once more, weak and useless. My fingers claw at nothing. The hands on me don't move. My stomach twists violently. I think I might vomit underwater. I think I might choke on that too.

Please, not like this.

The fight drains out of my muscles without my permission. The burning dulls into something heavier, deeper. A crushing pressure wraps around my ribs and squeezes. It feels like my chest is folding in on itself.

My heartbeat staggers, then slams hard enough to hurt.

The world dims. The blue light above me blurs into a pale smear. Sound disappears completely, replaced by a low, distant ringing.

I am dying.

Blackness creeps in from the edges of my vision, slowly swallowing the light inch by inch. My thoughts begin to blink out. Panic. Pain. Fear. All of it fading under the weight of the dark.

Then even the fear slips.

I don't feel the water anymore. I don't feel anything. I just hear his voice in my head.

And I let it carry me into the dark.

Chapter 23
Seth

I'm already standing when the first man reaches for his gun.

I fire twice. One round hits his chest. The second punches through his skull. He drops before his weapon clears the holster.

Screaming erupts across the club. Dancers throw themselves to the floor. Customers overturn tables and crawl for cover. Velvet curtains tear loose as another man fires toward us, the rounds shattering glass along the wall.

Beau moves with precision. He fires once into a man's shoulder. The guard staggers sideways, still trying to raise his weapon. Beau adjusts and fires again into his neck. The man collapses, his body folding inward as he hits the floor.

Another guard rushes from the edge of the stage, trying to circle behind us. Beau turns, kicks a barstool into the man's knees, and fires at close range into his temple. The body slams backward, blood splattering across the wall.

A waitress screams and drops behind the bar, dragging herself along the floor to get out of the line of fire.

More movement in the back hallway.

I drop behind a couch and fire twice as another guard steps out with his weapon raised. The rounds catch him high in the chest. He stumbles forward and crashes face first onto the floor.

Gunpowder thickens the air.

Beau calls out, "Reloading."

I lean out from cover and fire toward the DJ booth. A guard jerks as the round catches him in the ribs. He drops behind the speakers, groaning.

A blonde stripper presses herself against a mirrored wall, shaking, her hands clamped over her ears as she sobs.

"Go," I tell her.

She slides down the wall and scrambles for the emergency door.

A man steps into the hallway with a sawed off shotgun raised at chest level.

Too slow.

I drive forward, closing the distance before he can steady his aim. I fire once into his throat and again into his chest.

He still manages to pull the trigger.

The blast goes wild.

Behind me, wood explodes and glass rains down. The force rips through the space where I stood a second earlier.

Beau slams into me and drives us behind an overturned booth as the shotgun clatters across the floor.

"Move!" Beau barks, hauling me with him.

Someone near the stage is still crawling, trying to reach a dropped pistol.

I kick the weapon away and shove the man back with my boot.

"Where the fuck is Dante?" I shout.

Beau lifts his head just enough to scan the room. His eyes move across the balcony, the hallway, the bar.

"Gone."

I look up toward the balcony. The mirrored glass overlooking the club is empty.

Dante has left.

I lean into the microphone clipped inside my jacket.

"Travis, he's coming out the front. Gray jacket. Blue pants. Shoot him if you see him."

For a second there is nothing but the bass vibrating through the speakers and the sound of people crying.

Then a single gunshot cracks from outside.

Beau and I stop moving at the same time.

The club falls into a broken quiet. Bodies lie scattered across the floor. Music still thumps through the speakers, warped and muffled beneath the sound of groaning.

I run for the exit and shove through the front door.

Travis stands near the SUV with his gun raised. His hands are shaking. His face has gone pale. His eyes are locked on the man collapsed near the curb.

Dante lies on the pavement, writhing and clutching his foot. Blood soaks through his designer pants and pools beneath him.

"I think I got him," Travis says, breathless. "Holy shit. I got him."

Beau steps past me and lets out a low whistle.

"Well, damn. You're officially not useless."

Dante screams and tries to drag himself away across the asphalt.

I holster my gun and walk toward him.

His mouth opens as he tries to speak.

I kick him hard in the stomach.

"We're taking a ride."

His eyes widen. "I'm not going anywhere. Do you know who I work for?"

I grab him by the collar and haul him closer.

"Yeah, that's why you're going to take me to Elliot's manor."

"Fuck you. I'm not telling you shit."

He thinks this is a negotiation.

He's wrong.

A slow smile spreads across my face.

"That's what they all say."

Chapter 24

Brooke

Something hurts.

Pain, distant and dull, blooms somewhere in the center of me.

Then sound creeps in.

A thick, wet noise. A sharp exhale. The slap of skin against skin. It echoes strangely, like it is traveling through water before it reaches me.

Pressure follows.

My chest caves inward. My body reacts before my mind does. A violent jolt runs through me as something heavy drives down on my sternum. My ribs protest. Another impact. Then another.

Where am I?

The question drifts through slowly, like it has to fight its way up.

A voice breaks through next. Muffled at first. Then closer.

"Come on. Come on. Breathe."

Hands. That is what the pressure is. Hands pressing down, hard enough that my spine feels it against the tile beneath me. The floor is cold. I register that now. Cold and unyielding against my back.

Another shove.

Then heat.

Air is forced into me.

It tears down my throat like fire. My airway spasms violently. My body bucks without permission, rejecting it.

My sense of taste slams back all at once.

Chlorine. Metal. Blood.

I cough, and water erupts from my mouth and nose in choking bursts. It splashes against my lips, my chin, the floor beside my head. My throat feels shredded raw.

My ears ring, then clear in fragments. I hear my own coughing. I hear someone swearing under their breath. I hear water lapping softly somewhere nearby.

The pool.

Memory flickers. Blue light. Hands in my hair.

My sense of smell follows. Chlorine. Sweat. Damp fabric. The faint, metallic tang of blood.

Another breath shoves its way in, this time on its own.

It hurts worse than the first.

My lungs drag in air unevenly, like they don't trust it yet. Each inhale stutters. Each exhale trembles.

My fingers twitch against the tile. Sensation creeps back into them in painful pins and needles. My legs feel heavy and distant, but they are there. My skin feels tight and cold, soaked fabric clinging to me.

Sight comes last.

Light bleeds in through half-opened eyes. Fluorescent panels above me fracture into halos. The world tilts. Shapes move at the edge of my vision.

A face leans over me.

"Good," the voice says again, closer now, shaking. "Good. Stay with me."

My heart slams hard enough to make my chest ache.

Then the memory hits fully.

Water filling my mouth. My lungs burning. Kristie's voice on the screen.

My stomach clenches violently. My hand jerks toward my abdomen.

Air scrapes in again.

Miles is kneeling beside me. His hands tremble where they hover near my chest. His face is pale, a bandage wrapped tight over one eye. He looks like he might fall apart if I stop breathing again.

I cough harder. My chest aches from the inside out, every breath shallow and painful, like my lungs are bruised. My head pounds viciously, pressure building until it feels like it might split open.

"Brooke," Miles whispers. "Brooke. You're okay. You're breathing."

I am, but barely.

Everything feels wrong, heavy and delayed. My limbs refuse to respond the way they should. My vision swims, edges blurring in and out like a screen about to go dark.

Then hands grab Miles and rip him away. Guards haul me by my arms. My body feels like deadweight, useless and dragging, while my mind floats somewhere above it, watching without permission.

Everything after that fractures.

And slowly, I slip away again.

I wake up choking.

Not on water, but on air that burns on the way in. My lungs spasm violently, dragging breath into themselves like they don't trust it yet. Each inhale scrapes, shallow and incomplete, like my chest forgot how to open all the way.

I roll onto my side and retch.

Water comes up. Just enough to scorch my throat and make my eyes flood. I gag hard, coughing until my chest aches, like something inside me was beaten. My head throbs in slow, nauseating pulses. Even with my eyes closed, the room refuses to stay still.

My body feels wrong, dense and sluggish. Like it has not fully come back to me yet.

Drowning doesn't end when breathing starts again.

It lingers in the muscles. It lingers in the head. It lingers in the way the heart hesitates between beats, unsure whether it should continue.

I don't know how long I blacked out.

I try to sit up.

The world lurches violently.

I grab the edge of the cot and hang on. My ears ring in hollow waves. My vision blurs and narrows. I swallow hard, my throat raw, tasting chlorine and bile and fear all at once.

Then the cramping starts.

It is sharp enough to steal the breath I just fought to reclaim. I freeze, dread locking me in place.

No. Not now. Not here.

Another wave hits, tighter and more insistent. My stomach clenches hard, muscles pulling inward like they are trying to tear something loose from inside me.

I hit the floor with a dull thud, pain shooting up my legs as the concrete leeches heat from my skin. I curl over myself, arms locked around my middle, breathing through clenched teeth.

I crawl.

Each movement lags, like there is a delay between thought and action. Sweat breaks out across my back. My vision tunnels until the edges darken completely.

I reach the wall and drag myself upright. My legs shake violently beneath me.

Another cramp rips through me, twisting, relentless and cruel.

And then I feel it.

Warm, thick liquid moving between my thighs.

My breath catches painfully in my throat.

I don't want to look. I already know. My body knows. Every instinct inside me is screaming the same truth.

My hand moves anyway.

I press it between my thighs, shaking, terrified of the confirmation I am about to give myself.

When I pull my hand back and see the blood, bright and unmistakable and smeared across my fingers, something inside me fractures completely.

"No," I whisper.

Then louder, breaking. "No. No. No. No."

My hands shake so badly I nearly collapse again. I press my thighs together instinctively, like pressure might stop it, like my body might listen if I beg hard enough.

Tears spill freely now.

"I'm sorry," I whisper. To Seth. To our baby who never had time to exist.

I try to walk.

Each step is slow and careful, hopeful in the most pathetic way. Like if I move gently, the universe might change its mind. Blood slides down my inner thighs as another cramp slams through me, stealing my vision entirely.

I make it two steps.

Then three.

The room tilts sharply. My ears fill with static. My legs give out beneath me.

I don't feel the impact. There is only the sudden absence of ground, the sickening disconnect as my body lets go.

Darkness closes in fast.

"Brooke," Miles's voice cuts through the haze, sharp with panic. "Brooke, stay with me. Please."

Then everything goes black.

I wake up on the cot again.

Breathing still hurts. Each inhale catches shallow in my chest, like my lungs never fully recovered from what they were forced through. My head feels heavy, stuffed with cotton and echoing sounds that arrive a beat too late. My body feels emptied out, hollowed down to something fragile and exposed.

The physician stands beside me. I don't look at him. I keep my eyes fixed on the ceiling, tracing cracks in the concrete.

The question slips out anyway. "Did I lose it?"

He glances at the chart.

"Yes."

The word lands, sinking deep into my chest and staying there. I stare upward, waiting for something else to follow. An explanation that changes the meaning. A silence that suggests uncertainty.

Nothing comes.

"The amount of bleeding you experienced," he continues, "combined with oxygen deprivation and physical trauma, made the outcome unavoidable."

I swallow hard.

"Oh," I whisper.

It is the only sound my body seems capable of forming.

The physician turns away, already finished, already moving on to whatever comes next.

I lie there staring at the ceiling, lungs aching, chest caving inward, knowing something has been taken from me that I will never get back.

Chapter 25

Seth

We take him to an abandoned storage yard twenty minutes out. Corrugated metal units sit rusted and half collapsed while weeds push through the cracked concrete. The place has no cameras and no neighbors.

Travis stands near the open doorway, looking around the interior of the unit like he just realized what kind of night this is going to be.

Dante sits zip tied to a metal chair bolted into the floor. His breathing has already started to speed up as he looks between the three of us.

Travis clears his throat. "Are you guys going to torture him?"

Beau and I answer at the same time.

"Yes."

Travis blinks.

He shifts his weight and rubs the back of his neck. "I don't think I'm built for this. My stomach is too weak. I can't watch."

Beau jerks his thumb toward the outside of the building. "That's why you're supposed to be the lookout in the getaway car."

Travis nods quickly. "Cool. Thanks. Yup, I'll be out there."

He pauses and looks back at Dante.

"Good luck, Dante."

He takes two steps toward the door, then stops again.

"Actually, fuck you. You're a piece of shit."

Then he turns and jogs out of the storage unit toward the car.

The second Dante hears the door slam outside, Beau steps forward.

He doesn't wait for introductions.

Beau drives his fist into his face with full force. Dante's head snaps sideways. Blood sprays across the concrete. Before he can recover, Beau grabs his shirt, yanks him upright, and hits him again. The crack of bone shifting carries through the room. Dante gags, breath ripping out of him in a wet wheeze.

"I'm going to reset your expectations," Beau says calmly, hitting him again. "There's no negotiation happening here."

Dante chokes on blood and spit.

"There's just pain," Beau adds, letting him slump back against the chair. "And how fast you decide to stop it."

Beau steps back.

"Now, where is Elliot's manor?"

Dante's shirt is soaked through with blood. The gunshot wound in his foot has drained the color from his face, leaving his skin gray and slick with sweat. Every breath comes shallow and frantic, but his teeth stay clenched like he believes he can hold himself together through pure stubbornness.

I light a cigarette and watch him.

Dante blinks through the blood running into his eyes and forces himself to focus on Beau again.

"You think you're getting shit out of me?" he rasps. "Go fuck yourself."

Beau reaches into his pocket and pulls out his phone. A second later the opening riff of "Hunted Down" by Soundgarden rolls through the warehouse.

I exhale smoke slowly.

Beau always likes music when he works.

Back when we were deployed overseas, he used to blast it before interrogations. Loud enough to drown out the screaming.

Beau tilts his head slightly.

"That wasn't an answer."

Dante lets out a weak laugh that turns into a cough. "Even if I told you, you wouldn't make it out alive."

Beau walks toward him without responding.

He grabs Dante by the hair and yanks his head sideways. Dante tries to twist away, but the zip ties hold him tight against the chair.

The knife flashes once.

Dante's scream tears through the music as Beau slices clean through the cartilage of his ear. Blood pours down the side of his neck while the severed piece of flesh hits the concrete with a wet slap.

Beau picks it up and holds it up between two fingers, studying it for a moment.

Then he leans down until his mouth is next to Dante's remaining ear.

"Since you're not hearing us clearly," Beau laughs, "I had to check for myself."

Luke's presence flickers faintly at the back of my mind, not loud yet. Just watching.

Dante's scream tears through the warehouse.

"MY EAR. YOU CUT OFF MY FUCKING EAR!"

His body thrashes violently against the zip ties. The metal chair rattles against the bolts in the concrete as blood pours down the side of his neck and soaks into his collar. His breath comes out in broken, panicked gasps while he tries to twist away from Beau.

Beau holds the severed ear between two fingers, turning it slowly like he is examining a strange coin. Blood drips from it in thick, slow drops that hit the floor beside Dante's boots.

Dante gags and shakes his head, trying to focus through the pain.

Beau laughs as he holds the severed ear close to his mouth.

"Can you hear me now, Dante?"

He flicks his wrist and tosses the ear forward. It slaps wetly against Dante's cheek and slides down into his lap.

Dante gags again, his stomach heaving.

I step forward behind him.

Dante lifts his head slowly, one eye already swelling shut.

"You're wasting your time," he rasps.

"No," I say. "You're wasting mine."

I exhale smoke toward the ceiling and let my gaze drop to the table positioned directly in front of him.

Blades. Pliers. Lighter. Needles. Belt. Wire cutters. Bone saw. Salt.

Everything is laid out with intention. Nothing hidden. Nothing accidental.

His eyes track each item despite himself. His shoulders tighten. The chair creaks softly as he shifts.

"I'm not afraid of you," he spits, forcing the words out.

I step closer. "Yeah. That's fair. I'm sure you've seen a lot of guys like me, tall, tattooed, pissed off, making threats they never follow through on."

I lean down until we are eye to eye. "But I'm not most men, Dante. I'm a man of my word."

He says nothing.

"I assume you know who I am."

He swallows. "Seth Kincaid."

I nod once.

"Then you know my family history too."

"I know enough," he says, trying to straighten like his name still means something. "I'm Dante Valero. You know what happens to me if I talk."

"I do," I say. "I just don't care."

He scoffs, then breaks into a cough that bends him forward, pain ripping through him.

I crouch in front of him. "What you don't know is I'm about three weeks off my antipsychotic medication. I haven't slept. My girlfriend is missing. And my patience is pretty fucking thin right now."

I let the words sit.

"I need to find this manor. The faster you talk, the faster we wrap this shit up."

Dante turns his head away. "Fuck you."

Luke stirs closer.

"Stop asking, Seth."

I stand and move behind Dante, pressing the lit cigarette to the back of his neck.

The reaction is immediate. His flesh hisses as his scream fractures halfway through as his breath fails him, body jerking against the restraints. I hold the cigarette there until the skin blisters and splits, until his legs kick uselessly and the chair rattles against the bolts.

Then I pull it away and take a slow drag.

"One of the side effects of me being unmedicated," I say calmly, watching him shake, "is hallucinations. Impulsive behavior. Poor judgment."

I flick ash onto the concrete.

"When that happens," I continue, "I tend to get creative with my methods of torture."

I step back into his line of sight and tap the edge of the table once.

I pick up the knife. "And actually, right now, I'm hallucinating my dead brother standing behind me, and he's giving me ideas. None of them are quick or painless."

Luke's grin presses against the inside of my skull.

I drive the knife into the soft space just above his collarbone, pushing until I feel the blade scrape bone. Skin splits with a wet, tearing sound. Blood surges immediately, running down his chest.

Dante screams. The sound bounces off the walls.

His body jolts violently against the restraints, muscles spasming beneath the blood. His chest heaves, breath breaking into shallow, frantic bursts.

"FUCK," he gasps, voice cracking. "Shit, if I tell you, they'll kill me!"

The knife stays where it is, trembling faintly from the way his body shakes.

I press down just enough to remind him what comes next.

"They're going to kill you anyway," I step into his line of sight. "You're already dead. But I can give you options. A slow death or a quick one. Your choice."

He shakes his head hard. "You fucking idiot, I can't. Elliot has..."

I backhand him across the face. The chair rattles beneath the force. Blood sprays from his mouth, hitting the concrete in wet streaks.

Before he can recover, I grab his face, fingers digging into his jaw, forcing him to look at me.

"You don't get it," I snap. "I'm not fucking around. I will flay your skin off piece by piece if it brings me one inch closer to finding her."

Luke purrs approval.

"You're wasting time," he whispers. "Start with the eyes."

"I'm going to ask one more time," I say evenly. "Where is the manor?"

Dante coughs and spits. "You'll never get in..."

I don't blink.

I walk to the tool rack and take down the bone saw, its serrated edge catching the light.

"That foot is already useless," I turn it in my hands. "Not worth saving, is it?"

His breath hitches. "No. No. Wait. Wait."

I crouch beside his leg, the one Travis has already blown apart. The boot is soaked through, leather split and glued to what used to be skin. Blood has dried in thick black crusts around the laces. The foot inside is no longer shaped like a foot. It is swollen, split, bone pressing white through torn muscle.

It twitches when I touch it.

"You're lucky," I say quietly. "I'm doing you a favor."

"No. Fuck. Don't. Elliot will kill you."

His voice cracks into something desperate.

I grab his ankle. The joint shifts wrong in my grip. I set the saw just above the worst of the damage, teeth resting against skin that is already split open.

Dante starts screaming before I even move.

Then I push down.

The first drag of the blade splits what is left of the flesh. It doesn't glide. It snags and tears. The teeth chew through skin and fat in jerking strokes that vibrate up my arm. Blood spills instantly, pumping out in heavy bursts that coat my hands and the concrete beneath us.

He thrashes against the restraints, chair legs scraping uselessly against the floor.

I saw deeper.

Muscle parts in stringy strands. Tendons stretch stubborn and white before snapping one by one under the grind of metal. The sound is wet and fibrous, like tearing soaked rope.

He is shrieking now, voice shredding itself raw.

When the blade hits bone, the vibration changes. A hard, jarring resistance.

I press harder.

The saw skips once, screeching against the bone before finding purchase. Then I drive it back and forth with steady force. Bone dust mixes with blood, turning into a pale, gritty paste that splatters across my forearms.

It takes longer than it should.

The crack comes halfway through. A sharp, violent snap that echoes in the room as the bone splits unevenly. The lower half sags, held only by shredded tissue.

I keep sawing.

Beau stands in the doorway, arms crossed, watching without comment.

Luke leans against the far wall in my head, smiling like this is a homecoming.

The final strip of tendon stretches thin, trembling under tension, then tears with a wet rip.

The foot tears free in my hands.

I place it in Dante's lap, setting it down slowly so he can see exactly what it is.

For a moment he just stares at it.

Then the scream comes.

Blood surges from the mangled stump where his leg ends, pumping out in violent bursts that splash across the concrete floor. The torn flesh hangs in ragged strands around the exposed bone, slick and glistening under the warehouse lights. Muscle spasms uncontrollably as his body tries to process what just happened.

Dante's screams collapse into broken, choking sobs as he stares down at his own severed foot resting in his lap.

I grab the salt container and tear it open with my teeth.

I pack it into the wound with both hands.

Not a sprinkle. Fistfuls.

I grind it into the exposed muscle, into the open marrow, forcing it into every torn space.

The sound that rips out of him doesn't sound human. His back arches so hard the chair lifts off the ground for a second. Veins bulge along his neck. Spit and blood spray from his mouth as he convulses.

"Now," I say, my hands still slick with him, "we can talk."

I wrap the stump tight with gauze, pulling hard, cinching it down until the bleeding slows to a sluggish seep.

He seizes again under the pressure.

I lean in close enough that he can feel my breath over his face.

"No more pretending, you've been to the manor. You know where she is."

"I will tell you. I swear—I will talk—Just please."

I burn the cigarette into the side of his face. "Now!"

"North of Eugene," he gasps. "Off the 58. Gravel path. Front entrance."

I turn to Beau. "You think he's lying?"

Beau shakes his head once. "He's leaking from every hole. He's not lying."

I press the knife gently under Dante's jaw.

"Anyone else at the manor?"

"No. Just guards. Elliot is there. That's it. I swear."

I hold the blade there for another beat, then lower it.

"Pack him up."

We keep Dante alive, but barely.

His wrists are cuffed behind his back, metal biting into torn skin already swollen and raw. Zip ties cut deep into his ankles, one of them wrapped just above what used to be his foot. The bloody gauze around the stump has gone stiff and black, soaked through hours ago. The jagged end of his shin presses forward at an unnatural angle, wrapped tight but still leaking.

A strip of duct tape covers his mouth, sealed into sweat and blood. He makes guttural, wet sounds in the back seat. His whole body twitches with every bump in the road.

Travis drives. His hands lock on the wheel. His jaw stays tight. He doesn't look in the mirror.

I turn in my seat. "Directions."

Dante nods frantically, muffled pleas leaking behind the tape. I grab his jaw and rip it off.

He gasps for air like a drowning man. "Take the next right," he stammers. "Then the service road. No headlights once we're off the main road. They'll see you."

We follow the directions.

The pavement disappears beneath us, replaced by dirt and gravel. Pine trees press in from both sides, branches clawing at the vehicle. The tires crack over loose rock like bones snapping underfoot.

"Keep going," Dante says, his voice climbing. "There's a lodge at the end. Looks abandoned. It's not. Cameras. Motion sensors. Heat tracking in the trees. If you stop too early, it will trigger the perimeter."

"Where's the cutoff?" I ask.

"Past the fence line. There's a boulder with a red 'X' carved into it. Ten yards past that is the safe zone. That's where you park."

He looks around the car, panic shaking his voice. "I got you here. Okay? I did what you wanted."

Luke's voice slides into my head like static.

"He still thinks there's a deal coming. Show him what you really are."

The trees thin, and the manor comes into view. The exact one from the footage.

It sits there like it has been waiting for us.

Details Travis pulled on Dante flood my mind. Black Ridge Club. Payments routed through shell accounts. Girls moved in and out for years. Shipped, traded, disposed of. Dante's fingerprints on all of it.

He is not just a coward with a gun to his head.

He is a pipeline.

"This is it," Dante says too fast. "This is the place. I swear."

I open the door and step out. Cold air hits my lungs hard enough to sting.

Dante twists in the back seat, panic flooding his face. "Okay, asshole. You said if I helped—"

I yank the door open and grab him by the front of his jacket.

"Out."

He tries to brace himself against the seat. It doesn't help. I drag him out of the car and slam him onto the gravel beside the road. He hits the ground hard, breath leaving him in a broken grunt.

Dante scrambles halfway upright, blood still drying across his face. "Wait. Wait. I told you where it is."

I look down at him and think about the footage Travis pulled. I think about the girls who never walked back out of the places Dante delivered them to. The ones he dropped off like shipments.

"I don't have time to let you die slow. So this is going to be quick."

He tries to speak again. "Wait, no, just le—"

I raise the gun and fire.

The bullet tears through his skull. His head snaps backward as blood and bone burst out behind him and spray across the gravel and the side of the car. His body collapses immediately, lifeless before it even finishes hitting the ground.

Smoke drifts faintly from the barrel in the cold air.

"Jesus Christ," Travis mutters from the car. "Fuck, Seth. Is anyone's skull safe from a bullet around you?"

I don't answer.

I walk back to the door and shut it.

Because no, it is not. Not if they had a hand in what happened to her. Not if they fed her into this place.

Beau steps out from the other side, gun in hand. His eyes stay on the manor.

So do mine.

I rack a fresh round into the chamber.

"Let's go get my girl."

Chapter 26
Brooke

I keep thinking about Seth as a kid.

Ten years old. An age when most children worry about school or friends, not being chained in a basement by their father.

This one probably feels a lot like it.

The thought keeps circling in my head while I sit here surrounded by concrete walls, blood and despair. Richard used to drag him downstairs and leave him there in the dark as if fear was some kind of lesson a child needed to learn.

I'm an adult and I can barely breathe through this.

I try to imagine what it must have felt like for him. The cold floor. The silence after the door closed above him. The knowledge that the man who was supposed to protect him was the one who locked him down there.

Seth lived through that kind of terror when he was a child.

And somehow he still grew into the man I love.

Somehow he still became loyal, protective, and capable of loving someone like me with a devotion that still feels almost impossible.

The basement around me stays quiet except for the slow shifting sounds of people trying to rest.

When I finally look up, I notice Miles sitting on the edge of his cot across the room.

He is still awake.

His back curves forward slightly as his elbows rest on his knees. A strip of gauze covers the side of his face and an eye patch is wrapped tight around his head. The white fabric has already soaked through in places where blood bled into it earlier.

He doesn't look at me right away. He simply sits there breathing slowly, as if he is concentrating on the effort of holding himself together. He looks up when he hears me.

Something shifts in his expression. Like he already knows.

"I lost it."

Miles's mouth opens, then closes. His good eye fills instantly.

"I'm so sorry," he says.

For a second, neither of us speak.

Pipes creak overhead. Someone coughs from the far corner.

"I don't feel anything," I admit quietly. "Not the way I should."

Miles looks at me.

"I feel like something got ripped out of me and now there is just space where it used to be."

He swallows.

"You're allowed to feel that."

"I don't have time to."

Tears spill down my face before I can stop them. I wipe them away hard with the back of my hand, irritated with myself for letting them exist at all.

"There is no point in crying now," I sigh, my voice tight. "It's better this way. Better now than whatever way they plan to kill me tomorrow."

Miles shakes his head.

"No," he says. "We are going to survive."

I almost laugh at that.

I look at him properly then.

The patch strapped too tight around his skull. The faint tremor in his hands that he keeps tucking under his thighs so I won't see it. The way his spine stays straight anyway, like dignity is the last thing he has and he refuses to give it up.

"On the hunt, we can grab branches, rocks, anything. We aren't going to let them just kill us out there."

"They will kill us," I say.

"They are going to try."

Then he shifts forward and lowers his voice.

"If they move us," he says, "you stay near me. If you see an opening, you take it. You don't wait for anyone's permission. You don't wait for me."

My chest tightens at that.

"You do not get to martyr yourself."

He gives a faint, crooked half smile.

"Wasn't planning on it."

The next night, before the hunt begins, they call my name.

The physician's office smells the same, bleach, metal, blood, and antiseptic. He unwraps my arm carefully, examining the swelling, the bruising, the ugly angles of my wrist.

It still hurts. The constant dull pulse is a reminder.

Sophie appears in the doorway, arms crossed.

"Is she ready?" she asks. "For the hunt."

The physician doesn't look at her. "She shouldn't be running. She has significant internal bleeding."

Sophie scoffs. "Everyone's bleeding." She steps closer, gaze raking over me. "She's not special. She'll participate."

Then she turns and leaves.

The physician finishes rewrapping my arm without speaking. His movements are careful and efficient as he secures the wrap around my wrist and forearm. When he finishes, his hands remain there for a moment longer than necessary.

"I cannot help you," he says quietly.

I nod because I already understand that.

He glances toward the door before leaning slightly closer. Something cool presses briefly against the inside of my wrist as he finishes sealing the wrap.

A scalpel.

It sits hidden beneath the layers of fabric, positioned so I will be able to reach it if I need to.

My breath catches.

He looks me in the eye for the first time since I arrived here.

"I have seen what they do to people during the Hunt," he lowers his voice. "You do not want to experience it."

The words settle heavy in my chest.

"If they find you," he continues, "use it on yourself before they do their worst."

He is not offering me a weapon.

He is offering me a way out.

"Thank you," I say quietly.

He nods once.

"Good luck to you, Brooke."

I'm not going to use it on myself. If they want a hunt, I'm going to make them bleed for it.

After the physician finishes, the guards escort me back to the basement. A dress waits folded neatly on the cot.

It is soft cotton, pure white, sleeveless. It looks like something meant for a summer picnic or a ceremony. It is not armor. It is not meant for running. It is meant to be seen, exposed, easy to find in the woods.

Sophie stands in front of me, already dressed in black, her curved blades strapped to her thighs.

"I picked this one special," she smiles as she tosses a pair of white flats onto the cot. "It will make it easier for us to find you. You can't exactly blend into the trees."

I don't respond.

"Good luck," she adds lightly. "If I find you first, I will make it quick."

I hold her gaze for as long as I can before turning away to get dressed.

I sit back down on the edge of the cot to slide my feet into the shoes, and that is when I feel it. Warmth spreads slowly beneath the thin fabric, followed by a damp heaviness that makes my breath catch. The sensation is unmistakable, the sickening awareness that something is still happening inside my body whether I want to face it or not.

I look down.

Blood has already soaked through my underwear.

I press a hand there carefully and look back up at Sophie. "I'm bleeding. It is going to go through the dress."

She shrugs, completely unbothered. "You'll be bleeding more soon."

I hold her gaze for a second, calm enough that it almost surprises me.

If she tries to kill me first, the scalpel goes into her before anyone else.

I finish dressing without another word.

Sophie leads me out of the basement cells and up the stairs toward the game room. Each step feels heavier than the last.

The doors to the game room are already open.

Elliot stands at the center of the room like a host about to begin a performance. He is dressed in black from head to toe, boots polished, movements unhurried. A wolf mask rests in his hands, its empty eyes fixed forward. A chainsaw hangs at his side, the weight of it obvious in the way his grip settles around the handle. He looks pleased, almost reverent, like this is the part he enjoys most.

Asher lounges near the bar, also dressed in black, a fox mask tucked under one arm. He checks his crossbow with quiet precision, fingers running along the string, then the bolts lined up beside him. The tips catch the overhead lights. He smiles to himself as he works.

Knox stands closer to the wall, broad shoulders rolling slowly as if loosening up before a workout. A bear mask rests against his thigh. His axe is already in his hands, freshly sharpened, the wide blade reflecting light with every subtle shift of his stance.

Sophie joins them last, dressed in black like the rest, a sheep mask dangling loosely from her fingers. The contrast makes my stomach turn. Her expression focused, almost serene.

The room feels staged, as if everything in it has been placed with intention for what is about to happen.

The others are brought in behind me, Miles, Emma, Sarah, and Jared. All of us are dressed in white. Standing together, we look like sacrifices lined up at the altar.

Elliot steps forward, smiling with ease. "Here are the rules. When the first siren sounds, you run. You hide. You do whatever you think will keep you alive. You will have a head start."

He begins pacing slowly, the chainsaw resting across his shoulders.

"When the second siren sounds, your head start is over. That is when the hunt begins."

He stops and glances toward the side door.

"There will also be armed guards positioned throughout the forest to ensure no one breaks protocol or tries anything clever. They are not here to hunt. They are here to make sure you follow the rules."

My stomach sinks.

Elliot turns back to us and raises an eyebrow.

"If you manage to breach the perimeter and make it past the gates, you're free. You win. You escape."

He smiles, wider now.

"No one ever has."

I can feel Emma trembling beside me. Her breathing is shallow. Her eyes dart from face to face, trying to decide who to fear the most.

"This game usually produces zero survivors," Elliot continues. "If you survive the hunt itself, and we find you, your execution will follow shortly afterward."

I catch movement near the corner of the room.

Enzo stands beside one of the side doors, dressed in all black, a cattle prod slung over his shoulder. He's smiling. Not wide, not performative, just relaxed, entertained.

I don't know whether to feel sick or furious.

Elliot turns his attention back to us.

"Any questions?"

Emma takes a shaky breath. "I—"

Elliot cuts her off without looking at her. "All right. On your mark."

My muscles lock in place.

"Get set."

My breath stalls in my throat.

"Go."

Chapter 27
Seth

We don't waste another second.

The gate to the estate comes into view fast. Big iron bastard, but the sensor is visible through the fence, cheap tech for rich psychos.

I shoot it twice.

Sparks fly. The gate unlocks with a hard metallic clunk.

We push through and everything goes cold.

The courtyard is lit by moonlight and security lamps. The manor rises at the end of the long gravel path, windows dark, front door looming.

Six guards.

Spaced wide. Trying to stay hidden.

Too late.

Beau moves first.

Quick, clean headshots. Two on the right drop before the others even turn.

I catch one flanking the hedges and drop him with a shot to the neck. Another crouches behind the fountain. Two to the chest. He slumps over without a sound.

A crack splits the air near my ear. Something punches hard into my side.

For half a second I think it is impact. Then heat blooms along my ribs. My body registers it as pressure, not pain. I look down just long enough to see fabric split and dark spreading through my shirt. A shallow graze.

I barely feel it.

Adrenaline swallows the rest.

I pivot toward the muzzle flash near the hedgerow and put a round straight through the shooter's forehead. He drops mid breath.

Beau catches the last one mid sprint with a slug to the spine. His body folds like wet paper.

"Six down," Beau says.

He jogs ahead, gun in hand, smoke still curling from the barrel.

I follow close, one hand briefly pressing my side.

When we hit the front, Beau raises the gun and blasts the door straight off its hinges. It buckles inward with a scream of wood and steel, smoke curling around the frame.

That's when I see it.

"Wait."

I grab his arm and yank him back.

A glint above the doorway. Mounted rig. Tripwire shotgun, hidden behind the molding.

"Fuck me," Beau mutters.

I raise my Glock and fire twice.

The mechanism snaps. A deafening boom rings out as the rig fires harmlessly into the ceiling. Splinters rain down. The hallway beyond fills with smoke.

We move in.

Gunfire erupts immediately from the stairwell.

Two on the ground floor. One on the second.

Beau dives behind a column and returns fire with his backup Glock, forcing the two downstairs into cover. I go left, staying low, my side burning now.

The guy on the landing leans out to aim.

Bad move.

One shot to the head.

Beau keeps the downstairs guards pinned while I creep up from the side and take them both out with two clean shots to the back.

"Clear."

"Fucking amateurs," Beau mutters.

We keep moving, clearing each room one by one.

Every door opens to nothing. Every space is empty. We check, clear, and lock them behind us.

One hallway has blood smeared across the floor, with drag marks cutting through it.

There are no bodies.

Then we find the door.

It is heavier than the others, reinforced with steel brackets and bolted from the outside, like whatever is inside is not meant to leave. I step back, plant my foot, and kick hard near the lock. The frame gives with a sharp crack, wood splintering inward as the door bursts open.

The smell hits immediately.

It is a rancid blend of iron, bile, and decay that coats the back of my throat and makes my eyes sting. It smells like something has been opened and left that way for too long, like the room itself is rotting.

A chain rattles overhead.

I look up.

A body hangs from the ceiling by the wrists, suspended at an unnatural angle. The head lolls forward, chin dropped to the chest, mouth slack and open like she tried to scream. The shoulders are bare and slick with dried blood. The entire lower half of the body is gone, severed at the waist, as if someone carved away everything below and stopped when they were satisfied.

What remains of the torso is still leaking.

Blood and dark fluid slide down the abdomen in slow, uneven trails, dripping steadily into a floor drain beneath it.

My stomach drops so hard it feels like freefall.

For a split second, my brain refuses to process anything except shape. Black hair matted with blood. Tattoos. Ruined flesh where legs should be.

Brooke.

I'm too late.

My breath locks in my chest, like my lungs seize completely. Heat rushes into my face, then drains out just as fast, leaving me cold and unsteady. My hands start shaking, fingers tightening uselessly around my gun as my pulse spikes into something wild and uneven.

I see her the way she looked the last time I touched her. Alive. Angry. Breathing. I hear her voice in my head, not screaming, not begging, just saying my name the way she always does when she needs me to focus.

I'm not there.

I picture her alone in this room, looking at that door, waiting for it to open. Waiting for me. I imagine her realizing I am not coming in time. I imagine the moment hope leaves her face.

My vision tunnels hard. The edges of the room darken. The smell of blood thickens until it feels like it is coating the back of my throat. My legs feel hollow and useless. I can't feel the floor beneath my boots.

I've seen death before. I've caused it. I've watched it happen slowly, deliberately, without mercy. None of that prepares me for this moment. None of it matters when the shape in front of me matches the nightmare I've been carrying since the second she was taken.

My heartbeat slams hard enough to hurt. My knees threaten to give out.

This is not just a body.

It is the end of everything I have built my life around.

Something inside me snaps.

I am going to tear every man in this house apart.

I don't care how long it takes. I don't care what it costs. I am not stopping at a bullet or mercy. I will rip them apart with my hands if I have to. Elliot first. Anyone still breathing after him next. I will make this place choke on what it has done to her.

I want them to feel it. Every second of it.

And when there is no one left to kill, when the house is silent, empty and soaked in blood, I am going to end myself too.

Because if she is gone, there is nothing left to live for.

Beau's voice cuts through the roar in my ears, distant at first, like it is coming through water. "Seth. It's not her."

I don't hear him.

My body refuses to accept it. My chest is too tight to expand, my heartbeat slamming erratically against my ribs.

Beau steps closer, firm now. "Seth. Look at the tattoos."

I force myself to breathe. Force my eyes to focus. Force my brain to catch up.

The ink is wrong.

Heavy black script curls along the ribs. A half finished design on the shoulder blade. Lines and symbols that don't belong to her, scars that don't match the map I know by heart.

Reality snaps back into place with a sickening jolt. Relief hits hard and ugly, immediately followed by something just as dangerous.

Rage.

Then the sirens start.

Red strobes wash over the walls in harsh, pounding flashes while alarms scream through the manor's halls.

I step into the hallway with my gun raised, heart punching against my ribs. "We need to move. We need to find her now."

Beau steps beside me, weapon up, eyes sharp and focused. We clear each corner, check every sight line, and start kicking down doors one after another. Guards spill out of rooms and side corridors, shouting into radios and grabbing for guns they are too slow to use.

They drop fast.

Two go down in the hallway in front of us, chest shots that slam them into the walls and leave them sliding to the floor. Another tries to cut across behind us from a doorway. Beau puts a round through his throat before he finishes raising his weapon.

"Outside," I say.

We hit the back exit and push into the night. The cold bites through the heat still running under my skin. The sirens bleed out into the open air, thin and distant over the grounds.

Two figures stand near the tree line, watching us.

One holds two curved blades in their hands, the metal catching flashes of red from the lights behind us. Beside them stands another figure gripping a chainsaw, the pull cord wrapped around their wrist.

As soon as they see us drop the last two men by the door, their attention shifts. The one in the sheep mask tilts their head, assessing. The one with the chainsaw jerks their chin toward the forest. The chainsaw roars to life, the sound ripping across the yard and swallowing part of the siren wail.

I raise my gun and fire.

The shots tear bark from the tree trunk near their shoulder. The one with the chainsaw curses, turns hard, and bolts for the deeper dark between the trees.

They scatter fast, moving in the opposite direction, vanishing into the forest on a line that doesn't lead back to the manor.

They're going to hunt.

I need to find Brooke in this forest before they do.

Chapter 28
Brooke

The siren explodes overhead, loud and mechanical, shaking the ceiling as red lights flash in time with the sound. Miles grabs my hand.

We run.

We bolt through the doors and into the night, our feet striking tile, then dirt as we plunge into the trees. The white fabric of my dress snags on thorns and branches almost immediately. Behind us, Elliot's laughter echoes faintly over the dying siren.

Miles stays close beside me. His breathing is rough, steady only because he forces it to be.

"They've set traps out here," he whispers as we sprint deeper into the forest. "Rope snares. Pits. Spikes. I heard them talking about it."

I nod and scan the ground with every step.

"How far does the forest go?" I ask.

"I don't know," he says. "But we need to keep moving. That siren won't last long."

The blood between my legs stays warm, slowly soaking into the white fabric. The dress clings heavier with every step, making it harder to move.

I don't know how much longer my body will hold out.

The second siren wails through the forest, vibrating through the ground beneath my feet and carrying through the trees without fading.

The sound marks the beginning of the hunt.

We run faster, pushing our bodies past what they want to give.

My lungs burn with every breath, and each inhale feels shallow and incomplete. My legs shake as I force them forward, muscles screaming with fatigue and strain. The hem of the white dress tears repeatedly as branches catch it and rip fabric away. My shoes slip on damp leaves and loose soil, making every step unstable. My chest aches with every breath, the taste of iron thick in my mouth as my throat dries out.

Jared breaks first.

He bolts forward, stumbling at the start before forcing himself into a run. Panic drives him harder, his breath ripping out in ragged pulls as he sprints across the ground.

"Jared, wait!" I shout.

He doesn't stop. He runs straight between two trees, head up, lungs ripping for air, throwing everything he has left into speed. Branches lash at his arms. His shoes tear through mud and dead leaves.

He never sees the wire.

Piano wire stretches between the trees, pulled tight enough to hum. It blends into the dark like a hairline crack in glass.

Jared runs straight into it.

The sound comes first. A sharp metallic twang. Then a thick tearing noise.

The wire catches him across the throat.

His body keeps driving forward. The force of his sprint presses his neck harder into the line, and the wire bites deep. Skin splits open instantly. Muscle parts under the tension. The wire carves through him as his own momentum drags him along it.

Blood bursts outward in a violent spray, misting the bark and spattering the leaves.

A strangled choke tears out of him, cut short as the wire slices farther back. His airway opens. His voice dies in his throat.

His knees buckle.

He hits the ground, the wire snapping loose and vibrating between the trees.

His hands claw at the dirt. Fingers dig into wet soil as his body tries to process what just happened. His legs kick wildly, heels gouging into the earth.

His neck gapes open.

The front of his throat hangs in torn layers. Blood pumps out in thick surges. It runs down his chest, soaks into his shirt, pools beneath his face.

Blood fills his mouth and spills over his lips. His jaw works uselessly, eyes wide and unfocused.

His movements slow. One hand twitches against the leaves.

Then his body goes still.

Emma screams.

The sound tears out of her chest and doesn't stop. She freezes for half a second, staring at what is left of him, then runs toward his body without slowing.

"Emma, stop!" Miles shouts.

She doesn't listen.

She makes it three steps.

An axe flies from the left and slams into the back of her skull.

The crack splits the air.

The blade punches through bone and buries deep, driving her head forward with brutal force. There is a sickening crunch as the metal splits through skull and sinks in.

Blood bursts out immediately.

It pours from the wound in thick, heavy streams, running down the sides of her face and into the soil. More blood pulses out around the blade itself, bubbling as it escapes from shattered bone.

A thin line of pink and gray matter seeps out from the split in her skull, mixing with the blood and dirt beneath her.

Her face hits the dirt hard enough to bounce once before going slack. Her fingers twitch once against the ground.

Then her body goes still.

My steps falter, and my stomach clenches violently as nausea surges. Miles grabs my arm hard enough to hurt and pulls me forward.

"We can't stop," he says.

Laughter echoes through the trees behind us.

We run deeper into the forest, weaving between trees and uneven ground. The terrain dips sharply, forcing us to slow for a moment as our footing becomes unstable. Branches scrape across my arms and face, leaving stinging lines and pulling loose strands of hair free. Pain flares through my shoulder from earlier injuries, spreading down my arm. My lower abdomen cramps again, making my breath hitch and my pace falter.

A low rumble rolls overhead.

The first drops of rain follow seconds later, sparse at first, tapping against leaves and skin. Then more come, heavier, faster, the forest darkening as the sky opens above us.

A loud snapping sound cuts through the noise of our footsteps.

Gunfire cracks nearby, sharp and close enough to make leaves fall from the branches overhead.

Miles grabs my wrist and pulls me hard.

We're still running when Miles sucks in a sharp breath.

"Brooke," he yells. "Keep going."

The crossbow bolt strikes him in the back.

The impact makes a dull, heavy sound as the bolt punches through muscle.

Miles gasps and stumbles forward, his steps turning sloppy as blood spreads across the back of his shirt. He tries to stay upright, tries to keep moving, but a second bolt hits lower in his side, driving in with brutal force.

The impact knocks him to his knees. He collapses forward onto the ground.

I drop beside him immediately.

"No," I grab his shoulders, trying to lift him. "No, please!"

Miles coughs, rain mixing with the thick blood spilling from his mouth. It streaks down his face and collects along his jaw as his breathing turns wet and uneven, every breath visibly harder than the last. His remaining eye locks onto mine, sharp despite the pain.

"Brooke, don't stop. Go!"

"I'm not leaving you," I strain to pull him up. My hands slip. My arms shake. "I'm not leaving you!"

"You have to...You have to go now."

"No," I shake my head. "I won't leave you here."

He reaches for my wrist with shaking fingers and manages to grab it. His grip is weak but desperate, slick with blood and rain.

"Tell Alonzo."

Tears blur my vision. I shake my head, breathing hard. I remember Mila on the floor at Amber's house, bleeding from her chest, telling me to go while she was dying. I remember refusing to leave her. I remember how staying didn't save her.

Laughter echoes again, closer now, cutting cleanly through the trees.

Miles pushes my hand away with the last of his strength. "Go! Now!"

My chest hurts so badly that breathing becomes difficult. My throat tightens until I can barely force the words out.

"Miles, I'm so sorry."

I stand up and run.

I don't look back.

Branches strike my arms, shoulders, and face as I force myself forward. My legs feel weak and unreliable, vision blurring from tears, exhaustion, and pain. My breathing comes in short, shallow bursts that burn my chest with every pull of air.

Someone whispers my name from ahead.

"Brooke."

Sarah crouches behind a fallen tree, her face pale and pulled tight with fear.

"I think I found the gate," she whispers. "Come on."

I run toward her, pushing my body harder than it wants to go. My feet slip on wet leaves as the rain starts to fall, heavier now, slicking the forest floor and turning every step into a risk.

The crossbow fires with a harsh, mechanical snap.

The bolt punches through the air and buries itself in the side of Sarah's head. Her body jerks once, like someone yanks an invisible cord, and then she drops beside the tree without a sound, her eyes still open and empty.

"Sarah," I gasp, the word tearing out of me.

Another click cuts through the rain.

The second bolt slams into my shoulder, driving deep enough that it feels like my entire arm explodes from the inside. Pain flares hot and blinding. The force spins me sideways and throws me to the ground, the impact knocking the breath out of my chest as the forest tilts around me.

Blood spreads rapidly across the shoulder of my dress. The bolt stays embedded. The pain is constant, radiating down my arm and into my chest in blinding waves.

I lie there, struggling to breathe, rain streaking through the canopy above as my vision swims. Footsteps move closer through the brush. Leaves crunch under slow steps as Asher walks closer. Rain darkens his clothes, plasters his hair to his forehead, but his smile stays easy.

He laughs openly now, the sound satisfied, like he has already decided how this ends. He stops a few feet away and kneels slightly, bracing the crossbow against his thigh as he reaches for another bolt.

"You did better than I thought," he chuckles. "You almost made it."

My shoulder throbs violently. The bolt pulls at my arm with its weight, sending sharp pain into my fingers. I writhe on the ground, trying to get my legs under me, but my body refuses to cooperate.

Asher slides the bolt into place. He watches his hands, not my face.

"You know what I like best about this part," he says. "It's when you stop begging and start realizing there's no one coming."

I drag in a breath that barely fills my lungs. My fingers dig into the mud, nails breaking as I try to push myself backward. My legs kick uselessly, slipping on wet leaves smeared with blood.

Asher laughs again and pulls the string back partway, testing the tension.

"You see," he continues, "you don't die right away with these. It just hurts longer."

He takes one step closer.

That is when I move.

I slide my hand under my wrist wrap and force my fingers around the handle of the scalpel. Pain rips through my arm, but I don't stop. I pull the blade free and twist toward him.

Asher is still reloading.

I swing low and fast, slicing into the back of his ankle where the tendon is exposed. The blade cuts through flesh and tendons in one clean motion.

Asher screams.

His foot collapses under him, and he drops hard to one knee. The crossbow slips from his hands and hits the ground. He grabs at his ankle, blood spilling between his fingers as his balance fails completely.

"You fucking—" His voice breaks.

I don't wait.

I crawl forward and drive the scalpel into his thigh. The blade goes deep. He screams again and swings blindly, striking my face with the back of his hand. Stars burst behind my eyes, but I hold on.

He reaches for my hair. I shove the scalpel in again, higher this time, twisting as I pull it free. Blood soaks through his pants.

Asher falls backward, scrambling with his good leg, trying to put distance between us. He drags the crossbow toward himself with shaking fingers.

I push it away.

He roars and lunges, grabbing my wounded shoulder. Pain detonates through my arm as he shoves me onto my back. His weight crushes the air from my lungs.

"I'm going to kill you—"

I bring the scalpel up and slash across his forearm. His skin splits. Blood runs freely. He recoils just enough for me to twist sideways.

Asher tries to stand, but his injured foot buckles. He crashes back down, grabbing at me desperately, fingers slick with rain and blood, his breathing ragged.

I drive the scalpel into the side of his neck.

The blade sinks in deep.

Asher freezes.

His mouth opens, but no sound comes out.

I pull the blade free. Blood erupts from his neck, spraying across my hands as I drive the scalpel into his eye. Resistance gives way. Blood pours down his chest and soaks into the dirt beneath him, darkening the ground as rain mixes with it.

His grip loosens, then his body goes slack and collapses onto his side.

I don't breathe.

I wait. I watch.

Only when the blood stops pumping in violent bursts and slows into a thick, heavy stream do I let air back into my lungs.

I pull myself away, wincing as pain flares through my shoulder. I sit back on my knees, chest heaving, arms trembling. I tear the bolt out of my shoulder, teeth clenched as heat and pressure follow it free.

The scalpel is still lodged in Asher's eye. I wrap my fingers around the handle and rip it out. Blood spills down his face as his body sags.

I wipe the blade on his shirt and turn toward the crossbow. I crawl, grab it, and hook it over my good shoulder. My arm screams, but my legs hold.

The forest stays alive with sound as the wind rises and the rain comes down harder.

I don't wait to find out who is still alive. I move forward, keeping one hand on the crossbow while the other stays ready.

I am done running.

I hear boots pound behind me. I turn and raise the crossbow, my arms shaking while pain tears through my shoulder.

Enzo bursts from the trees, stun baton snapping with sparks. He grins like he can't wait.

I step back, grab a bolt. My fingers slip from the blood and rain. The bolt drops.

He closes the distance fast.

I force the bolt into place and yank the string back until it locks.

Enzo lunges toward me.

I fire.

The bolt slams into his chest, knocking him forward with a guttural sound. He collapses but keeps moving, dragging himself across the ground with one arm while blood spills from his mouth as he reaches for the prod.

My hands shake while the pain in my wrist throbs.

I reload the crossbow, forcing my fingers to work.

I steady my aim and fire again.

The second bolt punches through his skull as he lifts his head, snapping it back. His body jerks once, then goes still.

I hold my breath without realizing it.

I lower the crossbow and stagger back, soaked through with sweat, blood, and rain.

Then I hear it, another set of boots approaching fast.

I spin with the crossbow raised, my finger tight on the trigger because I can't survive another fight.

"Easy," a low, familiar voice says.

I freeze.

"Seth?"

My heart stalls, then slams back into motion as he steps out from the trees.

Rain slicks over him, beading on the black fabric, streaking through the blood on his skin and dripping from the edge of his balaclava. For half a second, he looks unreal, like something my mind creates to survive this.

Those storm gray eyes lock onto mine.

The forest disappears, and so does the pain.

"I'm here, baby."

Chapter 29

Seth

We move at the same time.

I cross the distance in a few long strides just as the crossbow slips from her hands, hitting the ground with a dull, forgotten thud. I catch her as she reaches me, the impact knocking the breath from my chest. Rain slicks over us, soaking into our clothes as her arms lock around my neck with desperate strength. Her body shakes against mine.

I tear the balaclava from my face and kiss her.

Rain mixes with blood on my hands and smears across her cheek and jaw when I touch her. I don't care. I don't care about anything except the feeling of her weight in my arms.

She is alive.

That's all that matters.

I hold her tighter, one hand cradling the back of her head, the other braced between her shoulders. I press my face into her hair as rain pours harder around us and let myself feel it. The heat of her skin. The uneven pull of her breath. The reality of her here with me. Relief hits so hard it nearly takes my legs out from under me.

She presses her face into the side of my neck, her breath breaking unevenly against my skin.

I cup her face in both hands and kiss her again. Her mouth trembles beneath mine. She tastes like blood and rain. I slide my hand to the back of her neck and pull her closer, deepening the kiss as the storm soaks through both of us.

Footsteps break through the moment.

I pull away and turn in one clean motion, gun already up. I fire twice. The first shot catches the guard in the shoulder and spins him off balance. The second goes straight through his face. He hits the ground with a heavy, final thud.

Brooke flinches at the sound, her breath hitching, but her arms stay tight around me.

She doesn't let go.

Beau's voice cuts through the trees. "You two can reconnect later. We need to move. Now!"

I look down at her. Her eyes are wide and glassy, shock clinging to her like a second skin.

I press my forehead to hers for half a second.

Then I take her hand and we run.

We tear through the trees, my arm locked tight around Brooke's waist. Blood seeps from her shoulder, dripping onto leaves and roots, marking our path through the underbrush. I keep her pulled close, my body angled between hers and the gunfire cracking behind us.

Every shot I take is fast and precise. One guard drops with a round through the skull. Another goes down screaming after I shatter his kneecap and leave him where he falls. I don't give them time to recover. I don't give them time to aim.

"Watch the ground," Brooke gasps, her voice raw. "They set traps."

I tighten my hold on her and slow just enough to scan the path ahead. A faint glint catches my eye. Thin wire stretches between two trees. I yank her back a step and shift us sideways. I fire through the brush ahead. A man screams, then collapses out of sight before we even see his face.

The trees open into a clearing.

Boots thunder behind us.

I spin and fire twice. Another guard drops into the clearing.

Beau bursts in from the left, weapon up, moving with ruthless efficiency. He takes down two more guards before I can speak. The third turns to run. I catch him mid-step, one clean shot to the spine. He hits the ground face-first.

We keep moving.

We burst through a side entrance of the manor, the door slamming back against the wall as I take point. My pistol tracks the hallway, my arm steady as I clear corners and doorframes.

Brooke stays tight on my right. Her breathing comes ragged and uneven, each step a fraction slower than the last. Her weight shifts wrong, like she is compensating for pain she refuses to acknowledge.

A door creaks open ahead of us.

The physician steps into the hallway slowly with his hands raised, his palms open to show he is unarmed. His face has gone pale, and his eyes move between the gun in my hand and Brooke standing behind me.

I keep the pistol trained on him.

"Did he help you escape?" I ask.

Brooke looks at the physician. For a moment she doesn't move, her chest lifting as if she is about to speak.

"Seth, wait—"

The words catch before she finishes them.

Her hesitation is enough.

I pull the trigger.

The shot cracks through the hallway and the round tears through his skull. His head snaps back and his body collapses where he stands, hitting the floor with a heavy thud.

Brooke flinches hard at the sound, her shoulders tightening as she stares down at the body.

I pull her closer as we keep moving.

Behind us, Beau reloads smoothly as we reach the main corridor. Brooke lifts her hand and points, her fingers shaking.

A faint glint catches my eye near the frame. I follow it up and see the thin wire leading to a massive double-bladed axe suspended just inside the doorway, positioned to swing at head height. One clean arc would have taken someone apart. I fire twice into the mechanism. The chain snaps, and the axe drops, slamming into the tile with a metallic crash that echoes down the hall.

"Clear," Beau calls.

We push into the foyer. Through the glass walls, the courtyard is already alive with movement. Guards converge from every direction, weapons raised, shouting over one another.

I pull Brooke closer, one arm locked around her waist, keeping her upright and shielded against me. My other hand stays on the gun, firing as fast as I can line up shots.

Two rush in from the right. I put the first down with a round through the jaw, pivot, and drive a shot into the second man's chest before he can steady his aim. Beau handles the left with ruthless efficiency. Brooke stays low and close, her legs shaking with every step, but she doesn't stop.

We force our way forward through smoke, noise, and bodies.

We reach the front gate.

The SUV waits just beyond. Travis leans out from behind the wheel, his eyes wild as he spots us.

"Run," he shouts. "Get in the fucking car. Now!"

I look down.

Brooke is limping badly now. One arm hangs useless at her side.

I immediately slide my arm under her knees and lift her into my arms. She doesn't fight it. She wraps her good arm around my neck and holds on.

Gunfire cracks behind us again.

Beau tosses a grenade over his shoulder. The blast sends a shockwave through the clearing. I bend over Brooke, shielding her with my body, and keep moving.

We reach the SUV.

I wrench the back door open and lower Brooke inside, turning my body to block hers as shots snap past us.

Beau dives in the passenger seat, already shouting at Travis.

"Drive!"

The tires scream, gravel sprays. The SUV lurches forward hard enough to slam us back against the seats.

I look down at Brooke.

She doesn't cry. She doesn't blink. Her eyes stay locked on mine, wide and distant, like she is still half trapped somewhere else.

I kiss her.

She doesn't respond at first. Her body stays rigid, her breath shallow and uneven. Shock has flattened her expression, smoothed everything into something frighteningly empty. I pull back just enough to see her face.

"Brooke."

Her eyes focus slowly. She nods once, like it takes effort.

There's too much blood.

The white dress is ruined, soaked through in places and smeared in others, clinging where it should not.

I ease her back against the seat, bracing her carefully, forcing my breathing to slow even as my pulse slams in my ears. "I need to check you."

She doesn't argue.

I don't start gently. I hook my fingers into the fabric at her midsection and tear upward in one hard motion, ripping the dress open so I can see her stomach and ribs. I need to know if she has been shot or stabbed somewhere that will end her fast. My eyes scan every inch of exposed skin, searching for wounds, for blood that doesn't belong where it is pooling.

Nothing fatal.

Only deep bruises spreading beneath the skin.

I swallow and move on.

I start with her arms. Dark bruises line her forearms and biceps, finger-shaped and unmistakable. The sight twists something hot and violent in my chest. I move to her right wrist and see the bandaging immediately, wrapped too tight, dirty, uneven. Someone did it fast with whatever they had.

I unwrap it slowly.

Her hand is badly swollen. The wrist beneath it is worse, purple and distorted, the joint locked stiff from swelling.

My jaw clenches until it hurts.

I check her left arm next. More bruising. More damage. The anger keeps stacking, heavier with every mark, but I force it down. She needs me focused.

I move to her face. A bruise blooms under one eye. Scratches trace her jaw. Her lip is split. Her neck is mottled with bruises.

My hands shake. I keep them steady.

I check her legs. Scrapes cover both knees. Bruises line her thighs. She flinches when I touch her ankle, and I feel the way she shifts, protecting one side of her body without thinking.

I follow the blood instead of asking questions.

When I reach her shoulder, I see the wound clearly. The entry wound is swollen and angry, blood still seeping through the torn fabric.

I exhale slowly, my eyes never leaving it.

"He shot me," Brooke says quietly. "I pulled it out."

That pushes my anger over the edge.

I swallow it down because losing control won't help her.

I lift the hem of the dress and check the rest of her. Her thighs are smeared with dirt and blood, her skin cold beneath my hands. I move higher with intent, shutting everything else out, focused only on finding injuries, not on the way her body shakes under my touch.

Then I see it.

Blood soaks her underwear.

My breath stalls hard in my chest, like something has reached in and squeezed my lungs shut.

I blink once, then again, forcing myself to look for another explanation. I tell myself it has to be from her hip, her leg, anywhere else I can make it make sense.

It is not.

It is exactly what it looks like.

I don't ask her. I can't say anything.

I already know what it means.

Chapter 30

Brooke

Seth's voice cuts through everything, low with barely restrained fury.

"Beau. Call the doctor. Now!"

Beau doesn't argue. He is already pulling out his phone.

Seth's eyes move fast, cataloging every inch of damage. His hands check my arms, my ribs, then hover near my side again like he is forcing himself not to grab too hard.

"Anywhere else?" he asks. "Shot? Cut? Anything you didn't tell me?"

I shake my head.

His jaw tightens. The muscles along it jump. His grip closes just enough for me to feel how hard he is holding himself in place.

"Look at me," he says.

I do.

"You're here," he tells me. "I've got you. Stay with me."

I try to speak and fail. My legs won't stop shaking. The dress is heavy and cold as it clings to me, soaked through with blood, dirt, and rain. Every drop tapping against the roof of the SUV sounds too loud.

Beau shouts from the front seat. "Doctor's ready. We're going now."

Seth nods once, then wraps himself around me as we move, pulling me back against his chest. In the SUV, he holds me there, one arm locked over my middle, the other covering my bandaged wrist, his grip firm and grounding.

Even as I blink and breathe, everything still feels unreal. The headlights smear into pale streaks through the rain. Travis is saying something up front, but it barely registers. The only thing keeping me anchored is the violent, steady rhythm of Seth's heart against my spine.

By the time we pull into the gated medical facility, the shock still has not worn off.

I feel wired and hollow at the same time. It is like adrenaline is still buzzing in my veins, but my brain has disconnected. I am watching myself from above, floating somewhere distant while my body sits limp in Seth's arms.

The SUV stops.

Seth is already out, rain soaking his hair and shirt as he lifts me. He doesn't ask. He doesn't speak. He just carries me carefully, like letting me touch the ground again is not an option.

The door opens before he can knock.

A tall man in his late fifties stands there in a white coat over black scrubs, already moving aside.

"Bring her in," he says.

Seth carries me down a quiet hallway and into a room that smells faintly of antiseptic and metal. Machines hum softly along one wall. The lights are low but bright enough to make my head ache.

"You can lay her there," the doctor nods toward the bed.

Seth sets me down with careful hands, like he is afraid pressure alone might undo me. His fingers brush my hair back, then still when his eyes drop to the blood-darkened fabric at my waist.

"She's hurt," his voice stays controlled, but urgent. "She's pregnant. I–I saw blood down there. You need to check that now."

The doctor pauses for half a second, then nods.

"Okay," he murmurs. "We'll start there."

He washes his hands and pulls on gloves. Seth stays close, one hand braced at my side, the other gripping the edge of the mattress hard enough that his knuckles blanch.

"I need a timeline," the doctor steps in close. "When did the bleeding start?"

"Yesterday," my voice sounds detached. "After they drowned me. I woke up cramping. Then it didn't stop."

He nods once. "Do you know how far along you are?"

"No."

His eyes flick to Seth for half a second, then back to me.

"Any clots? Tissue?"

I swallow. "Yes."

He adjusts the bed slightly and folds the sheet down. He places a hand low on my abdomen, pressing gently, then deeper. His fingers assess the firmness, the tenderness. I flinch despite myself.

"Pain here?" he asks.

"Yes."

He nods again.

"Vitals are stable," he mutters more to himself than to us. "We'll confirm with imaging."

He wheels the ultrasound machine closer.

Seth leans down, his forehead brushing mine.

"You don't have to look," he holds my hand. "I'll do it."

I don't answer.

The cold gel hits my skin. The probe follows, pressing just above my pelvic bone. The doctor moves it with practiced control, angling, rotating, adjusting pressure.

The machine hums. The screen flickers with shifting gray shapes.

The doctor leans closer.

Seth leans too.

"Tell me what you see," Seth says quietly.

"I will," the doctor replies.

He adjusts the angle again. Presses slightly deeper. Studies the monitor in silence.

Seth feels it first. His hand around mine goes rigid.

The doctor freezes for a fraction of a second, then continues scanning, slower now. He traces the area again, confirming.

"There's no cardiac activity," he says finally. "Measurements are consistent with approximately ten weeks."

Seth doesn't move. He doesn't speak. His thumb brushes once over my knuckles.

The doctor keeps going. "The bleeding you described suggests this began prior to the drowning event. Your body has not completed the process. There's retained tissue."

Seth's grip tightens painfully around my hand.

"Are you sure?" he asks.

The doctor holds his gaze.

"Yes."

Seth's shoulders go rigid. Something dark flickers behind his eyes.

"What does she need?"

The doctor turns the screen away. "We'll need to perform a quick procedure to remove the remaining tissue. If we don't, she risks infection and hemorrhage."

Seth nods once. "Do it."

The doctor looks to me.

"Is that okay?"

I search for a reaction. Grief. Panic. Anything that feels proportional.

There is nothing.

"Okay," I say.

The doctor explains what will happen in simple terms. Cleaning. Making sure nothing remains. Monitoring afterward. The words drift in and out like they aren't meant for me.

I focus on Seth instead.

He stands so close to the bed his knee presses into the frame. His hands keep clenching and releasing at his sides, like he is holding something back with sheer force. His face is rigid, eyes glassy but locked on me, like looking away might make this real.

He leans down again, his mouth near my ear.

"I'm here," he whispers. "I've got you."

They position me and numb me. I feel pressure, movement, hands working where I can't see. I stare at Seth the entire time.

I watch his jaw tighten when the doctor begins. I watch him turn his head slightly, like he can't stand to look but can't leave either.

I feel nothing.

I don't feel pain, grief, or fear.

Just distance.

It is like I'm floating somewhere above my body, watching it happen to someone else.

Seth reaches for my hand again, and I let him take it. His grip is too tight, his fingers trembling. He presses his forehead to my knuckles for just a second, like he needs that contact to stay upright.

"I'm sorry."

I can't respond.

I don't know how.

I keep staring at his face instead, at the way this is breaking him in real time. His eyes are red now. His mouth is drawn tight, the muscles in his neck standing out as he swallows again and again.

He feels everything.

And I feel nothing.

That realization scares me more than the manor ever has.

I lie there, numb and quiet, watching the person I love fall apart for something my body has already let go of, and I wonder what is wrong with me that I can't cry.

I wonder if the numbness will ever leave.

I wonder if I will wake up one day and finally feel it all at once.

Chapter 31

Seth

The safe house has been silent for the last forty eight hours.

I sit on the edge of the bed beside her, watching the slow rise and fall of her chest. The room stays dim and enclosed.

She lies against the pillows, wrapped in black sheets, barely moving. Since the procedure, she hasn't said much. Sometimes her body trembles without warning. Sometimes she flinches when I touch her. Most of the time, she doesn't react at all.

She hasn't really slept.

She drifts in and out, minutes at a time, her body never fully letting go. Each time she slips under, I wait for it. The jerk. The breath tearing out of her chest. The panic snapping her awake like something has grabbed her from the inside.

I think she might finally be staying down this time. Her breathing evens out. Her muscles loosen just enough that I let myself lean back, let my eyes close.

An hour and twenty five minutes.

That is the record.

The second the thought crosses my mind, she screams.

Her body jolts hard, hands clawing, breath breaking into sharp, broken gasps as she shakes violently. I'm on her instantly, pulling her against my chest, wrapping my arms around her before she can fold in on herself.

"It's okay," I murmur, the words pressed against her ear. "You're here. You're safe. I've got you."

She shakes harder in my arms, her whole body trembling like she is trying to outrun something still inside her. Her heart slams against my chest, fast and out of control, and her fingers fist in my shirt, twisting the fabric like she needs proof I am here. That I am real. That this is real.

"I know," I whisper. "I know, baby. I got you."

Her eyes are open but unfocused, staring past my shoulder, glassy and distant. I shift her closer, one hand at the back of her head, the other flat between her shoulders, feeling every shudder move through her.

"Look at me," I say, gentle but firm. "Hey. Look at me."

She does not. Her gaze stays locked somewhere else, somewhere I can't follow.

Every time she falls asleep, this happens. Every time, she comes back fighting.

I keep talking anyway. About anything. About where we are. About the bed. About the walls. About how the door is locked and nobody can come get her.

"You're not there anymore," I say quietly. "That place is gone. You're safe. I'm right here."

Her shaking eases only slightly, never fully stopping. I stay there, sitting close, my arms tight around her. Rage burns hot and I have nowhere to put it. There is nothing left to destroy that will fix this. Nothing left to kill that will undo what has already been done.

I can only imagine what she endured in that manor, what they did to her, and what they forced her to watch. Some torture doesn't just leave marks, it fucks with your mind. I know what torture looks like. I have inflicted it many times. I have broken people down piece by piece and called it necessary. I don't flinch at violence.

But that place was different.

What we saw goes beyond control, interrogation, or punishment. It was systematic and intentional. It was sick. That says a lot coming from someone like me.

Whatever she went through in those five days didn't end when I carried her out. It followed her back here. It lives in her muscles, in her breathing, in the way sleep almost feels impossible.

That realization hits me in my chest.

Because if that shit disturbs me, then I can't begin to imagine what it does to her.

I watch her breathe.

And I think about the ultrasound. About how she closed her eyes before the doctor even turned the screen.

I didn't look away.

I stared at that monitor until my jaw ached and my eyes burned.

No heartbeat. No movement.

I never planned to be a father. I told myself people like me shouldn't make more life. But the second she told me she was pregnant, everything shifted. I let myself imagine it. Her smile. Our child. A future that is not just survival. That idea was what kept me moving while I hunted for her. Every sleepless night. Every trail. Every moment I expected to die. It was for her. For both of them.

I look at her face again.

She has not cried. Not once.

That scares me more than anything else.

I'm unraveling, and she is somewhere unreachable, sealed behind her own eyes.

I hate that I can't reach her. I hate it enough that I have to leave the room before I damage something that can't be fixed.

The kitchen lights are low, casting dull reflections across stainless steel. I stand at the counter longer than necessary, staring at nothing, then force myself to move. I fill a pot, set it on the burner, and watch the flame catch.

I lean back against the counter while it warms, breathing through the pressure in my chest. It feels like barbed wire wrapped around my lungs, tightening every time I inhale. I wait it out. I let the moment pass without letting it turn into something worse.

The meds have leveled the noise. That is the difference.

No shadow in the corner of the room. No reflection shifting in the steel behind me. No voice leaning in close to remind me I'm too late.

Luke has been quiet since I started taking them again.

Not gone.

Just silent.

Footsteps approach. I don't need to turn around to know it is Beau.

He stops a few feet away, then leans against the opposite counter, his arms crossed.

"You good?" Beau asks.

"No."

"You want a drink?"

"No."

"A distraction?"

I keep my eyes on the pot.

Beau shifts beside me. "We can make some scumbags disappear tonight. The kind nobody asks questions about."

I exhale slowly. "Not right now."

"Doesn't have to be tied to this," he says. "Just... something to burn it off."

I shake my head once. "If I start, I won't stop. And I need to be clear when I go back in there with her."

"Fair." Beau studies me for a second, then nods. "We've got time. We'll plan. And then we'll execute."

I nod once.

"They're going to pay for what they did," Beau says. His voice drops. "All of them."

The water finally begins to simmer. I tear open a packet, stir slowly, keep my hands busy.

Footsteps echo again, lighter this time. Travis appears in the doorway. His shoulders sag like sleep has been optional for too long.

"Is she still not eating?" he asks quietly.

"No."

Travis nods once, like he expects that.

"Beau's ramen is actually really good," he says. "She might be able to keep that down."

"Yeah, that's what I'm making her."

"Good."

He steps closer. "You want me to sit with her for a bit?"

"No." My answer comes out too fast.

Travis stops, raises one hand. "Okay. Well I'm here if y'all need anything... Not that you would—I mean—."

"It's okay," I rub the back of my neck. "I know."

What I don't say, what I can't admit even in my own head, is everything tearing through me at once. I want to reverse time. I want her nowhere near that manor. I want our baby back. I want to hear her laugh again. I want my Brooke back, not the fragile version of herself she wears now like protection.

None of it can be undone.

And I have no idea how we are supposed to move forward from this without losing each other in the process.

I push off the counter and drag a hand down my face, forcing myself to breathe.

"I need to be in there with her."

Travis looks at me for a long second. There is sympathy there, but something firmer sits beneath it.

"Then go," he nods. "She needs you. I'll handle everything else."

He turns to leave, and he speaks again.

"I'm digging through every corner of the Collective database. I'll find Elliot. Everyone tied to this."

His voice stays steady, but the anger underneath it is unmistakable.

I nod once and go to stir the ramen.

Krueger is on my heels immediately, his nails clicking softly against the floor. Luna follows too, quieter, sticking close to my leg like she always does when something feels wrong. They both watch me with that same fixed attention they have not taken off her since we brought her back. They know. Animals always know.

It has been hard on them. They are used to her hands on their heads, her voice, the way she pulls them close without thinking. Now she barely reacts at all. No petting. No cuddling. No acknowledgment that they are there, waiting.

The ramen is warm. I ladle it into a bowl, careful not to overfill it.

I grab a spoon and stand there a second longer than necessary, grounding myself in the simple motions before I carry the bowl down the hall. Krueger follows. Luna breaks off ahead of us.

When I go back into the room, Luna is already at the foot of the bed, curled tight but alert, her eyes locked on Brooke. Krueger pads in behind me and stops near my hip, watching quietly.

She is sitting up slowly. Her eyes are swollen and unfocused, distant, but she is upright. Her fingers hover near the blanket like she doesn't know what to do with her own hands.

She looks at me, and something in her expression splits me open all over again.

I sit beside her and dip the spoon into the ramen, holding it near her mouth.

"Brooke," I say quietly. "You need to eat."

She doesn't look at me. Her gaze stays fixed on nothing, like something is still playing behind her eyes.

I slide an arm behind her shoulders and ease her upright. She doesn't resist, but she doesn't help either. Her weight settles against me.

I bring the spoon back to her lips. This time, she swallows.

"Good," I whisper.

She says nothing.

I feed her another spoonful, then another. Her body accepts it without protest, like the choice has been taken away from her. Her arms stay slack in her lap. One wrist is wrapped in clean white gauze. The other hand rests against her thigh. Her shoulder has been stitched and dressed, and she winces every time it shifts even slightly.

Krueger inches closer, his nose lifting as if he wants to check on her, but he stops himself. Luna doesn't move at all.

I reach to adjust the blanket.

She flinches.

The reaction hits hard enough that I have to look away for a moment. She used to lean into my touch without thinking. Now her body reacts first, already bracing.

"I'm tired," she sighs. Her voice sounds thin and worn down.

"I know, just a little more, then you can rest."

I give her the last spoonful.

Her face tightens immediately. She gags, a sharp, broken sound tearing out of her throat. I'm already moving.

"Hey," I grab the bucket by the door. "Hey, right here."

I make it back just in time. She folds forward and throws up into it, her body shaking violently. When there is nothing left, it still doesn't stop. She keeps dry heaving, her breath hitching, her hands trembling.

I hold the bucket steady and keep one arm around her until it passes.

When she finally leans back against me, she is shaking all over.

"Seth."

"I'm here," I murmur. "I'm right here."

"They made them eat people," she whispers.

My eyes widen as I hold her.

"These weren't bad people," she continues. "They were innocent. They were taken to the manor. They did awful things to them. They killed everyone. Even Miles."

Her breath catches.

"Miles was a good person," her voice breaks. "He helped me when they drowned me. He saved me. He gave me CPR. Now he's dead. I had to leave him. Just like Mila."

Her body finally folds inward, grief crashing through what little strength she has left.

I wrap my arms around her and hold her tightly. Krueger lies down beside the bed, pressing his body against the frame. Luna creeps closer and tucks herself near her hip, close enough to touch.

I stay there, speechless, knowing there is nothing I can say that will touch the weight of what she survived.

"You don't have to pretend you're okay."

"I'm not pretending," she replies, her voice quiet. "I just don't know how to feel anything yet."

"That's okay."

Her hand lifts, hesitant, barely reaching. The contact is light, uncertain, but it lands hard anyway.

I slowly shift closer and pull her into my arms, like one wrong move could send her shattering. She doesn't pull back this time. She folds into me instead, her face pressing into my chest. A sound slips out of her, so small it almost isn't there. Not quite a sob. More like grief catching on the way out and losing its nerve.

I hold her tighter.

I kiss the top of her head and let the words stay where they belong, pressed into her hair instead of spoken aloud.

I would've died to keep her from this. I would've taken every second of it if it meant she didn't have to. Because watching her like this, hollowed out and trying to relearn her own body, carrying something I can't fix, feels unbearable in a way violence never has.

It feels like failing all over again.

I couldn't save Natalie. I couldn't save Luke. I couldn't save our baby. Each loss stacks on top of the last, a record of every moment I arrive too late or not at all. Now I'm here, holding Brooke, trying to keep what is left of her intact, and it still feels like I'm failing.

I close my eyes, my jaw clenched, as her breath slows against my chest.

Pieces of both of us died while we were apart.

And I don't know if we will ever get them back.

Chapter 32
Brooke

I wake to a dark, silent bedroom.

The space beside me is empty.

For a moment I stay still, my hand slides across the sheets where Seth should be. My chest tightens before my thoughts fully catch up.

It has been two weeks since I escaped the manor.

Two weeks of broken sleep and waking up disoriented, my hands clenched and my pulse racing before I remember where I am. It always takes a few seconds to recognize the room, the house, the quiet around me. I remind myself that I'm not in that basement. I'm not in that Manor.

My body still hurts. Some of it comes from injuries that are healing. The rest comes from memory.

Seth only leaves the bed this late when the panic gets to him.

He tells me he is checking the locks, the cameras, and the perimeter around the property. He probably is doing those things. But that is not the real reason he gets up.

He gets up because lying beside me makes him feel useless.

He thinks he is failing me.

I sit up slowly, careful with my abdomen and careful with the way my ribs pull if I breathe too deep. The sheet slips off my shoulder. The air is cold enough to tighten my skin. I grab his shirt from the floor and pull it on. It smells like him. Cedar, smoke, and something that belongs only to Seth.

When I stand, the room tilts for a second. The dizziness comes and goes. It is worse when I have not eaten enough. It is worse when I pretend my body is not still catching up to what it lost.

I slip out of bed and move into the hallway without turning on the light. My bare feet barely make a sound against the floor.

A thin strip of light stretches across the floor from the training room.

The door is cracked just enough for me to see inside.

Seth stands in the center of the room with his back to the door, his fists slamming into the heavy bag over and over. The chain rattles with every strike. The bag swings hard and snaps back toward him, and he drives his knuckles into it again before it can settle.

He is not wearing wraps or gloves.

Blood streaks across the leather where his knuckles have split open. His hands look raw, swollen, smeared red from hitting the bag too many times.

Beau stands off to the side with his arms crossed, watching him.

"You planning to stop before you break something, or is that the goal?"

Seth exhales. It's not quite a laugh. "Haven't decided yet."

"I'm serious."

"I know," Seth says. "Say it."

Beau takes a beat, studying him.

"I came to make sure you don't screw this up."

Seth hits the bag again. The chain rattles loudly above them.

"Screw what up?"

"Her," Beau replies. "You're letting her die."

Seth's fist stops mid swing.

"She's alive," he says finally.

"That is the bare minimum," Beau shakes his head. "Don't act like survival is the same as living."

Seth rubs his hand over his mouth, his jaw tight.

"You think I don't know that? You think I don't wake up replaying every choice that led to this."

Beau's voice lowers.

"I know you do. And I also know this part."

Seth goes still.

"I understand this better than anyone," Beau continues. "I know what it's like to lose the woman you love."

Seth's breathing changes.

"This isn't about guilt," Beau adds. "This is about what you do next."

Seth slams his fist into the bag again.

"So what the fuck should I do?"

"Stop hovering, stop deciding her life for her because you feel guilty. Stop making her stay stuck because you can't stand to see her in pain. Pain already happened. It already owns a part of her. The question is what you're gonna do now."

"I'm trying to keep her safe," Seth answers quickly. "I'm doing everything."

Beau snorts. "You're doing everything except the one thing that matters."

"And what's that?"

"She survived torture," Beau says. "She doesn't need a padded room. Let her be angry. Let her be pissed about it. Let her say she wants blood. Let her want revenge."

Seth exhales hard.

"She's not a victim," Beau affirms. "Don't let her be a victim. Don't let her decide she's only something that happened to her. She's more than that."

Seth shifts his weight, staring at the bag.

"She can't even eat without throwing up half the time."

"So you sit with her," Beau tells him. "You help her eat. And then you stop building her entire world around what she can't do yet."

Seth hits the bag again, harder this time.

"I want her back."

"She isn't going to be who she was."

Seth doesn't answer.

"She's going to be who she becomes after this," Beau continues. "You can stand beside her while she figures that out, or you can keep mourning someone who doesn't exist anymore."

Seth drags a breath into his lungs.

"I fucking hate myself."

"I know," Beau replies. "But hating yourself doesn't help her."

Seth drives his fist into the bag again.

"I should've gotten there sooner," Seth's voice hardens. "I knew something was off. My gut kept telling me something was wrong and I ignored it."

The bag swings back and he hits it again.

"John. Mary. Amber. Nick. They were around her the whole time and I didn't see what they were."

The chain rattles violently above them.

"They were a threat," Seth hits the bag again. "I should've taken them out the second I felt something was wrong."

Beau watches him for a moment.

"It happened," he says. "Now you make sure what they did doesn't define her."

Seth's breathing fills the room.

"You're not helpless," Beau continues. "Stop acting like you are. You want to help her? Then stop hovering and start training. Start planning. Start putting the rage somewhere useful."

"Training her isn't going to heal her," Seth sighs.

"No, but it gives her a language besides silence."

Seth stands there staring at the bag.

"I don't want to push her."

"You're not pushing her," Beau says. "You are offering her a way out of the place she's stuck. She can say no. She can say yes. She gets to choose. That is the point."

Choose.

The word lands heavy in the room.

The door creaks softly when I push it open.

Both of them turn.

For a second Seth just stares at me. His eyes flick over my face, down my bare legs, to the oversized shirt hanging off one shoulder.

"Brooke," he says quietly. "I didn't mean to wake you."

"You didn't."

Beau glances between us. His eyes linger on Seth for a moment.

"I'll leave you two to it."

He claps Seth once on the shoulder as he passes, then walks out of the room without another word. The door shuts behind him.

Now it is just us.

Seth takes a slow step toward me. His hands stay at his sides, uncertain, and that hesitation cuts deeper than anything I overheard.

"Are you okay?"

The word twists inside my chest.

Okay.

Like it is somewhere I can walk back to if I just try hard enough.

I open my mouth to give the answer I have been giving for days. The one that keeps him calm. The one that lets him believe I am healing.

It never comes out.

"I heard what he said," I tell him.

Pain flickers through his eyes. "He shouldn't have said that."

"He wasn't wrong."

The words fall between us before I can soften them.

Seth flinches anyway. He drags a hand through his hair, his fingers catching like he wants to rip something out.

"I'm trying," he sighs. "I don't know how to do this right."

I see how exhausted he is. The shadows under his eyes. The tension in his shoulders that never leaves anymore. He thinks he has to hold everything together for both of us.

"I don't want you to want the old me back."

His eyes snap to mine.

"I didn't mean it like that," he says quickly. "I meant I want you to feel like yourself again."

"I'm not."

My voice breaks.

Seth steps closer and this time his hands come up, hovering near my arms like he is asking permission without saying it.

"Tell me who you are," he murmurs.

My chest tightens.

"I don't know," I whisper.

The tears start before I can stop them.

They slide down my face slowly at first and then faster, my breathing falling apart as everything I have been holding back finally cracks open.

"I don't understand anything anymore," I sob, my voice shaking. "I feel broken all the time. Physically. Mentally. Emotionally. I feel like they ripped something out of me and left everything else behind."

Seth's face crumples, but he doesn't interrupt me.

"I see them every time I close my eyes," I continue, wiping uselessly at my face. "I see the basement. I see that room. I hear them talking. I hear them laughing."

My chest heaves.

"They live in my head now," I choke out. "They took a piece of my life that I will never get back."

My voice cracks completely.

"They took the one chance I might've had to..." I swallow hard, the words sticking in my throat. "...have a family with you."

The words fall apart halfway through the sentence.

Seth's jaw locks.

Now the sobs come harder.

"They took everything from me," I whisper.

Seth's arms wrap around me before I even realize I'm falling forward. He pulls me against his chest, holding me so tight it almost hurts.

"I'm sorry," he murmurs into my hair, his voice rough. "I'm so fucking sorry."

I clutch the front of his shirt, my hands shaking.

"I don't know how to fix this," I tell him through tears. "I don't know how I'm ever supposed to be okay again."

"You don't have to be okay."

His hand presses against the back of my head, holding me there.

"You don't have to be anything right now."

I pull back just enough to look at him, tears still running down my face.

"Do you think I'm letting myself be a victim?"

His expression tightens.

"No," he responds quickly. "I think you're hurt."

I hold his gaze.

"And what if I'm both?"

His mouth opens, then closes again.

He refuses to lie to me.

"I think they tried to turn you into a victim," he says finally. "And I think I've been trying to keep you safe from that."

He looks into my eyes.

"I'd do anything for you," he adds, his voice cracking at the end.

"I know," I whisper. "But you can't do this part for me."

His eyes shine.

"Tell me what you want, and I'll do it."

The room goes still.

My heart pounds against my ribs.

I feel the weight of everything I lost. Everything they took. The future that disappeared in that room. The version of my life that will never exist now.

And then I hear Beau's voice in my head.

Choose.

I inhale slowly.

"I want revenge, Seth."

Seth's throat moves.

"Brooke—"

"I don't want a speech," I cut in. "I don't want to be told I'm strong. I don't want to be told I'm safe."

I look up at him.

"I want to kill them."

Seth's breathing changes. He doesn't look shocked.

He looks relieved.

"Okay," he whispers.

That one word hits harder than any comfort he has tried to give me.

"I don't want to be the final girl anymore," I continue. "I don't want to be hunted. I want to be like you."

My voice steadies.

"I want to be the hunter."

Seth nods.

"Okay."

My eyes burn again.

Seth finally takes my hands in his.

"Tomorrow," his gaze stays on me. "We start tomorrow if you want."

"I do."

He leans his forehead against mine.

"I'm not okay," I tell him quietly. "I'm not healed. I don't know if I ever will be."

"I'm not asking you to be."

"Good," I whisper. "Because I don't have that in me."

He holds my gaze like he is memorizing every piece of me.

"I want them dead, Seth. All of them."

Seth nods and pulls me back into his arms.

I name them silently in my head.

Kristie.

Knox.

Sophie.

Elliot.

Grant.

John.

They hunted me.

Now I will hunt them.

And I will kill every last one of them.

PART TWO

Chapter 33
Brooke

By the time I pick up the knife, training has already become routine.

For weeks, I train for hours every day. I run left handed drills until my shoulder burns. I work on balance and footwork, repeating the movements until my body stops hesitating and starts reacting.

My right wrist stays locked in the brace, aching with every movement, a constant reminder of what I can't use yet.

Then I started gun training.

The brace on my right wrist stays strapped tight while the bones slowly knit back together. Seth doesn't want me touching a weapon with that hand yet, and Beau agrees.

So everything comes from my left.

The indoor range smells like oil and gunpowder. The room has concrete walls and hanging targets, with no windows and no distractions.

Beau doesn't stand in front of me like an instructor. He moves along the perimeter instead, his eyes fixed on my form. He watches for any hesitation, correcting me the moment my body falters.

"Again," he orders.

I raise the gun. My left hand grips firm. My right hand comes in just enough to support, careful not to put pressure through the brace.

"Too open," he adds. "You're presenting your whole torso like you want to get shot."

I adjust, turning slightly, angling my body so less of me faces the target.

"Better." His gaze tracks my stance. "You're not on a range. You're in a hallway. Or a stairwell. Or a parking garage. Nobody gives you space to square up."

I fire.

The recoil slams harder without my dominant hand. It snaps through my left wrist, travels up my forearm, and settles deep in my shoulder. My right hand absorbs what it can, but the brace still takes a dull, unwelcome jolt.

The round lands near the center.

Beau steps in and presses two fingers against my elbow, nudging it inward.

"Line your bones up," he instructs. "If your frame's crooked, the bullet will be too. Don't fight physics. Use it."

I reset and fire again closer.

He circles behind me.

"You're still thinking about it. You hesitate half a second before the break."

"I'm not hesitating."

"You are. You're asking your body if it's ready. That's how you lose."

He steps into my peripheral vision and points toward the far wall.

"Move."

I pivot left and fire.

"Your movement is loud," he adds.

He walks up beside me and demonstrates, shifting his weight without lifting his boots fully, gliding instead of stepping.

"You don't stomp. You slide. Control the sound."

I mirror him. Shift. Pivot. Fire.

The round strikes center mass.

"Good. Again. Keep your shoulders down."

My shoulder burns, the tremor in my left arm getting worse every shot. I tighten my grip anyway.

Beau steps close enough that I can feel him behind me.

"You're not here to win a gunfight. You're here to make sure one never actually happens."

He moves away again, his voice carrying in the room.

"You don't trade shots. You don't clear rooms. You appear where they aren't looking, and you leave before they understand what happened."

I shift left, pivot, fire.

"Again."

I move before he finishes the word.

"Faster."

I fire mid step, recoil knocking my arm slightly off line. I correct and fire again.

"Control your breathing," Beau says. "The shot happens at the bottom of the exhale. Always."

I force myself to slow it down. In. Out. Break.

The next round lands dead center.

Across the room, Seth leans against the wall, arms crossed, silent and watching. His eyes track every inch of me. When my shoulder flinches, his jaw tightens. When I correct it, he relaxes a fraction.

Beau tosses me a fresh magazine.

"Reload while you move."

I eject the empty mag and step backward at the same time, slamming the new one home without looking down.

"Eyes stay up," Beau snaps. "You look at your hands, you die."

I keep my gaze on the target and rack the slide by feel.

I fire.

The impact jolts through my arm. My shoulder screams. My grip starts to shake visibly now.

My arm trembles harder, but my stance stays set.

Beau stops pacing and faces me fully.

I shift, pivot, fire.

He nods once.

"Better."

When I finally lower the gun, Seth pushes off the wall.

"My turn."

Beau nods and backs off without a word. That is their routine, switching off like two halves of the same machine.

As he passes me, he pauses long enough to murmur, "Disappear before you pull the trigger. If they see you coming, you've already failed."

I nod.

Seth tosses a practice blade at my feet. "Pick it up."

I do, with my left hand. The grip still feels wrong, but less wrong than it used to.

He circles me once, then stops behind me. "You don't win knife fights with strength. You win by staying on your feet."

I tighten my grip.

He moves fast. His arm hooks around my waist, knife pressing lightly to my ribs.

"Dead," he says.

I elbow him, spin, and try to slash. He dodges and catches my wrist mid swing. His grip is firm but not punishing.

"Don't hold back," I snap, breathing hard.

"I'm not," he says. "But I'm not breaking your other wrist just so you can feel tough."

"I want to feel ready."

His gaze locks onto mine. Calculating, like he is weighing whether I can take what I am asking for.

"You sure?"

"Stop asking," I say. "Make me fight for it."

He lunges.

I dodge this time, barely. I get a slice across his forearm. He grabs my shoulder, twists me, pins me against the padded wall.

"Knives are personal," he mutters near my ear. "You want to survive a close fight? You've got to be meaner than the fuck trying to kill you."

"I am," I mutter through gritted teeth.

"Then prove it."

I shove backward, dropping my weight, catching his knee just enough to throw off his stance. I turn fast, blade up, my chest heaving.

His eyes flare for a second.

"Good," he says.

I stand there, knife in hand, my heart pounding.

"Again."

Sweat rolls down my temple as I slam my forearm against Seth's wrist, twisting the knife from his grip.

He steps back before I can finish the motion.

"Again," I say, my breath ragged. The right side of my body feels half dead, but I need this.

"You're still favoring your right," Seth points out. "Stop doing that. It'll get you killed."

I lunge again. This time he lets me get the blade, but as soon as I have it, he knocks me flat with a shoulder to the chest.

"Fuck," I hiss, staring up at the ceiling.

Seth crouches beside me. "You're moving better," he murmurs.

I push myself up. "Again."

I lunge. He blocks, disarms me, and sweeps my legs. I hit the mat hard.

Seth helps me up. His fingers ghost down my arm, checking the bruises, the joint stiffness. When he gets to my ribs, I flinch and he freezes.

"I hate this," I whisper, my breath hitching. "I hate how weak I feel."

Seth's arms wrap around me before I can finish. He holds me there while I shake, biting down hard enough on my lip to keep from crying.

"You're not weak," he says into my hair. "You're the strongest woman I know."

"I don't want to just be strong," I whisper. "I want to be ready. I want to make them suffer."

"You will. We'll make sure of it."

The door opens behind us.

Travis steps in quietly, his eyes going straight to me instead of the room. He pauses then crosses the training space and drops into a chair against the wall.

"You good?" he asks.

I let out a short laugh that scrapes on the way out. "No."

He nods once. "Fair."

Seth pushes off the wall near the mats. "We'll take a break."

Then he heads for the door without another word, giving us space.

I don't argue. My body feels heavy, like it has finally decided to feel everything at once.

Seth nods and steps outside.

"Look at you, GI Jane," Travis leans forward, his forearms on his knees. "These fuckers have no idea what's coming."

"Yeah." My throat tightens. "I'm just not sure it fixes anything. Revenge doesn't bring people back. It doesn't undo what happened."

He doesn't interrupt.

"I probably wouldn't have been a great mom anyway," I sigh. "I'm too fucked up, this isn't something you bring a kid into."

"Don't say that," Travis says immediately. "You would've been a great mom, Brooke."

I shake my head.

"No," he adds. "You really would have. Just because you've been through hell doesn't mean you'd repeat it. If anything, it makes you better at protecting the people you love."

I stare at the floor.

"Good things happen to bad people all the time," I whisper. "And good people get screwed for no reason."

He nods slowly. "Yeah. I had the same thoughts after I lost Mila."

That cracks something open in my chest.

My eyes burn. I look away fast and wipe at my face before anything can spill.

"I'm so fucking mad, Travis. Everything in my life feels fake now. My dad was part of it. That whole psycho murder cult. He killed other killers, apparently, but he was still involved. And my aunt and uncle knew. They lied to me my whole life."

My voice drops. "I don't even know who I am anymore."

He doesn't rush to fix it.

I swallow and shift. "How are you holding up with all this?"

He leans back in the chair, dragging a hand down his face.

"Surprisingly well, considering the circumstances," he says. "I've gotten used to being an accomplice and possible federal fugitive."

I huff.

"As long as me and Seth end up in the same cell, hopefully I won't be someone's bitch," he adds dryly.

"That's not how prison works," I mutter.

"Let me cope."

A faint smile tugs at my mouth despite everything.

"What about your parents?" I ask.

He shrugs. "I called them from a burner. Told them I'm traveling abroad and I'll probably be out there for a couple years."

"And?"

"And of course they were busy," he says flatly. "So they didn't ask many questions."

I nod once.

"How's Naomi? Have you talked to her?"

"Not really." His jaw tightens slightly. "We both think it's not safe. Especially with these Collective assholes. They're tying up loose ends with anyone who survived that hotel. That bartender, Dane, was found dead in his apartment."

He rubs the back of his neck.

"I don't want to put her in danger just to hear her voice."

"You could call from a burner," I suggest.

"Yeah, I might."

The door opens again.

Seth steps in, letting Luna and Krueger enter first.

Luna pads across the mats and curls in my lap. Krueger follows and presses against Travis instead, lowering himself heavily at his side.

Travis rests his hand on Krueger's head.

The dog leans into it immediately.

I watch them.

"You two have come a long way," I smile. "I remember when you were convinced he was going to maul you."

Travis scratches behind Krueger's ear, shaking his head.

"Yeah," he laughs. "I guess the hellhound's grown on me."

Krueger huffs and pushes harder into his hand.

"I know he definitely missed you, though," Travis adds quietly, not looking at me when he says it.

My chest tightens.

Seth stays near the doorway for a beat, watching me, then shifts his focus.

"Travis," he says. "Take the pets and give us the room."

Travis nods, pushing to his feet. He gives Krueger a scratch before guiding both animals towards the door.

"I'll let you know if I find anything else."

Luna pauses at the doorway and looks back at me. Krueger pauses longer, then follows when Travis calls him again.

The door closes behind them.

Seth steps forward.

His eyes move over me, taking in the way I'm standing, the tension in my shoulders, the way my left hand flexes around nothing.

"You ready to hit harder?" he asks.

I exhale slowly. "Yes."

"You know why I'm good at this," he steps closer. "It's not talent. It's not training. My body's been in fight mode since I was a kid."

He doesn't look away.

"I didn't get to run. I didn't get to freeze. It was hit or get hit. Win or get chained to a wall. That switch flipped and it never flipped back."

He taps two fingers lightly against my sternum.

"You," he adds, "your body went the other direction."

I stiffen.

"Since you were twelve," he continues. "You learned how to leave before things got bad. You got good at reading rooms, hiding, running, figuring out who to trust."

I swallow.

"And with this," he says plainly. "You got good at escaping, physically, mentally. You survived by staying one step away from impact."

He steps back and picks up the training knife from the mat. He tosses it to me without warning.

I catch it with my left hand.

"But you don't get to run anymore," he tilts his head. "They're not gonna stop hunting you."

The word lands heavier than if he had said us.

"They're not going to get bored. You can't outrun people like that. You have to kill them."

He moves in without ceremony, his hand striking toward my shoulder.

I block late.

He grabs my wrist, twists slightly, and forces me to adjust my footing.

"You stepped back before I even touched you." His grip tightens for a second. "That's flight."

He releases me.

"Again."

He comes at me faster. A straight jab toward my ribs.

I shift back automatically.

He stops immediately.

"See that?" His eyes drift to my feet. "You give up space before you have to. You retreat before you're hit."

He steps in again.

"This time you don't move unless you need to."

He lunges.

I hold my ground and knock his arm aside. My injured wrist throbs inside the brace, but I stay planted.

He nods once.

"Better."

He circles me slowly.

"You don't need to be like me." His voice lowers. "You don't need to enjoy it. You don't need to crave it."

His eyes darken slightly.

"But you need to switch."

He strikes low toward my hip.

I pivot and drive the knife toward his side.

He catches my forearm and redirects it, letting the blade pass harmlessly by.

"Let the anger guide you." He keeps hold of my arm. "Use it. It sharpens you."

He shoves me back hard enough that I have to step to keep my balance.

"But don't let it blind you. Blind anger swings wide. It chases. It overcommits."

He moves again, quick, forcing me to react.

I don't step back this time.

I step in.

I close the distance and press the knife toward his throat. He grabs my wrist mid motion and stops it inches from his skin.

We stand there, breathing hard.

"That," he says quietly, "is fight."

He releases me.

"Your body's going to want to run." He holds my gaze. "Override it."

He walks past me and turns.

"You don't get to freeze. You don't get to wait. You see the threat, you end it."

I adjust my grip on the knife.

He faces me again.

"They're coming for you. So next time, you don't back up."

He steps forward once more.

"You make them fucking regret it."

Chapter 34
Seth

She doesn't flinch when she lands the punch.

A few weeks ago, her wrist still needed bracing. Today, she cracks the training pad with enough force to make my elbow jolt behind it.

"Good," I say. "Now do it again."

Brooke's breathing is calm, sweat glistening at her collarbone. Her stance is tighter, her weight more balanced. I can tell she still favors her right side. She still guards that shoulder, but she has stopped treating herself like glass.

She hits the pad again, harder.

Fury drives every movement.

Beau whistles from the corner, where he is reassembling her Glock. "She's gonna break someone's jaw with that left hook. Not bad for a righty."

"Damn right," Brooke mutters.

I catch her eyes. "Reset your stance. Knife next."

She grabs the practice blade and circles me. Her steps are quick, her eyes locked on mine. I can see the calculation behind her movements now. It is not just fight or flight or panic.

She is starting to think like a killer.

Her lunge is quick and controlled. I deflect, step in close, and whisper, "Too high. Try again."

She doesn't get flustered. She doesn't freeze. She ducks out and comes back lower.

This time, she nicks my ribs. Barely, but it is enough.

"Fuck yeah," Beau says under his breath.

I give her a nod. "That would've cut deep."

Brooke steps back, breathing hard.

This isn't for praise.

This is for survival.

Later, we sit in the training room, just the two of us.

Travis and Beau are posted at the long table in the adjacent space, files spread and reshuffled as they chase every remaining thread tied to the manor and to Elliot. The sounds stay on the other side of the wall.

Here, it's quiet.

I press a cold water bottle against Brooke's wrist and watch the muscles in her forearm tense, then slowly loosen. She barely reacts, just a small tightening around her eyes before she forces it down.

"You overdid it again."

She shakes her head. "I'm good."

"You're healing, not invincible."

"I know I'm not invincible," she replies. "I want to be ready."

I study her face. The darkness in her eyes isn't fading. It is settling in, rooting itself, becoming part of her instead of something she fights.

"I get it," I say. "But if you tear anything, I'll tie you to the fucking bed until you learn patience."

Her eyes flick up to mine. "Don't threaten me with a good time."

A corner of my mouth lifts despite myself.

She just looks at me, sweat darkened hair clinging to her cheek, her breathing still elevated, that storm sitting right behind her eyes. I hold out my hand.

"Get up."

She takes it.

I don't let go right away.

Her palm is warm, already callused from weeks of training, stronger than it used to be.

We move into position again, closer this time. Her body is warm, tight with muscle and adrenaline. She has come so far in two weeks. She hesitates less, she is more in control. Her wrist is still healing, but the way she moves feels like contained violence waiting to break loose.

"Romance" plays low through the speakers, the beat slow and heavy, almost ritualistic.

"Try to disarm me."

She lunges fast. I grab her wrist and twist, stepping into her space. Our chests collide. Her knee goes for my ribs, and I catch it midair, pinning her leg between mine.

"You let him get this close," I say, my voice rough, "he's not here to talk. He's here to take something."

She stares up at me, breathless. "I'm not letting anyone take shit."

I don't let go.

She doesn't back down.

She shoves me. I grab her hips and spin her, pressing her back into the padded wall. My body cages hers. Her arms come up between us, gripping my shirt. Our mouths are too close.

"This isn't training anymore," she whispers.

"No," I murmur. "It's not."

My hands are on her before my mind catches up. My fingers slip beneath the hem of her tank top. Her skin feels warm and smooth as my palms follow the curve of her waist. Her breath hitches.

That tells me everything.

I should stop. I should remember every boundary I set and every promise I made about patience. I told myself she deserved time.

But desire has been tearing through me for weeks.

My hands keep moving.

They slide higher across her stomach while her breathing shifts under my touch. Goosebumps rise along her skin beneath my fingers. She doesn't stop me. She doesn't say anything.

Her silence says enough.

Her chest brushes mine. A slow exhale spills against my jaw, and that last piece of restraint snaps.

I grab her and kiss her hard.

The second her mouth meets mine, the urge surges to the surface. My hand slides into her hair, gripping tight and pulling her closer.

She kisses me back immediately.

Her mouth tastes like mint. Heat shoots straight through me as her lips open against mine. When I bite her bottom lip, she gasps softly, the sound cutting straight through my chest.

Her nails dig into my shoulders.

I haven't touched her like this since the night before she was taken. I haven't been inside her in weeks.

Every day since has felt like punishment.

Watching her train nearly breaks me.

Her tank rides up when she moves. The strength in her legs. The focus in her eyes. I stand there pretending none of it affects me while all I can think about is how she sounds when I stretch her open.

Fucking torture.

My hand drops to her ass, gripping a full fist of soft flesh and pulling her into me until there is no space left between us. Her hips press against mine, and she feels exactly how hard I am through the fabric, the thick line of my cock straining for release.

She doesn't pull away. She rolls her hips instead, dragging friction right where I am already wound tight and aching. She knows exactly what she is doing, and she does it anyway.

She isn't teasing. She's demanding.

Her thigh slides between my legs, pressing up, grinding against me with maddening pressure. The contact sends heat shooting straight through my spine. My entire body locks up, every nerve firing at once.

I groan into her mouth, the sound rough and uncontrolled, my grip tightening on her.

"You remember how I fuck you?" I growl into her ear, my mouth so close my words brush her skin. "Because I haven't stopped thinking about it."

She moans softly, the sound vibrating straight through my chest. Her arm hooks around my neck and pulls me closer.

My hand slides under the waistband of her shorts, just far enough to cup the heat at the top of her ass. I drag my fingers down, gripping her hard, exploring like I've been starving and finally found something to take. I barely hold myself back from tearing the rest of her clothes off right there.

"I have been dreaming about this," I mutter, my mouth brushing her cheek. "Every night."

She tilts her head back, her throat exposed, her lips parted. "Then don't stop."

I shove her bra up in one rough motion, baring the full weight and curve of her breasts, and the sight nearly takes me out. I drop my mouth to her collarbone and bite down, giving her a mark she will feel tomorrow. Her gasp breaks against my ear, and she arches into me like she wants more. Her nipples drag against my chest through my shirt, tight and sensitive, and her fingers claw at my back like she is fighting to hold on.

My control shatters.

If we keep going, I know exactly what I'll do to her. I'll slam her back against the padded wall and spread her open with my hands, lifting her by her ass and grinding her down onto my cock until her voice breaks. I'll push inside her with one long, hard stroke and feel her clench around me, tight and wet from how badly she wants this. I'll slide my hand over her mouth to muffle the sounds she makes while I thrust into her again and again, deep enough to make her forget everything except the way I fill her.

The image hits with brutal force, and my cock throbs so hard against her it feels painful. Every part of me wants her right then and there.

I am seconds away from fucking her exactly like that.

I want it.

No, I fucking need it.

My hands fumble at her waistband, dragging it down just far enough to get where I need. She is already soaked, already moving against me with raw urgency, like her body decided long before either of us admitted we were done waiting. The friction hits me hard, my teeth clenched, my hips pushing forward before I can stop myself.

She reaches between us with trembling fingers and pulls at the drawstring of my sweatpants. The second her hand slips inside, her warm skin closing around my cock, my breath leaves in one violent rush. I brace my forearm against the wall because my knees almost give out.

She wraps her hand around me, stroking my full length with pressure that makes my vision haze at the edges. Her thumb brushes over the head, catching the pre-cum there, spreading it in a smooth glide that has my hips jerking into her hold. I bite back a groan and fail, the sound rough against her throat.

She presses a wicked smile to my jaw and tightens her grip, dragging her fist down to the base, then up again in a way that sends heat tearing up my spine.

She keeps stroking me with agonizing slowness. She wants to see exactly how close she can push me before I snap.

I can't get a full breath. Every nerve I have locks onto the feel of her hand, slick with sweat, her fingers wrapped tightly around the thickest part of my cock. Another involuntary thrust escapes me before I force myself still, biting the inside of my cheek hard enough to taste blood.

"Fuck," I mutter, dragging my mouth along her jaw and up to her temple.

Her gasp tears free when my hand slides between her thighs. I push past the waistband of her shorts, past the soaked cling of her panties, and run two fingers along her warm, dripping slit. She is drenched. Her body opens for me instantly, her hips rolling into my palm like she has been waiting for this exact touch since the moment we walked in here.

"Are you ready for me?" I ask against her neck, sliding my fingers through her wetness, letting her feel just how easily she comes apart for me.

Her only answer is a broken moan, her voice shaking as I push one finger deep inside her. Her walls clamp around me, tight and hot, pulling me in. My cock twitches hard in her grip at the feeling, at the knowledge of how tight she will be when I drive into her.

I grab her waist and slam her back against the wall, grinding against her thigh while my finger fucks into her. I slide a second finger inside without warning, curling them just right, and she cries out, her hand spasming around my cock as her body jerks forward.

She barely has time to take a breath before I spin her around. I yank her shorts and panties down to her thighs, leaving her exposed and braced against the wall, her palms flat, her legs spread, her ass arched in a way that makes my cock kick.

I step in behind her, ready to take her—

"Yo," Beau's voice cuts in, shattering the moment. "Travis found something."

I freeze.

Brooke freezes.

I turn my head slowly, like if I don't see him, he doesn't exist.

Beau stands in the doorway, his arms crossed, with no shame. "Sorry to interrupt the fight to fuck pipeline, but it sounded important."

My jaw clenches so hard it aches.

I want to kill him.

"I swear to God," I mutter, "if you ever walk in on us again, I'll shoot you."

Brooke lets out a shaky laugh, covering her face with her hand.

Beau shrugs. "I'll add it to my list of near death experiences." He turns and walks off, still talking. "Don't take too long. Travis said the trail's fresh. Might be our only shot at pinning Knox down."

I look at Brooke and brush her cheek with the back of my hand.

"Later," I whisper.

Her eyes burn into mine. "Promise?"

I kiss her again, hard and fast. A promise. A warning. A fucking prayer.

Then I force myself to breathe.

I adjust myself back into my sweats, my jaw tight, blood still surging through every inch of me. Brooke's fingers tremble as I help slide her shorts back up. I tug her shirt down, covering the bite mark I just left on her.

Her eyes are still dark with want.

We could have finished what we started. My body is screaming for it. But timing is everything, and right now, we have some soon to be dead motherfuckers to hunt.

Chapter 35
Seth

Travis tracked Knox the same way he tracks everything else, by following the smallest digital trail until it led exactly where he needed it to.

A burner phone tied to a shell company.

The shell company tied to a trust.

The trust tied to old Portland money that likes to pretend it has nothing to do with what happened in that manor.

Offshore accounts bleed into family foundations. Property records surface under alternate spellings. A name that had been scrubbed from one system shows up buried in another.

Knox thinks it is gone.

Thinks the Manor is noise that will fade if he waits long enough.

He's wrong.

It leads to a house outside Portland and a routine he assumes no one is watching.

That is all we need.

We don't rush it.

Tonight, I train Brooke to watch people closely, to pick apart their habits, their blind spots, so she knows exactly when to strike.

We sit in the car and watch. Rain streaks the windshield in uneven sheets, warping the neon from the club sign into bleeding red and blue smears. The wipers drag back and forth in slow rhythm, never fully clearing the view.

Brooke sits in the passenger seat, hood up, seat reclined just enough to keep her face in shadow. Her eyes never leave the entrance.

She reaches into the center console and pulls out the bag of peach rings.

She opens them without looking away from the door. The plastic crinkles softly in the dark. She tosses one in her mouth and hands me one. We share the bag between us, the sour dust catching on our tongues while we watch a man who thinks he is untouchable step into the open like he owns the night.

Two men trail behind him, laughing at something he has said like he rehearsed it. He wears a dark coat open at the front, expensive and useless in the rain, shirt half unbuttoned like he wants to be looked at.

Brooke goes still beside me.

"That's him," she murmurs.

Knox pauses under the awning long enough to let someone light his cigarette.

"Look at him," I tell her quietly.

Brooke's eyes track every inch.

"See how he stands."

Knox exhales smoke and turns his back to the street completely. The club door behind him. Open sidewalk in front. No check. No sweep. No glance in the glass of the parked cars.

"He doesn't rush," I point out. "He doesn't look. He doesn't think he has to."

Brooke's hands curl slowly against her thighs.

"He never hunted anyone," I continue. "He had people brought to him. Delivered. Tied up. Begging. He thinks violence is something that happens on a stage."

Knox laughs again, too loud, and throws his head back.

"He likes spectacle," I mutter. "Noise. Screaming. Cameras. Witnesses."

A town car rolls up to the curb.

Knox doesn't check the driver. Doesn't scan the reflection in the window. Doesn't even glance at the street before stepping down off the curb.

"He thinks if something's coming for him, it'll look obvious," I explain. "Masked. Armed. Loud. He doesn't think it'll look like this."

Brooke doesn't move.

"He doesn't believe in quiet," I add. "He believes in performance."

Knox takes one last drag of his cigarette and flicks it into the street without looking. Open back exposed. Head tilted toward his phone.

"Watch his hands."

She does.

"He texts while he walks. Eyes drop. Chin dips. His whole body softens. That's when he's least aware."

Knox's thumb moves over his screen as he steps toward the car. The driver gets out to open the door. Knox doesn't acknowledge him. Just keeps typing.

"He expects protection," I tell her. "He expects people between him and anything ugly. That's what money buys."

The door opens.

Knox ducks inside without ever turning his head.

"That's ego," I say. "Not confidence."

The door shuts.

The car pulls into traffic.

Brooke's breathing shifts.

"You don't go for him when he's drunk and loud," I warn. "You don't go for him when he's surrounded by an audience."

I turn my head just enough to look at her.

"You take him when he thinks the show's over."

Her jaw tightens.

"Between door and car," I continue. "Between hallway and room. Between party and bed. Those seconds when he thinks he's safe."

The taillights disappear down the block.

Brooke stays quiet, absorbing it.

I lean back into my seat.

"Tonight, you don't touch him," I tell her. "You learn him."

"I want him scared."

I nod once.

"Oh he will be."

The second night, we didn't stay in the car.

We go inside.

The lounge feels exclusive and predatory at the same time. Black velvet booths curve along the walls, pulling people into the shadows. Gold trim catches the low light and throws it back in muted flashes. The air hangs thick with perfume, sweat, and expensive liquor.

"Kill4Me" plays through the speakers. Bass rolls through the floor in slow, heavy pulses. It feels like a second heartbeat under my boots.

We slip in through a side entrance Beau has already compromised.

Nobody notices us.

They never do when they're staring at themselves in mirrored walls and camera phones.

Knox is in VIP, surrounded by bottle service with three bottles already half gone. A clean white line stretches across the glass table in front of him. Two women drape over his body, one straddling his thigh while the other leans into his ear, laughing like she's being paid to.

His head tips back when he laughs.

Brooke goes rigid beside me.

I step in behind her, close enough that my chest brushes her back.

"He doesn't recognize you," I murmur near her ear. "But he'll remember what he did to you."

Her jaw tightens. I feel the tension travel through her shoulder.

We stay in the shadows near a structural column just outside the spill of VIP light.

We don't sit, order drinks, or speak to anyone.

Knox sprawls across the couch with one arm thrown over the backrest as if the entire club belongs to him. The girl on his lap drags her fingers through his hair while he bends forward and takes a line straight off the glass table. He doesn't bother wiping his nose. He doesn't even glance around the room.

He has no reason to.

I feel Brooke tense.

"That's your window," I say quietly.

She doesn't answer.

"Drugs make him sloppy," I continue. "Alcohol makes him loud. Both make him predictable."

Knox's head snaps up when someone approaches the table. For half a second, his eyes sweep toward the entrance of the VIP section.

Brooke is already watching him. Every movement. Every habit.

I shift closer behind her.

"Tell me what you see."

"He never looks behind him."

Good.

"He checks the doors," she adds, her eyes fixed on him, "but not the corners."

Better.

"He keeps his back to the wall," she says. "But only when he's sober."

I nod.

"That's instinct fighting ego. Ego usually wins."

Knox grabs his phone from the table. The girl slides off his lap. He pushes himself up from the couch and heads toward the restroom. He starts typing as he walks.

He never looks over his shoulder. He never feels us in the room.

Brooke's fingers tighten around my forearm.

"He doesn't think anyone followed him out of that manor," she whispers.

"No," I reply. "He thinks you're dead."

Her breathing sharpens. The softness leaves her eyes.

"And what do we do with men who believe that?" I ask quietly.

"We let them feel safe."

I lean closer, my mouth brushing her temple.

"Exactly," I murmur. "Because the moment a man feels safe... is the moment he dies."

Chapter 36

The drive home blurs together in a haze of bass, cocaine, and rain-slicked streetlights.

Knox leans back in the rear seat of the town car, collar open, head tipped against the leather. His jaw aches faintly from grinding. The inside of his nose still burns from the last line he has taken off the VIP table.

He thinks it's worth it.

The driver keeps his eyes forward as the estate gates slide open.

Gravel crunches under the tires while the car curves up the long drive. The mansion rises out of the dark beyond the hedges, tall windows glowing warm against the wet night.

Safe.

That word settles comfortably in Knox's chest.

The car stops beneath the covered entrance.

One of the guards steps forward and opens the door. Rain drips from the brim of the man's cap.

"Evening, sir."

Knox barely looks at him.

"Yeah."

He steps out, swaying slightly as his shoes hit the stone. The world tilts pleasantly. His heart still races from the cocaine, every nerve buzzing.

Frank, the night supervisor, closes the car door behind him while another guard moves aside to let Knox pass through the front entrance.

The doors shut with a soft click.

Inside, the mansion is quiet. Too quiet for this hour, maybe, but Knox barely registers it.

He rolls his shoulders loose and climbs the staircase two steps at a time.

By the time he reaches his bedroom, the cocaine high has begun to twist into heat under his skin.

He peels off his jacket and tosses it across a chair. His shirt follows.

The bathroom lights snap on automatically when he steps inside.

He turns on the shower. Steam is already beginning to fog the mirrors as hot water pounds down from the rainfall head.

Knox steps under it and groans softly.

The water beats against the back of his neck, washing away the smell of perfume and sweat from the club.

His mind drifts as the heat soaks into his muscles. He thinks about the blonde from the VIP section, the one with the short dress and the sexy smile who slipped her number into his hand before he left. She said she would meet him tomorrow night after his meeting. Knox imagines her on her knees already, mouth open, hair pulled back while he grips it. The thought makes him smirk under the spray.

His thoughts shift to the meeting scheduled for the next afternoon with Elliot. Elliot wants to discuss the fallout from the manor.

The water streams down his chest as another memory surfaces.

Asher.

Asher had always been the loudest one in the room. The first to grab a bottle, the first to cut lines across the table, the first to laugh when someone started screaming.

They used to party for days without stopping.

Now Asher is dead.

Knox frowns slightly as the thought lingers.

He still doesn't know who killed him.

Part of him wonders if it had been Seth.

Knox had seen the reports afterward. The bodies in the manor. The chaos that followed.

Nobody has ever managed to locate that place from the outside. The estate had been scrubbed from every record and buried behind shell properties and restricted access roads. Even most members of the Collective have never been there in person.

Everything burned afterward.

The physician is dead. The guards are dead. No survivors have surfaced. Knox has assumed the victims died in the fire.

That is the logical explanation.

Still, the question creeps in now and then.

What if someone had gotten out?

The steam thickens in the bathroom.

Knox closes his eyes and tilts his head back, letting the water pound against his face.

Then the lights go out. The bathroom drops into sudden darkness.

For a moment he doesn't move.

"Jesus," he mutters, blinking into the dark.

He reaches out and shuts the water off.

Silence swallows the room immediately.

Knox steps out of the shower and grabs a towel from the rack, wrapping it loosely around his waist.

"Hello?" he calls.

No answer.

He steps into the bedroom, water dripping down his chest.

"Frank?"

Still nothing.

The house intercom sits beside the bed.

Knox presses the button.

"Hello?"

Static.

He frowns.

"Frank, answer the fucking intercom."

Nothing comes back.

The silence begins to feel wrong.

Knox walks to the bedroom door and opens it.

The hallway beyond stretches long and dim, lit only by faint emergency lights along the baseboards.

His heartbeat picks up.

"Frank?"

Still nothing.

He moves toward the staircase.

His bare feet make soft sounds on the wood floor.

When he reaches the bottom of the stairs, the smell hits him first.

Knox steps into the foyer.

Two guards lie on the white marble floor. One faces the ceiling, eyes open and empty. A dark hole punctures the center of his forehead. The other sprawls near the door, his throat torn open by a gunshot.

Blood has pooled across the marble, spreading slowly outward in glossy red sheets.

Knox stares at them.

"Oh fuck."

The words slip out before he can stop them.

He turns and runs.

The towel nearly slips loose as he takes the stairs two at a time.

Knox rushes in the bedroom and yanks the nightstand drawer open. His hand closes around the handgun inside. He pulls it free and spins toward the hallway.

Two figures stand in the doorway.

They wear black from head to toe, gloves, fitted clothing, and skull masks that conceal their faces completely.

They had not been there a second ago.

"Who the fuck—"

One of them steps forward.

The other stays slightly behind, watching.

Knox lifts the gun and pulls the trigger.

Click.

Nothing.

He pulls it again.

Click.

His stomach twists.

The first figure raises a hand calmly and opens their palm.

A single bullet drops to the floor.

Then another.

And another.

One by one, they fall from their fingers and tap softly against the wood.
Knox's breath catches.
The first figure reaches up and pulls the mask down.
For a moment, his brain refuses to process what he is seeing.
A face he recognizes from the manor.
Brooke.
His eyes snap to the second figure.
The mask comes off more slowly this time.
Seth.
Knox's stomach drops as if the floor has vanished beneath him.
And for the first time, he was afraid.

Chapter 37
Brooke

Knox's eyes dart between us, panic finally breaking through whatever confidence he has left.

I tilt my head slightly. "Hey, Knox," I say calmly. "I'll give you a ten second head start."

For a second he just stares at me, like his brain can't decide if I'm serious.

Then survival takes over.

He bolts, feet pounding down the hallway, shoulders slamming into the wall as he tries to find traction on the tile. The sound of his breathing echoes, ragged and desperate as he runs.

I watch him go.

Then I glance at Seth.

I said ten seconds, I meant two.

My hand slides to my gun.

I draw the gun smoothly and raise it, lining up the sight with the center of Knox's back as he sprints down the corridor.

"Round one."

The first shot tears into the middle of his back.

The impact snaps him forward hard. His scream rips out of him as his knees slam into the floor. The towel around his waist twists loose as his body lurches, barely hanging on as he hits the tile. Blood spreads fast across the skin of his back, running down his sides.

His palms scrape uselessly against the floor, leaving smeared red streaks as his body folds in on itself.

He drags himself with one arm, choking and crying, making broken animal sounds while his legs refuse to cooperate. Blood pools beneath his chest and spreads across the hallway in slow, thick waves.

I don't rush him.

I follow slowly.

He keeps pulling himself forward, nails skidding on tile, shoulder jerking with each weak drag. He doesn't look back. He already knows I'm there.

I smile anyway.

"Round two."

The second shot hits lower this time.

His scream collapses into a wet gurgle as his body slams flat. His legs kick once, then twitch. His head lifts off the floor in a confused jerk, like his nervous system is still trying to figure out why nothing works anymore.

I step over his useless legs and come up behind him.

He is still breathing, but barely. Each inhale rattles through blood.

I raise the gun and aim at the back of his head.

"Final round... Game over."

The shot blows through his skull.

Blood and bone explode forward across the wall. His head snaps violently to the side before his body goes completely still. Brain matter splatters across the tile. The hallway fills with the smell of gunpowder, copper, and burned flesh.

I lower the gun.

I stare down at what is left of Knox, the man who darted me, dragged me, hunted me, and thought I had broken.

He was wrong.

Seth comes up beside me.

He pulls the machete from the gear bag.

"What are you doing?" I ask.

He plants a boot on Knox's shoulder and grabs a fistful of hair.

"For later."

He lines the blade at the base of Knox's neck and swings.

The first strike cuts through muscle and catches bone.

Knox's head shifts but stays attached.

Seth adjusts his grip and brings the blade down again.

The second strike finishes it.

The head comes free.

Blood spills across the floor in heavy streams.

Seth lifts it by the hair and drops it into a sealed evidence bag he has prepped. He twists it shut and cinches it tight with a zip tie.

Then he wipes the machete on Knox's towel and turns back to me.

I meet his eyes.

He looks at me like he is seeing me for the first time. Blood on my face, gun still warm in my grip, the shadow of my last shot still lingering in the smoke.

Pride burns in his expression, mixed with admiration and hunger. He steps toward me and grabs my wrist.

"Come on."

Then we are moving.

We scan the hallway, my weapon still raised, hearts still hammering. Seth keeps one hand on my back as we run. Past the bodies. Down the marble corridor slick with blood. Through the open foyer.

The front door slams behind us, the echo chasing us down the stone path as gunfire residue clings to the back of my throat. My heart pounds like it hasn't caught up to the fact that Knox is dead.

The SUV's headlights slice through the dark, casting long shadows across the trees as the engine growls low, the sound vibrating in my chest. Travis waves us in with wild eyes like the house behind us is seconds from detonating.

Beau sits in the passenger seat, sniper rifle in his lap, gaze locked on the treeline.

"Move!" he barks.

Seth's hand locks around mine and yanks me inside. The door slams. The tires screech. The SUV fishtails just enough to spit gravel as we speed into the black.

I haven't taken a full breath since the second Knox hit the floor.

My legs feel like rubber and lead at once. I'm still wired, still wound, still tasting the gunpowder on the back of my tongue.

Seth sits in the corner of the back seat, legs spread wide, chest rising hard with every breath. Blood-slicked shirt clings to every inch of him, soaked through and sticking to the sharp lines of his body. His eyes are dark, feral, locked on me. He looks like they haven't blinked in minutes.

His hands are flexing like he doesn't know what to do with them. Like the only thing stopping him from grabbing me is the thin shred of control he has left. Veins bulge beneath his skin, his pulse visible in the cord of his neck, like something caged inside him is pounding to get out.

He doesn't look at me like I'm fragile. He looks at me like I'm fire.

And I can feel that stare all over my body. My limbs ache, but I don't know if it's adrenaline or from the heat coiling low in my stomach from the way he is looking at me.

No words. Just hunger. Just pride. Just raw, blistering heat. The kind that gets under your skin and makes you ache until you do something about it.

I crawl onto his lap without thinking, like I have done a thousand times before.

His arms snap around me the second I move. One locks around my waist like a vice, the other curls up the back of my neck, hand threading into my hair and holding me there. His grip isn't rough. It's possessive. Like if anyone tries to take me from him, they will lose the arm they reach with.

My knees bracket his thighs. My body settles over his, and the blood between us smears instantly.

I kiss him.

Just tongue and breath and need. Just teeth and urgency and the ache of surviving. I kiss him because I don't know what else to do with the way my body buzzes. I kiss him because I need to feel something that isn't fear or rage. I kiss him because he has watched me kill and not once flinched.

Because he understands.

He kisses me back like he has been waiting for permission to break. His mouth is hot, lips bruising mine, tongue sliding past them as his fingers dig into my hip. His breath is ragged. I can feel how close he is to losing control completely.

The SUV roars over gravel, lurching through a sharp turn as we speed through the trees. Beau is yelling something from the front seat. Travis curses under his breath, something about being an accomplice to murder, about blood on the seats, about needing therapy.

None of it matters.

Seth's mouth is on mine, and I am still high on the kill.

He kisses me harder and messier. His teeth catch my bottom lip and pull, and I moan into his mouth, nails digging into the nape of his neck. His tongue slides against mine in rhythm with the grind of my hips over his lap.

That's when I feel it.

The thick, hot press of him straining against his pants. He is already hard. His cock pulses through the thin barrier of the fabric, the heat of it unmistakable. I grind down again, slower this time, dragging friction right along the length of him.

He groans into my mouth then again when he tears away and lowers his lips to my throat. His tongue drags over my pulse slowly, followed by teeth, just enough to make me gasp. His grip on my ass tightens like the urge to fuck me is crawling under his skin, ripping him apart from the inside.

"Please," Travis groans from the front seat, twisting halfway around with one arm still hooked on the wheel. "Please don't fuck in this car. I'm already on the run with you both. I'm already traumatized. Let's not stack it."

Seth doesn't look up. Doesn't pause. Doesn't give a single fuck.

He growls against my skin, mouth still on my neck. "You're about to be a dead man if you don't shut the fuck up."

My head drops back with a laugh that is part shock, part high, part fuck-it.

My blood still races. My thighs are slick with sweat and heat and leftover adrenaline. My face is smeared with dried blood. My lips are swollen from the kiss and from the aftermath of the kill. And I don't care about any of it.

"Okay, okay. We'll wait."

"Jesus," Travis mutters, throwing his hand up. "Brooke, you still have blood on your clothes. Chunks. You have literal chunks. This is unsanitary. Seth, I'm begging you. Wait until she showers, or until I'm out of the car."

Beau doesn't even turn his head. He smirks, voice calm and amused from the passenger seat. "Let 'em have their victory lap, Trav."

Seth's hand slides up the back of my spine, pushing beneath the hem of my top. His palm flattens over my skin, fingers splayed, tracing the curve of my spine. He doesn't stop until his fingertips reach the bottom edge of my bra.

I shiver. Every nerve ending goes tight and hot and ready.

His breath hits my ear.

"I'm not waiting long."

And I believe him.

Because I can feel it, the way I'm still trembling in his lap, the way his cock throbs against my center like it is counting down the seconds.

He sees the blood, the rage, the violence and it doesn't turn him off. It makes him harder.

I put a round in Knox tonight.

And the way Seth looks at me says he is ready for a few rounds of something else.

Chapter 38

Brooke

By the time we reach the safe house, my body is still humming with leftover adrenaline. My pulse feels too quick, my breath too shallow, like my nerves haven't caught up to reality yet. Even my hands feel different. I keep replaying the moment I pull the trigger, the strange calm that follows, the knowledge that I've reclaimed something that had been taken from me.

There's blood on both of us. Not as much as before, but enough that I can feel it drying against my skin. Seth drags me to the sink and rinses it off quickly, his hands rough and efficient as water runs pink over our fingers before clearing.

Seth takes my hand without a word and guides me through the house. His grip stays firm, pulling me past dim lamps and quiet hallways until we reach a door near the back.

"Come here," he says. "I want to show you something."

He opens the door, and heat washes over my skin.

The pool room glows under soft blue light. Water ripples gently beneath the surface, steam curling upward and catching along the glass walls.

I stare at it in disbelief.

"I've been here two months," I murmur, "and I never knew this was an indoor pool."

Seth laughs once.

"I know, this place has everything."

I turn toward him, and the sight of him nearly strips the breath from my lungs. The humid air clings to his shirt, outlining the muscle beneath. His tattoos cut across his skin in heavy black lines, each one stark against the strength in his chest and arms. He watches me with a hunger that makes my stomach tighten, the look that feels like a hand wrapping around my spine.

I don't look away.

He steps closer, cups my jaw, and lifts my face to his.

"Do you trust me?"

My breath shudders.

"With my life," I whisper.

Something eases in his expression. He kisses me, slow at first, then deeper, anchoring me to the present, to him, to the heat in his mouth instead of the memory of drowning.

He turns toward the speaker and taps the screen.

Deftones fill the room, drifting across the warm air and echoing off the water.

Seth pulls his shirt over his head. Dark ink stretches across his torso in heavy lines that follow the shape of powerful muscle. A second later his pants slide down his hips and drop to the floor.

I can't look away.

His body looks built for violence and desire. Every line draws my attention. His cock presses thick and heavy against his briefs before he pushes the fabric down and steps free.

He catches my stare and smirks.

"Your turn," he says.

Heat moves through my chest and lower. I lift my shirt and drop it. Seth's gaze follows every inch of skin. My bra comes off next. His eyes darken when they settle on my breasts.

My leggings slide down my hips. My underwear follows, leaving me bare in the warm air.

He looks at me like it is the first time, and then he takes my hand.

We step into the pool together.

Warm water climbs our legs while "Cherry Waves" pulses softly around us. Steam drifts across the surface as Seth moves closer.

My pulse quickens.

Water reaches my thighs, easing muscles that have been tight for hours. When it touches my hips, memory pushes back. The slow rise against my skin echoes too closely to another pool.

Seth feels the shift immediately.

His hands settle on my waist.

"You alright?" he asks quietly.

I nod even though my breath catches.

"We stop when you say stop," he says. "You control this."

"I know."

As we move deeper, water climbs my ribs and chest. The room smells clean and warm, nothing like the chemical bite of the manor pool, yet my nerves still react.

Seth draws me against him.

When the water reaches our collarbones, he kisses me again.

Then he lowers his voice.

"I'm gonna put you under, okay?"

My eyes widen.

He brushes his thumb across my cheek.

"I promise. This will help. It'll let you take back everything they stole."

My stomach twists.

Images slam into me. Sophie forcing my head under water. Elliot pressing down while I fight for air. Kristie smiling while bubbles escape my mouth.

The moment I almost died.

My breath trembles.

But this is not their pool.

This is Seth.

I nod.

He kisses me slowly, letting our breaths mix. Then his arm wraps around my waist and he guides us under.

Water closes over my head.

Music softens into vibration. Light fractures above us. My hair floats around my shoulders.

Seth's mouth stays on mine.

The kiss changes underwater. His hands move along my waist and ribs before sliding to my hips.

The last time I had been submerged, I felt terror.

Now I feel something else.

Every nerve wakes beneath his touch. My body is not bracing anymore.

It is choosing.

Seth opens his eyes.

Gray locks onto mine through the wavering light of the pool.

Underwater, everything about him looks different. His hair lifts slightly from his forehead, dark strands drifting weightlessly around his temples. The angles of his face soften beneath the shifting ribbons of blue light moving across the water. Tiny bubbles cling along the line of his jaw and the bridge of his nose before slipping upward toward the surface.

His eyes never leave mine.

The color looks lighter down here, storm gray turned almost silver by the light breaking through the water above us. His gaze holds steady and unblinking, intense in a way that makes my chest tighten even though I'm not breathing.

His hand tightens at my waist.

The muscles in his forearm flex beneath the water while he holds me against him, my body suspended in the warm weightlessness between the surface and the tiled floor. His other hand drifts slowly up my spine, fingers sliding through the floating strands of my hair before settling against the back of my neck.

The look in his eyes says everything his mouth can't underwater.

I'm here.

I'm not letting you go.

For a moment I forget about the burn building in my lungs.

All I can see is him.

His mouth still pressed against mine. The faint movement of his chest as he holds the breath we shared seconds earlier. The way the water bends the light across the planes of his shoulders and the dark ink stretching over them.

He looks almost unreal beneath the surface.

Dangerous.

Beautiful.

Mine.

The pressure in my chest finally returns, a slow ache spreading through my ribs as my body reminds me it needs air.

I squeeze his shoulder once.

His arm tightens around my waist and he pushes upward, cutting through the water as he lifts us both toward the surface.

The second our heads break through, air rushes into my lungs in a sharp inhale.

Our mouths are still connected.

He rests his forehead against mine.

"See," he murmurs, lips brushing my skin, "I got you. You're okay."

A shaky breath leaves me.

His mouth moves down my neck. His hands trace my spine and hips while water rolls down my skin.

My pulse jumps again when his cock nudges my abdomen beneath the surface. Hard enough that the solid weight of him is unmistakable even through the shifting water. The shaft presses against my stomach with slow insistence, the broad head dragging along my skin before settling again. Faint ridges of veins run beneath my palm when I reach for him.

The familiar size of him in my hand makes heat bloom low in my body.

When I stroke once slowly, a rough groan vibrates through his chest and into the water between us.

"I missed you so fucking much," he says. Each word scraping out of him with weeks of tension and need.

"I missed you too, but..." I whisper.

His eyebrow lifts as his hand slides along my waist.

"But?" he asks, voice soft but edged with heat.

"It's been awhile," I breathe. "You might break me."

His mouth curves into a slow, dangerous smirk. He lowers his head, lips brushing my jaw as his fingers grip my hips.

"You can take it," he murmurs. "You always do."

My arms rise around his shoulders, fingers sliding across the damp heat of his skin before locking behind his neck. I pull him closer until our chests press together. His heart hammers against my sternum, and the contact sends a rush through me that has nothing to do with the water surrounding us.

He lifts me easily, hands spreading across my hips. My legs wrap around his waist and cross behind him, pulling us tight together.

The position brings him directly against me.

The thick length of his cock drags through the slick heat between my thighs.

My body reacts instantly.

Weeks without him have left a dull ache inside me that I have tried to ignore. The moment his cock touches me again, that ache surges awake. My hips move before I can stop them, chasing the pressure that has been missing for far too long.

He tightens his hold on me and shifts his stance. Water moves between us as he adjusts the angle, his hands firm on my hips while he guides my body down.

The swollen head of his cock settles at my entrance.

God.

Just the weight of him there makes my body tremble.

He pushes forward slowly.

The stretch hits first. My breath catches hard in my throat as my body opens around him. My nails drag across his shoulders while he continues forward with patient pressure, forcing me to feel every inch as he enters.

It's been weeks. Weeks of tension sitting under my skin. Weeks of wanting him and pretending I could ignore it.

My body can't pretend now.

He eases in slowly, dragging his cock against nerves that feel raw from neglect. I sink lower, breath shaking, until the thick ridge near the head pushes past the tightest part of me and every muscle gives at once. A low sound breaks out of my chest.

The fullness builds slowly, spreading through my core until my entire body trembles from the sensation of him filling me. When he finally bottoms out, my forehead falls against his shoulder.

"Fuck," he groans. "See? I knew you could take all of me."

His chest swells against mine, breath shuddering as the velvet squeeze of my body milks an involuntary throb from him. I feel it, a heavy pulse that presses outward, claiming every inch of space he just filled.

"I missed being inside you."

I missed it too, more than I can say. My body proves it, clutching tight, rippling around him as it adjusts to accommodate his size. The thick head, the slight upward curve, the way the veins along the shaft rub my slick walls each time I move.

His hips move in slow thrusts that drag along nerves that have been starved for him. Each movement pulls another sound from my throat. My body responds immediately, tightening around him, refusing to let him go.

Water moves around us with every motion, small waves breaking softly against my ribs as his hips drive into me.

His mouth brushes my jaw and slides down the curve of my neck, lips warm and demanding against damp skin while my legs tighten around his waist. Each thrust pushes him deeper, the thick length of his cock dragging along nerves that have already turned unbearably sensitive.

His teeth graze my skin lightly before his lips follow, soothing it, then pressing harder.

The rhythm builds without warning.

Pressure gathers low in my stomach, spreading outward through my hips and spine with every movement he forces into my body. My fingers tighten across his shoulders while my nails scrape lightly down his back, trying to hold onto something while the sensation keeps building.

"Fuck... Brooke."

His voice breaks against my skin.

His hips snap forward again, harder this time. The sudden force makes my breath catch as the full weight of him drives deep inside me. The impact sends a sharp wave of sensation through my core, making my body clamp down around him.

"Don't move," he mutters, almost desperate. "Fuck, don't move."

But I can't help it.

My body reacts on its own, tightening, shifting, pulling him deeper every time he thrusts forward.

Then his body goes rigid.

His arms tighten around me, locking me in place, holding me exactly where he wants me as his forehead drops against my shoulder. A rough sound tears from his chest. His cock throbs inside me as he comes, thick heat spilling deep in slow, pulsing surges that spread through my core.

"Shit...I'm sorry," he gasps against my skin. "I missed you so much. I couldn't hold it."

His hands slide up my back, gripping tighter, like he needs to stay connected, like he is not ready for this to end.

"It's okay," I breathe, still shaking.

I find his mouth and kiss him slowly, swallowing the last of his apology. My lips move against his, soft at first, then deeper, letting him feel that I'm here, that I wanted this just as much.

"I missed you too," I whisper against his lips.

He exhales against my mouth and kisses me again, slower, deeper, his hands still locked on my hips, keeping me exactly where he wants me.

Steam softens the room while his dick remains buried inside me, still hard and throbbing. A familiar grin tugs at the corner of his mouth.

"Seth."

"I'm not done."

He guides me backward until the smooth tile of the pool edge presses against my back. His hands slide down my thighs.

One leg lifts over his shoulder.

Then the other.

The position opens me completely, my hips tilting upward as he steps closer between my legs.

"You ready?" he asks.

I nod, breath uneven.

He drives forward.

The new angle forces a gasp from my lungs. His cock pushes deeper than before, stretching me around the full length of him until my toes curl.

My body reacts instantly. Muscles tighten around him in sharp pulses while my back arches against the tile.

He lifts my hips higher, holding me exactly where he wants me.

Then he leans backward.

Water climbs toward my face.

"Seth," I whisper.

"Yeah baby."

The surface slides over my chin, then my lips, then the bridge of my nose. A second later it covers my eyes and the world goes quiet.

Sound dulls beneath the water.

He stays inside me while my legs hook over his shoulders.

He thrusts slowly.

Each movement strikes deep and heavy, the strange weightlessness turning every motion into a stronger surge of sensation. Pressure gathers fast in my stomach while my lungs burn for air.

A soft sound escapes me in a trail of bubbles.

Just before the tension breaks, his grip tightens and he hauls me upward.

My head bursts through the surface.

Air tears into my chest as he slams forward again.

The impact shatters the pressure inside me.

I come instantly.

My body clenches around him in violent pulses while my back arches against the tile. He groans low and drives forward once more, his cock throbbing as he comes again in deep surges that match the rhythm of my climax.

Water rocks around us.

Slowly my muscles loosen.

My legs slip from his shoulders, but he catches my waist.

"I told you I got you," he whispers. "Always."

We stay there breathing hard while music hums softly through the room.

Eventually he pulls me into his lap on the pool steps. My back rests against his chest while his arms wrap around me. He eases his cock back inside me, settling there while the water rocks gently around us.

For a moment my mind returns to the drowning.

Then the memory shifts.

His arms around me. His breath on my shoulder. His heartbeat against my spine.

The water lifting my body instead of dragging it down.

None of it feels like death.

It feels like rebirth.

"I love you," he murmurs.

I lean into him.

"I love you so fucking much, Seth."

"You still coming?" he asks quietly.

"A little."

"Good."

A tired laugh escapes me.

"Sadist."

"Only for you."

Silence settles between us.

"I thought I lost you," he says finally.

"You didn't. You never will."

I turn to face him. His length slips free of me and we both groan softly at the loss.

"You saved me."

"You didn't need saving tonight."

We stay in the pool until the heat fades and our breathing slows.

Finally he kisses me softly.

"Let's clean up and go to bed."

I let him lift me from the water.

Tonight was healing.

I killed the man who hurt me and made love to the man who always saves me.

It is us choosing each other.

And choosing what comes next.

Chapter 39
Seth

The sun has just begun pushing through the trees when we step into the clearing above the safe house. Thin bands of light cut across the damp ground and catch on the dew clinging to the grass and branches. Pine needles stick to the bottoms of our boots as we stop near the bunker entrance.

Brooke rolls her shoulder once and glances at me.

"How did you know the pool thing would help?" she asks.

I look over at her. "Pool sex?"

She lifts a brow. "You know what I mean."

A laugh slips out of me. "I learned a lot of stuff in those psych classes."

Her mouth twists. "You really paid to take classes at Stratford just to watch me."

"Hell yeah."

She shakes her head, still looking a little stunned by it. Brooke never fully understood how far my obsession goes.

When we first started dating and she told me she was in therapy, I spent nights researching every technique those therapists use and every way I could reinforce it outside those sessions. I paid attention to details she assumed no one would notice. I learned which nights her nightmares hit the hardest and which music helped calm her afterward. I memorized the exact way she liked the apartment arranged so nothing will feel out of place when she came home.

I even learned what snacks Luna loves so she wouldn't make noise when I slipped into the apartment at night and watched Brooke sleep.

And when the manor broke her, when the miscarriage hollowed something out of both of us, I went back to that same instinct. I spent nights digging through anything I could find about trauma recovery, physical retraining, exposure therapy, anything that might pull her out of the hell they forced her into. I needed something practical to give her besides sympathy and empty reassurances.

Brooke stands in front of me now in the clearing, watching me like she is still trying to figure out what I have planned.

"Southpaw day," I say, tossing the mouthguard to her.

She catches it with her left hand and pushes it into her mouth without looking away from me.

My jaw tightens before I even realize it.

She has no idea how hard it is to stay focused.

Every time she shifts her weight, I see her naked. Every breath she takes reminds me of last night, her legs wrapped around me, her nails in my back, her cunt squeezing around my cock while she bites my shoulder to keep from screaming. Her thighs shaking when she comes. The way she says my name when I slide back inside her after the second round.

I have not gotten over it.

But this morning is not about sex. It is about control.

She throws the first punch.

Left jab. Fast. It clips my jaw. I let it land. Not because she surprises me, but because I need to see what she will do after.

She follows through.

Left leg comes up into a kick. Wide and off-balance. But she puts weight behind it. She is still figuring out how to move with her left, but she is learning fast. Too fast for most people. Exactly fast enough for me.

I catch her ankle and twist.

She hits the ground hard. Air leaves her lungs in a grunt, her back slamming into the dirt.

She gasps, but doesn't cry out.

I drop down before she can roll. Straddle her hips. Pin her thighs under my knees. Grab her wrists and slam them into the earth on either side of her head.

Her chest jerks up. Her tank top sticks to her skin. Her mouth is open. Her lips are already red and parted.

She looks good like this.

I lower my face to hers until our mouths are inches apart. “If I was Elliot, you would be dead.”

She bucks hard and almost throws me off.

I let her.

She rolls, scrambles to her feet, turning fast with her mouthguard clenched tight. She looks dangerous. That matters more than whether or not she is ready.

She needs to fight someone she trusts before she has to fight someone who wants her dead.

She comes at me again. More focused this time. Her punch lands clean in my ribs. I don't block it.

I smile.

She stands across from me, chest heaving. Her arms shake from adrenaline and effort. Her fingers twitch. Her mouth opens as she pulls air between her teeth.

She wants to get better. She wants to stop being a target. She wants to be the one people can't touch.

“That’s it.”

She spits the mouthguard into her palm and narrows her eyes. “You’re holding back.”

“I am,” I say, stepping in closer. “And one day I won’t.”

She doesn't back up.

My restraint cracks for one second.

I grab her jaw and kiss her.

Her mouth opens right away. Her body leans into mine like it can't decide if it wants to fight me or fuck me. Her hands go to my neck. Her chest presses to mine. I kiss her harder. Slide my tongue against hers. She moans into my mouth, and the sound goes straight to my dick.

She rolls her hips forward without thinking. Her body remembers what we did last night. So does mine.

I pull back.

“Do you want to keep going?” I ask.

She nods.

I press my hand to her chest and push her back three steps. "Then prove it."

She comes at me again.

This time her punch misses, but her knee follows fast. I catch her waist, twist us together. The second I touch her again, my brain goes back to her legs around my back, to her cunt dragging me deeper.

I force myself to stay present. We aren't done.

Not until she can fight and win.

And when she does, I will fuck her again the way she wants, hard, filthy, with nothing held back.

Two monitors sit at one end, wired into Travis's laptop. Another screen glows against the far wall, scrolling lines of code and location pings.

Travis stands at the head of the table, posture rigid, eyes locked on the data. He has that look he gets when he digs too deep and doesn't like what he finds.

Brooke sits beside me. Whatever exhaustion sits in her body has not dulled her focus.

Beau leans against the counter near the back wall, arms crossed.

Travis breaks the silence.

"I got into another Collective archive," he says. "Different build. Different security."

Brooke leans forward slightly. "Meaning?"

He taps a key and turns one of the monitors toward us.

Kristie Talbert's face fills the screen. Smiling like she is not a fucking demon.

Brooke goes still.

"She put out a contract," Travis says. "On both of you."

My jaw tightens. "Amount?"

"Two million each," Travis replies. "Dead only."

Beau exhales through his nose.

Travis keeps going. "One more condition. It has to be recorded. She wants proof."

Brooke's mouth curves. "She wants to watch."

Travis nods. "Yeah. Pretty much."

The room goes quiet.

I lean forward, palms flat on the slate. "Who else is in?"

Travis pulls up another screen.

Names. Handles. Flags. Locations.

"This is where Beau's assassin intel comes in," Travis types something. "Since Knox died, the Collective assumes you're actively hunting. That moved you from a minor problem to priority."

Beau steps closer and taps the screen. "These are confirmed entries. Ten so far."

Brooke scans the list, her eyes moving slowly over each name. "Any familiar ones?"

I nod once. "Elliot. Sophie. Don. Joe."

I barely pause on them.

"They're amateurs," I add. "Easy to deal with. Just harder to find."

My gaze moves lower on the list, then stops.

"And him," I tap the screen. "Rafe Calder."

Brooke looks up. "Who's that?"

"Claims he's a sniper," I scoff. "Has a reputation, but it's mostly noise. He hits what's standing still. That's about it."

Her posture shifts as she leans in slightly.

I keep reading.

"Sergei Volkov."

Beau exhales quietly. "Bratva. He's not just good, he's patient. He'll sit on a target for hours if he has to. Doesn't rush. If he's coming for you, you won't see it until it's already done."

Brooke's grip tightens against the edge of the chair.

"Who else?" she asks.

Beau scans the rest.

"Dmitri Sokolov," he says. "Another Bratva operator."

His finger moves down the screen.

"Diego Cruz. Cartel. Close range, fast, messy."

A pause.

"Jackson Reed. Ex-military. Thinks he's disciplined."

He keeps going.

"Ava Carpenter. Freelance. Quiet, but she leaves traces."

Another name.

"Ezra Kane. Independent. Tracks first. Executes second."

Beau's jaw tightens slightly as he leans back.

"I've crossed paths with a few of them," he says. "They're not competition. Just persistent."

There is a quiet edge under his voice now, something colder.

"That won't matter."

He glances back at the list.

"Most of them are amateurs."

I let out a short breath. "Good."

Travis frowns at me. "Good?"

"Yes," I say. "It means they'll rush instead of thinking."

Beau adds, "Hopefully they won't coordinate well. Everyone wants the payout. Everyone wants the footage."

Travis scrolls. "Some of these people specialize in capture."

Brooke doesn't look away from the screen. "Kristie wants me killed on camera."

"Yup," Beau says. "She wants spectacle."

Travis rubs his face. "If you don't disappear, they'll converge."

"Exactly," I reply. "We don't chase them. We don't hide from them."

Beau's mouth lifts slightly. "We bait them."

Travis looks between us. "You're talking about inviting ten killers into your orbit."

"Yes," I say. "On our ground."

Beau crosses his arms again. "If we seed movement and leak location noise, I can track who commits first. The aggressive ones will show themselves."

"And the careful ones," Travis adds, "will follow."

I nod. "Which means we choose the place, the timing, and the exits."

Brooke's voice is calm. "Okay, they want to hunt me. Let them come."

I squeeze her hand once. "The Collective sent killers for us."

Brooke smirks. "Then we collect their fucking heads."

Kristie's bounty pool is exactly what you would expect from a desperate politician with too much money and not enough patience.

Half the names Travis pulls up aren't professionals. They are amateurs who have managed to kill someone once and decide that qualifies them to start calling themselves hunters. A few are repeat offenders who have been caught before and somehow slip through the system again. Most of them have records thick enough to choke a prosecutor and are dumb enough to leave evidence behind every time they pull the trigger. They aren't careful. They aren't disciplined. Some of them have not even bothered to hide their last body.

It almost feels insulting.

Two million dollars on my head and this is the talent pool she pulls from.

Not a single legitimate hitman in sight.

Travis is combing through the Collective's archived security footage when he finds the first one worth mentioning. He rewinds the clip and turns the laptop so Beau and I can see the screen.

The man wanders through the frame like the cameras don't exist. Crooked grin, cheap leather jacket hanging off his shoulders, and a lazy uneven walk that looks less like an injury and more like a man who has never bothered learning how to move with control.

Professional killers scan their surroundings.

This idiot looks like he would forget his own name if someone doesn't remind him.

I lean closer to the screen and study his face for another second.

His name is Don.

Joe is always with him.

Don and Joe aren't professionals. They come as a pair. The Collective uses men like them when they want bodies without investing real resources.

They are sloppy and impulsive, violent in ways that feel personal instead of controlled. They move between perimeter work, intimidation jobs, and cleanup when someone else doesn't want blood directly on their hands.

Both of them were seen with Grant.

They're close enough to feel important and close enough to think they are untouchable.

They aren't.

We don't hunt them. We let them come to us.

Brooke goes out alone with no disguise and no visible backup. She chooses a public place with lights on and people everywhere. She doesn't act unaware. She moves through the world like she has not already been marked.

Don notices Brooke first. Joe follows his gaze. They trail her from a nightclub near the edge of town. Joe stares too long. Don never checks his mirrors. They peel off behind a liquor store, laughing like the night already belongs to them.

Their dumbasses never even check the car.

They climb in, still talking, still laughing.

I'm already in the back seat.

Joe shuts the passenger door and reaches down to the floorboard, pulling up a small bottle and a rag. He turns them in his hands while Don leans back in the driver's seat, watching the alley.

"That's her," Don says.

They keep talking not knowing I am three feet behind them. Don complains about the payout being split. Joe jokes about how easy this is going to be.

Don reaches for the ignition. Before the key turns, I lean forward and press the blade under his jaw.

Both of them freeze.

Joe slowly twists around in the passenger seat, eyes wide.

"Give me the keys," I demand.

Don's hand trembles as he pulls them from the ignition and passes them back over the seat.

I take them and slip them into my pocket.

Joe's gaze flicks between the knife and Don's throat. The bottle and rag are still in his hands.

"Both of you were seen with Grant." My voice lowers. "So you're going to tell me where he is."

Don swallows hard. His throat shifts against the edge of the blade.

"I don't know what you're talking about," he says, his voice thin.

I press the knife deeper. The skin splits and warm blood runs down my fingers.

"You better tell the truth," I say quietly, "or I'll carve it out of your throat."

Don's breathing turns ragged.

Brooke is not across the street anymore. She has already moved. By the time either of them realizes she's gone, she is standing just outside the passenger side window with her gun drawn.

They never see her.

Joe's fingers close around whatever he has been reaching for.

A shot cracks through the car.

Joe's head snaps sideways. Blood and bone explode across the dash and windshield. The force jerks his body, folding him across the center console. His legs kick once before going limp.

Don yells.

I grab his chin, wrench his head back, and drive the blade into his neck. The knife tears through muscle and catches, and the panic in his eyes is immediate.

He claws at the wheel. His feet slam uselessly against the pedals. I rip the blade free and bury it again, higher this time, twisting hard before pulling it out. Blood pours over my hands, flooding the space between us.

His scream breaks into a wet, choking sound.

I hold him there until the strength drains out of his body and his grip goes slack, then shove him sideways and let him collapse against Joe.

I lean back against the seat and exhale.

Brooke's voice comes through the passenger window, breathless and tight with adrenaline.

"Oh my God. Oh my God, baby, I'm so sorry. Is he dead?"

I turn my head toward the passenger side.

Joe is slumped across the console. Blood soaks the upholstery beneath him, spreading across the dash and dripping down toward the floorboard. Something warm clings to my hairline and slides down the side of my temple.

I glance back at Brooke through the glass.

"Part of his brain is in my hair," I sigh. "Yeah, baby. He's pretty fucking dead."

Travis has climbed out of the SUV and walks over to join her, stopping beside her as he looks through the glass at the mess inside.

He lets out a quiet breath.

"Well," he says dryly, "there goes our lead."

I reach into Don's jacket with fingers still slick with blood, pull out his phone, and wipe it off on his sleeve.

"Good," I scroll through the phone. "Then let's see who else wants a turn."

Outside, Brooke has already started back toward the truck with her gun lowered, Travis falling into step beside her as he looks over the scene.

He glances back at me. "Should we get rid of them or something?"

I step out of the car and take one last look at the bodies slumped in the seats.

"Nah, let them know."

I shut the door.

"This is what coming for us looks like."

Chapter 40
Brooke

Warm light pools across the room, casting a low golden glow over the rumpled sheets and the headboard behind him. "CPR" plays quietly from the speaker on the nightstand, the bass slow and soothing as the vocals drift through the air. The rhythm settles into a steady pulse that mirrors the heat building between us.

Seth leans back against the headboard, the sheets kicked completely off him and tangled near the foot of the bed.

I'm between his legs.

My hands rest on his thighs as I move over him, my mouth warm and slow around his cock while the music hums quietly behind us. His fingers are threaded through my hair, guiding the pace and watching every movement.

His thumb brushes along my jaw when I pull back for air, my lips sliding off him before I lean forward again. I take him deeper this time, my tongue dragging slowly along him as his grip tightens in my hair.

During training earlier, we made a bet.

I told him to stop holding back. If he is going to train me, he needs to treat me like someone who could actually kill me.

Whoever lost the sparring match has to go down on the winner.

Of course Seth won.

But this really isn't much of a punishment for me.

I love having his cock in my mouth more than anything.

I lean forward and take him deeper, my throat tightening as I force myself to relax enough to take more of him. The thick head of his cock presses deeper until my throat strains around the length of him, the pressure restricting my airway before I slowly pull back again.

I lift my head and wipe the corner of my mouth with the back of my hand, my other hand still wrapped around him.

"I'm sorry," I murmur.

Seth looks down at me, his brow tightening slightly.

"Sorry for what?"

I lean forward again and close my mouth around him, moving slowly for a moment before pulling back once more.

"I shot Joe too quickly. I didn't even wait for your signal."

For a second he just stares at me.

Then his hand slides to the back of my neck. With the other, he guides his cock forward and taps the head of it lightly against my lips, a crooked smirk pulling at his mouth as he does it.

"Don't apologize for that. You did exactly what I've been trying to drill into you. No hesitation."

I lean forward again and take him back into my mouth. My tongue moves slowly along the veins running down the shaft, tracing the ridges while I slide my lips lower around him.

His eyes flutter as his grip tightens slightly in my hair.

After a moment I pull back again, my hand still moving slowly around him.

"I want Sophie next," I say quietly. "I want to make her bleed."

Seth's expression hardens immediately.

"Don't worry, baby, we'll get her. And that bitch will drown in her own blood."

Something about hearing that sparks heat instead of fear.

After everything, I still want this.

I want him.

I finally pull away and sit back on my heels between his legs.

My back aches from training earlier, muscles tight and sore. The movement pulls the loose shirt higher up my spine, exposing the scars there.

Seth's eyes flick past my shoulder to the mirror on the wall behind me, catching the reflection of my back.

His jaw tightens as he reaches behind me, his fingers brushing along my spine before tracing one of the raised scars slowly.

I exhale softly.

"I thought I was going to die an anal virgin," I mutter.

Seth blinks down at me.

"The fuck?"

A small smile tugs at my mouth.

"You heard me."

His eyes drop to my ass. "Well...guess we should fix that then."

"I love how serious you are about it," I laugh. "I mean... I've never done it with—"

He cuts me off immediately. "You better not start telling me what you've done with anybody other than me. I don't want to know. Even if I already know, I don't want the fucking details. It makes me feel homicidal...more homicidal than usual."

I laugh, biting my lip. "Relax, Seth. You're the only man who has ever been inside me that mattered."

He tilts his head. "Better be."

"But seriously..." My voice dips. "I've only had your fingers. Never the real thing."

I hold his gaze for a beat, then slip my thumb between my teeth, biting down gently as I nod once.

"I want to try it."

His brows lift.

"Really?"

"Apparently, it takes a near-death experience to make me want to lose my ass virginity."

He sits up, brows lifting as he studies my face, like he is trying to decide whether I'm joking or spiraling. "You sure?" he asks. "Because the other night, you said you were afraid my dick might break you."

I roll my eyes. "Yeah, but it didn't."

His grin comes instantly. "Now it sounds like a challenge."

"I swear to God, Seth," I point at him. "If you try to go all the way in without prepping me first, I will beat your ass."

Seth laughs, the sound vibrating through the room. "Fuck, I love you." He leans in and kisses me, then pulls back and stands. "Lay on your stomach."

I turn slowly, my heart thudding harder with every second as anticipation settles in. I adjust, burying my face into the pillow, fingers curling into the sheets.

I hear the drawer slide open behind me. The soft rustle of supplies follows.

Then the quiet click of the lube bottle.

The cold hits first. A smooth, sudden slickness as he pours it over me. His hands follow immediately, spreading it with long, slow strokes. He takes his time, working it in from my hips down to the space between my cheeks, massaging it into my skin with steady pressure until my body starts reacting without permission.

I feel the heat of him behind me, close. His cock brushes the back of my thigh with every small shift of his weight. The contact makes my breath catch, my hips twitching.

"Your ass drives me insane," he mutters, his voice tight with restraint. "You have no idea what it does to me."

His hands don't rush. He keeps moving, spreading me open, then smoothing his palms back over my skin. His thumbs press in as he pulls me wider, holding me there for a second.

He exhales, then spanks me. Just enough to sting.

The sound cracks through the room.

My hips jolt.

"Had to," he says. "This is one of my favorite views on the planet."

"Pervert," I laugh into the pillow.

"For you, I am."

His mouth presses to my skin. Then a bite at the curve of my hip, sharp enough to pull a gasp from me.

His hands hold me open as he lowers himself.

Then I feel it.

The first pass of his tongue over me.

I jerk, a broken sound catching in my throat as the heat of his mouth hits me. He doesn't stop. He licks again, slower this time, dragging his tongue over the tight ring of muscle before circling it with obscene precision.

"Fuck," I breathe.

His hands stay firm on my ass, thumbs spread me wide, holding me open. His face is pressed between my cheeks, mouth hot, tongue moving in slow, deliberate passes that make it impossible to think straight. He doesn't rush. He works me, methodically, like he is paying attention to every reaction my body gives him.

I can hear my own breathing, feel my pulse pounding everywhere at once. My legs tremble against the mattress, toes curling as his tongue traces the same path again and again until the muscles there start giving way on their own.

The tip of his tongue presses in. Just enough to make my entire body jolt.

A sound tears out of me before I can stop it, half moan, half gasp, and I push back against him without thinking, hips lifting like my body has already decided this is what it wants.

He growls low, the vibration hitting me straight through the nerves already lit up. His mouth pulls away just long enough to say, "Keep this ass up for me baby."

His tongue returns to the same spot, slower now, firmer, pressing in and pulling back in a rhythm that makes my head spin. His hands never move from my ass, keeping me open, keeping me right where he wants me. I can feel how focused he is, like he is testing exactly how much pressure I can take before I come.

His hand slides between my thighs.

Two fingers drag through the slick there, spreading it, touching just enough to make my hips jerk again. He strokes my clit once, twice, then stays there, letting me feel the contrast. His tongue works my ass. His fingers remind me how wet my pussy already is.

My breath comes out in broken sounds against the pillow. Every nerve feels too close to the surface, like the smallest change will send me over the edge.

He presses his tongue in again, just a little deeper this time, holding it there for a second before pulling back. My fingers claw into the sheets as my body reacts, clenching, then easing.

He stays exactly where he is, working me open with his mouth while his fingers keep me soaked and sensitive.

Then he pulls back, and I feel him coat his fingers again. One thumb spreads me open while his slick fingertip circles the spot he just licked.

One finger pushes in.

I gasp, gripping the pillow tighter as my body clenches and then slowly gives way. He works it deeper until he is buried to the knuckle, then pauses, letting me feel it, letting my body adjust.

His free hand slides between my thighs, stroking once, teasing just enough to keep me open.

"You okay?" he asks softly.

I nod into the pillow. "Mhmm."

He kisses my lower back just above the line of scars.

Behind me, his cock brushes my thigh when he shifts, his breathing heavier now. His finger moves again, easing in and out in small strokes that make my hips twitch.

"Stay still baby," he murmurs. "Just breathe."

I do.

The stretch feels strange at first, unfamiliar, but not painful. He doesn't rush it. He lets me settle around him before moving again.

The rhythm starts slow. Small strokes that build heat little by little.

My legs spread slightly and he growls under his breath.

"Fuck, you're doing so good baby."

He slips a hand beneath my thigh, spreading me wider. He adds a second finger.

I gasp, my head tipping back.

"Too much?" he asks.

"No," I whisper. "Just... keep going."

"You like this more than you thought, huh?"

His fingers move deeper, stretching me further as he keeps the rhythm slow and controlled.

"That's it, baby," Seth murmurs, voice rough. "Let me stretch you a little more."

He scissors his fingers gently, coaxing my body open. The stretch makes my breath catch and my fingers claw into the sheets.

"You can take more," he says, voice darker now. "You want more, don't you?"

"Yes..." I breathe.

"Good girl."

My hips try to pull away for a second, but his hand settles firmly on my hip, holding me in place.

His mouth returns to my back, kissing the small of it before his tongue drags along the dip of my spine. I whimper, legs spreading wider as his fingers push deeper.

"Fuck," he groans. "I could come just from watching you take my fingers."

He bends over me, chest brushing my back as his fingers keep working me open.

"I'm gonna fuck this tight little asshole so good," he whispers near my ear.

My whole body hums, heat coiling low in my stomach as his fingers move steadily inside me.

Then he pulls them out.

I whimper at the loss, my body clenching like it wants them back.

Behind me I hear the slick sound of lube again and his low groan.

"Fuck, you're so wet."

His weight shifts behind me. The blunt head of his cock presses against my ass.

"You ready, baby?"

I nod hard, my face still buried in the pillow. "Yes."

He takes his time lining up, one hand on my hip. I feel the head of his cock press against me. His other hand moves down to spread me open just a little more.

Then he pushes in.

Just the tip.

The hot and sharp stretch hits instantly, enough to steal the breath from my lungs. My mouth opens but no sound comes out for a second.

"Fuck," he hisses behind me.

I cry out, a mix of shock and moan, the kind of sound that comes from my throat without warning. The burn is real, but underneath it is pleasure.

I exhale shakily. "Holy shit."

He pauses right away. One hand slides up my back in a slow drag. He bends over me, lips brushing the back of my neck.

"Breathe, baby."

I obey. I let myself exhale, let my muscles unlock one at a time. The tension drops out of my shoulders, and I focus on the weight of his hand on my back.

He eases in deeper.

Another inch, then another.

My thighs start to shake. My hands claw into the sheets, pillow bunched beneath my face. My body resists, then gives, then pulls tight again as he sinks deeper, every slow push forcing me to adjust. I moan loud into the pillow, overwhelmed and clenching hard around him.

He holds still, forehead pressed to my shoulder. "I'm not gonna last if you keep gripping me like this," he growls. "Tell me if you want me to stop."

"I'll kill you if you stop," I murmur.

He laughs and pushes in again.

I gasp when he bottoms out, hips flush to my ass, cock buried to the base inside me. The fullness is intense. A stretch that borders on too much, but not enough to make me stop. My body shakes from the shock of it, from the pressure and the heat and the way I can feel him in places I didn't know could feel anything.

"Still okay?"

"Yeah," I whisper. "Much better."

He smiles against my skin.

"Good. Because I'm not stopping."

He stays buried in me, holding still, giving my body time to adjust. His hand drags up my spine again, while his other hand shifts to grip the side of my thigh, keeping me open, keeping me grounded in sensation.

"You're so tight," he murmurs.

I swallow hard, every nerve lit up, every muscle on edge in the best way.

"Your dick is fucking huge," I breathe.

He grins. "Yeah. And you're taking me so fucking well."

Then he pulls back.

Just a few inches. Then pushes in again.

I moan loud as his hips roll forward again, not thrusting yet, just grinding deeper, working me open in controlled rhythm. The movement sends shockwaves through my core. My body clenches hard around him with every slow push, every tiny withdrawal.

My face stays pressed to the pillow. My hips rock back to meet him without thinking.

His hand slides to my ass again, gripping tight. His cock moves in slow strokes, building pressure with every motion, never pulling out too far, never pushing too fast.

I can't speak. I can only feel.

And I don't want him to stop.

"Oh my god...Se—Seth."

The words drag out of me in a broken moan I barely recognize as my own.

He chuckles, dark, low, rough in my ear, and does it again, rocking into me. Just enough to make me shudder and clench around him, my body trying to hold him there.

My arms give out and my chest hits the bed as he rocks into me again, this time with more weight behind it. Every roll of his hips pushes the stretch a little further. Every inch of him feels like it is carving a new space inside me.

The burn is still there, but it isn't pain anymore, it is pressure. Fullness. Power.

And I need more of it.

I hadn't known I could feel this full. I hadn't known I could crave it this much. That it would make me feel untouchable. Desired. Worshipped. Claimed.

His rhythm stays controlled, but I can feel the shift. He is starting to lose control. I hear it in the ragged catch of his breath, feel it in the way his hands dig into my hips like he needs to mark me from the inside out. His voice drops to a growl, filthy words muttered hot against my skin between thrusts.

"Fuck, baby. This ass looks so good taking my dick."

His hand tangles in my hair, yanking my head back just enough to bare my throat. He kisses it, then again, then bites hard. The sharp sting makes me moan loud into the mattress.

His thrusts stay deep, but the rhythm sharpens. The slaps of his hips against my ass fill the room, echoing through the wet sound of our bodies meeting over and over again.

He growls low and shifts his angle slightly, just enough to slam into a new spot inside me.

I gasp. My whole body jolts. I nearly come from that alone.

"Seth—"

"I know, baby," he rasps, voice strained.

His hand snakes down between my legs, moving fast. Two fingers find my clit, slick, throbbing, desperate for friction—and the second he touches it, I almost come off the bed.

"Fuck," I choke, body convulsing, hips jerking back against him.

"That's it," he thrusts harder now. "Come for me while I'm in your ass."

My breath shatters. My back arches. I am right there, right on the edge, about to break all over him.

"You gonna come for me, baby?" he grinds into me, hitting that spot again and again.

"Yes," I whimper. "Please—don't stop—"

I don't even realize I am shaking until he feels it.

His hand tightens on my hip.

He doesn't speed up. He doesn't break pace. He just keeps moving, burying himself to the hilt every time. The stretch still makes my legs shake, but now the burn bleeds into something hotter. Something addictive. Every time he pulls back, it feels like he is taking a piece of me with him. Every push forward fills me again, stuffs me full, until I can't tell where the ache ends and the pleasure starts.

"Fuck, Brooke," he murmurs. "I'm gonna fill your ass with so much cum."

The words wreck me. I whimper, I can't help it, because I can't form words anymore. Just sounds.

He stays deep, rocking into me with slow, perfect control. His cock drags along every hypersensitive inch, making my spine arch involuntarily. Then his fingers find my clit again.

I break.

My hips lift, chasing his touch, chasing him, needing more. I'm past the point of pretending I have control. I'm begging without words, my body speaking for me, and he groans like the sound of it physically hurts him.

The pressure in my core coils fast. It builds in seconds and detonates without warning.

My whole body locks up. Muscles tense, my back arches, and I scream into the pillow as the orgasm rips through me. My thighs tremble uncontrollably. The release comes in waves, each stronger than the last, drawn out by his deep, grinding thrusts that never let up.

"Fuck, Brooke," he groans.

I feel his whole body tense.

His breath catches in his throat, and his hands grip my hips tighter, hauling me against him as he shoves in hard, balls pressed flush to my ass. His cock twitches deep inside me and then he comes.

The first pulse is thick and hot. I feel it fill me in heavy spurts, warm liquid coating my insides as he empties himself completely. His cum spills around the tight seal of my ass clenching him, leaking out, sliding between my cheeks. He holds still, buried deep, his body shaking against mine with every pulse.

He doesn't pull out. Just stays there, his cock still throbbing, his jaw clenched against my shoulder, raw groans escaping his throat like he can't hold them back anymore.

The room goes quiet except for the sound of our breathing, both of us wrecked in the best possible way.

His forehead rests between my shoulder blades, skin damp with sweat. Then he wraps his arms around me, chest flush to my back, holding me like he isn't ready to let go.

"You okay?" he asks.

I nod, still catching my breath. "Yeah. I'm...good."

He kisses my shoulder, softer this time, his mouth lingering against my skin. "You did so good."

He stays inside me, not even trying to pull back. He lets my body relax around him naturally. Lets the tension bleed out of my limbs until all that is left is the warmth of him surrounding me, inside and out.

My muscles still tremble.

His lips brush the top of my shoulder again. "Now I've been in every part of you."

I let out a breathy laugh, turning my head just enough to catch his eyes. "Yeah...you're the only one who has."

He smiles down at me, lazy, proud, completely undone, and I see it in his face. The satisfaction. The hunger.

I never let anyone in like this.

Not even close.

Not until him.

Chapter 41
Brooke

Krueger moves ahead of me without making a sound.

He doesn't trot the way most dogs do. His body moves through the woods with a low, predatory rhythm, shoulders rolling beneath thick fur while his head stays low and his ears turn toward every small shift in the trees around us.

The forest behind the safe house is still damp from the night before. Pine needles cling to the ground in dark patches, and the cold morning air fills my lungs with the scent of wet soil and pine resin.

Seth and Beau are back at the clearing near the bunker fueling the cars before we move out. Beau had already completed a full perimeter sweep this morning, and nothing has tripped the wires and nothing has moved on the cameras.

Still, I bring my gun.

And the knife.

Some habits never go away just because someone tells you it is safe.

Krueger drifts ahead of me along the narrow trail, occasionally glancing back over his shoulder to make sure I am still following. The leash hangs loose in my hand, mostly unnecessary.

I need the air.

Training has been brutal the last few days and my body feels every bit of it. My shoulders ache from hours of drills and my thighs burn from running hills and sparring sessions that push me harder than the last.

My ass is still sore from yesterday.

But it was absolutely worth it.

I stretch my hips a little while I walk, trying to loosen the stiffness in my lower back and legs. The soreness is not enough to slow me down, but it is enough to remind me exactly how much Seth pushed my body the night before.

Krueger pauses a few yards ahead and looks back at me.

"Yeah, yeah," I murmur. "I'm coming."

When he circles back toward me, I crouch and brush my hand along the thick fur at his neck. His tail sweeps slowly through the leaves and pine needles.

For a few minutes the woods feel quiet.

Almost normal.

Then a rifle shot cracks through the trees.

The trunk behind me explodes in a violent burst of bark. Wood splinters tear past my shoulder and scatter into my hair.

I drop flat against the ground.

Krueger growls and sprints. One second he stands beside me and the next he vanishes into the trees, his body cutting silently through the underbrush as he disappears toward the ridge above the trail.

Another shot tears through the air.

Dirt erupts inches from my hand.

I roll behind the thick base of an oak and press my back against the trunk. My heart slams hard enough that my vision pulses with it. I force myself to inhale slowly and release the breath with control before panic can turn into something useless.

A third shot cracks through the woods.

The bark above my head bursts apart and splinters rain down across my shoulder.

I drop to my stomach and begin crawling, dragging myself through damp soil and pine needles while keeping thick tree trunks between me and the slope above. My elbows burn as they scrape across roots and gravel. My palms slip through mud while branches brush across my back.

Another shot rings out.

The sound drives straight through my chest.

I flatten myself against the ground and listen.

Then I see it.

A faint flicker through the branches higher up the ridge. A glass lens catches light for half a second, followed by the subtle shift of dark fabric pressed against the bark of a tree.

I draw my gun and lean just far enough around the trunk to fire once toward the glint.

I'm forcing him to move.

The shot cracks through the woods and shreds a cluster of leaves above his position. A branch snaps somewhere deeper in the canopy.

Silence hangs in the air for a moment.

Then his rifle answers.

The bullet slams through the trunk inches from my hip.

He is close.

The shooter stays patient.

So do I.

I crawl again, moving from one tree to another while keeping my body tight to the earth. My breathing slows as the fear in my chest hardens into something colder and more focused.

If he wants me, he will have to come lower.

The woods go quiet.

Too quiet.

Then a scream tears through the trees.

The sound is short and wet and cut off halfway through.

Something heavy crashes through branches higher up the ridge.

A deep, savage snarl follows.

Krueger.

My head snaps up toward the slope.

Leaves shake violently while branches crack under the weight of struggling bodies. A man's voice breaks into a choking sound that hovers somewhere between a scream and a gargle.

Then the snarling grows vicious.

I scramble to my feet.

Seth appears between two pines at the same moment, moving fast toward the ridge. Beau comes from the opposite direction with his gun already raised.

"Stay behind me," Seth says.

I climb the slope with them.

We find them about twenty yards up the ridge.

The sniper lies on his back against a fallen log with his rifle twisted beside him in the leaves.

Krueger stands over him.

The dog's jaws are buried deep in the man's throat.

Blood sprays across the forest floor as Krueger wrenches his head sideways and tears deeper into the wound. The sound of tearing flesh carries through the trees.

The man's hands claw weakly at Krueger's neck while his body kicks against the ground in fading panic. His arms tremble without enough strength to push the dog away.

Blood pumps through the shredded opening in his throat in thick bursts while he tries to drag air into ruined lungs.

Krueger only releases him when Seth gives a sharp command.

"Krueger."

The dog steps back reluctantly while his chest heaves and dark blood drips from his muzzle.

The sniper tries to breathe.

The sound comes out as a wet bubbling choke.

His eyes are wide with panic while blood fills his throat and floods into his lungs.

I step closer and look down at him.

His throat has been torn open into mangled muscle and shredded skin. Every attempt to inhale forces more blood through the ruined tissue while his chest struggles uselessly for air.

He is drowning in it.

Beau steps beside me and raises his pistol.

The shot cracks once.

The man's head snaps sideways and his body goes still.

Silence settles over the forest again.

Krueger stands beside the body with his shoulders tense and his blue eyes locked on the corpse as though he will gladly tear into it again if Seth allows it.

Seth nudges the fallen rifle with his boot.

“Rafe,” he mutters.

Beau crouches beside the body and searches the sniper’s vest while Seth pulls a phone from the man’s pocket and unlocks it using the man’s thumb.

One message thread is still open.

Confirm the kill. Footage preferred.

The contact photo fills the top corner of the screen.

Kristie.

She has sent someone into the woods to kill me.

Krueger leans against my leg, solid and breathing hard with lingering aggression.

I straighten.

“I'm not giving this bitch another chance to try and kill me.”

Seth looks at me instead of the body.

“She wants to take me out,” I continue. “I’ll get her first.”

Somewhere far from this clearing Kristie Talbert is probably shaking hands and promising safety to voters who have no idea she has just tried to have me executed in the woods.

She won't get another attempt.

“Got something,” Travis says without looking up.

Seth crosses the room and stops beside him while Beau leans against the wall near the weapons locker with his arms folded.

I move to Travis’s other side and watch as he pulls up the data feed.

Names and face matches scroll across the screen along with heat signatures, IP locations, and drone footage from the hotel that is still circulating across different servers.

Then the killer pool appears.

A list of aliases. Status updates. Bounty notes.

"Jesus," I mutter.

Five names remain on the screen.

Five hunters still in play.

Travis taps the header.

"She upped the price. Five million each."

My stomach drops.

"Ten million if they get both of you and stream it live. No editing. No delay. Just full-on torture porn for the highest bidder."

Brooke Sinclair and Seth Kincaid.

Dead or dying on camera.

Seth lets out a slow breath through his nose.

"She's getting impatient."

"She's getting desperate," Beau says. "The more we kill, the more expensive it gets. She is hemorrhaging money trying to make an example."

"The problem is that they aren't coming for revenge." My eyes stay on the screen. "These new ones don't give a fuck about what happened at the manor. They are here for the payout."

I stare at the screen and the numbers blinking beside each name.

"None of these people care about us," I scoff. "They don't know us. We're just names with dollar signs."

"Yeah," Travis says. "That's the point."

"They aren't the real threat," I say. "They are tools. Hired hands. They aren't the ones writing checks."

Silence stretches across the room.

Then Seth speaks.

"You're talking about Kristie."

I nod.

"She is the one who wants us dead. If we take her out then the rest of the board loses the person pulling the strings."

Seth's jaw tightens.

"She is a high-profile mayor in California. We aren't talking about picking off some nobody in a back alley."

"I know. That is why we don't make a scene."

Seth nods once.

"Go on."

"She's a public figure," I say. "People watch her every move. If she dies suddenly everyone looks closer."

"So what is the alternative?" Seth asks.

"She doesn't die publicly...She just disappears."

Seth leans back slightly and studies me.

"There is no crime scene," I continue. "There is no body to find and no evidence pointing anywhere. One day she is campaigning and smiling for cameras. The next day she's gone."

Beau folds his arms.

"That kind of disappearance makes headlines."

"For a while," I say. "There will be search parties and press conferences. Then the story fades and she becomes a missing person with no answers and no closure."

Seth keeps his eyes on mine.

"Killing her would eliminate any bounty for us."

"Yes," I add. "No one can retaliate properly. The people funding her will start looking over their shoulders instead of pointing fingers at us."

He considers that before giving a small nod.

"That, I can work with."

I lean back slightly and smile.

"I have some ideas."

Chapter 42

Seth

We had to leave the Oregon safe house.

The shooter is enough of a warning. He probably watched Brooke for hours before he took the shot. Kristie sent someone to finish what the manor failed to do.

We pack within the hour.

The drive north is not quiet.

Traffic clogs the highway for miles. Headlights stretch ahead of us in a slow line while rain streaks across the windshield. Travis grips the steering wheel like it is trying to escape him. His voice fills the car the entire time.

"I'm just saying this is insane. Someone tried to shoot her. That is a real thing that happened today. A sniper. A professional sniper."

"Travis," Beau says.

"What?"

"Shut the hell up."

Travis lasts about thirty seconds before he starts again.

"I'm just processing the situation out loud. Some people need to talk through trauma."

"Do it quieter," Beau mutters.

In the back seat, Brooke is the calmest person in the car.

Considering it is her umpteenth near death experience in the last few months, she handles it better than anyone.

Luna sits curled in her lap the entire drive. The cat tucks herself into the crook of Brooke's arm. Brooke strokes her absentmindedly until her movements slow.

Eventually her head tips sideways and comes to rest against my shoulder. She falls asleep like that.

Her breathing turns slow and steady while the highway lights pass over us in quiet flashes. One of her hands stays curled loosely around Luna's back while the other rests against my arm.

Krueger lies across the rear cargo area behind us, watching the road with alert eyes.

The Washington house is different.

It is not a shack. It is not a bunker. It is nothing that screams hiding.

From the outside, it looks like a private mountain home owned by someone with money and good taste. The structure sits back from the road among tall pines that block most of the surrounding view. A timber frame supports the high roofline. A thick stone foundation wraps the lower level. Wide windows face the forest but reflect the darkness outside, making it impossible to see inside from a distance. A wraparound deck circles the front of the house.

Nothing about it suggests danger. Nothing about it suggests the kind of people who are about to live there.

Security hides in the bones of the place. Reinforced doors disguised as custom woodwork. Cameras embedded into the beams. The driveway curves just enough that anyone coming up it will be visible for a long time before they reach the house.

You have to want to find this place. You have to know where to look.

It will do.

What stays with me is how natural it looks with Brooke in it.

I watch her move through the house like she belongs there. Luna in her arms. Krueger pacing at her side. She checks the back door. Tests the window latches. Moves down the hall and clears each room without being told.

She doesn't hesitate, doesn't look over her shoulder waiting to be hurt. She looks like someone who has decided she won't be caught off guard again.

I am proud of her for that. I just don't want it to be all she ever has.

I know how to live in blood. I know how to plan violence and carry it out. I know how to end someone and make sure there is nothing left that can be traced back.

What I don't know is how to give someone a quiet life without contaminating it with what I am.

And I want to.

Brooke Sinclair deserves a life that is not paid for in blood.

She deserves mornings that don't start with surveillance reports. Nights that don't end with body counts.

I don't know how to build peace.

I only know how to defend it.

So I stand there and watch her set Luna down on the couch, watch Krueger settle near her feet, and decide that whatever it takes, I'm going to make sure she doesn't have to keep doing this forever.

We move toward the dining room in silence.

Beau stretches out on the couch, boots crossed at the ankles. Krueger sprawls across the floor beside him. Travis paces near the window, phone in hand, thumb moving fast.

Then he stops.

His posture shifts.

"She's coming to Washington."

That is all he has to say.

The next name on our list is handed to us without effort.

Kristie Talbert.

Travis turns the phone toward us.

Kristie smiles back from the screen, standing beside a red and blue campaign bus. The slogan beneath her name makes my jaw tighten.

The National Coalition for Safer Communities.

"She's stopping in Spokane," Travis says. "Press event. Touring sites affected by vigilante violence. She's using it for votes."

"She's campaigning to be the governor of California," Brooke raises a brow. "Why Washington?"

"Image rehab," Travis answers. "Multi-state healing initiative. She's softening the ground before someone starts digging into her finances."

"Then we end the campaign." Brooke doesn't blink. "We'll just make her disappear."

I wait, because Brooke has the rest of the plan ready.

"While she's on the campaign trail, she's going to have to get her makeup done in a trailer or something. We take her from there. We take her out to a lake. We dump her body."

I watch her as she says it. Her voice stays calm and calculated.

Travis swallows. "You want a location with water and no people."

Brooke turns to him. "Can you pull up where exactly the event is going to be?"

Travis moves his thumb fast again. The map loads. He zooms, scrolls, and tilts the screen like he is reading the terrain with his eyes.

"There's a lake a couple of miles out from there," Travis says. "It looks secluded on the map. There's a narrow access road and not much around it."

Brooke's mouth twitches. "Perfect."

We put the plan into motion.

The lot the next morning is full of people who look busy and tired. Lighting crews adjust panels. Sound guys argue about levels. Staff walk fast with clipboards and radios. Everyone has a lanyard and a purpose.

We get lucky.

Kristie wants to look accessible, relatable. Boots-on-the-ground leadership. So instead of booking a suite at some five-star hotel, she opts to stay on the campaign bus overnight between stops.

Optics over safety.

It makes her easier to kill.

By the time we return to the crowd, Kristie is already at the microphone, and her voice is climbing.

The crowd is small but loud. Local press, bored college students, a few diehard supporters sweating through their red-white-and-blue polos. The kind of crowd that makes campaign managers nervous. Too small for someone running a national redemption tour. Too few bodies to drown out the wrong question.

Kristie Talbert stands on a makeshift stage under a banner with her name printed in bold serif and bullshit. Stars and Stripes with slogans that mean nothing. Her handlers have polished everything. Flags on both sides, lighting soft, podium centered like it gives her authority.

She looks exactly like the kind of woman who has spent decades in country clubs and closed-door fundraisers. Auburn hair styled into a smooth, shoulder-length blowout that barely shifts in the wind. Pearls at her throat. Navy sheath dress cut modest and expensive. Mid-fifties, polished, the kind of matriarch voters find reassuring. Her makeup is flawless. Her smile is not.

It stretches too tight across her teeth. Her jaw works slightly before each answer. She looks composed, but it's effort. I can see the strain even from here.

I stand next to Brooke under the shadow of a tree, baseball cap low, sunglasses on. Beau leans against the trunk beside us, arms crossed, chewing gum.

"I've seen school assemblies with better turnout," Beau mutters.

Brooke doesn't look away from the stage. "Don't jinx it."

Kristie takes the mic again, voice syrupy with practiced charm. "Thank you all for coming out," she says. "Despite the media's appetite for distortion, I'm grateful for the voters who still value facts over fiction."

"Here we fucking go," I say under my breath.

The press asks a few planted questions. Softballs. "What inspired your national safety initiative?"

"How do you respond to recent criticisms?"

She swats them away with rehearsed empathy and vague language about unity, reform, and restoring trust.

Then a younger reporter steps forward. He looks nervous. He clutches his mic too tight.

"Mayor Talbert," he says, voice unsteady, "do you still stand by your statements that your son was innocent, given the allegations from Brooke Sinclair and the evidence recovered in Stratford?"

Kristie's smile freezes for half a second before settling back into place.

"There was never sufficient evidence linking Nicholas to any murders," she says evenly.

The reporter swallows. "With respect, ma'am, several witnesses placed him at multiple crime scenes, including the death of his high school girlfriend, and—"

"Allegations," she cuts in. "Not convictions."

The crowd shifts.

"But he's deceased," the reporter presses. "Which makes a trial impossible."

She steps away from the podium, heels striking hard against the stage.

"My son cannot defend himself because he is dead," she says, her voice tightening. "That does not make him guilty."

She sweeps her gaze across the crowd, then leans back into the microphone.

"What we do have is a confirmed mass casualty event at the Everspring Hotel. A national manhunt for Seth Kincaid. Federal agencies are pursuing him across state lines for what can only be described as a massacre."

Murmurs ripple outward.

She points toward the press row.

"That vindicates my son. The real killer has already been identified."

Brooke doesn't move.

"Seth Kincaid is a wanted man," Kristie continues. "Law enforcement nationwide is actively searching for him in connection to the Everspring killings. That is fact."

She lets it settle.

"And Brooke Sinclair," she adds, tone sharpening, "is either dead or actively aiding him. If she is alive, she is not a victim. She is an accomplice."

A current of tension runs through the crowd.

"We know who was behind the tragedy at Stratford," Kristie says. "And yet you continue to question my son."

Her composure thins.

"My son, Nicholas Talbert was a good man."

Brooke shifts beside me, her knuckles tightening around the strap of her bag.

"He volunteered in community outreach," Kristie presses. "He mentored younger students. He had plans to pursue public service. The so-called evidence surfaced after he could no longer speak for himself."

The reporter tries again. "What about the footage from Stratford that showed him entering the property the night—"

"Context matters," she snaps. "Selective editing does not create truth."

Her voice rises.

"You want a villain? You have one. His name is Seth Kincaid."

I lean closer to Brooke. "She just put a target on both of us again."

Kristie steps forward, abandoning the script entirely.

"My son was targeted," she adds. "Smeared. Used as a scapegoat by people who needed a monster."

Phones lift higher.

"I will not allow his name to be dragged through the mud," she states. "He cannot defend himself but I will."

Her aide moves toward her, whispering urgently.

"Seth Kincaid will be found," Kristie says, her voice going cold. "And anyone who aided him will answer for it."

The aide tries again, but she pulls away.

She steps down from the stage without another glance at the podium. Her heels strike the stairs too hard. The microphone squeals behind her.

The crowd erupts with overlapping questions.

She ignores them.

Then she storms off the stage and heads straight for the trailer, heels striking hard, posture rigid with fury.

Travis's voice comes through Brooke's phone. "Makeup trailer is on the east side of the lot. She's probably moving there."

Brooke looks at me once. "Now."

We move with the flow of staff crossing the lot. We don't rush. We walk like we have jobs to do and deadlines to meet.

The makeup trailer sits behind two equipment vans. A small set of steps leads to the door. Light glows inside. A makeup artist stands near the entrance, talking fast, trying to soothe Kristie's rage.

Kristie's shoulders are stiff. Her face is tight. Her eyes are bright with anger.

The door shuts behind them.

Beau peels off toward the vehicles and disappears into shadow.

I stay a few steps back from Brooke, watching the lot and listening for anyone moving our direction.

Brooke climbs the steps and opens the door without waiting.

I follow.

The makeup artist turns, startled. “Who are you?”

Brooke closes the door, steps in, and puts a needle in the woman’s neck before she can raise her voice. The makeup artist makes a short sound, tries to turn, then sags. Brooke catches her and lowers her behind a chair.

Kristie spins toward Brooke, eyes wide. “What the fuck?”

Brooke moves fast, grabs her wrist, and puts the needle in her before she can scream.

Kristie tries anyway. The sound comes out warped. Her knees buckle. Brooke holds her up until her body stops cooperating, then sets her into the chair.

Kristie’s head tips to the side. Her eyes fight to stay open and lose.

I scan the trailer, then the small back hallway. “Clear,” I say.

We wrap her in a dark jacket from the rack and secure her arms. We use the back exit Travis flagged. Beau meets us behind the trailer with the vehicle ready.

We load her and leave the lot before anyone realizes her trailer has gone quiet.

The lake road is narrow and empty. Trees press close. The farther we drive, the less the world exists.

When Kristie wakes, her eyes open to dark water and the low hum of an engine. She tries to sit up. She can’t.

Her hands are zip tied behind her back. Duct tape covers her mouth. More duct tape wraps her arms, legs, and ankles tight enough to make movement pointless. Her body jerks. Her breathing hitches against the tape. Her eyes go wide, then furious, then terrified again.

Brooke leans closer so Kristie can see her face.

"Hi Kristie."

Kristie's muffled scream turns frantic.

Beau arranged the boat ahead of time. It is waiting for us when we arrive. Once we're aboard, he guides it father out, carrying us away from the shore until the lights on land shrink into small points in the distance. The water is dark. The air is cold enough to sting my face. The engine hum stays low, and the lake stays quiet, which makes every sound feel louder.

Kristie's eyes dart between us, then to the water, then back to us again.

I sit on the bench with my elbows on my knees, watching her without empathy. She earned this.

Brooke sits beside me, posture calm, gun resting on her thigh, eyes fixed on Kristie's face. She looks the way she looks right before she pulls a trigger, quiet and focused.

Beau cuts the engine when we reach the middle.

The boat rocks gently. The sound of water against the hull turns into a slow rhythm.

Brooke leans forward.

"Did you enjoy watching me drown, Kristie?" Brooke asks. "Because I'm about to enjoy watching you."

Kristie makes a muffled sound through the tape and tries to scoot back, but the tape on her legs turns it into a pathetic scrape.

Brooke keeps her eyes on her. "When we toss you into this lake, you'll sink fast. Even if the tape loosens, the zip ties won't. You won't be able to swim up. You won't be able to paddle. You're going to sink and die."

Kristie's eyes go wider. Her breathing goes frantic under the tape. I watch her throat move as she tries to swallow around panic.

Brooke tilts her head slightly. "Do you know what it feels like to drown, Kristie?"

Kristie screams behind the tape.

Brooke's mouth tightens. "It hurts. It's not peaceful. Your chest burns. Your lungs fight. Your brain screams at you to breathe, and you can't. You think you're about to explode from the inside."

She pauses, and her gaze doesn't soften.

"But I woke up after," Brooke continues. "I had to live with it. I had to live with the pain in my lungs. I had to live with the memory. You don't get that part."

Brooke's eyes flick down to the water, then back to Kristie. "You're going to die at the bottom of this lake, and nobody's going to find you."

Kristie's eyes squeeze shut for a second, then open again.

Brooke's voice drops lower. "Silver lining, you're going to see your son real soon."

Kristie jerks her head, a furious denial that turns into fear again immediately.

"When you get there," Brooke smiles, "tell him I sent you."

I shift forward and plant my boots, watching Kristie's eyes as they lock on mine.

I drag Kristie toward the edge of the boat. The hull rocks as her weight shifts. Beau steadies the boat with his stance, keeping us balanced.

Kristie twists and tries to kick, but her ankles are locked. The tape around her legs holds. Her breathing turns frantic and ragged under the duct tape. She makes a sound that is half sob and half scream.

Brooke steps closer and rests her hand on Kristie's cheek, almost gentle.

Kristie's eyes lock onto Brooke's face. The fear in them is raw. Brooke doesn't look away.

Beau glances at me. "Now."

Brooke pushes Kristie over the edge.

She drops into the lake with a heavy splash.

The water swallows her quickly. Her body bobs once, then starts to go under. The tape and the zip ties do exactly what Brooke says they'll do. Kristie's head disappears, and the water closes over her.

The lake goes quiet again.

Brooke stands at the edge of the boat, staring at the dark surface. Her shoulders are still. Her hands don't shake.

I watch the water for any sign of her. I don't see anything. I don't hear anything except the small lap of water against the boat.

Beau starts the engine.

The boat rumbles back to life, and we begin to move.

Brooke stays looking at the spot where Kristie went under, like she is making sure she doesn't come back up.

I step closer to Brooke and slide my hand into hers and squeeze once.

Beau steers us back to shore.

I don't feel anything for Kristie. I only feel for Brooke. I feel rage for what they did to her. Now I feel the simple satisfaction of seeing her get revenge.

Chapter 43
Seth

Takeout containers crowd the table, grease bleeding through the bottoms and soy sauce staining the wood. Beer bottles sweat onto coasters nobody bothers to use. The fireplace crackles low, filling the quiet spaces between conversations.

Open cartons sit between us, lo mein tangled in glossy noodles, fried rice packed tight with egg and green onion, half-crushed dumplings leaking oil into the corners, and a container of orange chicken picked apart between bites.

Steam curls out of the carton in my hands while I watch it drift into the air. For a moment I thought about the lake. About dark water closing over Kristie's head while her lungs fight for air.

The missing Kristie Talbert is already trending online.

Beau lifts his beer with a grin.

"Welp, her political career went under pretty quickly."

Travis barks out a laugh. "You are absolutely going to hell."

Beau takes a drink without breaking eye contact. "Have you seen the current state of the world? We're already there."

Brooke leans back in her chair, tucking one leg beneath her. Luna is sprawled across her lap, front paws planted against Brooke's stomach as she stretches her head toward the open carton. Brooke keeps one hand loosely around Luna, absentmindedly holding her back from shoving her face into noodles. She smiles, and it's not the polite version she uses in public. It's the real one.

Travis raises his bottle next. "They're really gonna need campaign reform."

"Shut up," Brooke laughs, shifting her carton slightly out of Luna's reach as a black paw reaches for a dangling noodle.

Luna tries again, stretching higher, claws catching lightly in Brooke's sweater, and Brooke nudges her back without even looking down.

Beau reaches across the table and steals the last dumpling from the carton without asking.

"Hey," Travis snaps.

"Too slow," Beau replies.

"You always eat the last piece."

Beau shrugs and pops it into his mouth. "You're squatting in my house."

"I mean, we are all wanted men at this point, so my options are limited."

Brooke rolls her eyes as Luna shifts in her lap and tries to climb onto the table. Brooke slides her forearm gently across the cat's chest and guides her back before she can reach the cartons.

"You two are exhausting," she laughs.

"And yet," Travis says, pointing his chopsticks at her, "you keep us around."

She shrugs and adjusts Luna so the cat stretches comfortably along her thigh. "Well you two are pretty useful."

Beau smirks at Travis. "Hey, he came in clutch. He shot a guy in the foot so we could find you."

Brooke looks at Travis. "Aww, really, Trav?"

Travis lifts his hands defensively. "It was partially an accident, but I definitely needed to shoot him so we could track you down."

I lean back in my chair, a beer hanging loose in my hand.

My eyes settle on Brooke again.

When she catches me staring, she lifts her chin slightly. "What?"

"You good?"

She holds my gaze a second longer than usual. Luna stretches toward the carton again, and Brooke lifts it higher without breaking eye contact.

"Yeah."

"Really?" I ask.

Her jaw shifts as she swallows. "I'm not spiraling, Seth."

"That wasn't the question."

"I'm fine," she says again, quieter this time, scratching lightly behind Luna's ear to distract her. "I'm not turning into a homicidal maniac."

I study her face for signs I recognize from myself. The distant look. The hunger. The tilt toward something darker.

"I can live like this," I tell her. "I don't want you to."

Her expression changes, but she doesn't flinch. "I'm not doing this because of you. I'm doing it because they don't get to keep breathing after what they did."

I understand her.

I kill because it feels necessary. She kills because it feels justified.

Still, I lean forward slightly, lowering my voice. "If you ever feel it pulling you somewhere you don't recognize, you tell me."

A faint smile touches her mouth as Luna finally gives up and settles fully against her stomach. "You'll be the first to know."

"Good."

Travis clears his throat in an exaggerated way. "Are we done with the emotional check-in, or are we doing a healing circle next?"

I flip him off.

Brooke keeps her eyes on me for another second before looking away, stroking Luna's back while the cat purrs.

Travis wipes his mouth with the back of his hand. "Actually I want to know something. How did you two psychos meet?"

Brooke shifts in her chair, curiosity replacing whatever tension had been there.

I glance at Beau.

He leans back and stretches his arms behind his head. "You want the sanitized version or the one that got us flagged."

"Flagged version," Travis says.

Beau nods once.

"2019," he begins. "We were attached to a joint task force overseas. Officially we were providing perimeter security for contractor operations. Unofficially we were babysitting people who had better lawyers than morals."

His tone stays even, almost bored.

"Most of the job was routine," Beau continues. "Convoys. Warehouses. Equipment moving through places where nobody outside the military was supposed to be paying attention. Contractors handled a lot of the infrastructure. They had their own security teams and their own paperwork."

I lean back in my chair and stare into the fire.

"At first it looked normal," I say. "Then people started disappearing."

The room stays quiet while he speaks.

"Laborers," Beau continues. "Drivers. Villagers who lived too close to the wrong road. Migrant workers moving through the area. Nobody important enough to trigger an investigation."

I can still see the place when I close my eyes.

Dust blowing through broken fences. Diesel generators humming all night.

"We started noticing trucks moving at odd hours," I add. "Vehicles that never showed up on official manifests."

Beau nods.

"They were moving people," he says. "Civilians. Some local. Some from other countries. None of them there voluntarily."

Brooke's hand stills slightly against Luna's back.

"They had a compound," Beau continues. "Concrete building on the edge of a supply route. Guards posted outside. Contractors with government badges and private security patches."

The fire cracks quietly behind us.

"There was a basement," I say. "They kept them chained down there."

Beau gives a short nod.

"We reported it, command told us to stand down," he adds. "They said the contractors were operating under separate authority and the situation was not our jurisdiction."

I watch the fire for a moment before speaking again.

"We went back anyway."

Beau rubs a hand over his jaw.

"It was supposed to be reconnaissance. We planned to document what was happening and pull the civilians out quietly."

His mouth twitches slightly.

"That part went according to plan."

"We cleared the basement first," I add. "Cut the chains. Got the civilians outside the compound."

The fire pops behind me.

"Once they were clear," he says calmly, "we dealt with the rest of the building."

Beau leans forward with his elbows on his knees.

"There were eleven contractors on site. They were armed. They tried to fight."

"They all died," I lift my gaze from the fire. "We made an example."

Beau nods once.

"We gutted two of them and hung the bodies from the outer gate."

"Another one lost his head," I smirk. "We put it on a post facing the road."

"The rest we left where they fell," Beau continues. "Anyone passing through the area would see exactly what happened there."

"By morning the whole region knew that compound was gone," I lean back again. "Command was not pleased."

Beau gives a quiet laugh.

"Internal review. Pattern of insubordination. Excessive force. Extreme conduct."

"They removed us from the task force," I add.

Beau shrugs slightly.

"They preferred to handle the problem quietly," he says. "Administrative separation. No medals. No prison."

He lifts his bottle slightly.

"Now we freelance. I'm an assassin."

His eyes flick to me.

"And he's a serial killer."

I look at Brooke while the room processes the story.

She doesn't look shocked or afraid. She looks like she understands exactly why we did it.

Travis exhales slowly and drags a hand down his face. "Crazy how two killers have more morality than people running governments."

Beau lifts his beer, "Exactly."

Brooke reaches across the table with her free hand and brushes her fingers against my knuckles. I turn my hand and catch hers.

After we finish eating, Beau goes to do his routine perimeter checks with Krueger.

Brooke stacks the empty containers without being asked, rinses her hands at the sink, and says, "I'm going to go take a shower."

She walks upstairs barefoot. The water starts running a minute later.

Travis and I stay at the table.

He pulls his laptop closer and flips it open, blue light catching in his glasses. The house feels quieter without Beau's dry commentary filling it.

"So you want the good news or the weird news?" Travis asks.

"Start with good."

He types for a few seconds, eyes scanning fast.

"The pool's gone."

"Completely?"

"Domains scrubbed. Admin account deactivated." He glances up. "No active bounties."

I lean back in my chair.

"That was fast."

"Well Kristie's dead," he continues. "No one's getting paid now."

"Or someone higher up shut it down."

He hesitates. "That's the weird part."

I look at him.

"It didn't collapse," he adds. "It closed. Clean. Like someone flipped a master switch."

"Grant or Elliot"

"Probably."

Travis clears his throat.

"Is Brooke okay?"

"She's okay."

He doesn't look convinced.

"I mean," he says carefully, "she went through so much. In that place. For a week. And she lost the—"

He stops himself.

"I'm sorry."

"It's fine."

"It just seems... normal," he murmurs. "For her. The sniper. Kristie. None of it shakes her. She wasn't even that scared in the woods."

I let out a quiet breath through my nose.

"No," I reply. "It's not normal."

He looks up.

"Brooke's not normal," I add. "I'm not either."

The fire cracks softly.

"After you go through enough shit," I continue, "your body runs out of ways to react. Fear doesn't hit the same."

He nods.

"She's good. And I'm always going to make sure she's good."

That isn't bravado. It's a fact.

Travis studies me for a second, then gives a small nod.

His expression shifts a second later, like something has just clicked in his head.

"Wait right here," he says. "I've got something."

He crosses the room and digs through his bag. I watch him move things aside until he finally pulls something small out of the bottom.

He walks back over and holds it out to me.

"You left this at the hotel," Travis says. "I figured you probably needed it."

I look down at what is sitting in his palm.

The ring.

The engagement ring I was supposed to give Brooke.

For a second the room around me fades and I'm back in the hotel ballroom, blood on the floor, everything falling apart before I ever get the chance to ask her.

I take it carefully from his hand.

"How did you get this?" I ask.

Travis rubs the back of his neck.

"Well, after I finally got out of that freezer, I was running around the hotel trying to find you and Brooke," he explains. "I ended up stumbling into the room where they took your body."

He pauses for a second.

"And that's when I saw the ring."

I close my hand around the ring and slip it into my pocket. I'll give it to Brooke when the time is right.

"Thank you Trav," I nod. "For everything."

He blinks. "Whoa."

"What?"

"I get a thank you now." He leans back in his chair. "And a nickname?"

I narrow my eyes at him.

His grin spreads. "Can I give you one?"

"No."

"Sethy?"

"Don't push it."

He laughs.

I push away from the table and stand. Travis glances up for a second. We exchange a quick nod before I turn and head for the stairs.

Upstairs, the shower has gone quiet. I go to the bedroom.

Brooke is already in bed when I open the door, Luna curled along her ribs.

I reach into my pocket before anything else and pull out the ring.

For a moment I just look at it again.

Then I cross to the dresser and open the top drawer. I move a few things aside and set the ring carefully in the back where it'll stay hidden and safe.

Not yet.

Soon.

I close the drawer and turn back to the bed.

I toe off my boots, strip down, and slide under the covers beside her.

She shifts immediately, fitting herself against my side like she has been waiting for me. I wrap an arm around her waist and pull her closer, pressing my mouth against the curve of her neck.

Her hand finds my chest. My palm settles over her hip. I hold her a little tighter.

One day soon, when the kill list is finished and the world finally stops hunting her, I will take that ring back out of the drawer and ask her to be with me for the rest of our lives.

Chapter 44
Brooke

I'm still in the manor.

The ground presses cold and wet beneath my palms, and the mud glues itself to my skin in heavy streaks. Pine needles cling to my forearms as I struggle to push myself upward. Pain throbs through my shoulder where the crossbow bolt tore through me, and the sensation crawls down my arm in steady electric pulses that make my fingers twitch uncontrollably. Miles lies motionless behind me with his blood soaking into the forest floor, and his body doesn't move or respond.

I try to crawl forward with every ounce of strength I have left, but my legs refuse to cooperate. My arms buckle beneath my weight, and every inch forward feels futile and hopeless.

Asher steps out from between the trees with his crossbow already raised and aimed at my head. Elliot follows with the chainsaw balanced in his hand. The motor roars awake with a jagged snarl that vibrates through the ground and through every bone I have. Sophie moves to his left with her curved blade catching the dim light that filters through the branches. Knox stands behind them with his axe held loosely at his side while he watches me.

They form a half circle around me.

Elliot tilts his head with a slow smile that carries nothing except cruel satisfaction. He lifts the chainsaw, and he lowers the snarling blade toward my face.

I scream as the world shatters open around me.

I lunge upright in bed with my breath tearing through my chest and my hands clawing at the sheets as if the fabric can stop a blade.

Seth reaches me before I can even inhale.

He wraps his arms around my body and pulls me tightly against his chest. One hand cradles the back of my head while the other presses firmly against my spine, holding me together while the nightmare shakes every part of me.

"Hey, breathe," he murmurs into my hair with quiet patience. "Breathe baby. You're here with me, and you're safe."

My heart slams against my ribs with frantic force.

"I was still there," I whisper with shaking breath. "All of them were there, and I couldn't move or fight or breathe."

He tightens his arms around me.

"I got you," he holds me tighter. "You're safe with me."

I let my forehead rest against his chest until the tremors inside my body soften into something manageable.

After a long minute, I pull away from him.

"I need to move."

His eyes search mine with slow concern. "Where?"

"I need to clear my head," I say. "I'm going to the gym."

He studies me for several seconds before he nods. "Alright, I'll stay here."

I press a kiss to his shoulder, slide out of the bed, and dress quickly. My feet move silently down the hallway while the house settles into stillness.

The punching bag waits in the corner of the gym. I wrap my hands slowly and step toward it.

The first punch lands with a deep, hollow thud that echoes through the quiet room. I throw another punch and then another. Each impact sends a sharp spike of pain down my injured shoulder, but the burn only fuels the motion. I keep hitting until sweat collects at the base of my neck and my breath grows loud enough to drown out my thoughts.

I picture Elliot's grin, and my fist slams into the bag. I picture his eyes, and my knuckles sting with the force. I picture the chainsaw, and my breath grows ragged.

He feels like an infection that refuses to leave my mind. Sophie, Grant and John live there too. They lodge themselves inside the darkest corners of my thoughts, and they wait for me whenever I close my eyes. Killing them won't fix this.

I can put a bullet in Elliot's head. I can carve Sophie open. I can watch Grant bleed out on the floor. It won't matter.

They will still be here.

In my sleep. In the dark corners of my head. In the split second before I relax.

They don't just die and disappear. They stick.

And if I am still waking up like this years from now, then in some twisted way, they already won.

I step back from the bag with my chest rising too fast and my hands trembling from adrenaline.

My phone rings with a sharp sound that slices through the room.

I wipe my face with the back of my hand and answer without checking the number.

"Hello, Brooke," a distorted voice says. "Wanna play a game?"

I freeze for a breath and scan the gym, checking each shadow and every corner.

"Cute," I reply. "Are you Jigsaw or are you Ghostface?"

"Neither."

"Seth?"

"Nope."

"Who the fuck is this?"

"You shouldn't be asking who I am," the voice taunts. "You should be asking where I am."

My jaw tightens hard enough that I feel it in my ears. I step into the hallway slowly and my nerves climb fast.

"Bad dream?" the voice asks, and the mocking tone crawls under my skin instantly.

I move toward our bedroom with steady steps. If this turns out to be Seth, he is about to piss me off. I stop in the doorway and look in. The blankets on his side are still raised around him. I stay where I stand because nothing about the room feels right. I reach toward the dresser and grab my knife, letting the weight settle into my palm as my heartbeat picks up.

"Are you planning to ask about my favorite scary movie?" I ask slowly, "or are you planning to try to kill me? Kristie doesn't have money to pay for bounties since she's dead, and you will join her if you choose to fuck with me."

The voice pauses for several seconds.

"I like your fire," the voice says finally, quieter now, almost amused. "Let's see if you can find me, because you're very cold right now."

I step into the hallway with my pulse rising, knife steady in my hand.

"Cold," the voice says.

I turn left first and check the guest room. The bed is empty. The blinds are closed. The closet door sits slightly open. I push it wider with the tip of the knife and find nothing.

"Still cold."

I move down the hall, slower now, listening. I check the bathroom next. The shower curtain is open. There is no one inside.

"Freezing."

My jaw tightens. I step back into the hallway and head toward the stairs.

"Cold."

I move closer to the top of the stairs outside the gym.

"Still cold."

I start down, one step at a time, my hand sliding along the railing as the second floor opens into the main level below. My eyes sweep the space automatically, checking the couch, the windows, and every corner.

"Better," the voice says. "Not by much."

I step off the last stair and cross the living room, passing the long couch and the wide windows that look out toward the dark line of trees. The glass reflects my movement back at me, knife in hand, shoulders tight. The house is quiet, but something about the silence presses against my skin.

"Warmer."

I pause near the kitchen and glance toward the back door, then toward the hallway that leads deeper into the house. My pulse starts to pick up.

I turn toward the back hallway. I reach the hallway and slow my steps, every nerve pulling tight.

"Warm."

I pass the laundry room and find it empty. I check the storage closet and find nothing there.

"Warmer."

I stop in front of the basement door. My fingers tighten slightly around the knife.

"Hot."

I push the door open. The staircase down disappears into shadow. I descend slowly, the steps creaking beneath my weight as the tension thickens with every step. My breathing stays controlled, but my pulse is loud in my ears.

"Burning."

I step off the final stair and onto the basement floor. I flick on the lights, and the room fills with harsh brightness that cuts through every shadow.

The figure stands in the far corner with his tattooed arms crossed over his chest in a posture that shows complete confidence and control. He wears only gray sweatpants that cling low on his hips, exposing the deep line of muscle that frames his abdomen. A faint trail of dark hair runs from his navel downward, disappearing into the waistband of the sweats and drawing my eyes lower before I force them back up.

The black skull mask covers his face entirely, but everything below it is unmistakably Seth.

He looks relaxed and confident and completely aware of the fear he has manipulated inside me.

My breath catches despite the rush of irritation through my chest.

He tilts his head slowly in a gesture that carries wicked amusement. He lifts his phone to his mouth, his voice deep and distorted as it comes through the mask.

"You're on fire."

Chapter 45
Seth

I stay in the corner of the basement while the lights light the room and wipe out every shadow. The mask keeps my breathing even. I need a clear read on her before I put my hands on her.

Brooke stands near the last step with her knife in her hand. Her face is calm. Calm in a way that only comes after the violence starts making sense. Brooke is not surviving anymore. She is not shaking or second-guessing or flinching at the weight of what she has done. She has passed that point. She has learned how to choose violence and live in it. She doesn't carry the kills like guilt. She wears them like armor.

Watching her become that makes me hard as fuck. My cock pushes firmly against the front of my sweats while I study the woman standing in front of me. She looks stronger like this. Like the world has finally stopped trying to break her and she has decided to break it instead.

I press play on my phone.

"Ambrosia" rolls through the speakers.

"Seth—"

"Come here, Brooke. Now."

She walks toward me. She doesn't look away from the mask. She stops right in front of me, close enough for me to hear her breathing and feel the heat pouring off her skin. Her pulse hammers in her neck like it's trying to break free.

I take the knife from her hand and grab the hem of her sports bra. The thin fabric stretches beneath my fingers as her breathing shifts. I slide the blade beneath the band between her breasts and cut straight through the center.

The fabric splits.

Her tits fall free.

Her chest lifts with quick breaths while the cool air tightens her nipples. The sight pulls a heavy pulse through my cock.

I have to stop myself from just grabbing her and bending her over the nearest surface.

I drop the ruined bra and lower the knife to her shorts. I hook the blade under the waistband and drag it through the fabric in one clean line. The shorts fall down her thighs. Her panties slide with them and pool around her ankles.

One second she is standing there in gym clothes. The next second she is standing naked in front of me in the basement, breathing hard, eyes wide, and waiting for my next move.

Her hands hang at her sides. Her fingers curl like she doesn't know where to put them. She doesn't cover her chest. She doesn't close her legs. She doesn't take a single step back. She lets me look at her. Another hard rush of heat moves through my body, and I know I could do anything to her right now, and she would take it because she trusts me.

That kind of trust always does something to me that is difficult to explain to anyone who has not lived inside my head. Most people want safety from the people they love. Brooke gives herself to me knowing exactly what I am capable of, and that level of surrender means everything.

I grab her torn bra from the floor and stretch the fabric into a strip. I lift it toward her face. Her eyes stay on the skull mask up until the moment the cloth covers them. I wrap the strip around her head and tie it firmly at the back.

She sucks in a sharp breath, and I can feel the panic hit for a second before she forces it back down and stays exactly where she is. She stays because she trusts me more than whatever instinct tells her to step away.

My cock is rock hard, and I wrap my hand around myself for a brief second just to keep from losing it right there. I squeeze once, force my breathing back under control, then let go.

I slide the edge of the knife along her hip, the cold steel grazing her skin as I move it slowly up the curve of her waist and over her ribs. When I reach her breast, I let the flat of it pass over her nipple, dragging it lightly until her breath catches and the bud tightens beneath the chill.

I don't take the blade away.

I trace it higher, gliding it up the center of her chest and along the line of her throat, just enough pressure for her to feel it without breaking skin.

My mouth drops to her breast at the same time.

I close over her nipple and suck, slow at first, my tongue pressing and flicking against it as her body reacts. Her breath breaks, chest rising sharply as I pull harder, keeping the rhythm steady while the cold edge of the knife lingers at her neck.

I ease off just enough for the air to hit her nipple, then take it back into my mouth, holding her there while the blade stays pressed lightly to her throat.

Then I lift the blade higher and bring it to her mouth. She sticks out her tongue without me asking and runs it up the length of the metal, tasting it.

She knows that turns me on.

I press the blade between her lips until the handle rests against them. Her chest moves with a small adjustment as she balances the weight.

"Crawl to me, Brooke. Follow my voice."

She drops to her knees slowly. Her palms meet the concrete. Her knees follow. Her whole body trembles from the mix of fear and arousal, and that mix sharpens the dark, possessive edge inside me into something that feels almost dangerous.

I step backward across the floor. I move toward the wall.

Her blindfolded head angles toward my voice while she crawls forward. Her shoulders stay tense but lower slightly as she continues moving.

She trusts that I won't let her run into anything. She trusts that if I hurt her, it will be the kind of hurt she likes, the kind she wants.

"Keep crawling, baby. Come to me."

She follows the sound of my voice on her hands and knees. Warm air moves across the knife handle between her lips as she crawls closer.

Every inch of distance she closes makes my control strain, because the urge to grab her hair and drag her the rest of the way is loud in my head. I force myself to hold back and let her earn it.

My shoulders hit the wall. I plant my feet and wait for her.

"Right here," I say when her fingers finally bump against my toes.

She stops crawling.

Her head tilts upward under the blindfold as if she is trying to look at me.

I reach down and wrap my fingers around the handle of the knife. I pull it slowly from between her teeth. Her lips stay parted for a second after the blade leaves, and her breath catches in that gap like her body wants me to fill it with something else.

I tilt her chin up and take her in, blindfolded, kneeling, naked, with her hands resting on her thighs and trusting me completely in a concrete basement after everything she has survived. The sight hits me hard enough that my cock twitches again inside my sweats from how badly I want her.

"That's my good girl," I murmur, letting her hear every bit of praise in my voice.

Her thighs press together slightly. Her breathing deepens in a way that tells me she understands exactly what that title means between us.

I flip the knife in my hand and drive the blade into the wall beside my hip, forcing it deep through the drywall and into the wooden stud behind it.

The metal sinks in with a heavy crack. The handle juts out near her shoulder.

I reach to the side and pull a length of rope from the hook mounted on the wall beside the tool rack. I left it there earlier when I set up the basement, knowing exactly how I plan to use it.

Brooke doesn't move while I work.

I grab her wrists and tie them behind her back, tightening the rope until her shoulders roll back and her chest pushes forward for me.

Her breathing grows heavier, but she holds her ground and lets me take her there, fear still clinging to her skin while she keeps giving herself to me.

I move behind her and drag her backward by her bound wrists until the handle presses into the base of her spine, forcing her back into a deep arch. Her lips part on a quiet sound that shoots straight through me and tightens every muscle in my body.

I step in front of her again and push my sweats down. My cock is fully hard, and the pressure throbs painfully low in my stomach. Her blindfolded face tilts toward the sound, and her lips open before I touch her.

"Open your mouth."

She obeys immediately and lifts her chin.

I slide my fingers along her jaw and hold it firmly while I lean in closer. I watch her lips part wider, blindfold tight over her eyes.

I gather spit in my mouth and let it fall directly onto her tongue. She makes a small sound from the back of her throat as it lands, but she doesn't pull away.

"Keep it open."

Her tongue stays out, glistening, waiting.

I place my hand behind her head and guide her forward until her lips wrap around the head of my cock. Her tongue presses against me slowly, and the warmth of her mouth steals a breath straight out of my chest. Her jaw relaxes. Her throat works to take more. The blindfold heightens every one of her reactions, and each one hits me hard.

I tighten my grip in her hair and pull upward.

She rises off her knees with a soft sound, her body lifting until her feet find the floor. She stays bent forward, her mouth still wrapped around me as I keep my fist buried in her hair to hold her there.

My other hand slides to the center of her back.

I step closer and guide her backward toward the wall, forcing her to move with me while she stays folded over in front of me.

Her feet shuffle across the floor as her mouth stays locked around me. When her ass brushes the knife handle she gasps.

The vibration runs straight through my cock.

I lean over her. I place both hands on her hips. I spread her ass apart slowly. Her breath shakes. Her body tightens. I push her backward until the handle presses between her cheeks and then slides against her entrance.

Her entire body jolts, and her mouth tightens around my cock.

I watch every inch of her react.

She trusts me fully in this position. She trusts me blind, bound, exposed, and pinned against a knife handle that only moves when I move her.

I adjust my grip on her hips and lower my voice.

"Good girl."

Her body trembles against my hands, and the sound of her breath shakes through the space between us. The knife handle presses against her, but I don't push her onto it yet.

I wait long enough to feel her legs tighten and her hips shift with equal parts fear and desire. That is the line I need. That is the moment that tells me where her mind truly is.

I spread her again, slower this time. Her thighs open wider. Her spine arches harder. Her chest lifts with a sharp inhale that she tries to control. Every reaction comes from trust, not panic.

My cock throbs in her mouth, and I pull back from her slowly, letting her lips release me so she can breathe. She takes air in one quick rush. Her blindfold stays tight, and her head tilts slightly as she waits for my next move.

"Stay exactly where you are," I say. My pulse hits hard enough that I feel it in my jaw.

I place one hand on her hip. I place the other on her lower back. I guide her backward inch by inch until the handle aligns perfectly with her entrance. She feels the shift instantly. Her hips jerk. Her toes curl against the concrete. Her throat releases a strained sound she can't hide.

The moment the tip presses against her, she freezes for one breath.

Her body braces and opens at the same time, and the duality of it nearly breaks my control. Her chest rises in one long inhale. Her thighs loosen enough for me to continue.

I push her back slowly.

The handle stretches her inch by inch, and her entire body reacts with raw, uncontrollable tension. Her breath stutters. Her legs shake. Her hips roll forward slightly, then back again, and she lets out a sound that is part shock and part need.

Her head drops forward. Her bound wrists pull at the rope. Her knees spread wider. Her breath pushes out in a slow, uneven stream.

I move her another inch.

Her mouth opens around a silent gasp. Her spine arches so sharply that her shoulder blades press against my chest. Her thighs tremble without rhythm. Her body clenches around the intrusion like she doesn't know whether to retreat or take more.

I guide her hips.

She takes the next inch with a low groan that makes me harder. My cock aches with the kind of pressure that nearly forces my hips forward. I push her farther until the handle fills her completely.

She shakes in my hands.

I lean over her and press one hand between her shoulder blades to keep her steady.

"That's it baby. You can take it."

Her hips roll forward slightly, instinctively trying to adjust to the stretch.

I move her forward and back onto the handle once more.

She gasps. Her entire body jolts. Her voice finally breaks through her restraint.

"Seth," she breathes. Her tone carries need, fear, trust, and surrender all layered in one.

I hold her steady and lean down until my chest presses lightly against her back.

She exhales sharply and pushes back against the handle.

She takes the handle fully, and her entire body shakes against my hands. The sound of her breath vibrates through her chest in fast, uneven waves.

"You like that, don't you baby?"

She inhales sharply and nods.

I keep one hand on her hip to hold her in place. Her skin feels hot beneath my palm. Her knees press wider, trying to adjust to the pressure and stretch. The blindfold forces every sensation to hit her without warning, and she absorbs all of it because she trusts me to guide her through it.

I grip the back of her head firmly. Her blindfolded face tilts upward. Her breathing breaks on a soft gasp.

"Open."

She obeys immediately. Her spine arches. Her bound wrists tighten behind her back. Her knees spread wider to balance herself on the handle buried inside her.

I bring my cock to her lips again. Her tongue touches the head, and her breath warms the sensitive skin.

I push forward slowly until her mouth wraps around me again.

She moans the moment I slide in.

The vibration travels through my dick and settles deep in my hips. Her throat works to take more of me, and each movement of her mouth rocks her body against the handle buried inside her. The blindfold keeps her locked inside the sensation, and every small shift of her hips sends another tight pulse through her body. Her breathing grows uneven. Her muscles tighten around the intrusion while her mouth continues working over me.

I hold her head with both hands and control the pace. She follows every movement with a hungry, desperate focus that makes my control strain. Her trust in this position, blind and bound and balanced on a knife handle, feeds directly into the pressure building inside me.

Her mouth tightens around me. Her hips roll again.

Her mouth moves over my cock in slow pulls while her body trembles around the handle buried inside her. Each tremor runs up her spine and into my hands. Every sound that escapes her pushes heat deeper into my stomach and tightens my grip in her hair.

Her hips rock again, harder this time. Her breath breaks into a sharp gasp around me.

I watch the reaction travel through her body. Her thighs tighten, back arches deeper. Her mouth clenches around me as the pressure inside her builds too fast for her to control.

Her orgasm hits her without warning.

She jolts violently against the handle. A broken cry slips from her throat around my cock while her cunt convulses around the intrusion. The movement forces her hips to grind down harder, and I watch her slick arousal spread along the matte black handle where it disappears between her thighs.

She shakes through the release, her legs struggling to hold her upright while the waves tear through her. Her mouth tightens again around me while her body pulses uncontrollably around the handle.

I groan at the sight.

Her slick coats the metal where it enters her, glistening under the basement lights each time her hips jerk through the aftershocks.

Her mouth continues moving over me while the last of the tremors run through her body.

I pull out of her mouth slowly.

Her breath rushes across my skin while she tries to steady herself. Her lips stay parted, chest lifts and falls quickly while her thighs tremble around the handle still buried inside her.

Her body can't stop shaking. Her feet slide slightly against the concrete floor while she tries to keep her balance. Watching her struggle through the aftershocks sends another surge of heat through my body that forces my jaw to tighten.

I wrap my hand around her hip again.

I lift her slowly off the handle, inch by inch. Her legs shake harder as the handle slides free from her body. Her breathing turns ragged and uneven.

When the handle slips completely free, she nearly collapses forward. I catch her immediately with both arms and hold her against my chest.

Her breath hits my throat in fast, uneven bursts.

"You got me so hard baby." My voice shakes from the effort it takes to keep control of myself.

I keep one arm around her while my other hand slides down to her ass. My palm lands against her skin in a sharp smack that echoes off the basement walls.

Her body jolts.

A soft cry slips from her throat as the impact ripples through her hips.

I rub the heat back into the spot slowly with my hand, feeling the warmth bloom beneath my palm. Then I spank her again, harder this time.

Her back arches immediately.

The sound of the second smack rings through the room, followed by a broken breath that escapes her lips.

I slide my hand lower.

My fingers move between her legs.

The moment they touch her I feel the slick heat coating her skin. She is soaked, her arousal still spreading slowly down her inner thighs from the orgasm that just tore through her on the handle.

"Fuck," I breathe under my breath.

I press my fingers against her entrance.

She gasps the second I push inside.

Her body tightens around them immediately, still sensitive and pulsing. I slide my fingers deeper, feeling the way her walls flutter around them while she tries to catch her breath.

"You're so fucking wet."

I move my fingers slowly inside her, feeling the heat and slick tension still lingering there. Her hips rock slightly against my hand.

Her blindfolded head tilts back against my shoulder while her breathing comes out in shaky bursts.

I curl my fingers inside her once.

Her entire body reacts instantly. Her legs tremble harder, and a soft sound breaks from her throat as her hips push forward against my hand.

I let out a low breath against her ear.

I pull my fingers out slowly, watching the slick shine stretch between them before it breaks. Then I bring my hand back to her ass and spank her once more.

The impact snaps her hips forward again.

I turn her around and guide her to the workbench. Her chest presses down. Her hips lift easily when I pull them up. Her knees part as if her body has been waiting for this exact position.

I step closer, and my cock slides between her legs, coated in the heat still dripping down her thighs. Her breath hitches. Her hips push back with a small, desperate movement. I push into her slowly.

Her body stretches around me. Her cunt tightens instantly, and the force of that first squeeze almost makes me come right there. I have fucked her more times than I can count, and it still feels like the first time every time. That split-second stretch. That impossible pull. That perfect moment when I bottom out and feel every muscle inside her flutter.

I push deeper. She is tight. Fuck, she is always tight. No matter how many times I have been inside her, she never gets used to the size of me. Her body fights to take it, then molds around me. She grips me like a vice, her cunt milking every inch, squeezing down. I can feel her still clenching from the last orgasm, nerves twitching around me, drawing me deeper, tighter. It feels fucking perfect. Every time with her does.

Her knees buckle, and I hold her hips to keep her steady. Her body clenches around me again, harder than the first time, and the pressure forces heat up my spine.

I set the rhythm, driving into her in controlled, hard thrusts that force her chest harder into the workbench with every movement. Her bound wrists pull against the rope behind her back as her body struggles to keep up, her thighs trembling while her breath breaks into low, uneven gasps that fill the room.

I watch myself slide in and out of her.

Every thrust disappears into her heat, then drags back out slow enough for me to see the way her body stretches around me before pulling me back in again. Her slick coats me, catching the light each time I move, and the sight of it locks my focus in place. I adjust my angle just enough to watch it more clearly, to see exactly how she takes me, how her body opens and then clenches down again.

She starts to lose control of it.

I feel the shift the second it happens.

Her body tightens around me in quick, building pulses, each one sharper than the last. Her hips push back against me without thought, chasing the pressure, trying to meet every thrust before I even give it to her. Her breath hitches and stutters, breaking apart as the tension climbs too fast for her to control.

"Ohhh fuck—Seth," she gasps, her voice raw, strained, pulled straight out of her.

I tighten my grip on her hips and drive into her harder, deeper, holding nothing back now. The impact forces her forward against the bench, then pulls her back into me again. Her knees spread wider to keep her balance, her body opening under the pressure as she takes everything I give her.

I keep watching it.

The way I fill her. The way she tightens every time I bottom out. The way her body keeps reacting like it can't decide whether to hold me there or take more. The sight drags something darker through me, something that pushes my control right to the edge.

I feel her start to unravel around me.

"Come, baby." My voice low despite the heat building in my chest. "Come on my dick like you came on that knife."

That is all it takes.

Her entire body seizes, then breaks.

The orgasm hits her hard and fast, ripping through her in a violent wave that travels from her core through every part of her body. Her cunt clenches down around me in sharp, wet spasms that steal the breath from my lungs. She cries out against the workbench, her voice breaking as the force of it pulls her apart in my hands.

Her thighs shake uncontrollably. Her back arches as far as the rope allows. Every muscle in her body tightens and releases in rapid, uncontrollable bursts while she rides through it, unable to stop the way her body keeps reacting.

I hold her there through it and feel every pulse, every clench, every second of her coming undone around me.

I follow right after her.

I thrust deep and hold myself inside her as heat shoots through me in hard, uncontrollable pulses. My hips jerk against her until every last pulse empties. My breath hits the back of her neck in uneven bursts. My hands stay locked on her hips while I try to steady myself.

She stays against the workbench with her chest rising fast and her thighs trembling. Her blindfold holds every reaction in place, and her body tells me exactly how much this moment changes her.

I pull her upright slowly and keep myself inside her until her breathing returns to normal.

She leans against me.

I hold her there and feel the last of my control settle back into place. When I pull out, I don't rush. I watch myself slide free, watch my cum spill out of her slowly, trailing down her inner thigh.

The tension in her shoulders softens beneath my hands. When I feel her body finally settle, I untie her wrists. I reach up and untie the blindfold. The fabric slips away, and her eyes blink against the light before locking onto mine. I pull the skull mask off and drop it onto the workbench beside us.

She turns toward me slowly, as if she is still adjusting to being able to see again. Then her hands come up and she pulls my face down into a kiss that lands harder than anything that has happened in the room before it. Her mouth moves against mine with a fierce urgency.

She is not hiding anymore. Not her violence. Not her need. And fuck, it turns me on even more. Seeing her stop hoping someone will save her and start hunting the ones who try to break her, my final girl is not just surviving anymore.

She is fucking lethal.

And watching her step fully into that version of herself while choosing me in the middle of it sends a dark, burning heat through my chest that only she can pull out of me.

I cup her jaw and kiss her back until she finally pulls away, her breath shaking against my lips.

"How did you get down here so fast?" she asks. "I swear I saw you in the bed."

"I propped pillows under the covers," I reply. "You really fell for that?"

She stares at me, eyes narrowing. "Seriously?"

"Yeah, baby, you are going to have to start checking bodies," I sigh. "I told you."

"Always check the bodies." We say it in unison, the words hitting at the same time, a broken echo of the rule I drilled into her.

"That is how Amber got you with that CPR dummy," I remind her.

She grimaces. "Yeah, please don't remind me."

Her gaze shifts back to me, suspicion creeping into her voice.

"Wait. How did you know where I was?"

I lift my phone slightly.

"There are cameras around the house. All I have to do is check them from my phone."

Her brows pull together. "You've been watching me on cameras?"

"I'm always watching you, Brooke."

A slow smile spreads across her face. She shakes her head and gives my chest a light shove. "Creep."

Her eyes drop to the floor, taking in the shredded remains of her sports bra and the torn waistband of her shorts. She lets out a rough breath that carries amusement and disbelief.

"Well, you destroyed my clothes," she says. "How am I supposed to get upstairs like this?"

I shrug. "Wear my sweats. I will carry you up there. Travis and Beau are probably asleep, but even if they aren't, I will block the view."

She narrows her eyes. "Then what are you going to wear?"

"Nothing," I glance down, then rock my hips, letting my cock swing slightly as if proving the point. "I don't care if they see my dick. It's impressive."

She laughs hard at that, the kind of laugh that loosens her shoulders and settles her back into her body. She steps into my sweats and pulls them on. They hang low on her hips and swallow her legs.

I slide my arms under her and lift her with no effort. She wraps her arms around my neck, and I shift her so her breasts stay covered pressed against my chest. Her head drops against my shoulder as I carry her to the stairs. She feels warm, soft, and calm. She feels like herself again.

I hold her closer as we move through the quiet house.

"The only person who should be in your dreams is me," I murmur by her ear.

She presses her mouth to my throat in a slow kiss that says everything she doesn't answer out loud.

I carry her upstairs to bed.

And she sleeps through the night.

Chapter 46
Brooke

We found the party before we ever set foot back in Oregon.

Travis worked through the Collective databases, routing everything through a VPN chain so long it made my head hurt. He pulled vendor contracts, encrypted invites, and travel manifests disguised as charity coordination.

Elliot is hosting a private event in Portland.

Grant is on the confirmed list.

So is Sophie.

Knox is dead. Kristie is dead. They know that. They know someone has taken them out. If they have any survival instinct at all, they should assume we are coming.

"They're either setting a trap," Travis explains over the call, "or they're so arrogant they think you won't come back here after everything that happened."

Seth leaned back in his seat. "Well they're fucking wrong."

The three of us drive down.

Beau handles the wheel for most of the trip while Seth and I sit in the back. The highway cuts through miles of forest and wet asphalt, the sky hanging low and gray above the road. Travis stayed behind at the Washington house with Luna and Krueger so someone could keep eyes on the network and warn us if anything shifts.

"You three get caught," Travis says, "I will absolutely deny knowing you."

"You will absolutely go down as our accomplice," Beau replies.

"Yeah," Travis admits. "So don't get caught."

The closer we get to Oregon, the tighter my chest feels. This is where everything starts unraveling. The manor. The victims. The bodies.

If Elliot is arrogant enough to host a party after all of that, he either believes we are dead or believes he is untouchable.

Neither of those things is true.

We roll into the outskirts of Portland just after dark. We check into a seedy motel on the edge of town. The carpet feels damp under my shoes. The air smells like old cigarettes and cheap cleaner.

Nobody comes looking for us here. That's the only comforting part.

The next day we locate Sophie.

That afternoon, Sophie walks out of the hotel with a driver escorting her to the curb. A black SUV idles at the front entrance, polished and spotless, sitting like a prop in front of the revolving doors.

She wears oversized sunglasses and walks down the steps with the slow confidence of someone who believes nothing bad can ever happen to her.

Every part of that ease raises the tension in my chest.

The SUV pulls away from the hotel and drifts toward the boutique district, stopping in front of a shop with dark windows and a gold logo on the glass. The store looks high-end, with tailored mannequins in the front and frosted glass hiding the back rooms.

We sit in the car across the street and watch the entrance through the windshield. Traffic moves around us, horns sound here and there, and an occasional siren passes in the distance that has nothing to do with us.

She spends almost forty minutes inside the boutique. I picture her in front of a bright mirror, turning side to side, smoothing the fabric down over her hips, maybe laughing with a stylist, acting like she is not a sadistic murderous bitch.

Our car idles between a delivery van and a dark sedan, the engine humming low enough to blend with the background noise of passing traffic. Sophie's SUV remains parked directly outside the boutique entrance in the alleyway.

The engine runs as the driver opens the door and steps out, lifting his phone to check the screen before bringing it to his ear.

"She's been inside forever," I say.

Seth glances toward the boutique entrance. "She'll come out soon."

I shift my focus back to the driver.

He moves a few feet away from the SUV, and his jacket falls open as he walks. The gun at his side is easy to spot now. An inside-the-waistband holster sits on his right hip.

Seth sees it at the same time I do.

The driver paces along the curb with a cigarette in one hand and his phone in the other, drifting farther down the sidewalk as he scrolls. He pauses every few steps to type, then keeps walking without once looking back at the vehicle.

From the back seat, Beau finally speaks.

"What's in the cooler?"

Seth lets out a quiet breath that almost passes for a laugh.

"A gift," he says. "For Sophie."

Beau looks at the cooler and smirks.

Seth shifts his attention to the SUV across the street. "It's time."

I nod.

We both step out before the driver even thinks to turn around. Seth crosses the street with calm confidence, blending into the flow of pedestrians. I head in the opposite direction along the sidewalk, then circle back behind the parked SUV. I slip behind the SUV and press the release beneath the rear hatch. The trunk pops open with a soft click. I lift it just enough to slide inside and lower it quietly behind me. I shift across the cargo space and lower myself flat against the floor behind the folded seats.

The passenger door opens.

Seth slides into the seat before the driver reaches the door.

The driver climbs in, still distracted by whatever is on his phone. He shuts the door and tosses the device onto the center console before finally turning his head.

"What the f—"

Seth moves before the sentence finishes.

The knife drives forward beneath the man's ribs.

The driver's eyes widen as the blade punches into him. Air bursts from his lungs in a wet gasp. His hand drops toward the holster at his hip.

Seth twists the knife deeper.

The man's shoulders jerk as pain tears through him. His fingers brush the grip of the gun but never close around it.

Seth rips the blade free and drives it into him again with brutal force.

Blood spreads across the front of the man's shirt and soaks into the seat. His mouth opens twice as if he means to shout. Only a choking sound comes out.

Seth grabs the back of his collar and forces him forward against the steering wheel.

The driver slumps there with his forehead resting just above the horn.

From the trunk I watch Seth wipe the blade against the man's sleeve before sliding the knife back beneath his jacket.

Then he shifts the body slightly so it leans naturally toward the wheel, like a driver bent forward to check something on the dashboard.

I stay perfectly still in the cargo space and watch the boutique entrance through the narrow strip of glass behind me.

Twenty minutes later Sophie steps outside.

Even from this distance I feel my chest tighten when I see her.

Her dark hair hangs loose around her shoulders and a black coat wraps tightly around her waist. Sunglasses rest on top of her head as she steps onto the sidewalk.

She looks relaxed and comfortable. That's about to fucking end.

She pauses near the entrance while a clerk hands her a white shopping bag. They speak briefly. Sophie smiles.

The sight of that smile makes my jaw tighten.

Seth watches her through the side mirror.

She turns and walks down the sidewalk toward the SUV without scanning her surroundings. Her heels strike the pavement in steady, confident steps. She opens the rear door and climbs inside.

For a moment she notices nothing.

She places the shopping bag beside her and adjusts the sleeve of her coat.

Then she looks up.

Her eyes move toward the front of the vehicle.

The driver's body still leans forward over the steering wheel. Blood slides slowly down the side of his neck and onto the console.

Her body freezes.

Seth turns in the seat and looks directly at her.

Recognition strikes her immediately.

Her hand flies toward the door handle.

Seth presses the central lock button and the mechanism clicks loudly through the SUV.

She yanks it again.

Panic spreads across her face.

"What the fuck—"

She twists toward the opposite door.

Locked.

Her breathing begins to speed up.

Then she hears my voice behind her.

"Miss me, Sophie?"

She turns just as I pull the plastic bag tight over her head.

Her reaction is immediate. Her hands fly upward as her body jerks violently against the seat. Her heels slam against the floor while she twists beneath my grip.

The plastic tightens over her face every time she tries to inhale. Her fingers claw at the bag as panic surges through her.

I brace my knee into the seat behind her back and hold the plastic firmly in place.

"Surprise, bitch. I bet you thought you'd seen the last of me."

She fights harder.

Her elbow smashes against the door panel while her nails scrape across my wrists.

Each breath sucks the plastic tighter against her mouth.

Seth reaches forward and shoves the driver's seat lever down. The seat drops back hard as he grabs the man by the collar and hauls his body across the console, forcing the weight of him into the backseat beside Sophie. Blood smears across the leather as the corpse collapses against the door.

Seth slides behind the steering wheel, adjusts the seat forward, and starts the engine. The SUV pulls smoothly away from the curb and disappears into traffic. A few cars back, Beau falls in behind us.

No one outside notices anything.

Inside the vehicle, Sophie's movements begin to weaken. Her hands keep clawing at the plastic but the strength behind them fades quickly. Sophie's body sags forward.

I keep the bag tight for several more seconds. Her fingers slip from my wrists and her head drops against the seat. I drive the needle into her neck and press the sedative in. Her body goes limp almost immediately.

I loosen my grip and pull the plastic away from her face.

Sophie collapses sideways across the seat, unconscious. The boutique shopping bag has fallen to the floor and several pieces of clothing spill halfway out.

Seth glances at us through the rearview mirror.

"Is she out?"

"Yes."

He nods once and turns onto the main road.

In the back seat, Sophie's chest rises slowly with each breath. I lean back and watch her.

This time she isn't escaping her karma.

We bring Sophie back to the motel once the sedative drags her under completely. Her head slumps against the seatbelt, mouth slack, eyes rolled half-open in that empty, drugged way.

The dog crate sits in the middle of the bedroom floor, metal bars dull under the yellow light, hinges rusted near the base.

Seth carries her in first. Her limbs hang loose, dead weight in his arms, her head lolling against his shoulder. He sets her down on the bed and steps back while I check her pulse and watch her eyes for any sign of awareness.

We drag the crate into the bathroom and wedge it beside the tub. The thing is old and ugly, but the latch holds firm when I test it.

Seth lifts her again and eases her inside the crate. Her body folds awkwardly, but he forces her knees up and shoulders down until she fits, spine bent, cheek pressed against the steel floor. I grab her wrists and guide them through the front bars, one at a time, until both arms stick out past the metal.

Her hands dangle in the air, fingers limp and palms up.

I wrap zip ties around each wrist and cinch them tight to the bars. The plastic digs into her skin, pinning her bones against cold metal so she has nowhere to move once she wakes up. I test the restraints by pulling her hands toward me. The bars don't give. Her arms stay locked in place.

I go to the sink and pull open the drawer where the motel keeps its repair tools. A small hammer sits inside, the metal head worn and stained, the handle scuffed from use.

I take it and walk back.

She is still out.

Her wrists hang through the bars of the crate, zip ties cinched tight, leaving them exposed with nowhere to go.

I crouch beside her and take a second to look at her right wrist. It looks fragile. Too fragile for everything she has done. I adjust my grip on the hammer and line it up carefully over the joint.

I bring it down.

The impact lands with a dull, cracking sound. Her wrist collapses sideways against the bar, bending at an angle it is not meant to bend. The joint gives under the force, bone shifting beneath the skin.

She comes awake screaming.

Her body jerks violently inside the crate, shoulders slamming into the sides as her legs kick against the floor. Her eyes snap open, spit gathering at the corner of her mouth as the sound tears out of her.

She tries to yank her right arm back through the bars. The zip tie holds.

The motion only twists the broken joint further. The skin around the wrist swells fast and mottles deep, and the hand hangs limp, fingers spasming and curling.

"What the fuck?!" she screams, voice cracking. "WHAT THE FUCK?!"

I ignore her. I shift my attention to her left wrist.

That hand still moves, fingers clawing at the air, nails scraping against the metal like she can find a grip where none exists.

"Stop," she yells. "Stop, Brooke. Listen to me. You need me alive. I'll call off Elliot. I'll—"

I raise the hammer again, this time over her left wrist.

Her eyes lock on the motion. Terror finally replaces that smug arrogance.

"Brooke, wait, please!" she shouts. "You want Elliot, remember. You want him more than me. Use me. Use my access. Use my—"

I bring the hammer down.

The second impact sounds worse, because she feels every millisecond of it. Bone cracks under the blow, and her left wrist snaps sideways against the bar, matching the ruined angle of the right. The skin puffs up in an instant, veins standing out, the hand twisting as nerves fire.

Her scream goes higher, shredding her voice.

She tries to curl into herself, but the crate gives her nowhere to go. Her shoulders heave. Her fingers twitch and claw at nothing. Both hands now hang broken outside the bars, destroyed and useless.

I watch her fight against the restraints, watch realization hit her through the pain.

Those hands held me under water. Now they will never hold anything again.

Sophie curls inside on her side, wrists zip-tied and pulled through the bars, ankles bound, hair a mess around her face. Both wrists hang outside the crate, twisted at angles, and she screams every time the broken bones shift against the metal. She still manages to look smug through the tears and spit.

"You fucking bitch, you psycho bitch!" she cries, voice hoarse and cracking. "You think this changes anything. You're completely fucked, Brooke. Elliot will check in. He knows my schedule. He'll realize I'm gone, and he'll come for me."

I lean against the doorframe and cross my arms, watching her test the bars with her shoulder.

"Nobody's gonna come for you," I say. "You belong to us now, Sophie."

Her eyes flick from me to Seth, who leans against the sink with his arms folded. He watches her like he is waiting for something worth reacting to.

"You really think you're safe now," she scoffs. "Huh, Brooke?"

I say nothing.

She turns her attention to Seth and smiles. "Seth, you should've seen her at the manor. Did she tell you everything? Did she tell you how she begged for Elliot's cock? Your precious little Brooke offered her pussy to him. She said she wanted to please him."

Seth's gaze slides to me for a second.

We already went through this. I told him exactly what happened in that room, how I planned to use Elliot's ego and his body to get close enough for a knife or a distraction. I told him I was willing to make him believe anything if it meant getting out alive.

I hold Seth's eyes and don't look away.

He pulls a cigarette from the pack in his pocket and places it between his lips. He lights it, takes a long drag, and then walks closer to the crate. Sophie tries to shift back, but the space is too tight. Seth exhales smoke directly through the bars into her face. She coughs once and glares up at him.

"You're gonna need to try harder, you stupid bitch," he says, voice calm and bored. "I already know exactly what happened."

Sophie's nostrils flare.

Seth leans a little closer. "I'm going to make sure you and Elliot feel every single thing you put her through, and more. You wanted a show at that manor. You're getting one now."

Sophie stares at him with pure hatred. Her lips curl back over her teeth.

She spits toward him, aiming for his face. The spit lands near his boot instead, flecking the floor at his feet.

"That is why your fucking bastard baby didn't survive."

Hatred rolls through me in one clean, vicious thought, and every part of me agrees she deserves to die screaming in that cage. Every instinct in my body tells me to draw my gun and put a bullet through her skull, to erase her voice and everything she has ever done. I keep my hand away from the weapon and force myself to calm down, because killing her now will waste what I want from her and what we still plan to do to Elliot.

I step forward before I really think about it. Metal scrapes across the tile as I grab the side of the crate and drag it toward the tub. The weight strains my arms, and the sound scrapes through the bathroom.

"Lift it," I say to Seth.

He stubs the cigarette out on the cracked sink edge, sets the butt aside, and steps in beside me. He hooks his hands under the bottom of the crate and lifts it easily. Sophie yelps as the crate jolts up.

He sets the crate down inside the tub. The metal leaves marks on the porcelain.

Sophie's breathing picks up.

"What are you doing?" she demands. Her voice has lost a small layer of control. "Brooke, I'm sorry."

I reach for the faucet and turn the handle.

The pipes rattle before water rushes from the spout, clear at first, then slightly discolored from the old system. It splashes against the tub floor and around the bottom of the crate.

Sophie jerks away from it as far as the cramped space allows.

"Brooke," she snaps. "I'm sorry, okay. Please, I only did those things because they wanted me to."

I watch the water level climb slowly around the base of the crate.

"There's nobody else at this motel," I say. "You can scream as much as you want. Nobody will hear you. Nobody will come for you."

She presses her back against the rear bars, trying to lift her knees.

Seth leans against the wall near the door, arms folded again, eyes steady on her.

"Hope you can hold your breath," he chuckles quietly.

Her eyes fly to him again. "If you leave me here, Elliot will find me."

"Elliot will have his hands full later," Seth says. "He'll have enough to worry about when we arrive."

The water reaches her calves.

Sophie shifts again, trying to keep her feet under her. The crate doesn't give her much room. Her shoulder knocks against the bars, and the metal rattles.

"You can't do this," she says, voice climbing. "You're reckless if you think you can walk into that party and walk out again. Grant will be there. Security will be everywhere. You'll get killed before you reach the door."

"That sounds like planning advice," Seth nods. "I'll keep that in mind."

The water reaches her knees.

She tries to lift them higher and presses against the top of the crate, but there is too little space. Her movements grow smaller as she realizes each shift makes less difference.

Sweat gathers along her hairline.

"Brooke, listen to me," she shouts, focusing on me again. "You want revenge. I understand that. I understand wanting him dead. Elliot deserves every single thing that is coming. You don't have to kill me for that."

I step closer to the tub and look down at her.

"I don't want revenge, Sophie. I want you to suffer. I want you dead."

She tries to push her body up to keep her head higher. The motion only lasts a few seconds each time.

Her breathing turns shallow and fast.

"Brooke please. I'll drown if you keep doing this," she pleads.

I raise an eyebrow. "You tried to drown me first."

Her mouth opens, then shuts again.

The water climbs to her waist.

She bends her knees tighter, pressing her back harder against the bars, trying to keep her chest above the surface. Her wrists stay tied. Her ankles stay bound. Her movements grow jerky.

"Please," she begs finally, voice cracking. "Brooke, think about this. You're a good person. I'm sorry."

I watch her eyes, not the water.

"You'll never touch anyone again," I smile. "You'll never hurt anyone again."

Her jaw clenches, and she swallows hard.

The water reaches her ribs. Her breathing hitches every time the surface rises higher.

Seth checks his watch casually. "We shouldn't be late. It sends the wrong message at these events."

The water keeps rising. It reaches the base of her chest, then the top of it. She strains upward, trying to gain another inch.

"Turn it off!" she yells. "Turn it off, Brooke. You made your point. You win. Turn the water off!"

Her voice cracks on the last word.

I let it run a few seconds longer, watching the line near her chin.

Then I turn the handle and shut it off.

The tub is nearly filled. The water reaches almost to the top of the crate. Her knees press against the metal ceiling. Her neck strains upward to give her nose room.

She pants, each breath shallow and quick.

Her nose hovers barely above the surface. Each slight movement sends ripples across the water, touching her lips.

Her eyes are huge now.

I crouch so she can see my face clearly. Her gaze locks on mine.

"We're going to go get Elliot at his party," I say. "We're going to handle him, and then we're going to come back for you."

Her throat works as she swallows.

"If you hold still, you'll keep breathing long enough for us to finish," I add. "If you panic, you'll speed everything up. The choice is up to you."

Seth opens the bathroom door and steps out into the main room.

I stand up and follow him, glancing once more at the crate in the tub. Sophie's chin trembles as she fights to keep her nose above the line.

I flip the bathroom light off and close the door.

Seth walks toward the bed where our clothes are laid out for the party. He picks up his shirt and looks over at me.

"Time to crash a party."

Chapter 47
Seth

Brooke stands in front of the mirror while she changes, and the red halter dress slides into place. It fits her a little too well, the fabric clinging to every curve. She is really testing every string of restraint I have left by wearing that while we are on a kill mission. The sight of it pulls up the memory of that other dress she wore before.

Almost two years ago. A crowded club with loud music and cheap liquor. Brooke stared at me while she danced with some idiot.

I couldn't remember his name now. I honestly didn't give a fuck.

I killed him not long after that. The timing was unfortunate for him, and his judgment was worse. You danced with the wrong woman once and suddenly your life expectancy dropped to zero.

The dress still irritates me a little when I see it again. That memory never quite fades. At least this time she is walking in with me, not grinding on some asshole's dick.

She pulls the wig on carefully, adjusting it until it sits just right. The hair is a deep chocolate brown, cut with bangs that soften her face and shift her features enough to make her unrecognizable.

I lean against the dresser and watch her make small adjustments in the mirror. The disguise works.

"You good?"

She nods once. "I think so."

I step in behind her, close enough that my chest brushes her back. Her eyes stay on mine in the mirror as I slide my hand beneath the hem of her dress.

"Tell me if this gets distracting."

She lifts her chin a fraction. "It already is."

My fingers trace the back of her calf and move higher, following the line of her leg until the silk gathers under my knuckles. The dress rides up as I guide my hand along her thigh, my thumb pressing into warm skin before I reach the holster strapped tight against her. I check the buckle first, then the strap, testing the tension. My palm lingers, heat bleeding into me, and I adjust the angle with care.

"You tighten this yourself?"

"Yes," she says as her body reacts.

I slide my thumb along the inside of her thigh and tug the strap once more, slower this time. "You did fine, I just want it perfect."

"Of course you do," she says.

I lean in closer, my mouth near her ear. "If you have to draw, it needs to be clear and clean. No fumbling."

"I won't."

I guide my hand higher for a final check, just enough to feel the tension in her muscles, just enough to make my pulse spike. Then I withdraw, forcing distance back into the room even though my body protests.

"Same rules," I meet her eyes in the mirror. "You stay close. You don't wander. If anything feels wrong, you look at me."

She turns her head and faces me fully, confident beneath the heat. "I always do."

I lift another car from the airport garage without anyone noticing, which says more about money than security. It is a dark graphite Mercedes S Class, understated in the way only truly expensive cars are. Quiet enough that you can forget how dangerous it really is.

Before I even turn the key, I check it inch by inch. I pull panels, run my hands along the seams, check the wheel wells and the undercarriage. There is no tracker under the dash. There is nothing wired where it shouldn't be. Nothing blinking or humming. The trunk is deep and wide, lined in clean black felt. Big enough for a body.

I miss my Impala. I always will. But since I can't have it, I figure I might as well enjoy borrowing from people who have many cars and dollars at their disposal.

Travis feeds me every checkpoint the Portland Police Department and the FBI have set up in the area. He lists troopers posted along the highway, unmarked units parked near the main exits, and federal vehicles tucked far enough back to feel clever. Beau follows us in a separate car, staying several lengths behind so we can split if something goes wrong or if one of us gets pulled over.

We avoid every checkpoint he names. We use back roads that skirt the main arteries, timed merges that drop us into gaps in traffic, and side streets that keep us away from plate scanners.

I keep my grip firm on the wheel and my foot heavy on the gas. We have a narrow window to work with, and every mile feels like it matters. Elliot is confirmed for tonight's event at Saints & Sinners. After that, he will disappear again behind money, private security, and locked doors that will take more time to crack.

I refuse to let that happen.

Saints & Sinners glows from half a block away, its gold light spilling onto the sidewalk through a wide glass frontage. Music pulses hard enough that I can feel the beat through the pavement when we roll past. Security stands along the entrance in tailored black suits, earpieces snug against their ears, eyes scanning.

I park down the street and shut off the engine, watching the entrance while Beau eases his car into a dark space a little farther back.

I slick my hair back with my fingers and adjust my jacket. I am clean shaven, collar open, the fit intentional without drawing attention.

"Remember," I say quietly. "We blend."

Brooke nods once.

She checks her reflection in the darkened window of the car. She doesn't look like the woman they hunted. She looks composed. She looks untouchable.

Beau's voice comes through the earpiece. "The back alley is quiet. The delivery door has a keypad. I don't see obvious cameras, but I wouldn't rely on that."

Travis follows. "Interior feeds are partial due to lighting interference. The VIP level is elevated with limited sightlines. If Elliot is there, he won't be on the main floor."

I open Brooke's door and offer my hand. We walk toward the entrance together. We join the line and move forward at an easy pace. Bass rolls through the building and up into my chest. Laughter spills out from the doorway.

The bouncer gives us a brief glance. Brooke hands over the invitation Travis spoofed. He scans it, nods once, and lifts the rope.

The club closes around us as soon as we step inside.

Black marble floors reflect bodies in fractured angles. Gold accents catch the light in brief flashes. Blue and purple strobes cut faces into shifting sections. The bar runs along one wall, bottles stacked high and backlit.

An elevator sits behind frosted glass with two guards posted in front of it. They are armed, but their posture lacks discipline.

"Five guards on the stairs and two at the elevator," I murmur to Brooke. "All carrying."

She nods without breaking stride.

We drift deeper into the crowd. Brooke moves in front of me with an easy confidence that draws every eye for a second and then moves those eyes away again. People notice her enough to enjoy the view and then turn back to their own problems, which means no one stares long enough to memorize her features.

"Seven Nation Army" starts to play, the opening notes punching through the speakers and rolling under the noise of voices.

I step in closer and slide my hands down to her hips, fingers settling against the fabric of her dress. She starts to move against me, rolling her hips with intent that stays balanced between performance and hunger. She presses back into me with intention, giving every person watching a clear story about who we are and why we are here.

I let her dance, let the rhythm carry her movements while I scan over her shoulder, counting guards and security positions between bodies. The closeness sells the cover, and anyone paying attention will see a couple locked on each other instead of the room.

My dick starts to get hard from the way she rolls her hips on me, and she knows exactly what she is doing. My erection doesn't care about mission windows or kill plans, and the pulse of the hunt threads through it and makes everything sharper. Brooke always does this to me, and the fact that we are here to take someone out only makes the pull worse.

I keep my focus where it belongs, scanning the room, tracking movement, waiting for Elliot to show himself.

The music slows, the rhythm darkening into something heavier. Every movement around us becomes harder to track, shoulders brushing, drinks sloshing, laughter splitting the tension wide open.

Then something changes.

I don't see it at first. I feel it, the kind of shift that tells you the predator has just noticed the prey.

I lift my gaze to the upper level.

Low couches sit beneath softer lighting, shadows stretching longer up there and moving slower than the floor below. A glass railing frames the space, reflective enough to distort movement, like everything is happening a half second behind reality.

And Elliot sits at the center of it.

He leans back against a wide couch, one arm stretched across the backrest like he owns the room. Drinks sit untouched in front of him. Two men flank him, both too still and too aware for this kind of setting.

I feel Brooke stiffen beside me the second my focus locks.

She follows my line of sight, her eyes narrowing as she finds him.

"That's him," she says under her breath.

Elliot leans forward slightly and says something to the man on his right, his gaze drifting over the floor out of habit.

Then he sees her.

Recognition hits clean and immediate, and his posture tightens just enough to give it away.

Brooke doesn't look away. She holds his stare from across the club, her chin lifted and her expression stripped down to nothing. The wig softens her features and blurs the edges, but it doesn't hide what matters.

She wants him to know. She wants him to remember.

Elliot leans back again, and smiles.

That is when it clicks.

Not just him.

I drag my attention off Elliot and start scanning the room.

Movement at the bar to the left catches my eye. A man leans against it with a drink in his hand, his posture loose like he doesn't have a reason to be there.

But I recognize him.

Diego.

Across the floor, closer to the dance crowd, another one stands just outside the shifting lights. He isn't dancing or drinking. He is watching.

Jackson.

My pulse shifts.

I look again.

They aren't together.

They are placed.

Brooke's fingers brush mine for half a second.

Then she speaks, low.

"Three o'clock."

I follow her line of sight.

A woman stands near the railing on the opposite side of the room, angled just enough to watch the floor without drawing attention to herself.

Ava.

Brooke's voice comes again, quieter this time.

"And behind her."

I shift my focus slightly.

There.

Half hidden near the hallway entrance, someone leans against the wall with their head down like they are scrolling through their phone.

But they're not.

Ezra.

I go still.

They're spread out across the club, watching and waiting.

This is not a party.

This is a setup.

Elliot leans forward again, resting his elbows on his knees, that same pleased, mocking expression settling into place.

Then he picks up a microphone.

"Well," he says, his voice smooth and unhurried, like he has all night to enjoy this. "I was starting to think you wouldn't show."

The room doesn't react. Most people don't even notice.

But I do. Because now I can feel it.

Too many eyes. Too many angles. Too many ways this can go wrong.

Elliot leans back again and lifts one finger, not a signal anyone else will catch, just enough.

Brooke doesn't move. She stands beside me, steady, locked on him.

Then I see it.

A faint red beam cuts through the low light.

It doesn't sweep or search.

It lands directly on Brooke's chest.

Chapter 48
Seth

I move before my brain catches up.

I slam into Brooke and drive her sideways just as the shot cracks through the club.

Pain tears across my shoulder as the round grazes through it, but not enough to slow me down. I push through it and keep moving.

The room erupts.

Glass shatters, and someone screams. A man drops, clutching his neck as blood sprays across the marble. The music cuts out mid-beat, and for half a second everything stalls.

Then the panic hits.

Bodies surge in every direction as people shove, trip, and fall. Drinks hit the floor and shatter underfoot while someone disappears beneath the crowd.

I roll, come up fast, and scan.

Jackson is already shifting, trying to adjust his angle.

He doesn't get the chance.

Beau fires from outside, and Jackson's body snaps back before dropping out of sight as the beam cuts out completely.

Gunfire cracks again, but this time it is sloppy.

One of them fires too fast and misses, the round tearing into a man trying to run. He drops instantly. Another shot follows and hits a woman near the bar, and she collapses before she even understands what happens.

They can't track us.

We are moving too fast.

Brooke drops low and slides under a table just as another shot tears through the space where she had been standing. The table flips from the impact, glasses shattering around her as she comes up on one knee.

I pivot in the opposite direction and cut through the crowd, forcing a bad angle while I bring my weapon up.

A guard moves in from the right, trying to intercept. I fire once. The round hits him clean, and he drops immediately. Another guard pushes forward behind him. I adjust and fire again. He spins and collapses against the bar, taking bottles down with him as they shatter across the counter.

More shots follow from above.

They're rushing now. They're missing.

Brooke rises from behind the table with her gun already up, her eyes locked on the second level. She finds Ava. Brooke fires once, and the shot hits her square in the chest. Ava staggers, shock flashing across her face.

Brooke fires again.

The second round drives her backward over the railing, and her body tips before crashing down onto a glass centerpiece below. The impact shatters it instantly, shards scattering as her body hits the floor and goes still.

Brooke shifts again.

Ezra tries to retreat toward the hallway. I see it the same second she does.

She fires first.

The round catches him mid-step, and his body snaps back into the wall before sliding down, leaving a dark smear behind him.

I turn left. Diego is pushing through the crowd, using bodies as cover while trying to disappear. I track him through the movement and fire.

The shot lands clean.

He folds hard and goes down, taking two people with him as he hits the floor.

Another guard comes at me from the side, weapon already raised. I close the distance and fire twice. The first round hits his chest, and the second drops him before he can pull the trigger. A third guard tries to flank from behind.

I turn, catch the motion, and fire without thinking. He goes down mid-step.

Gunfire snaps again from above, wild and uncontrolled. A round tears past my head close enough that I feel the air shift. Another strikes a man behind me, dropping him instantly.

Beau keeps firing from outside, each shot landing with brutal precision. A guard on the stairs drops before he can raise his weapon. Another staggers and collapses, clutching his throat. A third tries to run and doesn't make it more than a few steps.

I move through it, ignoring the burn in my shoulder, keeping my focus locked on what matters.

Elliot.

I find him halfway down the stairs. He pauses just long enough to take in the damage, the bodies, and the panic as it spreads through the club.

Then he runs.

He cuts through the VIP hallway, slams into the side door, and disappears into the private garage before I can line up the shot.

"Garage," Brooke says, breath catching, panic bleeding into fury.

We tear through the hallway. People scatter as the alarms finally catch up to the violence. Red light pulses across the exit, washing everything in flashes of chaos.

We hit the valet ramp just as Elliot comes into view.

He moves fast, cutting through the panic. He reaches his car, yanks the door of his black Lamborghini open, and drops into the driver's seat.

Then I hear that fucking engine roar to life, echoing through the garage as he slams it into gear and guns it toward the exit.

"Shit," Brooke breathes. "He's getting away—"

A valet attendant runs straight into my path, keys clutched in his hand, heading for a sleek black Porsche idling near the front.

I grab him by the front of his jacket and shove him hard into the concrete. He hits with a grunt, the keys slipping from his hand. I snatch the keys to the car, rip the driver's door open, and drop into the seat.

Brooke is in the passenger side before I can even tell her to move.

I start the engine and floor it. The tires scream as we launch out of the garage, just in time to see Elliot's Lamborghini explode up the ramp ahead of us. He clips the front end of a sedan near the curb, sending it spinning into the intersection. Metal shrieks. Glass bursts across the pavement. Drivers slam their horns, swerving, panicking as everything falls apart.

"There," Brooke points. "That's him."

The tires bite hard, launching us forward. I weave through the chaos, nearly clipping a car that swerves too late. A light pole goes down behind us with a burst of sparks. People are still running from the club, screaming, shoving each other, trying to survive.

But all I can see is Elliot.

He drives that Lamborghini like he thinks it will save him. He tears through intersections, ignores every light, cuts across oncoming traffic. He forces an SUV into a fire hydrant that explodes upward in a geyser of water. He doesn't look back.

Every time I see his car twist through another red light, my grip on the wheel tightens.

I hate him. The sound of his voice. The smugness in every word. The videos he made. The footage of him torturing his victims. What he did to my girl won't go unpunished. He doesn't get to vanish into the night. He doesn't get an easy exit or a clean death.

He is mine.

Elliot cuts into a side street, buildings closing in. The street narrows. I keep after him, bumper to bumper. Brooke doesn't speak. Her eyes are locked on his car.

Elliot glances back, just once. His eyes meet mine in the rearview.

And he fires.

The shot lights up his car. The bullet cracks through our windshield, spiderwebbing the glass dead center. The cabin fills with the scent of powder and burning plastic. I line up my shot, lean just enough, and fire at his rear tire.

The bullet hits home.

The car jolts violently, skidding sideways in a spray of sparks. Elliot fights the wheel. I see it. The exact second he knows he has lost control.

The Lamborghini slams into a concrete barrier at full speed. The front folds in, steel twisting. The hood crumples. The windshield shatters in a single violent burst. One headlight bursts outward in a spray of debris. Smoke billows from the engine.

I hit the brakes and skid to a stop twenty feet behind him. I step out with my gun raised. I want him to crawl. I want him to beg. I want him to know what it feels like to lose control and choke on it.

Elliot fucking Grant is going to die.

For a moment, all I hear is the ticking of overheated metal and the hiss of smoke curling out from under the hood.

We move fast, weapons raised, eyes locked on the wreck. Elliot's body hangs halfway over the steering wheel, his tailored blazer soaked with blood. It has poured down his shirt, splattered across the shattered windshield, smeared with the pattern of his face where it slammed forward.

Then the driver's door flies open.

He collapses out of the car and hits the pavement hard. Blood spills from his mouth and nose in thick, dark streams. He coughs wetly, twists onto his side, and rolls to his knees, hands shaking. His face is cut open, jaw split along one side.

He raises the pistol and fires blindly.

Rounds slam into the side of our car. The windshield fractures again. A headlight explodes with a sharp pop, glass bursting across the street. Brooke drops low, fires back with clean shots. One hits him in the shoulder, spinning him, blood trailing mid-air. He stays upright.

Then he runs.

He limps toward the open street, dragging one leg, leaving a broken trail of blood across the pavement. His other arm dangles, dislocated or worse. He doesn't look back. He just moves.

We jump back into the car. I floor the gas.

The tires scream, and the frame jolts as we launch forward.

He tries to cut through the intersection. He makes it halfway across the crosswalk before I reach him.

The front end of the car smashes into his body with the full force of the engine behind it. His body snaps backward, limbs whipping out of sync with each other. His spine folds against the hood. I hear bones break in rapid succession. His head slams into the windshield. The glass collapses inward, webbing instantly with cracks.

He rolls up and over the top of the car, thuds onto the roof, and bounces off the back, slamming onto the street like a dropped carcass.

I brake hard and skid to a stop. Smoke pours from the front grill. Fluid pools under the car.

Brooke is already moving, hair lashing in the cold air.

I step out and approach what is left of him.

Elliot twitches on the pavement. Blood spills from his mouth in long ropes, his lips peeled back from shattered teeth. One leg is ruined, bent at angles that shred muscle. Bone pushes out through one thigh, the skin split and gaping. His shoulder is caved in. One arm lies folded under his chest. Chunks of flesh are missing from where he skidded across the asphalt.

He opens his mouth to speak, but all that comes out is wet breath and blood.

I bring my boot down on his wrist. The bones shatter instantly, tendons snapping beneath my heel. The scream that comes out of him barely makes it past the blood clogging his throat.

I grab what is left of his expensive jacket and drag him across the pavement. His legs leave two thick red smears trailing behind. One of his shoes has come off, and the bare foot twists limp, shredded at the heel. His femur juts fully out of the torn skin. His broken arm flops with each pull, bone sawing against the ground.

He gurgles, choking on blood and broken teeth.

I reach the back of the car and pop the trunk. The latch clicks and the lid lifts, hinges groaning under the strain.

"Kincaid, you piece of shit," he rasps. Blood bubbles at his mouth as he tries to crawl backward. "Don't put me in there!" He claws at the asphalt with one hand that barely works, fingernails scraping uselessly against the pavement.

I grab him and haul him up. His body sags in places it should not, weight shifting wrong as bones slide against each other. I shove him into the trunk without slowing. He hits the metal hard, lands twisted on his side, and starts screaming. The sound is shrill and broken, panic tearing through every breath.

I slam the trunk shut.

The steel dulls the noise just enough to make it tolerable.

I stand there for a second, listening to the muffled pounding and the sounds he makes when he realizes no one is coming. Then I walk back to the driver's seat. My hands are slick with blood. I wipe them on the inside of my jacket, dragging my palms along the lining until the fabric darkens.

Brooke is already in the passenger seat.

I slide in beside her and glance over.

She looks radiant. Her eyes are bright, lips parted in a slow, satisfied smile she doesn't bother hiding. Her head tips back against the seat as she lets out a long breath, the kind that empties something heavy from her chest. Her thighs press together beneath her dress.

I tighten my grip on the steering wheel.

She shifts in her seat, adjusting herself, and a soft sound slips out of her throat. She bites her lower lip, not to stop it, but to draw it out longer.

I chuckle. "You're going to make me pull over."

She laughs.

The sound of adrenaline still flooding her system. She liked watching me do it. She likes what I did to him. She likes that he begged. She likes knowing he is still back there, breathing hard, panicking, screaming into a box that won't open.

Her body makes that part very clear.

I take the next turnout without easing up much. Gravel snaps under the tires as I cut the wheel. The car slides before it catches, headlights sweeping over trees and brush before landing on a narrow overlook carved into the mountain. There are no streetlights, no traffic. Only a rusted guardrail and a drop beyond it that vanishes into black.

The engine idles low. I shift into park and shut the engine off.

"Get out."

She looks at me with her breath caught. "Out here?" she asks, barely above a whisper.

I don't answer. I open the door and step into the cold night air. She follows quickly, her heels crunching over gravel as she trails behind me.

We move around the back of the car. The paint gleams under the moonlight, streaked only with road dust and blood. The brand new trunk shifts, metal groaning with a hollow echo. A muffled scream kicks up from inside, followed by several frantic bangs. He is panicking now, kicking at steel he is too broken to bend. It's pathetic.

Brooke stares at the trunk, her eyes wide but focused. Her lips part slightly, breath coming out slow. She looks satisfied. She looks turned on. Nothing about her posture reads as fear. This is power, and she likes how it feels when it belongs to her.

"Hush" starts playing from the speakers, like it has been waiting for this exact moment.

I step in close and wrap my hands around her hips, my fingers digging into warm skin as I pull her against me so she can feel exactly how hard I already am.

She doesn't flinch when I lift her and set her on the trunk.

From inside, Elliot slams his fist against the lid again.

"Let me out!" he shouts, his voice muffled and frantic. "Let me the fuck out!"

He hasn't passed out yet, and he hasn't given up.

Good.

She looks down at the trunk beneath her instead of at me, staring at the metal like she can see straight through it into the dark where he is trapped. She knows he can hear everything.

I step between her legs and drag my hands slowly up the inside of her thighs, spreading her wider as my palms move over heated skin. Her breath hitches hard when my thumbs brush closer to where she is already wet. I push her dress up inch by inch, exposing her completely to the cold air and to me.

She is not wearing panties.

Her thighs tighten instinctively, but I force them apart again and keep them open with a firm grip.

Her throat works as she swallows, and she nods once without lifting her eyes from the trunk. Her fingers curl over the edge of the metal behind her, and her nails scrape across the paint as she anchors herself.

The car shifts again beneath us.

Inside, Elliot pounds harder.

"Let me out!" he yells. "You fucking bitch!"

I let one hand slide higher between her legs and press two fingers against her slowly, feeling the slick heat waiting for me. She sucks in a breath so hard that it stutters in her chest. I drag my fingers through her, spreading her open while I watch the way her hips lift.

She is already soaked.

I circle her clit with my thumb while my fingers push inside her at the same time, stretching her carefully. Her head tips back and her chest rises with a shaky inhale. Her legs try to close around my arm, but I keep them open and slide my fingers deeper, curling them slightly until her body reacts.

She gasps and grabs the trunk harder.

"Don't stop," she whispers.

I drop to my knees between her legs while keeping my fingers inside her. I pull her closer until she sits right at the edge of the trunk, her ass hovering over his face through layers of steel.

I flatten my tongue against her and drag it slowly while my fingers pump inside her.

She cries out, and the sound is not quiet.

Her hips jerk forward into my mouth while her body clenches around my fingers. Her breathing turns messy instantly. I work her with my tongue in long strokes, then circle her clit while curling my fingers inside her, rubbing that place that always makes her lose control.

Her thighs start shaking.

Her hands slide on the metal before gripping again.

"Oh fuck," she gasps.

I suck her clit into my mouth while my fingers move deeper, slower, then faster, stretching her open and filling her at the same time. Her hips start grinding against my face in short, desperate movements.

The car rocks under us. Inside, Elliot screams again.

"Brooke!" he yells. "I'm going to fucking kill you!"

She hears him, and I feel it in the way she tightens around my fingers.

I drive my fingers harder into her and curl them firmly while my mouth stays on her, licking and sucking until her whole body starts trembling.

Her stomach tightens visibly. Her breathing breaks apart into gasps.

She is dripping onto my mouth.

"Please," she whimpers. "I'm going to come."

I push in deeper and work her faster, relentlessly now, with my fingers curling and uncurling inside her while my tongue keeps circling her clit without mercy.

Her thighs clamp around my shoulders. Her back arches. Her hips buck forward.

Right then, Elliot makes another sound from inside the trunk, and it comes out thin and weak. He is running out of fight or oxygen.

She comes hard.

Her body locks around my head, squeezing my fingers as wave after wave tears through her. Her hips slam forward. Her chest heaves. Her mouth opens in a sound she can't control while I keep my fingers inside her and my mouth on her, riding every wave.

She shakes violently. Her moans come out broken and high.

I stay there and hold her through it, feeling every pulse, every clench, every desperate aftershock around my fingers while my tongue never leaves her.

She is still trembling when I finally slow my fingers and pull them out of her gradually, watching her wetness shine in the light, knowing he hears every sound she makes while she comes on top of his coffin.

I slide my hands up her sides and hook my fingers under the neckline of her dress. I shove the fabric down hard and slow, scraping it over her skin until her tits spill free. They are full and heavy in my hands, nipples already tight from the cold and from the way she just came apart for me. I lean down and take one into my mouth. I suck hard, my tongue working her nipple while my hand closes around the other breast and squeezes. I roll her nipple between my fingers until she gasps and arches, pushing herself into my mouth.

Her back bows, her chest pressing into my face, her hips rocking. I can feel my cock straining behind my zipper, aching and thick and pissed off from waiting.

I pull back just long enough to undo my pants and free myself in one sharp motion. My cock slaps against my stomach, heavy and leaking, and I make sure she sees it. I want her eyes on it. I want her to feel the way my body is coiled and ready when I step between her thighs. Her pussy is still pulsing, wet, hot, and open.

I grab her hips, line myself up, and drive into her in one brutal thrust.

She cries out, her head tipping back as her hands fly out to grip the edge of the trunk. The sound she makes is half laugh, half sob, completely broken, and it hits me straight in the gut. I bury myself all the way in, bottoming out in one stroke. Her body stretches around me and clenches hard, tight enough to make my breath stutter.

I pull back and slam into her again. Each thrust knocks her spine into the metal with dull, hollow impacts. The trunk groans under her, echoing every hard movement. A thin, useless muffled scream punches up from beneath us.

She wraps her legs around my waist, heels locking behind me, dragging me in deeper. Her dress is shoved up around her hips, her tits bare and bouncing with every drive of my body. Her mouth falls open, lips red and wet from biting down too hard. Her breath comes in ragged pulls, every exhale breaking apart around my name.

Her voice cracks when she tries to speak, and the sound falls apart in her throat. Her thighs twitch around me, squeezing tight like she is trying to hold me there. She is already close again. Her body is shaking, worn thin and overstimulated, but it still clings to me like the only thing it knows is the way I fill her.

"You like that, baby," my mouth brushes her ear, my voice low and rough against her skin. "You like being fucked like this, right on top of him. Huh?"

She doesn't answer with words. She bucks up hard instead, grinding herself down on me, her whole body shuddering as she chases the friction. Her nails dig into my shoulders. Her breath breaks apart against my neck.

The trunk thuds again beneath us.

"Let me out!" Elliot shouts, his voice hoarse now. "I'll fucking gut you fuckers!"

I laugh softly against her throat and tighten my grip on her hips.

"I wouldn't waste my breath if I were you, Ellie," I call out, not even raising my voice. "You might run out of oxygen before I come."

The trunk goes silent for half a second, then rattles harder, frantic and uneven.

The car creaks under the force of it. The suspension rocks. The metal thuds again beneath her, weaker this time.

I drive into her harder, faster, pushing her forward so her hands slam against the roof for balance. One hand comes up to her breast, squeezing and tugging it roughly, while my thumb rolls over her nipple until she gasps. My other hand locks on her hip, fingers digging in deep enough to bruise, keeping her exactly where I want her.

I fuck her like I mean to mark her from the inside, like I want her to feel me for days. Her head tips back. Her eyes flutter shut. Her moans break down into whimpers that turn into curses and my name, over and over, breathless and wrecked.

"Don't stop," she begs, her voice wrecked.

She shatters around me with a cry that tears straight out of her lungs. Her nails rake down my back. Her hips jerk forward uncontrollably. Her body locks around me, pulsing and spasming, dragging me deeper every time she clenches.

I hold her there and keep fucking her through it.

She gasps my name and rocks against me, meeting every thrust.

Her stomach flexes with each uneven breath. Her breathing breaks apart into short, uncontrolled sounds that spill out of her mouth. She is losing the ability to regulate anything except the way she moves against me.

I grab her thighs and haul her closer to the edge of the trunk, forcing her legs wider and opening her up. Her dress bunches at her waist, the fabric biting into her skin. She gasps when the angle changes, when I drive deeper, when her whole body jolts with every thrust like she can't escape the sensation even if she wants to. Her body reacts before her mind can catch up.

She doesn't need to think. She just needs to feel. She needs to be ruined on top of the same piece of shit who chained her up and tortured her, who thought he could touch her and walk away breathing.

No fucking chance.

Her nails dig into my shoulders, hard enough to bite, grounding herself by leaving marks.

"Set—Seth," she moans, my name pulled apart by the way her breath keeps stuttering.

I lean down until my forehead presses to hers, my teeth clenched so tight my jaw aches.

I want to mark her badly enough that the bruises outlast the memory of his hands. I want every inch of her to remember it is me who takes her back. I want her to remember it is me who makes her come on top of him while he screams into the dark. I want her to remember it is me who makes her feel safe enough to fall apart like this, knowing I will tear his ribs open before I let him touch her again.

"Come for me again, baby," I say as I thrust harder. "Let him hear how good you feel."

Her body locks up around me. Her thighs quiver as they tighten. Her breath catches sharp and high in her chest as she comes. Her hands claw into my shoulders as she shakes. Her pussy clenches so hard around me that my vision blurs and I almost lose control right there.

I grit my teeth and pull out fast, grabbing the base of my cock before the pressure drags me under. It throbs hard in my fist, every muscle in my body screaming to finish.

I want him to hear it all. I want him to know he is nothing. That she came on top of him while I buried myself inside her, while I made her forget every second of pain he ever caused. And when I'm finished, when she is safe and spent in my arms, I'm going to tear that trunk open and show him what the fuck consequences look like.

No begging. No mercy. Only pain.

She drops to her knees without asking, her hands sliding up my thighs as she leans forward and takes me into her mouth.

I suck in a breath through clenched teeth.

Her lips are warm and swollen from everything I just did to her. Her mouth works me slow at first, then deeper, her tongue dragging along the underside of my cock like she knows exactly how close I already am. Her eyes stay locked on mine the entire time, dark and blown wide, daring me to come down her throat.

Her throat flexes as she takes me deeper.

I thread my fingers through her hair and tighten my grip, holding her exactly where I want her while she hollows her cheeks and takes me deeper. Her lips stay sealed around me, her tongue moving slow, she knows exactly how to pull it out of me. Her body still trembles from her orgasm, small aftershocks running through her, but she doesn't pull away. She stays there and takes it like she wants everything I give her.

The pressure builds fast.

It drags tight through my body, heavy and impossible to ignore, until it snaps.

My grip locks in her hair as I drive deeper, a rough breath tearing out of my chest as I come. My release hits her hard, flooding her mouth in thick, pulsing waves. I feel it spill across her tongue, feel the way her throat flexes around me as I fill her, each pulse heavier than the last.

I hold her there and watch it happen, watch the way her lips stay wrapped tight while her breathing breaks through her nose. My cum fills her mouth completely, gathering behind her cheeks as I keep going, slower now but just as intense, dragging every last pulse out.

It keeps coming. Until there is nothing left.

I ease my grip just enough to pull back, watching the way my release lingers on her lips before she closes them again, holding everything I give her.

She doesn't swallow.

She keeps it there, cheeks full, her chest rising and falling as her eyes lift to mine, like she knows exactly what she is doing to me by holding it.

I already know what she is going to do.

I pop the trunk.

The scream comes instantly, hoarse and panicked, ripping out of Elliot the second the lid opens and cold air hits his face. He is still alive, blood smeared everywhere like he has been rolled in it. His eyes go wild when the light hits him.

Elliot screams.

The sound tears out of him, his head snapping back as panic and pain hit all at once.

Brooke turns slowly, then leans forward and spits straight into his mouth.

My cum and her saliva mix.

Hot and thick, it lands past his lips, forcing its way in as it blends with the blood already coating his face, some of it spilling back out as he chokes on it.

"Enjoy your last meal, motherfucker."

Elliot tries to scream again. It doesn't sound human anymore. It sounds like what happens when fear finally understands it is out of options.

Brooke slams the trunk shut.

I zip my pants without rushing, then look at her.

Her chest is still rising fast. Her eyes are wild and bright.

I smile at her before I can stop myself.

God, I love her.

I pull her into me and pick her up as she wraps her legs around my waist, her body still coming down in uneven waves. She presses her forehead to mine, her hands sliding into my hair.

She is here. She is alive.

That is all that matters.

I kiss her hard. She kisses me back like she understands exactly why it happened this way.

I pull back just enough to look at her.

"Let's go torture this piece of shit."

Chapter 49
Brooke

We drag them back to the abandoned warehouse in silence.

Elliot's cage waits in the center of the concrete floor, welded from thick steel bars and bolted directly into the slab.

Beau shoves him through the open door.

Elliot hits the ground on his back. His ruined leg strikes the floor with a wet smack. He tries to catch himself with his hands, but his palms slip in the blood already spreading beneath him.

The limb doesn't look like it belongs to a living person anymore. Skin hangs in torn strips. Bone pushes through the muscle in a jagged white arc.

Beau crouches in front of the cage and studies the damage like a mechanic inspecting a bent axle. He reaches out and flicks the exposed bone with two fingers.

Elliot screams.

The sound rips out of him raw and violent. It bounces off the warehouse walls and echoes back across the concrete. His entire body jerks. He claws at the floor, trying to drag himself away from the pain, but the rest of him refuses to cooperate.

Blood sprays from his mouth as he coughs. Elliot spits a thick mouthful of it near Seth's boots.

"Fuck you," Elliot rasps. "Just shoot me."

Seth smirks and glances at Beau.

"So many men have told us that around this point."

Beau gives a small nod. "Yeah. They always want the shortcut."

Seth looks back down at Elliot.

"I can shoot you," he says calmly. "But it won't be somewhere clean. It'll be somewhere that hurts like a bitch. And you won't die fast."

Elliot glares up at him with his jaw clenched.

Seth crouches to his level.

"You want to know why I don't do quick endings?"

Elliot stays silent.

"Back when we were overseas, we had a guy begging the same way you are. He wiped out half a village and still thought mercy was on the table."

Seth glances over his shoulder.

"Where did you shoot that one, Beau?"

Beau scratches his jaw.

"His nuts."

Sophie sucks in a quiet breath.

Beau continues, completely unfazed. "He dropped screaming. It took him a long time to die."

"And then there was the asshole who raped those women and children," Seth adds.

Beau glances at him. "Yeah. You handled that one."

Seth's mouth twitches slightly.

"Ah, yes, I let him find out what it feels like to get penetrated against your will."

He looks back at Elliot.

"You want to know where I shot him, Ellie?"

Elliot's breathing turns shallow.

Seth leans closer.

"Because that is exactly where I would shoot you."

Elliot swallows hard.

I remember him telling me about that.

A Marine squad had gone rogue. They wiped out an entire village. They shot the men first. Then they lined up the women and children.

They raped them.

Seth and Beau found what was left.

Beau pinned their leader into the dirt. Seth took a rifle and forced the barrel inside his ass before he pulled the trigger.

I didn't know that kind of brutality was possible until Seth said it out loud.

From what he told me, the man didn't die quickly. He screamed and bled out slowly.

Honestly, he got exactly what he deserved.

I wish I had done the same to Nick.

I stand and kick Sophie's cage door. Her jaw stays clenched. The color has drained from her face until her skin looks gray and waxy. Sweat gathers along her hairline.

She leans against the bars, her eyes unfocused for a moment.

Across the room, the industrial tub waits against the far wall. It is deep and stainless steel, the kind used for equipment or bodies depending on the facility.

I turn the valve.

Water roars out of the hose and crashes into the empty basin. The noise fills the warehouse and echoes through the metal beams overhead. Warm mist hits my face as the tub begins to fill. The smell of chlorine mixes with rust and blood. The water level climbs slowly, turning the steel sides into a dull mirror beneath the warehouse lights.

Behind me, I hear the blender.

Seth stands at a scarred metal table, the cheap plastic pitcher in front of him. The motor whines loudly over the rush of the water, blades tearing through whatever he packed inside. The mixture inside looks pink and thick. He holds the lid with one hand and watches it spin, his attention steady, his shoulders relaxed.

The smell reaches me even from across the room.

The blender whines harder for a second, then cuts off. Seth lifts the lid and looks into the pitcher. He doesn't make a face. He reaches for two dented metal cups and starts pouring the pink sludge, careful so nothing spills.

I shut off the water when the tub sits nearly halfway full. The echo softens to a low slosh. I wipe my hands on my thighs and walk back toward the cages.

Sophie watches me. Her eyes flick from the tub to the blender to the cup in Seth's hands. Fear sits under her skin, but shock blurs it.

Elliot stares too, jaw clenched, breath coming in short, shallow pulls. Sweat and grime streak across his face. His pupils look blown, more from pain than anything else.

Seth hands me two cups.

The liquid inside looks thick and frothy. It clings to the sides of the metal, a soft pink that would look harmless in any other context.

I walk to Sophie's cage first.

Her fingers curl around the bars as I approach, knuckles pale.

"You should drink," I hold the cup up to the gap in the bars. "You need protein if you want to make it through tonight."

Her gaze drops to the cup, then back to my face.

"What the fuck is that?" she whispers.

"It's a protein shake. You always gave them to us in the manor."

Her throat works as she swallows.

She reaches through the bars and takes the cup from my hand with both of hers, the metal rattling softly against the cage.

"Don't make me pour it down your throat," I add calmly. "That would be a waste of everyone's time."

She lifts it to her mouth and takes a small sip.

Her face changes instantly.

She gags and jerks the cup away, spitting the pink liquid onto the concrete. It hits in a wet splash and spreads in a pale smear between the bars. Her whole body shudders. She holds the cup out like it might bite her.

"What the fuck is that?!" she chokes. "What is that?"

I laugh before I can stop myself.

"What's wrong Sophie? You don't like sucking on Knox anymore?" I chuckle. "That's surprising."

Her eyes go wider. She stares at the cup like it has turned into a bomb.

"No. No, no," she whispers.

Sophie makes a broken choking sound and slams herself backward into the cage.

"Funny, you swallowed plenty of him before." I tilt my head slightly. "You were a lot more enthusiastic then."

Her stomach rolls hard, and Sophie makes a choked, strangled sound from the cage as she turns her head and spits, her shoulders tightening while she tries to force it back down.

Seth walks forward. Something frozen and dark swings from his hand before he drops it hard against the concrete directly in front of the cages.

Sophie screams. Elliot recoils violently against the back of his cage.

What is left of Knox's head rolls sideways across the floor with a wet crack. The lower jaw is missing completely, ripped away beneath the nose. Frozen flesh has started collapsing inward from decay, the skin gray and split in places where freezer burn and rot have eaten through it. One eye socket is empty. The other still holds part of a clouded, sunken eye buried in blackened tissue. Clumps of dead hair stick to the side of the skull where frost still clings stubbornly to the skin.

The smell hits seconds later. Rotting meat beneath chemical cold.

I shift my focus to Elliot as I walk toward him, the cup still in my hand, my steps slow and certain as the space between us closes.

He notices. His breathing changes first, growing uneven as his eyes drop to the cup before lifting back to mine. His leg lies twisted beneath him, useless. He watches me, tracking every step.

I stop in front of his cage and hold his gaze, letting the silence sit there long enough to settle into him before I move. Then I lower myself just enough to meet his eyes through the bars.

I lift the cup.

His head pulls back on instinct, but there is nowhere for him to go, nowhere for him to escape what is already coming.

I tip it forward.

The contents pour through the bars and onto his head, thick and wet as it hits his hair and spreads over his face. It clings for a second before sliding down, dragging across his skin in slow streaks, catching in his lashes, smearing over his mouth.

Elliot screams as he gags violently, thrashing against the bars while the liquid runs into his mouth and nose. He tries turning away, but it only smears deeper across his face. He spits and chokes, panic finally breaking through whatever composure he had left.

Sophie makes another broken sound from the other cage.

I rise back to my feet and watch him. Seth steps up beside me.

"You both loved to play games," I smile. "You should be grateful we came prepared with refreshments."

Seth moves closer to the cages, his tone calm.

"I'll be nice," he says. "One of you gets a choice. I'm going to make it long and painful either way, but one of you can volunteer and at least die before you watch what I do to the other."

The silence that follows presses in around us.

"So, decide."

Sophie's breathing comes out fast and shallow. Her fingers tighten around the bars. Her eyes move from Seth to me to the tub and the blender, taking everything in while her brain tries to find a way out that doesn't exist.

Elliot speaks before she can.

"Do her first," he blurts. "Take Sophie first."

The words come out fast, almost tripping over each other, like his mouth can't wait to shove her in front of him.

Sophie's head snaps toward him.

Her face crumples for a second, disbelief pushing through the pain.

"Elliot," she shouts. Her voice sounds thin and broken. "Are you fucking serious right now?"

I laugh, the sound low and mean and completely sincere.

"See, Sophie," I step closer to her cage. "See how fast the man you served throws you under the bus. You were nothing but a toy to him."

I smile at Sophie's face, watch the realization sink all the way in, then turn my head.

"Beau, get the lye."

Beau pushes off the table without a word. His boots click across the concrete as he heads toward the metal shelves along the wall. Glass clinks softly while he moves bottles aside, searching for the white bag.

I face Sophie again.

Her hands still grip the bars. Her knuckles have gone pale. Her eyes shine wet, furious and terrified, locked on Elliot like she wants to rip his throat out before we can.

"Well, you heard the man, Sophie," I say calmly. "Ladies first."

Chapter 50
Brooke

I got the idea from one of my favorite revenge horror movies, the kind that never really leaves your head once you see it. The setup had stuck with me for years, the image of someone forced to balance over something that would eat them alive the second they slipped. It felt right for Sophie.

The industrial tub sits against the wall, stainless steel, deep enough that you could lose a person in it without much effort. Four thick wooden planks lie across the top, two near where a chest would land and two near the hips and thighs. They are spaced just narrowly enough that a body can lie across them, but not comfortably, and definitely not safely. Hot water already fills the tub halfway. Steam rolls up in steady waves, turning the air thick and humid.

Beau hauls Sophie out of the cage with no sedation. Her face looks pale and clammy, but her eyes are clear and pissed off. She twists hard in his grip, teeth bared.

"Get your fucking hands off me!" she snarls.

Beau doesn't look impressed. He rolls her onto her stomach on the floor and pulls her arms behind her back. The rope slides around her broken wrists and ankles, tightening into a clean hogtie before she can twist away. She thrashes anyway, muscles jerking, breath coming out in harsh bursts.

"You should save your energy," Beau scoffs. "You'll need it."

Together, we lift her and carry her to the tub. Four wooden planks stretch across the width of it, spaced a few inches apart. Steam rolls up through the gaps in slow, thick waves. Beau lays her across them on her stomach, her body perpendicular to the boards. One plank sits under her shoulders, one beneath her abdomen, one at her hips, and one under her knees.

The wood creaks as her weight settles. The structure holds, but not comfortably. The gaps between the planks leave parts of her unsupported, forcing her body into a strained, uneven line. Heat curls up around her face when she exhales.

She tests it immediately, shifting her weight. The planks answer with low groans and a slight dip that brings her closer to the steaming surface.

"You might want to be still for this," I say.

That gets her attention. Her breathing stutters, then slows just enough. She makes smaller movements now, careful ones. Each one earns a soft creak from the wood and a subtle drop toward the water below.

Seth sits at the metal table nearby with both their phones in his hands, Sophie's in one and Elliot's in the other. Screens glow against his fingers while he scrolls through message threads and location logs. He looks calm and patient, like he is reviewing paperwork before a meeting.

Elliot watches everything from his cage, hands locked around the bars, jaw clenched so hard the muscles jump. His ruined leg stretches out in front of him, but his eyes stay sharp with anger and fear.

I crouch in front of Sophie so we are almost eye level, the tub between us.

"Here is how this works," I say. "You tell the truth and maybe you die faster. You lie and things change."

She swallows. Her throat bobs against damp skin.

"Where is Grant?" I ask. "And where is John?"

She lets out a weak laugh that sounds thin. "Fuck you."

"You don't have enough time for that," I say. "Answer the question."

"They're going to kill you," she rasps. "You're not going to get to them. They're going to get you."

I don't respond.

I plant my hand on the back of her head and shove her face straight into the hot water.

Her scream cuts off under the surface. Bubbles rush up around her ears. Her whole body lurches against the ropes. The planks groan as her weight shifts across them. The water climbs over her skull and cheeks, covering her completely. The heat hits her skin and steals her breath.

"Let's see if you can last a minute."

I hold her there while she thrashes, counting silently in my head. Her legs jerk and pull against the hogtie. Her shoulders strain against the plank beneath them. The wood flexes with every violent movement, but it holds.

Twenty seconds.

Thirty.

Her movements slow and turn sloppy, driven by instinct instead of control.

Forty-five.

Bubbles surge harder. Her body convulses.

At fifty-five I yank her head back up.

She comes up choking, water pouring from her mouth and nose. She coughs so hard it sounds like something might tear.

"You made it almost a minute," I chuckle. "Not bad."

Her hair sticks to her face in wet clumps. Her eyes are red and wild. Water runs off her chin and drips back into the tub.

"Where is Grant?" I ask again. "And where is John?"

"I told you," she coughs. "You're wasting your time. They move constantly. Nobody knows where they are."

Seth's voice cuts in from behind her.

"Lie."

I hook my boot under the plank supporting her knees and kick it out from under her.

The wood cracks loose and slams to the concrete. Sophie's legs drop a few inches, dragging the rest of her body down with them. She screams and tries to twist, but the remaining three planks barely hold her.

"You just lost stability," I murmur "Try again."

"Fuck you!" she gasps. "Grant's got the police on his side. John moves around like a ghost. You'll never find them before they get to you."

"Then why haven't they killed me yet?" I ask. "You have so much confidence in them, but are they here to save you. No."

I raise my voice slightly.

"Seth, pour the lye."

He stands, grabs the thick plastic bag Beau pulled earlier, and rips it open across the top. The white granules pour into the tub in a heavy stream. The reaction comes fast. The water hisses and turns cloudy, bubbling up in thick, milky waves. Heat rolls off it strong enough that my face prickles.

Sophie smells it before she registers it. Her nose wrinkles. Her eyes widen.

"What is that?" she screams.

"Motivation. Now. Where is Grant and John?"

She stares into the tub like it might jump up and grab her. Her fingers curl uselessly against the air, searching for something to hold.

"They were arguing," she says quickly. "Seattle came up a lot. They move constantly. I never get full details."

"Seth?"

"Partial truth," he replies. "Seattle is in their messages. So is Denver. So is a gala with Victor Voss. She is picking pieces."

I knock the plank under her hips away.

It shoots sideways and slams to the floor. Sophie's body dips again. Now only two planks hold her, one under her abdomen and one under her shoulders. Her ribs press hard into the wood as her midsection sags between them. Her face now hovers inches above the lye-clouded water. Steam hits her skin directly. Her eyes squeeze shut for a second.

"Stop," she sobs. "Please stop. You already have enough."

"We barely started," I say. "Where is Grant?"

"He doesn't tell me anything," she cries. "I was collateral. I only killed people because Elliot made me do it."

"Not an answer," I press. "Try again."

I press down on the plank near her shoulders with my hand, forcing it to flex. Her body lowers another inch. The heat hits her fully then. She flinches and tries to arch away. The position makes her wrists scream and her hogtied limbs strain, but there is nowhere for that pain to go.

Seth's voice comes from behind her again.

"She texted someone four days ago. She told them they would join Grant at a VossTech gala. She mentioned big donors, big launches, in two weeks."

I lean closer to Sophie's face.

"Let's play a game. You tell me what you know and you get to die watching less of what happens to Elliot. You lie and you cook slower."

Her eyes fill, more with rage than regret.

"I don't know the location!" she shouts. "I swear to God I don't know. Grant said Victor was hosting a gala. Grant is going to be there. That is all I heard."

"Where is the gala?"

"I'm not sure," she says. "He only said VossTech. He said donors. He said security. He didn't say which building."

In the cage, Elliot slams his hand against the bars.

"Shut the fuck up!" he shouts. "Don't tell them anything. Keep your fucking mouth shut."

Sophie flinches at his voice.

Her body trembles on the two remaining planks. The steam licks at her face and arms. Her muscles lock, trying to hold her torso up, trying to keep her mouth out of the water. Her shoulders shake violently. Her injured wrists spasm against the rope.

"You heard him," I tell her. "He never cared whether you lived through this. You were always disposable."

Her eyes fill fully then, tears mixing with sweat.

"They'll kill you," she whispers. "Grant will hunt you until you are dead."

"He already tried," I sigh. "Last chance. Give me everything."

She breaks.

"Grant is going to be at Victor Voss' gala," she says, words spilling fast. "They're planning something big. I don't know the venue. I don't know the address. I only know he said that is where he takes the board and the donors, and that is where he wants to make his point."

Seth scrolls again, checking for anything she might be hiding.

"She's telling the truth now," he says finally. "Nothing in here has the location. Just the name, the timing, and Victor."

Sophie sucks in a breath like that information might save her.

It will not.

The heat licking at her skin has already started to bite. Her cheeks redden. The steam burns her eyes. Her muscles shake from effort. The angle forces her spine to arch, her ribs grinding into the planks that cross her chest. Every second upright costs her something.

"Here is the part you didn't understand when you tortured innocent people," I lean in close. "There is no version where you walk away clean. In fact, you won't walk away at all."

Her arms tremble so violently that the planks rattle. A raw sound tears out of her throat. She is caught between the strain on her joints and the heat rising against her face.

Eventually, one of them wins.

She tips forward.

Her face breaks the surface of the lye-clouded water.

The scream tries to come out and immediately turns into a choking, gurgling sound. She jerks back instinctively, but the position drags her into it again. The reaction is immediate. Her skin reddens along her cheeks and lips. She thrashes, trying to wrench herself upright again, but her muscles have nothing left.

I watch her fight with every weak inch she has. Her head lifts halfway, then sags again. The rope cuts into softened skin at her wrists and ankles. Her sobs turn hoarse and broken.

I kick away the plank under her shoulders.

The last support shifts. Her body tilts, balance gone.

"You can't hold yourself up forever," I say quietly. "You really should have chosen a different side."

Her chin hovers over the surface, trembling. Her breath comes out in wet, ragged gasps. Her arms shake like they might snap.

I place my boot against the final plank.

"Game over, Sophie."

I push.

The plank slides free. Sophie's body drops into the tub, swallowed by the white, hissing water. Her scream tears out once, then collapses into something wet and broken as the surface surges over her face.

The water reacts immediately.

It foams and churns around her like it has been waiting.

Her arms jerk violently, skin turning pale and slick as it begins to slide apart under the heat. I watch patches of her flesh loosen and peel, curling away from her body in thin, ugly ribbons that drift through the cloudy water.

She arches hard, instinct driving her spine up even while the ropes drag her back down. Her legs kick beneath the surface, sending waves crashing against the steel sides of the tub. Every movement only drags more of her through it, spreading the damage faster.

Her face breaks the surface for a heartbeat.

Her lips are already wrong, swollen and tearing as she tries to scream again. What comes out is a choking, bubbling sound instead. Pink foam spills from her mouth and runs back into the water. Her eyes find mine in that moment, full of terror and understanding that finally lands too late.

She goes under again.

Her chest bucks, forcing out a thick, broken gurgle. Her shoulders convulse. Then her whole body starts to lose rhythm.

I watch her skin come apart in places, watch the shape of her change as the water eats at her. Her stomach looks like it is collapsing inward. Her chest sags and warps as the surface layers give up. Her hair floats loose around her head, dark strands sticking to her face and drifting away again in the steam.

The thrashing turns sloppy. The sloppy movements turn into weak jerks.

Her hands claw at nothing, fingers slipping through skin that no longer holds together, leaving red smears that vanish into the white churn. Her head rolls to the side and stays there, mouth open, eyes still staring even as her body stops working.

The water keeps bubbling around her.

I stand there and watch until the violent movement fades. I watch until the surface calms and the steam thins.

Only then do I step back and breathe, not because I'm shaken, but because the rage finally has somewhere to settle.

Behind me, Seth remains silent. He doesn't interrupt or hurry me. He stands there, letting me witness the conclusion of something that started the moment Sophie decided to fuck with me.

I straighten slowly and wipe my hands on my jeans. Then I turn away from the tub.

Some parts of me go under with her. The parts that wake up choking. The parts that flinch at water.

What remains feels unbreakable, darker, and deadlier.

Chapter 51

Seth

"Go ahead," I smile as I step closer. "I'm right here. Take your shot."

He stinks of rot and panic. He's slumped in the chair because that's the only way he can stay upright at all. One shoulder sags lower than the other. His left leg jerks when his nerves misfire. His mouth works around blood and spit, but nothing worth hearing comes out.

I tilt my head and study him. "Let's make things fair, I don't enjoy mutilating people who can't fight back." I lean in until my face hovers inches from his. "That's your thing." I tap his chest once, light, almost friendly. "So here's your chance. Hit me."

He tries.

The effort wrecks him. His broken arm twitches uselessly, bone scraping inside torn muscle. His other arm shakes when he tries to lift it, wrist bent wrong, skin split wide where white bone pushes through. A whimper tears out of him before he can stop it.

I laugh. "Oh yeah, that's right. You're too much of a pussy to hit me."

I grab his arm before he can pull it back. My hand closes around what is left of his wrist, fingers locking just below the joint. He sucks in a breath and shakes his head, eyes squeezing shut as his body tries to curl inward against the chair restraints.

"Now you know what it feels like."

I twist.

The bone gives with a wet crack. Another shard punches through skin, longer this time, slick with blood. His scream fills the room. His body jerks against the chair, straps biting into him, legs kicking without coordination.

I lean in close, my mouth near his ear, and smile.

"That was just the warm-up."

Behind me, Brooke moves toward the speaker.

"How about some music Elliot."

I already know what she is doing. The first notes slide into the room.

"Goodbye Horses"

Elliot hears it immediately. His jaw locks so hard his teeth grind. His chest hitches and stutters, breath cutting in short, panicked pulls. A sound tears out of him that is not quite a scream and not quite a word.

I grin. Brooke has always had a dark sense of humor, and I fucking love her for it.

I step closer, slow enough that he feels every inch disappear. I want him tracking my movement. I want him counting seconds.

He tries to straighten in the chair.

His body refuses. Both legs are now broken. The ankle is shattered. His knee jerks uselessly. His torso tips sideways, caught by straps before he can fall. Something grinds inside his chest when he moves. We both hear it. His face tightens, and a strangled sound rips out of him as his lungs fight for a rhythm they can't find.

I press two fingers to his throat.

His pulse hammers under my touch, panic doing half the work for me.

I lean in.

"You know what's funny?" I murmur. "This is the first time we've met in person."

His eyes flick toward mine, unfocused and terrified.

"I've hated people before, I've hated them enough to take my time. Enough to remember their faces. But I've never hated anyone the way I hate you."

I straighten just enough to look at him properly. Blood coats his mouth.

"You put Brooke through hell. You thought you were breaking her." My smile widens. "All you did was make her stronger."

I lean closer again.

"So here's how this works," I continue. "Everything you did to her, I'm going to make you feel. Then I'm going to do it again. And then I'm going to do it a third time, just to be sure it really fucking hurts."

His eyes fill, terror finally registering.

"I've done a lot of things," I add. "I've taken my time with people who begged. I've learned exactly how much a body can handle before it gives up, and exactly how to stop it from doing that."

I lean closer.

"And I've been excited before. But you're special."

I move my hand from his arm to his face and cup his jaw, fingers digging into the hinge where bone meets bone. He tries to pull away, but the straps hold him tight. His breath comes fast and shallow, lips trembling, teeth chattering as his body understands what is coming before his mind catches up.

"So just know," I tighten my grip. "I'm going to end you. Not fast. We're going to take our time. We're going to enjoy this."

Elliot cries out.

"And when it finally gets too much," I add, lowering my voice, "the last thing you're going to see is her standing over you, smiling."

I hit his jaw hard and fast.

The sound is a sickening crack that echoes in the warehouse. His mouth snaps open at the wrong angle. Teeth clack together before one skids free, clattering to the floor. Blood pours down his chin as he screams, the sound mangled and uneven, his body thrashing uselessly against the restraints while the song plays on, filling the room.

I laugh quietly.

Elliot tries to yell. It comes out wrong.

His jaw hangs at a crooked angle, blood pouring down his chin and soaking into his collar. His tongue drags clumsily against broken teeth as he forces the words out, every syllable chewed to pieces by bone that no longer works.

"Cuh... Cuh-linn," he mumbles. Spit and blood spray with it. "Colin's gonna find you." His eyes roll, unfocused but burning. "He's gonna fuckin' kill both of you." He sucks in a wet breath and keeps going, voice slurred and thick. "Gonna make it worse. Worse than this." Another broken sound tears out of him. "Make you watch her die first." His mouth twists, trying to smile. "He'll fuck her in front of you too."

I sigh.

"Oh yes," I say calmly. "Your brother Grant." I tilt my head. "Or Colin, since you want to be personal about it."

I crouch down so we are eye level. I want him looking at me when I say it.

"I've got plans for him too," I go on. "A lot of them." I glance back toward Brooke for half a second, then return my attention to Elliot. "If he comes for us, he saves me the trouble."

I straighten and rest a hand on the back of the chair, leaning in close enough that he can feel my breath against his ruined mouth.

"He'll be doing me a favor. He can come all the way here to die instead of me hunting him down." I smile again. "That sounds convenient as hell."

Two hours pass.

I keep track because I want him to know I have time. I want him to understand that this isn't a moment of rage or a loss of control. This is patience. This is intention.

By the end of it, the floor is slick. Blood has pooled and dried and pooled again. His breathing has gone ragged and uneven, his chest hitching in short, panicked pulls that never quite fill his lungs. I tear muscle where it screams the loudest and then move on before his body can give up. I make sure he stays conscious. I make sure he feels every second. I talk while I work.

He cries. He begs. He sobs until his throat is shredded and all that comes out are wet, broken sounds.

Eventually, I stop. I step back and look at him.

"You know what the funny part is," I say, voice calm. "I expected more."

His head lolls forward, chin slick with blood. One eye has swollen shut. The other tracks me weakly.

"I thought you were going to be ruthless," I go on. "I thought you'd be slightly intimidating."

I shake my head. "You're not. You're just a weak pussy little bitch who liked hurting people who couldn't fight back."

He tries to speak. His mouth works around broken bone and split skin. Nothing useful comes out.

I lean in a little closer. "You're not who you thought you were. And you're definitely not who I thought you were."

I yank him upright again when he starts to slump.

"Not yet, bitch," I chuckle against his ear. "You're staying awake for this part."

He twitches in my grip, blood coating his face, soaking into his shirt, painting the floor. He earns this. Every fucking second of it.

"Here's what's going to happen next," I tell him. "Your body's about to get real confused. Shock's knocking on the door, but we're not letting it in yet."

I stab him low. Not deep enough.

He howls and arches against the chair.

"That one won't kill you, painful though."

Another stab.

"I'm avoiding anything important. See, I want you to last. Your body's going to start shaking soon. Muscles firing without permission. You'll feel cold even though you're bleeding everywhere."

His legs twitch. Then they stop listening to him altogether.

I feel it when his strength drains. The fight leaks out of him as his nervous system misfires. His breaths hitch, then stutter, like something inside him is unplugging piece by piece.

I straighten, letting him slump at last, his body folding in on itself as the shock finally starts to settle in.

I don't rush the next part. I've got time.

I crouch next to him and slap his cheek.

"Hey. No naps yet, champ. We're just getting started."

He flinches. Useless, blind reflex. I watch the muscles in his jaw seize up. He wants to scream again, but he's saving it. Or maybe he's lost his voice with all the fucking screaming already. Either way, I'm not done.

"Now, your liver's here." I jab the blade into his right side. Not deep. "Not touching it, don't worry. Wouldn't want you bleeding out too fast. But the nerves in that area? Fireworks. You're about to fucking feel them."

He tries to move. I drive my boot into his knee. He shrieks.

"Your body's going into shock," I explain. "You've lost so much blood, your organs are going to stop functioning. But don't worry. You're not quite there yet."

I sit him up, grab his other hand and stretch his arm out straight. I plunge the blade through the meat of his back, twist it, and pull. Muscle separates. A scream tears out of him.

He starts coughing. His own blood floods his mouth and sprays the floor in strings of red.

"Your body's fighting to stay awake. It thinks you still have a chance. Spoiler alert: You don't."

I tilt his chin toward me. What's left of his face is an oozing mess. Blood slicks his cheeks, his nose, his open mouth.

"I want you to know why you're dying? You're dying because you are a pathetic piece of shit. You thought you could hurt her. You thought you were invincible."

He moans. That's all he has left.

I stab him again. Below the ribcage this time.

"Wrong," I whisper. "You're just a corpse now."

I wipe the blood from my knife onto his shirt and look down at what's left of him in the chair. His body twitches in uneven pulses, his chest rising in shallow pulls that never seem to reach all the way in, like every breath stops halfway and dies there.

I glance at Brooke. "He's crashing."

Brooke is already moving.

She reaches for the metal table beside us, her hand closing around the syringe. The tray rattles softly as she pulls it free, the needle catching the light for a split second before she turns back to him.

She steps in, grabs his shoulder to hold him still, and drives the needle straight into his chest.

The plunge is clean. The liquid disappears into him in one push.

His body reacts instantly.

He jerks against the restraints, hard enough that the chair legs scrape across the floor. His head snaps back, his mouth falling open as a broken gasp tears out of him. Blood bubbles up over his lips, spilling down his chin as his lungs fight to catch up.

Some people think adrenaline turns you into something stronger. It doesn't.

It wakes everything up. It forces your body to feel every bit of what it's going through, every nerve firing at once, every signal hitting faster and harder than it should.

It won't save him.

It makes sure he feels it.

The panic comes first, flooding his face as his breathing speeds up, his chest pulling harder even though it isn't working. Then the pain follows, catching up all at once, dragging through whatever is left of him as his body lights up under it.

I let him feel it.

Let the fear rush in before the oxygen does. Let the pain catch up with what's left of his brain.

His eyes shift past me.

They land on Brooke.

Something ugly twists across what's left of his face. He forces the words out through his ruined jaw.

"I should've killed you," he slurs at her. "That first night."

Brooke smiles. "Shoulda, woulda, coulda."

I smile slowly, letting him see every inch of it as I stand to my full height.

"And see, like I told you." My voice drops as I hold his stare. "She is the last fucking thing you'll ever see."

I move behind him. I lean down and wrap my hands over his eyes, clamping his skull in place.

"You don't even deserve to look at my girl."

Then I shove both thumbs in.

His sockets cave under the pressure with a wet pop, soft tissue collapsing beneath my thumbs. His scream cuts loose a second later, loud, high-pitched and feral.

It fills the room. And I love it.

Blood pours fast. I feel it slip down my wrists. He thrashes, head jerking back, body jerking forward, blind and fucked, hands clawing the air like he thinks someone might help him.

I crouch again, close enough that he can hear me through the fog.

"You're not going to last much longer," I say softly. "You're already dead."

His lips twitch. Both eye sockets are nothing but hollow red pits, leaking and twitching.

I straighten up and look at her like we're deciding what to eat for dinner.

"So, what do you wanna do with him?"

Brooke doesn't even blink.

"Cut him up. Leave the pieces for Grant."

God, I fucking love her.

My hand finds her waist. She leans into it like muscle memory, like this is just another day, like mutilating the bastard who ruined our lives is as routine as brushing our teeth. The music in the background is upbeat and disgustingly cheerful, which makes it even better.

I glance back at Elliot. His face is a mess of blood, snot, and swelling. I flash him a wide grin, all teeth and malice.

"You hear that, Ellie?" I taunt. "We're going to turn you into a fucking puzzle."

He gurgles something. Might've been "please," might've been "fuck you." Hard to tell with no eyes and a jaw that barely hinges.

I saunter to the corner of the room, where the chainsaw is waiting. I grip the handle. I squeeze the starter. It coughs, then growls, then roars to life with a violent purr. I turn back toward him, stepping into his line of what used to be vision. He is slumped in the chair, twitching, broken, drenched in his own fear.

"Welcome to the last few minutes of your miserable fucking life."

I lift the saw, letting the roar fill the silence between us.

"This is gonna hurt," I say, dragging it out slow. "Really, really bad."

I grin down at him.

"Let's make some noise."

Chapter 52

Brooke

We left Elliot and Sophie in pieces in the warehouse.

The building disappears behind us, swallowed by trees and distance, and I don't look back. The smell clings anyway. It sticks to my clothes, my hair, the inside of my lungs.

Beau doesn't ride back with us.

Right after we finished, he wiped the blood from his hands and said he had somewhere to be. A contract he already took before all of this. Another hit.

He said it wouldn't take long and he'd meet us back in Washington.

Then he grabbed his gear and disappeared into the dark like he always does.

Seth and I packed up our things, took the car, and got back on the road.

Seth drives the way he always does after something like this. Fast enough to put space between us and what we've done. Careful enough not to draw attention.

The road rumbles beneath the tires, a low vibration that settles into my bones. Oregon stretches out in long, dark seams of highway, broken by trees and the occasional porch light flickering in the distance.

My adrenaline drains slowly. What's left behind feels heavy and dull, sinking into my shoulders and down my spine. I watch Seth's hands on the wheel. His knuckles are split and swollen, streaked with dried blood that has turned nearly black.

The highway blurs past the window, but my mind stays behind in Oregon.

Miles' voice comes back to me without warning. The promise I made to him in that goddamn manor.

My stomach twists.

Oh my God, Miles.

I am supposed to tell his husband. I squeeze my eyes shut and try to pull the address back from wherever my brain buried it.

River something. River Drive. River Avenue. River Road.

I press my fingers to my temple, angry with myself for not remembering something that matters that much. He trusted me with that. The only friend I had in that sadistic place, and I can't even keep the one promise I made to him.

My throat tightens, but I force the tears back. I pull my phone out and scroll through addresses in Oregon, hoping something will jog it. That is when I see another Oregon address sitting there.

Samantha's.

For a second I just stare at it.

If we are going to live like ghosts from now on, maybe it is time. She has probably seen the news. She is probably worried about him. I glance over at Seth behind the wheel and wonder if he will finally be ready to meet her.

"There's something I want to do before we get back."

"What?"

"We're probably not coming back here," I say. "Once we leave."

"Yeah."

Trees blur past the window. "I don't like the idea of people just wondering what happened to you. Thinking you vanished."

His jaw tightens. "We're wanted people, Brooke. Everyone should wonder."

"I know," I look over at him. "But this is different."

He exhales slowly. "You're talking about my mom."

"Yes."

"She gave you her address?"

"Yes."

He nods once. There is no big reaction. Just a small shift, like something inside him clicks into place.

"She might've seen the news," I say. "Your name was everywhere. If I were her, I'd be scared you were hurt or dead."

Silence fills the car again. The road keeps humming beneath us.

"You really think she cares?"

"Yes," I reply. "She just needs to know you're okay."

He drums his thumb against the wheel once, then stills it.

"How long?"

"Five minutes," I say. "Ten, max."

He exhales through his nose, a quiet release that sounds more tired than resistant. "Give it to me."

I unlock my phone. I read the address slowly. Seth enters it without comment, one hand on the wheel, the other tapping the screen. The GPS recalculates and speaks up, announcing our turn.

The drive stretches on. The highway narrows. The forest thins. Houses begin to appear, spaced far enough apart to suggest privacy instead of safety.

Seth slows as the house comes into view. He doesn't signal. He doesn't turn into the driveway. He pulls to the curb across the street and lets the car idle.

He doesn't say anything. He just looks.

The house is ordinary. One car sits in the driveway. The curtains are drawn halfway. A single light glows in what looks like the living room.

I break the silence. "Do you want to come in?"

He exhales through his nose, eyes still fixed ahead. "No. Not now." After a moment, he adds, quieter, "Maybe after we finish all this."

I nod, "Okay."

Neither of us moves.

"She just needs to know you're alive," I say gently. "That's all."

Another pause stretches between us. His fingers tighten around the steering wheel.

"Tell her I'm okay."

I look at his hands. I see the dried blood ground into his knuckles and the tension locked through his shoulders. I don't say that he is hurt in ways she can't fix.

I open the door and step out, then close it softly behind me. I make it halfway across the street before I stop.

I look back.

Seth is still there. His posture hasn't changed. His grip on the wheel stays firm. His gaze is fixed forward, caught somewhere between the windshield and the house beyond it. He doesn't follow me.

He isn't ready yet.

I walk up to the door and knock once, firm but careful, then let my arm fall back to my side.

The door opens almost immediately.

Samantha stands there like she has been waiting just behind it, shoulders tight, eyes already glassy and braced for the worst. When she sees me, something in her face breaks.

"He's okay," I say before she can ask.

She exhales sharply and grabs onto me, pulling me into a hug that feels both desperate and thankful. "I've been watching the news," she says into my shoulder. "Every update. Every press conference. Every time his name came up, I thought that was it. I thought I was going to lose him again."

"He was injured. But it's Seth. He can handle more than most people."

She pulls back just enough to look at me, eyes red, mouth trembling. "Thank goodness."

She steps aside and lets me in. The door closes softly behind us.

The house smells like clean laundry and something warm cooking. It smells safe. The normalcy presses in on me, bright and gentle in a way that almost hurts. This place hasn't been touched by the things Seth and I carry in our bones.

Footsteps move through the hallway.

A girl appears first, talking into her phone, voice animated as she complains about something. She slows for half a second when she notices me standing there.

Samantha glances toward her. "That's my daughter, Elise."

The girl lifts a distracted hand in greeting before continuing down the hall, already back in whatever argument is happening on the other end of the call.

A boy follows a few seconds later, rolling his eyes like he has heard the same complaint a hundred times.

"And that's my son Ryan."

Ryan flashes his sister an exaggerated look before disappearing after her.

Neither of them stops. Neither of them asks who I am. I am just another adult standing in their house, easy to overlook.

My eyes drift across the room.

They catch on a photograph.

It sits slightly crooked on the bookshelf, like it was moved and never placed back quite right. I step closer and pick it up.

A man with kind eyes and a tired smile stands beside her. Elise and Ryan are tucked between them in the picture.

"That's my husband," Samantha murmurs.

I glance over. She is not looking at the photo. Her gaze stays fixed somewhere past the wall.

"He's the one who helped me when I ran from Richard," she continues. Her voice remains calm, but something heavy sits beneath it. "He was a lawyer. He worked with a shelter for women escaping domestic violence. He made sure they had somewhere safe to land."

In the photograph his arm rests around her shoulders, protective without looking possessive. Like he understands exactly how to love her.

"He died of cancer two years ago."

"I'm sorry," I say quietly.

The words feel small, but I mean them.

She nods once, then looks past me for a second like she is deciding how much to say.

"I told Elise and Ryan they had a brother," she says. "I told them he died when he was little. That they never got to meet him."

Something tight settles in my chest.

Her gaze shifts back to mine.

"After everything that's been on the news about Seth, I've been hesitant to tell them the truth," she continues. "I don't want them to get the wrong impression before they even meet him."

Her voice softens, but it doesn't waver.

"I want them to meet him first. I want them to see who he actually is. I know he's a good person." She pauses, then adds, quieter, "And I think they'll love each other."

I nod, even though something in the back of my mind reminds me that Seth and I are barely holding onto this life as it is. We are one mistake away from losing it completely, and there is a real chance this is the last time we will be able to come here for a long time.

Her expression softens again.

"It's mostly just us now." Her gaze drifts towards the old photos. "I don't have any other family."

I lower the frame back onto the shelf, my fingers lingering against the edge a second longer than they should.

The question slips out before I think about it.

"Why do bad things happen to good people?"

Samantha finally looks at me. Her smile is soft and sad in a way I recognize too well.

"Maybe people like that aren't meant for this world. Maybe this world isn't built for people who try to be good."

That is a truth I don't want to carry yet.

Samantha glances toward the door.

"He's outside?"

"Yes," I reply. "He told me he isn't ready yet."

She nods, like she already knows that will be the answer. She moves closer to the window and looks out toward the street. Her eyes land on Seth sitting in the car, posture rigid, hands on the wheel like he is holding himself in place.

"But, he didn't want you worrying." I add. " He wanted you to know we're okay."

Her eyes flick up to mine. "You're leaving?"

"Yes. We'll probably be gone for awhile."

She nods slowly. "I understand. You don't have to explain it to me. But wait... I want him to have something."

She turns and disappears into another room. I hear a drawer open, then close. When she comes back, she is holding a photograph in both hands, careful with it.

She presses it into my palm.

"That's him," she says softly. "The day he was born."

The photo shows Seth as a newborn. His little face is red and his tiny body is wrapped in a hospital blanket that nearly swallows him whole. A ridiculous little orange pumpkin hat sits crooked on his head. Samantha is smiling in the picture, fully smiling in a way that shows she has no idea what horrors will one day come for her son.

"When he's ready," her voice breaks. "I'll be here."

She pulls me into another hug, slower this time, lingering. "Tell him I love him. No matter what."

Samantha doesn't let go right away.

Her hands stay on my arms. She searches my face one more time.

"Thank you," she says quietly. "For coming. For telling me. For loving him."

I nod.

Her mouth tightens, but she doesn't cry. She just nods once, the way people do when they are trying not to fall apart. She steps back and opens the door for me.

At the threshold, she pauses.

"Wherever you end up, please keep in touch."

"I will, I promise."

She leans forward and hugs me one last time. When she pulls away, she straightens her shoulders.

The door closes behind me with a soft click.

The night air hits colder now. I stand on the porch for a second, letting my breath even out. Through the window, I can see Samantha move back into the house. I can hear her kids laughing.

I walk down the steps slowly. Halfway across the street, I glance back.

Seth is still in the car, exactly where I left him. He doesn't look at the house. He doesn't look at me until I open the door.

Back in the car, the door closes with a muted thud. Seth's eyes go to my hands before my face. I place the photograph gently in his lap.

He picks it up and studies it in silence. His thumb brushes the edge once.

"She okay?"

"She's worried," I reply. "But she understands."

He nods. He doesn't say anything else. He starts the engine and pulls away from the curb.

The house fades into the dark behind us.

Neither of us looks back.

Chapter 53

Grant fastens the last button of his shirt and rolls his shoulders as if testing the fit. The bedroom mirror bends his reflection, but the distortion doesn't bother him. He smooths his hair back into place and adjusts his cufflinks with steady hands.

The bed behind him is ruined. The sheets are twisted into knots. Blood stains the headboard and trails across the wall in uneven arcs. He studies the pattern with mild irritation, already calculating what the cleaner will charge.

He lets his gaze rest on her for a moment longer than necessary.

She almost had the right look. Dark hair. The same stubborn glare Brooke carries when she refuses to yield. That resemblance was the reason he kept her longer than usual.

Almost.

Brooke would've fought with purpose. Brooke would've understood that fear is a currency.

Grant exhales slowly as an older memory surfaces. Richard had always preferred to turn the end into theater. After they were caught, he liked to make it a contest of chance. He would load a single round, spin the cylinder, and slide the barrel inside them. The sound of the chamber clicking into place used to make them tremble harder than anything else. Richard enjoyed the suspense. He enjoyed watching hope rise and collapse in the space of a breath.

Grant never cares for suspense.

He believes in control. He believes in deciding when something ends instead of letting probability toy with him. Grant likes to watch them scream in agony.

He glances at the blood again, then checks his watch. Elliot's party should be ending soon. If the trap works, Brooke and Seth are already dead.

He pulls out his phone and leaves a voicemail.

"Sorry I missed the party. I was having a bit of fun."

A pause, faintly amused at himself.

"How'd it go? Did they take the bait?"

He picks up his jacket and drapes it over his arm.

"I should be able to make the after party if you've got them secured. Things got a little messy here. You know gunplay gone wrong... for her at least...Call me back."

He slips the phone back into his pocket.

Grant turns off the light and closes the door behind him without another glance at the bed.

His secure phone buzzes in his pocket. He checks the screen and sees the flag he assigned to Elliot's events.

Multiple shots fired at a private party. Several fatalities are confirmed. Witnesses evacuated. Security feeds interrupted. Host currently unaccounted for.

Grant reads the message twice. The elevator doors open onto the lobby while his brain adds implications. He replies with a demand for clarity, fingers tight around the device. The answer arrives before he reaches the car.

Private cameras cut mid event. On-site storage drives corrupted. No verified footage of final minutes. Elliot not seen leaving by any exit.

Grant tries Elliot's personal phone. Then the burner, then the phone he uses for women. Then the one he uses for deliveries. All four drop straight into dead silence. Either powered off or buried somewhere signal can't reach.

He spends the next two hours hunting.

By two in the morning his office sits dark, city light bleeding along the windows and leaving most of the room in shadow. Files and maps lie open across his desk, dotted with routes, accounts, and names that mean nothing without the idiot who should be answering his calls.

At 3:14 a.m., his main phone vibrates once.

No alert sound plays. No banner slides across the top. The device just lights up on the desk, a flat blue rectangle pushing a small pool of color into the darkness.

Grant knows it will be one of Elliot's burners before he picks it up.

He unlocks the screen and sees a single text message.

Elliot: Come and get the last pieces of your brother.

Grant lets his jaw clench until it hurts.

He closes the message and taps the location tag.

Coordinates lead to a pin in the warehouse district at the edge of the industrial corridor. No movement shows. Just a dead dot sitting in a part of town where nobody calls the police.

Grant switches to a city system and pulls up the radio log. A call had come in five minutes earlier from a trucker who had seen a door hanging open and lights burning inside a supposedly vacant building. Dispatch had marked it as suspicious activity and started routing it to a night patrol car.

Grant redirects it before the officers clear their current traffic stop.

"Unit twelve, stand down on that warehouse check," he says over the line, voice calm and clipped. "Detective Grant will handle. Possible connection to ongoing investigation. Per command, no additional units respond until requested."

The dispatcher confirms.

His position might be bought, but the badge still opens all the doors that matter.

By the time he reaches the warehouse, the signal from Elliot's phone has vanished entirely. The building squats at the end of a narrow lane, siding streaked with old rain, graffiti clinging to one side. The main door stands slightly open, not forced, not broken, just ajar. That detail tightens something in his gut more than shattered locks ever would have.

He pushes the door open fully and steps inside.

The smell hits him before he reaches the center of the room. It carries copper, chemical burn, and rot, all of it layered together and settling heavy in the back of his throat.

The overhead lights are on. They buzz as they cast a flat, unforgiving brightness across the concrete. The space has been cleared out with intention, leaving nothing in the center except what he is meant to see.

Grant steps inside.

His gaze moves first to the left, drawn to the industrial tub.

The liquid inside has turned cloudy and gray, thickened into something that barely moves. What remains in it no longer resembles a person. The surface of the skin has broken down, pale and uneven, sloughing in places where the lye has eaten through it. Patches have separated completely, exposing darker tissue beneath, the skin softened and dissolving. Strands of hair float loose across the surface. The smell coming off it intensifies the closer he gets, sharp and chemical, layered over decay.

Grant's jaw tightens.

His attention shifts forward.

Three cardboard boxes sit in a neat row in the center of the floor, their seams crisp and the tape laid down in clean, deliberate lines.

He stops several steps away and looks at them.

For a fraction of a second, a weak part of his mind tries to reframe it. It suggests a joke. It suggests a setup. It suggests Elliot stepping out from behind a pallet, laughing, cameras rolling, ready to say, "Got you, brother. Just testing your response time."

That thought collapses almost immediately under the weight of the text and the boxes in front of him.

Grant walks to the first box and crouches beside it.

He lifts it slightly, testing the weight, then sets it back down with care. He reaches into his pocket and pulls out a slim knife. He cuts the tape and folds the flaps back.

Inside, someone has packed a section of Elliot. Flesh and bone have been wrapped tight in clear plastic, padded with paper. Enough shape remains that Grant can tell exactly which part of his brother he is looking at. Enough damage shows that he can tell whoever did this wasn't rushed. The exposed edges have been cleaned enough that nothing drips.

The muscles around his eyes tighten involuntarily.

He closes the box.

The second crate weighs less but shifts differently when he touches it. Whatever lies inside doesn't sit as one piece. When he opens it, he sees why. Loose sections slide against each other, bone flashing through ruined meat.

His fingers tremble once on the cardboard lip. He presses his palm against his thigh and holds it there until the movement stops. He moves to the third box. He already knows what it contains.

He lifts the lid.

The smell hits harder now. Elliot's head lies inside. The rot and metal tang roll up into Grant's face. The cut at the neck shows layered work, some clean, some rough.

This is a message arranged piece by piece.

Grant looks down at his brother's face and sees every failure layered there. Every time he indulged that arrogance. Every time he let Elliot treat operations like games. Every time he listened to John's cautious voice saying not yet, not this way, not like that.

He forces himself to hold the stare of what remains.

Eventually he folds the lid back down and stands. The room sways for one heartbeat, then steadies as anger fills the space.

He calls the retrieval unit first, giving the address and a quiet code that guarantees haste and silence. Then he calls the erasure crew, the ones who know how to make a crime scene look like nothing important has ever happened there.

He watches them arrive. He watches them work. They lift each wrapped section and slide them into sealed black bags. When they take the head, one of the men pauses for half a second before his training wins and his hands keep moving. The skull knocks against the lip of the container with a dull, unmistakable sound.

No one speaks to Grant. No one makes eye contact longer than necessary. They know who pays them and know better than to ask questions about brothers or boxes.

When the last bag leaves the floor and the last crate has been folded flat, Grant's hands feel too hot and his wrists pound with the pulse he can't slow. The feeling in his chest doesn't resemble grief. Grief implies softness. This feels like something hard poured molten and held there until it burns everything it touches.

He steps outside into the cold and shuts the warehouse door behind him. The night air carries exhaust and distant sirens.

He pulls out his phone and dials the number. John picks up before the second ring finishes.

"What?" John's voice comes through flat and bored. "This better be important, Grant."

Grant stares at the dark warehouse door and tightens his grip on the phone.

"I just collected my brother in pieces. Three boxes on a floor. You want to guess who did that, or do you want me to spell it out for you?"

"I heard Elliot's party went sideways. I figured he was hiding with whatever was left of his pride. I didn't realize we had moved into the gift basket phase."

"Seth did it," Grant's voice hardens. "Seth and that bitch of a niece of yours that you fed to my brother. They walked out of there breathing because you and the rest of those fucking bastards decided she should be a test case instead of a corpse. You all decided Seth needed a show trial and a public execution instead of a clean shot. You kept them alive for optics. Now my brother is in bags."

"The Collective made those calls, not just me," John says. "They wanted Brooke in the manor. They wanted Seth on death row. I followed the vote, just like you did. The one thing that came from me alone was simple. I told you not to let Elliot kill her. I told you he'd fuck up. You ignored that. He played with her anyway. He got what he had coming."

Grant's grip tightens on the phone.

"I don't give a fuck!" Grant snarls. "This is your fucking fault! I want both of them dead and whoever else they're working with!"

"You're the one who started this," John shoots back. "You brought in Kristie and Victor. You vouched for Elliot. Look at your scoreboard now. Kristie is dead. Elliot is dead. You're standing on one leg, and that leg is Victor Voss."

"Victor is more than enough," Grant retorts. "His money gives me leverage."

John gives a low, humorless laugh.

"You stupid son of a bitch. He uses you because you're his lapdog. When you stop being useful, he will move on. You keep calling him leverage. He calls you a tool."

Grant looks back at the warehouse, jaw tight.

"I'm done waiting for permission," Grant growls. "I'm going to find Brooke and Seth. I am going to take her apart slowly. When I'm finished, I will send you both their heads. Then we will see whose stock rises."

"You sound desperate, Grant."

"If you get in my way again, I won't stop at them. I'll come for you. I'll come to your house. I'll put Mary in a box just like Elliot."

John's voice drops, all pretense gone.

"I will put you in the ground myself. You want to come at me, then do it."

Grant's mouth twists with rage. "Keep telling yourself that. When I deliver Brooke and Seth, you will be standing there with nothing. And when I decide you go next, nobody will step in."

John gives a low, humorless laugh. "You haven't delivered anything. You lost the hotel. You lost the manor. You lost your brother. Stop boasting and start finishing. Until then, you're just noise."

The line goes dead.

Grant lowers the phone and feels his hand finally steady. He puts it away and pulls out his department handset, the one tied to the detective badge he has bought.

He opens the bulletin system and pulls up the files on Seth Kincaid and Brooke Sinclair. He adds their suspected roles in the Everspring Hotel massacre, the Portland party shooting, the warehouse mutilation, and the other bodies that will never hit a public report. He tags them as primary suspects in multiple homicides, kidnappings, and organized dismemberment. He notes their history of escaping secure locations and killing armed opponents.

He writes the classification.

Seth Kincaid and Brooke Sinclair are to be considered a psychotic serial killer couple with extreme risk to officers and civilians.

He sets the alert to nationwide. He selects every distribution list he can touch, including city departments, county agencies, state patrol, federal task forces, and cross border partners.

Under engagement protocol he types exactly what he wants.

Officers should treat both suspects as active lethal threats. Use of lethal force upon contact is authorized. Attempted capture should only occur when overwhelming tactical advantage exists. If that advantage doesn't exist, officers are ordered to shoot to stop and are permitted to shoot to kill.

He attaches the warehouse coordinates, the time stamp on the burner message, and a brief description of the scene that will make any cop pay attention.

Then he sends it.

Confirmations start rolling in. Departments acknowledge receipt. Task forces log it. Liaison units tag it active.

Grant locks the phone and leans against the hood of his car. The engine ticks in the cold. The sky over the city looks calm.

Brooke Sinclair is alive.

Seth Kincaid is breathing.

Now every badge in the country has permission to end that, but Grant intends to end them first.

Chapter 54
Seth

Brooke's voice breaks above me.

My head is still between her thighs. She lies on her back across the bed with her thighs draped over my shoulders while my hands hold her hips in place. The sheets are twisted beneath her and her fingers are buried in my hair while my tongue moves slowly across her clit.

Her hips twitch against my mouth.

I hum quietly against her and let the vibration roll through her while my tongue slides lower.

"Seth," she moans.

I reach beside the bed and pick up the small vibrating toy.

She feels it the second it presses between her legs.

"Oh my—"

I slide it inside her.

The vibration hits instantly. Her body jolts beneath me as her hips lift against the sensation.

"Oh—fuck—right there."

I keep my mouth on her while the toy hums deep inside her, the vibration building with every small movement of my hand. My tongue works steadily across her clit while the toy pulses inside her.

Her breathing breaks into uneven gasps while her thighs tighten around my shoulders.

Then she comes.

Her body tightens hard around the toy while her hips lift against my mouth. A broken sound slips out of her throat as the orgasm rolls through her.

I keep the toy inside her while I slow my mouth.

My tongue traces one last pass across her clit before I pull back.

I sit up between her legs.

Her chest rises and falls quickly while she watches me.

My eyes move over her body while her breathing slowly settles. Her chest lifts and falls against the sheets.

My gaze settles on her nipples.

The barbells that used to sit through them are gone.

I reach out and drag my thumb slowly across one, pressing over the exact place where the piercing had been. The skin feels smooth beneath my fingers, but I can still trace the faint line where it closed if I press just enough.

"What?" Brooke asks when she notices me staring.

"I miss your piercings."

My thumb presses harder before I pull my hand back.

She exhales, her voice quieter when she answers. "Grant took them out before he brought me to the manor."

The words land, and something in me turns violent.

He saw her like this.

Grant stood over her and looked at her body. He put his hands on her tits. He touched her. That fucker took out her piercings like he had the right to decide what stayed and what didn't, and then he dragged her into that place.

My jaw tightens until it aches.

Elliot died screaming.

I remember every second of it. I remember the sound of it. I remember how long it took. I remember cutting into him, the way the blade bit and tore, the way his body came apart piece by piece while he was still alive long enough to understand what was happening. I remember packing what was left of him into boxes.

It still isn't enough.

Grant is still breathing. And he will die in agony.

I lean forward and press a slow kiss against Brooke's stomach, letting my mouth move upward along the center of her abdomen while I force the rage into something I can control.

Earlier, when Travis went out to get supplies, I had him pick up a sterile piercing kit for me.

I already knew I would fix this.

I lift my head and look at her again.

"Do you want them redone?"

Her brows pull together slightly. "Yeah," she says after a second. "But I can't exactly walk into a shop right now and get them done."

"You know I have my piercing license. I got it when I opened the shop."

"Oh," she says, a little surprised. "Okay... I didn't know that."

I hold her gaze for a second longer, then I reach beside the bed and grab one of the pillows.

She looks at it.

"What are you doing?"

I place it over her face.

"Hold this over your head."

She laughs softly beneath the pillow.

"Seth?"

"Keep it there."

"Why?"

"Just trust me."

She sighs into the pillow but keeps it pressed over her face.

"That usually means you're about to do something weird."

"Probably."

I slide out of bed and reach into the nightstand drawer. The kit sits exactly where I left it.

Before I touch anything else, I glance back at her.

Her body is still loose from everything I have just done to her. The toy sits abandoned on the bed beside her thigh.

I step back to her.

My hand closes around it, then I slide my other hand between her legs, parting her just enough. She inhales the second I touch her, her body reacting immediately.

"Seth—"

I press the vibrator back inside her.

Her back arches, a broken sound slipping from her throat as her hips lift off the mattress. I hold it there for a second, making sure it is exactly where I want it, feeling the way her body tightens around it.

"Stay," I tell her quietly.

She nods, breath uneven, her fingers gripping the sheets.

I pull my hand away and turn back to the nightstand.

The sterile needle remains sealed in its packaging while I pull on a pair of gloves and set the jewelry out. I reach for the clamps and taper next.

Behind me, she shifts against the mattress, her breathing soft but unsteady as her body reacts on its own.

I tear open the sterile packet and move back beside her.

The cooler air in the room makes her nipples tighten immediately.

My fingers settle around one, rolling the bud slowly between my thumb and forefinger before positioning the clamp. I ease it into place with care, tightening it just enough to hold firm.

She inhales sharply beneath the pillow.

My hand slides between her legs and grips the base of the toy still buried inside her. I pull it halfway out before easing it back in slowly.

Her hips lift immediately as the vibration hums deeper inside her.

My mouth lifts slightly. I drag my thumb slowly across the other sensitive peak, then fit the second clamp in place, adjusting it until both sit secure against her skin.

"What are you doing?" she murmurs into the pillow.

"Relax."

I move the toy once more, pushing it in slowly until it is seated deep inside her again. The vibration settles into a steady pulse.

Both of my hands return to her chest. I quickly clean her nipple with an alcohol pad. One hand steadies her breast while the other positions the needle. My fingers roll the clamped nipple once, testing the exact spot where the old piercing used to sit.

The tip of the needle rests against her skin.

I push it through.

Her body jerks beneath the blankets and a sharp sound breaks through the pillow.

"Ah—fuck."

The sound carries pain and pleasure at the same time.

Her hands tighten around the pillow while her breathing grows heavier.

I guide the taper through immediately after, following the fresh channel to keep it open and smooth. Her body reacts again, a strained sound slipping from her throat as the pressure shifts.

I follow the taper with the barbell, feeding the jewelry through in one steady motion before removing the taper and twisting the ends into place. A thin line of blood forms around the entry point. I wipe it away with a gauze pad.

Her nipple swells slightly around the metal, the clamp still framing it.

The sight of it makes my dick harder.

Her hands still clutch the pillow over her face while the toy continues to vibrate deep inside her.

I clean the second nipple with alcohol and roll it slowly between my fingers again, adjusting the clamp slightly before lining up the needle.

Her body reacts immediately. Her hips shift beneath the blankets, the vibration still working inside her.

My fingers steady her breast and I push the needle through.

Her back arches against the mattress and a long moan pushes through the pillow.

"Oh my god... Seth."

I guide the taper through the new channel, keeping the motion quick before sliding the second barbell into place and removing the taper. My fingers tighten the jewelry until it sits secure against her skin before releasing both clamps.

Her chest rises and falls steadily now while both nipples sit pierced and perfect.

My thumbs brush lightly across them once.

She shudders beneath my hands.

I reach down and wrap my fingers around the toy again. I pull it out slowly.

Her hips drop back onto the mattress as the vibration disappears.

"Okay," I say quietly. "Take the pillow off."

She pulls it away and immediately looks down.

Her eyes widen the second she sees them.

She stares at the barbells for a long moment before lifting her gaze back to mine.

"You're insane."

"For you, always."

My hands settle on her thighs while I look at them again.

Her legs open slightly on the bed.

"They look good. Thank you."

"Yup," I say quietly. "Now let me admire my handiwork."

The metal glints faintly under the light while her nipples remain stiff around the fresh piercings.

"You're thinking about how they look while you fuck me."

"I am."

She smiles slowly.

"Then what are you waiting for?"

I slide my hand slowly up her thigh while the other pushes my sweats down.

The knock at the door cuts through the room. It is loud enough that both of us freeze. Brooke's body stiffens beneath my hands while her breathing shifts. Her eyes snap toward the bedroom door. Another knock follows. She sits up slightly on the bed, her legs still parted around my hips.

"Who is it?" she asks.

I step back from between her legs and pull my sweats up first, dragging the fabric over my hips. The movement forces my cock forward against the front of the material. I exhale quietly and slip a hand inside the waistband, shifting my dick upward until it sits flat against my stomach instead of jutting outward through my sweats.

It still presses firmly against the cloth, but at least it is less obvious.

Brooke slides off the bed at the same time, her attention already fixed on the sound outside the room.

I cross the bedroom and reach the door.

Beau waits in the hall, shoulders tight. Travis stands behind him with a tablet tucked against his chest, his jaw clenched, dark circles under his eyes like he has been staring at the same screen for too long.

"Living room," Beau says. "You both need to see this."

Brooke pulls on the first clothes she can reach, then follows me down the hall. We gather around the television on the wall.

Travis flicks something on the screen. The television feed shifts to a breaking news banner. A reporter stands in front of a graphic with two photos side by side.

My old booking photo.

Brooke's Stratford photo.

Bold text beneath them calls us a nationwide manhunt.

"Turn it up," I say.

Beau grabs the remote and raises the volume.

"...authorities are asking the public to be on the lookout for Seth Kincaid and Brooke Sinclair," the anchor says. "The pair is now wanted in connection with the Everspring Hotel massacre, multiple kidnappings, and a series of homicides involving dismemberment. Investigators believe they may be operating as a psychotic serial killer couple, responsible for a growing number of violent crimes across several states."

Brooke's fingers tighten on the back of the chair in front of her.

The screen shifts to footage from different angles. Grainy shots from Everspring security cameras play first, catching blurred figures and streaks of motion. Still images follow, rows of body bags lined up outside the hotel while emergency lights wash everything in red and blue. Then they pull an old photo from the campus vigil for the Stratford students.

The anchor keeps talking.

"Some online communities have already begun referring to the pair as 'The Stratford Slashers,'" she says. "The name references both the Stratford student homicides and the dismemberment patterns present in later crime scenes."

Travis lets out a breath that sounds half horrified and half impressed.

"I mean, at least they gave you guys a cool serial killer name," he says quietly.

Brooke shoots him a look that could cut through bone.

"Really? That is the part you focus on."

Travis lifts his hands in front of his chest. "I'm just saying what everyone else is thinking," he mutters.

"Law enforcement sources confirm that both suspects are considered armed and extremely dangerous," the anchor continues. "Officers have been instructed to treat any contact as a lethal threat. If you see them, you should not approach. You should call the tip line immediately."

A message bar crawls along the bottom, listing a reward amount and a federal number in bold white text.

"Fucking fantastic," Brooke says quietly. "They made it sound like we planned the Everspring massacre."

"They needed a story that made sense to people who watch this shit over dinner," I glance at Brooke. "Serial killer couple sells more fear than the truth ever will."

Beau exhales through his nose and points at the screen. "Listen to this part."

The feed cuts to another talking head, some former profiler with too much hairspray and a practiced frown.

"Based on current evidence, this fits a pattern of pair bonding around violence," she says. "He has military training and a history of aggression. She is the survivor of multiple mass homicides who appears to have fused her attachment to him with participation in his crimes. Together they present an extreme risk. Law enforcement will likely prioritize neutralization over capture."

Brooke's mouth pulls tight. She turns her head just enough to meet my eyes.

"Wow, they really psychoanalyzed us."

Travis shifts uncomfortably beside the couch. "I mean... I can't say they're exactly wrong."

Brooke raises an eyebrow.

Travis lifts his hands defensively. "But also, context matters. You guys are killing people, but it's justified. And you are killing bad people."

He pauses.

"Like... really bad people."

Beau walks out the room.

"Travis," Beau's voice carries down the hallway, "stop talking."

"Seth. Office. Now."

I walk down the hall and push the office door open.

Beau stands by the desk with his arms folded. He waits until I shut the door.

"I need your help with something," he says.

"With what?" I ask.

"Mercer."

The anger comes back the second I hear his name.

My fingers flex at my sides. I keep my face neutral.

"He was supposed to be my last hit," Beau says.

I look at him.

"He slipped me," Beau adds. "Got away before I could finish it."

That alone is enough to tell me how bad the situation is.

Mercer is not sloppy. Mercer is not careless. Mercer is smart.

He is tactical in a way that makes most men look like amateurs, and when we were still in the Marines he has a reputation that only a handful of people ever earn. He was one of the most vicious killers in the unit.

Besides us.

"He knew I was coming for him," Beau continues. "Which means he knows the contract is still open. And Mercer is not the type to sit around waiting for someone to try again. He is the type who hunts the person hunting him."

Beau looks straight at me.

"So before I get the chance to recalibrate and go after him again, he is most likely going to come for me."

Mercer is what happens when the military takes a violent ego and gives it structure. He learns the rules well enough to bend them. He learns the language of brotherhood well enough to hide behind it. He's the guy who volunteers first, then makes sure someone else pays the cost.

He likes pressure. He likes watching people crack. He likes testing boundaries until you either fight back or fold.

Me and Beau clocked him early. I mean we are no saints, but Mercer's kind of cruelty isn't about orders or missions. It is personal entertainment. He never says the quiet parts out loud, but everybody hears them anyway.

The worst part is that Mercer can perform competently when it matters. He can shoot. He can move. He can plan. He can make it look clean. When you try to warn someone about him, you sound paranoid because Mercer knows how to keep his record polished while he dirties everything else.

I look at Beau and keep my voice low. "Fuck. I always hated that asshole."

Beau holds my gaze. "Now you can kill him. I need backup for this."

"Beau," I sigh. "Brooke is in the other room. We are already on a nationwide manhunt list. Every move we make is a risk. We can't start taking side work."

Beau's jaw tightens. "This is not side work. This is a threat coming at us."

I look at him. "You have people. You always have people."

"None that I trust more than you," Beau replies. "I need your help, Seth."

That lands harder than Mercer's name.

Beau doesn't ask often. Beau doesn't beg. If he says he needs me, it means he has already run through every other option and hated the results.

"Mercer has backup," Beau continues. "At least two. Possibly more. He isn't moving alone."

My eyes drift to the desk. My mind pulls up Brooke's face without asking.

I swallow.

I owe Beau my life.

That debt is not something you pay back with words. Beau has pulled me out of situations that should have ended me. He has done it without ever saying it out loud, but I keep the score anyway. I keep it because I'm not stupid. When you owe someone like Beau, you don't forget it without becoming the kind of man I refuse to be.

Still, guilt burns in my chest because I know what this will look like from Brooke's side.

I disappear again.

I choose violence again.

I choose someone else's need over her peace again.

Brooke has been through too much to be treated like that. She has earned truth in blood. Every secret I keep from her feels like stealing something.

I drag a hand down my face. "She'll know something is off."

"She'll know if you act weird," Beau replies. "So don't."

I let out a slow breath. "That's not helpful advice."

"You want helpful?" Beau folds his arms. "Mercer is already moving. Someone most likely sent him to kill me."

My stomach twists.

I could say no. I could stay.

And then Mercer would show up anyway, and I would have to live with the fact that I left Beau alone against a man who has always loved stacked odds.

I rub a hand over my mouth and stare at the floor for a beat.

"How soon?"

"Tonight," Beau pushes off the desk. "We go in quiet. We end it fast. We come back."

I nod once, slow, because my body has already decided and my mind is still trying to fight it.

"If anything shifts, we leave." I hold his stare. "If I say we're done, we're done."

Beau nods. "Fine."

I move toward the door, then stop with my hand on the knob.

Behind it, Brooke is still in the living room. She's still waiting in that soft, fragile space we keep trying to build inside chaos. If I walk back in there and lie to her face, part of me will hate myself for it.

If I don't go with Beau, part of me will hate myself for that too.

I stand there, trapped between loyalty and love, and neither one feels clean.

I open the door and step back into the hall with Beau right behind me. The quiet in the house feels different from the tension in the office.

Brooke looks up from the couch the second we come back in. Her eyes move between us.

"What's going on?" she asks.

"Me and Beau are going to check in with a couple of his connections," I say. "See if we can get ahead of the Mercer problem before it turns into something bigger."

Her brows pull together slightly.

"Can I come?"

"No."

The answer comes out fast, but I keep my tone calm.

"It's not like that," I add. "We're not walking into anything. We just need to ask a few questions. These are people who only trust us, so I don't need backup."

She holds my gaze for a second, reading it, trying to decide how much of that she believes.

"I should at least come in the car."

I shake my head.

"No."

Her expression tightens.

"Seth—"

I step closer before she can keep going and cup her face, pulling her into a kiss that cuts off whatever she's about to say.

She softens against me for a second before I pull back.

"I'll be back," I murmur. "Three hours. Max."

Her eyes search mine.

I can see it.

The hesitation. The part of her that doesn't like this, that doesn't trust it, that doesn't want to let me walk out that door again.

"Three hours?"

"Three hours."

She exhales slowly, like she is forcing herself to accept it.

"Fine," she relents, even though it isn't.

I brush my thumb along her jaw once, then step back.

"Lock the doors after we leave."

Her lips press together, but she nods.

I turn before I give myself a reason to stay.

Chapter 55
Brooke

I pace the length of the house until my calves burn and my pulse thuds behind my eyes. Krueger paces with me, his nails clicking against the concrete in an uneven rhythm, stopping when I stop and starting again the second I move. Every few steps, he glances up at me like he is waiting for orders I don't have.

The lock turns.

Krueger freezes first. His head snaps toward the door, ears perked, whole body tensing like a loaded spring.

The door opens and Beau steps through. Seth follows a second later, slower, one hand braced against the wall for balance. There is dried blood along his hairline and down his neck.

My chest drops and lights up at the same time.

"What the fuck?" My eyes drag over the blood on his face. "What the actual fuck happened to you?"

Seth tries to smirk. It looks wrong around the split in his lip. "Beau's idea of foreplay."

"Very fucking funny." I turn to Beau, jabbing a finger at him. "You dragged him into whatever the hell that was and forgot to mention the part where someone almost cracked his skull open."

Beau shuts the door behind them and looks down at me. Six foot five of calm, broad-shouldered bullshit, trying and failing to keep his face neutral. The muscle in his jaw twitches once.

"If I'd told you anything, you would've tried to come," Beau folds his arms. "And you would've blown it before we got within ten feet of Mercer."

"That's not the point," I glare at him. "The point is you let me sit here with nothing. No details. No warning. You let me wonder if both of you were dead while you pulled whatever stunt you pulled."

Seth sinks onto the couch with a rough exhale, fingers pressing against the side of his head. He watches us with tired eyes and way too much patience.

"You tell him, baby," Seth mutters.

I whip my head toward him. "Don't fucking start. I didn't know there was a plan. I didn't know you were baiting anyone. I just watched you walk out of this house while we're on a nationwide fucking manhunt."

Seth lifts an icepack to his temple. "I'm aware. I got the memo."

Krueger trots over to Seth, sniffs his jeans, then his arm, then his face, like he's checking for missing pieces. Seth scratches behind his ear, and the dog leans into it with a happy grunt.

I turn back to Beau.

"You didn't think for one second that maybe I deserved to know what the fuck was going on?" I stare between them. "You had me sitting here counting the many ways things could go wrong. I didn't even know what I was waiting for. I just knew you both were gone."

Beau draws in a slow breath and keeps his eyes on mine. He looks like he wants to smile and knows better.

"Seth's fine. He's been injured worse than this. My doctor checked him already. No fracture. Just a concussion risk and a fucked-up lip."

Seth flips him off again without looking.

Beau ignores the gesture.

"I almost got a concussion," Seth mutters. "For a plan I wasn't fully briefed on."

"If I'd let anyone in on the full play, Mercer would've known," Beau leans against the counter. "He watches people for a living. He would've read it on Seth the second he saw him. He would've put a bullet in his head before I could move. This was the only way to get close without getting him killed."

I stare at him, breathing hard.

"You still could've told me something. Not the whole thing. Just enough that I wasn't sitting here in the dark like a fucking idiot."

"I told you enough to keep you here," Beau says. "I didn't tell you enough to get you killed."

My hands curl into fists at my sides.

"You're an asshole, Beau!"

"I know that," Beau glances toward Seth before looking back at me. "But if it wasn't for me you two lovebirds would have been in body bags. Mercer's dead, everyone's safe now."

The words land, but I refuse to let them soften anything yet.

I shift my glare back to Seth.

"And you. You walked out with him and didn't tell me what it was. You didn't tell me you were stepping into something dangerous."

Seth gives an unhelpful half smile.

"I had questions. Then Mercer's guy hit me in the face and the conversation ended."

Beau snorts once.

"For the record, I didn't send you into a trap. I had the situation completely in control."

I exhale slowly, shoulders finally dropping a fraction.

"Don't ever leave me sitting here like that again."

The fear still burns. It still sits under my ribs. The rest of it shifts.

Relief can sit in the corner for now, because I am not finished with this conversation.

I walk over to the couch where Seth sits with the ice pack pressed against his temple.

"I'm not done being mad."

"That's good then." Seth looks up at me. "It means you still love me."

My jaw clenches. I hold his stare for another beat, then let out a tight breath.

"I'm going to shower. I've been sweating my ass off, having panic attacks, thanks to you two geniuses."

Seth's mouth curls into a crooked smirk. He shifts on the couch and tries to lean in for a kiss, the ice pack sliding away from his temple. I turn my head just enough that he catches my cheek instead of my mouth.

"Nice try," I say, standing up.

I head for the stairs before either of them can respond. Krueger follows me a few steps, then stops and pads back to Seth like he can't decide who needs supervision more.

My legs feel heavy as I climb, every muscle aware of how long I have been pacing and waiting and imagining worst case scenarios. The second floor hallway feels too quiet.

Two years ago, I was a regular college student. I worried about finals, rent, and whether I could keep pretending I was fine after my parents died. My biggest fear was wasting my life, not losing it in a shootout or bleeding out on some concrete floor with my name on a warrant.

Now I am a wanted woman. The police have my face on every screen. A psycho murder cult wants me alive long enough to torture me. Every safe house feels temporary. Every quiet moment feels like a countdown to impending doom.

Dr. Feldman would have a field day with this. She would probably write a paper about me if she could. Layers of unresolved grief, chronic trauma, attachment issues, moral injury, all wrapped in felony charges and a body count that keeps growing.

I'm going to need therapy until I die. And that is only if I actually live long enough to sit on some couch again and talk about how fucked up I am.

The water hits my shoulders hard and hot, loud enough to drown out everything else for a minute.

I stand there, letting it run down my spine, over my abdomen, between my thighs, trying to wash the adrenaline out of my skin. My palms press flat against the tile. My forehead rests against the wall. Steam fills the small space until my reflection blurs in the glass.

My chest still feels tight. My thoughts still run in circles. Every worst case scenario replays on a loop behind my closed eyes. Seth on concrete. Seth bleeding. Seth not coming back.

I drag the conditioner through my hair with shaking fingers and rinse it out too fast. I scrub at my body like friction can erase what today has done to my nervous system. My skin is already sensitive from stress and pacing and too much cortisol, but I keep going anyway.

I want peace. But I don't think peace is coming.

This is the life I signed up for. I chose Seth knowing exactly what he is capable of, knowing what follows him, knowing that loving him means living inside danger. I accept all of it. I accept him with blood on his hands and ghosts in his head.

I guess being on the run comes with him.

That doesn't mean I have to like it.

I still have every right to be pissed.

I shut the water off and stand there dripping for a second, listening to the quiet rush back into the house. My heartbeat finally slows enough that I can breathe without it stuttering.

I wrap a towel around myself and wipe the fog from the mirror with my forearm.

My eyes look tired.

I make my way down the hall barefoot, damp hair clinging to my back, towel tucked tight around my chest. The bedroom door is cracked open. "N.h.i.e." is playing softly in our room.

Seth is already inside.

He is laid back on the bed, shoulders pressed into the mattress like he owns the space, hips positioned right at the edge. His feet are planted on the floor, knees spread just enough to keep himself open, exposed. His sweats hang low on his hips, barely there, the fabric pushed down far enough to show the full length of him.

One hand rests behind his head, relaxed, almost casual. The other is wrapped around his dick, working himself with slow, unhurried strokes like he has all the time in the world.

He looks up when I step in. His mouth tilts.

"Hey."

My pulse jumps straight into my throat.

He is still bruised. There is dried blood along his hairline, streaked down toward his temple, catching in the edges of his stubble. His lip is split, slightly swollen. The ice pack sits abandoned on the nightstand, already forgotten.

He doesn't stop touching himself.

My towel suddenly feels too heavy. And my pussy feels too wet despite the anger sitting in my chest.

"What are you doing?" I ask, even though the answer is obvious.

His eyes drag over me, slow and thorough, taking in every inch of damp skin. "Trying to take my mind off the concussion. Doctor's orders."

I snort despite myself.

"That is not what he said."

He gives one slow pump of his hand, deliberate enough that I can see the way his grip tightens, the way his cock jumps slightly in response. "He said to avoid stress."

My gaze drops before I can stop it.

He is so thick and hard. The head flushed darker, already slick, catching the low light every time his hand moves. My stomach tightens as I watch him, heat pooling low and fast, my body reacting before I can even pretend I'm still just angry.

My thighs press together for half a second before I stop myself.

I should still be pissed. I am still pissed.

But the way he looks right now, bruised, blood still on him, sitting there like he knows exactly what he does to me, it makes my pulse spike harder.

My gaze drops again, slower this time. I track the movement of his hand, the steady drag of his grip, the way his body responds to it. His stomach tightens, his hips pushing up just enough to chase the friction.

I can feel it between my thighs, already slick, already aching for him. My body gives in before my brain can catch up, pulling me toward him like a magnet, like it doesn't care about anything except the way he feels inside me.

I want him.

I want him inside me, deep enough to shut everything else out. I want to feel him stretch me open, make me forget the fear, the waiting, the way my chest locked up when I thought he wasn't coming back.

Focus, Brooke. Don't let him off that easily. Don't fall for his cock sorcery.

"I almost lost you today."

His expression softens immediately.

"Baby—"

"And you're in here jerking off."

He lifts his shoulders in a half shrug. "Multitasking."

I step closer toward him.

Seth's breathing has gone heavier now, slower, his chest rising deeper with each inhale. His hand keeps moving, like he is testing how long he can hold himself back.

"Don't ever make me imagine life without you again," I say.

His jaw flexes.

"I won't."

I stop between his knees and let my towel fall to the floor. The fabric drops at my feet, leaving nothing between us.

He looks up at me, eyes dark and blown wide, his teeth sinking into his bottom lip as he keeps stroking himself, slower now, like he is trying not to lose control too fast.

"You still mad at me?"

"Yes."

"But you're standing in front of me naked."

"Yeah."

He lets out a quiet breath as he smirks. "That feels like progress."

I reach down and wrap my hand over his, stopping his movement.

His breath catches.

"You don't get to scare the shit out of me and then act surprised when you know I need you," I murmur.

His throat works.

"Fair."

I slide his hand away and replace it with mine, closing my fingers around him, feeling the heat, the weight, the way his body reacts instantly to my touch.

His head tips back immediately, eyes closing for half a second like his body has been waiting for that exact contact.

"And Beau," I add. "I'm still going to murder him later."

Seth groans softly. "He already knows."

I stroke him slow and firm, watching his stomach tighten under my hand, the muscles in his abdomen pulling with each movement.

"You're lucky I love you," I tell him.

His eyes open again, locked on mine.

"I know. That's the only reason I'm still breathing."

My grip tightens.

He hisses quietly and lifts his hips a fraction closer to me, chasing the pressure, both of us still riding the edge of everything that almost went wrong today.

"Still mad?"

"Yes."

A low sound rumbles out of his chest. His thumb brushes over the head of his cock, spreading the pre-cum that has already gathered there. Then he swipes it up with his thumb and lifts his hand toward my mouth.

He presses his thumb to my lips, and I suck it clean, tasting him while his eyes stay locked on mine. His throat works as he watches me, something darker settling in his expression.

"Good," he murmurs. "Show me how mad you are."

Chapter 56

Seth

The house smells like garlic, whiskey, and burnt onion.

Travis claims it's "caramelizing."

I call bullshit the second the smoke detector chirps.

"I'm telling you," Travis says, fanning the pan with a plate, "this is how chefs build flavor."

"Flavor of what," Beau raises a brow. "Ash?"

"Okay Gordon Ramsay, let me see you make some dope ass chili," Travis sarcastically shoots back.

Beau snorts, "I'm good on your dope ass chili, I'd rather not have diarrhea tonight."

Brooke laughs into her hoodie sleeve, curled up on the couch with a blanket half on her legs.

The weight in her shoulders has shifted. Not completely gone, but lighter and looser. I haven't seen her sit still this long in weeks. Not since Hollow Pines. Not since the hotel. Not since the kill list started getting shorter.

It isn't the same Brooke I first met. It isn't the girl from the diner. But it is a version of her that isn't clenched in fight-or-flight every second.

And fuck, I love her.

Even if this version is sharper. More dangerous. More like me.

She glances over and catches me staring and smiles.

"Alright, it's done," Travis declares, holding up a ladle like a trophy. "My award winning chili."

Beau makes a face. "It looks like prison food."

"That's rich coming from you. You put maple syrup on eggs."

"It's fucking delicious and it's culinary innovation, dickbag."

Brooke laughs under her breath.

"Babe, you're not eating?"

"Waiting to see if it kills Beau first." I say as I watch Beau get a bowl.

"Appreciate you," Beau mutters, already digging in.

We eat. It isn't bad. It isn't great either, but no one cares.

The TV plays the local news softly in the background.

I grab the remote, turning the volume up.

"—Kristie Talbert still missing after a month long search—"

We all look up. The footage shows the makeup trailer. Crime scene tape.

Travis spoons another bite into his mouth and mumbles, "Damn shame. Wonder if we'll ever find out what really happened."

Brooke lets out a small laugh.

I lean back and let the voices fade under the crackling fire.

For a moment, everything feels... peaceful.

A faint, rhythmic beeping cuts through it.

Travis's head snaps toward his laptop on the coffee table. The sound repeats, sharper this time, urgent in a way that makes the energy in the room shift before any of us even understand why.

"That's not normal," he says, already moving.

His fingers fly across the keyboard, pulling up the Collective database. Lines of code flicker across the screen before a notification window forces itself to the front.

"Shit," Travis mutters. "It's a live feed."

My chest tightens.

"What kind of live feed?" Brooke asks, her voice already shifting, already knowing the answer isn't going to be good.

Travis doesn't respond right away. He clicks into it, eyes scanning fast, jaw locking.

"Private stream. Restricted access. This is... this is coming from inside their network."

The beeping stops.

The silence that replaces it feels worse.

Beau raises a brow, "Put it on the TV."

Travis nods once and moves quickly, connecting his laptop to the screen. The TV flickers, then the feed fills the entire wall, stretching wide and impossible to ignore.

No one sits down.

No one speaks.

The room seems to hold its breath.

The video stabilizes.

My mother's face fills the screen.

Samantha's eye is nearly swollen shut. Blood crusts along her hairline, dried in dark streaks that trace down her temple. Her lips tremble so badly that her teeth click when she tries to speak. Her hands are bound behind her, her shoulders pulled tight, and her whole body shakes hard enough to rattle the camera.

"Seth," she cries. "Oh God, Seth."

Something inside my chest tears open.

I can't move. I can't speak. My lungs lock as if they have forgotten how to work.

Behind her, just out of frame, a voice drifts in.

It is Grant's voice, calm and measured, and he is enjoying every second of this.

"Here's your last chance, Samantha," he says. "Tell your boy the truth."

She sobs, her shoulders curling inward as much as the restraints allow. "I love you so much. I never stopped. I swear to you, I never stopped."

The edges of my vision blur, and the room narrows until there is nothing left but the screen.

"I'm so sorry," she sobs, her voice breaking apart. "I'm so sorry for leaving. I didn't protect you from him. I regret it every day. I didn't know you were alive."

She looks down for a second, then forces her gaze back up, terror flooding her eyes. "I thought you were dead. I thought Richard killed you. That's why I didn't come back. I thought I had already lost you."

Grant's voice cuts in again.

"Time's running out."

Brooke shifts beside me, close enough that I can feel the heat of her body, but she doesn't touch me. She doesn't speak. She just watches.

Samantha leans forward as far as the ropes allow, and her voice drops, softer now, like she is talking to a child.

"You'll always be my baby. My little boy in the pumpkin hat."

Every memory I buried comes back at once.

They didn't come in order. They didn't give me time to breathe. They hit hard and fast, stacking on top of each other until I couldn't separate one from the next.

I saw the park. Luke ran ahead while I chased him, both of us yelling while she called after us to slow down. I heard her laugh, clear and real in a way I hadn't let myself remember.

I saw the floor of our old place. Colored pencils scattered everywhere. My hand moved across the paper while she sat beside me, guiding my fingers, showing me how to shade, how to add depth, how to make something look real.

I saw her waiting outside school. Every time. She never missed it.

It kept coming, faster, heavier, until it landed on the one memory I had kept buried deeper than the rest.

IHOP.

My eighth birthday. Right before she left.

I sat across from her in the booth. She slid the box across the table, smiling, like she couldn't wait for me to see it.

I opened it and saw the model car.

A '67 black Chevy Impala.

She told me it looked fast enough to outrun the world. Like maybe I could too someday.

I held it in my hands and understood, even then, that it was more than just a car. It mattered because it came from her.

And she was everything to me.

My throat tightens so hard it feels like it is closing.

Grant steps into frame.

The gun is already in his hand. He presses the barrel against her temple, forcing her head slightly to the side while his grip remains steady.

Samantha's eyes lock onto the camera.

She knows what is coming.

"I love you, Seth," she whispers, her voice barely holding together. "I'll always love y—"

The gunshot explodes through the speakers.

Her head snaps sideways, and blood sprays across the screen in a violent burst that paints the frame red before her body drops out of view. The camera shakes, then falls and hits the floor with a jarring crack.

The image tilts.

All that remains in view is the hardwood and a smear of blood spreading slowly outward.

The feed doesn't cut.

Grant's shoes step into frame. He crouches, picks up the camera, and his face fills the screen again. His expression is calm, and he watches me like I am part of the experiment.

"Now you know I'm not fucking around."

He tilts his head slightly.

"You and Brooke are next."

The screen goes black.

The room stays frozen.

The remote slips from my hand and hits the floor, the plastic cracking against the hardwood as the sound echoes too loud in the silence.

No one moves.

No one speaks.

I stare at the dark screen as if it might change if I keep looking, as if she will come back, as if this could still be undone.

My hands feel numb. My chest feels hollow.

Something in my body starts to shut down. My fingers go still, my jaw locks tight, and my breathing turns shallow, like it can't fully come in. The room dulls around me, sounds fading, vision narrowing until all I can see is the empty screen. I can't swallow. I can't blink. I can't move. My body just... stops.

I manage to force one word out.

"Mom."

Chapter 57
Brooke

My body doesn't know what to do with what just happened.

I want to scream, to sob until my throat shreds itself, to grab something heavy and throw it hard enough to break, but none of that comes out, because it all stays locked inside my chest, burning and building with nowhere to go.

Seth doesn't move.

The television still glows across the room, the image frozen on a smear of red that has no right to exist outside of a nightmare, yet it fills the space, like it has not just carried the last seconds of his mother's life into this room while we stand there and watch it happen.

His eyes are open, but he's gone, not looking at anything in front of him, not tracking movement, not reacting, because they stay fixed somewhere past all of us, somewhere I can't reach no matter how hard I try.

"Oh God," I whisper, and then I am already moving before the sound has fully left my mouth.

I drop to my knees in front of him and bring my hands up to cup his face, feeling the coldness of his skin under my palms, the unnatural stillness of him as my thumbs drag along his cheekbones in a grounding motion that I hope will pull him back into his body and remind him that he's still here and not alone.

"Seth," I say, my voice shaking despite everything in me trying to hold it together. "Seth, baby."

Nothing.

The absence of a response heightens my anxiety.

I swallow hard and force myself to try again, louder this time, pushing the words through the tightness in my throat. "Look at me."

His pupils don't shift toward me, and his breathing stays shallow and incomplete, like his body has forgotten how to draw air deep enough to keep him alive.

Beau is at my side almost immediately, dropping into a crouch with a controlled urgency that contrasts sharply with the chaos inside my chest, his eyes moving over Seth's face with precise focus as he assesses what's happening.

"Hey, man," Beau says. "Seth. Stay with us."

Behind me, Travis swears under his breath before the words unravel into something louder and more frantic, his hands dragging through his hair as panic takes over. "Fuck. Fuck, fuck, fuck. He's catatonic. Jesus Christ."

I tighten my grip on Seth's face, my heart slamming hard enough against my ribs that it makes me feel sick, and I force myself to stay anchored to him instead of the rising panic. "Seth," I say again, steadying my tone even as everything inside me shakes. "You're here. You're with me. I need you to look at me."

For a long second, nothing changes, and that nothing threatens to crush me.

Then his jaw tightens just slightly, a faint shift that would be easy to miss if I hadn't been watching him this closely.

Beau catches it. "That's it," the encouragement clear in his tone. "Good. Stay there. Stay on him."

Travis is already moving, pacing once before rushing toward his laptop, flipping it open with shaking hands as his fingers fly over the keys. "I'm finding that fucker right now."

I lean closer to Seth until my forehead presses against his, forcing my breathing to slow, so he can follow if he can hear me at all. "Breathe," I murmur over and over, refusing to let the word lose its meaning. "I'm right here. You hear me? I'm not going anywhere."

His eyes flicker faintly, the smallest sign of movement that still feels like everything.

I drag my thumbs beneath his eyes, wiping away the tears that have gathered there without him seeming to notice them. "Come back to me," I whisper, the plea slipping out before I can stop it. "Please."

His breath hitches once, then again, slightly deeper the second time, and the change is enough to keep me from falling apart.

Beau nods beside me, his focus locked on Seth. "That's it. Stay there."

I hold his face like it's the only thing keeping him from breaking apart completely, like letting go would mean losing him for good.

"Seth," I repeat, stronger this time. "Breathe with me."

I exaggerate every inhale and every exhale, pressing my forehead against his chest so I can feel what his lungs are doing, searching for any sign that he is still fighting his way back.

For a moment, there is nothing.

Then I feel a faint hitch beneath my skin, barely there but real enough to catch onto.

"There," I whisper, my voice breaking anyway. "Do that again."

His jaw flexes, and a muscle ticks beneath my fingers, the smallest shift that still manages to crack through the fear that has locked me in place.

I slide one hand down to his wrist, then to his hand, finding his fingers loose and unresponsive in mine, warm but disconnected, like they belong to someone else.

"Come on," I murmur.

I guide him toward the bedroom one slow step at a time, moving carefully so he can follow, and he does, his body responding to my movement without resistance, without awareness, which feels worse than if he had fought me because it means he is not choosing this at all.

His shoulder brushes against the doorframe as we move through it, and he doesn't react in any way that suggests he feels it.

"Easy." My voice comes out quiet, even though I'm the one barely holding myself together.

I sit him on the edge of the bed and drop down in front of him again, my knees pressing into the carpet as my hands come back to his face, firmer this time, anchoring him in place so he can't drift away from me again.

"Hey," I tighten my hold, forcing his attention to me. "You're here."

There is no immediate response, and the silence stretches too long.

"I need you here," my voice cracking despite every attempt to control it. "With me."

His eyes flicker again, just slightly, like something inside him is trying to reconnect, and then they finally focus, slowly settling on my face.

My breath catches in my chest.

"Brooke," he says.

The word comes out flat and hollow, stripped of everything that sounds like him, but it is still him.

Relief hits so hard that my hands start to shake.

"I'm here," I lean closer like he might disappear if I give him any space. "I'm right here. I'm not going anywhere."

His shoulders drop, not in relief but in collapse, like whatever has been holding him upright has finally given out, and he nods once.

I ease him back onto the bed, moving carefully so I don't jolt him, and he lets me guide him, lets me pull the covers over him, lets me climb in beside him while his body stays tense under my arm, his muscles locked even in stillness.

I curl into his side and press my ear against his chest, needing to hear his heartbeat to reassure myself that he's still here.

His pulse races beneath my cheek, uneven and erratic, stumbling and surging in a way that makes my chest tighten, but it is there, and that is enough for now.

I close my eyes and match my breathing to his, forcing my body into a slower rhythm, refusing to let myself break while he needs me like this.

Samantha's face keeps cutting through the dark behind my eyes, replaying over and over again, her voice echoing in my head, her last words pressing into me.

I had only seen her twice, and somehow that had been enough to understand how much she loved him, enough to hear the truth in her voice when she spoke about regret and loss, enough to feel the impact of her absence already settling into the space around us.

Her arms around me on that porch replayed without warning, the way she held on, the way her voice cracked when she whispered that she was grateful

I loved her son, and the memory hit me hard enough that my heart sank all over again.

A tear slips free before I can stop it, and I wipe it away quickly and quietly, because I don't have the luxury of falling apart right now.

He needs me present, steady, holding him together in a way I'm not sure I can maintain for long.

Outside the room, voices rise and clash, breaking through the fragile quiet I am trying to hold onto.

"We go now," Travis demands, his voice tight with fury. "We find Grant before he disappears."

"That is exactly what he wants," Beau fires back. "He wants us reactive and sloppy. You want to get Seth killed on a night like this?"

"He just executed his mother on live," Travis snaps. "You want to sit on that?"

"I want us alive," Beau replies. "I want Seth alive. Running out there like that gets us all buried."

Their argument circles in repetitive bursts, but I force myself to tune it out, keeping my attention where it needs to be.

On Seth. On the way his jaw tightens when their voices rise. On the subtle shift in his breathing when Travis swears. On the tension that still lives in his body even as he lies there.

The adrenaline that has carried me this far begins to drain out of my system, leaving behind a heavy exhaustion that settles into my limbs and makes everything feel harder to hold together. My arms ache, my legs feel heavy, and my head throbs with the aftershock of everything that has just happened.

I whisper his name under my breath, repeating it quietly, just enough to keep him tethered to me.

Time passes.

Then his voice breaks through the quiet again.

"I'm okay."

The words are quiet and flat, but they are real.

My heart stutters in response.

Seth's throat works before he speaks again.

"I just need a minute."

I lift my head slowly, searching his face, taking in the way his eyes have closed and his breathing has deepened slightly.

"Okay," I whisper. "I'm here."

I settle back against him, letting my body finally give in to the exhaustion as I focus on the steady rhythm of his breathing and the sound of his heart beneath my ear.

When his breathing evens out, mine follows. Sleep comes quietly, pulling me under before I can fight it.

I fall asleep holding him, because letting go feels like it will break everything.

My arm slides across the bed and meets cold sheets.

I sit up immediately, my heart already racing, and for one brief second I try to convince myself that he has only gone to the bathroom and that I have barely been asleep.

The clock on the nightstand tells me otherwise.

An hour has passed.

Panic climbs up my spine.

"Seth," I whisper as I push myself out of bed.

The bathroom is empty, the light off, the door standing open with nothing inside.

I move down the hallway barefoot, checking every room with quick, panicked movements, but the living room is empty, and there is no sign that he has been there at all.

I knock on Travis's door.

He opens it almost immediately, his expression shifting the second he sees my face. "What's wrong?"

"Have you seen Seth?" I ask, the words coming out too fast. "He's not in the room."

Travis's face tightens. "No."

That is all it takes.

We move at the same time, heading down the hall to Beau's door. Travis knocks once, and Beau yanks it open, already half dressed.

"Have you seen Seth?" I ask, my voice unsteady now.

"No," Beau's eyes flick past us down the hallway, and I can see the moment he understands. "Fuck."

We don't say anything else. We run.

Cold air hits my face as we rush outside, and my eyes go straight to the driveway.

One car is missing.

My stomach drops hard enough that it feels like falling.

"No," I breathe. "No, no, no."

He didn't wake me. He didn't leave anything behind. He didn't take his phone.

He just left.

Alone.

My hands start to shake as everything clicks into place at once, the manhunt, his face everywhere, every cop and every federal agent looking for him.

And he has walked straight into it.

"He's going after Grant." The certainty settles into me immediately. "By himself."

Travis swears under his breath, and Beau drags a hand down his face, his expression tightening with a look of dread.

I stand there staring at the empty space where his car should have been, knowing exactly what this means.

Whatever restraint he had left died with his mother on that screen.

Chapter 58

Seth

I lost track of how long I was on the road.

Time stopped meaning anything the second the screen went dark, and it never started again, because everything stayed frozen on the moment her head snapped to the side, on the sound of the gunshot tearing through everything, on the way her voice cut off mid-word.

Everything after that feels wrong.

The road stretches in front of me, endless and empty, but I don't remember getting on it, I don't remember passing anything, and I don't remember making a single decision that lead me here. My hands are on the wheel, locked tight, my fingers digging in so hard they hurt, but the pain doesn't register the way it should because it gets buried under everything else pressing against me.

I feel all of it at once.

I see her every time I blink, and the image shifts between the way she looked at the end and the way she looked when she said my name, when her voice softened, when she tried to comfort me even as she knew what was coming.

My throat tightens so hard it burns, and I drag in a breath, it gets stuck in my chest like my body has forgotten how to do something as basic as breathing.

I should have been there.

The thought doesn't come quietly, it repeats over and over, crashing into everything else until it becomes the only thing that makes sense.

I should've been there.

I shouldn't have been watching from a distance, standing in a room while a screen showed me the worst moment of my life. I should've been in that room with her, I should've been between her and him, and I should've killed him before it ever reached that point.

My foot presses harder on the gas, and the engine growls beneath me as the car pushes faster, but the speed does nothing to ease the pressure building inside my chest.

I hear the gunshot again, and it doesn't fade or soften, because it keeps replaying in perfect clarity, like it is still happening and will never stop happening.

I hear Grant's voice right before it, calm and controlled in a way that makes everything worse, because there was no hesitation and no urgency.

He enjoyed it.

I want to kill him.

The thought settles into me with a clarity that cuts through everything else, and it doesn't feel reckless or impulsive, because it feels like the only thing left that makes sense.

I don't want it to be quick, and I don't want it to be clean, because I want him to feel exactly what he took, piece by piece, second by second, without anything to shield him from it.

I cross into Oregon without noticing the exact moment it happens, the sign flashes past and disappears, and nothing outside this car holds long enough to matter.

I don't plan where I am going, and I don't make a conscious choice to turn, but my body does it anyway, following a path it already knows.

I don't want to go there, but I do anyway.

Her house comes into view, and something in my chest cracks open in a way that almost makes me stop breathing entirely, because the sight of it pulls everything back into focus at once.

Police cars line the street, their lights flashing in harsh pulses of red and blue that wash over the house, the yard, the windows, turning everything into something distorted and unreal.

Medics move, not rushing, not panicking, because there is nothing left to save, and the officers stand in clusters with the kind of grim efficiency that only shows up when it is already too late.

They found her.

I slow just enough to see the yard, and that is when I see them.

Two smaller figures stand near the sidewalk, wrapped in blankets, their bodies folded inward under grief too heavy for them to carry. They are crying so hard they can barely hold themselves upright, their shoulders shaking, their voices breaking in a way that cuts through everything else even from this distance.

My half siblings.

My jaw locks so tight it aches, and for a second my grip on the wheel loosens, just enough to make the thought surface.

If I stop, I will get out, and the moment I step into that yard with my face already burned into every system they have, every cop out there will see a target instead of a person. They won't hesitate, and they won't ask questions. I will be dead before I make it halfway across the grass, and my siblings will watch it happen.

I already know it, because there is no version of me that will stay in that car if I let myself think about it for even one second longer. I will walk straight toward them without stopping, without thinking, pulled by something stronger than reason, and I won't make it back out again.

I will try to say something I don't know how to say, something that can never come out right, and I will feel all of it at once. Everything will break open in a way I won't be able to control, and there will be nothing left to hold it together.

I can't do that.

My grip tightens again, harder than before, my hands locking back into place as I force the car forward.

I keep driving.

The house disappears behind me, but it doesn't leave, because it stays in my chest, in the back of my mind where everything continues to replay whether I want it to or not.

The grief doesn't fade, and it doesn't soften into something manageable, because it shifts into something colder, something harder, something that doesn't ask for release.

It becomes something I can use.

Grant didn't just kill her. He made her speak, he made her apologize, and he made her say she loves me while he stood there with a gun pressed to her head.

He took his time, and he made sure I watched every second of it.

My hands shake again, from the force of everything building inside me with nowhere to go.

I press harder on the gas, and the car surges forward, the engine straining as the road blurs beneath me, but it still doesn't feel fast enough.

I don't have a plan, and I don't need one, because the outcome has already been decided somewhere deeper than thought.

I know exactly what I'm going to do when I find him, and the certainty of it repeats over and over in my head, steady and unchanging.

I'm going to make him suffer.

I keep driving, and the world narrows until it is just the road, the engine, and the sound of my own breathing trying to stay even against everything working against it.

Then the passenger seat shifts, and the movement breaks through the narrow focus I've locked myself into.

I didn't look at it at first. I already know.

Luke sits there, one arm draped casually, head tilted, a smile on his face like a bad joke that never dies. He looks solid. Real enough that my hands tighten on the wheel.

"Well," he says, glancing ahead at the road. "Kind of ironic, right. Both our moms. Headshots."

He lifts his hand and presses his index and middle finger straight against his temple, thumb cocked. He makes a quick, sharp gunshot sound under his breath. Then he flicks his thumb down like he's pulling the trigger.

My chest tightens.

"Go away."

He chuckles softly. "I mean, sure, my mom did it to herself, but still. Very poetic. Family tradition, maybe."

"Shut the fuck up Luke!" I snap.

"I'm losing count," he continues. "Seriously, I am. You keep stacking them up, and it's getting hard to keep track."

My vision pulses at the edges as I force myself to keep my eyes on the road.

"How many people is it now?" he tilts his head slightly as he studies me, "that you thought you could love and save?"

The words land heavy, they hit something that is already cracked open.

"You couldn't save Brooke," he adds. "She barely made it out of that place alive."

My jaw tightens as my grip shifts slightly on the wheel.

"You couldn't save your baby."

My hands falter for a fraction of a second before tightening again.

"You couldn't save your mother."

Pain in my chest twists so hard it feels like it might tear.

"You couldn't save Natalie."

My breathing stutters as the names stack on top of each other.

"You couldn't save me."

His smile widens, like he is enjoying every second of this.

"You can't save anybody, Seth."

My hands start to tremble on the wheel, not enough to lose control, but enough that I feel it, enough that it bleeds into everything else.

"So stop pretending," his voice lowering just slightly, just enough to make it feel closer and heavier. "Stop acting like you're something you aren't."

My vision sharpens, then blurs, then sharpens again as I try to force focus back into place.

"Let the rage do what it is supposed to do," he continues. "Let it burn everything else out of you until there is nothing left but what you actually are."

"Shut up," I snarl, the words coming out harsher this time as I try to force him out of the car with the sound of it.

He leans back again, that same expression still fixed in place, but something about him flickers for a second, just enough to remind me that he isn't really there.

Even then, his words don't fade. They stay in my head exactly the way he said them, repeating and digging in deeper every time I try to push them out.

My vision darkens as I grip the wheel harder, my knuckles paling under the strain while I force my focus forward, but it doesn't matter because everything is already spiraling in a direction I can't stop.

I think about the file I pulled up before I walked out, and the details come back in fragments that sharpen as they settle. Names, locations, schedules, a list of people who think they are untouchable. Most of it blurs together now, but one detail stays clear and burns brighter than the rest.

Victor Voss.

He is hosting a gala tonight, and the image forms in my head with unsettling clarity. It is black tie, set inside a building made of glass and steel, with money layered so deep it turns into arrogance. The room will be full of people who believe they exist above consequence, above fear, above anything that might reach them where they stand.

The guest list is exactly what it should be. Collective members, donors, men and women who fund unspeakable crimes, all wrapped in layers of private security built to keep people like me out.

Grant will be there.

My breathing turns uneven as my thoughts fracture and collide, refusing to slow down.

I see his face in my head. I see the moment he realizes I am there. I see the shift in his expression when he understands what that means. I see the way his body will move when I put a bullet through him, and I see the way he will hit the floor.

I don't care if I die tonight, I only care that he does. The thought doesn't scare me. It settles into place like it has always been there, waiting for everything else to fall away so it can take over completely.

The road stretches ahead of me, dark, empty, cutting through the night like it is leading me exactly where I need to go. There is nothing behind me anymore, and there is nothing left that can pull me back.

I press harder on the gas and drive, already gone from anything that might have tried to save me.

Chapter 59

Brooke

The panic burns itself out somewhere past the freeway on-ramp, but the aftermath lingers, settling into my body in a way that feels worse.

Beau drives while I stare straight ahead, my hands locked together in my lap so he won't see them shaking. I press my fingers together hard enough that the joints ache, focusing on the pain because it is easier than focusing on everything else.

It took more than it should have to get him in this car.

Beau didn't want to leave. He kept saying Seth would come back eventually, that someone needed to be there when he did, and that walking out now could make things worse.

I told him I would go alone if he didn't come with me.

That was the only thing that worked.

Travis gave me everything before we left. Locations, access points, entry routes, and the name of the event Victor Voss is hosting tonight. His hands moved fast across the keyboard while he explained it, his voice tight, his eyes flicking between the screen and me like he was trying to decide if he should say more and choosing not to.

He stayed behind without arguing. Someone had to be there if Seth came back.

"I led them to her," I say.

Beau's eyes flick toward me for half a second before returning to the road. "What do you mean?"

My throat tightens, and I swallow against it, forcing the words out anyway. "After the warehouse. After we killed Elliot. I made Seth take me to Samantha's house."

Beau's jaw shifts slightly. "Grant has resources. He finds people. That wasn't you."

"It was. He had to know where to look. I walked him straight to her."

Silence fills the car. The road stretches ahead in a long, dark line, the headlights cutting through it without making it feel any less empty.

"Don't do that," Beau says finally. "Don't put that on yourself."

I shake my head, my gaze fixed on the windshield. "I can't get it out of my head. Her face. Her voice. The way she was talking to him."

My chest tightens again, sharper this time.

"She had to apologize," I continue. "She had to explain herself. She had to tell him she loved him while she knew she was about to die."

My voice cracks.

"She didn't deserve that. And he shouldn't have had to see it."

Tears spill before I can stop them, and I swipe them away fast, angry at myself for letting them show because weakness feels dangerous right now.

Beau doesn't look at me, but something in his posture shifts.

"I've seen some pretty fucked up things." His voice loses a fraction of its edge. "I know exactly where Seth's head went. Mine would've gone there too."

I turn toward him despite myself. "What happened to your parents?"

He doesn't answer right away. His grip on the wheel tightens slightly.

"You want the long story or the short one?"

I glance at the GPS. "How long until we get there?"

"About three hours."

"Then give me the long one."

He nods once, keeping his eyes on the road as the headlights carve a narrow path through the dark highway.

"My father ran a network," he starts after a moment. "Not the Hollywood version of organized crime. This was the kind of operation that moved real money through real ports. Containers, weapons, people, things that disappeared into shipping routes and never showed up on a ledger."

He adjusts his grip slightly.

"My mom came from another family that did the same kind of work on the other side of the world. Different crews, different continents, same business. Their marriage was supposed to end a war between those networks."

His jaw shifts as if he is grinding something down.

"It didn't."

"There were four of us," he continues. "Me and three younger siblings. Two brothers and a little sister. Things started getting tense when I was about ten. Deals were falling apart, shipments disappearing, people pointing fingers behind closed doors. My parents decided it would be safer if I wasn't around while the adults figured out how not to kill each other. One of my dad's contacts moved me out of the country."

"Where did you go?" I ask.

"A training compound in Colombia," he says. "Kids like me got sent there when their parents decided it was safer to turn them into weapons than leave them exposed."

He keeps his eyes on the road.

"I spent years there learning how to survive," he continues. "How to shoot, how to track, how to disappear. I thought maybe I'd never have to go back to the family business if I got good enough at something else."

The tires hum against the pavement. He shifts in his seat, adjusting his grip on the wheel.

"When I was eighteen, my parents asked me to come home for a truce dinner. Both sides of the family were supposed to be there. Cameras, security, a big show of unity. The kind of thing that told the rest of the world nobody was about to start a war."

Streetlights streak across the windshield. His thumb taps once against the steering wheel.

"I brought her with me," he adds.

I angle toward him, resting my shoulder against the seatback. "Her?"

"My girlfriend," he continues. "I never brought her around them. I knew better. But she wanted to meet my family. She thought if we were going to build a future, she needed to understand where I came from."

I drag my nails lightly across my palm, grounding myself in the sensation.

"I should have told her no," he says. "I should have left her out of it completely."

His fingers drum once, then go still.

"I was supposed to sit at the table with them," he goes on. "My mom told me to move one of the cars in the driveway before dinner started. It was blocking the entrance and some of the guests were complaining. I grabbed the keys and walked outside."

The engine dips as he eases off the gas for a curve.

"I heard the first shots before I even reached the car."

I turn fully toward him now, my breath catching without warning.

"By the time I got back inside, it was already over," he murmurs.

My hand slips from my lap and presses against the seat beside me.

"They didn't just kill them," Beau continues. "They made sure the bodies told a story. Hands were cut so nobody could hold power again. Rings were taken so no one could pretend the old bosses were still in charge. Faces were destroyed so nobody could build shrines for them later."

A car passes in the opposite lane, headlights flashing across his face.

"My brothers died under the table. My sister died in my mother's lap."

I swallow hard and look away for a second, staring out at the blur of trees.

"My girlfriend died in that house with them."

My fingers curl into the fabric of my leggings.

"They wiped out everything tied to them. Blood, alliances, attachments. They made sure nothing survived that could grow into a problem later."

He shifts his shoulders slightly, like he's trying to shake something off.

"That was the first time I realized loving someone could get them killed."

The words settle heavy, pressing into the quiet between us.

Losing your family like that was already unimaginable, but losing the person you loved at eighteen, in a room that was supposed to mark peace, felt like a different kind of devastation. There was no time to process it, no space to say goodbye.

For a second, my mind betrays me and goes straight to Seth.

To the way he looks at me like I am the only thing keeping him here. To the way everything in him burns too hot, too fast, too absolute. To how easily something like this could happen again if we aren't careful, if we slip even once.

I press my lips together and force the thought down.

It explains something about Beau that I had not fully understood before, the distance, the control, the way he moves through the world like attachment comes with a cost he has already paid once.

"I saw her before one of my father's men pulled me out," Beau continues. "He shoved me into a car and drove like hell. The whole time he kept telling me how lucky I was."

I shake my head slightly. "Wow."

"They said I didn't have to take over the family anymore," Beau sighs. "They said I could walk away from all of it."

I glance at him again. "Did you believe them?"

"For about five minutes," he says. "Then the rest of them started talking."

His jaw shifts as he exhales through his nose.

"They started talking about how useful my name still was," he continues. "How many alliances it could repair. Which prisons I would have to visit to show loyalty to the right people."

He adjusts his grip on the wheel again, knuckles brushing the leather.

"That's when I realized they weren't trying to save me. They were just moving the pieces around again."

The road curves, and he follows it.

"I didn't want any of it," Beau adds. "Not the titles, not the wars, not the family business. I wanted something that belonged to me instead of my bloodline."

I tilt my head slightly. "So you joined the Marines after that?"

"Yeah, part of it was getting out. Part of it was making sure nobody ever got that close to me again."

Silence stretches for a few seconds, filled only by the low rumble of the engine.

"And part of it," he admits, quieter now, "was that I didn't really care if I lived through it."

I shift in my seat, pulling my legs in closer.

"They thought it was temporary. They figured I would come back trained, disciplined, useful. They thought the military would turn me into a better weapon for them."

I glance at him again. "And that's where you met Seth."

A faint smile touches his mouth.

"Yeah, turns out he and I have a lot in common."

He taps the steering wheel once.

"Different reasons. Same appetite for violence. Same understanding that the world doesn't fix itself. Sometimes you burn the problem out."

The road rumbles beneath us while trees blur by on either side, and the world keeps moving like nothing is wrong.

"So when I say I understand Seth," Beau adds, "I mean it. Shit like that changes you."

I turn back to the window, watching the dark slide past.

"He's going to do something terrible."

"Yeah," Beau agrees.

I drag my sleeve over my hands, folding them tighter. "And we can't stop him."

Beau lets out a quiet breath. "That part we can agree on."

I stare ahead, voice steady. "I'm going to do something terrible too."

Beau looks over at me then. "Are you ready for this? Because what you're planning to do isn't something you just come back from."

"I haven't come back since I left the manor. I'm not the same person."

He nods once in acceptance.

The rest of the drive stretches long and quiet.

My thoughts drift back to Seth. I picture his face when the screen went black, the way his body went empty, like something vital had been unplugged. I know him well enough to understand what that moment did to him.

He can't let this go.

He has lost too much in too short a span of time. He thought he was going to lose me. We lost the baby. And now he has lost his mother in the most brutal way possible, with no goodbye, no chance to reconcile, and no chance to hear those words without a gunshot following them.

There is no version of Seth that witnesses that and stays the same.

I feel it settling into place with sick certainty. He's going to lose himself. Whatever thin strip of humanity he still holds onto is about to burn away.

And I am terrified of what he will become.

Three hours later, Beau slows the car and pulls off the road. Trees crowd around us, thick enough to hide the vehicle from the drive beyond. Up ahead, iron gates rise out of the dark, framing a mansion that glows softly against the night.

We move fast after that. Beau handles security like it is instinct. One guard drops without a sound, and another follows moments later. The booth opens, and the gate slides wide.

We slip inside.

The house looms closer with every step, and I can hear conversation drifting through the air, along with the clink of glass and low laughter, all of it untouched by what is about to happen.

I reach the front door and lift my balaclava just enough.

The door opens.

A maid freezes when she sees me, confusion flickering across her face before she steps aside automatically.

An older woman with gray hair approaches from inside, and the moment her eyes land on me, recognition hits hard enough that she physically recoils. Shock spreads across her face, her posture locking as she takes me in, clearly understanding exactly who I am.

I smile.

"Hello, Mrs. Grant."

Chapter 60
Seth

I come back to myself standing in blood.

It slicks the marble floor in wide, uneven smears, footprints layered over footprints where guests tried to flee and failed. Red tracks curve, overlap, and stop abruptly where bodies fell. Glass crunches under my boots when I shift my weight. It is everywhere. In my treads. On my hands. Up my sleeves.

Somewhere behind me, something crackles and pops. A fire alarm is going off, shrill and useless, competing with the low electrical buzz of damaged lighting overhead.

I blink.

I barely remember parts of it.

Bodies fill the room in obscene arrangements. Folded at angles the body isn't meant to bend. Draped over tables that were set for champagne and hors d'oeuvres less than an hour ago. Linen is soaked through, floral centerpieces crushed flat and dark with blood. A violin lies snapped in half near the stage. A crystal chandelier still sways, scattering light over the carnage like a spotlight.

I count without meaning to.

Five.

Ten.

Twenty.

Thirty at least.

Bodies cover the marble and the carpet between the tables.

The security team went down first.

I had the rifle waiting before I ever walked in. It was already positioned, already sighted. I took the guards before anyone inside understood what was happening. Two at the entrance. One at the service corridor. One near the glass wall overlooking the city.

I took their radios next.

No calls went out.

After that, everything broke open.

The shotgun handled the ones who got too close. The rest I handled however I had to. It didn't happen clean. It didn't happen in order. It happened fast and loud and angry.

People ran the moment the first blast echoed through the hall. Some tried to hide behind tables. Others sprinted toward the exits.

The doors locked automatically when the system triggered.

They only trapped themselves inside with me.

None of it slowed me down.

I scan the room one more time and finish counting.

Thirty bodies. Maybe more.

A man slumps against a banquet table near the wall. What is left of his face is unrecognizable, skin split, bone showing through in places. I remember him because I made him bite the wooden table first. I remember pressing his mouth down until his teeth met the edge. I remember the sound when they shattered. Then I kicked. Again. And again. I didn't stop when he dropped. I stopped when there was nothing left to give.

Another body lies on its side a few feet away, throat opened by the jagged edge of a champagne bottle. I remember the sound more than the movement. The wet gurgle. The frantic hands clawing at nothing. The bottle breaking in my grip. I remember stepping over him and using what was left, shoving it into someone else's eye socket, pushing until it resisted, then pushing harder until it did not.

Luke stands near the wreckage, hands clasped behind his back, posture relaxed, like he is walking through a private gallery curated just for him.

"Beautiful," his eyes bright, almost reverent. "You finally stopped pretending."

I step over a body without looking down.

He smiles wider, teeth flashing white against the red-streaked light. "You see it now? This is who you are when you stop lying to yourself."

I don't answer. I'm too busy taking inventory.

Two bodies near the bar have shotgun wounds blown clean through their backs. Exit wounds the size of fists. One of them slammed forward hard enough that his face shattered a glass display. Teeth and crystal litter the floor beneath him. Another lies facedown, spine twisted, blood pooled so thick it looks black. I remember the recoil. I remember not lowering the gun afterward.

A woman in a designer gown is slumped against a pillar, throat gone. A man near the stage is missing an arm below the elbow. I don't remember taking it, only the sound he made when he realized it was no longer there.

They deserved it.

Every one of them.

These people were not innocent partygoers. They were donors and facilitators. Predators wrapped in money and charm. They smiled at galas and preyed on people like Brooke. Like my mother.

I step forward and then I hear it.

Victor Voss drags himself across the floor, leaving a wet trail behind him as his body struggles to move through the blood he has already lost.

His expensive suit is torn open and soaked through, the fabric clinging to him in heavy, dark patches. One arm hangs useless at his side while the other trembles so badly he can barely pull himself forward. His face is swollen and split, his eyes nearly closed beneath bruised, broken skin.

He looks small now, stripped of everything that once made him untouchable.

He no longer resembles the tech billionaire genius he claims to be.

Victor Voss is the richest member of The Collective, and his money funds half the monsters in this room while his influence keeps people like them protected when bodies start piling up.

His daughter was Amber Voss.

My brother's lovesick little lapdog. The one who killed Mila. The one who betrayed Brooke and put a knife in her.

I walk toward him with the shotgun aimed steadily at him.

"Please," he gasps, his voice wet and broken as he struggles to breathe. "I don't know where Grant went. He left early. I swear."

I press the barrel under his chin and tilt his head up so he has no choice but to look at me. His entire body shakes under the pressure, and his breath stutters unevenly against the metal.

I think of my mother's face on that screen, bruised, crying, apologizing for something that was never her fault.

"You're going to give me everything you have," my voice is flat and stripped of anything human. "Anything tied to the Collective. To Grant. Contacts. Ways in."

"Yes," he sobs immediately. "Yes. Anything. Please. Just tell me if I do, will you let me live."

"You're not in any position to negotiate," I tell him, "but it won't hurt your chances."

I hold my hand out.

"Your phone."

He hesitates, and that hesitation costs him.

The barrel presses harder into his skin, forcing his head back another inch.

He fumbles the phone out with shaking fingers and hands it over, his grip unsteady and desperate.

"Unlock it."

He does.

I don't move the gun.

"Open your banking."

His breathing stutters harder now, panic bleeding into every movement. "I can't, there are limits, there are approvals."

I press the barrel harder into his throat, cutting off whatever excuse he thinks will save him.

"Well, you better figure out a way to make it work because that piece of shit took my mother's life." My voice drops lower and colder with every word. "So now, I'm gonna drain every dime from the fucking Collective, and I'm gonna kill all of you."

His eyes widen, terror finally breaking through whatever composure he has left.

"I can send some," he stammers. "Ten million. Maybe more. I need access codes."

"Do it."

His hands shake so badly that he fumbles the screen twice before finally getting into the account.

I pull my burner from my pocket and unlock it, turning the screen toward him.

"Wire it to this account."

His eyes flick to the numbers. He doesn't question it. He knows better.

It is one of my offshore accounts. Clean enough to move through without immediate flags, buried under layers I built long before tonight.

I watch everything.

I watch every number, every transfer, every confirmation as it happens in real time.

"Twenty."

"I can't move that much at once," he says, his voice breaking. "There are flags, there are systems, it will trigger audits."

I press the barrel harder under his chin, forcing his head back. His breath stutters.

"Look around you," I respond. "Does it look like I give a fuck about your audits."

His eyes flick across the room, landing on the bodies, the blood, the destruction.

"Twenty," I repeat.

He swallows hard, his throat working against the barrel still pressed to it. "Okay. Okay."

It takes longer than it should.

There are multiple screens and multiple confirmations, a second account, and a workaround that he has clearly used before.

He knows how to move money like this.

Of course he does.

While he works, I reach into my pocket and pull out a slim drive.

I take his phone from his shaking hand long enough to connect it and start the extraction. Data begins transferring immediately, pulling contacts, accounts, message threads, and routing paths tied to The Collective.

He watches me do it, breathing uneven, but he doesn't say a word. He doesn't dare.

Finally, the transfer goes through.

My burner vibrates in my hand.

I glance down.

The confirmation sits there. Twenty million wired in. The transfer is fast enough for now and temporary in a way that doesn't matter.

It is a start.

When he finishes, I nod once.

"Thanks."

I pull the trigger.

The blast tears through the ballroom, deafening and absolute. His head disappears in a violent spray that paints the wall behind him. Bone and blood and something soft spatter the marble. His body collapses and goes still, face-first into the mess he helped create.

Luke claps slowly, the sound sharp in the silence.

"Proud of you," his voice warm. "This is the Seth I knew and loved."

I lower myself into one of the chairs.

The shotgun rests across my knees, speckled with blood. My hands are still shaking, but my breathing begins to even out in slow, uneven pulls, like my body is trying to remember how to function after forgetting.

I pull the drive free from his phone and slide it into mine.

The transfer starts immediately. Files begin to populate, lines of data stacking over each other as everything copies over. I watch just long enough to catch the structure. Names. Numbers. Threads layered over threads. Patterns start to push through the noise. Routes. Timing. Conversations that cut off too clean or redirect too fast.

The realization hits.

Grant didn't just disappear from the gala. He could have doubled back. He may not have even been here to begin with.

Brooke.

Her face hits me without warning. The way she cups my face like she is holding me together with her hands. The sound of her voice when the screen goes black. The way she stays steady for me when everything else collapses.

I left her alone.

The chair scrapes loudly as I stand, the sound cutting through the room and echoing off marble and glass. I step over bodies without looking down, my focus narrowing until there is only one thing left that matters.

Then I hear it.

Sirens.

Faint at first, buried under the ringing in my ears, but they build fast. Too fast.

They are closer than they should be.

Luke tilts his head, listening with a grin that spreads slow and wide. "You should stay. Finish it. Maybe go out in a blaze of glory."

I ignore him.

My brain shifts.

Everything inside me snaps into something colder, cleaner. I move fast without rushing, scanning the room, tracking sightlines, exits, angles. The main entrance is exposed. The side corridors will already be compromised once they breach.

There is a service hallway behind the bar.

I move toward it, stepping through blood and broken glass, keeping low. My boots leave prints, but it doesn't matter anymore. The scene is already beyond saving.

The sirens cut closer.

Doors slam somewhere down the hall. Voices cut through the noise, sharp and closing in.

"Clear the perimeter."

"Move, move."

They're here.

I slip into the service corridor and press myself into the shadow behind a structural column, just out of direct sight from the main hall entrance. My breathing slows on instinct, my grip on the shotgun loosening just enough to stay silent.

The ballroom doors burst open.

Officers flood in.

They move with precision, weapons raised as they sweep the room. One of them halts mid-step, and even from here I see the exact moment it registers the bodies and how many there are.

"Jesus Christ," someone mutters.

"Call it in," another says. "We've got multiple DOAs. This is a mass casualty."

They spread out, stepping carefully through the blood, checking pulses that aren't there, calling out positions, confirming what I already know.

One of them reaches Victor Voss.

"Victim is—" He stops. "Fuck. That's Voss."

The name carries.

It changes the tone immediately.

"Get this locked down," someone else says. "No one in or out. We need—"

I move.

While they focus forward, I slip back through the service corridor, silent, controlled, using the noise they are making to cover my exit. I don't rush. I move like I was never here.

By the time they realize what they are looking at, I'm already gone.

I step outside into the cold air and keep walking until I reach the car.

My hands are steady when I open the door, but the moment I sit behind the wheel, the adrenaline starts to shake loose inside my chest.

I pull away from the building and drive.

I don't remember leaving the city. I remember the road. Headlights cutting through darkness. My hands locked on the wheel while mile after mile stretches out in front of me.

Eventually the traffic disappears and the buildings thin out.

The world begins to feel abandoned.

I pull into the empty lot of a closed gas station and shut off the engine.

For a moment I just sit there, breathing.

I reach into my pocket and pull out my burner phone. It's clean, and no one has the number. Not Brooke, not Beau, not Travis, and nothing ties it back to them.

My hands still shake as I dial Brooke first. It rings once, then twice, then a third time before the call drops with no answer.

I hang up and dial again, faster this time, like that will change something.

It doesn't.

I switch to Beau, but the call rings out and ends without an answer. I stare at the screen for a beat before tapping Travis's number.

It rings once before he picks up.

"Travis," I cut in, my voice sharp and tight. "Where is Brooke?"

There is a pause.

"Seth, where are you?" Travis asks, his words coming fast now. "You ran out in the middle of the night. We've been trying to—"

"Where is Brooke?" I repeat, louder this time. "She's not answering her phone."

I hear him exhale.

"They left."

My chest drops.

"They left?" My grip tightens around the phone. "Where the fuck did they go?"

"They went to look for Grant."

My stomach twists.

"At the gala? I'm here right now. He's not here."

"They didn't go to the gala," Travis sighs.

Then—

"They went to the Grant family estate."

My pulse spikes.

"Where is it?" I demand. "Send it. Now."

"I don't have the exact address yet," Travis replies. "I'm still pulling it. They moved fast. I barely caught it before they were gone."

"Did they check in?"

"No. Nothing since they left. Phones are either off or out of range."

A cold pressure settles in my chest.

"Then find it," I snap.

"I am," he says. "But if they're already there, you're not going to beat them. You need to get back here so we can track them properly."

I don't answer right away.

Because he's right.

If I drive blind, I lose them completely. If I go back, I get eyes, access, control.

I hang up.

Luke appears beside me like he has always been there, watching.

He smiles.

"Perfect. Now you get to find out what it feels like to be too late again."

I'm already moving.

The engine roars to life. Tires scream against asphalt as I turn the car around too hard, too fast.

I drive like I can outrun what is coming. Like I can still get there in time. Like I have not already been too late once tonight. I don't know what I am going to find when I get there.

I only know I can't be late again.

Chapter 61
Brooke

Colin Grant's family had gathered tonight to plan Elliot's funeral.

They sat around the long dining table with drinks half finished and folders spread across polished wood. They had also come together to discuss revenge. Elliot's death demanded it in their world. They intended to decide who would pay and how.

They expected a strategy meeting.

They didn't expect me.

Grant's mother, Evelyn, whimpers as I cinch the final knot around her wrists.

The rope cuts deep enough that the skin has already turned pale. She twists instinctively to test it, and the chair groans under her weight.

Thomas, Grant's father and former police chief, sits at the head of the table. His posture remains stiff. His jaw sets as he watches me move.

Daniel, Grant's youngest brother, sits near the wall. His knees slam together so hard the chair rattles against the floor. He tries to force himself still when he sees me looking at him.

"You have no idea what you just did," Daniel's voice shakes despite the attempt at confidence. "You have no idea who you just fucked with."

I ignore him.

Gina sits across from him.

Grant's second wife was younger and perfectly styled, but her mascara had smeared into uneven streaks down her cheeks, her breathing came in shallow bursts, and her eyes tracked every movement I made.

Thomas Grant finally speaks.

"You untie us right now," he says, his voice cold. "You don't understand the kind of trouble you're in."

Evelyn Grant nods frantically. "Our son will destroy you for this."

Daniel laughs once. "You're dead already."

Beau finishes tightening the final restraint and steps back. None of them notice him leave the room.

I pick up Gina's phone from the table.

My hands remain steady.

I open FaceTime and tilt the phone so the camera captures the entire room.

The call rings once.

Then Grant answers.

"Hey, Gina," he says casually. "I'll be there soon, what's up?"

Then his eyes focus.

His expression changes instantly.

"What the fuck?" he snaps. "What the fuck is this?"

I step into the frame.

"Hello, Colin."

For half a second he freezes.

Then the rage erupts.

"You stupid fucking cunt," he snarls.

Thomas leans toward the phone, straining against the ropes. His head jerks toward the screen.

"Colin, get every cop you have over here right now."

Evelyn twists in her chair, panic creeping into her voice.

"Where are the guards?" she demands.

Beau answers from the other room.

"I killed them."

The room goes still.

Daniel lets out a short laugh that sounds forced.

"You two should run while you still can."

I let the silence sit for a moment before I speak.

"You could call every police officer and federal contact you have, Colin," I say calmly.

Grant's eyes burn into the screen.

"You're fucking right I am," he snaps. "I'll have the police there in minutes, you stupid bitch."

I let that sit for half a second, then shake my head slowly.

"You and I both know that's not true. Your family estate is about twenty minutes from anyone else, including the police."

His expression flickers.

"And right now," I continue, "your entire department is probably busy cleaning up what happened at Victor Voss's gala."

His face shifts, not much, but enough. Shock cuts through the anger for a split second before he tries to bury it.

I tilt the phone slightly, letting him see the room again. His family. Their fear. The way everything is already slipping out of his control.

"On our way here, we caught the news," I add. "Seth must have done his worst."

My gaze locks on his.

"Your family is next."

The room goes quiet.

Daniel's breathing picks up, fast and uneven. Thomas's confidence cracks, the weight of the situation settling into his posture. Gina starts to cry, soft at first, then harder when no one stops her.

Grant's voice explodes through the speaker.

"You touch them and I swear to God I will kill you!" he screams. "I'll skin you alive. I'll make you beg for death!"

Evelyn leans forward in her chair, her face twisted with fury.

"He's going to kill you, you stupid little bitch."

I meet her stare without blinking.

"You're in no position to make threats, Mrs. Grant. And just so you know, I've already killed one of your pathetic, sadistic sons. I had him cut into so many pieces they're gonna have to reassemble him in his fucking coffin."

The words settle into the room.

Thomas's jaw sets. Gina starts crying harder.

"You fucking bitch," Grant snarls.

I stop behind the chairs.

The knife slides free from inside my jacket. It is a long hunting knife. The blade catches the light as I turn it once in my hand.

Daniel sees it first. His bravado slips.

"Hey." Daniel jerks against the ropes, panic bleeding into his voice. "You don't want to do this."

Thomas straightens in his chair.

"You put that down." His stare hardens on the knife in my hand. "This won't end well for you."

I ignore him. I start walking slowly behind the chairs.

"I learned a lot about your family recently."

The knife rests loosely in my hand as I pace behind them.

"You're old money. Generations built on stealing from people who never had a chance. You profit off poverty. You profit off people's desperation. You destroy lives quietly so yours can stay clean and spotless."

Thomas glares at me.

"You have no idea what you're talking about."

I step closer to his chair.

The tip of the blade presses lightly against the center of his chest, right over his heart. I let it sit there for a moment, watching the shift in his breathing.

Then I move again.

"Your money helped build the manor. The one Elliot used. The one where innocent people were tortured and killed while your family signed checks, dined on elegant cuisine, and looked the other way."

Evelyn starts shaking her head.

I stop behind Gina.

"Your father had the right titles and money." My gaze drifts over her shoulder. "So you grew up untouchable."

The knife lifts slowly.

"You learned early that no one was going to stop you. Not law enforcement. Not the courts. Not anyone who might have asked questions."

The blade slides gently across the side of Gina's neck. Her entire body stiffens as the cold steel presses against her skin.

Grant's voice snaps through the speaker.

"You shut the fuck up!"

"That's how you get to play detective."

The edge of the knife traces a slow line just beneath Gina's jaw before I pull it away.

"No training. No initiation. No consequences. Just nepotism."

Daniel swallows hard.

"You were never there to help people," I say. "You were never there to uphold the law. You helped other killers cover their tracks. That is what the Collective needed you for."

Thomas's composure cracks.

"You don't know anything about us."

I step behind him again.

"And Colin, you were the detective Samantha thought would help her. She thought you would help her get the boys away from Richard."

Grant's face tightens on the screen.

"You set her up," I continue. "You helped Richard fake his death."

Grant shouts something through the phone, but I keep talking.

"That woman spent years believing her son was dead," My grip tightens around the knife handle. "You broke her spirit and then you killed her."

The room goes silent.

I move again, circling the table slowly.

"And now, I hope she's at peace."

Daniel starts breathing faster.

"And hopefully wherever she is... She sees exactly what I'm about to do."

Grant explodes through the phone.

"You fucking stupid bitch!" he shouts. "I'm coming for you and I will fucking gut you!"

Daniel finally breaks.

"Please," he pleads. "Listen, we can fix this. We can pay you."

Evelyn starts crying. Gina sobs harder.

Thomas's voice loses its edge.

"You don't have to do this."

Grant continues screaming through the phone.

"I will rip Seth apart in front of you!" he yells.

I shake my head slowly.

"I don't care about any of your bullshit threats."

My grip tightens slightly around the knife.

"I have no sympathy for you people."

I look directly into the phone.

"My sympathy died with Samantha."

I tilt the blade slightly so the light runs down the steel.

"This isn't justice. This isn't about right or wrong."

I look around the table at all of them.

"This is revenge."

Grant's voice explodes through the speaker again.

"I've already called the squad on you," he adds. "They'll be there in minutes."

I nod once.

"I figured. Your family will be dead before then."

Evelyn gasps. Daniel jerks violently against the ropes. Gina begins sobbing again, her breathing turning frantic. Thomas stares at me in disbelief.

Fear spreads across the room.

Grant's voice drops into something colder.

"I promise you, you will die screaming."

He leans closer to the camera.

"What you did to my brother will seem like mercy compared to what I do to you. I'm going to have each of your limbs chopped off so that you're nothing but a fucking torso!"

His voice grows more vicious with every word.

"I'll have every member in the Collective take turns raping you within an inch of your life. You'll beg for merc—"

"I'm done talking, Colin," I smile. "Choose who goes first."

The room freezes.

Grant's rage collapses instantly.

"No," he begs. "No, no, please. I'll give you anything. I'll call off the manhunt. I swear."

"Choose."

His voice breaks as he spits another insult at me.

"Okay," I shrug. "I'll choose for you then."

The knife moves before anyone can react. I step behind Daniel and drive the blade clean through his throat. The steel punches through flesh and muscle with a wet, violent sound.

Blood erupts from his jugular instantly.

It sprays across the table and the floor in thick bursts as his body convulses violently against the ropes. His heels hammer the floor while choking sounds tear out of him.

Grant yells through the phone.

I pull the blade free.

Daniel's body jerks once more before slumping forward. Blood continues pouring from the hole in his throat.

I look into the phone.

"Guess you're an only child now, Grant."

Across the table Gina is still crying, her mascara smeared across her cheeks.

I walk slowly toward her.

She shakes her head desperately.

"Please," she whispers.

I stop beside her chair.

"Usually I would have sympathy for someone like you," I murmur.

She sobs harder.

"But you knew what kind of man he was."

Her breathing stutters.

"You knew he killed his first wife to be with you."

Her eyes widen.

"You knew what he was doing in the manor and you turned the other way because he gave you credit cards, vacation homes, and access."

I tilt the knife slightly.

"And now the consequences have come."

The blade flashes once.

I drag the blade clean across her throat.

The edge bites deep and opens her skin from ear to ear in one brutal motion. Flesh parts instantly under the pressure of the steel. A thick burst of dark blood surges from the wound and spills down the front of her dress.

Gina convulses against the ropes.

A wet choking sound tears out of her as blood floods her mouth and pours over her chin. It splashes across the table and drips steadily onto the floor.

Grant yells through the phone.

Her body thrashes once more, heels scraping violently against the floor as her lungs try to pull in air that never comes. Then the strength leaves her. Her head sags forward. Her body jerks once.

Then she goes still.

I step away from Gina's body and wipe the blade once against the side of my jacket.

Grant's voice tears through the phone speaker. He is screaming now. The rage has collapsed into something raw and hysterical.

"You fucking bitch!" he shouts. "I will kill you. I swear to God I will kill you!"

I ignore him. Instead I walk back toward the duffel bag sitting near the edge of the dining table. I unzip it slowly.

Grant's father watches me with wide eyes.

I reach inside the bag. Then I pull it out.

Seth's bat.

Barbed wire coils tightly around the barrel. Nails jut out along the metal at uneven angles, bent and rust stained from use. The weight settles into my hands the moment I grip it.

Grant's voice cracks through the phone again.

"Stop! Brooke stop."

"No."

Thomas's composure shatters.

I rest the bat loosely against my shoulder.

"Seth has told me many ways he's killed people," I tell them.

Grant keeps shouting through the phone, but I talk over him.

"He said a bullet in the head is actually the kindest."

I walk slowly toward the head of the table.

"Usually you're dead before your brain can register the pain."

Grant's mother begins sobbing harder.

"But this," I say, lifting the bat slightly in my hand, "is not kind."

The barbed wire glints under the overhead lights.

"It doesn't end things quickly."

I step beside Grant's father.

"You feel every single hit."

"Brooke please," he shouts through the phone. "Please don't do this."

I look at the screen.

"Grant, you killed my parents."

I tilt the bat once in my grip.

"You killed Seth's mother."

Grant's voice breaks completely.

"Don't."

I shrug, "So it's only right that I do this."

"No!" he screams.

"Eye for an eye, Colin."

The bat swings.

The bat connects with the side of his face with a wet, cracking impact that sounds wrong for a human skull. Bone gives way instantly. The barbed wire bites deep, tearing through skin and muscle as the nails punch inward. Blood sprays across the dining table in a hot arc, splattering the white tablecloth, dripping down the polished wood.

Blood pours from his mouth in thick, choking streams, soaking his collar, his chest, the rope holding him upright.

Evelyn shrieks.

I swing again. The bat hits his temple. His body convulses, legs kicking uselessly against the chair as the ropes keep him upright, forcing him to take it.

Grant is howling through the phone.

I barely hear him.

One final swing caves in the side of his skull completely. There is no sound this time. Just a heavy, final slump as his body goes slack in the chair, head rolling forward, blood pouring freely onto the floor beneath him.

I lower the bat slowly. Blood drips from the nails and barbed wire, splattering softly against the tile.

Grant's father is dead. And Grant felt every second of it.

I walk toward Grant's mother. She sees it coming. Her whimpering turns frantic, breath hitching as her whole body strains against the ropes. Her eyes flick to the phone on the table like it might save her.

Grant's voice breaks through the speaker, hoarse and panicked now, stripped of rage. "Please! Please don't do this. Please. I'll do anything. I swear. I'll disappear. I'll give you—."

I stop in front of her chair.

"Seth didn't even get to ask you not to do what you did to Samantha. He didn't get to beg."

Grant yells. "Brooke, please. Please. She did not—"

"Samantha didn't deserve any of it," I cut in. "She didn't know Richard was evil. She didn't know what you and Richard were capable of."

I lean closer to his mother. She's crying openly now, tears sliding down her face into the blood on her collar.

"But you knew," I continue. "You knew exactly what your sons were. You knew what your family did. And you are going to die with that knowledge."

I lift the bat.

"I'm sorry, Evelyn. But this is for Samantha."

I swing.

The bat crashes into her skull with a wet, crushing sound. Bone caves in immediately. Blood sprays across the wall behind her in a wide, uneven fan. She screams once, a thin, broken sound that dies before it fully forms.

I swing again.

The barbed wire tears into her face, ripping skin loose, nails punching deep. Her head snaps sideways, neck twisting, chair rattling violently as the ropes hold her upright. Blood pours down her chest in thick streams.

Grant is screaming now. Not threats. Not promises. Just raw grief tearing itself apart through the phone speaker.

I bring the bat down again.

Her jaw shatters. Teeth scatter across the floor. Her mouth opens and closes uselessly as choking sounds spill out.

One more swing caves in the side of her head completely.

Her body goes slack.

I lower the bat slowly, breathing steady, arms heavy, blood slicking my hands and dripping to the floor. The room goes silent except for Grant screaming through the phone. There is no one left alive to shield him from it.

While all of this happens, Beau moves through the house.

I smell it before I see him again. Gasoline burns the back of my throat with every breath. By the time I straighten, the mansion stinks of blood, bile, and fuel, layers of rot and fire waiting to meet.

Grant is still screaming through the phone. Threats. Rage spiraling into hysteria now that there is no one left to hear it but me.

I lift the phone closer to my face and look straight into the camera.

"Don't worry, Grant. You'll meet them all soon in hell."

I end the call.

Beau steps up beside me, eyes scanning the room once, taking in the bodies, the blood, the ropes still creaking faintly as they settle.

"You ready?" he asks.

I nod.

We walk out together.

The night air hits hard, cold against skin that still feels hot. Beau strikes the match without ceremony and tosses it back through the open doorway. The flames catch instantly.

Whoosh.

The sound is violent and greedy. Fire races along the gasoline trails like it has been waiting for permission. The mansion lights up behind us.

As we walk back to the car, neither of us speaks. There is nothing left to say.

I am not proud of what I did. But I don't regret it either. There is no coming back from this.

The old Brooke would have felt fear, remorse, and guilt. She would have shaken apart under the weight of what she had done. She would have questioned herself until nothing of her remained.

That version of me died at the hands of their sons.

I glance back once.

The fire has already taken hold of the house. Flames climb the walls and burst through the windows as glass shatters and heat rolls outward in violent waves. The Grants are gone along with their walls, their money, their power, and their bloodline.

Everything they built ends here.

I turn away from the fire and walk into the dark, leaving nothing behind but ashes and the promise that Colin Grant is next.

Chapter 62
Seth

I kill the engine before I step out of the car.

The door slams behind me as I move toward the house, my focus already locked in. I take the steps fast, clear the entry in seconds, and shove the front door open.

I scan the room without breaking stride, clearing corners, checking the hallways, clocking anything that could be a threat.

A gun snaps up.

"Holy shit," Travis blurts, lowering it a second later. "Dude. We thought you went off the rails. We weren't sure if you were gonna come back."

"I needed space," I snap.

Travis lets out a breath and drags a hand over his face. "Well, you could've gave us a heads up, man, before going all rogue. Tell me you didn't just walk into that gala blind."

"I handled it."

"Handled how?"

"I killed Victor and everyone there."

Travis freezes for half a second, then blinks like his brain needs to catch up.

"Jesus Christ... Okay."

Travis exhales through his nose, already pivoting.

"Fine. You said you had something."

I reach into my jacket and toss the drive across the room. It slides across the table and stops near his laptop.

"That's Victor's," I say. "Everything he had on the Collective is in there. Find Grant."

Travis grabs the drive, still staring at me like he is recalibrating. "Yeah. Yeah, I'm on it."

"Where is Grant's family estate?"

"It's three hours out," he says. "And they've already been there."

My head snaps toward him.

"What?"

"Brooke and Beau," he says. "They're already on their way back."

Something hits my chest hard enough to make it difficult to breathe.

"Why did you let her leave?"

Travis lets out a short, humorless laugh. "You think I'm about to fight with Brooke? I'm just as scared of her now as I am of you."

My jaw locks.

"What happened? What did she do?"

The door behind me opens.

Brooke steps inside first.

Her clothes are streaked with blood, dark and dried in some places, fresh in others. It marks her hands, her sleeves, the front of her shirt. She carries herself differently, like something inside her has settled into place and locked there.

Beau follows her in, steady as ever, the smell of smoke and gasoline clinging to him.

Travis goes quiet.

Everything in me locks onto her. She meets my eyes and doesn't look away.

Relief hits so hard it makes my head spin. Rage follows right behind it.

I move straight for Beau.

"What the fuck were you thinking?" My fist already tight. "Why would you take her out there?"

He keeps his eyes on mine. "Would you have preferred she went alone?"

I stop, but my hands still want to swing.

Brooke steps between us and shoves both her hands against my chest, hard enough that I take a step back. "Enough."

I keep my focus on her. "You want to explain what the fuck you just did?"

"What needed to be done," she replies.

"What needed to be done?" I repeat. "You should've stayed here. You should've answered your phone."

She looks at me like I've lost my mind. "We're on the run, Seth. I'm not answering a number that I don't recognize in the middle of a manhunt."

My mouth opens, but nothing comes out.

"You left," she continues. "You walked out without saying where you were going. You left your phone. You could've been dead or in cuffs for all I know."

Heat crawls under my skin. "You should have stayed here. And I'm not done with you, Beau, for letting this happen."

Travis glances up from the table, trying very hard to look invisible. Beau exhales and shakes his head once.

"Your girl walked into that mansion and erased Grant's bloodline for you and Samantha," Beau scoffs. "Maybe you should calm the fuck down."

The room goes quiet except for Travis pretending to type. Beau steps back and gives us space but keeps listening. I grab Brooke's hand, turn away from both of them, and lead her upstairs without asking.

The office door shuts behind us with a solid click.

"You don't make any more moves without me," My voice comes out flat and hard.

Her glare sharpens instantly. "I'm sorry, Seth, but you don't get to tell me what the fuck to do when you're the one running around like you have a death wish."

"You're acting like you're fucking invincible. You're lucky you're alive. He could've had squad cars ready to empty a clip in you. You're the one acting impulsively."

Her eyes narrow, heat flashing. "I'm acting like someone who's done watching Grant stack bodies while we hide. I'm acting like someone who refuses to sit in a house while other people pay for the shit he started with us."

"Here's the problem, Brooke," I step closer, keeping my eyes locked on hers. "I don't want to add you to the list of people Grant wants to kill just to get inside my head."

She steps closer, her voice rising. "You have no idea what he put me through taking me to that manor. He sent people to kill us. And now your mother is dead because of him." Her voice cracks, then hardens again. "Every time we hide, he hurts someone else. I'm done waiting around for him to finish us off."

"I'm trying to keep you alive," My jaw tightens. "I'm trying to keep you out of a fucking morgue, and you're walking yourself straight toward a body bag."

She lets out a humorless laugh. "You keep saying that, like it gives you the right to decide everything. Stay here, Brooke. Wait here, Brooke. Hide here, Brooke. I'm done sitting still while you go play executioner alone. I don't need your protection. I can protect myself just fine."

"I don't know what part of this you're not getting." A humorless scoff leaves me as I shake my head. "I'm a real killer, Brooke. I'm not new to this shit like you. I'm not doing this for play. I plan and I execute. I don't act impulsively."

Her head snaps toward me.

"Then what the fuck was that when you left?"

For a second I don't answer.

Okay, maybe that was impulsive.

I was barely holding it together when I walked out. My head felt like it was packed with glass and noise. Half of what happened after that blurs together when I try to replay it.

I barely remember it.

"I don't need a bodyguard, Seth." She steps closer again, her eyes locked onto mine like she's trying to force me to understand. "I need a partner. I need you to trust me when I say I can walk into a room and do what needs to be done. I need you to stop treating me like I'll shatter every time someone points a gun at me. I went to Grant's family home and avenged Samantha for you."

"I didn't need you to avenge shit!" I shout. "I needed you to stay here. I needed you to stop charging in like an impulsive, stubborn idiot who doesn't think of the consequences."

Her mouth trembles for a second before it hardens again. "Wow, Seth, you're really a fucking hypocrite."

I lean down until my face is inches from hers. "Listen carefully, Brooke, because I'm not repeating myself. You're done running solo. You don't leave this house without me beside you. You don't move on anything unless I say we move."

"If I keep waiting for you, he keeps breathing," she fires back. "He keeps hunting. He keeps sending people after your family and everyone linked to us—"

"Brooke, shut the fuck up." I step closer, close enough to feel her breath hit my mouth. "If you leave this house without me again, I'll chain you to that bed and make damn sure you stay put."

Her eyes flare. "Fuck you, Seth."

Something in me shifts from anger into something darker with her name carved into it.

Her lip curls, disgust written all over her face. "You can bark orders all you want. I'm still going to kill him. I'm done running while the man who ruined our lives keeps breathing. I'll finish this with or without you."

She tries to push past me toward the door.

That tears through whatever restraint I had left.

I close the distance in one step, grab her by the throat, and slam her back against the wall. My hand wraps around her neck, squeezing just enough to hold her in place and remind her exactly who she's talking to. Her breath hitches, but her gaze doesn't flicker.

"Brooke," My voice edged with barely controlled rage. "You act like you forgot who the fuck I am and what I'm willing to do to keep you alive."

Her fingers curl around my wrist, nails digging into my skin. Her eyes burn into mine, full of rage and something that looks too much like need for how hard we're fighting.

She lifts her chin a fraction against my hand and holds my stare.

"Then prove it."

Chapter 63
Brooke

His hand wraps around my throat, tight enough that I feel my pulse hammering against his palm. His breath hits my mouth in short bursts. I look up at him, anger still burning, desire right behind it, both twisting together until it aches in a way I can't separate.

His jaw moves like he's grinding something down, his eyes dark and raw, every part of him exposed.

I understand what this is. This is the only way he knows how to keep himself from falling apart.

The edge in his stare wavers for half a second. His fingers twitch against my neck, grip tightening before it eases just enough to let me breathe.

Then he slams me back into the wall, and the impact knocks the air from my lungs. His mouth crashes into mine, teeth clashing, lips bruising under the force. I kiss him back just as hard and bite down on his lip until I taste blood.

He hisses and pulls back, eyes blazing, and his hand drops from my throat.

I shove against his chest and twist away, forcing the office door open as I move into the hallway. I barely make it three steps before he catches me.

His hands lock around my waist and I yelp as he lifts me clean off the floor. My stomach flips as he throws me over his shoulder like I weigh nothing.

"What the fuck, Seth?" I snap, fists pounding against his back as I twist against him, in a futile attempt to break free.

He doesn't slow down. He doesn't answer.

His hand lands hard against my ass, then his fingers hook into the waistband of my leggings. He drags them down just enough for cool air to hit skin already overheated. My ass and pussy are fully exposed as I hang over his shoulder.

A sharp, helpless gasp escapes me.

"Seth—"

His middle and ring fingers press between my legs, finding me soaked. He drives them inside in one hard motion while he keeps walking. My body jolts against his shoulder, breath punching out of me in a broken sound.

"Oh, fuck," I choke, nails digging into his back.

He curls his fingers deep, rough and possessive, like he is claiming something he refuses to lose. Every step he takes forces them deeper, the movement relentless. My body rocks against him, hips twitching with every push.

He slows just enough to drag his fingers out and drive them back in with controlled precision. Heat builds fast, anger dissolving into something desperate and aching that I can't hold back.

"Say it," he demands.

"I need you, Seth," I breathe, the words pulled out of me.

His grip tightens. He thrusts once more, then pulls his fingers free and slaps my ass hard enough to sting.

He kicks the bedroom door open without breaking stride.

He throws me onto the bed, and my back hits first, the air ripping out of my lungs in a sharp rush. I barely have time to react before he moves.

He grabs my ankle and flips me onto my stomach in one forceful motion. My cheek presses into the mattress as I try to push up, but his weight and grip keep me in place.

The dresser drawer slams open.

The duct tape tears loudly through the room as he yanks it free.

He grabs my wrists and drags my arms behind my back. I twist, trying to pull free, but he forces them together and wraps the tape tight around them, once, twice, pulling it snug until my shoulders strain and my fingers flex uselessly. The tape bites into my skin.

He fists a hand in my hair, yanks my head up. He tears off another strip and presses it over my mouth, sealing the argument there, every word I still want to throw at him trapped under adhesive and heat. The tape bites at the corners of my lips when I try to spit a curse at him.

His hand grips the back of my neck for a second, holding me there. I feel him shift away just enough to unbuckle his belt. The metal clinks loud in the quiet room. He pulls the leather free and loops it around my throat, snug but not crushing, a solid band of pressure that keeps me perfectly aware of exactly how close his control is to snapping.

I feel the heat of him pressed against the backs of my thighs as he shoves my leggings the rest of the way down, leaving them tangled around one ankle. The air feels colder against my exposed skin, sharp against the heat already building under my nerves.

In the mirror across from the bed, I catch him behind me. His body is tight, muscles rigid, jaw locked, desire and rage tangled so completely I can't tell the difference.

He pulls down his pants and grips himself. His dick is fully hard, thick and veined. The head is dark and swollen, a sheen of pre-cum already gathering at the tip. His fist closes around himself in one slow stroke, as if he is testing how much pressure he can take before he snaps.

His eyes meet mine in the reflection. He grips the belt and pulls me back slightly, arching my spine. My bound wrists strain behind me as he steps closer, his thighs pressing against mine.

He lines himself up, then he drives into me in one hard thrust.

My cry smothers against the tape.

He pulls out and slams back in, deeper, the sound of skin meeting skin loud in the room. His grip tightens on the belt, keeping my head tilted back, controlling the angle as he moves.

Each thrust is hard and unforgiving. The veins along his cock press against me, stretching me, filling me completely. My body jerks forward with every movement, wrists bound, mouth sealed, forced to take everything he gives.

The mirror reflects everything. His body driving into mine. The tension in his arms as he holds me in place. The belt tight in his fist. My back bowed, legs trembling, breath breaking uselessly behind the tape. Our clothes hang twisted and half stripped, fabric clinging to overheated skin.

It's raw. It's brutal.

It is exactly what we both needed.

I watch it all in the mirror, every filthy detail laid out in front of me. The brutal snap of his hips. The way my spine bows each time he drives into me. The way my breasts bounce with the force. The way the duct tape seals over my mouth, pushing my sounds back into my throat until they spill out as frantic, muffled cries I can't control. Tears blur my vision. My hair clings to my face. Sweat coats my skin. I look wrecked, used, and undone.

His eyes stay locked on my reflection, tracking every shift in my expression. The tightening in my jaw. The tremor in my thighs. The way my body tightens each time he hits deeper. He watches me come apart under him, piece by piece, reaction by reaction, as if he is cataloguing my undoing.

"You wanted me to prove it," he pants, voice thick and low as he drives in again, harder, forcing another sound out of me against the tape. "Now I'm showing you who the fuck I am."

Heat floods through me, anger tangled with humiliation, tangled with something hotter that I can't stop. I hold his gaze through the mirror. My glare dares him to push further.

My body tightens around him, clenches hard, despite everything I try to hold back. I feel the pulse of it grip him. I see the moment he feels it. His jaw locks. His breath cuts off. A rough curse slips from him before he can swallow it.

His rhythm breaks, then turns rougher.

"Fuck," he growls, thrusting harder, deeper, chasing the reaction he just pulled out of me, chasing the way my body keeps giving him more.

He moves like he needs this, like he needs me undone and shaking and unable to think of anything except him.

My climax hits fast and violently, stealing my breath in one rush that leaves me shaking. I scream into the duct tape, the sound trapped and broken in my throat, my body locking as the release tears through me. My legs shake under the force. My muscles seize. Pleasure crashes through me in waves that blur my vision and bow my spine until I feel like I'm going to snap.

He keeps driving into me, relentless and focused, fucking me through the aftermath like he needs to force me past every limit I thought I had. He moves with a need that feels dangerous, a need that tells me he is trying to outrun something inside his head. Using me is the only way he holds himself together, and I take everything he gives because it keeps him here.

I take every thrust. I take every drag of sensation. I take every second that lasts longer than I can handle. Even while I shake and gasp and fall apart,

I know he is watching. He knows what he is doing to me. He knows how completely he owns every part of me.

Only when my legs start to tremble uncontrollably, oversensitive and wrung out, does he pull out.

I gasp against the duct tape, spit collecting at the seam over my lips, my chest rising and falling in harsh drags of air. My body feels dazed, twitching with aftershocks.

He strokes himself once and leans over me. He spits into his palm and fists himself tighter, stroking with a rough need that makes his breath catch. His other hand clamps around my thigh, holding me open and keeping me exactly where he wants me.

Then he moves with quick force. He grabs my hips with both hands and drags me up. My ass lifts into the air. My thighs shake under me.

He grips the belt with one hand and lifts my head. My eyes rise to the mirror.

I see everything. I see myself, mouth stretched under the tape, cheeks wet, hair tangled, eyes wild. I see him behind me, chest moving rising and falling, dick thick in his fist, gaze locked on my reflection. His free hand spreads me wider, his thumb pressing into my hip with bruising force.

He spits again, letting it drip between my cheeks. It lands hot on my skin. He spreads slowly.

I flinch from the contact, not from fear, but from the anticipation of what I know he plans to do. I know how deep he will go. I know how far he is about to push me.

My voice strains under the tape, my breath shaking, my body already tightening again for him.

He groans behind me, a low filthy sound that only comes out when he has lost every layer of restraint. Then he pushes into my ass.

The burn hits instantly, stretching and intense.

My scream tears into the tape as he drives in inch by inch until he is fully inside me. My chest hits the bed. Every muscle shakes while my body fights to adjust to the pressure and the size of him. I feel stretched to the limit. I take all of it.

My body opens for him, hungry for his cock, hungry for him. Every nerve fires at once. I shake under him, overwhelmed by the force of it.

He leans over me with his weight pressing into my spine, the heat of his chest settling across my back. His voice breaks behind my ear, low and rough as his hand grips the belt around my neck and snaps my head up toward the mirror. "That's right," he growls. "Take it."

His hips slam forward without warning.

The sound fills the room. Skin against skin. Loud, punishing thrusts. It hits and reverberates around us. My body jerks forward with every thrust. My legs struggle to hold me up. He doesn't slow. He doesn't pull back. He doesn't give me a moment to breathe.

He fucks me like this is the only way he knows how to feel.

Hard. Deep. Relentless.

Each thrust sends heat through my bones and forces a cry into the tape. Tears gather in my lashes as pain twists with pleasure until I can't tell one from the other. I crave the next movement even as my body shakes from the last.

His breath breaks apart behind me. His hips drive into mine with force that punches air from my lungs. His rhythm stays brutal, and every movement lands deep inside me, dragging another helpless sound into the tape.

He releases the belt and my head falls forward, but nothing feels easier. His hands clamp around my hips with a grip that allows no movement except the one he chooses. He pulls me back onto his cock with rough strength, using my body like he needs this to settle the anger inside him. He moves with need that leaves me shaking. And my body answers every move.

My second climax crashes through me with violent force, tearing a muffled scream into the duct tape. My entire body convulses. My vision blanks white. My cunt clenches around nothing while my ass tightens hard around him, pulsing in helpless waves that make me gasp. Every muscle in me locks as I break apart under his weight, twitching uncontrollably, unable to stop the way my body keeps giving him more.

His thrusts turn erratic, deeper and rougher, driven by the way I clamp down on him. I feel him thicken inside me. I feel the tension race through his body. Every muscle above me tightens at once. He growls my name, guttural and strained, and slams into me one last time before he comes, spilling hot and deep while his hands lock on my hips like he is anchoring himself to me.

He stays inside me. His breath drags heavy against my ear. His chest presses into my back. One hand grips my ass, fingers digging in. The other slides up my spine, like he can't pull himself away.

He doesn't let go.

Even when the room stops spinning. Even when my legs stop trembling. Even when my throat burns from screaming into the tape. Even when aftershocks keep rolling through my body in relentless waves. I feel him everywhere. I feel the stretch of him inside me. I feel the way my ass keeps fluttering around him, oversensitive and spent.

Then he collapses onto me, his full weight folding over my back. His chest rises and falls against mine in harsh pulls of breath. His forehead rests beside my neck, skin hot against my shoulder. The duct tape is still sealed over my mouth, slick with spit and sweat, but I don't move.

I listen to his breathing. I listen to the silence. I let the aftermath settle over us while he stays wrapped around me like he is afraid to let the moment end.

Then I feel it.

A drop of something warm lands on my skin. Then another. It isn't sweat. It isn't spit.

My eyes lift to the mirror in front of us, the glass fogged around the edges from our bodies, from the heat, from everything that just tore through us.

Seth's face is half hidden behind me. His hair sticks to his forehead. His jaw stays locked so tight I can see the muscle jump beneath his skin.

But I see his eyes.

They are red. They are wet.

Tears slide down his face in silence, tracking over his cheeks and falling one by one onto the back of my neck. Each drop feels heavier than the last.

He isn't making a sound. He's crying without realizing it, like his body started bleeding emotion before his mind could catch up. His chest keeps rising and falling against my back, while his arms stay wrapped around me like he might fall apart if he lets go.

Something inside him broke and the pieces were too small to pick up.

Chapter 64
Brooke

When he finally pulls out and shifts to the side, I stay still, my cheek pressed to the mattress, my breath dragging in and out like my body is trying to remember how to function.

His hand rests on my hip for a moment, then slides up my back. I feel the change in him before he moves.

He reaches for my wrists first.

The duct tape peels away in harsh, ripping sounds, each pull sharp against my skin. He works fast, but I feel the guilt in every careful touch. My hands fall free, fingers curling into the sheets on instinct.

Then he turns me gently, his thumb brushing my jaw as he peels the tape from my mouth. The adhesive tugs at my skin. When it's gone, I suck in a full breath for the first time since he taped me, the air hitting my lungs.

He lies down beside me, close enough that our shoulders touch. Neither of us speaks. Sweat cools on our skin. Our breathing stays uneven. The room still feels like it is vibrating from everything we just did.

He finally exhales. "I'm sorry."

I turn toward him and push the hair from his face, my fingers brushing the bruise forming along his cheekbone. "I'm sorry too."

His eyes close like those three words land exactly where they need to, like they hit something already breaking.

I take a breath. "I know you might not be ready… but we need to find your siblings."

His eyes open slowly.

I keep going.

"Samantha told me her husband died a few years ago. She didn't have any other family. Since your brother and sister aren't with her… they're probably in foster care by now. And after what I did to Grant's family…" I pause, my voice tightening. "He'll come for them next."

Seth stares at the ceiling like he is trying to erase what he just saw. But I catch the shift in him, the way his breathing changes. He knows I'm right.

"How are we going to get them?" he asks. "There's a fucking manhunt for us. We can't just show up at some social worker's office and ask nicely."

I sit up and reach for the leggings he ripped earlier, still on the floor, useless.

"I have an idea," I say.

He doesn't ask what it is. He just stands and pulls his pants up. "I need a minute."

He doesn't look back as he leaves the room.

The door shuts behind him hard enough to rattle the wall.

I sit there alone in the dark. My legs tremble from exhaustion. I know he is spiraling. I know that I push. But I don't regret it.

We can't afford to sit in silence and grief. Not with more innocent lives hanging in the balance. Not with Grant still breathing.

I get up, adjust my clothes, and walk out of the room.

Travis is in the kitchen, hunched over his laptop, a half-drained cup of coffee sitting beside him. His focus stays locked on the screen, fingers moving in short bursts across the keys. He hasn't been sleeping. Not since the video. Not since we watched Samantha die on screen.

I step inside. He looks up, his eyes landing on me first. His gaze sharpens slightly as he takes me in, then flicks past me toward the hallway.

"You and Seth make up?" he asks, his eyes flicking past me again toward the hallway. "Based on the noise, I'm guessing yeah."

My gaze darts from the floor to him. "I don't know. I don't know what's going on right now, but I need your help."

He sits up, alert. "With what?"

"I need you to search the Oregon CPS database. Two minors. Elise and Ryan. They're Samantha's kids. Seth's half-siblings."

Travis's jaw shifts. "You think they're alive?"

"They have to be," I reply. "Grant would've killed them on that call if they were there. Their dad died a few years ago, and she didn't have any other family. So they're all alone."

He leans forward, pulling the laptop closer. "If she didn't name a guardian, the state would've stepped in fast."

"That's what I'm worried about. If they're in the system... Grant could easily find them. And after what I did to his family, he'll be looking."

He is already typing, his eyes flicking across the screen. "Got it. Give me a second."

The silence stretches as his fingers move. Then—

"Found them. Elise Roberts, fifteen. Ryan Roberts, fourteen. Jefferson High in Portland. Emergency foster placement with Patricia DeWitt. Samantha updated her paperwork two years ago, listing her as a backup guardian. Looks like CPS honored it."

My heart thuds. "We have to get them. Grant will come for them if we don't."

"We have to move quickly," Travis sighs. "I guarantee you if Grant's people are digging, they'll be found. They're vulnerable, Brooke."

"I know...That's why I have a plan."

Travis looks at me sideways. "What kind of plan?"

"I need Naomi."

His brows lift. "Naomi?"

"She has reach. She still has followers, the TikTok audience. If she frames it like a contest or a fan meet-up, we can get the kids to come to her without tipping off anyone watching them. If we roll up in person, we risk getting flagged. But if it's Naomi, it just looks like content."

"You want to bait them with influencer clout?" he mutters. "That's crazy as fuck, but it might actually work."

"I need you to call her. She trusts you."

Travis sighs, then nods slowly. "Alright. I'll call her."

Chapter 65

Seth

I still hear that gunshot. I still see my mother fall backward. The blood was already spreading by the time her body hit the floor. I couldn't move. I keep replaying what she said before it happened.

I never stopped loving you.

I'm sorry I didn't protect you.

I didn't believe it before. Not until I saw her die for it.

And now the weight of it just sits on my chest like punishment. I never should've doubted her in the first place.

I thought she abandoned me. That she chose herself and ran.

But she didn't run. She was lied to.

By Grant.

By Richard.

And if I had just listened to Brooke, if I had gone to her house and heard her out, I would've gotten one moment with her. I would've been able to hug my mother for the first time in almost twenty years. I would've met my siblings instead of seeing them outside the house next to police.

I should've just gone.

I should've given her a chance.

Instead, I'm sitting here with blood on my hands, knowing she died thinking I didn't love her.

And I hate myself for that.

My eyes drift to the picture on the nightstand. The one Samantha gave Brooke the last time we went to her house.

It shows me as a newborn, lying against her chest with a tiny pumpkin hat on my head. Samantha is smiling down at me in the photo like I'm the only thing in the world that matters.

I stare at it longer than I should.

I hear the door open downstairs. A familiar voice follows. I sit up slowly and pull on my shirt. I don't rush. I don't really want to face any of them yet. But I make myself move.

By the time I reach the stairwell, Brooke is already hugging Naomi in the foyer. Naomi looks thinner. Worn the hell down. There's a haunted look in her eyes like she hasn't slept in weeks.

"You okay?" Brooke asks her gently.

Naomi gives a crooked little shrug. "Survived a hotel massacre, so... yeah. I guess I'm as good as I'm gonna be."

Brooke gives her a knowing smile. "Not my first rodeo with a massacre."

Naomi's eyebrows lift. "Shit. Yeah. I forgot who I was talking to for a second."

"I'm sorry about your friends," Brooke's voice softens.

"Yeah," Naomi looks down for a second before meeting her eyes again. "I am too."

Brooke nods once, then cuts right to it. "I asked Travis to bring you here because I need your help. Really, your influence."

Naomi looks between them, guarded. "With what?"

Brooke takes a breath. "Seth has two siblings. Their mom, Samantha, was murdered. We traced the kids to a foster home, but Grant is probably already looking for them."

Naomi's expression freezes.

"We need a way in," Brooke leans in slightly. "Quietly, without police or social workers or raising any alarms. If you staged some kind of TikTok contest or influencer meet-up at their school, it might give us a shot at finding them without tipping anyone off."

Naomi blinks. "So you want me to help you kidnap two children."

Brooke doesn't flinch. "Technically, yeah. But they're his family. And they've got no one left. Samantha is dead. They're next."

Naomi's voice sharpens. "I just watched people get massacred at a hotel. I've been trying to keep a low profile since. I thought if I went off-grid, they wouldn't come for me too."

"I know," Brooke's expression softens. "I hate asking. But this is our only shot. If we wait too long, they won't be there anymore."

"I wouldn't ask you if we had any other option," Travis rubs a hand across the back of his neck before meeting Naomi's eyes again. "But you're the only one who could pull something like this off without it looking suspicious."

Naomi crosses her arms tight around her chest. "And you think they'll just show up to some random TikTok contest?"

Brooke's voice softens. "They're kids. They're online. They're probably watching you already. We just need a way in."

Naomi stares at her, her jaw set. After a long pause, she mutters, "Wow, I'm going to commit a felony with three people I met at a hotel. Great."

Brooke smiles, and it is the first time I have seen her relax in days. "Thank you, seriously."

I'm still standing at the top of the stairs. Quietly watching, trying to listen and process. Beau catches my eye and motions for me to follow him toward the office. I drag my feet behind him. Once we are in the office, Beau turns around and leans against the desk, his arms crossed.

Beau looks me dead in the eye. "I'm not apologizing for taking her."

I shake my head. "Didn't think you would."

"She did what you couldn't do. What you weren't ready to do."

My jaw shifts. "I know."

"She did it for you," Beau adds. "For Samantha. For every fucked-up thing Grant ever did to both of you."

I run a hand through my hair. "Yeah."

"She's not just surviving, Seth. She's doing what we do. What you taught her to do."

I stay silent. I let it settle in. I let it burn a little.

Beau doesn't stop.

"I know what it's like to lose your parents. I know how grief fucks you up. It makes you want to shut down. But you can't afford to shut down right now."

"I'm not shutting down."

"You're spiraling."

"I'm trying not to fucking kill everything in my way."

"Well, we don't have time for you to fall apart. The kids need us. Brooke needs you. You can break later. Right now, we've got a mission."

I stare at him, my pulse pounding.

He claps me once on the shoulder. "Let's go get your siblings. Then we kill Grant. Then you can lose your shit, curl up in a ball, whatever the hell you need. But not now."

I nod slowly. Not because I'm okay.

But because he's right.

"Let's go get them."

It's just after six a.m. when we hit the road. Southbound this time, out of Washington and deep into Oregon. The van hums steady beneath us, every mile dragging us closer to a place I wasn't sure I was ready for. It's a six-and-a-half-hour drive with no music and no distractions. Just the muted rumble of tires on asphalt and the occasional whisper of wind slipping in through the window.

No one really talks. Brooke sits beside me with her knees tucked up, scrolling through the latest news on her phone. Travis drives while Naomi keeps her headphones in, probably rehearsing whatever the hell she is going to say once we get there.

And me, I stare out the window. I watch the trees blur. I replay Samantha's voice in my head. The moment she looked into the camera, her lips trembling, her eyes locked on mine before the screen went black. I haven't spoken about it. I just keep seeing it. Over and over, like the footage carved itself into my brain.

I clench my jaw and force my thoughts back to the plan.

We are going straight to Jefferson High School. Travis says Elise and Ryan are enrolled under their foster placement. It is a public high school with weak security, so we have a decent shot if we move fast.

By the time we reach the outskirts of the city, it is just after noon. We pull into a strip mall parking lot across the street from the school and switch vehicles, trading the van for a nondescript SUV Beau wired and stashed. It is less obvious and easier to ditch if things go sideways.

From the top of the lot, we have a clear view of the school entrance. The bell hasn't rung yet, but kids are already gathering out front. Some wait on rides, others hang around like they don't want to go home. It is all backpacks, skateboards, Bluetooth speakers, loud voices, the usual teenage noise.

Naomi takes a long breath, then flips down the visor mirror and reapplies her lipstick. She tightens her hoodie, brushes her hair to one side, and gives a small half-smile.

"Ready?" Brooke asks her softly.

Naomi shrugs. "As I'll ever be."

Brooke hands her the mic tucked under her collar and shows her the hidden signal trigger disguised as a playlist remote. One tap to speak to us. Two taps to abort. Naomi opens the door.

She walks straight into the chaos like it is just another brand deal. Confident. Camera-ready. The crowd notices her almost immediately. A couple of girls point first. Then recognition spreads through the front of the school.

"Oh my God, Naomi Mills?"

"That's her. That's Naomi!"

Within seconds, she is swarmed. Teens shout her name with their phones raised high. A few push in for selfies. Some are already live-streaming. She smiles, poses, says a few words, and waves to a group hanging by the steps.

I hate how easy it is. I don't remember being this impressed by anyone when I was a kid. But it works.

Then I see them.

Two kids stand off to the side of the crowd. They aren't part of the chaos. They just watch.

Elise stands stiff, her arms crossed over her chest. Her curly hair hits her shoulders. She's tall for her age, and has piercings along her ear and nose. She looks like our mom just with a harder edge.

Ryan stands a little behind her. His dark hair falls into his eyes. He looks skinny and restless. He doesn't look like Samantha or me, but his eyes are hers. The same soft brown that used to watch me from the kitchen window while I played in the yard.

My pulse hits hard.

"That's them," I say. "Front right. She's in the red hoodie. He's next to her."

Beau leans forward. "I see them."

Naomi spots them too. She starts moving toward them through the crowd, calling their names low enough that only they can hear.

I turn and scan the street. That's when I see it.

A black van with tinted windows and no plates.

It pulls in from the cross street, idles for a second, then rolls to the curb across from the school. Two men in black step out. Their movements are quick. One checks the street. The other adjusts something under his sweatshirt.

"Company," Beau says sharply. "Two o'clock. Black van. Armed."

"Shit," I mutter.

Brooke is already clicking the comms. "Naomi. We've got a situation. Get them now. You need to move."

Naomi doesn't hesitate. She turns to Elise and Ryan. "You need to come with me right now," she says. "You're not safe."

Their eyes widen in shock and confusion. Elise steps back. Ryan looks ready to run.

The two men start crossing the street.

"Naomi," Brooke snaps. "Move. Now!"

Naomi reaches forward and grabs Elise's wrist, then Ryan's.

A gun comes out.

The first shot cracks through the air.

Screams tear through the schoolyard. Students drop to the pavement and dive behind anything they can find. Phones hit the ground. Chaos erupts.

Naomi doesn't flinch. She yanks both kids toward her and runs.

Brooke throws it open from inside the SUV.

Naomi runs full speed, dragging the kids behind her. Another shot fires and sparks against the curb beside them. A third shatters the rear window of the SUV.

Naomi dives into the open door with Elise and Ryan. Brooke pulls them in and covers them with her body.

Travis hits the gas.

The men break into a sprint, trying to close the gap.

I climb halfway out the window and fire. Travis peels out of the lot, tires screaming against the pavement. A bullet slams into the back of the SUV, but we are already turning onto the street.

In the rearview mirror, I see the men dive back into the black van.

"They're tailing!" Travis shouts from the front.

We weave through traffic.

And just like that, it is us and them, burning south with two kids in the backseat who have no idea who the hell we are or what kind of war they just got pulled into

Chapter 66

Seth

"Get down!" I bark.

Brooke shoves Elise and Ryan into the footwell and curls over them like a shield. One arm is braced against the seat, the other is wrapped around Naomi. Naomi tucks in tight, eyes wide, fingers digging into Brooke's jacket.

Travis floors it. The engine roars and the tires shriek as we rocket out of the lot. For a second, we're airborne, weightless, and then it all slams back down. My shoulder hits the door. My jaw snaps shut, hard enough that I taste blood.

They're behind us immediately. The way they move, tight, fast, with no wasted effort, I know this isn't random. They're trained. And they're going to get someone killed.

Brooke's back is turned toward the window, her whole body curved over the kids. Naomi's hands are still shaking. Elise is frozen. Ryan's face is buried in his knees. They didn't sign up for this. They're just kids.

My brother and sister.

Fuck.

Beau leans out the passenger window and fires.

The first shot sends glass spraying. The second hammers metal. I watch the recoil jerk his arm and correct. He doesn't pause. He just keeps shooting.

The SUV fishtails into the turn. I brace with my boots, lean out the shattered back window, and line up. My heart's pounding, but my hands are steady. I squeeze the trigger twice. The inside of the SUV erupts with sound. My ears go fuzzy. The second shot slams into their windshield and leaves a web of cracks that splinter outward.

A round punches into the rear. Another one tears straight through the glass behind me. Shards spray my neck. I feel blood but ignore it. I've bled before.

But if one of those bullets hits Brooke, if Elise takes one to the back of the head, if Ryan dies right here in this SUV trying to outrun the kind of world I've been neck deep in for years, I'll never come back from that.

"Faster," I snap. "They're lining up a shot."

Travis weaves through the narrowing street, threading between parked cars. The SUV clips a side mirror, sparks fly. They don't slow.

Another crack of a shot. This one skims past Beau.

He jerks, growls, blood slicking down his cheek in a bright red streak.

"You hit?" I yell.

"I'm good," he mutters, wiping it across his jaw with the back of his hand.

I'm watching that SUV. It closes in. I can see the passenger reaching, weapon drawn, angling for Travis. They want to end this quickly. Kill the driver, flip the SUV, pick off whoever survives.

"Hold it," I shout. "Two seconds."

Travis gives me a window.

I lean out farther. Wind tears at my face. My shoulder is screaming, but I block it out. I focus. I aim.

I find the driver's eyes just before I fire.

The bullet hits him right in the forehead. His head jerks back. The van swerves violently. One tire climbs the curb. Then the entire vehicle lifts, flips, scrapes along the asphalt with a howl of metal on pavement.

It slams into a light pole, then rolls again.

On the second roll it clips a parked car, metal grinds, sparks spit, and something underneath ruptures. Fuel sprays and catches. Then the fire hits. The explosion rocks the SUV, a bloom of orange and black that lights up the inside like a flashbang. Heat sears through the broken window. Travis doesn't slow. He guns it harder, wheels screeching as we put distance between us and the wreckage.

"Stay down," I bark. "Nobody moves."

Still nothing from the back. I can't tell if they're frozen or hiding or crying.

We take backroads. Travis zigzags, throws in a few loops. Beau reloads in silence, his cheek still bleeding.

I watch Brooke. She's still folded over the kids. Naomi is sitting up now, muttering something low, her hands running over Elise's arms. Elise doesn't move. Ryan's eyes are still locked on the floor.

I tell myself they're alive. That's enough.

But it doesn't feel like enough.

Not when I dragged them into this. Not when my blood is on the seat and Beau's cheek is split open and Brooke's heartbeat is still trying to crawl out of her skin. Not when Elise and Ryan, kids I never even got to meet properly, just watched bullets tear past their heads because I showed up in their life a decade too late.

Once I make sure no one follows us and the road stays empty, we get the kids off the floor and into their seats. They move without a word, too stunned to fight it, too quiet for kids their age. We still have hours before we make it back to the house, and the silence stretches the whole way. I keep my eyes on the road or anywhere but them. I don't say anything. I don't trust myself to.

We arrive at the house, I throw the SUV door open and climb out first, gun still in hand, my eyes scanning the dark treeline out of habit. There is nothing but trees, gravel, and the weight of what we just outran. My chest is tight. My hands won't unclench.

Brooke slides out next, protective until the end, one hand still gripping Naomi's arm, the other hovering near Elise like she is afraid the girl might bolt.

I catch her wrist. "You hurt?"

She looks up fast, startled. Her eyes are wide but focused. "I'm okay."

I step closer and kiss her. I feel her hands grip my jacket, and I breathe her in like it might settle the guilt inside me.

"I need to check you," I mutter.

"I'm fine. You're the one who got glass in your neck, asshole." She brushes the small shards of glass off my shoulder.

"I've had worse," I smirk as I look her over again anyway.

The back door creaks open.

Brooke turns immediately, her attention shifting.

"Elise, Ryan, come on. You can come out now."

They don't move.

Ryan's face is pale. He just sits there in the seat, legs curled under him, arms wrapped around his chest like a makeshift shield. Elise is frozen stiff beside him, her posture rigid, her jaw clenched. She looks ready to fight or run. Probably both.

Brooke moves toward them with slow steps, her voice softening. "It's okay. You're safe. You can come out."

Elise eyes her warily, like she's waiting for a lie.

"Where did you take us?" she asks, her tone sharp. "Are we being kidnapped?"

Brooke doesn't flinch. "No. We're here to protect you."

"And who are you?" Elise snaps. "I don't even know who the hell you are."

Brooke nods once. "Fair. But I know who you are. And I know what your mom wanted."

That gets a reaction. Elise's eyes flicker, like something cracks beneath the surface. But she still doesn't move.

Naomi steps forward. "This is a safe house. It's hidden, monitored, locked down. No one can get to you here."

Elise looks between all of us like she is trying to find the trick. She slowly gets out of the SUV. Ryan finally shifts. He unbuckles, climbs out of the SUV, and stands beside Elise, saying nothing, just staring.

Beau walks past. "If we're done traumatizing them in the damn driveway, we should probably take this inside."

"I've got them," Brooke says. She moves slowly, gently placing her hand on Elise's shoulder. "Please."

Elise stares at the ground, then lets herself be guided.

Inside, the house lights click on one by one. They take in the house. One long hallway leads to bedrooms, an armory, med supplies, and a main room with a couch and a stocked fridge.

It's not their home. But it's better than the morgue.

I hang back. I can't look at them. Not yet. Because I don't know what to say. I'm the reason they were in that car. I'm the reason they almost died in it.

Brooke meets my eyes across the room.

I nod once. She's got this.

I'll protect them with everything I have. But she's the one who knows how to make them feel safe.

I stay silent.

My hands still smell like gunpowder.

Ryan sits closest to the end, his shoulders hunched, his eyes flicking between faces. Elise stays tight next to him, her posture defensive, ready to fight or flee if we so much as twitch wrong.

I should've said something. Introduced myself. Told them I was their brother.

But what the fuck am I supposed to say? Hi, I'm the dead kid your mom cried over for twenty years, and now half the country wants me dead. Welcome to the safehouse.

Brooke sits on the edge of the coffee table.

"You're safe here, I know it doesn't feel like it right now, but you are."

Elise's arms stay locked across her chest. "You literally just kidnapped us."

"Not exactly."

"You shot people."

"They were coming to kill you," Brooke says.

"Right." Elise rolls her eyes, but her voice cracks at the edges. She is scared. She is trying not to show it.

"I'm not asking you to trust us yet," Brooke leans forward slightly. "But I need you to listen."

Elise glares at her. "Why?"

Brooke looks at me. Then back to them.

"Because Seth is your brother."

Elise recoils. "What?"

Ryan's eyes shift to me.

"Half-brother. Samantha was his mom too."

"No." Her voice is sharp and defensive. "My mom said her first son died in a fire."

"She thought he did," Brooke speaks gently. "His father made her think that. He took him and hid him."

Elise blinks hard. "Do you know who killed my mom?"

"Yes," Brooke answers.

Elise's voice shakes. "Why would someone kill her?"

"To hurt Seth."

I want to say I'm sorry. That I would've taken the bullet meant for her if I could. But I just stand there.

"This doesn't make sense," Elise says, tears welling up.

"I know." Brooke holds her gaze. "But it's the truth."

Travis steps in. "They were coming after you two next. And we stopped them."

Elise turns toward him, narrowing her eyes. "Why do you care about us?"

"Because you're his family," Brooke isn't looking at me now. She is focused on Elise, talking like this is a bomb she doesn't want to set off.

Elise looks at me with disbelief.

"He hasn't even said anything to us."

She isn't wrong.

Brooke speaks up. "This is hard for him too."

Elise snaps, "He didn't even know her."

I flinch.

"He did," Brooke says firmly. "That was his mother too."

Brooke glances at me. I step forward.

"I knew about you two," I finally admit. "But I didn't feel like it was my place to be in your lives."

Elise stares at me like she wants to believe it, but doesn't know how.

"I don't trust you."

I nod. "That's fine."

"This whole thing is fucking crazy."

"I know."

She turns back to Ryan, who still hasn't spoken. Still hasn't blinked much either.

But they don't get up.

I'm not the one who can win them over, not tonight. But I'll keep them safe. Even if they never forgive me for it.

Brooke doesn't say anything as she stands. She just reaches for my hand and gives it a small tug.

I follow her down the hall.

Her grip stays tight until we are out of view. She stops in the kitchen, by the sink.

I lean back against the counter. My head feels like a fucking war zone. My hands are still trembling and my jaw won't unclench.

She turns to face me.

"She doesn't hate you."

"She should."

"No," She shakes her head once. "She's terrified. And everything she believed just got flipped on its head."

I laugh under my breath. It sounds wrong. "Yeah. Join the club."

Brooke reaches up and touches the cut on my jaw. Her thumb skims the edge of a bruise I hadn't even registered yet. "You okay?"

"You asking physically or...?"

"Don't dodge it."

I look at her. The lights are low, but I can still see the smudge of dried blood on her sleeve. Her eyes aren't as panicked anymore. She has that calm again. That cold, steady survival instinct she leans into when everything else goes to hell.

"I don't want them to see me like this."

She frowns. "Like what?"

"Gun in my hand. Blood on my face. A killer."

"You saved their lives."

"I shouldn't be the one who had to."

Brooke steps closer. Her fingers slide down to my wrist. Her touch is grounding, but it doesn't stop the spiral. Nothing can right now.

"I wanted to look at them and say something," I admit. "Anything. But I couldn't. It's like, every time I opened my mouth, all I could think about was her. And how I was too fucking late."

Brooke leans in until her forehead touches mine. "You're not too late for them."

I close my eyes.

Her hand slips behind my neck, her fingers threading through the hair there. "You showed up. You pulled them out. You protected them."

"They don't want to be around me."

"They don't know you yet."

I open my eyes again.

"Then what if they do get to know me, and they still don't want to be around me?"

Brooke doesn't flinch. "Then we try again. And again. Until they understand who you really are."

I don't ask her who that is. I'm not sure she knows. I damn sure don't.

Her lips brush mine. But there is nothing soft about the way I kiss her back. It isn't about sex. It isn't even about comfort. It is the only way I know how to come back to reality.

When we break apart, I rest my forehead against hers again.

"You scared?" I ask.

"Yeah."

"Of me?"

"No." She traces the line of my jaw with her knuckle. "Of losing you."

She steps back before I can say anything else and glances toward the hallway. "We should make them something to eat. Or at least bring them water. Naomi's probably trying, but..."

I nod.

Brooke touches my face one more time, then turns away.

I watch her go. Still tasting gunsmoke. Still carrying the guilt of my mother's death.

But with her, I can pretend I am something better than what I thought I'd be.

Chapter 67
Brooke

Naomi and I lead the kids down the hallway of the house. Elise walks behind us stiffly, her jaw tight, her arms crossed. Ryan trails behind, clutching the strap of his backpack like it's the only thing anchoring him. Neither of them has said much since we got here.

"Okay," I keep my voice soft. "So this is your room. There's another across the hall, whichever one you want to sleep in is fine. We've got extra hoodies and sweatpants. It's nothing fancy, but they're clean. Hopefully they'll fit."

Elise says nothing.

"If you need anything," Naomi adds, standing beside me, "seriously, just ask. Food, blankets, toothpaste. Whatever."

Still nothing. Elise glances around the room like she's trying to find possible exits. Ryan sits slowly on the edge of the bed, his eyes distant.

"You're safe now," I add. "We promise."

Elise blinks at me, but the rest of her face doesn't move.

Naomi shifts uncomfortably.

"Well. We'll give you guys a minute to get settled," I force a small smile that no one returns.

We step back and leave them in the room, the door clicking shut behind us. As soon as we're out of earshot, Naomi exhales like she's been holding her breath since we left the car.

"Jesus," she mutters. "They're so shook."

"I know."

"I'm shook. I still can't believe I just participated in a kidnapping. At a high school. On TikTok Live."

I turn to her. "Wait, was it actually live?"

She makes a face. "No. I just recorded it. But still. That footage exists. It could be evidence."

I sigh and run a hand through my hair. "This is so fucking crazy."

Naomi nods grimly. "Yup."

"But if you hadn't done what you did, those kids would be dead right now. You saved them."

She glances at me, quieter now. "Yeah, thanks."

I arch a brow. "So was it for the kids, or was it for Travis?"

Her eyebrows shoot up. "What?"

"I mean, you did cross state lines and commit a felony. Just wondering if Travis asked you nicely or if it was more of a 'whatever you need, I'm yours' kind of vibe."

She stutters and blushes instantly, looking away.

I grin. "It's okay. If you two are... you know."

She fidgets. "We're taking things slow. I don't even know what this is yet. I mean, are we just trauma bonding? Or is it real? I don't know. Surviving a massacre together does weird things to your brain."

I nod. "Trust me, I get it."

Naomi's voice softens. "He's the only one who protected me at the hotel. Everyone else was screaming or running or just... dying. But Travis stayed."

"Travis is a great guy," I glance toward the hallway. "He deserves the best."

She smiles faintly. "Yeah."

Footsteps echo down the hallway before either of us can say more. Travis rounds the corner, still in his hoodie, dark circles under his eyes but more grounded than earlier.

"How are the kids?" he asks.

"As good as can be," I rub the back of my neck. "They're quiet."

He nods like he expected that. Then his gaze slides to Naomi. "Can we talk? Somewhere private?"

"Sure." She pushes away from the wall and walks with him.

I watch them disappear down the hall together, and something in my chest softens.

Travis is the only person who's never left me. When the world exploded after Stratford, he stayed. When it got worse at Everspring, when people we trusted turned on us, when Uncle John betrayed me and Mary covered it up, he was still there. Not just watching my back. Fighting beside me. Protecting people. Surviving.

And now here he is, trying to let someone in. It feels like hope. A weird, tentative kind.

He deserves that.

I walk down the hall to the bedroom.

I find Seth in the dark.

He's sitting on the edge of the bed, his elbows on his knees, his fingers laced tight like he's holding himself together with tension alone. His head hangs low.

"Seth?"

He doesn't lift his head.

I shut the door gently and step closer. My chest is already tight. I know that look on him.

"Are you okay?" I ask.

He exhales like the breath has been trapped in his ribs for hours. "I don't even know how to answer that."

I sit beside him. I just look at him. His hands. His jaw. The faint bloodstain still on his shirt collar. I don't know how to fix this, but I know I need him to know he's not failing.

"You've been a better brother to them in one day than most people manage in a lifetime," I lean my head on his shoulder. "You got them out. You kept them breathing. You protected them, even when they didn't know they needed it."

He lets out a quiet sigh.

I look down. "It's not your fault, you know."

His fingers twitch once, like he wants to believe me but can't. "Then why does it feel like it?"

I could tell him it's survivor's guilt. That grief scrapes the inside of you raw and leaves nothing behind but blame. But he knows that already. And he's not just grieving the people he lost. He's grieving the life he never got.

I reach for the chain around his neck. His hand stills for a second when my fingers brush the vial, like the contact pulls him out of whatever he's stuck in. The small glass rests warm against his skin, the darkened chain worn from never leaving his neck. My blood.

"I love that you never take this off," I whisper.

His jaw tightens slightly. "They tried to take it when they brought me into the hospital. I almost tore the place apart trying to get it back."

I look back down at it, my fingers steady around the glass. "When I drew my blood, I didn't know it yet. But I was already pregnant."

He goes completely still.

I lift my eyes to his. "So that's me. And our baby. Both of us. Right there."

He raises the vial slowly, holding it between his fingers. His thumb drags over its surface in a slow, absent motion, like he needs the contact to keep from spiraling.

"That was the only thing I thought about when I was bleeding out in that hotel. When I could barely see or breathe or move. This. You. Our baby. It was the only thing that kept me alive."

I press my lips to his shoulder.

"I'm glad you made it back to me," I whisper.

"I just don't know what to do now."

"You keep going," I press my hand against his chest. "With me."

But part of me still hurts. Something inside me still bleeds quietly where no one can see.

I draw in a breath and let it out slowly before the words start.

"They told me you were dead."

Seth turns toward me.

The memory hits before I can stop it. Elliot standing there in the manor, his voice calm when he said it. Seth's dead. The floor tilting beneath me. My lungs locking. My body collapsing before I even understood what was happening.

Then the basement.

My stomach twisting in sharp waves that stole the air from my chest. Blood soaking through my dress while panic tore through me because I thought I was going to die in that place.

And worse than that, I knew the baby was dying with me.

"I didn't believe them at first. But when I did, when I believed you were gone, I wanted to die."

Seth's eyes don't leave mine, but something changes in them.

"I didn't think I wanted to be a mom," I admit. "Not before."

I glance down for a second, my fingers tightening around the edge of his shirt, then force myself to keep going. My throat tightens.

"But after I thought you were gone, the baby was the only piece of you I had left. The only thing I could protect."

I shake my head.

"I fought so hard to keep it safe. I did everything I could." My voice cracks. "But it wasn't enough."

Tears burn behind my eyes. I blink them back hard, but one slips free anyway. I wipe it away quickly.

"I'm sorry," I whisper.

Seth goes still beside me. For a moment he just stares at the ground. He reaches for me, pulling me into him until my face presses against his chest.

"That's not your fault," he says quietly. "It was mine."

I look up at him.

"I should've never taken you to that hotel," he continues. "We should've left the country the second I knew that PI was on us. I should've gotten you out before any of this started."

His voice drops lower.

"All of it is my fault."

I shake my head immediately.

"No, it wasn't your fault, Seth."

I draw in a slow breath.

"I think the world is just a fucked up place," I tell him. "And we keep getting fucked by it."

The corner of his mouth twitches, but the guilt doesn't leave his eyes.

I reach into my hoodie pocket and pull out my phone.

"There's this song. I play it when I think about the baby. It makes it hurt a little less."

I open Spotify and queue the track.

"Sienna."

The soft intro fills the quiet around us.

"I didn't want to forget," I whisper. "So I gave it a song. Something to hold onto."

Seth watches me place the phone between us and let the music play low. He closes his eyes. For the first time in hours, maybe days, he takes a full breath.

I lean my head against his shoulder. His hand closes around mine.

And the music does the crying for us.

Chapter 68
Brooke

It's been three days since the kids got here.

For three days, the house has echoed with quiet footsteps and doors that close too softly. They stay in their room together like if they separate, something else will be taken from them. They eat when I bring food to them. They shower when I remind them. They don't explore the house. They don't ask questions. They don't trust us.

I can't blame them at all.

Ryan watches everything like he is storing information away for later use. Elise doesn't talk much, but her eyes say enough. She studies us constantly, assessing and calculating, waiting for one of us to prove her instincts right. I can feel her suspicion even when she's silent.

Seth and I wake up tangled together in the kind of sleep that only comes after too much adrenaline and not enough time to grieve. His arm is wrapped around my waist, holding me close like I might vanish if he lets go. For a few seconds, everything feels almost normal, which makes it worse when reality comes rushing back in.

The feeling fades quickly.

We get dressed without talking much. I tug on a tank top and jeans. Seth pulls on his shirt, and grabs his phone from the nightstand.

We walk into the living room and find Travis and Naomi on the couch. They are sitting close to each other. Travis' arm was slung behind her shoulder. The space between them feels electric in a way that is hard to ignore. Naomi's top hangs half off her shoulder. Travis looks rumpled and wide awake at the same time. They both straighten when they see us, like they were caught doing something they weren't supposed to.

"Morning," Travis says, rubbing his neck.

I arch a brow at them. "You two okay?"

Naomi clears her throat before answering. "Yeah. Just... talking."

Seth's attention shifts past them toward the hallway. "Have you seen the kids?"

Travis shakes his head slowly. "Not for a few hours."

Something tightens painfully in my chest, and my first instinct is to tell myself they're fine. My second instinct is to stop lying to myself.

"They usually don't come out without Brooke," Naomi adds quickly. "I figured they were sleeping."

Seth turns toward the hallway without another word. I fall into step beside him because I already feel the change in him, the way his shoulders set and his pace tightens.

He knocks on the door firmly. "Elise," he calls. "Ryan."

There's no answer.

He knocks again, harder this time. "Hey. It's Seth."

Silence answers him again, and my pulse starts to climb. A cold wave moves through my body. He opens the door slowly, and everything inside me drops.

The room is empty.

The beds look untouched. There are no shoes by the door. There are no backpacks on the floor. The window remains locked from the inside.

"No. No, no, no." I rush past him and check the bathroom. The bathroom is empty. I open the other room down the hall. That room is empty too.

We rush back into the living room. The security monitors glow in the corner of the living room. Travis is at the keyboard within seconds, fingers moving fast and precise. The footage rewinds, and the house feels like it is holding its breath with us. Naomi stands behind the couch tense, like she is waiting for the moment the screen confirms our worst fear.

We all lean in. There they are.

It is early morning, an hour ago. Elise moves first. She has the keys in her hand, and the sight of that makes my stomach twist. Ryan follows her. They pause at the door like she is listening for something beyond the walls, like she is checking for danger before she moves.

Then they're gone. The van backs out of the driveway and disappears down the road.

Seth slams his hand into the wall. "Fuck."

I grab his arm before he can move again. "Hey. Hey. We can track them."

He nods once, jaw tight and eyes already focused. His breathing is shallow, and his stare is locked on the screen.

"They won't get far. I'm not losing them, not after everything."

The tracker pings sharply on the screen.

Travis is already pulling up the live signal. Seth grabs a gun off the rack by the hall closet, checks it once, then shoves extra ammo into his pocket. I grab the keys and my phone, hands moving on muscle memory because my mind is too loud.

The sky is still dark when we climb into the Jeep. Seth drives fast, hands tight on the wheel, shoulders set like he is bracing for impact. I watch the tracker like it might disappear if I blink. They are fifteen miles ahead of us, moving west.

The tracker leads us to a small grocery store just off the highway. The building looks worn down and half-forgotten, which makes sense because Elise wouldn't choose a crowded store with cameras on every corner. She would choose somewhere quiet, somewhere that feels invisible.

Seth turns into the lot and pulls into the far corner without speaking, angling the Jeep so he can see the entrance clearly. The engine ticks as it cools. One of his hands rests on his thigh. The other looks empty, but I know the gun is within reach.

"They're inside," I say, watching the van parked crooked near the side of the building.

He nods once. "I see it."

"I'll go in."

His eyes meet mine. "Two minutes. If something feels off, you get out."

I nod and step out and cross the lot. The automatic doors stall before sliding open. Inside, the air smells old and sour, like refrigerators that haven't been serviced in years. The tile is cracked. The fluorescent lights hum overhead.

An older man sits behind the counter with a crossword book open in front of him. He glances at me once, then back at the page like he has seen every kind of trouble and decided none of it is his business. A scratched shotgun is mounted beneath the counter, within reach.

I spot Elise and Ryan near the snack aisle with a basket between them. A couple canned things. A bag of chips. A jar of peanut butter. Elise scans the aisles, shoulders tight, eyes moving. Ryan keeps grabbing whatever he can reach and dropping it into the basket without thinking.

Relief hits hard enough to make my vision blur for a second.

"Elise," I say carefully. "Come on, we need to go."

Ryan looks relieved. Elise doesn't. Her jaw locks, her whole body going rigid like she has already decided I'm the problem she needs to get away from.

Then she runs.

"Help me!" she shouts as she sprints toward the counter. "This is the woman who kidnapped me!"

The clerk startles, knocking his stool back as he pushes to his feet. My stomach drops, not because of what she said, but because of what it could trigger. Police. FBI. Grant. A call that puts our faces on a screen. A mistake we don't get to fix.

The front window explodes inward.

The clerk's head snaps back as a bullet tears through it. He collapses instantly, blood spraying across the counter and the crossword book.

Elise screams.

"Get down now!" I shout.

Automatic fire rips through the storefront. Glass and shelves explode around us. The lights stutter, buzzing harder, and the noise drills straight into my skull.

I grab Ryan and shove him behind an aisle endcap. "Stay down. Both of you. Don't move."

Elise drops beside him this time without arguing. Her hands clamp over his shoulders, pulling him down with her. It takes a dead man for her to listen.

Boots hit the tile inside the store.

Two masked men move through the shattered entrance. A third stays outside, firing in controlled bursts that keep us pinned. They don't rush. They move like they know exactly what they're here for.

I crawl toward the counter, keeping low, and reach behind it. My fingers close around the shotgun. It is old and heavy, but it is loaded.

"Keep down," I whisper. "Stay low."

The first masked man moves down the cereal aisle, weapon raised, checking each row with slow precision. I press myself flat against the tile in the next aisle over and wait until he passes.

Then I shift, aim low, and fire.

The blast tears through his shin. Bone gives out. He screams and drops hard, his rifle clattering across the tile and skidding out of reach. He drags himself forward, fingers slipping in his own blood as he reaches for it.

I pump the shotgun and rise into a crouch.

He keeps crawling, leaving a thick smear behind him. His breathing turns wet and uneven. The second man's shadow cuts across the shelves a few aisles over, searching, closing in.

I step in behind the first one.

He stretches his fingers toward the rifle.

I fire.

The shot drives through his back at close range. His body jerks, then collapses over the weapon he never reaches.

The second masked man shouts and shifts position. The one outside keeps firing through the broken windows, glass still raining down in sharp bursts.

The second man inside charges down the opposite aisle, trying to flank me. I drop back behind a shelf and wait, forcing myself to breathe through the noise.

He steps into view between two displays.

I fire again.

The blast catches him high in the torso and throws him sideways into a rack of canned goods. Metal crashes. He doesn't get back up.

Movement flashes at the entrance.

The last man pivots, trying to retreat. Seth appears in the doorway at the same time, gun already up, moving fast, locked in. The masked man turns toward him. For a second, the angle lines up wrong.

I fire first.

The shot hits him from the side and spins him into the doorframe. He drops hard and doesn't move again.

Smoke hangs in the air. The clerk lies behind the counter, motionless. Blood spreads across the cracked tile. My arms start to shake as the adrenaline burns off, leaving everything cold and hollow. He didn't deserve to die for a basket of chips and a panicked lie.

Seth steps inside, sweeping the store, gun still raised. He moves past the bodies, then slows.

His gaze drops to the nearest one. He crouches, yanks the mask off.

There's a pause. Then his jaw tightens.

"...Sergei," he mutters.

His expression goes colder, something shifting behind his eyes that I recognize immediately. The pool. The way they moved. The way they watched.

"They're not random." He stands again his expression flattening. "They were in the pool."

I look back toward Elise and Ryan, still curled into each other behind the aisle.

"They came for the kids..

Seth's grip tightens on his gun.

"There were three outside."

"That makes six," I answer. "There were six of them."

His eyes flick over me again. "Are you hit?"

"I'm fine."

His gaze shifts toward the kids, and his face tightens in a way that makes my stomach knot.

I look at Elise and Ryan. They still crouch near the counter, pale and shaking.

"You wanted to leave," I gesture towards the bodies. "This is what followed you."

Ryan starts crying softly.

Elise looks at me differently now. The change is subtle but real. She no longer looks at me like I kidnapped her. She looks at me like she understands what almost happened and understands who would have paid for it.

"Stay behind me," I tell them. "We're leaving. Now."

They don't argue.

Seth and I reach for our phones at the same time.

I unlock mine first. Nothing looks out of place. No unfamiliar apps appear. No strange notifications pop up.

Seth checks his next. His jaw tightens as he scrolls quickly through the screen before shaking his head.

"They weren't tracking our phones. Which means it was theirs."

I look at the kids.

Their phones.

"They tracked you through these," Seth says, holding one up briefly before dropping it on the floor.

He brings his boot down on it hard. The screen explodes under the pressure.

I grab the other one and slam it beneath my heel. Glass shatters and the phone bends under the weight until the screen cracks open and the battery shifts loose.

"If they were tracking the signal," I say, grinding my heel down again, "these would have led them straight to us."

Elise watches the broken pieces scatter across the floor. Ryan wipes his eyes with the sleeve of his hoodie.

We move to the bodies, and I hate how practiced this feels. I collect the phones from the men inside the store. Blood smears across one screen as I wipe it clean Seth brings in the ones from outside and drops them onto the counter beside the dead clerk.

Six phones sit there. One of them vibrates in my hand. Incoming FaceTime call. The name on the screen makes my pulse spike hard enough to hurt.

Grant.

I look up at Seth. Seth grabs it before I can react. He answers it.

Grant's face fills the screen, sitting like a smug bastard in some wood-paneled room, flanked by two other Collective members. One of them is smirking. The other is sipping a drink like this is a normal conference call.

Seth keeps the camera low, pointed at the blood-soaked tile and the dead men cooling around it.

"Nice try," Seth says coldly.

Grant's eyes flick, recognizing the scene.

"You sent six," Seth continues. "You should've sent more."

The smirk fades from the guy on the left. Grant's smile stays.

"For now," Grant replies smoothly. "Just wanted to remind you, you're not ghosts. You're visible. Traceable. Killable."

Seth flips the phone around and shows his own face, and I can see the fury in his eyes even through the small screen.

"Enjoy your last days," Seth's jaw tightens. "I'm going to send you and John straight to Hell."

Then he ends the call. We stand in the silence. Then Seth tosses the phone into the clerk's sink behind the counter and smashes it with the butt of his shotgun.

Outside, the parking lot is a mess of broken glass and blood. The Jeep is still parked at the far end. Three bodies sprawl near the curb, and the air tastes like smoke and metal.

Seth walks over, gun still in hand, and plants his boot on one man's shoulder. The guy tries to groan, mouth smeared with blood, leg barely hanging on. Seth presses the muzzle to the base of the guy's skull and pulls the trigger. The blast echoes off the empty storefronts. Red mist hangs in the air for a second before it falls away.

We don't get to leave risks behind us.

We get the kids into the Jeep fast. Elise stops for half a second before sliding into the backseat, Ryan right behind her. The doors shut. Seth is already in the driver's seat. The engine turns over and we pull out before anyone has time to look twice.

The van sits where they left it. I glance at it once, then look at Seth.

"We're gonna have to get Beau to come back for the van," I say.

Seth doesn't take his eyes off the road. "He will."

The drive back is quiet. Elise and Ryan stay huddled in the backseat, not speaking, not looking at us. I keep one hand in Seth's, the other braced against the door, eyes fixed on the empty stretch of highway ahead.

I check the rearview more times than I want to admit. Each time, I catch Elise watching us, quick glances toward the front when she thinks I won't notice. She keeps looking at Seth, like she can't decide if he's the threat or the only reason she's still alive.

When we pull up to the house, Seth cuts the engine. Elise shifts first, crossing her arms, trying to build that attitude back up like armor. I don't give her the space to settle into it.

"Don't," I turn in my seat just enough to face her. My voice cuts through the car. "I'm not in the mood for the whole smartass routine tonight."

Her jaw tightens, but she doesn't say anything.

I take a slow breath, forcing my voice to stay calm. "I understand what you're going through is hard. I know you've lost both of your parents. I know we're strangers to you. And I know none of this makes sense yet. But what you don't get to do is put all of us at risk because you want to play the defiant teen card."

Ryan's gaze drops straight to his lap. Elise keeps staring at me like she wants to push back, but her hands give her away, shaking where they're tucked under her arms.

"When my parents died, I didn't make reckless decisions. I didn't run into traffic or go knocking on danger's door just to prove I could. I survived. I made smart moves. Because that's the only way to make it out of this kind of shit alive."

I lean slightly over the center console, making sure she can't look away from me.

"And this will be the last time either of you pulls something like this. I'm not risking Seth for you. Not again."

I nod toward the front seat, toward the blood dried into Seth's shirt, and I force myself not to think about how much worse it could've been.

"You think this is normal? You think people out there are playing fair? Those men weren't there by accident. They were waiting. Waiting to take you or kill you. You wouldn't have made it another mile."

I look between both of them.

"We are here to protect you. Whether you believe that or not. But let me make one thing clear. This man, your brother, means everything to me. And I won't sacrifice him for anything or anyone."

Elise opens her mouth like she's about to argue, but I hold her gaze until she shuts it again.

"Are we clear?"

A beat passes.

Then two small nods.

"Good."

I open my door, Seth is already out on the other side, moving without a word, scanning the perimeter before shifting his attention back to them.

I pull Ryan's door open and step back just enough to give him space to move. Seth opens Elise's side at the same time.

"Out," he says.

They climb out slower now, the fight gone quiet, replaced with something closer to shock.

Seth stays close behind them, positioning himself between them and the open drive without making it obvious. I fall in on the other side, closing the gap so there's nowhere to slip through. We move them forward together, straight toward the house, no pauses, no chances to second-guess it.

We aren't giving them room to run again.

Chapter 69

Brooke

Four weeks later, the house doesn't feel like it's holding its breath anymore.

I'm in the kitchen with a mug that has gone cold in my hands, listening to the soft scratch of pencil against paper drifting in from the living room.

Elise is sitting on the floor with her back against the couch, sketchpad balanced on her knees. One leg is tucked beneath her, the other bent, foot flat on the rug. Her shoulders are pitched forward with concentration. She presses too hard when she draws. I notice that early on. The graphite smears under the side of her hand, darkening parts of the page she probably doesn't intend to shade.

Seth stops when he sees her.

He doesn't announce himself or comment right away. He just stands there, quiet, watching the movement of her hand like he is studying a mechanism rather than a picture.

After a few seconds, he clears his throat.

"You using an H for that?" he asks.

Elise stiffens, but she doesn't look up. "Yeah."

"That explains it," he points to the pencil beside her sketchbook. "It's going to look flat unless you compensate with pressure. Try a 2B."

She finally glances at him, suspicious and assessing. The same look she gave me during the first week. Then she reaches into the pencil case, fingers lingering for a second, and switches pencils.

Seth sits on the edge of the coffee table instead of the couch. He doesn't crowd her. He doesn't hover. I didn't realize how much that matters until I feel my chest ease watching it.

"You're still pressing too hard."

Elise bristles. "I'm not."

"You are," he replies calmly. "You're digging into the paper instead of letting the graphite do the work."

She glares at him, jaw tight, then looks back down. Her grip loosens anyway. The line softens.

She doesn't comment on the difference, but I can tell she notices it.

"What are you drawing?" he asks, not demanding, not prying. Curious in a way that doesn't feel invasive.

She pauses then tilts the sketchpad just enough that I can see it from the kitchen.

It's Samantha.

Seth exhales under his breath.

"That looks just like her," he says.

Elise's voice is careful. "I know."

He shifts, crouching so he is level with her instead of above her. His hands rest loose on his knees.

"I used to sketch in class when I was a kid. Drove my teachers crazy."

Her eyes flick up. "You draw?"

"I did...Before everything else. Then it turned into tattooing."

Her forehead creases. "You're a tattoo artist?"

"Yeah," he answers. "Turns out people are a lot less mad when you draw on their skin if they asked you to."

That earns a small sound from her, halfway between a scoff and a laugh. She catches herself and looks back down at the page like it slipped out by accident.

"Mom used to draw too," she says after a moment. "She said it helped her think when her head got loud."

Seth's gaze shifts to her hands, to the way she's pressing the pencil harder than she needs to. He nods once. "Yeah. That sounds right."

Elise hesitates, then glances up at him. "She used to draw pictures of you, too. When you were little. She kept them up in her art room."

Something tightens in Seth's expression, small but there. He doesn't look away. "She did?"

Elise nods, then drops her eyes back to the page like she said more than she meant to. She doesn't start over this time. She keeps going, adding detail, darkening lines, building on what's already there instead of erasing it.

I lean against the counter and watch them both. Nothing is being fixed here. No one is saving anyone. But something is starting to take shape anyway, quiet and real, without anyone forcing it.

At the table, Ryan sits shoulder to shoulder with Travis. The laptop screen throws pale light across Ryan's face, reflecting in his eyes as lines of code scroll past. It might as well be another language to me, but to him it looks like a puzzle waiting to be solved.

Travis doesn't rush him. He explains each step for Ryan to follow.

"So if I change this," Ryan asks quietly, pointing with one careful finger, "it reroutes the request?"

"Yeah," Travis replies. "You're not forcing your way in. You're just telling it to knock somewhere else."

Ryan nods, absorbing that. He leans closer, reading every line twice before touching the keyboard. His fingers hover for a second, then he types, like he is afraid the wrong keystroke might break the whole thing. The screen refreshes. A new window opens.

Ryan's shoulders lift just slightly. "It worked."

Travis smiles. "Told you. Systems don't like being bullied. They respond better when you listen to them."

Ryan keeps staring at the screen, unblinking. Then he glances up at Travis, searching his face.

"I didn't mess it up."

"No, you did it right."

Ryan nods once. His hands settle on the keyboard.

I watch from the kitchen and realize something small but important. Ryan doesn't just need reassurance or praise. He needs proof. He needs to see that when he follows the rules of a system, it behaves the way it is supposed to.

Travis gives him that without making a big deal out of it.

Ryan types again, a little faster this time.

In the kitchen, Beau has taken over breakfast without asking. He moves through the space opening drawers. Eggs crack cleanly against the counter. Butter melts.

Naomi leans against the counter, watching him with mild curiosity. "You're actually good at that."

He glances back briefly. "I have layers."

She hums. "It smells good."

"I will accept the compliment."

From the table, Travis looks up from the laptop. "Since when do you cook?"

Beau slides the spatula under the eggs and flips them neatly. "Since I learned that food is a useful bargaining tool."

Naomi smiles. "That explains a lot."

Travis watches for a second longer than necessary, "You know he kills people for a living, right?"

Naomi freezes. Her head snaps toward Beau. "I'm sorry, what?"

Beau doesn't even look up. "Only on days that end in Y."

Naomi stares at Beau for another beat, then lets out a slow breath. "I thought you were just... helpful."

"I am helpful," Beau says. "The other thing is a separate skill set."

Travis shakes his head and goes back to the laptop. "Who do you think you are? Liam Neeson. This isn't Taken."

Beau scoffs, "I'm way more efficient of a killer than he was in that movie."

Naomi pours herself coffee, still looking at Beau like she's recalibrating her understanding of reality. "I'm going to pretend none of this was said."

"Healthy coping mechanism," Beau replies. "Highly recommend."

I watch the exchange and finally see it for what it is. Beau isn't flirting because he wants Naomi. He is flirting because Travis notices. Beau enjoys the reaction more than anything. Chaos with intention. Loyalty buried under provocation.

I carry my mug into the living room and sit beside Seth on the couch. He shifts just enough to make room, his arm resting along the back cushion behind me.

He looks down at me. "You okay?"

"Yeah."

Elise finishes her sketch and sets the pad on the table without a word. She doesn't look at anyone when she stands. She just walks down the hall, shoulders squared, carrying something she doesn't want inspected.

Ryan follows a minute later. He pauses by Travis's chair, "Can I try the other thing later? The one you showed me."

Travis looks up, surprised. "Yeah. Whenever you want."

Ryan nods once and disappears after his sister.

The room settles. I lean over and reach for the sketchpad. I turn to the last page.

Elise. Ryan. Samantha.

All three of them are together. Elise is leaning into her mother's side. Ryan is half asleep against her shoulder. Samantha's hand rests over both their backs. Like nothing bad has ever happened. Like nothing ever will.

My throat tightens until it hurts.

I close the sketchpad and set it back on the table. The drawing stays where it belongs, untouched. If anything in this house deserves to survive what comes next, it is that.

Seth walks our bedroom. He sits at the foot of the bed with his shoulders tight, eyes fixed on nothing.

I move closer, keeping my voice low. "They're adjusting."

He doesn't look at me right away. His jaw ticks once.

"Elise isn't there yet," he mutters. "Ryan's easier. I think he wants to like me. He just doesn't know how."

"They're both just... processing, but they're watching you."

He lets out a breath that sounds like it scrapes his throat on the way out.

"And you're doing better than you think," I add. "You've been patient. You've been honest. You're a good brother."

His mouth twists, like the words taste wrong. "Last time I was a brother, I taught him how to sharpen a knife and lie without blinking."

"Luke made his own choices. He was only ten months younger than you. You couldn't have changed him, even if you'd tried."

Seth's fingers flex at his sides.

"I was on the same path."

"But you made different decisions. You never wanted to be like him."

He finally looks at me, and his eyes are tired in a way that never fully goes away.

"No matter how much you taught him," I continue, "and no matter how much you warned him, he was still the one who picked the worst version of himself."

Seth stares at me like he is trying to push the guilt out through his skin.

"You've chosen to be better," I add. "Elise and Ryan might not get it yet, but I see it. They're starting to. Give it more time."

He doesn't answer, but his expression shifts. It softens slightly, like he isn't fighting it as hard as he was.

Before I can say anything else, the door opens.

Travis steps in, already holding the tablet in his hand. His expression is off, tight in a way that makes my stomach drop before he even speaks.

"There's another one. Another Live feed."

Seth's head turns immediately. Mine follows a second later.

Travis walks straight over and puts the tablet into my hands.

The screen flickers once.

And then his face fills it.

John.

He smiles like he is looking at something he already owns.

"Well, well, well. If it isn't my favorite niece."

I don't say a word. My grip tightens around the edges of the tablet until my fingers start to ache.

"You've really outdone yourself this time," John eyes move slightly, like he is taking in more than just me. "The Vosses. The Talberts. You and Seth did what the Collective needed. You cut out the rot that was making us weak."

Seth steps in behind me, close enough that I feel the heat of him at my back. He doesn't touch me. He just watches.

John's smile sharpens. "Elliot and Grant thought the Collective was a business. They wanted contracts and surveillance and leverage. They wanted control they could measure and sell. That's not what we are."

His tone drops, almost reverent.

"The Collective exists to keep the world in order. Predators on top. Prey beneath. Fear as a currency. Blood as proof."

My stomach turns, but I keep my face still.

"You two have reminded everyone what real killers look like," John continues. "You don't negotiate. You don't beg. You don't back down."

He leans closer to the camera, his eyes locked on mine.

"You were touched by it, Brooke. You've killed in pain. You've killed in love. Now look at you."

His smile spreads wider.

"A weapon shaped by fire. Just like Seth. You two weren't the problem. You're the correction. You are what the Collective needs to survive what is coming."

The frame jolts slightly, like he's moving.

"You did what I needed you to do," he adds, satisfaction threading through every word. "You exposed the weak ones. You made the fractures visible. You made people pick a side."

Behind me, Seth's breathing shifts.

John's voice softens, almost gentle. "Tell me, doesn't it feel righteous? Doesn't it feel good knowing you are no longer the victim?"

I hold his gaze through the screen. I don't blink. I don't answer.

Then I reach forward and cut the feed.

The screen goes dark.

My hands are shaking when I lower the tablet. My pulse is too fast, my skin cold, like he reached through the screen and took something with him when it ended.

All I can think about is him watching from somewhere else, smiling like he already won.

Seth doesn't say anything right away. He steps around me and takes the tablet from my hands, turning it over once in his grip like he might snap it in half.

I glance toward the hallway where Elise and Ryan are sleeping, and my chest tightens for a different reason. We brought them into this. We dragged them into it, even if we didn't have a choice.

“I’m tired of waiting,” I say. “We need to end this. I can’t keep living like this.”

Seth nods once. “Then we finish it.”

I move, my hand closing around my gun on the nightstand.

“Travis, we need to find Grant and John. Now”

“We don't need to find them,” Travis turns the screen toward us, his expression uneasy. “They already know where we are.”

Chapter 70
Seth

The room goes still.

Travis drags a hand over his mouth, then nods toward the screen. "The Collective database is acting like a coordination board. Grant posted a job, and it wasn't subtle. Contracted killers picked it up."

He taps the screen, pulling up another window. "Dmitri is one of them, along with a few others I'm still working to identify. They're meeting first, then they're moving to this location."

Brooke exhales slowly. "Shit."

"Yeah," Travis says. "He is close. Tacoma. That is where the login cluster keeps landing."

Brooke looks at me. "The kids have to go."

I nod. "Now."

Travis nods once. "Naomi and I can take them to the bunker in Oregon."

Brooke meets his eyes. "Okay, be ready to leave in thirty minutes."

Everything after that shifts into motion.

Brooke wakes Elise and Ryan and tells them we are leaving. Elise starts to argue, then takes one look at our faces and stops. Ryan says nothing, but the way he moves makes it clear he understands enough to be afraid. Bags are packed, the van is loaded, and Travis sends something to my phone.

"I scrubbed the rest of the signal," he says. "But this one stayed."

A blinking dot appears on the map.

Grant is already moving.

I watch the dot track across the screen. This is how he moves through the world, convinced that nothing can touch him.

My father was the same. Inside that house, he believed he owned everything under that roof. He broke Luke and me down and called it discipline. He thought he was building soulless killers.

I killed him because men like that don't stop.

Grant is no different. He hides behind authority and money while he destroys people who can't fight back. He killed my mother. He dragged Brooke into that manor and thought he would walk away from it. Now he thinks sending hired killers here will fix it.

Grant is still breathing.

I'm about to end that

I tighten my grip around the phone as the tracker keeps moving.

Naomi stops pacing while Travis keeps working and Beau is already moving through the room. I check my weapon and grab the rest of my gear, running through everything in sequence.

Brooke moves past me to grab her jacket, and I stop her before she can get too far. My hand comes up to her jaw and forces her to look at me, and I kiss her once before letting her go.

We go back to getting ready.

Bags are thrown together, shoes are pulled on, and the van is ready in minutes.

Brooke pulls Travis into a quick hug, then Naomi. She wraps her arms around Elise and Ryan, holding them tighter than she probably means to before letting them go.

They climb into the van, the doors shut, and the engine turns over.

We step back.

I watch the van roll down the hill until the red glow of the taillights disappears behind the trees. Brooke stands in the doorway.

"You okay?" I ask.

She nods once.

I step closer and tilt her chin upward so I can see her face.

"I'm scared," her voice hardens. "But I'm ready to end this shit."

"We will."

I hand her a pistol and point toward the staircase.

"You take the landing. You stay there."

"And if something happens to you?"

"You get out and find Beau. You stay alive."

Her jaw tightens. "I'm not leaving you."

"You promise me you won't freeze."

She swallows. "I promise."

I kiss her once and step back.

"Go."

She starts up the stairs, then pauses halfway and looks back.

"What are you doing?"

"I'm grabbing another mag," I say, already turning toward the stairs. "I want more ammo on me just in case."

She nods once, then continues up. By the time she reaches the landing, she is already lowering herself flat, positioning over the railing with the kind of focus that tells me she is locked in.

I move into the bedroom and go straight to the nightstand. The drawer slides open. I grab another magazine and check it before slipping it into my pocket. My hand goes back in for another, fingers brushing against something small and solid.

I stop.

The ring box.

For a second I just stare at it sitting there. I pick it up, turning it once in my hand. If we make it through this, I am not waiting again.

I'm asking her.

I shove it into the pocket of my cargo pants and push the drawer shut.

Then I move.

I head back into the living room and crouch behind the couch with a knife in my hand instead of a gun. A blade makes less noise when it opens someone up.

The house creaks around me while I wait. A loose branch drags across the roof when the wind shifts. I slow my breathing and listen for anything out of place.

Then gravel crunches under tires.

Headlights sweep across the front wall and cut through the broken slats of the blinds. Doors open outside. Boots hit the driveway, heavier than before. The men speak in low, clipped voices as they move toward the porch.

Two gunshots break the quiet.

The sound carries through the trees, followed by the thud of bodies hitting gravel. Beau doesn't miss. When he fires, people drop.

But this time, it doesn't stop them.

Gunfire erupts all at once.

Automatic rifles tear into the house from outside, not aimed, not careful, just ripping through everything. Wood explodes. Glass shatters inward. Bullets punch through the walls, chew through the couch, and tear into the floor. The sound fills the entire space and is loud enough to drown out thought.

I drop flat behind the couch, pressing myself as low as I can. Splinters rain down over my back. A round tears through the cushion inches from my head, and another punches through the wall behind me.

They aren't trying to get in clean. They are trying to wipe the entire place off the map.

I can't see Beau. I can't hear him over the gunfire.

I can't see Brooke either.

The rounds keep coming, ripping through the second floor, tearing across the ceiling, and spraying through the landing where she just moved.

For a second, my head goes somewhere I don't want it to go.

If one of those rounds hit her—

I shut it down.

I stay flat. I wait it out. I listen.

The gunfire slows, then stops.

Silence doesn't follow. Boots hit the porch again, and they move fast and aggressive while closing in.

The handle jerks. The lock holds for one second before something heavy slams into the door. The frame groans. Another hit follows, harder. The wood cracks. A third impact blows it open. The door bursts inward.

The first man enters low, rifle sweeping, clearing angles as he moves. His partner follows tight behind him, covering the opposite side.

The first one tracks toward the couch, and his barrel dips slightly.

I move.

The blade cuts across the back of his ankle.

He reacts fast, twisting, trying to pull away, but the tendon gives. His leg folds and he drops hard, and a sharp grunt breaks out of him as the rifle slips from his grip.

He reaches for it immediately.

I grab his vest and drag him back before he can get control. The knife drives into his ribs, angled up. He slams his elbow toward my head, and it clips my shoulder enough to sting but not enough to stop me.

I stab again.

He chokes, still fighting, still reaching. Blood runs down his chin as his fingers scrape toward the rifle.

I wrench his head back and drive the blade under his jaw.

His body jerks once, then drops.

The second man pivots, and his weapon is already coming up toward me.

A gunshot cracks from above.

The bullet tears through his upper chest and knocks him sideways into the wall. He stumbles and tries to bring the rifle back up.

Another shot follows.

This one takes him through the head. Bone and blood hit the wall behind him as his body collapses across the doorway.

I glance up.

Brooke is on the landing, flat against the floor, with her arm extended through the railing and her gun steady as she tracks the entryway.

She is alive.

The tightness in my chest loosens just enough for me to breathe again.

Outside, more gunfire answers, and Beau fires again.

Then one of them moves through the doorway.

He is different and faster.

Dmitri.

He takes in the bodies in one glance. His rifle comes up, but I am already moving. I knock the barrel aside as he fires, and the shot punches into the wall behind me.

We crash into each other.

The rifle drops between us.

He goes for his boot.

I see it a fraction too late.

The blade comes out and drives straight for my side. I twist, but it still catches me. The edge slices across my ribs, shallow but enough to burn. Pain hits, but I stay on him.

I drive forward, and my blade meets his. Steel slams together.

We lock there for a second, and we are both pushing and trying to take control. He doesn't rush, and his eyes stay on mine, calm, like he already knows how this plays out.

He moves first.

The knife comes low and fast. I block it, but he shifts and slams his shoulder into me, driving me back into the wall. My grip slips.

His blade comes up again.

I catch his wrist this time, stopping it inches from my throat. His arm strains against mine, pushing down and trying to force it through.

Blood runs warm along my side.

I don't give him space. I drive my forehead into his face.

Bone cracks, and his grip loosens.

I wrench his arm aside and bury my knife into his stomach.

He grunts, and his breath leaves him, but he doesn't drop. His hand snaps back up, and the blade cuts across my shoulder.

We are still moving and still fighting. I twist the knife and drag it upward through his abdomen. His body folds slightly as his breath catches.

I pull the blade free and drive it straight into his throat.

His eyes go wide. His body jerks once, then goes loose.

I shove him off me and he hits the floor hard.

For a second, all I hear is breathing, including mine, Brooke's above me, and Beau somewhere outside.

Blood spreads across the entryway in a thick and dark pool.

Beau's voice carries in. "Two down out here."

I step over Dmitri's body and move toward the doorway. Two men lie near the truck with rifle wounds punched through them. One of them twitches, and Beau finishes him.

Beau scans the truck again. He steps inside through the side door, and his rifle is still up.

"He's not here."

Fuck.

Grant never planned to be here.

My phone vibrates in my pocket. I pull it out and check the screen. The tracker dot moves across the map, and it is not coming toward the house. It is heading for the highway. Right toward the van.

Beau looks at the tracker. "Fuck!"

Brooke is already moving down the stairs and dialing Travis.

The line rings. No answer.

"Travis!" Brooke's eyes fill with panic when it goes to voicemail.

The dot keeps moving, steady, and it follows the same road the van took.

"He's behind them."

It locks into place. Grant never wanted us dead here. He wanted us far enough away that we couldn't protect them.

I grab the keys and move for the truck, and Brooke and Beau are right behind me.

The engine roars to life. Gravel sprays as we tear out of the driveway.

Chapter 71

The van's headlights cut a narrow path through trees and the empty shoulder. Twenty minutes have passed since they left the house. Naomi keeps checking the mirrors, then the kids, then the mirrors again. Travis keeps both hands on the wheel, eyes forward, trying to drive normal when nothing feels normal.

Elise sits rigid in the back seat, shoulders lifted and arms folded tight. Ryan leans forward between the seats, tracking every passing sign and every break in the tree line. Krueger paces in the limited space behind the back row, leash clipped to a metal anchor in the cargo area. He tries to push toward the doors anyway, but the leash stops him short each time. Luna sits in her carrier on the seat near Naomi, eyes open, body still, ears turning toward every sound.

Naomi exhales hard. "I hate this."

Travis doesn't look at her. "I know, I'm sorry I dragged you into this."

Naomi smirks, "It's okay, at least I get to spend more time trauma bonding with you."

Travis slowly reaches for her hand. Naomi laces her fingers in his.

The road is quiet and dark until red and blue lights flash in the mirrors.

Travis's grip tightens on the wheel.

Naomi turns in her seat, eyes wide and fast."Shit, is that the police?"

"Fuck," Travis says.

The patrol vehicle closes the distance. The lights stay on. The vehicle stays close, holding their bumper in its glare.

Krueger lifts his head and growls. He surges forward again and hits the end of the leash. The clip snaps him back. He fights it anyway, muscles tight, body twisting, trying to get between the kids and whatever is behind them.

Naomi's voice goes sharp. "We should pull over."

Travis shakes his head once. "No."

Naomi stares at him. "Travis, we can't run. We've got two kids back here."

Elise sits up straighter. "What's happening?"

Ryan's voice comes out quiet. "Are we getting stopped?"

Naomi turns toward them, forcing her tone down. "It's okay. Nobody moves around. Just stay calm."

Then she looks back at Travis. "It might be highway patrol. It might be nothing. If we don't stop, we make it worse."

Travis scans the shoulder ahead, then the trees, then the rearview. The patrol car stays close enough to fill the van with colored light. The pressure doesn't let up.

Travis signals and eases onto the shoulder.

The van rolls to a stop. The engine drops to idle. The road goes quiet in a way that makes every small sound stand out.

A door slams behind them.

Footsteps crunch on gravel.

A flashlight beam sweeps across the rear windows, then moves forward. It pauses on the kids. It pauses on Naomi. It pauses on Krueger, who snaps his teeth at the air and growls again.

Travis swallows. He lowers the driver window halfway.

The man outside moves slowly. The badge catches the flashlight glare. He leans in close enough that his breath fogs the glass edge.

Travis recognizes his eyes first.

Grant smiles.

Naomi freezes beside Travis. Elise's stare locks on the window. Ryan's face goes pale in one fast shift.

Grant raises a gun and presses it against Travis's temple through the opening.

"Don't move. Don't reach for anything."

Travis holds the wheel with both hands. His knuckles go white.

Naomi's voice shakes. "Travis."

Grant's gaze slides to her. "You're going to do exactly what I say."

His eyes move to the back seat. Elise and Ryan don't speak. Both of them watch his hands.

Grant pulls the driver door open. Cold air rushes into the van. "Everybody out," he says. "Now."

Naomi starts to speak. Grant cuts her off. "Out."

Travis steps out first, slow and careful. His shoes hit gravel. He keeps his hands visible. Naomi climbs out next with her hands up, forcing herself to breathe. Elise climbs out stiff and furious. Ryan follows, eyes darting between the patrol car and the trees.

Krueger tries to jump out behind them. The leash yanks him back hard. He growls and thrashes, trapped by the clip in the cargo area.

Three men step into view around him, all armed. One stays near the patrol car. One stays near the shoulder, watching the road. One moves closer, his gun angled toward the kids without a tremor.

Naomi's eyes widen.

Grant's smile stays calm. "Turn around," he says to Travis.

Travis hesitates for half a beat. The gun presses closer to his head. Travis turns. A man grabs his wrists and cinches zip ties tight. The plastic bites into skin. Travis flinches once and forces himself still. Naomi is next. She jerks when the zip ties snap shut, then steadies her breathing and lifts her chin.

"Kids," Grant says.

Elise shakes her head. "No."

One of the men seizes her arm and forces her hands back. Elise fights once, hard and fast. The gun moves closer to her chest. Elise freezes, breathing through her nose, eyes bright with rage and fear. The zip ties snap shut around her wrists.

Ryan's breath turns shallow. Naomi twists toward him as much as she can. "Ryan, stay with me."

Ryan's eyes stay locked on Grant as another man grabs his wrists. The zip ties tighten. Ryan doesn't cry. His lower lip trembles anyway.

Grant nods toward the trees. "Walk," he says.

Travis's eyes flick to the shoulder and then to the dark beyond the road. "Where are you taking us?"

Grant steps closer, gun still up. "Deep enough that nobody hears you."

The men move in tight around them, guns trained, forcing the group away from the shoulder and toward the tree line. Travis tries to angle his body toward the kids. One of the men shoves him forward.

"Keep moving!"

They step off the gravel and into the brush.

Leaves and twigs snap under their shoes. Cold air cuts through their clothes. The patrol lights stay behind them, flashing through branches until the trees swallow the road.

Naomi stumbles on uneven ground. One of the men grabs her arm and yanks her upright.

Elise tries to twist her bound hands behind her back, testing the zip ties. The plastic doesn't give. She clenches her jaw, refusing to let anyone see her hands shake.

Ryan walks with his shoulders hunched, eyes wide, trying to keep his footing. Naomi presses her shoulder against him whenever she can, trying to keep him close without making the men suspicious.

Grant stays near the front, guiding them deeper. He doesn't need a flashlight. He moves as if he already knows where the ground dips and where the branches hang low.

Travis keeps looking for a break in the trees, any opening where he could run. Every time his weight shifts, a gun moves with him. Every time he slows, a hand shoves him forward again.

They walk deeper. The trees thicken. The ground grows softer and slicker underfoot. Travis's wrists ache where the zip ties cut into skin.

Grant stops after several minutes and lifts a hand. The men halt with him, guns still raised.

They stop in a small clearing where the trees thin just enough to show the sky. The ground dips there, soft with damp leaves and exposed roots. The road noise is gone. The flashing lights are gone. Everything that could've helped them disappears behind the trees.

Naomi and the kids stop too, bodies stiff, breath loud in the quiet. Grant takes a slow step closer. One of the men adjusts his aim to match the movement. The barrel follows Travis's head as if it is attached.

"You know," Grant says, "it took me a minute to figure out who they were working with to hack into The Collective's database."

Naomi swallows hard. The man behind her presses the gun closer to her head, and Naomi freezes again.

"But then it clicked," Grant continues. "The timing. The way every problem kept turning into an advantage for them. The way you all knew to be in the right place at the right time."

Travis's lips part.

Grant tips his head, watching him. "You're the one behind the screen. The one who made doors open. The one who made evidence vanish. The one who made my family easy to find."

Naomi's breath hitches. Her eyes squeeze shut for half a second, then open again.

Grant's smile widens. "Now you're at the wrong place at the wrong time."

He leans in closer to Travis's face. "You gave her the information to kill my family."

Elise makes a sound through her teeth. The gun near her shifts immediately.

"Quiet!" the man warns.

Elise shuts her mouth. Her eyes stay locked on Grant, hate so bright it looks reckless.

Grant straightens and looks at all of them. "Family is important, right?"

Naomi starts sobbing, "Please don't do this."

Grant ignores her. "I already took everyone they love."

Travis's face tightens. Ryan's eyes go wider. Elise's throat works as if she is trying to swallow something that won't go down.

Grant's tone stays even. "Except for you four."

Travis's head lifts a fraction. His voice comes out rough. "They're just kids."

Grant stares at him for a moment. "I don't give a fuck."

Naomi shakes her head hard. Tears run down her face anyway. She keeps wiping them with her shoulder because her hands can't move.

Grant takes one step back, then points his gun toward Naomi. Then he shifts it toward Elise and Ryan.

"You," he says to Travis. "Or them."

Ryan's breath starts coming fast. Naomi leans closer to him. Elise's chin lifts again. Her mouth trembles. Travis's shoulders shake once. He forces them still.

Grant lifts his free hand and points at Travis's chest. "Decide."

Travis looks at the kids.

Ryan's eyes are fixed on him. He doesn't speak.

Elise's face is tight with fury and fear, both fighting for space. She shakes her head once.

Travis's mouth opens. It closes again. His eyes squeeze shut for one beat, then open, glassy and raw.

"Grant," Travis says. His voice cracks on the name. "If you want to hurt Brooke, do it to me."

Grant laughs, like he has been waiting for that line.

"Oh, I will," he says. "Don't get it twisted. You're all dying. This is only about order."

Naomi makes a small sound that turns into a sob. The gun at her head doesn't move.

"Me," Travis says. The word scrapes out of him. "Take me."

Grant's expression shifts with interest. He looks entertained.

"Wow," Grant chuckles. "You think that's noble?"

He steps closer, "It isn't."

Travis's breathing turns ragged. "Please."

Grant's voice drops. "You're picking yourself because you don't want to watch. You're trying to escape what I'm going to do to them."

Naomi's sobbing gets louder. Ryan starts crying. Elise's shoulders shake hard.

Grant straightens again. "That's not as heroic as you think."

Travis swallows hard and lifts his chin, forcing himself to stay upright even as the zip ties cut deeper into his wrists. Blood has already slicked the plastic where he has struggled against it.

Grant keeps the gun trained on Travis's chest. Grant reaches into his jacket with his other hand and pulls out a knife.

Naomi screams Travis's name.

Grant steps closer without lowering the gun. The barrel stays aimed at Travis's heart while the knife flashes forward.

The blade drives into Travis's side.

Travis's body jerks violently against the restraints. A raw sound tears out of his throat as the steel sinks deep into muscle. Grant rips the knife free and drives it in again, lower this time, forcing it between Travis's ribs. Blood spills instantly, running down Travis's shirt and dripping onto the ground.

His knees buckle.

One of the men beside him grabs his shoulder and yanks him upright so Grant can keep stabbing.

Grant twists the blade before pulling it out, then plunges it back into Travis's abdomen with brutal force while the gun remains fixed on his chest. Travis gasps and chokes, his body convulsing against the zip ties while blood soaks through his clothes and pools beneath his boots.

Grant pulls the blade free and goes again, higher this time. Travis chokes on his breath. His face twists. His eyes go unfocused for a second, then snap back, wild with pain.

Naomi and Elise scream, Ryan cries so hard he can barely breathe.

Grant doesn't rush. He watches Travis's face each time.

When Travis sags, the man holding him tightens his grip and forces him upright again.

Grant crouches slightly, bringing his face level with Travis's. "This is the part Seth and Brooke don't understand," he says quietly. "You can be smart and still be powerless."

Travis tries to lift his head. He can't hold it. His breathing turns shallow and uneven. His mouth opens as if he has something to say, but his body stops cooperating. His shoulders drop. His weight goes heavy in the man's grip.

Naomi makes a broken sound that doesn't resemble words anymore.

Grant stands and wipes the blade on Travis's jacket.

Then Grant steps toward Naomi.

Naomi backs up a half step, even though there is nowhere to go. The gun at her head forces her to stop. Her eyes are wide and wet, and she is shaking hard.

"Please," Naomi pleads. "Please."

Grant looks past her to the kids, as if he wants them to see everything.

He lifts the knife.

Naomi's breath hitches. Elise fights the zip ties again, wrists twisting, plastic biting deeper. Ryan sobs and tries to step toward Naomi, but the man with the gun shoves him back with a hard hand to the shoulder.

Grant's voice stays calm. "Now you're going to show me what you're willing to lose."

He angles the knife toward Naomi's throat, close enough that she can feel the cold metal.

"Don't move. This is going to get messy."

Chapter 72
Seth

Beau drives fast with both hands locked on the wheel. His knuckles are pale under the dash lights. His jaw is clenched so tight I can hear his teeth grind when he breathes. He keeps swearing under his breath.

Brooke sits in the passenger seat with my phone in her hand. She keeps refreshing the tracker screen until her thumb slips from sweat. The dot is gone. The app keeps loading and failing. Grant either killed the tracker or switched vehicles. Either way, he did it on purpose.

I sit in the back seat and keep my knife in my hand. My mind keeps dragging up images I don't want.

Brooke's voice goes tight. "There."

Beau brakes hard enough that my shoulder hits the seat. Headlights sweep across a van on the shoulder, angled wrong, silent, dead. The driver door is cracked open, and that small gap looks staged. The hazard lights are off. The whole thing feels like bait.

Then we hear Krueger. His barking tears through the night from inside the van, furious and trapped. It hits my nerves like a wire pulled too tight.

Beau throws the car into park. We are out before the engine settles. Brooke has her gun up. Beau has his rifle up. I keep my knife ready.

We move to the van first.

I listen past Krueger's growling, past the engine ticking as it cools.

A voice carries through the woods. Then another. Then Naomi makes a sound that is half protest and half fear.

Brooke moves first.

She steps off the shoulder into the brush, gun up, breath shallow. Beau follows immediately, rifle raised, eyes scanning the dark. I follow them with my knife in my hand, keeping my steps quiet.

The forest swallows the road light fast. Leaves crack under our boots. Branches slap our sleeves and faces. The voices get clearer, we hear some sort of struggle. Naomi's voice tightens, and then it cracks. We slow at the edge of a clearing.

Then we see it.

Travis is on the ground near a tree, wrists zip tied behind his back. Blood spreads beneath him, soaking into the leaves and dirt. Too much blood. His face has gone gray under the moonlight, and I can't tell if he's even alive.

Brooke's hand flies to her mouth, covering it before the sound can escape. I feel the way her body locks up, the way everything in her wants to run to him.

Beau shifts slightly, his voice cutting in under his breath. "No. Brooke, wait."

Her shoulders tense harder.

Naomi is on her back a few feet into the clearing, her wrists zip tied behind her. Dirt and leaves cling to her skin where she must have fought. Her leggings are gone. Grant stands over her, one hand still at her hip, the other holding a revolver.

Elise and Ryan are farther back, zip tied and shaking. One of Grant's men stands near them with his rifle raised to their heads, watching them like they are already dead. Another stands off to the side of Grant, scanning the trees, waiting for movement.

We stay low at the edge of the clearing, watching, waiting, trying to line it up so we can take every one of these fuckers out without giving them a chance to put a bullet in Naomi or the kids.

Grant tilts his head, looking down at Naomi.

"Here's how we're gonna play this."

He spins the revolver in his hand.

"We're gonna play Russian roulette."

My grip on my knife tightens.

"I'm gonna stick this in your cunt," he crouches slightly, lowering the gun, "and I'm gonna pull the trigger until your luck runs out."

Naomi's scream cuts through the clearing.

That's our window.

Beau fires.

His rifle cracks once, and the man near the kids drops before he can turn. Beau fires again, and the second man goes down just as fast. Brooke fires once as well, hitting the third man and the sound overlaps the second shot. The clearing fills with echoes and the smell of burned powder.

Grant jerks upright, startled, head snapping toward the noise. His hand leaves Naomi for half a second, and that half second is all I need.

I sprint.

He turns toward the movement, trying to find a target, trying to decide who to shoot first. He sees me too late.

I hit him hard and drive him to the ground. His hands come up fast, clawing at my throat and jacket, trying to shove me off. I punch him once in the face. I punch him again. I hit him until blood spits from his mouth and his eyes blink too slow.

Brooke fires again.

Grant's hand jerks, and he screams. She shot his hand, and the sound is ugly. He tries to curl that hand against his chest, but his body is still fighting me.

He bucks under me and twists, trying to throw me off. His good hand scrapes the ground, searching.

A knife flashes in his grip. He drives it into my hand.

Pain explodes up my arm. My fingers spasm, and the knife in my other hand almost slips. Blood runs hot and fast between my knuckles.

I slam my weight forward anyway and hit him again with my free fist.

Grant uses my split second of pain to wrench his body sideways. He shoves hard and scrambles out from under me. He gets to his feet and runs, clutching his damaged hand close while his other hand pumps for speed.

He crashes through brush, and keeps going.

Brooke drops beside Travis the moment Grant breaks away.

She presses both hands to Travis's bleeding body. Her hands start shaking as soon as she makes contact, but she keeps pressure, teeth clenched, eyes locked on him.

Naomi crawls toward Elise and Ryan with her hands still bound.

Beau moves to the kids first. He keeps his rifle up with one hand and cuts Elise's zip ties with the other. He cuts Ryan's next. He gets Naomi's wrists free right after. Naomi immediately wraps her arms around both kids, holding them close, shaking too hard to hide it.

I push myself up, cradling my bleeding hand against my chest. My skin feels too hot and too cold at the same time. My heart hurts in my ribs.

Brooke looks up at me. Her face is smeared with blood that isn't hers. Her eyes are wide and wet.

"Go!"

I don't move fast enough.

"Go!" Her voice breaks on the word.

My eyes flick to Travis. His breathing is thin. Brooke is pressing down with both hands, refusing to let him slip away. Naomi is holding the kids close, whispering to them, trying to keep them from falling apart.

Beau looks at me and gives one short nod. Letting me know he has them, that Brooke won't be alone.

Grant is still running.

If Grant disappears, he will do this again. He will keep coming until he wins.

I make the decision. I turn and chase the sound of his footsteps.

My wounded hand burns with every heartbeat. I keep moving anyway, because letting him vanish is worse. I can hear him ahead. He is loud now, crashing through the woods. The trees thin and the road appears again.

Grant bursts out first and heads for his vehicle.

I sprint to the truck. The keys are still in it. I get in and start the engine with my good hand.

Grant's taillights jump ahead as he peels off. I follow right behind him.

He fires first. His arm hangs out the window and muzzle flashes light the road. The first shot shatters my side mirror. Glass snaps across the cabin and bites my cheek. The second shot punches through the windshield and misses my head by inches. I duck and keep driving.

He fires again.

The bullet rips through the passenger side window. The smell of gun powder fills the car. I keep the wheel straight and push harder. The road curves.

Grant takes it too fast.

I take it faster because I can't let him widen the gap. I close the distance.

He glances back, and I catch his face in the mirror. His eyes are wide. His mouth is open. He is not laughing now.

I hit his rear. His car fishtails. Tires scream. He flips. Glass and sparks tear through the dark as the car rolls, then slams down onto its roof. Metal grinds against asphalt before it finally comes to a stop.

I brake hard and shove my door open before my car even settles. Smoke curls up from the wreck. The engine ticks. Something inside hisses.

For a moment, everything goes quiet. Then I see movement.

Grant drags himself through the shattered window, coughing, one arm hanging wrong while the other claws at the ground. He pulls himself free and hits the pavement hard, rolling before trying to push himself up.

I move in fast. I grab the back of his shirt and rip him off the ground. He twists and swings with his good arm, catching me across the jaw. My head snaps to the side, but I don't slow down.

I hit him back harder.

Bone cracks under my fist. He stumbles, but he stays on his feet. He shoves off me and runs straight for the trees.

I watch him disappear into the dark for half a second, then I go after him. Blood runs down my hand and drips from my fingers, but I keep moving. I can hear him ahead of me. He is loud and uneven, crashing through brush without control.

I close the distance fast.

He stumbles and goes down hard. I hear the impact, hear him curse as he tries to scramble back up.

I come through the brush just as he turns.

He has a knife in his hand. He lunges. The blade comes straight for my throat. I knock his wrist aside and drive into him. We hit the ground together, rolling through dirt and leaves while he tries to get on top. He slams a knee into my ribs. Pain cuts through my side, but I stay on him. He swings the knife again. The blade slices across my arm, shallow but hot.

I grab his wrist and slam it into the ground once, then again. The knife slips from his grip and disappears into the leaves. He goes for my throat instead, fingers digging in as he tries to choke the air out of me.

I drive my forehead into his face. His nose breaks under the impact. Blood pours immediately. His grip loosens.

I roll on top of him and start hitting him. The first punch lands and I see Brooke in that manor, dragged inside while he stood there and let his brother torture her.

I hit him again.

The next one lands and I see the footage, her parents, the way Grant stood there with my father and John while they murdered them, like it was just another job.

I hit him again.

My mother's face flashes through my head, the way she looked into that camera right before he took her from me.

I don't stop.

Then I see Travis on the ground, blood spreading under him.

Each hit lands harder than the last, everything in me coming out with it. The anger, the loss, every thing he did that he never had to answer for. His head snaps side to side, blood spilling across his face, his body slowing under me.

I could kill him right here.

It would be easy.

Too easy.

My fist stops mid-swing. I stare down at him, breathing hard, blood running from my hand onto his shirt.

No. He doesn't get that.

I grab his collar and slam his head into the ground.

Once.

Twice.

The second impact takes the fight out of him. His body goes loose under my hands, his eyes unfocused, breath uneven. I watch him for a second to make sure he is out.

Then I reach down, grab both of his wrists, and wrench his arms behind his back. I tear a strip from his shirt and bind them tight, pulling it until there is no give.

He groans once, barely conscious, but he doesn't fight.

I haul him up by the back of his collar. His weight drags heavy, his feet barely keeping up as I pull him through the trees. Branches hit his body as I drag him forward. His boots catch on roots and rocks, but I keep moving, forcing him back toward the road.

By the time we break through the treeline, he's half-conscious and barely upright.

I shove him against the side of the truck and grab his jaw, forcing his head up. Blood covers his face. His eyes struggle to focus.

"You don't get an easy ending," I tell him.

He tries to speak, but nothing comes out.

I drag him to the back door, shove him inside, and make sure he stays down. Then I slam the door shut and move around to the driver's side.

Tonight is not the end.

Tonight is the beginning of his suffering.

Chapter 73
Brooke

"Please," my voice breaks in my throat. "Please, Travis. Don't do this. You can't leave me."

My hands are slick with blood. I press down harder. Naomi is on the ground beside me, shaking, her jacket piled under her palms, already soaked through. She keeps whispering his name, over and over, and she sounds terrified of stopping.

Travis's face is gray. His lips have a blue tint. His eyes flutter without landing anywhere.

Beau drops into a crouch on Travis's other side and presses two fingers to his neck. His jaw tightens.

"His pulse is slowing. We're moving now. My doctor is ten minutes out."

My breath catches so hard it hurts.

"No." Panic bleeds into my voice. "No, no, no."

Beau grips my shoulder, firm. "Brooke. Look at me. You can't freeze."

I swallow hard and nod.

Beau turns his head toward the trees. "Elise. Ryan. Move. Now."

They stare for a beat, shock locking them in place, then Naomi's voice cuts through it.

"Go! Do exactly what he says."

They move.

Krueger is barking back near the road, frantic and furious, and the sound slices through my nerves.

Beau and I lift Travis together.

Travis groans. It's barely audible. The sound knocks the air out of me.

"I've got you, I'm right here. Please stay with me."

I think of Mila for half a second, and then I push it away because I can't handle it. I survived losing her because Travis stayed. Because he kept me going. Because he kept showing up even when I didn't deserve it.

I can't do this again.

We move him across leaves and dirt toward the vehicles. Beau moves fast, clearing the way, calling instructions back over his shoulder.

Beau opens the back door of the van. "Careful with his right side."

We lay Travis across the back seat. I climb in with him. Naomi and the kids climb in beside me, pressed tight because there isn't room for anything else.

Beau gets in the driver's seat and starts the engine. Gravel spits under the tires as he turns us around.

Naomi keeps pressure on Travis's side with her jacket and her forearm. Her face is streaked with tears.

"Travis. Please keep your eyes open, please!"

I lean over Travis and press my forehead against his for a second.

"Please," I whisper again. "I can't lose you."

My phone vibrates in my pocket.

I don't look. I can't look. I keep both hands on Travis, one pressing down, the other gripping his wrist even though his pulse feels faint.

Beau drives fast. The road jerks under us. The headlights cut through trees and darkness. Naomi's breathing turns ragged every time Travis's body shifts.

We hit another patch of gravel and Beau brakes hard.

Headlights swing across a different clearing. A truck is already there, parked off the road. A man steps into the light wearing gloves and a headlamp. A bag is slung over his shoulder. Another person is behind him with a second bag and a folded stretcher.

Beau is out before the engine fully stops. He yanks the back door open.

"Stab wounds," Beau says. "Multiple. Blood loss."

The doctor nods once. "Bring him in."

They don't waste time. They pull the stretcher out onto the ground and flip it open. Naomi and I climb out, hands still pressed to Travis, then we help lift him. Beau takes most of the weight. The assistant grabs the other end.

Travis groans again, then goes quiet.

They get him onto the stretcher and drag it onto a tarp spread across the dirt. The doctor kneels and cuts Travis's shirt down the middle with trauma shears. Fabric falls away. The blood loss looks worse under the headlamps.

"Multiple stab wounds," the doctor states. "Upper abdomen and flank. Possible liver involvement."

The assistant moves quickly, connecting the tubing as the machine begins its steady mechanical rhythm, and the blood flows through the line and into the container.

I stand at the edge of the tarp, hands clenched so tight my nails bite into my palms. Naomi is beside me, fingers hooked around my arm.

The doctor presses hard against Travis's side. Travis twitches.

"Stay with us," I whisper, stepping closer. "Travis, look at me. Please."

His eyes flutter. They don't focus.

The portable monitor beeps.

Then it slows.

Beau stands at the foot of the tarp, watching everything. He looks tense in a way I don't see often.

"Pressure's dropping," the assistant says.

"Fluids," the doctor orders. "Now. Prep blood."

A needle goes into Travis's arm. Another line goes in. The doctor moves fast.

Blood starts welling again from one of the wounds.

"Damn it," the doctor mutters. "He's bleeding internally."

My breath turns into a sob I can't stop.

"No, no, no!" I cry. "Please!"

"I need room," the doctor says sharply.

"I'm not leaving!" I snap, tears spilling hard now.

Beau steps in, hands on my shoulders, firm. "Brooke. You breaking down doesn't help him."

I don't fight him when he guides me back a step. I can't take my eyes off Travis anyway.

The doctor inserts a tube. Travis jerks, then goes still.

The monitor slows again.

The beeps spread farther apart.

"Travis," I sob, and my voice breaks completely. "Please. Please don't leave me. Please."

My knees buckle. Beau catches me, holding me upright while I shake and cry. My whole body feels out of control.

The doctor presses two fingers to Travis's neck. "Come on," he murmurs. "Stay with me."

Seconds drag.

Then the monitor stutters.

Beep.

Beep.

Beep.

The rhythm comes back, weak but present.

The doctor exhales once. "He's still here."

I cry harder, forehead pressed against Beau's shoulder, shaking so badly I can barely stand.

"I'm not done," the doctor adds, already moving again. "He's not stable. He's alive, but he's critical."

Alive.

The word lands and my lungs finally pull in air.

I look at Travis. Pale and unconscious but still breathing.

"Hold on," I whisper through tears. "Seth is going to finish this. And you're going to be here when we get you out of this."

My phone vibrates again.

This time I notice. The screen is smeared with blood where I touched it earlier. My fingers don't cooperate at first, but I swipe it anyway.

"Seth?"

"I've got Grant," Seth says.

The pressure in my chest eases just enough that I can think again.

I sink onto the ground beside the tarp, close to Travis's shoulder, eyes locked on the monitor.

"Is he alive?"

There's a pause on the line.

"Yeah," Seth replies. "For now."

My grip tightens around the phone. My jaw clenches so hard it aches.

"Good." My voice is colder now. The shock hasn't left me, not really, but something sharper has slid underneath it. Something focused. "Because I'm not done with him."

The doctor moves past me again, adjusting lines, checking vitals. Travis doesn't wake. He's still pale. Still fragile. But he's here. He's alive.

"As soon as he's stable," I continue, eyes never leaving Travis's face, "I'm coming back to the house."

Seth doesn't interrupt me.

"And when I get there," I add, "I'm going to make it as painful as possible."

"I'll wait."

The call ends.

I lower the phone slowly and set it on the ground beside me. My hands go back to Travis, one resting over his, the other lightly against his arm like I'm afraid he'll disappear if I let go.

If Travis dies from this, I don't know how I will survive what comes after.

But I know exactly what I will do.

I will make Grant suffer until his last breath.

Chapter 74
Seth

Grant is strapped to the table, wrists and ankles locked down so tight the circulation in his hands is already compromised. His fingers are tinged purple. It will slow the bleeding later. His chest rises fast and shallow, panic starting to chew through whatever arrogance he walked in with.

He still smiles at me.

"You're such a fucking disappointment, Seth," Grant mutters once I pull the gag down just enough for him to speak. His voice is rough, but there's satisfaction in it. "Richard always said it."

I don't answer. I step closer instead. I want him to watch. I want him to understand how much time exists between now and the end.

"You like to talk," I murmur calmly. "That's going to be a problem for you."

Grant laughs. It sounds wrong in this room. "Watching your mother realize she was going to die. That was fun."

I look at him fully now.

"You're gonna pay for that," I tell him. "I promise you that."

Grant tilts his head. "I regret nothing."

"Yeah," I glance around the room before looking back at him. "And now you're here."

I reach for the gloves and slide them on slowly. Latex snaps against my wrists.

"You tortured Brooke," I continue. "You stabbed Travis in front of my brother and sister. You put guns to their heads."

Grant spits. It hits my boot.

"I'd do it again," he bites out. "Watching you unravel was worth it."

"You wanna know how I killed my father?" I ask.

That shuts him up.

"I beat him to death," I continue. "It wasn't quick, and it wasn't clean. I took a tire iron and kept swinging until there was nothing left of his fucking head but bone and pulp."

Grant's breathing stutters.

"He was a piece of shit," I add, stepping closer. "And so are you."

I stop right in front of him.

"So when you talk about him," I murmur, "you should remember that."

I move to the workbench and pick up the long knife. Built for this kind of damage. I turn on the torch and hold the blade over the flame.

The metal darkens, then reddens, then glows.

Grant starts to struggle. His body knows before his mind catches up.

"Fuck," he grits out. "Listen to me. The Collective will tear you apart if you kill me."

I turn off the torch and walk back to him.

His eyes flicker. Rage tries to surface.

"Oh really," I tilt my head slightly. "That's not what John said."

I grab his shoulder and drive the glowing blade into his side.

Flesh sizzles. The smell hits immediately. Grant screams, his body arching violently against the restraints, veins standing out in his neck as shock collides with pain.

I leave the blade there long enough to cauterize.

Then I pull it free.

The wound seals instantly. No blood. Just ruined flesh.

Grant sobs. His whole body shaking as his brain tries to process pain it can't escape.

"I'm not starting slow," I tell him. "I don't reward fuckers like you with patience."

I set the knife down carefully and lean in close enough that he has to look at me.

"You're going to live through this. Every part of it."

Grant's eyes are wild now.

I straighten and step back, already cataloging what comes next. What can be taken. What can be damaged without killing him. How long the human body can be kept on the edge before it breaks completely.

I have waited a long time for this.

Grant watches me like this is still a contest, like he is waiting for his turn to speak because he assumes he is going to get one. Blood runs from his mouth and down his chin, but his lips still try to pull into something smug when I stop moving and just look at him.

He coughs, and it turns wet halfway through.

"Your... father..." he manages, dragging in a breath that doesn't come easy. "Always thought you were weak."

I step closer.

He swallows, throat working through it, chest hitching. "He thought Luke had potential," he forces out. "If his mother hadn't... fucked him up before he was even born. Drugs will do that. Ruins the wiring."

I don't speak.

Grant takes that silence and runs with it, even though it costs him.

"He told us you were a liability," his voice breaking under the strain. "Said if it came down to it... he'd choose Luke."

He lets out something that tries to be a laugh and fails, turning into another cough.

"Funny... how that worked out."

I stop directly in front of him.

"I heard about the babysitter," Grant says, quieter now, each word pulled up through pain. "Natalie. That was her name, right?" He pauses, sucking in air. "Richard didn't even bother moving the body. Just left her down there... with you."

His eyes drag over my face, hunting for a reaction.

"You cried for days," he adds, voice rough and uneven. "Locked you down there with her. That was when he knew... you were weak. Like your mother."

A broken sound slips out of him, something close to a laugh.

"It felt good... putting a bullet in her head."

My hands curl into fists.

"And Brooke's father," Grant goes on, slower now, words starting to slur at the edges. "He really thought they could take down The Collective." He coughs again, blood spilling from his lips. "There is no leaving. There never was."

His eyes sharpen for a second, fighting to stay focused.

"Her dad begged. Her mom screamed." He drags in another breath. "They were lucky... we didn't find little Brooke that night."

He leans forward as much as the restraints allow, even though his body shakes with it.

"If we had...Richard and I would've taken our time with her." His mouth twitches. "Wouldn't that be ironic... if your father broke in your girl before you got to her? He liked breaking pretty little things... like her."

I exhale once, slow.

"I know what you're doing," I say calmly. "You're trying to make me end this faster."

I lean down until we're eye level.

"Fuckers like you always think provocation equals power," I continue. "You say the worst thing you can imagine and hope it buys you a quick death. But you'll never get that from me."

Grant's smile tightens but doesn't disappear.

"You're not pissing me off," I tell him. "You're making me more innovative."

I straighten and step back, giving him space just long enough for it to register. I turn toward the table of tools.

"I will be the last thing you see before you die, Grant. But it's going to take a while."

I pick up a wrench and test its weight.

"And until then, I'm going to hurt you in ways you didn't know a body could survive."

Chapter 75

Brooke

Travis hasn't moved in several minutes.

The monitor beside him keeps its rhythm, a steady pulse that tells me his heart is still working, but the rest of him looks emptied out. His skin is pale against the hospital sheets. His mouth hangs slightly open. His lashes rest too still against his cheeks.

The doctor's words replay whether I want them to or not. He is not out of danger. The next few hours will decide everything.

Naomi has not left his side. She dragged her chair close. Her hand stays wrapped around his, thumb moving slowly over his knuckles in the same small circle. She hasn't checked her phone or slept. She hasn't said a single word about how tired she must be.

She just stays.

Every time I look at her, I think of Mila.

I think of the way Travis moved that night. He saw the threat and stepped in front of me. Protecting the people he loves is not something he debates. It is something he does.

And he is lying here because of the world I dragged him into.

The guilt settles deep in my chest until it feels hard to pull in air. I lace my fingers together and press until my knuckles ache, trying to redirect the pressure somewhere else.

"I should have—" I start, but I stop. There is no version of that sentence that fixes anything.

Naomi looks up at me. Her eyes are red.

"Don't...Don't turn this into something it isn't."

"He keeps getting hurt because he's standing next to me."

"He's here because he chose to be," she replies. "He protects the people he loves. That includes you."

The doctor steps in again, checks the monitors, adjusts the IV line, presses lightly at the bandages under the sheet. He studies the numbers for a moment longer than I like, then looks at us.

"He's still unstable," the doctor explains. "We're doing everything we can, but the next few hours are critical."

I nod, swallowing back the burn in my throat.

When he leaves, something shifts inside me.

Naomi sees it.

"You need to go," she says quietly.

"I don't want to leave him."

"You're not leaving him," Naomi squeezes Travis's hand. "I'm here. I'm not moving. If anything changes, you'll know."

I glance toward the hallway where Elise sits with Krueger at her feet, his leash wrapped tight in her hand, while Ryan sits beside her holding Luna close against his chest, just as Beau comes back in and hands them each a bag of chips without saying a word.

"The kids should stay here," Naomi adds. "Whatever you're about to do, they don't need to see that."

"Yeah."

She nods once.

"Go."

I lean down until my mouth is close to Travis's ear.

"Don't check out on me," I murmur. "You're not leaving yet."

His breathing shifts slightly. It might be reflex. I choose to believe it's not.

I press my lips to his temple and straighten before the grief can take over.

Beau meets my eyes and gives a short nod, like he already knows what I'm about to do.

I turn and head out before anyone can say anything else.

The drive back feels off in a way I can't shake. The road stretches out in front of me, headlights cutting through the dark while my grip tightens on the wheel. My thoughts won't settle. They keep circling the same place, grief and anger twisting together, building into something that won't let me sit still.

Every mile drags me closer, but it still feels like it's taking too long.

By the time I pull up, my jaw is tight enough to hurt.

I step out and head straight for the house. The safe house door shuts behind me. The basement door is already unlocked.

I take the stairs slowly.

The smell hits first. Burnt flesh, thick, foul, sour, layered over with bleach that does nothing to hide it. It clings to the air, settles in the back of my throat, makes every breath feel heavier.

Seth stands near the table with his sleeves rolled up, his hands controlled, his focus locked in.

Grant is strapped down.

What is left of him is barely recognizable.

His fingers are gone. His toes too. The ends are sealed over, cauterized into blackened ruin, the skin around them swollen and split. His chest rises unevenly, every breath dragging through him like it is being pulled out instead of taken in. Sweat and blood coat his skin, and his entire body shakes in small, constant tremors that he can't stop.

He lifts his head when he sees me, and even that small movement costs him.

His mouth pulls into something that tries to be a smile, but it breaks halfway through.

"Well," he rasps, voice shredded and uneven, catching between breaths. "Looks like the gang's... all here."

He coughs as soon as the words leave him, a wet, choking sound that forces his body to jerk against the restraints. Blood spills from the corner of his mouth as he tries to breathe through it.

I step fully into the room. I move around the table slowly, my boots quiet against the concrete, giving him time to watch me, to understand that I am not in a rush.

"You know, Grant," I say, "you've taken a lot of things from me over the years. My parents. My freedom. Maybe the last piece of my sanity."

I stop where he can see me clearly.

"That's why I don't feel bad about what I did to your family," I continue. "I enjoyed every blow."

Grant's mouth twitches. His face tightens, and a strained sound slips out of him before he can stop it. He tries to speak, drags in a breath that doesn't come easy, and chokes on it.

I keep going.

"Before I even drove down to their house, I wasn't completely sure they were bad people," I admit. "I just assumed they had to be, to raise two sadistic fucks like you and Elliot. Turns out I was right."

A smile pulls at my mouth.

"Your brother pissed himself before I killed him," I add. "Your wife cried. Your mother begged. I'm pretty sure your father shit himself."

I give a small shrug.

"All pathetic, just like you."

Grant jerks against the restraints, the movement tearing through his body. A broken groan rips out of him as pain floods through whatever nerves are left intact. His breathing turns uneven, shallow, desperate, but he still tries to push through it.

He spits out words between breaths, voice breaking apart as he forces them through the pain, each sentence dragging itself forward like it is fighting to exist.

"Your mother..." he chokes, a wet cough cutting him off before he tries again. "We carved her open... ear to ear. She wouldn't stop screaming..."

His chest stutters. He swallows hard, like it burns.

"Your father... we gutted him," he continues, words slurring. "Took his eyes... made sure he saw it coming before we did."

He lets out something that almost sounds like a laugh, but it collapses into another strained breath.

"They were so fucked up..." he rasps. "You couldn't even have an open casket..."

His head tilts slightly, eyes trying to lock onto mine, even as his body trembles under the strain.

"We should've found you that night," he mutters, voice dropping. "Taken turns... forced our way into your tight little cunt while we strangled the life out of you..."

He coughs again, harder this time, blood spilling from his mouth as his body jerks against the restraints.

I laugh.

The sound cuts through everything else in the room.

"Grant," I sigh, shaking my head, "these weak attempts to intimidate me or piss me off aren't going to work. I don't give a fuck anymore."

I step closer until I'm right beside his face.

"You're dying," I tell him. "Maybe tonight. Maybe tomorrow."

I glance at Seth, then back at Grant.

"But guess who decides."

I tap my chest once, then gesture toward Seth.

"Me and him," I smirk. "The two people you tried to destroy."

Grant's eyes shift, struggling to focus. The pain is still there, but something else starts to surface under it.

Fear.

"Your life is in our hands," I continue. "We decide if you take your next fucking breath."

I lean in close enough that he has no choice but to look at me.

"So tell me," I whisper, "who's the god now?"

Chapter 76
Seth

I watch Brooke the moment it happens.

I smile at the recognition. This is the look she gets when fear stops negotiating and clarity takes over.

I light a cigarette because my hands need something to do. The flame catches, the ember glows, and I take a slow pull. Then another. I step closer and pass it to her.

She inhales.

I can see it ground her, pull her fully into her body.

She steps forward and presses the lit end straight into Grant's eye.

His body bucks against the restraints so hard the table rattles, a noise tearing out of him that is not language anymore.

I hand her a knife.

"What do you want to do first?" I ask.

"Hmm," she turns the blade in her hand. "Why don't you give me some ideas?"

I tilt my head and look at Grant. At the panic spreading across his face now that he understands we're not fucking around.

"Well," my eyes flick back to him. "Didn't he say he was going to rape you if he found you that night?"

She nods. "Mm-hmm."

"Then let's take away his ability to rape anyone."

She smiles.

Grant's face finally breaks. The arrogance collapses into raw panic.

"No," he gasps. "No, no, no."

"Oh, yes," she glances at the table. "Give me the shears."

I retrieve the heavy shear cutters and place them in her hand.

Brooke smiles.

Grant sobs now. The sound fills the room and then cracks under its own weight.

She looks up at me. "Is there anything to cauterize it?"

My mouth curves before I can stop it. I reach for the torch and feel the heat still trapped in the metal.

"I still want him alive," she murmurs. "Dickless. Ballless. Pathetic."

Grant tries to curl in on himself even before she lifts the shears. His scream rips out fast, strained and frantic. He knows exactly what she is about to take from him.

I stay where I am and watch her.

She isn't breaking him to prove a point. She is removing the last thing he ever used to hurt anyone. She is taking back every inch of power he stole.

Grant thrashes against the restraints, the straps biting into his wrists and ankles as his body jerks and twists. He is stripped down to nothing but his underwear, leaving him exposed in a way that makes the fear hit harder. His thighs tremble. His heels scrape against the table, dragging uselessly for leverage he can't find. His panic fills the room in broken, uneven sounds that echo off the concrete walls.

Brooke steps in, she grips the waistband and yanks his underwear down, forcing him fully exposed, leaving him with nothing left to hide behind.

The blade comes up next. She positions it at the base of his groin, right where the skin meets the root of his dick.

A sound tears out of him, raw and broken.

Then she cuts.

The shears part his flesh in a single, brutal motion. It opens the skin around the entire organ, slicing through the shaft and the thin tissue that encases both testicles. Blood pours immediately. Thick, hot, pulsing streams run down her wrist and coat the inside of her palm. His nuts split open as she drags the blades downward. Both testicles spill free, still attached by connective tissue for a moment before she severs everything with a decisive finish.

As a man, watching that hits me in a place instinct tries to guard. Everything below my belt pulls tight fast, like my body thinks I'm the one getting sliced open. It should make me sick.

It doesn't.

Because it's Grant. Because the bastard earned this. Because seeing the one thing he shoved into every victim he ever took get hacked off him feels so goddamn right I almost smile. He spent his whole life acting like that shit made him powerful. Now it's gone, useless, bleeding out like the rest of him.

And I'll be honest. Watching him lose it makes me feel fucking good.

What was once his dick and balls drops from her hand onto the floor. The severed penis, the emptied pouch of the scrotum, and the testicles lie in a mangled heap, glistening under the overhead light.

Grant's body jerks so violently the chains rattle. His voice cracks. His breath comes in wet, broken gasps. He doesn't pass out. He feels every inch of the raw, exposed wound where his genitals used to be.

Brooke takes one step back.

"There," Brooke smiles. "Now no one will ever have to feel you inside them again."

I get the blowtorch and ignite it.

The blue flame roars to life. I step toward the open wound between his legs, and the heat hits him before the flame does. His scream tears straight up through his chest. It climbs in pitch. It shreds into something thin and animal-like.

I pressed the flame to the bleeding tissue. The wound sizzles. The edges curl and blacken. The smell thickens. His body bucks so hard the table shifts an inch. He is crying now, choking on his own breath, but I continue until every open vessel is sealed shut in a blistered, ruined mass of charred flesh.

I turned off the torch. The room goes quiet except for his rasping breaths. What remains between his legs is nothing but a blackened crater, cauterized and destroyed, the final proof of exactly what we took from him.

Brooke straightens, I step closer and reach out. Wipe a smear of blood from her cheek with my thumb. Her eyes flick to mine.

I've never wanted her more than I do right now. Not just because of what she's done. But because of what it cost her. What she gave up to be this, here, now, with me.

And I'll never let anyone touch her again.

She leans in, whispers something to Grant. He's barely conscious, barely alive. But I watch his eyes twitch. He hears her. Whatever she says, it's meant to be the last thing his mind clings to.

She turns away from him. Looks at me. "That's enough for now."

I nod, wrapping an arm around her waist. We walk upstairs, leaving the door open. Letting him hear our steps, our silence, our calm. Because he knows now, he is nothing to us.

I want to ask about Travis. I already know the answer, I can see it on Brooke's face, but I need to hear her say it. I need the truth out loud, even if it kills me.

"He's alive," her voice cracks. "Still not stable. Naomi's with him. Beau and the kids stayed. I told them to call me if anything changes."

I nod, because talking feels dangerous. The truth sits heavy in my chest, and I can feel it pushing up, trying to force its way out. I don't want to admit that I'm scared. I don't want to say out loud that I keep seeing the amount of blood he lost, and my brain keeps doing the math that men like him don't survive that kind of hit.

I have seen enough bodies to know it.

And it scares the hell out of me.

I'm not supposed to care this much. Travis isn't some deadweight rookie. He's family now, the real kind, the kind you bleed for without thinking. The idea of losing him feels devastating.

"Grant's not gonna last much longer," I tell her. "A few more hours, maybe. If we do anything else, he'll bleed out. Even cauterized."

Brooke doesn't flinch.

She looks at me and says, "Then let's not kill him like that...Let's bury him alive."

That pulls a grin out of me. I kiss her once. This version of her, the one who can calmly sentence a man to hell, is the one I always knew existed. The one who matches me bone for bone.

"I'll get the shovel."

We load him into the back. Duct tape around the wrists, just in case. I secure the restraints tighter. His fingers are already gone. His toes too. He won't crawl far. But I'm not leaving anything to chance.

He's barely awake. Slack-jawed, wheezing, eyes glassed over.

There was a heavy, reinforced wooden crate in the basement. It's been sitting down there. Built for exactly this. The wood is scarred, the metal bands dulled with age and use. The hinges creak when we drag it free. Beau built things like this for men who thought they were untouchable. Men like Grant.

We haul him through the tree line, boots sinking into damp earth. The forest is cold and dark and quiet. Grant is quieter at first. Breathing wrong. Short pulls of air through busted ribs. His jaw is swollen and crooked, blood dried dark against his chin and throat. He watches the hole as we dig it, eyes tracking every movement, every shovel of dirt, every widening inch. He studies it like he's trying to memorize the shape of what's about to erase him. Then he finds his voice again.

"You think you can kill me?" he spits, blood spraying with the words. "The things I've done, the people I've killed. I'll be remembered forever."

Brooke doesn't look at him. She keeps digging. Her shoulders rise and fall with effort. Dirt streaks her arms. Her jaw is set. She doesn't give him even a glance. That denial hits him harder than anything else we've done so far.

Grant laughs, harsh and wet, coughing halfway through it. "You're a fucking bitch, Brooke," his eyes locked on her. "Just like your whore of a mother. I'll make sure someone finishes what we started. I'll make sure they kill you right in front of him."

That's when I stop digging. The shovel drops into the dirt.

I cross the distance in two steps and drive my boot into his jaw hard. The impact lands clean. His mouth snaps sideways. Teeth clack together. The scream that tears out of him afterward is broken, garbled, barely recognizable as human.

He collapses back against the restraints, choking on blood and spit, jaw hanging wrong, eyes wild.

"I'm tired of hearing you fucking talk," I snarl.

We lower the crate into the hole. The wood scrapes against dirt as it settles. The fit is tight. Grant thrashes when he sees it, panic finally punching through whatever bravado he had left. His breath turns fast and shallow. His chest heaves. He tries to say something else, but it comes out as a slurred whine, jaw useless now, words dissolving into noise.

We don't rush. We secure him inside, cinch the straps. Weight pressing in from every side.

I look down at him. "Any last words?"

Grant opens his mouth to say something.

I shovel dirt straight into his face. It cakes his eyes. His nose. His mouth.

I slam the lid down on him.

The first scream hits the wood hard enough to make it shake. The sound vibrates up through the ground, into my boots, into my bones. Something slams against the inside again and again.

I pause with the shovel in my hands.

I think about my mother. About my father turning men like Grant loose on the world. About Brooke dragged through hell because men like him needed to feel powerful. About Travis bleeding out on the ground while Grant watched and smiled.

Out of everything I've done, I know this is one of the worst ways to die. And Grant deserved all of that.

I shovel dirt onto the crate. The screams turn muffled and desperate. Then rhythmic and uneven. Then panicked breathing beating against wood, slower each time.

Brooke takes a turn. Her shovel lands with force. Dirt thuds down in heavy clumps.

By the time the hole is filled, the forest sounds normal again. Wind through branches, leaves shifting. Night insects starting up like nothing happened. Nothing left to mark what's underneath.

Brooke wipes her hands on her jeans. I can see in her shoulders, the tension that hasn't released yet. I step toward her, already reaching for her.

Her phone rings.

The sound slices through the quiet.

Brooke freezes. She looks down at the screen and I see the worry in her face before she even says anything. She doesn't answer. Her fingers curl around the phone.

"Brooke."

"I can't," she shakes her head once. "I can't hear it if it's—"

"Then don't," I take the phone from her hand and shove it into my pocket. "We're going there."

She looks up at me, eyes wide and glassy.

The truck doors slam and I'm behind the wheel before my brain catches up to my body. The engine roars to life. Gravel sprays as I throw it into gear and punch the gas hard enough to snap her back against the seat.

The road blurs. Trees streak past. The speedometer climbs into numbers I don't register. My hands don't shake. My vision doesn't blur. Everything narrows to the road and the thought of Travis on a table somewhere, dying because of us.

Brooke presses her forehead to the window, breathing hard, whispering Travis's name like a prayer.

Nothing about this feels like hope.

It feels like a race we're already losing.

Chapter 77
Brooke

It's been two weeks.

Two weeks of hell dressed up as silence. Two weeks since we ended Grant, since the ground swallowed him whole, and the world kept moving. It doesn't bring back the people he took from us. It didn't undo the damage. It left a space where rage used to sit, and that space hurts worse.

The air smells like flowers and damp earth.

Everyone here is dressed for mourning, but not the way I'm used to. No black. Seth and I are both in white. It feels wrong and right at the same time. As if saying this isn't about darkness today, even if darkness brought us here.

My eyes burn. I stopped trying to wipe the tears away ten minutes ago. They just keep coming, sliding down my face without permission. I lean into Seth's side, pressing my shoulder against his arm, grounding myself in the familiar weight of him. His hand tightens around mine. I feel it before I see it, the slight hitch in his breath, the warmth of a tear landing on my knuckle.

The service blurs. Words float past me, kind ones, hollow ones, sentences about loss and love and remembrance. I hear them, but they don't stick. All I can think about is how unfair it is that grief keeps finding new ways to hurt. How even when you think you've bled out enough, there's always more.

Seth's thumb rubs slow circles against my palm. He's here and I'm here. That feels like the only solid truth left.

People cry quietly. Some bow their heads. Some stare straight ahead like they're afraid that if they look down, they'll fall apart completely. I recognize that feeling. I live in it.

The tears finally slow, not because I feel better, but because my body has nothing left to give. My chest aches with every breath. I swallow hard and lift my gaze to the name etched into the stone near the casket.

Samantha Roberts.

This isn't a funeral for the life we lost on the run. This isn't for the chaos or the blood or the war we've been fighting.

This is for her.

For the woman who loved Seth even when she thought she'd lost him forever. For the mother who carried guilt for years and still chose love. For the voice on the screen that told him the truth too late. For the baby in the pumpkin hat who never stopped being hers.

We're watching the funeral from the car, parked far enough away that no one notices us. Seth sits beside me in silence, jaw clenched, eyes locked on the crowd. Elise is in the backseat next to Ryan, both of them quiet, both of them staring out the window like they don't know how to be here either. Krueger's head is in Ryan's lap. Luna's curled against Elise's arm.

It's Samantha's friends and coworkers who organized the service. Her old nursing colleagues, a neighbor, the friend who briefly took in the kids when the cops showed up. They're the ones who gave her this moment. A proper goodbye.

The drive back to the house feels off. Seth keeps his eyes on the road. One hand on the wheel, the other resting against his thigh, knuckles pale from how tight he's holding himself together. His silence says more than anything he could say out loud.

I glance back.

Elise leans her forehead against the window, face turned away, her jaw clenched like she's trying not to cry again. Ryan sits next to her, staring at nothing. It looks like no one's blinked in twenty minutes.

I lean back against the seat and let the road pass.

My mind drifts to Travis. He's finally stable. He woke up two days ago, still in pain, still hooked up to enough machines to terrify me, but he's alive.

He's not out of the woods. His body's healing, but his soul's been through the wringer with the rest of us. He can talk and sit up for short stretches. He cracked a joke yesterday about how he's two and 0 for stabbings. I told him it wasn't funny. He said it kind of was.

Travis isn't just my friend. He's my brother in every way that matters. The only family I had when I had nothing. The one person who never gave up on me, even when I didn't know who I was anymore. Even when I didn't want to be found. He's the one person who made me believe there are still good people in this fucked up world.

And I'm not ready to lose him. Not now, not ever.

When we pull into the driveway, the kids are quiet. No one moves until Seth kills the engine.

Elise gets out first. Her cheeks are still streaked with dried tears, but she doesn't wipe them away. Ryan follows, slower. He didn't speak, didn't look up. They pass us without saying a word.

Then Elise stops and turns.

Her mouth opens like she wants to say something, but no words come out. Instead, she walks straight up to Seth, and then throws her arms around him.

Sobs break loose like they've been waiting in her throat for hours. She buries her face in his chest and cries like it's the only thing left she knows how to do.

Seth freezes. His eyes flick to me like he's asking for instructions. I'm sure he's never had to deal with a grieving teenage girl. I understood her pain more than she knows.

I nod.

He wraps his arms around her, slow and careful. He holds his little sister like she might shatter if he squeezes too tight.

From where I stand, I see it shift in him. His face tightens, his jaw locking as he looks down at her, and then the control cracks just enough. Tears slide down his face. He doesn't wipe them away.

He just holds her tighter.

Ryan steps closer and wraps his arms around both of them. His head drops against Seth's side. He doesn't say anything, but I see the tears.

Three of them, tangled in a grief they didn't choose, mourning the same woman from different lifetimes.

They didn't grow up together, but they have each other now. None of them say it out loud. But they all lost their mother. They all gained a sibling. Maybe something like peace is possible.

Inside the house, Beau's waiting with a laptop and a half-finished beer.

He looks up. "We need to talk."

Seth and I drop onto the couch, the weight of the last few weeks hanging off our shoulders like soaked clothes.

"It's never gonna be safe for you two unless we fake your deaths," Beau says. "Right now, the government presumes you're both dead. That's good. Let's make it official."

Seth doesn't speak. He just nods once.

"I got people," Beau continues. "Family ties. They've got access to morgues. All we need are bodies close enough to pass for you, add some DNA, burn it in a car or a house. Fire's the most efficient way to erase identity."

Seth nods slowly. "Okay. Let's do it."

"But first," I say. "I need to see Mary."

Seth looks up, tense. "You think she knows where John is?"

"I don't know. But if she does... I need to end this. I need to end him."

Seth nods once. "I'll gas up the car."

We leave the kids and the pets with Beau, and make the trip to Fresno. It takes most of the day. When we reach the house, I know something's wrong before we even stop the car.

The mailbox is overflowing. The grass is overgrown. Flies buzz against the inside of the windows like something's rotting. Seth sees it too. I can feel it in the way his body tenses beside me. He gets out first and walks up to the front door and I follow.

The smell hits before we're even inside. I pull my jacket up over my nose and mouth, breathing through the fabric, but it doesn't help much.

Seth kicks the door open.

And there she is.

Aunt Mary, decomposing on the living room floor. Skin bloated and blackened, maggots burrowing into her neck. I can't tell what the cause of death was. Pills? A razor? Her face is too far gone to read.

I step forward.

Seth grabs my wrist. "You don't need to see that."

"I do."

He lets me go.

She's my last blood relative. My mother's sister. The only person who knew what really happened to me as a child and did nothing.

Part of me wants to believe she deserved it. That this was karma. That she died regretting everything. But another part of me wonders if she was just weak. Another woman eaten alive by men like John, Richard and Grant.

I turn away. My eyes burn from more than just the smell.

There's a sheet of paper next to her body. Curled and stained at the edges. I crouch and pick it up carefully.

It's a letter addressed to me, in Mary's handwriting.

I read it silently.

Brooke,

I was supposed to protect you.

You were the only blood I had left, and I let The Collective get you. Just like I let them get my sister.

I told myself I saved you. I thought I did. But I didn't.

I know they're going to hurt you. And if you do come out of this alive, your rage will kill me. And I deserve it.

So I'll do what I was supposed to do. Even if I burn in hell for eternity.

I'm sorry, I wasn't strong enough to save you.

– Mary

I stare at it, not sure how I feel. It was a combination of sadness, guilt, fury and pity. She was the last biological relative I had. Now there's only me.

Then the house phone rings. I walk over and answer it with a shaky hand.

"Hello?"

"I knew you'd come."

My mouth goes dry. "You can see me?"

"Always."

"Did you kill Mary?"

"Does it matter?" John says softly. "She died the moment she realized she failed you."

My grip tightens on the receiver.

"I think I loved your aunt," he adds. "She lasted longer than any other woman I've been with."

Something in my chest twists.

"You sick son of a bitch," I snap. "I'm going to find you. I don't know where you are yet, but I will. And when I do, I'll kill you."

A quiet, amused chuckle slips from him.

"Stay sharp. It's the only way you'll survive." He pauses. "Goodbye Brooke."

My chest tightens.

The line goes quiet.

Seth walks over and takes the phone from my hand. "You okay?"

"Yeah, let's go."

We didn't stay long after that. There's nothing left here. Seth burned the letter after I read it twice, the words still fresh in my head as the paper curled in on itself and turned to ash. We scrub the place of fingerprints. Mary's body gets reported anonymously.

By the time we're on the road again, the sun's setting behind us.

This isn't closure. This isn't peace.

It's a pause.

Chapter 78
Seth

Three months pass like minutes.

The fake deaths stuck.

That's the thing about the system. It doesn't dig very deep when the bodies are burned, the dental records line up, and no one important keeps pushing. If you stage it correctly, mix in DNA, and let the fire erase what is left, people accept the version of events placed in front of them. It's easier to believe in a tragic accident than to entertain the idea of something calculated. Brooke and I, the Stratford Slashers, finally met our end in a fiery crash on a mountain road.

We used a wrecked SUV in the mountains. One male, one female, unclaimed morgue bodies, close enough in height and build. I set the fire myself. Brooke slid her old bracelet onto the female corpse's wrist. I left my knife and one of my rings in the ash. That was enough. A few weeks later the manhunt officially ended. Kincaid and Sinclair, presumed dead. No longer active threats.

Elise and Ryan were never officially found. A few missing kid flyers went up to make it look thorough, but no one hunts very hard for two teenagers without a recognizable last name or political value. The world forgets quickly when the narrative loses traction.

Now we are ghosts living under new names.

On paper, under the names Devin and Veronica Rhodes, Brooke and I are legally married. The records say we signed the documents in a quiet county office months ago. The paperwork makes us ordinary. It makes us legitimate. It makes us harder to find.

I chose the last name.

Rhodes was Natalie's last name. She always felt like an older sister to me, the only person I could trust as a kid. Using her last name makes it feel like she is still here in some small way. It makes it feel like I carried something of her forward instead of letting everything she was disappear.

I still intend to give Brooke the ring. I still intend to stand in front of people who know our real names and promise her something that isn't built on forged documents and contingency plans. I still intend to give her a wedding that doesn't require aliases.

For now, the paperwork will do.

We have a new house. Two stories tucked deep in the forest, fog rolling across the ground most mornings. We're still in Washington where the roads narrow and strangers rarely pass through.

The kids have new identities too. Travis built them from scratch. Immunization records, transcripts, a paper trail that stretches back years. He enrolled them in a private school that doesn't ask many questions and doesn't keep staff who enjoy digging through families' histories.

Travis is back on his feet as well. He moves without the limp now. He spends most nights hunched over his laptop, breaking through encrypted networks and siphoning money.

The Collective database ended up being more useful than they ever intended.

Travis drained millions out of the Grant family accounts. Elliot's money, Grant's money, the family trusts, the shell corporations that funded their operations. He pulled it out piece by piece and routed it through offshore accounts before anyone realized what was happening.

Combined with what I took from Victor Voss's account, we had enough to keep all of us afloat for a very long time.

Poetic, in a twisted way.

The same system they used to control people is the system that ended up paying for our freedom.

We're comfortable now, safe and bored sometimes. But that's what survival is. It's not exciting. It's not some high-adrenaline chase. It's quiet. It's homework and dinner before bed and grocery runs in sunglasses. Burner phones, quiet alarms and daily routines.

Brooke has been going to therapy every week. She says it helps. I believe her. She laughs more now. The nightmares still come, but the weight that used to sit on her chest all the time is finally starting to loosen.

And now I've started therapy.

Brooke said I should try it. She said if I don't at least try, I'm never going to know if it could truly help with the bullshit that lives inside me.

So now here I am. Sitting in our home office, camera off, mic on. Laptop balanced on the edge of my desk. The therapist's voice playing in my ears.

The name on her screen says Dr. Morales.

"Good afternoon, Devin," she greets. "How has this week been?"

"Quiet."

"Is that good or bad?"

"Good."

I lean back in my chair.

"So where we left off at the end of the last session," she begins. "You described yourself as someone who survived a lot of fucked up shit. I want to understand the parts of you that don't feel much. The parts you have called wrong."

I shift slightly in the chair and watch the black square where my camera would be.

"My childhood wasn't complicated," I shift my attention from the floor to her face on the screen. "It was violent."

She waits.

"My father believed abuse was the same thing as discipline. If something went wrong in the house, he decided someone needed to bleed for it."

Her pen starts moving.

"He kept everything quiet. No screaming. No neighbors calling the police. Just rules. You followed them or you didn't."

"And if you didn't?"

"He liked turning things into games. He would take my brother and me down to the basement and tell us to fight. Said it would toughen us up."

Her pen pauses.

"What happened during those fights?"

"We fought until one of us couldn't get up anymore."

"And then?"

"Then he chained the loser down there."

She sits very still.

"He would leave us there for twenty four hours. Sometimes longer. Said it built character."

The room on her screen stays quiet while she listens.

"He made us watch him do fucked up things," my jaw tightens at the memory. "Sometimes he made us do them too."

She looks up from her notes.

"I was raised in cruelty, it stopped shocking me," I add. "I started seeing it as part of how the world works."

I lean back slightly in the chair.

"And once your brain learns to see the world that way, it doesn't turn off."

She nods once.

"So you learned to stay alert."

"I learned how to read a room before anything happened. The way someone walks. The tone in their voice. If you pay attention long enough, you can see violence before it starts."

"And that helped you survive."

"I stopped assuming people are safe," I answer. "I assume they're dangerous until proven otherwise."

Her pen moves again.

"I want to ask how you experience empathy," she replies evenly.

"I understand it," I say. "I just don't always feel it."

"Give me an example."

"If someone dies and they aren't mine, I don't care."

That is the cleanest way to put it.

"And if they are your loved ones?"

My jaw tightens.

"Then it's different."

Different means I would burn the world down without a second thought. Different means I wouldn't sleep until every fucker that hurt Brooke was gone.

"I don't usually care when people die."

"Most people don't," she replies. "The difference is intensity. When you do care, how far does it go?"

"It doesn't have a limit."

"Is that devotion or control?"

"You think those are different?"

"Yes," she answers calmly. "Devotion protects. Control eliminates uncertainty. Which one drives you?"

Devotion and control are one in the same for me.

"Devotion."

She lets that sit.

"Have you ever enjoyed hurting someone?" she asks.

"Yes."

I don't pull punches.

"For what reason?"

"Because it worked."

"Worked how?"

"It stopped the people that hurt me or tried to. It silenced the noise in my head. It made fear disappear."

The first time I felt it was when I bashed my father's skull in. It made me feel untouchable for a moment. It made the chaos easier to deal with.

"So violence regulates you."

"It used to."

"And now?"

"Now I don't need it as much."

That's true. It's also not the whole truth.

"That's not the same as not wanting it."

"I don't wake up looking for it. And that's new."

"What changed?"

"Responsibility."

"Explain."

"I have two teenagers who depend on me. I have a wife who believes I can be more than what I was built for. I can't afford to be reckless."

If I lose control now, it doesn't just cost me. It costs them.

"So you restrain yourself for them."

"Yes."

"Is that morality, or strategy?"

"I'm not sure," I admit. "I don't want them to see that part of me."

Because once you see it, you can't unsee it. Once you understand how easy it is to hurt someone, something in you shifts.

"Because you're ashamed?"

"Because I don't want them to learn it."

"Devin," she murmurs, "do you believe you are fundamentally broken?"

"Yes."

"Why?"

"Because normal people don't think the way I think."

"Explain what you mean."

I lean back in the chair and stare at the dark screen while the silence stretches between us.

"I don't wonder whether someone deserves to live." My thumb drags over my knuckle. "I decide whether their actions justify it. I look for leverage before I look for emotion. When someone threatens the people I care about, my first thought is how easily their body would break. I don't feel disturbed by that. I feel focused."

"Do you experience remorse or regrets?"

"Yes."

"About what?"

"My mother."

I look down at the desk in front of me. The framed picture of me and Samantha sits beside my laptop. I stare at it for a moment.

"I didn't talk to her before she died."

Dr. Morales doesn't interrupt.

"I thought she abandoned me," I continue. "I thought she chose to leave and start a new life without me. I believed that for most of my life."

My eyes stay on the picture.

"But that wasn't the truth."

The silence stretches between us.

"She tried to find me," I sigh. "Someone lied to her and made sure she never could."

My fingers rest lightly against the frame.

"By the time I understood what really happened, it was too late."

Dr. Morales speaks carefully.

"And that is where the remorse comes from."

"Yes."

I keep looking at the picture of a woman who looks relieved just to be holding her son.

"I spent years believing the wrong story about her," I frown. "And she died before I ever gave her the chance to tell me the truth."

"That must be difficult to live with."

No shit.

"And then there's my brother. I hallucinate sometimes, that's why I take medication."

Her pen stops moving.

"You experience hallucinations?"

"Yes."

"What do you see?"

I rest my elbow on the desk and look down at my hands.

"I see my brother sometimes."

Her expression shifts slightly.

"Do you know why?"

"I don't know," My gaze drops to my hands. "Maybe guilt."

"Guilt from what?"

"From killing him."

Her eyes stay steady on the screen.

"I killed him in self-defense," I admit. "But I still see him. He shows up when the worst parts of me start pushing forward. When the violent instincts start coming back."

She nods slowly.

"And before that?"

"Before my brother died," I answer, "I used to see my father."

"You hallucinated your father?"

"Yes."

"When did that begin?"

"When the same urges started surfacing. Whenever the part of me that wants to hurt people started coming out, he would appear."

She writes something down.

"So the hallucinations are connected to violent thoughts."

"Yes. My brain reminds me exactly what happens when I let that part of myself run unchecked."

"Do you believe you were born this way," she asks, "or shaped this way?"

"Both."

"If you had grown up somewhere safe, do you think you would still crave control?"

"Maybe."

"Let me ask you something harder," she continues. "Do you believe you deserve love?"

"No."

"Why?"

Because ever since Brooke met me, her life has been turned upside down. She lost her friends. She lost whatever version of normal she had left. She survived things most people wouldn't make it through. Two years of violence, cults, kidnappings, funerals, blood. All of it tied to me.

"Because I don't know how to give someone peace. But Broo–Veronica saw the worst parts and didn't run."

"And you?"

"I stay too."

There is no version of this where I leave.

"Last question for today," she gives a small smile. "If the past never comes for you, if no one knocks on that door, who do you want to become?"

"Everything my father wasn't."

"Define that."

"Predictable, safe, loving. The man who fixes things around the house. The one who shows up to school conferences. The one who doesn't need a contingency plan for every grocery run. The man who loves his wife in every way."

"And do you think that is possible?"

"Yeah."

"Good... Same time next week?"

"Yeah."

"Camera on?"

"Maybe."

The call ends.

I sit there for a long moment after the screen goes dark.

Then I stand up and walk toward the sound of voices in the other room.

Elise is sitting cross-legged on the floor with a sketchpad in her lap, tongue between her teeth in concentration. Ryan's next to her, half-watching, half-scrolling through something on a tablet Travis modded to run off-grid. Brooke's in the kitchen, barefoot, hair tied up, voice low as she talks to Travis on the phone. She paces as she listens, relaxed, absentmindedly twirling the cord of the charger plugged into the wall.

They look... settled.

Elise glances up and catches me staring.

"What? Do I have something on my face?"

"No," I reply. "Just trying to figure out if that's supposed to be a raccoon or you."

Ryan snorts. Elise rolls her eyes, but there's no bite behind it.

"It's Krueger, actually. I see you decided to be a D1 ragebaiter today."

I walk over and crouch beside her. "I'm your big brother, I believe that's part of the job description."

"So annoying," she mutters, shading in the picture.

"Oh I can be worse."

Ryan lifts the tablet. "I found that movie you were talking about. The crazy Korean one."

"The revenge one?"

He nods. "Yeah. Travis said it was too violent for me. Which means it's probably amazing."

I smirk. "Oh we're definitely watching that later."

Brooke turns around from the kitchen and gives me that look, the one that says she heard everything. She hangs up and walks toward me, winding her arms around my waist. Her cheek presses against my chest.

"You good?" she asks.

"Yeah."

Her brows lift. "And?"

"It went well."

Brooke watches my face like she's waiting for it to crack. Then she exhales and slides her fingers into my back pockets.

"You didn't punch the screen."

"Not this time."

She leans in and murmurs, "Proud of you."

I rest my chin on the top of her head.

Travis comes through the front door. He stops just inside the living room, surveys the scene, kids on the floor, Brooke wrapped around me, "After the Storm" playing low from the speaker.

"So, this is what domestic bliss looks like, huh?"

Brooke doesn't even turn around. "You should know. How many times has Naomi been at your place this week?"

Travis smirks. "Well what can I say, the whole almost dying for her really did the trick."

Elise eyes him warily as he lowers himself onto the rug beside her and reaches for her bowl of pretzels.

"Touch it and die."

"I literally almost died, you know. Took seven stab wounds to the torso for you guys."

Elise rolls her eyes. "You're gonna milk that forever, aren't you?"

"Yup." He grabs one anyway and pops it into his mouth. "Perks of martyrdom."

Ryan tries to stifle a laugh. I just shake my head.

This house still has secrets. Trauma embedded deep in all of us. But the laughter drowns it out now.

And somehow, I believe we might actually be okay.

Chapter 79
Seth

For months she had been asking for a full back tattoo.

Every time we passed a shop window she slowed down to study the work behind the glass. Every time she noticed my machines sitting unused in the drawer she brought it up again.

She wanted one from me.

I told her the truth from the beginning. A full back piece hurts like a bitch. The needle runs across bone, muscle, and nerve endings for hours without stopping. The vibration spreads through your body until your skin feels swollen and irritated everywhere the machine passes.

She listened to all of that and shrugged.

"I've survived worse."

That ended the discussion.

I lay everything out across the worktable with the same routine my hands had followed for years. The sterile needles stay sealed until the last moment. Ink caps sit in a straight row while I fill them with black and deep red. Alcohol wipes, gloves, wrap, and paper towels stay arranged within reach.

My hands move through the preparation like muscle memory. Tattooing had always done something to my head that nothing else managed. Once the machine started buzzing, the world narrowed down to a few controlled details.

Skin. Ink. Pressure. Precision.

Everything else faded.

Tonight I get to tattoo my girl again.

She steps into the room wearing a red slip dress. Thin straps rest over her shoulders while the soft fabric drapes across every curve of her body. The material brushes lightly against her thighs when she moves.

The overhead light traces the smooth line of her shoulders and back.

My eyes move across her once before I force my attention back to the equipment.

She walks past me and switches on the speaker. The system hums softly as the playlist loads.

Then she drags a chair into the center of the room. The legs scrape slowly across the wood floor.

She turns the chair backward and straddles it, resting her forearms along the backrest while leaning forward slightly.

Her back stays completely exposed.

I pause while looking at her.

"You sure you don't want to pick the design?"

She shakes her head.

"I want you to."

That answer settles heavier in my chest than it should.

"Something that represents everything I survived," she adds quietly. "Something that feels like me."

My eyes move across the scars scattered along her back. Every one of them marks something we have walked through together.

I nod once.

"Okay."

I grab a pencil and begin sketching. The lines form quickly while she waits. I adjust the proportions twice before widening one section slightly.

When I turn the sketch toward her she leans forward to see it.

Her entire expression changes.

"I love it."

"This will take hours," I tell her. "Six at least."

She laughs softly.

"I think you're forgetting how little pain bothers me when you tattoo me."

My mouth lifts slightly.

"You enjoy it too much."

She looks back over her shoulder.

"I only enjoy it when it's you."

I pull on gloves and begin preparing her skin. The antiseptic wipes across her back in slow passes. She inhales sharply when the cold liquid touches her skin, and the muscles along her shoulders tighten before relaxing again.

I measure the center of her spine, spread the stencil gel, and press the design into place, smoothing it down carefully as my fingers brush her skin.

My pulse picks up every time I touch her.

I switch on the tattoo machine. The buzzing vibration fills the room.

The first hour passes without problems. The needle moves steadily along the stencil lines while my hand follows the shape I drew earlier. Her body stays still while the outline slowly begins forming beneath her skin.

Then she starts moving.

At first the movement barely registers. Her shoulders roll once before settling again. Her hips shift slightly against the chair.

I lift the machine.

"You okay?"

"Mmhmm."

She adjusts her position again.

The opening bass of "Angel" spreads slowly through the room.

She leans forward a little more.

That small movement causes the slip to shift along her hips.

The fabric parts just enough for me to see the curve of her ass.

My eyes follow the line of her spine downward before I force my attention back to the tattoo.

"You're fidgeting."

She smiles faintly.

"Am I?"

"Yes."

I reset my grip on the machine and continue outlining the next section.

The motor hums steadily in my hand while the needle moves through her skin. The rhythm usually locks my focus in place.

Then she moves again.

This time her hips tilt forward slightly. The slip tightens across her ass and lifts along the back of her thighs. That movement exposes the seat beneath her.

And the wetness between her legs.

My brain locks onto that image immediately.

The machine hovers above her skin while the needle continues vibrating in the air.

I lift it away and breathe slowly through my nose.

"Brooke, if you want a break you can say that."

She turns her head and looks over her shoulder.

Her expression looks wide and innocent.

"I don't want you to stop."

Her lips curve slightly.

"Am I making it hard for you to focus?"

Her hips tilt forward again. The slip slides higher along her ass. The view between her legs becomes clearer.

That ends my patience.

I set the machine down on the tray. The metal rattles softly against the surface.

She stands slowly. Her eyes stay locked on mine.

Her fingers catch the hem of the slip and lift it upward. The fabric moves slowly along her body.

Her pussy appears first beneath the rising cloth. Then the smooth line of her stomach comes into view. The dress continues upward until the curve of her waist appears.

Her breasts lift free of the dress while she raises it higher. The soft weight shifts while the fabric slides over them. Her nipples tighten slightly when the cooler air touches her skin.

The slip clears her head and falls to the floor beside her feet. She stands completely naked in front of me.

I'm already rock hard inside my sweats.

Her eyes drop immediately to the outline pressing against the fabric. Her lip catches between her teeth while she studies it.

But she doesn't reach for me. She touches herself instead.

She steps forward until she stands between my knees. The warmth of her body fills the narrow space between my legs while I look up at her.

Her fingers slide slowly down the center of her stomach. They move past her navel and continue lower until her hand slips between her thighs.

I lean forward without thinking. I watch her spread herself open with two fingers while her slick glistens under the light.

Her other hand rests against my shoulder for balance. Her breathing deepens while her fingers begin moving slowly over her clit.

I lean forward and press my lips against her stomach. Her skin feels warm beneath my mouth.

She inhales softly when my lips move upward along the flat line of her abdomen. My mouth brushes across her skin while I follow the path her fingers took seconds earlier.

Her hips shift slightly while she continues touching herself.

My hands slide along the outside of her thighs while I stay there between them, breathing her in.

"Fuck," I mutter quietly.

Her fingers keep moving between her legs.

Then she lifts her hand.

Her fingers glisten. She holds them in front of my mouth.

My lips part and she pushes two fingers past them. Her taste fills my mouth immediately. My tongue moves slowly along the length of her fingers while I suck them deeper.

Her breath catches above me.

I keep my eyes on hers while my tongue drags along her skin, cleaning every trace of her wetness from them.

When I finally pull back she slides her fingers out of my mouth. She looks down at me like she knows exactly what she is doing.

Watching her touch herself like that erases every rational thought from my head.

"Brooke, if you keep doing that I'm gonna come in my pants."

Her lips curve slowly.

"Then take them off."

The control she has in that moment irritates me almost as much as it turns me on.

I shove my sweats down far enough to free my dick. The cool air brushes across the sensitive skin and pulls a breath from my chest.

She reaches down immediately.

Her slick fingers wrap around the head of my cock and stroke once, spreading her wetness across the tip.

My breath catches.

Then she turns around and straddles my lap with her back against my chest. Her thighs slide across mine while her ass brushes against my length.

I grip the arms of the chair to stop myself from thrusting upward. Even that light contact makes my hips twitch.

Her body settles against me while the warmth of her skin presses against my stomach. She reaches between her legs again and wraps her fingers around my dick before guiding the tip toward her entrance.

The head slides slowly through her soaked cunt.

My breath leaves my lungs slowly while she lowers herself down my shaft.

Her body descends gradually while her pussy stretches around me. Heat surrounds my shaft while she continues settling lower.

By the time she sits fully on my lap my dick is buried deep inside her.

A low moan escapes her throat while her hips roll slowly.

"Fuck," I groan near her ear. "You love distracting me."

Her fingers slide down her body again while she begins rubbing her clit.

"Yeah," she whispers. "You look so hot when you're focused."

My hands close around her hips.

"I want you to keep going," she murmurs. "While you finish the tattoo."

I look toward the machine resting on the tray.

"You realize if I ruin a line you're stuck with it forever."

She laughs softly.

"I trust you."

I exhale slowly and reach for the machine again.

The tool feels heavier in my hand now because she's sitting on my lap with my cock buried inside her.

I press my palm against the small of her back to steady her.

"Stay still."

"I am still."

Her hips shift slightly. The movement drags her walls along my shaft.

My jaw tightens.

I lower the needle toward her skin and the machine buzzes back to life. The sound fills the room again while I resume the linework. Years of practice keep my hand controlled even while my body struggles to focus.

Her breathing deepens behind the sound of the machine.

I wipe away excess ink and lean closer to check the line. I dip the needle into the ink cap again and continue working.

Her walls tighten around my cock again.

"You're doing so good," she murmurs.

My breath slows through my nose.

"Don't play with me right now."

"I'm not."

My hand pauses briefly.

"Brooke."

"Yes, Seth?"

"If you keep doing that I won't finish this tonight."

She laughs quietly.

"You always finish your work."

Her fingers slide down her stomach again. Her pussy clenches around my dick.

My grip tightens.

"Jesus Christ."

"You feel so good inside me," she moans.

That fucking does it.

I set the machine down and grab her hips.

I lift her slowly until she rises along my cock before pulling her back down again with more force. Her body reacts immediately, tightening around my dick while her breath leaves her chest in a broken gasp. I begin moving beneath her while my hips push upward.

The slow thrusts quickly build into a deeper rhythm.

Eventually I stop again.

"Get up."

She freezes slightly.

"Seth—"

"Now."

She lifts slowly. Her body rises along my shaft inch by inch.

The slick sound fills the room.

I grab her waist, stand, then turn her around and bend her over the worktable. Her palms strike the surface while her back curves and her ass lifts behind her.

I watch myself push back inside her.

My dick slides through her soaked folds before sinking deeper, and her wetness spreads across my shaft every time I move. The sight of her slick coating me while my length disappears inside her again makes my stomach tighten.

I watch it happen again.

My cock pulls free slowly before driving back inside.

Tattooing must be a kink for us.

The first time I tattooed her we ended up fucking on the shop table before the ink even dried.

My hips slam forward again, the force pushing her into the wood hard enough that it rattles beneath her hands. The rhythm builds quickly, the sound of skin striking skin filling the room while her moans slip out between breaths.

My hand slides into her hair and closes into a tight fist at the base of her scalp. I pull her head back toward me until her spine curves deeper and her throat stretches along my shoulder.

She gasps when I draw her closer.

I lean forward and bite lightly into the side of her neck, making her shudder.

"You wanted this, huh?" I murmur against her throat.

She nods quickly, her fingers tightening along the edge of the table while her body pushes back against me.

My free hand slides down the line of her thigh before lifting her leg onto the table beside her. The new angle opens her wider and pulls a rough breath from my chest when my cock pushes deeper inside her.

"Seth," she gasps, her voice breaking apart. "Fuck... you're so deep."

"You wanted it," I murmur between thrusts. "So take it."

My hips drive forward again and at the same moment my palm cracks across her ass. The sound snaps through the room and her body jerks beneath me while the table shudders from the force.

My hips pull back and slam forward again, and my hand strikes the same spot across her ass the instant my cock fills her again.

Every thrust pushes deep into her and every thrust ends with another hard slap against her skin. I watch her ass bounce under my hand each time I spank her, the movement sending a tight squeeze through her pussy that makes my dick thicken even more inside her.

My eyes stay locked on where our bodies join while my hips keep moving.

The wet sound fills the room with every thrust, louder than the music still playing through the speaker behind us.

I tighten my grip in her hair again. Her head tips back while my hips continue driving into her.

I pull back slowly so she can feel every inch of my cock slide out of her. My free hand moves between her legs and spreads her open while I watch myself push back inside.

Her pussy swallows my dick again, tightening the deeper I go.

My hips snap forward harder when the memory hits, dragging a broken sound from her throat.

"You remember our first time?"

She nods quickly.

My hand slides down and smacks her ass again while I drive forward.

"Yes, Seth—" she gasps.

Another thrust pushes deep into her followed by another hard slap.

Her legs tremble beneath the force.

I drive into her again, harder this time, watching how well she takes me. My hand comes down across her ass again as I push deeper.

The crack echoes through the room while my cock drags slowly out of her.

Her pussy tightens around me again.

That squeeze destroys the last piece of control I have left.

"Fuck," I groan.

My hips slam forward one more time, burying myself as deep inside her as I can reach.

Then I come.

My body locks against hers when the first pulse hits, heat flooding through my cock while it throbs inside her tight walls.

I hold her there by the hair while my release fills her.

Another pulse follows.

Then another.

My hips stay pressed forward while my dick jerks inside her, spilling deep while her body trembles beneath my hands.

A low groan leaves my chest.

"Jesus Christ," I mutter.

My breathing slows while the final pulses empty inside her.

Her body sags weakly against the table while her chest rises and falls in uneven breaths.

I stay buried inside her for a moment longer, feeling the way her pussy still tightens faintly around my shaft as the tension drains from both of us.

"Now you're gonna sit still, let me finish this tattoo while my cum leaks out of you."

She groans softly.

I slowly slide out of her and a thick line of my release follows, spilling from between her thighs and sliding down the inside of her leg.

I watch it for a second.

Then I smack her ass once more.

"Okay," I reach for the wipes beside the machine, "sit back down."

I nod toward the chair.

"You still have hours left."

The tattoo still isn't finished.

And I always finish my work.

Chapter 80
Brooke

The machine finally goes quiet.

For six hours the needle has carved through my skin, through scar tissue and memory, tracing lines across my back that burn with a deep, pulsing heat. Now the only sound left in the room is the faint bass of the playlist and the steady rhythm of Seth cleaning his tools.

He sets the tattoo machine down with careful precision and peels off his gloves. His eyes stay on my back.

"You good?"

My throat feels dry. "Yeah."

My muscles tremble when I shift. The pain is not as sharp anymore.

Seth steps closer, his hand hovering near my waist before finally resting there.

"Don't twist too fast."

"I know."

He helps me stand. My knees feel weak from sitting so long while he worked.

He guides me toward the mirror on the far wall of the bedroom. The heat from the lamps has fogged the glass.

Seth wipes it clean with his forearm.

I look up.

The skull stares back at me from my reflection.

It is solid black, its hollow eyes deep and dark. Roses surround it, heavy petals layered around bone. Vines and thorns curl through the design, threading through my scars instead of hiding them. The tattoo stretches from my shoulder blades to the base of my spine.

My past is still there. It is just no longer the only thing people will see.

"I love it," I say quietly.

Seth's mouth lifts slightly. "It looks good on you."

I raise my hand but stop before touching it. Heat radiates off my skin and makes my breath hitch. The pain grounds me. It reminds me that I am here, standing in this room, not trapped in that manor with people hunting me for sport.

I catch Seth's reflection behind me in the mirror. His eyes are darker than usual. Pride and something more possessive lingers there, softened by a look he rarely lets anyone see.

He steps forward and kisses me.

His mouth is warm, and my body leans into him before my mind can catch up. For a moment I let myself exist inside that kiss and nowhere else.

Then the memory surfaces.

Miles.

If I don't make it, tell him I loved him. Tell him so he's not sitting there thinking I left him or waiting for me to come home.

His voice had been calm even though he believed he was about to die.

Our address is 24781 Riverbend Lane. Eugene, Oregon.

The numbers slam back into my mind.

24781 Riverbend Lane.

I pull away from Seth.

"What?" he asks immediately.

I step back from the mirror. My back protests, but the pain barely registers now.

"Miles."

Seth's jaw tightens, but he stays silent.

"He gave me his address before the hunt," I continue. "He told me that if one of us didn't make it, I should tell his husband."

The words feel heavier now that I say them out loud.

"I forgot," I admit.

Shame scrapes through my chest.

I should have gone sooner. But we had been hunted. We had been running and bleeding and surviving hour by hour. When it finally ended, when the noise stopped and the danger pulled back, my mind did something worse than panic.

Entire memories lock themselves away where I can't reach them.

Seth steps closer and studies my face.

"Do you want to go now?" he asks.

"Yes."

"I'll drive."

The house looks beautiful. Wind chimes by the door click softly in the breeze like the world never broke.

I stand there for a second with my hand half raised, because knocking means making it real. Then I knock.

Footsteps come quickly. The door opens.

A man with tired eyes and dark hair looks at me with polite confusion. He isn't rude. He just has no idea who I am.

"Hi," he says. "Can I help you?"

My mouth goes dry. "Are you Alonzo?"

He nods once. "Yeah. That's me."

"My name is Brooke."

"Oh my God," he murmurs under his breath.

My throat tightens. "I'm sorry to show up like this. I didn't know how else to do it."

His eyes sharpen.

"I wanted to tell you," I say quickly, the word tumbling out before I can stop it. "about your husband Miles."

The rest comes rushing out with it.

"We were taken to this manor with other people. They were hunting us. It was..." My voice catches, but I force myself to keep going. "It was horrible."

Alonzo stares at me, trying to piece together what I'm saying.

"We were held there," I continue. "Miles saved me more than once. He kept me alive when I shouldn't have been."

He lifts a hand slightly, like he wants to interrupt, but the words are already spilling out.

"I saw him get shot."

His face tightens, but I keep going because stopping now feels impossible.

"He died trying to help me escape," my voice cracks. "Everything was chaos. People were dying and I—"

"Wait—," he interjects.

My hands shake, so I lace them together.

"I'm sorry," I whisper. "I just needed you to know he wasn't alone. He fought. He mattered. He—"

"Brooke?"

The voice comes from behind him.

My entire body freezes.

Alonzo turns his head slowly, and his expression changes in a way that finally makes sense.

Miles is there in a wheelchair.

Alive.

He's behind Alonzo in the hallway, hands resting on the wheels like he pushed himself closer the second he heard my name. The same man that survived with me in that manor, the same man that told me to keep breathing when I wanted to give up.

My knees go weak.

Miles looks at me like he can't decide if I'm real. "Oh my god, Brooke. You're alive!"

I can't get air into my lungs. My mouth opens and nothing comes out at first.

"Miles," I finally manage, and it sounds like a question because my brain can't accept it as fact.

Alonzo steps aside. His hand reaches back and rests on Miles's shoulder.

My eyes burn. "I thought you were dead."

Miles's throat works as he swallows. "I know."

I take one step forward, then another. When I reach him, I drop to my knees right there in the entryway.

My hands find his arms. My forehead presses against his chest.

"I'm sorry," I choke. "I'm so sorry. I saw you get shot and I thought I left you there."

Miles's hand comes down on my shoulder. "You didn't leave me." His voice shakes, "You survived."

I pull back, wiping my face with my sleeve, embarrassed and wrecked at the same time. "You were shot."

"I was, I couldn't move my legs at first. I thought that was it." He glances at Alonzo, then back at me. "I played dead. I waited. When it got quiet, I crawled. I found one of their cars and drove until I passed out."

A broken laugh slips out of me and turns into a sob. "Oh my God."

Miles's mouth twitches. "Yeah."

Alonzo crouches beside the chair, eyes bright. He looks between us like he's trying to understand the whole story.

I nod. "Your husband is amazing. He saved my life."

Alonzo's hand tightens on Miles's shoulder. "Thank you."

Miles looks up at me.

"Are you okay?"

The question almost breaks me again.

"I'm alive," I reply.

"Good." Miles nods slowly. "I'm glad you made it out."

I swallow hard.

"There's something else you should know," my voice hardens. "I made them all pay for what they did. Every one of them."

Miles holds my gaze for a long moment. Then he nods.

"Good," he murmurs. "They deserved it."

I look at him, still half convinced I might wake up and find this is a dream.

"You were right."

"About what?"

"That we would survive."

Miles nods once. "We did." Then he glances down at the wheelchair and back at me with a tired smile.

"And the bastards who did this didn't."

Chapter 81

Brooke

My therapy session with Dr. Feldman is quieter than the others.

Nothing erupts, and nothing unravels. The truth settles in me, and it finally feels quiet.

Surprisingly she still wanted to treat me after everything. After the headlines, the murders, the fire that was supposed to end it all. When I reached out months later, using a new name, and a story so close to the truth it barely qualified as a lie, she didn't hesitate. She looked me in the eye through the screen and said, "I know who you are, Brooke. I'm still here. And your secret is safe with me."

The screen loads. Her face appears like it always does, serene, patient, a soft lamp glowing in the corner behind her but everything feels different. Or maybe I do. I sit cross-legged on the couch, fingers knotted in the hem of my sleeve, but not because I'm unraveling.

Dr. Feldman waits, as she always does, without pressure just giving me space.

I exhale slowly. "I still have nightmares about the manor."

She nods, and doesn't write it down.

"I still miss the girl I was before everything," I sigh. "Not in a sad, desperate way. Just... sometimes I grieve her. The version of me who didn't know what it felt like to kill someone, or be hunted, or tortured."

Dr. Feldman's voice is calm. "Do you wish she could come back?"

I shake my head. "No. She wouldn't survive this world. I think she had to die for the rest of me to live. But sometimes... I miss not knowing. I miss the version of life where monsters were abstract. Where survival wasn't a strategy."

"That's an honest answer," she responds. "Painfully so. You've carried a lot of guilt about who you had to become."

"Because part of me liked it." I meet her eyes through the screen. "Not inflicting pain. But the control, rage, the vengeance. I'm not ashamed of surviving. I'm just scared of what parts of me survived with it."

Dr. Feldman leans in slightly. "Do you think those parts define you?"

"I think they protect me, but they don't have to lead."

She studies me for a moment, then nods. "And now?"

I look down at my hands, then toward the window. "Now I want a life. One that's real. Even if it's strange or messy or hidden. Even if we have to build it from nothing."

"That's good," she says. "The desire to reclaim something normal. The key is redefining what normal means for you."

I laugh under my breath. "I don't think normal even exists anymore. But peace? Safety? Love? I think those can still happen."

"And Seth?" she asks gently.

I smile a little. "I choose him. Every version of him. The broken one, the violent one, the one who would burn the world down for me. He's mine. And I'm his. That'll never change."

Dr. Feldman watches me carefully. "And do you feel safe with him?"

"Yes," I smile. "Undoubtedly, he's the only person I feel completely safe with. He knows who I am. He doesn't ask me to pretend. He's the only person who never looked away from my flaws."

She nods. "That sounds healthy."

"It feels like it," I reply.

Dr. Feldman closes her notebook softly. "You've done the work, Brooke. You clawed your way out of something most people couldn't survive. You lost things. You let parts of yourself die. But you're still here. You're still choosing love, you're choosing yourself. That isn't only healing. That is transformative."

I blink hard, trying to fight back tears. "Thank you."

"You don't owe me gratitude," she says. "You did this. I'm just glad to be here to witness your journey."

I nod.

Dr. Feldman watches me for a moment, then her tone shifts, gentler. "Before we end, tell me one thing you're going to do tonight that is for you."

I stare at my screen, thinking of a hundred answers that sound good and mean nothing.

"I'm going to breathe, I'm going to let myself feel okay for five minutes without worrying.

"Good," she says. "Keep it small. Keep it real. And Brooke, when the urge to punish yourself shows up, name it. Don't feed it."

I swallow. "I'll try."

"I know. We'll talk again soon."

The call ends.

The screen goes dark, and for a second I just sit there with my phone in my hand. I set the phone down on the couch and stare at the blank television screen.

Footsteps come down the hall.

Seth appears in the doorway, shirt sleeves pushed up, hair a mess, eyes locked on me in a way that says he has been listening for my tone since the call started.

"You done?" he asks.

"Yeah, I'm done."

He comes closer and stops in front of me. He doesn't touch me yet. He studies my face first.

"How bad?"

"Not bad," I say. "It was good. Annoyingly good."

His mouth twitches. "That's my girl."

He shifts his weight and looks me over again, like he's trying to decide what will keep me from spiraling tonight.

"What do you want?" he asks, voice low. "Tea, a shower...my dick?"

I snort once, because of course he would say that.

"Something else actually."

Seth's brows lift slightly. "Talk to me."

I stare at him for a second, and I can feel my pulse pick up. A need that won't settle.

"You wanna know something fucked up?"

His eyes narrow just a little. "Always."

"What if we go dig him up," I look up at Seth. "Grant. I keep seeing his face in my dreams. I keep thinking about him under the dirt. I want to look at him and know how really dead he is."

Seth holds my gaze for a beat, then nods once like it's a simple plan.

"Okay...I'll get the shovel."

That should scare me, how fast he agrees. It doesn't, it calms me.

He turns toward the back closet and pulls it out, the one we kept for practical reasons and never talked about. He slings it over his shoulder like it weighs nothing. I grab my jacket and my boots without thinking.

Outside, the night air is cold and clean. Gravel crunches under our steps. My thoughts won't stop replaying it, the way we buried him fast that night, adrenaline in our veins, hands shaking, blood drying on our skin. We dug. We dropped him in. We covered him up. We left.

Tonight we come back.

The forest smells damp. The ground looks undisturbed in the way nature always does, even when it is hiding rot.

Seth grabs the shovel. I take a flashlight. We walk in together, following a path neither of us ever marked. That night burned itself into my head.

We reach the spot.

We didn't leave a marker. But we remembered exactly where we put him.

Seth plants the shovel into the earth and starts digging. I kneel beside the hole and help clear dirt as it comes up, hands working fast, breath coming short.

The dirt is heavier than I remember. It resists in stubborn clumps. The cold makes the soil hard, packed tight. Every time the shovel bites down, it sends a jolt up my arms.

Minutes pass, maybe more. My sense of time turns useless.

Then the shovel hits something solid.

Seth stops immediately. He doesn't speak. He just changes the angle, digs slower, careful now. I crouch and brush loose soil aside with my gloved hands, peeling dirt away in small, shaking motions.

Then we see the crate. Seth hops in and pries it open.

Grant isn't a man anymore.

He is a ruined thing beneath the earth. His skin is darkened to a sick, mottled gray, split wide in places where it has pulled apart, sagging in others where the tissue has collapsed inward. What is left of his face barely holds its shape. His mouth is stretched open too far, lips torn and peeled back, teeth exposed in a permanent, broken grimace that no longer resembles anything human.

There are holes eaten straight through him where insects burrowed deep and stayed. The flesh around them is soft and caved in, wet with decay. Parts of him look hollowed out, like something worked through him from the inside and left nothing worth keeping behind.

Rot clings to him. The kind that glistens under the dirt, where the body has started to break down into something unrecognizable. The sour, putrid smell hits hard. I breathe through my mouth so I don't gag, but it barely helps.

I stare anyway. I need my brain to see it. I need the truth to land where the fear kept living.

Seth looks down at what's left of him. His expression stays cold.

Then Seth unzips his jeans and pisses into the grave.

"Rest in piss, motherfucker," he says.

I laughed, a real one. Head thrown back. That sharp, dangerous joy that made my chest twist.

Seth glances at me. "Better?"

"Yes," I reply.

We don't give Grant more attention than that. We start filling the hole back in. Dirt thuds down. Leaves fall. The ground starts looking ordinary again. The forest takes its secret back.

When we finish, Seth presses the shovel into the dirt once more, firming it down. He wipes his hands on his jeans and turns toward the Jeep.

I follow him through the trees, the flashlight beam bouncing with every step. My chest still aches, but it feels quieter now. It feels manageable.

Seth keeps walking like nothing happened, like we didn't just open the earth and look at something that used to terrorize our lives. He reaches the Jeep first and opens the rear door.

I stop a few feet behind him and cross my arms, watching him dig around in the back like he's looking for a jacket.

"I think my methods of torture might be better than yours at this point," I taunt.

Seth pauses and glances over his shoulder. "Excuse me?"

"I'm just saying. I did a lot of the killing. And torturing. Like... a lot."

He turns more fully toward me, mouth twitching. "Oh so you think you're a better killer than me?"

I smirk, "I don't think. I know."

He gives a dry laugh, then faces the Jeep again. He grabs the duffel we tossed in the back, unzips it, and reaches down.

He pulls out the black skull mask.

The scratched edges catch the flashlight beam. That mask has seen too much of us.

"Interesting," he murmurs. "Let's see if your survival skills are still intact, final girl."

I grin, biting my lip. "You gonna give me a head start?"

Seth flips the mask once in his hand, then looks at me. "You still fast?"

I raise my brows. "Are you asking because you care, or because you want to watch me run?"

His mouth curves. "Both."

My pulse jumps.

He slips the mask on.

"Run."

Chapter 82

Seth

A better killer than me, huh.

I fucking love her so much.

I have to admit, she's made progress fast, faster than most people I trained with ever did.

She runs like she means it. Her boots pound over the forest floor in hard, even hits. Her ponytail snaps behind her with every stride, cutting through branches. This isn't play. This is muscle, adrenaline, and survival fused together. Every movement says the same thing. She doesn't want to be caught.

But I know she does.

I keep my distance at first. Close enough to keep her in sight, far enough to let her feel that pulse of fear climbing up her throat. I don't make a sound. Just shadow and breath. Watching. Stalking.

Her body moves like a weapon, cutting through the trees, agile as hell, but I know her rhythm. I know the way she'll veer left when the slope dips. The way her footwork falters when she's thinking too hard. I track every pivot, every staggered breath.

She has no clue how close I am.

The night air is thick with pine and earth and the faint scent of her perfume. I watch her duck under a low branch, and hear the scrape of bark against her sleeve. She picks up speed on the hill, boots kicking up wet leaves. A fallen log comes up ahead and she vaults over it like she has done it a thousand times.

God, she is fucking fast.

But not faster than me.

I pick up speed. Branches lash my arms. Mud kicks up onto my jeans. I don't care. All I see is her.

The way she moves like she wants to escape but knows she won't. I let her go a few more seconds. Just long enough for her to think she might make it.

Then she slips.

Her boot hits mud at the wrong angle and she loses speed. It isn't a full fall, but it is enough.

I lunge.

One hand catches her hip and the other locks around her waist. I yank her back into me so fast it knocks the air out of both of us. We hit the ground hard, dirt and wet leaves spraying out around us.

She gasps, sharp and breathless.

I pin her with my weight, knees braced on either side of her thighs, one hand spread over her ribs. She shifts beneath me, not fighting outright.

I lean close. My voice stays low. "I got you."

Her eyes flash up at me and she smiles. "Or did I get you?"

I glance down.

Her hand is between us.

A knife is angled up at my stomach, close enough that I can feel the cold of the blade through my shirt. She kept it hidden until the last second, tucked tight against her body where I wouldn't see it until I thought I already won.

I go still for half a beat.

Then I laugh once, breathless, because of course she did.

"Clever girl."

She keeps the blade steady and her eyes stay on mine. "You told me to keep my knife on me, even when I'm with you."

My hand slides to her wrist, not forcing it down yet, just holding her there, feeling the strength in her grip. I keep my weight careful so I don't press into the blade.

"So everything I drilled in you finally stuck."

She smiles wider. "Yeah, but you can always drill more."

My throat tightens. The mask is still on my face, but I can feel my grin under it.

I lean closer until my breath hits her mouth. "You're asking for trouble."

Her knife doesn't drop. Her body still arches, chasing contact, daring me to do something about it.

I lift my hand to the mask and pull it off, because I need her eyes on mine. I need her to see my face and understand this is real. I drop the mask into the dirt beside us.

Her knife stays between us, angled up at my stomach. I reach down and grab the blade. The edge bites into my palm and splits skin. Blood slides warm over my fingers.

I don't flinch.

Her eyes widen, just a little, and her breath catches hard.

I close my hand tighter around the knife, forcing it away from my body. Then I bring that same bloody hand up to her mouth and trace across her lips with my thumb.

Down her chin. Down her throat.

A red trail follows my touch. She swallows under it, pulse jumping against my fingers.

I keep my hand at her throat, not squeezing, just holding her there.

I lean in and kiss her. Hard and deep, like I am claiming the moment back. The taste of my blood hits my tongue. She makes a sound into my mouth and it turns into a shiver through her whole body.

I shift my weight and roll her with me, taking her hand and pinning it above her head. Leaves stick to her hair. Damp earth smears her cheek.

Her breath comes fast. Her eyes stay locked on mine.

I press my mouth to her ear. "I'm going to drill everything I've got into you."

Her laugh breaks out, breathless and unsteady, and her body softens under me like she is already saying yes.

My hand slides down her abdomen as I hold her beneath me, but she stays on her back with her eyes locked on mine. My weight presses her into the forest floor, keeping her exactly where I want her. My fingers catch the waistband of her leggings, and I yank them down past her hips in one rough pull, exposing her legs to the cold night air. The chill hits her instantly, and goosebumps rise fast.

She moans, breath shaking.

I stay over her, my chest hovering above hers, close enough to feel her warmth rise to meet me. I push her thighs apart with my knee and drag my fingers between her legs. Heat floods my hand, and her body trembles hard.

I undo my belt with one hand, spit into my palm, stroke myself once to line up, and grip her hips firmly enough to guarantee she will remember this.

Her body tenses beneath me.

I thrust into her fully, driving her into the ground.

Her cry tears through the trees, as her hands fly up to grab at my shoulders. She clutches my shirt, pulling me down, her legs falling open wider under my weight.

"Ooohhhh Seth," she moans, voice breaking apart.

I cover her mouth with my bloody hand because I want to feel every sound she pushes out against my skin. Her teeth graze my palm, and her back lifts from the ground as she tries to take me deeper.

I growl and drive into her again, meeting her eyes the entire time.

She sobs into my hand as her body tightens around me with enough force to shake my control. Her legs wrap around my hips, pulling me closer, refusing to let go.

She tries to speak, but the words collapse against my hand.

I grab her hair and pull her head back slightly, forcing her to look at me while she arches for more, her entire body open beneath mine and completely at my mercy.

I start pounding into her, every thrust hitting hard enough to shove her deeper into the earth beneath us. Her moans tear out of her without control, like she can't tell where the hurt ends and the pleasure begins. Her nails drag across my arms, searching for something to hold on to.

I release her mouth and catch both her wrists in one grip, dragging them above her head and locking them there. She gasps the moment I drive into her again, deeper and harder. Her back arches, her thighs shake around my hips, and her breath splinters with every impact.

She completely loses it.

Her entire body convulses under me, legs trembling so violently she can barely keep them around me. Her breath cracks apart, her chest rising fast. When her orgasm hits, it slams through her with full-body force, shaking her from head to toe. Her eyes roll back, her mouth falls open, and a broken moan pours out of her.

"Fuck, fuck, fuck," she gasps, voice wrecked.

I drop my mouth to her ear, teeth grazing her skin before I speak, my voice low and rough.

"Keep coming for me like that and you won't be able to walk right in the morning."

Her body reacts instantly, a broken moan slipping from her lips like that is exactly what she wants.

I don't slow down. I chase my own edge with my hips snapping into her in a hard, relentless rhythm. Every muscle in my body strains for release, and when it hits, it crashes through me with the same force I drive into her.

I stay buried deep inside her, spilling into her while she still shakes beneath me. Her breath stays broken, her thighs trembling around my waist, her chest rising fast. I slide my free hand down to her sternum and press my palm over her heart, feeling it slam against my skin.

We stay like that for a long moment, bodies tangled, breathing hard, completely wrecked. The forest around us feels unnaturally quiet, almost aware of what we have done, like it stands there watching us come apart together.

I roll her over in one movement, shifting from above her to beneath her. Her gasp hits my throat as she climbs on top of me, straddling my hips with quick, hungry determination.

Her hands spread across my chest as she steadies herself. Her breath comes fast, and her hair falls around her face in a wild, tangled curtain. She reaches for the hem of her top and pulls it over her head, tossing it aside. The moment her skin is bare, I see the blood from the cut on my hand smeared across her breasts, streaked over her neck, and staining the corners of her mouth. The sight hits me hard. She looks dangerous, beautiful, and fully fucking mine.

I grip her hips firmly.

"Still think you're the better killer?" I ask near her ear.

She laughs, rough and breathless.

"Maybe. But I know I'm the better fuck."

My grin presses into her throat.

"Then round two better prove it."

She lowers herself onto me, sliding down my length with a gasp that shakes both of us. Her thighs tighten around my waist as her palms drag up my chest. Every movement smears more of my blood across her skin, turning her into something feral and intoxicating.

"Fuck. Ride me, baby," I grunt, my voice harsh with need.

She moves with purpose, dropping her hips and grinding against me in a rhythm that grows faster with every breath. Her nails dig into my shoulders for leverage. Her body trembles from the intensity of each thrust, and her moans rise louder as she loses control.

"Scream all you want, no one will hear you," I growl, my voice hitting her like a command she has been waiting for.

She sinks down harder, taking everything I give her. Her scream cuts through the trees. Her head tips back, her body arching above me, chest rising fast, breath already gone. Her thighs clamp tighter around my hips as she rides me, faster now, chasing something she can't slow down.

"Oh god, Seth," she moans, voice breaking apart.

I drive my hips up into her, meeting every drop of her body with force. The impact snaps through both of us. She claws at me, dragging my shirt down my arms, gripping my neck, grabbing anything she can reach. Her movements turn frantic, losing rhythm, turning into pure need as she bounces against me harder, deeper.

I slide my hand from her waist to her throat, my fingers pressing over the blood streaked across her skin. Not tight. Just enough to hold her there. To ground her. To make her look at me.

Her eyes lock on mine instantly. Her breath stutters.

"Stay right there," I murmur, guiding her pace, controlling the angle as she moves.

Her muscles start to tighten around me. I feel it immediately. The way her body begins to pulse, the way her rhythm starts to break. Her thighs shake harder, her movements stutter, her voice catching before it can fully form.

She's right there. I feel it building in her before she even realizes it herself.

I drag my hand back to her hip and slow her down. Her body reacts instantly, a frustrated sound breaking from her throat as her pace is forced to shift.

"Seth—" she starts, breathless.

"Are you about to come?" I ask.

Her body clenches around me again, answering for her.

I tilt my head slightly, watching her lose it in real time.

"I didn't give you permission to come yet."

She whimpers at that, her hips trying to pick the pace back up, but my grip tightens, holding her in place. I slow the movement between us, pulling out slower, pushing back in deeper, dragging every inch out of it instead of letting her rush through it.

Her head drops forward, her breath shaking as the tension builds instead of breaking.

I lean up, closing the space between us, and kiss her.

My mouth moves against hers while my hips keep that slow, controlled rhythm, forcing her to feel every second of it instead of letting her escape into it. Her hands slide up my neck, gripping tight, her kiss turning desperate, needy, like she is trying to pull more out of me.

I pull back just enough to look at her.

"You gonna be my good girl and ask me if you can come?" My voice low against her lips.

Her body tightens hard around me again, her control slipping further with every second I hold her there.

"Come on, baby," I murmur against her mouth, barely moving inside her, keeping her suspended right at the edge. "Ask me."

Her breath breaks, her voice barely holding together as she tries to speak, her body still trapped right at the edge I put her on.

"Seth," she gasps, voice trembling. "Please—please let me come."

I slide my hand from her waist to her throat, my fingers resting over the blood I left on her skin. I hold her there, guiding her, keeping her focused on me. She moans at the contact, her breath stuttering.

Her muscles tighten around me. Her thighs shake harder. Her voice catches in her throat. She reaches the point where sound barely forms.

I feel her pussy clench around me. The way her body fights it. The way she tries to hold on even when she cannot.

"Come on my dick," I demand. "Right fucking now."

The command hits her at the same moment everything in me snaps. Her body tightens around me with a brutal squeeze, and the sound she makes breaks straight through my control. Her orgasm hits with violent force, and mine slams into me at the exact same second. The two of us come together so hard it feels like the world narrows to nothing but heat, breath, and the way our bodies lock against each other.

I release inside her with a groan against her neck, my body shuddering under the intensity of feeling everything she feels at once. The dual climax rips the breath from my lungs and leaves her shaking on top of me, both of us losing control in the same instant.

Her legs tighten around my waist, pulling me deeper as if she can drag every last pulse out of me. Her teeth sink into my shoulder, and I let her take as much as she wants. I feel the tremor of her release drag through her muscles, squeezing me in perfect rhythm with every wave crashing through mine.

I stay buried deep inside her because I can't pull away. I want every aftershock. I want the heat of her wrapped around me while she trembles through the final pulses of her orgasm. Her heart slams against her ribs when I touch her chest. Her skin is warm and damp. She looks perfect.

I press my forehead to hers, still inside her, breathing hard. My hand slides under her thigh to feel the last of the shaking, the warmth, the way she clings to me like her body refuses to let the moment end.

Her laugh comes out rough.

"That might've been better than therapy."

I smirk against her mouth.

"Told you I'm good for your mental health."

"Don't let it go to your head," she murmurs, still breathless.

"Too late."

I brush her jaw with my thumb, then cup her face. She leans into it.

She reaches for the mask on the ground and traces the edge with her fingertips.

"Keep it," she whispers. "Might need a rematch."

I grin at her.

"You're not going to be able to walk tomorrow."

She smiles like she wants that.

"Then carry me."

I kiss her again, slow at first, but softness never stays between us for long. Neither of us wants it to.

Chapter 83
Brooke

The dining table is covered in pencil shavings, scratch paper, and half-empty water bottles.

Elise has her chemistry book open. Ryan is hunched over his notebook, chewing the end of his pencil. Ryan's hand is on Luna's head under the table, scratching the spot behind her ears that makes her eyes half close. Luna stays draped across his lap. Krueger lies on the floor with his body tucked close to my feet, watchful and calm. His ears flick every time someone shifts. He doesn't miss anything.

Seth sits between them with a pen in his hand. He looks at the worksheet like it's a problem he can solve with enough patience and enough blunt force.

"Okay," he taps the page. "This is what they want. Strong acids dissociate more completely in water. Weak acids don't. That difference changes pH, and that changes how fast reactions happen."

Elise squints at the numbers. "Why do I have to learn chemistry again? This stuff makes me feel stupid."

"It's not you," Seth drags the book closer and flips the pencil between his fingers. "It's the way they explain it. Look."

He writes a few steps out, slower than he normally does anything, and slides the paper toward her. His pen taps the equation again.

"This part is the whole problem. If you understand what's dissociating and what isn't, the rest is just math."

Ryan leans in. "So HCl is strong, right?"

Seth nods. "Yeah. Hydrochloric acid is strong. It breaks apart easily in water."

Elise points at another line. "And this one?"

"Acetic acid is weak," Seth circles part of the equation as he speaks. "It still reacts, but not the same way. That's why the pH changes differently."

He pauses and looks up at both of them, like he's deciding how to translate this into something they'll remember.

"If you mix the wrong stuff, somebody passes out." His eyes drop back to the worksheet. "If you mix other wrong stuff, somebody won't wake up."

Elise's eyes narrow. "That's not helpful."

A faint smirk pulls at Seth's mouth. "It is helpful. It just depends on the situation."

Ryan lifts his head. "Is that going to be on the test?"

Seth's mouth twitches. "It should be."

I shoot Seth a look over my wine glass.

He glances at me like he can feel it. "What?"

"You know what," I narrow my eyes at him.

He points his pen at the book again. "I'm teaching them chemistry."

"You're teaching them crime," I mutter.

Elise snorts before she can stop herself. Then she covers it with a cough like she's embarrassed she laughed.

Seth finally looks amused. "Acids deteriorate flesh," he flips his pen, still looking at the page. "That's chemistry. Not crime."

I lower my glass slowly. "Seth."

He turns his head just enough to meet my eyes. "What? It's true."

Ryan makes a noise that might be a laugh. "That is so gross."

"It's accurate," Seth shrugs and taps the worksheet again. "Accuracy gets you points."

Elise stares at the worksheet again. "I hate this."

"No, you don't," Seth replies. "You just don't understand it yet."

Ryan points at a problem. "So is this one a strong acid or a weak acid?"

Seth leans closer and starts explaining. Elise finally solves the problem and shoves the paper toward Seth like she's challenging him to tell her she's wrong.

Seth scans it and nods once. "Correct."

Elise sighs with a small smile. She tries to hide it, she can't.

Ryan leans back and stretches. "Thank God."

Seth closes the book and stands. "Go brush your teeth. Go to bed. You've had enough brain damage for one night."

They gather their stuff and drag themselves down the hall, still arguing about whether chemistry is evil or just unfair. Their voices fade behind their bedroom doors.

The house settles.

The quiet that follows isn't the same kind of quiet it used to be. It isn't empty. It isn't waiting to swallow me. A blanket left over the arm of a chair. A pair of Ryan's socks abandoned near the hallway. A pencil on the table that nobody picked up.

I stare at it all for a second, and a feeling of contentment washes over me.

After my parents died, I spent years telling myself I didn't need anyone. I learned how to carry grief by myself. I learned how to swallow loneliness and call it independence. I learned how to smile at people and keep the important parts locked away.

Then Seth showed up and changed everything.

Then Travis, Naomi, Beau, and somehow these two kids, Seth's siblings, crashed into our lives and refused to leave.

This isn't the family I imagined when I was younger. It's not picture perfect. It's not safe in the way normal people mean safe. It's rough around the edges and insane.

But it's mine.

And I love it.

Seth comes back into the living room after checking the locks. He turns off the last lamp in the kitchen and leaves only the soft light by the couch. Then he sits beside me, grabbing my feet and placing them in his lap.

"You wanna pick the movie?" he asks.

"You can pick it."

He grabs the remote and scrolls through options, stopping on something with a screaming woman on the cover and a title that looks like it was written to be obnoxious.

I glance at him. "You picked this on purpose."

Seth's mouth twitches. "Maybe."

Krueger lifts his head and settles it back down. Luna hops off the chair and climbs onto the back of the couch, tail flicking once as she watches us.

Seth hits play.

The opening scene starts with heavy music and a dark hallway.

I lean into Seth without thinking. His hand rests under the blanket on my thigh, thumb lazily stroking, his other arm stretched behind me. I'm just starting to drift when his phone buzzes on the coffee table.

He picks it up, sees the name, and grins. "Travis."

He answers and hits speaker. "You better not be calling to interrupt. Brooke was just telling me how good I am with my tongue."

I slap his chest, half-laughing, half-mortified.

Travis groans. "For fucks sake I don't know why I still talk to you."

"Because you miss us," Seth mutters.

"'Miss you' is generous. I'm calling because I have something you're gonna want to hear."

"What?"

"I found him," Travis replies.

Seth shifts under me. "Who?"

"John. He's in Florida. Island off the coast. I traced a dummy shell account back to a private villa. There's a yacht. Security. He's not hiding, he's recruiting."

Seth glances at me, heat gone cold behind his eyes.

"Wanna go to Florida?"

I meet his gaze and smirk.

"Hell yeah."

Chapter 84

Seth

We ride the boat in silence while the engine hums low beneath us.

The sound stays muted enough to blend with the water moving against the hull. Warm night air clings to my skin and clothes. The scent of Florida water hangs heavy in the dark, brine from the ocean mixed with the smell that settles into coastal ground.

Brooke sits on the bench in front of me with her gun resting across her lap. Her attention stays fixed on the horizon where the black line of the island cuts into the sky. She twists the suppressor onto the barrel of her pistol in one quick motion.

Beau handles the wheel with quiet confidence. His shoulders remain loose while he guides the boat through the water with small adjustments.

The private island appears first as a dark shape stretching across the water. As we move closer, the outline of the villa becomes clear. The structure rises behind a wall of palms, larger than any house built for simple living. A few windows glow with soft interior light that spills across the stone exterior. The place carries the polished weight of money and privacy.

I scan the shoreline again.

Only a handful of guards move near the dock and outer path.

That isn't an oversight. That's arrogance. Someone here believes distance and money are enough to keep them safe.

They're wrong.

Beau cuts the engine before we reach the dock. The sudden quiet settles over the boat while it glides the rest of the way forward on momentum. The hull brushes against the wood, and the dock answers with a quiet creak before the water steadies us.

Brooke reaches and squeezes my forearm once.

I answer with a single nod.

Beau steps out first. His boots land on the dock without a sound. He moves into the darkness along the palm line and disappears between the shadows without saying a word.

Time stretches while we wait.

I focus on the island and listen carefully for anything out of place.

A dull sound carries across the water from the direction of the house. The noise fades quickly and the island returns to silence.

Beau's voice comes through my earpiece. "Front is clear."

Brooke exhales once and steps onto the dock. I move with her.

We cross the yard toward the villa, keeping close to the palms and the darker edges of the property. The back entrance comes into view quickly.

The door is unlocked. Brooke pushes it open and steps inside. I follow with my knife already in my hand.

The hallway is dim and quiet. A heavy candle scent hangs in the air, trying to cover the stale odor of sweat and blood.

We move through the house one room at a time. Brooke keeps her breathing quiet and her steps light. She knows how to move through a space without drawing attention.

Light spills from beneath a door at the end of the hall.

Voices come from inside. Men, talking and laughing.

The laughter cuts off when a wet cracking sound breaks through the room. A girl lets out a weak cry.

Brooke's eyes harden. She opens the door and we enter together.

Two men stand inside the room.

A young woman is tied to a chair in the center. Her wrists are bound behind the backrest and her ankles are secured to the legs of the chair. One of her eyes is swollen shut. Blood runs from her split lip down her chin. Her head hangs slightly forward as if she is struggling to stay conscious.

One man holds a knife streaked with fresh blood.

The other leans close to the girl's face, speaking to her in a quiet, mocking voice.

Brooke raises her pistol.

The first man turns his head at the movement.

Brooke fires before he can react.

The suppressed shot cracks through the room. The girl flinches violently in the chair, the legs scraping against the floor as her body jerks. The bullet punches through the man's chest. He drops where he stands.

The second man snaps toward Brooke, his hand flying for the gun at his waistband.

I throw my knife.

The blade leaves my hand in a straight line and sinks into the side of his throat. His body locks up as the steel drives deep. He grabs at his neck, choking as blood pushes between his fingers. He stumbles backward and collapses hard against the floor. His legs kick once before the movement stops.

Brooke moves to the girl immediately. When she reaches the chair and sees the ropes, she holsters the pistol and pulls a knife from her pocket.

"It's okay," Brooke whispers. "We're getting you out. Stay quiet."

The girl tries to speak but only a thin breath escapes her mouth.

Brooke cuts through the ropes at the girl's wrists first. Her arms fall forward, shaking from the strain. Brooke slices the rope at her ankles and steadies her as she slumps forward.

"You need to listen to me," Brooke says firmly.

The girl nods quickly, eyes wide.

"Go outside," Brooke continues. "There's a man named Beau waiting near the dock. He's here to get you out."

The girl stares at her for a second, trying to process the words.

Brooke grips her shoulder once. "Go. Now!"

The girl pushes herself to her feet and moves toward the door, unsteady but moving.

I retrieve my knife from the floor and wipe it on the dead man's shirt. I don't look at their faces again. I keep my focus on the hall.

Brooke steps back beside me.

We move down the hall. Low music pulses behind the next door. Someone turned the volume up enough to shake the walls.

Brooke opens the door.

The smell reaches me before anything else. It carries the thick metallic weight of blood that has already begun to dry.

The overhead lights buzz faintly while the scene comes into focus.

A girl lies on the tile floor.

She can't be older than twenty. Her skin has already gone pale beneath the harsh white lighting, and her eyes remain open, fixed on the ceiling as if she had been staring there when everything ended. Blood has pooled beneath the back of her head and shoulders, spreading across the white tile in a dark stain that has begun to thicken along the edges.

Her body sits twisted at an angle that immediately explains how she died.

But that is not the worst part of what I'm looking at.

A man is between her legs.

His pants hang halfway down his thighs while his hips move slowly against her corpse. The motion shifts the girl's body slightly across the floor with every push forward. The man grunts each time he forces himself into her.

A wolf mask covers his face.

For a moment my brain refuses to accept what it is seeing. My grip tightens around the knife until the handle presses hard into my palm.

He turns his head toward us slowly, like we interrupted him.

"I got this," Brooke says quietly beside me.

Before I can respond, she moves.

She rushes him.

The man snarls and pushes himself off the corpse while yanking his pants upward with one hand. His other hand reaches for the knife lying beside the girl's shoulder.

Brooke is already moving.

Her blade flashes into view as she pulls it free while charging toward him.

They collide near the center of the room.

The man swings the knife toward her head in a wide, desperate arc.

Brooke drops beneath the swing and drives her shoulder into his chest hard enough to send him sliding backward across the tile. His shoes skid through the blood on the floor as he struggles to stay upright.

His hand shoots out and grabs a fistful of Brooke's hair before yanking her forward with enough force to pull her off balance. His other hand comes across her mouth with a violent slap that cracks through the room.

Her head snaps back from the impact.

The second his hand connects with her face, I move.

I close the distance in two strides and drive my shoulder into his back, slamming into him hard enough to break his balance. My hand grabs the collar of his shirt and jerks him away from Brooke before he can swing again.

Blood appears along Brooke's lip as she steadies herself. Her arm drives forward.

The blade punches into his chest. The knife sinks deep between his ribs while he screams behind the wolf mask.

I step fully behind him and grab his shoulder to hold him upright.

My knife comes across his throat in one clean motion.

The steel cuts deep.

I pull hard and feel the blade drag across muscle and cartilage before catching briefly against bone. Then the flesh opens under the pressure and blood erupts down his chest, spraying across Brooke's arm and the front of my shirt.

The man staggers forward with a choking sound trapped in his throat.

For a moment something darker inside my head pushes forward.

I want to drive the knife deeper. I want to keep cutting until his head separates from his shoulders and rolls across the same floor where he violated her.

But there isn't time for that.

The man collapses between us. His body strikes the tile with a heavy thud while he chokes on the blood flooding his airway.

Brooke rips her knife free from his chest as he falls.

The wolf mask turns sideways against the floor. His legs twitch once before he goes completely still.

Brooke and I both look down.

The girl still lies on the floor. Her empty eyes stare at the ceiling.

My hands tighten around the knife.

Brooke steps over the wolf mask man like he's trash. She keeps her gun up as we move back into the hall.

We take the stairs fast and quietly.

The top floor is warmer, and it smells like expensive linens. Light spills from the end of the hallway. Voices drift out, casual and smug, like they're in a private club.

Then I hear a girl scream. It isn't a startled scream. It is pain. It is panic. It is the sound of someone realizing nobody is coming to help her.

Brooke's grip tightens on her gun. Her eyes flick to mine.

I nod once. We move.

We reach the doorway and stop just long enough to take inventory.

John is in the center of the room. He's wearing the goat mask again. Four other Collective members stand nearby, all of them wearing animal masks. Their knives catch the overhead light every time they shift.

A girl is laid across the Collective symbol on the floor. Her arms are pinned back. Her legs are forced apart. She's crying and thrashing, and the only reason she is still moving is because they are letting her.

They talk over her like she isn't human.

One of the masked men laughs and says something to the others. Another replies, still calm, still entertained. Their voices sound normal. That is what makes it worse.

John lifts his hand slightly, and the room settles like they're trained.

"Before we begin," John smiles, "let's make a toast."

The girl's scream turns into a choked sob.

John tilts his head like he's listening to music.

"I'll go get the wine," he adds.

He steps away from the group and walks toward the hall, unhurried, confident that nothing in this villa can touch him.

Brooke watches him go. Her body changes without her moving. Her focus narrows. Her breathing turns quiet.

She leans toward me and whispers, "I'm gonna follow him."

I keep my eyes on the room. "Go."

Brooke slips back into the hallway and follows John at a distance. She moves close enough to keep him in sight, far enough that he won't feel her presence until she wants him to.

I step into the room without drawing attention to it. My pistol is already in my hand with the suppressor threaded on the barrel. Sound carries too easily in a place like this, and every second we waste inside this house increases the chances someone comes looking.

The masked men don't notice me right away. Their attention stays fixed on the girl. The men stand around her as if she is a centerpiece.

That arrogance is about to kill them.

I raise the pistol and fire twice.

The first shot hits the closest man in the upper chest. His body jerks backward and the knife in his hand drops before he can lift it. The second man takes the next round a fraction of a second later. The bullet punches through his sternum and drives him back a step before he collapses.

The suppressed shots are short and controlled, but the room changes immediately.

The third man snaps his head toward me. He tries to pivot, tries to bring the knife up, and tries to move around the girl without stepping on her.

He's too slow.

I close the distance and grab him by the head.

My hands clamp against both sides of the mask and I twist with everything I have. His neck gives under the pressure. The break runs through my arms and into my hands as the vertebrae snap. His body loses strength instantly and drops against me before sliding to the floor.

The fourth man comes at me without thinking.

He charges across the room with the knife raised and his weight thrown forward. The swing is wide and desperate. The blade catches the fabric of my sleeve and cuts through the cloth without reaching skin.

I step into him instead of backing away.

My shoulder slams into his chest and drives him into the wall. The impact forces the air out of his lungs in a harsh grunt. His knife arm drops just enough.

I drive my blade into his abdomen.

The knife sinks deep beneath his ribs and I feel the resistance of muscle give as the steel pushes through. His body stiffens and a strangled sound pushes through the mask.

I pull the blade free and stab him again.

The second thrust lands higher. His body jerks once and then the strength drains out of him. The knife slips from his hand and hits the floor with a dull clatter while he slides down the wall.

I step away from him and turn to the girl.

She's shaking so hard the symbol beneath her looks like it's moving. Her face is wet with tears. Her mouth opens, but she can't get words out.

"Stay still," I tell her. "You're safe now."

She nods fast, terrified, trying to obey.

I crouch beside her and cut the restraints quickly, guiding the blade so it never touches her skin. The ropes fall away from her wrists first. The skin there is raw and swollen from the pressure. Her breathing comes in uneven pulls as her body tries to recover from panic.

She curls inward, arms folding toward her chest as if she can make herself smaller.

"Look at me, stand up," I whisper. "You need to move."

She pushes herself to her feet and sways. Her entire body shakes hard enough that her teeth knock together.

"Go downstairs," I point toward the hallway. "Beau will help you."

She hesitates for half a second, then turns and runs. Her bare feet slap against the floor as she disappears into the hallway.

A moment later Beau's voice comes through my earpiece.

"Any other girls?"

The girl answers him somewhere below us. Her voice trembles through the connection.

"It was just three of us they brought in here."

Beau responds immediately. "Go to the boat."

Her footsteps move quickly down the stairs, then fade toward the dock and the open water.

"Beau."

"Yeah?"

"After you get them on the boat, grab the spare fuel."

A brief pause follows.

"How much?"

My eyes stay on the hall.

"As much as you've got," I respond. "We're burning all this shit down."

"Copy that," Beau replies. "I'll bring them up."

The house goes quiet again.

I scan the door and hear movement somewhere down the hall. A cabinet door opens. Glass shifts against glass. Someone moves around with the casual pace of a man preparing for a celebration.

I remain in the center of the room.

The bodies lie across the tile where they fell. Their masks have slipped out of place, jaws tilted sideways and ears pressed against the floor. Blood spreads slowly beneath them.

Then footsteps return in the hallway.

John walks into the room carrying a bottle and glasses as if he is entering a private dinner. He steps through the doorway mid-thought, the bottle balanced casually in his hand.

Then he sees the room.

He stops, lowering the bottle slowly. John turns his head, taking in the scene piece by piece. Then his gaze settles on me.

I stand in the center of the room with my pistol lowered but ready, my knife still wet in my other hand.

Brooke steps in behind him. She closes the distance without rushing, gun aimed at the back of his head. Her voice is low and calm.

"Hello John."

John doesn't move at first.

He exhales once, and the goat mask tilts toward me like he's trying to make sense of the impossible.

"So," John sighs, "you found me."

Brooke shifts her aim a fraction closer. "Yeah, I told you I would."

Chapter 85
Brooke

John freezes in the doorway, wine bottle hanging in his hand.

The glasses tilt and clink softly, a stupid sound that doesn't belong in a room full of bodies.

Seth stands in the middle of it, blood on his knuckles, gun lowered at his side. Four masked men are on the floor, limbs bent wrong, knives scattered near their hands.

I step in behind John and keep my gun trained at the back of his head.

"Put it down," I demand.

John exhales and sets the bottle and glasses on a side table, slow and careful. He turns just enough to speak without looking at me.

"I let you guys be, I left you alone. What's the point of finding me?"

My voice comes out flat and clear. "As long as you're alive, you're a threat."

Seth's gaze stays on John's hands.

John's voice cuts in. "So, you finally learned, haven't you?"

His right arm shifts beneath the cloak.

I catch the movement immediately. His fingers flex near his wrist, slowly dragging something down from inside the sleeve.

Metal glints beneath the fabric.

Seth sees it too.

I fire.

The suppressed shot cracks through the room, and the bullet punches through John's hand just as his fingers close around the knife. Skin splits. Knuckles burst open. Blood sprays across the front of his cloak in hot, messy streaks. The blade slips from his ruined grip, clatters across the tile, and spins away.

John jerks violently, clutching his mangled hand beneath the cloak while blood runs through his fingers and patters onto the marble.

I fire again.

The bullet tears through his left kneecap.

The joint blows apart beneath the fabric. Bone cracks. Blood bursts through the torn material and splashes across the floor as his leg folds wrong.

He screams behind the goat mask, but somehow he stays standing for half a second, swaying on the one leg still holding him up.

So I shoot the other one too.

The next round punches through his other knee and destroys whatever kept him upright. His legs buckle beneath him, useless and shaking, and he slams onto the marble hard enough to make the room echo.

His injured hand hangs at his side, shredded and dripping. Blood runs down his wrist, over his fingers, and onto the tile in thick drops.

Then his other hand reaches up and tears the goat mask off before throwing it aside.

The mask hits the tile beside him with a dull clack.

Now his face is exposed. The same face I grew up seeing across dinner tables and in quiet living rooms. The same calculating eyes that watched everything when I was a kid.

Without the mask, the performance disappears.

He was never really my uncle.

Just a man bleeding out on the floor with both legs ruined and fury burning in his eyes because he understands exactly how this will end.

Beau walks into the room carrying a red fuel canister in each hand. His eyes flick once toward John sprawled across the floor, then toward Seth. Without a word, he sets one of the canisters beside him.

Seth grabs it.

Beau turns and heads back downstairs to the girls, leaving us alone with John.

John's expression shifts for the first time. His chest rises and falls unevenly, but he lifts his chin anyway, still trying to control the room with his voice.

"Do you want me to beg, niece?" John asks. "Do you want me to beg for my life?"

My voice stays calm. "It wouldn't do you any good."

John's mouth curves into a thin smile. Blood stains the edges of his teeth. His eyes remain locked on mine.

"You will never be free of me. I'll live inside your mind forever. You're still my creation. You're the weapon I carved out of trauma and fear. You survived because of me." He points at me with his bleeding hand, fingers trembling. "You're not the victim anymore, Brooke. You're a killer now. Just like me. Just like your father. Just like Seth."

Seth holsters his gun against the tactical belt at his waist, then slides the bloodied knife back into its sheath before grabbing the canister.

He unscrews the cap.

The sharp smell of gasoline floods the room.

John finally glances at Seth then back to me.

"And it felt good, didn't it?" he continues, his voice lowering as blood runs freely down his wrist. "Killing all those people to get to me."

Seth steps forward and dumps the gasoline over him.

The liquid drenches John's chest and pours across his ruined legs. It soaks into the fabric of his cloak and splashes across the marble beneath him.

John flinches hard as the fuel runs into his wounds. His eyes snap back to mine.

Even now, bleeding across the floor and reeking of gasoline, he studies my face as if he expects to find satisfaction there. Some trace of pride. Some reaction that proves he still owns a piece of me.

I pull the lighter from my pocket and strike the wheel with my thumb. The flame catches, small and bright above the metal casing.

I hold his gaze while the flame flickers in my hand.

"Actually, John... I don't feel a goddamn thing."

I toss the lit lighter at him.

The gasoline ignites instantly.

Fire races across his body in a violent burst of orange and white, swallowing the front of his cloak before he can draw another breath. Flames climb his chest, curl over his shoulders, and catch in his hair.

John screams.

The sound rips through the villa, raw and animalistic, nothing polished left in it. He thrashes against the marble, but his ruined knees buckle uselessly beneath him. Burning fabric melts against his skin. The gasoline spreads beneath him in a bright, hungry pool, crawling outward in thin streams of fire.

The smell hits next.

Smoke. Fuel. Burning hair and flesh.

His skin darkens and splits beneath the flames. Blisters swell across his jaw and neck before bursting open from the heat. Parts of his cloak fuse to his body while the fire eats through layers of fabric and skin together.

John twists in agony, his mouth open around another scream. For the first time, there is no performance in his eyes. No control. No lesson. No power.

Just terror.

For a few seconds, I watch him burn.

Then I raise the gun.

My sight settles between his eyes while flames claw up the side of his face.

The shot tears through the room.

The bullet punches into the center of his forehead with a wet, brutal crack. His head snaps back from the force, and the back of his skull bursts open against the heat and smoke. Blood, bone, and tissue spray across the burning marble behind him, hissing where it hits the flames.

For a split second, his body stays locked in place, fire rolling over his face and neck.

Then everything gives out. John collapses hard onto the floor while the flames keep eating through what is left of him.

The room goes still except for the crackling fire.

Seth steps closer and his shoulder settles against mine. His eyes move over my face, searching for any crack in the calm.

"You alright?"

"Yeah," I reply.

I close my eyes.

I didn't shoot him out of mercy.

I shot him because I was done listening to him scream. Done letting him take up space in the world. Done letting him be the shadow at the center of every ruined thing inside me.

That bullet wasn't forgiveness.

It was closure.

For the first time in years, the pressure inside my chest is gone. No scream presses against my throat.

Seth reaches down and grabs the fuel can Beau brought upstairs. He starts pouring the remaining gasoline across the floor around John's burning body. Fuel splashes over the marble and spreads beneath overturned chairs and shattered glass while the fire crawls outward in bright waves.

"Let's go."

We move through the villa quickly, checking corners and clearing each doorway as we go.

The stairs creak under our boots as we go down. We don't talk until we hit the bottom floor and see Beau.

He's in the living room near the back entrance with another gas canister resting beside his leg. Beau looks up when we enter. His expression stays flat, but his jaw is tight.

"I have someone waiting at a rendezvous point," he says. "They can take the two girls from there."

Seth nods once.

Beau continues. "You and Brooke wait somewhere near the coast. I'll take them to the point. I'll come back for you. Then we take the plane out."

I look around at the expensive furniture and the soft lighting and the quiet walls. I think about the girl upstairs, the one that was already dead.

"First," I say. "Let's burn all this shit down."

Beau's mouth twitches slightly like he already knew that was coming.

"Yeah, good thinking, Sinclair."

He nudges the extra canister toward me with his boot.

I pick it up.

We move through the house again, opening every door and clearing every room. Closets, bathrooms, storage spaces. Each time a door swings open my chest tightens because I expect to find another girl inside. We don't.

Seth moves ahead of me, pouring gasoline in heavy streams across the hardwood floors and rugs. The fuel spreads quickly beneath furniture and through the open doorways.

I take the other canister into the main room and circle the space. Gasoline runs down the curtains and across the door frames. I tilt the container higher and let it spill over the walls and furniture.

I want this place to burn fast.

Upstairs, smoke already drifts down through the stairwell from John's room.

Seth glances at me once as we move for the door together.

The smell of gasoline sticks to our clothes as we step out of the villa.

We don't stop. We put distance between us and the house, boots hitting the path as we move toward the dock.

Behind us, Seth flicks the lighter.

The small flame appears for half a second before he drops it.

The gasoline ignites instantly.

Fire races across the floor and climbs the curtains in seconds. Heat pushes outward as smoke begins to gather along the ceiling.

The villa finally looks like what it is.

Hell.

Seth and I break into a run for the dock while the fire behind us roars to life, growing louder with every step.

Beau already has the girls inside the boat.

He reaches out and grabs my arm as I climb in. Seth steps in behind me.

The boat pulls away from the dock while flames burst through the villa windows and begin to consume the roof.

I watch the fire swallow the house. I stare at it until distance softens the details. The fire keeps rising. Smoke rolls over the water.

Seth's arm settles around my waist and pulls me closer while the fire spreads across the roof.

Beau steers toward the coast.

Seth turns his head toward me. His face is smeared with sweat and smoke.

"You hungry?" he asks.

I blink at him because the question feels strangely normal after everything that just happened.

"Yeah," I smile. "A little."

Chapter 86

Seth

The bell over the diner door dings when we step inside, and the sound feels ridiculous after what we've done.

Brooke keeps her sunglasses on anyway. I keep my cap low. We look like we walked out of Hell. Smoke still lives in our clothes. There is ash in the seams of her hairline. I have a smear at my jaw I missed when I wiped my face.

The hostess barely looks up.

"Two?" she asks.

I nod once.

We slide into a booth near the window. The diner is warm in that familiar way, heat turned too high and the smell of old coffee and pancakes hanging in the air. The place reminds me of Lorraine's Diner, the same worn booths and steady vibe of a place that never really closes.

Brooke wraps her hands around the menu even though she already knows what she wants.

I pull my phone out and check it.

"Beau said the pilot will be there in an hour. We eat. We don't need to rush."

Brooke lets out a breath that almost counts as relief. "Cool. Maybe we can sightsee."

I lift my eyes, and see she is trying to be funny.

"We're technically dead. We don't want anybody to recognize us."

Brooke snorts and nods. "Right."

The waitress appears with two waters and that tired late night voice. "What can I get you?"

I don't even open the menu. "Coffee. Black. Eggs, fries, bacon."

Brooke smiles.

"Turkey sausage," she says. "Pancakes. Extra syrup."

The waitress scribbles and walks off.

Brooke looks at me. "Where are we gonna go after this?"

I lean back and scan the room without making it obvious. My posture says relaxed. Even though my eyes say I will kill anyone who looks at her wrong.

"It's up to you."

Brooke swallows. "I guess, figure out what peace looks like for people like us."

I smile. "I like the way you think."

The food arrives fast. The coffee hits the table with a soft clink, then the plates. Eggs glistening. Fries piled high. Bacon crisp. Brooke's pancakes are golden brown and fluffy, syrup already threatening to run.

She cuts into them anyway. The first bite makes her shoulders drop a fraction. The rush of sugar and heat hits her.

We eat without speaking. It is quiet between us in a way that doesn't feel empty. It feels like we're learning how to be normal.

Brooke glances up and catches me watching her.

"You're staring."

I don't look away. "I like what I see."

She laughs under her breath. "Yeah? With blood and ash all over my face?"

"Yeah...Especially with that."

She reaches for her water. "You're insane."

I take a bite of bacon. "I know."

A small record player sits on the edge of our table by the window. One of those diner decorations people bring back because nostalgia sells better than plastic menus. The casing is scratched, but the needle arm still sits in place.

I lean slightly toward it and look at the small playlist cards stacked beside it.

Most of the titles are the usual filler.

Then I see it.

"Lovesong"

For a second I just stare at the card.

Out of all the songs that could have been sitting there tonight, it's that one. After everything that just happened, after the fire and the blood, this is the one waiting on the table.

It feels absurd.

Then the television above the counter flashes bright and I realize something else.

It's New Year's Eve.

I completely forgot.

My hand moves without me thinking, slipping into my pocket out of habit. My fingers brush against something solid and familiar.

I freeze.

You've gotta be shitting me.

I pull it out slowly, already knowing what it is before I even look.

The ring box.

These are the same pants. The ones I shoved it into before everything went to hell and we had to leave the safe house.

I stare down at it for a second, my grip tightening around it.

Of all the times. Of all the places.

And somehow, it's still here.

It feels like the universe lined something up just for this moment.

I reach over and press the button. The speakers crackle.

Then the opening of "Lovesong" by The Cure drifts through the diner. The steady bass line settles into the room and Robert Smith's voice follows a second later.

Brooke blinks in surprise.

Then her mouth curls.

"Awww," she smiles. "This is my song."

"It's our song now," I tell her.

She shakes her head, smile widening.

The diner noise fades as the song wraps around us.

She looks at me and laughs quietly.

"Who would have thought we'd end up back in a diner together, after everything we survived?"

That is when it hits me.

The certainty.

I have never been so sure of anything in my life. Not a shot. Not a kill. Not survival.

Her.

I think about New Year's Eve, exactly a year ago. The hotel, the rose gold ring that never made it to her finger. The interruption. The chaos. I remember the nerves that night, the way my hands shook, the doubt that crept in even though I love her more than anything in this world.

I don't feel that now.

Not even a trace.

I keep my eyes on hers. I don't blink.

"I knew from the moment I saw you."

Brooke's smile stalls, caught between wanting to tease me and wanting to cry. She just watches me like she is trying to understand what I am about to do.

I reach into my pocket and pull out the ring box.

Brooke's gaze drops to it, then lifts to my face.

"I've loved you since the moment I saw you, Brooke. Even when you didn't know I was there yet. Before you looked at me. Before you even said my name."

Her eyes gloss. She tries to blink it away.

I reach for her hand and lace our fingers together. My thumb rubs over her knuckles.

"We've been through hell together, Brooke. We've bled together. We've killed together." A faint grin tugs at my mouth. "I've stacked a lot of bodies for you."

She lets out a quiet laugh while she wipes at the corner of her eye, and my chest eases at the sound.

"I've taken a bullet or two for you," I add.

I shake my head once, staring down at our joined hands for a second before looking back at her.

"I kept waiting for the right time to ask you this. Every time I thought I had it, something went to shit."

I let out a breath through my nose.

"And then it hit me. The perfect moment is whenever I'm with you."

I hold her gaze, not looking away.

"I don't need everything to fall into place first."

My grip tightens slightly around hers.

"I just need you."

The words scrape something raw out of my chest.

"I want the rest of my life with you."

I open the ring box, letting her see it before I say anything else.

The rose gold catches the diner light, warm against all the grime and exhaustion. There is still a fleck of my blood on it, dark and dry in a place most people would never notice.

"Brooke, will you marry me?"

She looks at the ring for a second before lifting her eyes back to mine, as if nothing else in the room exists.

"Do you even have to ask?" Her lips tremble around the smile trying to break through. "Yes, duh."

The tension leaves mt chest all at once with a breath I hadn't realized I was holding.

I take the ring out of the box and reach across the table for her hand. My thumb rubs over her knuckles before I slide the ring onto her finger. The warm metal looks beautiful against her skin. Mine, finally, where it always should've been.

Outside, headlights sweep across the window as a car pulls into the parking lot and idles.

I glance toward it, then back at Brooke.

"Time to go."

Before either of us moves, the television above the counter crackles louder. The screen flashes bright colors as the New Year's broadcast cuts in. The crowd on the TV starts counting down, voices rising together.

Ten.

Nine.

Brooke lifts her hand, and the ring catches the cheap diner light. She gives me a look that says 'You did that' and she isn't letting me forget it.

"Okay," she murmurs. "Husband."

My mouth quirks. In that moment I feel the happiest I have ever felt.

"Soon baby," I squeeze her hand and stand. "Let's disappear first."

Eight.

Seven.

Six.

Brooke grabs the front of my shirt and pulls me down.

Five.

Four.

Three.

She kisses me hard, her hands sliding into my hair as the last numbers echo through the diner.

Two.

One.

I kiss her back just as fiercely. I hold onto her like I'm not letting anything take her away from me again.

The television erupts with cheers behind us as the new year begins.

"Lovesong" continues playing while we leave the diner.

Me and my final girl survived it all.

That's the only ending that ever mattered.

Epilogue One

Brooke

One Year Later

The reflection in the mirror barely looks like me.

I'm wearing a black lace dress, fitted like sin and stitched to my bones. The gown hugs every curve, off the shoulders, with a slit that shows my leg when I move. The train rests behind me in a dark spill. A single black rose sits above my left ear, pinned into loose waves.

My eyes look darker than usual, and calmer too. I still look haunted, but I finally feel at peace.

"Damn, Morticia," Travis's voice cuts through the silence as he steps into the room behind me, already lighting a joint. "Look at you all ready to marry Gomez."

He offers it to me without ceremony.

I take a long drag, hold it, and exhale slowly. "Sure am."

He grins. "Seth's definitely giving John Wick meets American Psycho. It's terrifying. And kinda cool. But mostly terrifying."

I smirk, still watching myself in the mirror. "If we didn't already get fake-married once, this would feel insane."

"Oh, it still does." Travis leans against the wall beside me, taking another hit. "The priest Beau got for this thing? I'm ninety percent sure he's one of Beau's hits. The man looks like he's being held hostage."

"He probably is," I say casually.

"Some things never change," Travis mutters with a laugh, blowing smoke toward the ceiling. "This whole thing is like a fever dream."

I turn to face him, narrowing my eyes with mock suspicion. "And what about you? You've been dating Naomi for how long now?"

Travis blinks, then squints at me through the haze. "Is this a setup?"

"Just asking." I step closer, lowering my voice. "You two are disgusting together, by the way. In love, happy, cute. It's sickening."

He rolls his eyes but can't hide the smile tugging at his mouth. "We may or may not be moving in together next week."

"What?" I gasp, then launch myself at him, throwing my arms around his neck. "Trav! I'm so happy for you!"

He hugs me back tightly. "You deserve this too, you know."

I feel it then, that sharp little pinch behind my ribs that used to mean I didn't believe it. That I didn't trust it. But this time, I did.

This time, it feels real.

Travis pulls back and gives me a look, the kind that says he is pretending not to get choked up. "Now let me walk you down the aisle to your serial killer husband before he decides to murder the priest out of impatience."

"Wouldn't be the first time someone's died at one of our family gatherings." I loop my arm through his. "Try not to cry."

"No promises."

We step outside just as the opening notes of "Nothing's Gonna Hurt You Baby" drift through the speakers.

It's dusk, that magic hour where the sky bleeds soft purples and blues behind the mountains. The wind moves through the grass in soft waves. The aisle is black velvet, lined with glass pillars and low black candles flickering against the dark.

The altar glows like a portal to another world. A massive heart of black roses rises at the center. Fog curls up from the lake like ghosts' breath. A blood red neon sign glows through the mist. Til Death.

It feels dramatic. Gothic. Completely unhinged.

Exactly the kind of wedding I always imagined.

The guest list is small. Only the people who matter.

Miles sits beside his husband, Alonzo. Naomi sits next to them with Elise and Ryan beside her. All of them are dressed in black. All of them hold bouquets of black stemmed roses.

My little found family.

The only family I ever really needed.

Beau stands beside Seth with his arms folded across his chest, playing the role of best man with the same calm confidence he brings to everything else. Seth's best man and hitman.

And Seth...

Seth looks like sin in a suit.

Black on black. No tie. His collar sits open just enough to show the edges of the tattoos climbing up his neck.

His eyes search for me.

And the second he sees me, he smiles.

The kind of smile that says he would break every law in the world just to kiss me.

The priest standing between us looks terrified.

I notice it immediately.

I kind of love that.

I feel perfect.

I feel alive.

And I walk toward my ending.

Or actually, my beginning.

The wind lifts the hem of my dress as Travis walks me down the aisle, his arm steady under mine. When we stop in front of Seth, Travis gives my hand one last squeeze before placing it into Seth's.

For a second, the three of us stand there together.

Travis looks at Seth, then pats him once on the back, the kind of handoff that says more than anything either of them could put into words.

Take care of her. I know you will.

Seth gives him a small nod. Then Travis steps back and returns to the others.

The priest clears his throat.

His hands shake as he opens the book.

From the side, Beau watches him carefully with his arms still folded, his expression promising violence if anything goes off script.

Then Seth reaches for my hands.

His palms are warm and scarred. I lace my fingers through his without thinking.

My heart is loud in my ears, but it is not frantic.

It feels settled.

Like it finally understands where it belongs.

I look up at his face.

The last of the daylight catches along the edge of his jaw and the curve of his cheekbone. His dark hair falls loose across his forehead, slightly wind-tossed. The collar of his black shirt sits open at his throat, the ink along his neck visible above the fabric.

His gray eyes stay locked on mine.

The rest of the world could disappear and he wouldn't notice.

There is something different in his expression tonight. The usual intensity is still there, that dangerous focus he carries everywhere, but something softer sits underneath it now.

Relief.

Possession.

Love.

His thumb moves slowly across the back of my hand, rough skin against mine.

For a second I just take him in.

This man tore the world apart for me. This man held me together when I was splintering. This man has seen me at my worst and never flinched.

If love is a choice, I've made it a thousand times already.

Every scar. Every dark thought. Every terrible choice that somehow led both of us here.

And the strangest part is that nothing about it feels wrong.

If anything, it feels exactly the way it was always supposed to be.

The priest asks if we're ready to begin.

Seth answers before I can. "Yes."

The priest nods and gestures to Seth. "You may begin your vows."

Seth doesn't look at any notes. He never does anything by script.

He looks at me.

"I don't say things pretty," he begins. "You know that. I just tell the truth."

A quiet breath moves through the small crowd.

"I didn't grow up believing in forever. I didn't believe in fate. I didn't believe in mercy. I believed in surviving and that was it."

His thumb presses into my knuckle, grounding himself as much as me.

"Then I met you. And everything I thought I knew stopped working."

My throat tightens.

"You saw me for exactly what I am and you stayed. You didn't try to save me. You didn't try to fix me. You chose me."

His voice drops lower.

"I promise you this. I will never lie to you. I will never leave you. I will never make you feel small to make myself feel bigger."

Tears blur my vision.

"I will protect you. I will fight beside you. I will build something new with you even if we have to do it a thousand times over."

He exhales slowly.

"You're my wife. You were before today. You will be after this. You're mine in every possible way."

He squeezes my hands.

"I love you more than I can ever express in words. I've already killed for you... a lot. I almost died for you and I'd do it again. Now I want to spend the rest of my life loving you."

My eyes stay locked on his as I blink back tears. He looks nervous underneath all the confidence, I know this matters more to him than anything else ever has, and it shows.

The priest turns to me. "Brooke."

I take a breath and lift my chin.

"I didn't believe in love," I admit. "I was raised to endure."

Seth's fingers tighten.

"I thought love was something that happened to other people. Not me."

I shake my head slightly. "Then I met you."

A quiet laugh slips out before I can stop it.

"You never pretended to be good. You never pretended to be gentle. You showed me exactly who you were and trusted me to decide."

I swallow.

"I choose you. Not because you saved me. Not because you'd burn the world for me."

I meet his eyes. "But because you see me. All of me. And you don't ask me to be less. You helped me find my voice."

Tears well up, I keep going.

"I promise to stand with you when it's hard. I promise to tell you the truth even when it scares me. I promise to build a life with you."

I smile through the tears. "I finally found my home and that's you. You're my home. And I'm never leaving."

Seth looks at me as if my vows healed something inside him.

The priest clears his throat again, visibly overwhelmed. "Do you, Seth, take Brooke—"

"Yes," Seth says immediately.

A soft ripple of laughter moves through the group.

"And do you, Brooke, take Seth—"

"Yes."

The priest blinks, then exhales. "By the authority vested in me, you are now husband and wife."

Seth doesn't wait for permission.

He pulls me in and kisses me like he's sealing a promise. His hand cups my jaw, thumb brushing once near my cheekbone. He pulls back just enough to look at me, eyes locked on mine.

"Hey, wife."

My smile comes easy. "Hey, husband."

He kisses me again, shorter this time, then rests his forehead against mine for a heartbeat before letting me go. When we turn, the people who stayed are still there. The ones who survived with us. The ones who chose us.

Beau whistles low. Elise wipes her eyes. Ryan smiles and stands a little taller. Miles squeezes his husband's hand. Naomi smiles through tears while Travis tries to quickly wipe away his own while clapping.

Seth leans down, voice low. "Still glad you said yes?"

I laugh and press my lips to his again. "Always."

The music fades behind us as we drift from the warmth of the ceremony, fingers laced. We follow the path around the edge of the property, past trees strung with soft lights. For once, there's no plan. No blood. No body count. Just us, walking into a life that doesn't feel borrowed anymore. The stars above are real. The calm in my chest is real. It's just me and the man beside me, his hand in mine, his vows still echoing in my head.

Then he straightens and murmurs, "I've got a gift for you."

I blink. "What?"

He doesn't answer. He just takes my hand and starts walking, guiding me away from the lights and the warmth and the noise. The music fades behind us as we cut around the edge of the property, past trees strung with soft lights.

His grip stays firm. He leads me toward the parking lot, where a row of cars sits under dim lights.

Then I see it.

The long hood comes into view first, the black paint catching the last stretch of fading light. The shape of the body sits low and aggressive against the gravel, unmistakable even from several steps away.

My breath catches hard in my chest, and my feet stop moving before I realize it.

Seth turns his head toward me immediately. He watches my reaction closely, studying my face as if that matters more than the car sitting in front of us.

Parked just ahead of us is a 1969 black Barracuda.

My mouth opens, but my brain doesn't catch up fast enough to find words.

"You didn't," I finally manage.

"I did. It was yours before everything went to hell. It's still yours."

My eyes burn. I swallow, because I refuse to cry right now. Not after surviving all of it. Not after finally getting something good.

Seth presses the keys into my palm. His fingers close over mine for a second. "You ready to take it on the road?"

I walk to the driver's side like I'm afraid it'll vanish if I move too fast. I open the door. The smell hits me first. Leather, old car and something expensive.

I slide in and grip the wheel.

Seth gets into the passenger seat and shuts the door. He looks over at me with that same look he gave me at the altar.

I turn the key.

The engine wakes up. The sound fills my chest.

I smile so wide it almost hurts.

Seth watches me, then his mouth twitches. "Let's not die before our honeymoon, okay?"

I laugh once.

Then I floor it.

The tires bite and the Barracuda surges forward, and for a second I forget to breathe.

The parking lot lights streak past. The property falls away behind us. I keep both hands on the wheel. My grip is tight. My smile spreads across my face.

Seth braces one hand on the dash as we hit the road. "Jesus."

"You know you love it when I scare you," I remind him.

He looks over at me, and his eyes soften in a way that still catches me off guard.

The engine growls when I push it. The car responds instantly. The road opens into a long stretch with trees on both sides and nothing in front of us. Headlights carve through the dark and the world feels simple for the first time in a long time.

We take the curve and the Barracuda grips the road like it was built for nights like this. The window is cracked just enough to let the cold air slide in.

Seth's hand lands on my thigh. His thumb presses once.

Then he reaches for the stereo.

The cabin fills with the first notes of "Sextape" by Deftones. He turns it up and finally looks at me. Not a quick glance. He holds my gaze for a beat, eyes dark and warm, like he is reminding himself we made it, together.

I keep my eyes on the road, but my throat tightens anyway. "You okay over there?"

Seth watches me for a second longer than necessary. "You look good driving this, Mrs. Sinclair."

A laugh slips out of me. "I love my wedding gift, Mr. Sinclair."

The name sits in my mouth and it doesn't feel borrowed. It feels right.

We didn't take his last name. Seth would never carry that name into a new life with me. Not after everything his father did.

His father killed my parents. His father built nightmares and called them lessons. Seth carried that name like a scar for most of his life.

So we left it behind. We took mine instead.

Sinclair was a choice. It meant a clean line between what came before and what comes next. It meant we don't have to drag the past forward with us.

We are finally free from our past.

Whatever we were before this doesn't matter now. What matters is this. His hand in mine. Our vows in the air between us.

Everything we survived led us here, exactly where we belong. Living a dream we never knew could exist.

Seth the killer, my stalker, my lover, is finally my husband.

And I'm his wife.

Two lost souls who found each other in this lifetime.

And if there's another one after this, we'll find each other again.

Epilogue Two
Seth

Two Years Later

The smell of burnt flesh never leaves.

Doesn't matter how long I spend in the shower, how much citrus cleaner I use, or how many times I replace the fucking filter on the incinerator. It clings. It gets under the nails, into the fibers of your clothes, into your goddamn bloodstream.

I stand over the steel chute, watching the last chunk of meat curl and blacken under the flames. The incinerator roars beneath my fingers, a low, hungry growl that always sounds too eager.

This is my role now.

Beau pulls the trigger.

I erase the body.

We have a system, one that works because it never changes. Beau likes the action, the kill, the chaos, the gleam of adrenaline in the blood-slicked moment. Me? I handle the aftermath. The cleanup. The parts most people don't have the stomach for.

I am the ghost who makes the bodies disappear.

The cleaner.

Not glamorous. Not easy. But necessary.

Especially when Beau is the one doing the killing.

I glare at the table, where what is left of the guy's ribs still steams in a shallow pan of blood.

"Would've been done an hour ago," I mutter, peeling off a glove with my teeth, "if you hadn't carved him up like you were fucking Picasso."

Beau leans against the far counter like we are on break from a fucking barbecue, wiping down his blade with a piece of the guy's shirt. "Art takes time, brother. I was in a groove."

"Yeah? Well, your groove just cost me another shirt."

He smirks, like he enjoys pissing me off. "I'll get you another."

I don't bother answering. Just reach for the tongs and start shoveling the last of the bones into the fire.

The heat licks up the edges, curling the flesh, blackening it in waves. It is hypnotic if you look too long, how easy it is to reduce a person to ash. Nothing but heat and smoke and bone dust.

The silence settles in again, broken only by the hiss of the furnace.

It should be disturbing, what we do. But it isn't. Not anymore. We aren't butchers. We're erasers. Making the world a little quieter, a little safer, one bastard at a time.

And today's bastard deserves it.

I watch the last piece collapse into glowing charcoal before I swing the incinerator door shut and twist the dial all the way to max. The machine roars back to life behind the steel panel.

I peel the last glove from my hand and drop it into the burn bin before stepping outside into the cold night air.

The first thing I see is the back of the car.

The taillights catch the light spilling out from the garage behind me, the red lenses reflecting across the polished black paint. Chrome runs along the edge of the bumper and the trunk line, clean and bright against the dark finish.

My '67 Impala.

I asked Beau and Travis to go get it for me. The car has been sitting in the underground garage at Travis's old apartment building ever since we disappeared, tucked away where no one would notice it. Travis looped the security cameras years ago just in case we ever needed to come back for anything important.

I walk closer, the long hood stretching toward the front of the property, the paint polished enough that the faint glow from the street lights slides across the surface.

Then I notice her.

Brooke sits on the hood.

Her legs are crossed at the ankles. One hand rests beside her on the metal while the fingers of her other hand drum lightly against the hood. The small rhythm echoes softly through the quiet night.

Her eyes stay on me the entire time.

She wears all black, but something about her tonight looks different. Her hair is pulled back away from her face, leaving her features bare. There is no makeup, no armor, no attempt to look like anything other than herself.

Just Brooke.

My gorgeous fucking wife.

I keep walking until I reach the front of the car. My hand slides up to her jaw and I lean in, pulling her toward me before she can say anything. My mouth presses against hers with a hunger that has nothing to do with violence and everything to do with the simple need to feel her there.

When I pull back, she cocks her head, half amused. "You know your sister's gonna be pissed, right?"

"She'll live," I say as I unlock the car.

I move around to the passenger side first and pull the door open for Brooke. The interior light catches the ring on her finger as she slides in and shuts the door.

I circle around the front of the car and slide behind the wheel.

The leather seat creaks under my weight, familiar in a way that settles in my chest. My hands wrap around the steering wheel, the worn grip fitting against my palms exactly the way it always has.

Beau climbs into the back a second later, dropping into the seat behind us while letting out a low whistle under his breath, as if we didn't just reduce a man to dust.

I turn the key.

The Impala rumbles to life, the engine vibrating through the frame with a deep, steady growl that echoes through the quiet road.

I shift the car into drive and pull away from the curb, the tires crunching over gravel as we head toward the road that cuts through the trees. The headlights slice through the darkness ahead while the engine settles into a smooth rhythm beneath us.

A minute later Brooke reaches across the console. Her fingers slide into mine. I lace our hands together and rest them between us while steering with the other.

The road curves through the trees before the house finally comes into view. Soft light glows through the windows, warm and steady against the dark woods around it.

Before I even bring the Impala to a full stop in the driveway, the front door swings open.

Elise stands in the doorway, her mouth pulled tight in the same expression she always wears when she knows we were out doing something she probably doesn't want to know about.

But tonight, she isn't alone.

On her hip is a ten month old baby girl with wild dark curls and storm-gray eyes that cut straight through me every single time I look at her.

She squeals the second she sees us. Her whole body twists with excitement as she points at Brooke and me, little fingers grabbing at the air.

Our daughter.

Mila.

And just like that... everything I'd ever burned, buried, and bled for... is right there waiting.

Elise stands in the middle of the marble foyer barefoot. Her eyeliner wings stretch sharp and her entire presence carries the unmistakable energy of someone who has decided the night is already ruined.

"I told you I needed to be out of here twenty minutes ago," she snaps while shifting Mila higher on her hip as my daughter squirms and whines for freedom.

Brooke raises both hands immediately. "I know. I know. I'm sorry. They were taking their time cleaning up."

"Not you, Brooke." Elise's tone softens the instant she looks at her. "You can do no wrong in my eyes. This asshole," she says while jabbing a perfectly manicured finger directly at me, "is the reason I'm late. Again."

Beau rolls his eyes. "Here we fucking go." He turns on his heel and walks back toward his car, dragging his phone from his pocket as he answers a call.

I lift both eyebrows and lean against the doorframe, already preparing myself for whatever argument she plans to start next.

"And where exactly do you think you're going?"

Elise doesn't answer right away. She gives the most exaggerated eye roll I have ever seen, the kind only a teenager can pull off.

Then she groans and shifts Mila toward me.

"Here. Hold your kid."

She passes my daughter over like she is handing off a particularly clingy purse. I take Mila, adjusting her against my chest with ease before pressing a kiss into the top of her curls.

She lets out a soft, satisfied sigh and settles immediately, her cheek resting against my chest while her tiny hand grips the front of my shirt.

"I'm going on a date," Elise announces while already stomping toward the hallway like the discussion is finished.

"What?" I lift my hand and gently cover Mila's ears. "Who the fuck said you could go on a date?"

Brooke reaches over and smacks my arm, her eyebrows lifting in warning. "Seth. She's almost eighteen. She can go on a date."

"Thank you," Elise calls out while spinning around dramatically. "See? This is why I love her more. She doesn't try to lock me in a tower guarded by psychos."

I narrow my eyes at her. "That can be arranged."

Without even pausing she fires back, "It wouldn't be any worse than living under your fascist dickhead curfew."

I open my mouth, ready to respond, but she keeps going.

"You were probably late because you were fucking Brooke in the car or something."

I lift my hand and flip her off.

Brooke bursts out laughing beside me, barely managing to cover her mouth.

"On any other day you would be right," I mutter. "But not tonight."

Elise groans loudly and slaps both hands over her ears. "Oh my God, that's disgusting."

Mila squirms in my arms, completely uninterested in the argument happening over her head. Her small hands grab at the collar of my shirt while she lets out a quiet string of sounds that mean nothing and somehow still feel important.

Elise lowers her hands slowly, narrowing her eyes at me.

"Seriously though," she says, shifting her weight to one hip. "You two disappeared for hours. Again. Do you realize how suspicious that looks?"

Brooke leans against the wall beside me, her arms folding across her chest while she watches Elise with a tired smile. "We told you we had errands."

Elise snorts. "Your errands always involve coming home smelling like smoke and dead bodies."

I glance down at my sleeve and brush a bit of soot off the cuff.

Brooke doesn't even bother denying it.

"That is circumstantial," she says calmly.

Elise stares at both of us for a long moment before shaking her head in dramatic disappointment.

"You two are the most suspicious married couple in the history of suspicious married couples."

"Yet you still live here," I point out.

"Because you two are rich and I like getting paid to babysit the most precious girl in the world."

Mila lets out a happy squeal and claps her hands together like she agrees with that statement.

Brooke reaches over and brushes a curl away from Mila's forehead. "Where is this date happening?"

Elise immediately brightens. "Dinner and a movie."

"With who?" I ask.

She pauses just long enough to make my blood pressure spike.

"A guy."

My jaw tightens.

"A guy," I repeat slowly. "Very descriptive."

Elise rolls her eyes so hard it is a miracle they stay in her skull.

"His name is Mateo. He works at the bookstore near campus. He reads actual books and listens to music that existed before TikTok. You would hate him."

"I already do," I reply.

Brooke nudges my shoulder. "Be nice."

"I am being nice."

"You threatened to lock her in a tower five minutes ago."

"That was a reasonable suggestion."

Elise throws her hands in the air.

"I'm leaving before he changes his mind and chains me to a radiator."

She grabs her heels from the entry table and shoves her feet into them. Just before she reaches for the door, I glance toward the living room.

"Ryan."

Ryan looks up from the couch immediately.

"You're going with her."

Elise freezes halfway through opening the door.

"Excuse me?" she says slowly.

Ryan blinks at me. "What?"

"You're going with her," I repeat. "You sit three seats away. You watch the guy. If he says something stupid, you let me know."

Elise turns around fully now, staring at me like I just committed a war crime.

"That is insane."

I ignore her and reach into the inside pocket of my jacket. I pull out a small folding knife and toss it toward Ryan.

He catches it.

Ryan looks down at the knife, then back up at me.

"Seriously?"

"Seriously," I say.

Elise points at me. "You can't send a fifteen year old with a knife on my date."

"He's sixteen," I correct calmly.

"That doesn't make it better."

Ryan flips the knife open and closed once, testing the hinge.

"Honestly," he says with a shrug, "I was bored anyway."

Elise drags a hand down her face.

"This family is unbelievable."

She reaches for the door again and yanks it open.

"If you embarrass me, I will throw you out of the moving car," she tells Ryan.

Ryan stands and slips the knife into his pocket.

"I'll sit far enough away that your boyfriend won't notice me."

"You've got two hours, Elise. Don't make me send Beau after you."

"That's not funny," Elise groans. "He'd actually enjoy it."

She rushes over and kisses her niece's cheek, grabs her purse. Ryan follows as they run out the door.

As the door shuts behind them, I let out a breath and bounce Mila gently against my shoulder.

Brooke exhales slowly beside me.

Mila pats my chest with both hands and babbles something that sounds suspiciously like a laugh.

I look down at her and shake my head.

"Your auntie is absolutely going to give me a heart attack one day."

Brooke smiles.

"You say that now," she says while leaning in to kiss Mila's cheek. "Just wait until this one starts dating."

I look down at my daughter.

Then I look back at Brooke.

"No," I say firmly. "That is not happening."

She gives me a look that says she isn't even going to argue with me about that tonight.

Then she pushes away from the wall and stretches her arms over her head.

"Well," she glances toward the kitchen. "I should probably get the popcorn and snacks ready for our movie night."

"Good plan."

She walks toward the kitchen, and for a moment I just stand there with Mila in my arms and watch her go.

Brooke moves through the house with a confidence she never used to have. The tension that used to live in her shoulders has eased over the years. She still carries the scars, the memories, the darkness that shaped both of us, but she carries it differently now.

She owns it.

She finished her master's program last year. The degree hangs in her office even though the name printed on it is not the one she was born with. The paperwork might not tell the whole truth, but that doesn't change the fact that she earned it.

She did the work.

Now she runs therapy groups twice a week for trauma survivors. People who have been hurt, broken, and left behind by the world sit in a circle with her and talk about the things most people refuse to say out loud.

They trust her. They listen to her.

And somehow, against every possible expectation, she helps them.

I watch her disappear into the kitchen and feel something settle deep in my chest.

For a long time, survival was the only goal either of us had.

Now we have something else.

A home.

A life.

A family.

I look down at Mila, who has managed to grab a fistful of my shirt and is currently trying to chew on the fabric with complete determination.

For the first time in my life, I'm not just surviving, I'm raising a family. Being a brother. Being a father. Being a husband.

Being a brother to them still feels strange some days. Ryan and Elise move through the house with the restless energy of teenagers who finally understand they are safe enough to push boundaries.

Ryan is still quiet by nature, but he looks people in the eye now. He makes jokes. He lets me teach him how to fight and how to carry himself in a room without shrinking from it.

Elise still talks to me as if I personally invented every problem in the world, but the truth shows up in the small moments she thinks no one notices. She asks Brooke for advice now. She lets me teach her how to drive. Sometimes I catch her slipping into Mila's room late at night just to rock her back to sleep when she wakes up.

She loves it here.

Even if she pretends otherwise.

We didn't grow up together. We didn't even meet until three years ago. But somehow, we have made something out of the ashes.

Our chaos. Our house. Our family.

Brooke stands at the stove with her back to me, focused on the pot like the fate of the world depends on the popcorn not burning. Her hips shift slightly as she moves, her attention completely locked on the task in front of her.

Mila babbles in my arms while chewing on her fist, drool soaking into the front of my shirt without the slightest concern.

I walk up behind Brooke and slide an arm around her waist, pulling her gently back against my chest. The scent of coconut baby shampoo lingers in her hair.

"You're definitely going to burn it," I murmur near her ear while carefully handing Mila over to her with one hand.

Brooke lets out an annoyed breath. "That only happened once."

"Three times."

She elbows me in the ribs.

"Whatever."

Footsteps echo from the hallway as Beau walks into the kitchen.

"All right, I'm about to head out," he says while zipping up his jacket.

Brooke turns toward him, bouncing Mila lightly on her hip. "You don't want to stay for movie night?"

He shakes his head. "Not tonight. I have some things to handle."

Brooke raises a brow, "Normal things or assassin things?"

Beau shrugs, "A bit of both."

He steps closer and presses a kiss against the top of Mila's head.

"I still can't believe you two gave my goddaughter that long ass name," he muttered, grinning.

Brooke smiles. "Don't hate on my baby's name."

Mila Samantha-Marie Sinclair.

We named her after the women who saved us. Mila, Brooke's best friend. Samantha, my mother. Marie, Brooke's mother.

The names sit together now, tied to something new instead of the loss they came from.

Brooke shifts Mila higher on her hip and glances at Beau. "Well, it's still better than Beau."

Beau lets out a laugh under his breath. "That's not even my real name."

Brooke freezes. Her head slowly turns between the two of us. "What?" Her eyes narrow. "Seth. Did you know about this?"

"Yeah," I shrug. "With his family history and the line of work he does, I didn't expect him to go around using his full government name."

Brooke scoffs. "He's our daughter's godfather. I think I should know his real name."

Beau shrugs like the entire conversation is mildly amusing. "Beau is my alias. That's all you need."

"Mila has the best godfather in the world," I say calmly. "I trust him with my life. And with hers."

"Bullshit." Brooke shifts her weight and glares at him. "You're my daughter's godfather. I should know your full name."

Beau just grins.

"That's a story for another day, Sinclair."

Brooke shakes her head like the two of us are equally ridiculous.

He reaches out and claps a heavy hand against my back.

"You did good, Seth."

Then he gives Brooke one last wink before turning and walking out the door.

It still doesn't feel real sometimes. That I have a daughter. A family. A future that doesn't end in blood.

I dump the finished popcorn into the biggest bowl we have and shake the movie theater butter seasoning Brooke likes over the top.

"Travis said he and Naomi will be here in twenty minutes," Brooke says while setting Mila gently into her bouncer next to the couch. She tucks a soft blanket around her and places a teether in her hand.

Mila grabs it immediately and starts gnawing on it with complete focus.

I follow her to the TV room. "What's on the movie agenda?"

"Movies," Brooke says with a little smirk. "We're doing a Scream marathon."

I shake my head and set the bowl on the coffee table. "Very on brand."

Luna is already perched on the back of the couch like she owns the place, her tail wrapped neatly around her paws as she watches Krueger with mild judgment.

Krueger lies stretched out in front of the fireplace, his massive body blocking half the rug. His head lifts the moment Mila makes a noise, eyes tracking her every movement with the quiet intensity of a dog who has fully accepted his role as her personal security detail.

Brooke grabs two sodas from the kitchen while I dim the lights in the living room. When she comes back, we settle onto the couch the same way we do every Friday night.

She leans back into me, resting her head against my chest, and stretches one hand toward the bouncer to gently touch Mila's tiny foot.

Our daughter wiggles in response, letting out a small burst of babbling while kicking her legs against the blanket.

I wrap my arms around Brooke and pull her closer, holding her against me while the steady rhythm of her breathing gradually settles into sync with mine.

Five years later and I'm still hopelessly in love with the girl I once stalked across a diner.

I was never the hero of this story. I knew that early. I knew it the first time I chose violence because it felt easier than mercy, the first time I realized I could live with blood on my hands and still sleep at night. I'm what people call a monster. A villain. A killer. A man shaped by damage and consequence. The monster in me never disappears. But now he has a home.

And her name is Brooke.

Brooke never tries to change me. She sees the same darkness in herself and doesn't look away. She doesn't ask me to be better. She asks me to be honest. Somewhere between the bodies and the grief and the choices we couldn't undo, we learn how to carry that darkness without letting it hollow us out. We didn't become good people. We became each other's reason to start living.

I choose her and she chooses me.

I press a kiss to the top of her head and lower my voice so only she can hear it.

"I love you to death."

She tilts her head back to look at me, a smile pulling at the corner of her mouth.

"I love you too, even beyond that."

Mila shifts in her bouncer and lets out a soft sound that draws Brooke's attention immediately. Brooke leans down and picks her up, and I help settle her between us on the couch.

Mila rests her head against Brooke while one tiny hand grabs the front of my shirt.

The three of us sit tangled together in the kind of peace I never believed I'd earn.

Not until her.

Not until us.

And now?

Now I live for her.

THE END

Acknowledgements

This story started as a movie in my head. I kept adding to it, pushing it further, letting it get darker, until it turned into something real. Now it's three books, and I'm still trying to wrap my head around that.

It wouldn't be here without the people who pushed me to take this seriously.

First, Staci. You were the first person to read *All the Ways I'd Kill for You*, and the one who told me to stop playing around and actually publish it. You saw something in this before anyone else did, and you didn't let me doubt it. That changed everything. I'm so thankful for you and our many years of friendship.

To my Aunt Mia and my Uncle James, thank you for showing up for me the way you always have. Your support never wavered, and it meant more than you probably realize. And you both really are the best hype crew I could've asked for. (And no, they are not like Aunt Mary and Uncle John.)

To my son, you are the reason I kept going when things felt dark and hopeless. You kept me grounded when my mind wanted to spiral. I love you more than anything. And I hope you never read these books. If you do, there are several chapters I need you to skip.

To my Mom, Dad and Gram, thank you for raising me to love storytelling and encouraging my creativity. You let me grow up on horror movies, let me lean into the dark, the strange, and the unusual, and never tried to water that down. That shaped me more than you know.

To Susan and Meghan, thank you for everything you do behind the scenes. You've been there hyping me up, helping me stay organized, and keeping things moving when I felt stretched thin. I appreciate you both so much, and I'm grateful for our friendship even with the miles between us.

To my street team, thank you for riding this out with me. For the posts, the messages, the edits, the reactions, the chaos. You didn't just support these books, you helped bring them to life in a way I never could on my own. You all are so amazing and I wanted to acknowledge you all by name.

Abigale W., Tatyana A., Kyra S., Misty V., Brooke J., Nikkie W., Rose A., Mya S., Tiffanie W., Teressa O., Lauren G., Amanda L., Rebecca T., Marissa S., Cindy P., Sarah S., Aura, Dionnete N., Jamie S., Jacquelin M., Delilah C., Ashley J., April C., Asha W., Nessie N., Miyah, Katlynn L., Katie, Stephanie H., Melissa P., Ginger W., Kristan P., Nichole S., Amanda, Alana M., Heather D., Krista H., Debbie H., Kellie Q., Jodi B., Mimi, Rachael, Storm V., Fallon S., Louise M., Mariel W., Leisha, Deidra S., Paige, Stacy B., Jaime S., Alyshia J., Sarah, Denise C., Keioni M., Christy R., Kiare, Kay W., Keri H., Berenis M., Michele J.,Coyah T., Allie G.

And to every reader who stuck with this trilogy from beginning to end, thank you. Thank you for sticking with Brooke and Seth through every twist, every breathless moment, every bit of chaos that spiraled way beyond what either of them (or I) planned. Thank you for caring about these characters enough to follow them into the dark and for trusting me to tell the story in a way that earned your time.

Writing this book was a lot. It stretched me, pushed me, and pulled things out of me I didn't expect. And knowing you were on the other side of these pages, reacting, rooting for them, worrying, theorizing, made all the difference. There's nothing like having readers who feel the story as deeply as the characters do.

Your reactions matter. Your time matters. Your support matters.

And the fact that you chose to spend all of that on my work genuinely means the world to me.

Thank you for seeing the beauty in the chaos.

Thank you for letting Brooke and Seth live in your head a little longer.

I appreciate you more than you know.

www.ingramcontent.com/pod-product-compliance
Lightning Source LLC
LaVergne TN
LVHW100459110826
845146LV00002B/453

* 9 7 9 8 9 9 4 8 5 6 5 1 2 *